EXTERRA

A Different Kind of Love Story in Four Parts

*Te amo
para siempre—
Danu/Paulette*

By P. Egeli

Exterra

Tellwell Talent
www.tellwell.ca

ISBN
978-0-2288-1387-3 (Hardcover)
978-0-2288-1386-6 (Paperback)
978-0-2288-1388-0 (eBook)

TABLE OF CONTENTS

Dedication 7

Acknowledgments. 9

Book One: The Beginning. **11**

Chapter 1:   An Unlikely Beginning 13

Chapter 2:   The Flight. 19

Chapter 3:   Going Beyond 22

Chapter 4:   The Revealing. 25

Chapter 5:   The Real(?) World Intervenes 27

Chapter 6:   It Gets Complicated, Very Complicated 31

Chapter 7:   The Final Test 39

Chapter 8:   So, Now What?. 42

Chapter 9:   Surprisingly, Life Goes On. 47

Chapter 10: But Who Am I Now, and What Must I Do? 51

Chapter 11: Off to Work. 57

Chapter 12: When Death Can Be Love—Or Something Else As Tender . . . 61

Chapter 13: The Taking of a Life, Gently 68

Chapter 14: Now I Understand—A Little More About My Lover and
             My New Life. 71

Chapter 15: The Truth Shall Set You Free. Or Not 75

Chapter 16: No Buts, Only Ands 78

Chapter 17: Passion is the Same Passion for All?. 83

Chapter 18: A Walk in the Park. 93

Chapter 19: The Shark 99

Chapter 20: The Making 102

Chapter 21: Until the Dawn 107

Chapter 22: Journey into Darkness 110

Chapter 23: In Between 119

Chapter 24: The Invitation 124

Chapter 25: Danu Entertains Her Love Beneath a Large Green Tree 129

Chapter 26: Out from Between. 137

Chapter 27: Danu Comes Home to the Sea 141

Chapter 28: The Negotiations. 148

Chapter 29: More Questions and Some Difficult Answers 153

Chapter 30: Danu's Trust in Dagon Is Threatened 157

Chapter 31: Flying 166

Chapter 32: Surrender. 168
Chapter 33: Coming Back. 174
Chapter 34: Knowledge Is Power?. 177
Chapter 35: The Quickening 181
Chapter 36: A Small Bouquet of Spring Flowers 187
Chapter 37: And Then It Was Summer 190
Chapter 38: Preparations for the Dance 197
Chapter 39: Midsummer's Night Eve 200
Chapter 40: The Long Way Home 203
Chapter 41: The Calm Before the Storm? 208
Chapter 42: And so Danu Returns to Between With Dagon 216
Chapter 43: A Return to the Grove. 219
Chapter 44: What Is Good For One, Is Not Necessarily
             Good For the Other. 223
Chapter 45: Fall 226
Chapter 46: Everyone Dies, Eventually 231
Chapter 47: Winter: The Contract Is Signed And Danu
             Stays for Awhile. 238

Book Two: Exterra Saved. 241

Chapter 1:   Beginning In The Middle 243
Chapter 2:   A Desperate Intervention. 249
Chapter 3:   Living On 254
Chapter 4:   Back To Work, Back To Normal?. 261
Chapter 5:   Now What, My Love? 268
Chapter 6:   But It Is Spring Again 273
Chapter 7:   Back Where I Started From? 278
Chapter 8:   Who Will Come, Will Come. 280
Chapter 9:   But First We Must Talk 284
Chapter 10: Visitors 287
Chapter 11: The Reckoning 291
Chapter 12: Beyond Between 296
Chapter 13: Who Do You Love? How Do You Love Them? 298
Chapter 14: The Rejoining. 301
Chapter 15: The In-Gathering 308
Chapter 16: I Can See More Clearly Now... 311
Chapter 17: Further Into The Flow. 316
Chapter 18: Am I Trustworthy? 319
Chapter 19: Working On My Job Description. 327
Chapter 20: Close Encounter 333
Chapter 21: One More Night 336

Chapter 22: The Trial: What Should I Say? 340

Chapter 23: Life Goes On 346

Chapter 24: Another Sidhe Spring. 349

Chapter 25: The Net Tightens 355

Chapter 26: We All Do What We Have To Do 359

Chapter 27: Battle Plans 362

Chapter 28: I Plead Our Case And Am Taken By The Life Current 364

Chapter 29: Some Things Cannot Be Prepared For 369

Chapter 30: Now There Is A Tomorrow 374

Chapter 31: The Gift 379

Chapter 32: Gathering The Gifts Of Goodbye. 383

Chapter 33: Much, Much Later. 386

Book Three: Danu's World. 389

Chapter 1: My Story Begins Again 393

Chapter 2: The Meeting 396

Chapter 3: How I Love Thee 402

Chapter 4: Negotiations 405

Chapter 5: I Learn More Than I Want to Know 409

Chapter 6: Farewells 413

Chapter 7: We Fly Away 419

Chapter 8: We Have Only This Time, Maybe No More 424

Chapter 9: The Arrival 429

Chapter 10: How It Is 434

Chapter 11: Dagon Arrives 439

Chapter 12: Desolation 443

Chapter 13: Evening Comes and Leaves Softly. 447

Chapter 14: Revelations 449

Chapter 15: Safety? 456

Chapter 16: I Almost Grow Comfortable Here 459

Chapter 17: Redemption 463

Chapter 18: A Desert Retreat 466

Chapter 19: Sky Dancer 470

Chapter 20: Anticipation. 473

Chapter 21: Time to Talk 476

Chapter 22: We All Do What We Must Do. 484

Chapter 23: A Small but Significant Change 488

Chapter 24: I Want to Stay ... Below. 491

Chapter 25: Missing Pieces of the Puzzle. 500

Chapter 26: A Planetary Puzzle—With Disturbing Answers 505

Chapter 27: The Reckoning 512

Chapter 28: I Get a New Job Description 519
Chapter 29: The Cave of Pain 529
Chapter 30: The Leave-taking 533
Chapter 31: The Council of Life and Death and Love 537
Chapter 32: Preparations 542
Chapter 33: Danu's Banquet Plans 549
Chapter 34: The Last of the Chosen 557
Chapter 35: Three Banquets 562
Chapter 36: Other Lessons 565
Chapter 37: Back to the Business of Reviving a Planet 571
Chapter 38: Alone 573
Chapter 39: All Must Rise, Live, and Then 579
Chapter 40: What Must Be... 590

Book Four: Danu Crowned **601**

Chapter 1: Before the Beginning 603
Chapter 2: The Call 604
Chapter 3: Fiócara Leaves His Mark 610
Chapter 4: A Careful Balance 615
Chapter 5: Negotiations 621
Chapter 6: The Shadakon 632
Chapter 7: Midsummer's Eve 636
Chapter 8: We Bridge Across Sorrow—For Now 645
Chapter 9: The Refugees 658
Chapter 10: Return to the Cave of Green Tara 663
Chapter 11: Rebuilding Trust 669
Chapter 12: Reunions 682
Chapter 13: The Calm Before the Storm 687
Chapter 14: The Sidhe Females Arrive 691
Chapter 15: The Secret 695
Chapter 16: Danu Witnesses 709
Chapter 17: Not Dead, Not Alive 723
Chapter 18: The Healing 728
Chapter 19: I am Alive and Again Grateful 730
Chapter 20: We Are Sidhe—We Love Who We Love 735
Chapter 21: Much Later 740

DEDICATION

This book is dedicated to the women I knew who chose to live outside of the expectations of those who would define love in one way, or by one set rules. They loved themselves and went off to be pilots, adventurers, doctors, and wise women. Their daughters, maybe some of who are reading this book, were not taught to distrust themselves; nor did they compel themselves to love or partner according to the rules of whatever community they found themselves in.

In my own life, they include my grade school teacher, Mrs. Agnese Henry, who, when I asked why she didn't have a husband, said, "I had one and we loved each other. But he died. I don't need another one."

Didn't need a husband? That rocked my fourth-grade world.

ACKNOWLEDGMENTS

It was the living life force of this planet that took me in, as I wandered as an only and lonely child. Beings came to meet me—coyotes, birds of many sorts, and later, bottle-nosed dolphins that surfed beside me in the Gulf of Mexico. Later people encouraged me to ponder about our responsibility to life, and that it wasn't all blooming and growing and carrying on for us humans. It was a vast dance and we were but a part of it. Some of us could wake up to that fact, but mostly we humans forgot this again and again.

James Hershberger, my botanist and alchemical friend, would scowl at me when I asked what a plant that he was showing me was "good for." I finally got it: it's not all for us and we've made a mess of things and, hopefully, will have time to make some repairs to the much-torn web of life.

Finally, I thank everyone who told me to write (I was writing just a little bit at times). Those who read my early efforts and encouraged and gently helped me cull overused words and sentence fragments—Billy Jack, Ellory Littleton, Myra King, Vanessa at Tellwell, and my circle of friends who saw me to the finish line with this project: I thank you.

EXTERRA

The Beginning: Book One

CHAPTER ONE

AN UNLIKELY BEGINNING

I watched the planet rapidly grow in the viewing port from a small green orb to a clear view of the buildings of the spaceport directly beneath us. I felt the last moments of precise adjustments before our ship made landfall on Exterra––another earth-type planet where we were delivering cargo.

I had managed to avoid leaving the ship the last time we were here. Being a reluctant spacer tourist in ports like this had lost its meagre pleasure for me. It was finally quiet after most of the crew went landside. I craved being alone, to have time to think my own thoughts without the distraction of people moving and talking and thinking around me. I would dream my own dreams that I tried so hard to remember when I awoke. There was often the fading sense of finally being where I should be, among those who understood me without me having to accommodate them.

I had grown up on old Earth. Being on a ship was nothing like old Earth, of course––and I liked that. The ship had adjusted gravity and even a small swimming unit. I was sick of Earth and her offerings. Preserved parks, with the paths that kept all away from any remaining significant experience of "nature": carefully protected trees with precisely monitored underground watering systems; a few bears that watched through the fences around their small territories. We were still pretending that nature was still thriving outside the cities, but the pretence had worn thin with me.

From above old earth, one could see the sprawling cities that merged into each other in a solid blanket of light that kept out the stars. People down there were hustling for something, anything that might lift them up from their precarious position on the ladder leading nowhere.

I didn't want recreational sex, the fantasy of sexually explicit videos (Three Dees), designer drug vacations and the rest. Swimming in the seas of Old Earth was not a good idea. I did it anyway, and noted that few gulls flew now, and almost no fish swam amidst the garbage and plastic. Sunshine danced enticingly on the empty waves but the water was devoid of most life. I wasn't just sick of old Earth. I was heartsick for her.

I shipped out. I flew as a techno and didn't care where I went or if I would advance, or even if I saved my credits. They accumulated anyway because I wanted little that they could buy. Nothing bothered me much except dealing with my co-workers. It was eventually noted that I did not willingly partake in recreational off-ship opportunities. In time, this fact moved me into the active category of "needs monitoring," which meant I would eventually be called in for a talk.

I was summoned shortly after we landed on Exterra where we would spend a week unloading and taking on cargo before moving on.

I smiled unconvincingly and feigned forgetfulness about how long it had been since I went off-ship –– forgetful being a more desirable label than "paranoid traits" –– and stepped down to the planet's surface, shoreside, as I sometimes thought of it—a reluctant visitor.

I wandered, vaguely drawn to a carnival-like gathering of tents and colours, music and smells. The food smelled good, although some offerings were intriguing and sometimes unpleasant.. I had always tried not to be a conservative Earth-woman, but in truth I lost my own appetite quickly. Better not to eat in port anyway. I wandered on.

By continuing to walk, I eventually ended up in the exotic sex trade section of the fair. Blue and pink banners flew.

Various people stood behind the golden cords of electro-barriers, calling out to the passers-by, trying to strike a fast deal.

I was quickly closed in on by a guide. His job was to be able to assure the company that owned our fleet that I had voluntarily chosen what I might sign up for here.

Males preened, some in archetypal Old Earth outfits that hadn't changed since male strippers had arrived as cowboys or firemen at parties of housewives wanting to go slightly towards the edge for a night. Females also strutted, catcalled, and did what they could to advertise their wares without giving up much for free.

Nothing especially interested me. I'd had this conversation with myself before. I wished I was interested, knew that I was probably being observed, and wished I was a better actor. The truth was: I felt the same way about their offerings as I did about a stroll through a protected "wilderness area." Nothing of any significance would happen. I had tried setting aside my dislike of men before and usually ended up just paying them for the agreed upon time and returning to the ship. They were making a living, and I respected that. I just didn't want their wares. I felt apologetic unless they laughed.

Some did laugh.

As I walked on, I noted the banners were violet now. Those standing behind the slight but possibly lethal cords were more intense. The guide, who had kept pace with me, was insistent now. I didn't really listen as he rattled on, catching only fragments.

"No, no, no. This would not be appropriate for you! Perhaps something more ...?" He did not say safe but it was clearly implied. One man or, more accurately, "being" behind the barrier made brief eye contact that reminded me of a caged lion I had seen on Earth—unblinking and unreadable, and very aware of me. He had the eyes of an old, weary, but hopeful predator.

This section offered possibly more than temporary diversions. Here one could probably find final relief.

I lingered and looked around curiously. Some moved towards me, seemingly casually. Some didn't bother, having judged me as a passing tourist with not enough courage or desperation to find out what was being offered.

It was then that my eyes locked with a shock-like intensity with those of a tall, lean man. Perhaps it was because he was the first who seemed to see me, and he smiled an acknowledging faint smile. I could feel, hell, I could *see* the air between us tremble. I stood transfixed.

I was a lot closer to the fence. I didn't remember moving. I couldn't recall how that had happened, and worse, since I normally value thinking before acting, I found that I didn't care.

I didn't notice how he had approached so close to me either. He was looking down at me and smiling as if we shared a private joke. Or perhaps, an understanding.

Can fierce and reassuring be entangled in one look? It can. It was.

Time stood still. I know it probably hadn't, but time is subjective. I'd learned that during the long night watches, which were longer than possible by the clock. And brief times of joy are so fleeting that even as one experiences them, one is saying, "Goodbye, goodbye ..." And yet, everything around me was still and unmoving. It was as if I was poised between one moment and the next.

We were close enough to touch. We *were* touching without physically touching. I could feel his absolute attention and it was deep and quiet. I breathed as I had learned to breathe as a diver far beneath the surface, struggling to calm myself, knowing I was on the edge of something that demanded my full attention. An edge I had never believed existed.

I had the new realization that under certain circumstances, one might agree to ... anything.

"This may be confusing for you," he said wryly. His saying anything was thrilling. Just as the air had trembled, now the sound of his voice entered me like a sustained note. I knew we were attuning; he was tuning me. I knew I was open to the process, even though some part of my mind was shouting from behind a hastily shut door, *No! Danger. Danger! You don't know what you are doing!*

Thing is, I did know. I knew that those of the Old Blood, those who humans called vampires, had lived and thrived on Earth, and later found space travel an interesting way to extend their hunting grounds. I knew that my cynicism was no match for this.

He was glamouring me.

Unbelievably, I loved it.

He smiled again, somehow curving towards me, easily avoiding the barrier between us. "You know what Robbie Robertson said. 'You like it now. You'll learn to love it later.'"

How would he possibly know I valued what Robbie Robertson, a songwriter from the late 1900's, had said?

And then he shrugged and said, "Would you like to get away from this crowd?" He smiled again. "If that's what you want, you have to say yes. That's part of it."

At this point the fairground guide, long ignored by me, grasped my arm — the first physical contact he had attempted and the last. My look caused him to quickly drop his hand. I was of course, armed. But he was showing genuine fear, a dread for his own future that caused him to assert himself briefly, to come between me and what was coming into being here. He hastily produced an electronic pad and pen and wrote in the necessary details. He was documenting that I was voluntarily going to cross the line.

I would now have to sign that I had chosen to leave with this being and was freeing the company of any legal responsibilities. I would be a temporary visitor; the screen said I would be transferred to the care of a "Shadakon."

I hereby agree that in the event that I find it appropriate to my total experience of pleasure, I agree to surrender my physical life, the form read.

And I was asked to sign and initial one of two choices at the bottom—

Yes.

Not at this time.

I shakily signed and initialled the second choice, witnessed by a bored server who was circulating with a tray of assorted drinks. The crew behind the fence was playing what was probably a well-understood game of trying to get him a little closer. He skittered out of the way and carried on.

I signed to banish the guide. He disappeared with the tablet, but not without smirking briefly at me. "One of those, then," he muttered.

The Shadakon was still very close by and I knew he had taken in my reaction to signing out to whatever fate befell me.

"What is this?" I demanded, already knowing it was a futile gesture. This was not unexpected to him; this clause in fact referred directly to him and the incredible anticipation that was starting to build in me. Was this just business? How could it be anything but? I had just met him behind a thin encircling wire. I was a first-time attendee of the fair and had already put myself in the hands of … a vampire? *Had I lost my mind?*

I already knew that I had, but there was no fuzzy feeling of induced consent.

I felt more awake than I had in a long, long time, maybe since childhood when it was explained in no uncertain terms how I could and could not act. The questions I had asked as a child were already problematic for my parents. "Why didn't we help that man today?" I had seen him, thin and struggling to remain on his feet in the long line he was waiting in. "We didn't stand in lines. Why did he have to?"

I learned not to ask too many questions and certainly not any important to me. I gathered my own information from an early age. But I wasn't going to disappear into the night with this strangely desirable being—although it was still early afternoon—without getting a few answers first.

"We've got to talk, Player," I said with as much matter-of fact calmness as I could fake at the moment.

He studied me for what seemed to be a long time, though time was no longer predictable to me at this juncture.

"Don't pull back, pleasure-seeker. You knew and came to find me once you entered the gate. Do I not have your invitation within, as well as a signed contract?"

His voice was calming, educated, with a slight, unique accent. It brought to mind old Shakespearean plays I had suffered through in my studies long ago. His eyes held mine; they were like dark amber, with dancing lights. I knew that he was telling me the truth. I had felt the faint pull of attraction that had led me to his corner of the fair. It had grown and was continuing to grow into something I could not even imagine. Long before, I had given up on wanting someone, assuming that people lied about this as they did about so many things. I thought on this afternoon I had finally experienced ultimate hunger for something.

It might turn out that I was very wrong.

Still, I tried to hold onto what—up until a minute or so ago—was important in my life. I had been a lonely child, eager to test myself against the wider world. But the accomplishments I achieved had not brought more than momentary happiness. My parents had been relieved when I was accepted into the space fleet, after my other nomadic work as a diver. That my new career might end my life we all knew, but meanwhile it was prestigious. I learned to cover my curiosity and not ask unwise questions. They asked me nothing about my life. I gave them weather reports of every planet I visited—number of moons, colour of sky, strange folks I saw there, and no doubt they shared these details with their social circle and gained approval from having such a dutiful (at last) daughter.

As for friends, I supposed what I had had were passing acquaintances. They were people to have a meal with, with promises to re-join with them that faded away with time. I didn't miss them or wonder why this happened. I was—off planet—but, more than that, we had never really shared a common reality.

I owned some land in an ecological reserve in the rain forest of Pan America. Of course I could not live on it, and it might already have fallen to the increasing pressure to harvest the valuable timber since I left. It would eventually be a stripped hillside. If not now, later.

It did not take me long to run through the list of my holdings, but there was also my life that even in these last grey years, I had taken for granted. Early escapes into drugs and alcohol seemed to cost more and more the next day or week, and I learned to take what came on my own, without comfort of such distractions. Life was as it was for me. *But surely I was not forfeiting my life today, was I?*

"Your life is your own today. You are protected by contract."

I have always been a private person and have never appreciated others trying to second-guess my thoughts that I had chosen not to reveal or elaborate on in the first place. I had run into those who, for their own reasons, attempted to draw me out with remarks that seemed to imply rapport. "I see sadness in your eyes …" and the implied, "… *and I can fix that with my attentions.*" But this man or whatever was not guessing what was going through my mind.

He *knew.*

Yet he allowed me the politeness of some lapsed time before he responded to my line of thought. I sensed that what was growing between us was driving him on, too. Such calm. Meanwhile I felt my hands shaking and jammed them into my pockets.

"We can leave now," he said. And he held out his hand, a hand with long tapering fingers.

In one of many acts of courage I would take, I put my cold hand into his cool one and the shock of contact made me gasp.

CHAPTER TWO

THE FLIGHT

He laughed and I heard within, *"There's more, much more."*

His laughter was as cool and sure as his handclasp. And then we were rising up, the fence obviously no impediment to him. We rose over the heads of a stop-framed crowd, none of whom looked up to see us.

I felt keenly alive and somehow not surprised to be moving through the air. It was much like moving in the sea, only I could take deep breaths of air that had the taste of smoke and the body scents of the many people gathered here woven into it. We were moving, but he was not dragging me, I was staying aloft with no difficulty while holding his hand, although part of my mind was shouting in fear and incredibility. And then we outdistanced my rational mind.

The me who had longed on countless nights to leave the ship and float off into the night waters of deep space, was awake and laughed.

"… never … coming down …"

Some old rocker had sung that. Ah, Steppenwolf. I was able to easily pull that from decades-past times of listening to the Before Music. Before: when Earth and her inhabitants still believed in forever. Perhaps the singer had managed to not come down, but the rest of the planet's population had brought themselves very down. Families—very small families with at most one child if they won the draw—lived in very small places. Ecstasy, either induced or natural, was not practical. Nor was it tolerated.

We landed with a slight thump on a quiet street. My knees were weak but not with fear. I leaned against this stranger's arm and said with feigned formality, "I think it's time we learned each other's names."

I had signed the form in front of him of course, but I had scrawled it for the benefit of the company's records. Anyway, it seemed significant somehow that I give my name, after flying through the air with him, away from any safety and sanity that I previously might have comforted myself with.

And so I spoke my names to him, first, unused middle, and last. And then, acting on a feeling of strong and unexpected intuition, I said aloud another name that I had chosen in my youth, when I was researching many lines of enquiry about the nature of the universe and still believed that metaphysics might trump our inevitable fate. I had developed some skills, though I used them little these days. Still, giving this name seemed to be correct now, though I could not imagine how.

I had never before spoken it to another.

He regarded me for longer than his usual pauses. For my mortally slow thought processes? To consider what I had done? *Was it appraisal I felt? Approval?* Was the request for his name an unusual one, perhaps with unknowable connotations? This was not my world and probably not originally his. The Blood were scattered across the worlds that we had so far encountered. Now it was I who waited …

I waited.

"They call us Shadakon. That is close to the name of … my kind."

Where? When? How long? I resolutely pushed these questions aside.

"You called me 'Player,' a nice image," he said.

I got a flash of him, wearing a fedora in a smoky back room. "You humans' mythology of the vampire is partially true," he continued, "although history is always written to suit the teller."

Still no name. I thought.

He studied me again and for the first time I wondered if he could see into me as completely as I had thought.

"So you like to fly … are you so well-travelled that you are fearless in the air?"

I thought of my childhood dreams that had entertained but also tormented me. In them I had learned to move freely, to drop lightly to the ground from far above. The ship had had canned air and music, inescapable "music" with its subliminal commands telling us that we felt fine, that we were enjoying the exciting privilege of space travel. But I would simply sit there, only wishing to fly away.

God, how I hated those curving corridors, and how I loved the eye-aching emptiness of the deeps. Even the recreational free fall was in a confined space with metallic air and cumbersome required safety gear. But all the time, all of us, were in enforced togetherness, feigning civility while meanwhile the crew generated endless gossip and speculations. Some of it centred on me and the fact that no one entered my room. Ever.

But flying! I had yearned to fly since my earliest dreams in which I successfully willed myself off the ground. How could he know my joy that left my knees wobbly?

We had come to an outlying treed area that surrounded the spaceport. We were in front of a stone house, an anomaly in a time of more modern and lighter built buildings. There was an encircling barrier of cypress-like trees, blue green and pointing narrowly at the sky and defining a private space behind the house. He looked at my grin of joy, and said, "My name, one of my names which I still think of myself as, is Dagon." And with that he walked up the three stone steps and palmed open the door. He did not draw aside to let me enter, but instead stood at the entrance, with the afternoon sun making blue highlights in his thick dark hair. For the first time I saw the control, the patient fierceness.

Yet his voice was mild and he made a playful-seeming bow and flourish.

"This is my home. Please enter and be my guest if you so wish."

The sunlight caused a flicker of light to play off his eyes, although he did not squint nor look away. At this point in the stories, one still has the chance to get away. Or does one? I had the choice of euphoria or the predictable sameness that was my life. I had never wanted anything like this before; I finally knew how that felt.

His home was simple and uncluttered, with rich-coloured furniture—just enough to suggest a lived-in space. What was there was priceless. One wall featured a tapestry so intricate that it could only be medieval in origin. The colours were muted and rich, and the picture was that of a great hall with a banquet in progress. Even the hounds beneath the tables were depicted with great accuracy. The people were uniformly small by our current standards and all dark haired. Stepping back to study it, I saw a troubadour with his harp sitting on a low seat before what must have been a queen or highborn lady. He was tall and dark and lean. She was looking at him with undisguised attention.

Dagon came over beside me and we studied the picture. I looked from it to him and he put a finger lightly to his lips.

"Don't ask. Please. I only keep it to be reminded of how I survived and how far I've come. And how most things are still the same."

So we sat down and he offered me wine, which I had no thirst for.

And then he offered me bliss.

CHAPTER THREE

GOING BEYOND

Who got up first, who closed the gap between? I cannot say for sure, although it may have been me.

And now, I must unavoidably give evidence of my general dislike for a favourite human activity. I was pretty sure that kissing might be happening soon. Of course I had been kissed over the course of my life. The social kisses felt like an unhygienic waste of time. Being marked by saliva or the suggestion of it perhaps, claiming an acquaintance or friend, not unlike a cat might mark his place in your house. The cat, having made its point without concern for the effects on others, is uninterested in any consequences that follow.

My experience of supposedly intimate kissing was even less desirable. It felt too close, even though the other was often emotionally miles away from being with me, and yet, perversely, glued to my lips. I usually tried not to stiffen, but the other, intent on kissing, seldom noticed my politely unspoken lack of enthusiasm. This was just one part of my general withdrawal from erotic or sexual interactions. It generally got worse from there, especially with those who saw me as a challenge. I didn't want to be cured of not-liking an unpleasant activity.

I had finally arranged my life so that such interactions could be held at bay.

This man, this being, had kissed and touched throughout the history of his and my kind. I had seen the expression in the eyes of the lady he played to in the tapestry. But now nothing was the way it had been before for me. We were sitting close to each other. When had that happened?

When I wanted him so badly I thought no more thoughts, remembered nothing else in my life. He brushed my cheek lightly with his fingertips in a tango-like move that went down and lingered on my shoulder and then down my arm. We were dancing. There was brightness between us that shimmered and flared. We had all the time in the world. He ran his hand lightly down from my hair this time, and then tipped up my chin.

His eyes held me. The room grew transparent and the evening was around us. He kissed. I kissed. Was such a difference from my previous experiences possible? I could feel the edges softening between me and this stranger. The waves of pleasure broke high and higher upon my beach. My fortressed island was going under the waves.

He read my state of mind and smiled again. "You like it now; you'll learn to love it later."

I was under the surface now, but with no desire to breathe. Rapture of the deep—I would have given my last pearl of air to a passing fish. He swept me up and laid me down on a soft yielding substance. A tiny part of me registered—*fur? Is that fur?* For such an item would be an unthinkable luxury now, if it could even be found.

As I melted in, I saw his eyes above me. They looked almost sleepy, but for a moment I saw the panther poised over me and I looked back into its now golden eyes with no fear.

We intermingled after the first kiss in every way I thought was possible and some that I only learned that day. Later we may have been outside under the stars, perhaps above the ground, in the treed area around his house. I cannot swear to that or anything else that happened that night. I believe at one point I cried a strange high note and he laughed. I felt his presence in my mind and body and it was the same, the same ... incandescent yet not burning brightness. No pain, no awkward even momentary struggles with trapped legs or arms.

Or perhaps we were flying part of the time.

I had once seen a documentary about two eagles mating in the air. They fell spiralling and calling and pulling up and out to climb and do it again and again. I remember wind rushing by, although it just as easily could have been the blood rushing within me in this marathon of pleasure and more pleasure.

Eventually though, I felt that I might truly drown. I was more tired than I had ever been, even after weeks of pulling midnight watches. Even after months of midnight wakefulness, of struggling to solve why I was the way I was, I had eventually set aside those questions to find sleep. Now I was unable to maintain awareness. My inner light faded to grey. I was perhaps in an emergency, but no warning siren rang. I slid away toward an event horizon of nothingness.

I fell into a dream. In the dream I could not move and I struggled to draw breath from an empty tank. My legs were knotted and my hands were in painful fists. I was wrapped in a grey fog that swirled around me.

I was so thirsty! I could smell water nearby and knew all I had to do was to wake up and drink. I was so thirsty, so depleted. I faded further but carried that thought back up to consciousness later.

I awoke at twilight of the next day on the pelt of thick, cinnamon-coloured fur. Dagon was sitting beside me. He watched me as I struggled to come out of the dream, thirsty, needing ...

Then, abruptly, he wrapped me in his arms and gave me—what? Energy? Relief? I came up to a usual level of wakefulness and then continued to recover and take more of the energy such that it spilled out, luminescent in the space between our bodies. Like phosphorescence, it glowed in my hair and surrounded us in dancing motes of moonlight.

He fed me, although I would not have said that then. He offered unbelievable energy, and I took and took until he pushed us apart gently, frowning slightly.

I was getting a little better at reading him now. His gaze seemed questioning. I had no questions. I knew that he had taken from me at the end of our evening. He had tapped into my funded life energy and also that which his actions had raised in me. I awakened with the memory of the glory of our night's connection faded to dull grey.

I briefly touched my neck and he just shook his head. "It is rarely like that now. It is the life essence that we require. In our youth and, only rarely later, do we enact the old blood ritual." He continued to study me.

Perhaps he had a question but was not yet prepared to ask. Time would lead us to that question and answer—but not yet. My life was my own, yes? This would end with the deep disappointment of returning to the ship and moving on and on, yes? I did not ask myself these questions. The answers were no longer important.

I still sparkled with energy. For the first time in my life, I was completely happy.

CHAPTER FOUR

THE REVEALING

As the evening darkened, he lit candles in niches all around the room. There were two white flowers floating in a bowl of water that seemed to put out more and more scent as we moved into the night.

I wanted to move, to dance. After pacing around the room twice, he caught my arm and attention. Now it was he who was sinuously relaxed. He was laughing, kindly, at me; aware of the effect he had on me. He pulled me down to sit next to him.

"You do not ask. Are you not curious about the gift that you received?"

I shook my head. "I will not judge you. Or myself."

He raised an eyebrow. "Fair enough, simple ethics, milady? Perhaps there's something else you'd like to know?"

I heard his ironic tone and his expectations of the predictable questions—*how many people, how many women had he known? Taken what they unknowingly offered? How many had not survived his attentions?*

I did not ask any of these questions while he waited.

"I want to see you; to see your body in the light." I whispered. He looked directly at me.

"As you wish," he said. "But you must be willing to do anything that you ask me to do." There was something under-spoken in these words that I thought that I should pay attention to. But at this moment it eluded me.

In the paleness of moonlight and candle bright, he took off his loose shirt and shook out his long black hair, although when we had met at the fair I had not remembered it quite this long. As he turned slowly to show me what I had asked, I saw pale ridges of scars running here and there.

There was a large white star burst over his heart.

This man—this being before me—had been staked! It took all my years of space-time not to cry out, to let go of the fragile thread that tethered me to my old life and sanity. Fear circled me like the sharks I had met diving. This was no drug-induced reality that I was experiencing as I lay waiting somewhere for the dose to wear off. What I saw as I looked at him was real.

I touched him. There. He was cool and muscled under my hand.

He nodded. "Yes. Some things leave their marks. They thought I was undone." He smiled. "More inaccurate mythology. Now you."

My clothes came off in a lump that maliciously tripped me at the last moment. I briefly stood on one foot, clumsily ridding myself of my shoes and feeling the difference between his body and mine. I looked like I had been constructed out of every protein bar, sugared snack, and slack day of my life. If I was a swimmer (and I still was in a limited way), he was of the air—lean and strong. I shivered while he languidly removed his pants and unzipped his soft boots. He looked innocent of my mindset, but we both knew he was not.

"Come here, woman."

He was cool and pale. I was surprised and grateful that touching him brought me as much pleasure as being touched, and so I moved easily into exploring him. He lay relaxed but aroused and watched me. I took my time, and found myself in unfamiliar territory. I would at times have a wave of fear and stop, as if I had heard the branch crack nearby in the woods (or how I imagined that might have been in an earlier time). But nothing happened to justify my fears and so, alert but reassured by the continuing seeming safety, I would resume. No one before had ever allowed me to find my own rhythm. Always there was an overriding, shortcutting, of something that might have grown stronger if I could have found my own way. He drew me down over him. I rocked to the rhythm of my beating heart, its tempo increasing and increasing. And when I could stand it no more, I realized that he was subtly withholding, not giving into the growing energy between us.

He caught my eyes and hissed. "Yesss. You want your soon unstoppable release that will lead you to peace. But I must resist mine. My hunger is as great as yours is now. I want to take you! But I am abiding by your wishes, confused as they are, and that of the contract. Now you know a little more about me!"

There was a storm building within my body and I was crying out, and not caring that I did, beating on his chest, and maybe even trying to get loose, to stop what could not be stopped, when I came by my own efforts. My last thought, as the last waves crested over me was "Take it then!" And doubtlessly he did avail himself of my energy, for I awoke in the morning, and he was gone.

CHAPTER FIVE

THE REAL(?) WORLD INTERVENES

I awoke to pounding and an official voice on the other side of the front door. I struggled into a robe that I found across the foot of the bed, weighing my options to withdraw to the inner, window-free part of the house, when I distinctly heard my name and rank being called.

"Shit!" I opened the door, feeling as horrible as I no doubt looked.

They assessed me glumly.

"OK, no breach of contract at this time, but we need to talk to you. Not here …" The one speaking looked about nervously. "Ah … outside in ten minutes. We'll wait in the vehicle."

Damn right you will wait, I thought. I considered my options, already knowing that I would at least superficially cooperate. There were two of them, Tweedledum and Tweedledee—company cops. I knew I had missed my ship-out but I also knew that with my work record and unused shore leaves they couldn't really do anything to me. However, it would be well to keep my options open.

I found my clothing and put it on, noticing that it was rumpled and baggy on me. I rinsed my mouth, and thought longingly of the sunken tub in the back of Dagon's house that I could not get into for the immediate future. It also occurred to me, in a fleeting way, that I couldn't remember when I had eaten last, during however many days I had been here. Then I went out to meet them.

They insisted on taking me to a nondescript cafe, whose retro decor suggested cappuccino coffee—or at least a soya and algae analog. They put a menu in front of me and waved that I should order. While we waited, they got down to the business at hand.

"We are here to advise you that you are engaging in a high-level dangerous activity and further advise you to immediately quit the premises of the so-called—" He consulted his notes, "… Shadakon."

"Why are you bothering to do this?" I asked balefully.

"Our investigation has shown you to be on an ordered leave, with chronic stress and subsequent anti-social maladjustment. Your profile shows you to be within statistically significant parameters shared by other people who have upgraded their recreational contract to allow death by choice. As you know, the company has a lot invested in you …" His voice trailed off.

The soup I had ordered tasted like dead things, like a swamp maybe. I stirred it around as if I might put another spoonful in my mouth, but knew I couldn't.

They looked at me and my untouched cooling coffee and looked at each other and then at the compu-pad in front of them.

And then I understood the situation I was in.

Company men. Keeping things legit and properly accounted for. I had just received my second official warning. Duly noted and signed by me. These transactions were probably good business for this dump during slow afternoons. There was always a server available to witness as needed.

They noticed me glaring at them and the remains of their lunches.

"Anything else you have to say?" I asked, seemingly calm.

One of the men stared at me with a look of disgust and perhaps a dollop of righteous pity. "A woman like you doesn't have to … I mean, there must be something else at the fair that would turn you on besides this!"

I stood up, gratified to see the bowl of congealed soup and cups travelling leisurely outward for a long time before they crashed to the floor, and the table slowly rocking from where I had momentarily been. They jumped back, but not before giving me their last words of advice. "Change the damn contract to the first option Lady, to your acceptance of death by pleasure. He's got a copy ready. Save us all a lot of trouble. He'll be calling us to remove the body before the end of the week."

They left without looking back.

Ugly men. Ugly place. Bad thoughts.

I decided to walk around for a while. So I wandered, pondering. I identified one choice would be to go back to work if allowed. No doubt this would remain in my file, but I am good at what I do, and not focusing on my crewmates meant my mind was clear for work. However, it occurred to me that I might have been set-up somehow on this forced leave, on this planet. It could have been any one of my many colleagues who did not appreciate my continuing obvious disinterest. So it might shake down that I wouldn't be back in space other than as a paying passenger. I could maybe get a job as a hack maintenance worker on a shallow water algae or fish farm on old Earth.

I'd seen a few of these "farms" on my trips to the coast and during my earlier diving experiences. The giant, open-ocean cages held fish, bred to eat nonstop and grow fast. They were so damn stripped of their genetic fish wisdom that if they made it out of the cage, they'd swim around the outside perimeter, waiting to be fed and would be picked off or die of starvation.

Or I might qualify to work on an algae farm, putting in shifts doing repetitive scraping of the fast growing crop until a failure in my diving rig left me drowned and food for the remaining scavengers.

I was good enough at my work underwater or alone on a watch, no good at card games, team vids, small talk and the connections that was required to be a team player.

I might live on and on, stuck on Earth with its charms of crowding, food rationing, increasing solar radiation through the tattered ozone holes, ever-rising heat and pollution. Not much to do there except to work and partake of the remaining sins. Most people still used the cheaper opt-outs—alcohol and drugs, and computer hook-ups. Humanity would always have its means of small escapes.

My assessment of my choices left me feeling bleak. Space was the best I had managed, and I was often miserable in space. Always the feelings of being caged and watched, my behaviour shaped to suit others. Maybe I had already lived out the best part of my years. I still I wondered why my shipmates seemed content enough about their fates. *You don't miss what you never knew?* I wondered.

Or, I could let a nonhuman use me for food. All very legal of course, just the slightest whisper of implied suicide, no longer uncommon in us humans. Death by bliss? A pleasant ending at least.

I was starting to feel shaky and the low sun's glare off mirrored windows was evoking something that promised to be a very bad headache. I consulted my inner map, and made for Dagon's house, with an immediate plan to fall into the tub and be gathered enough to have a conversation with him before I would retreat into my now usual unthinking state. Or I could just let the evening proceed without providing the details I was struggling with.

Who was I fooling? Maybe myself. Certainly not him.

I stood at the door and realized that I had a lot of assumptions but no reason to believe that they were valid. I might not be welcome anymore.

Surely he would have sensed the earlier presence of the company men; it lingered unpleasantly in the air at his front door. And what made me sure that he was alone? I stood silently, headache hammering, seeking refuge in the panther's den.

Until the door opened and he was there.

"Welcome to my home, if you wish to enter," he said. There was no playfulness in his tone this time.

We faced each other until he backed away to allow me entrance and stood observing me. The glimmering light and my headache decided what I had in fact, already decided. It was cool and twilight in the room. One perfect blossom floated in a crystal bowl and filled the room with its essence. It smelled ... otherworldly. I could not even imagine how it had come to be here.

There were white flowers in the tub room that looked like what Earth's lilies once looked like. Their stamens were blood red against the white petals. The huge tub that I had so wanted to be in earlier was filled with warm water that gently swirled. I felt soiled by the rub and bump of contact with the people outside and particularly the men I'd had my unpleasant conversation with. I climbed in gratefully.

I stretched out in the water and sank below the swirling surface, bobbing up to breathe, then down to float almost weightless near the bottom. Exhale. Exhale. The in-breath came of its own volition. Until at some point, it wouldn't. I had seen a few people die. Always there was that last out-breath, sometimes as gentle as a sigh.

My skin softened in the water, my hair softened and floated around me.

It was longer. Long ago I had had long, windblown hair. My parents indulged me by not mentioning it during one of my last difficult summers with them before leaving home. But after that, my diving interests resulted in me having short, practical cuts.

And when I entered the Space Corps, I kept it short. It was just another thing that might draw unwanted attention to me. Wavy, auburn hair. I reached out and wrapped a tendril of dark red around my finger. Two wraps. I came out of the water.

There was a small mirror on the wall. Framed within it I saw a pale woman, without the sunburnt neck and wrist zones that most spacers have on land. There was a hint of cheekbone and hip that was not familiar to me. My hair hung to my shoulders. But I was too restless to focus over-long on this.

Dagon was obviously in the next room. I could feel the pull of his presence—and something else. Concern? For me? For him? I walked in, leaving the muddle of my clothes on the floor. He smiled at that.

"How quickly things change," he said mildly.

On a low table sat a carafe of red liquid, fresh bread and a plate of sautéed vegetables. There was a place setting for one. Dagon lounged nearby and waved me to sit. I poured and swirled the liquid in my glass. Plum wine. I breathed in sunshine and ripe fruit. *God! Plum wine. Where had these grown, how had he obtained this? The cost ...*

Lost in my reflections, I looked up suddenly to see him watching me intently.

"Drink." It was a soft-spoken command.

Instead I turned my attention to the vegetables. Barely cooked golden squash, some translucent onion.

It looked like the best of my past, before Earth's birthrate had peaked and all possible land was put into the most efficient crops—soya and high-pro rice and grains and endless yellow fields of modified canola and corn.

"Eat."

And so I tried, really tried, to honour the richness of this gift. I sipped without swallowing and tasted and felt the golden squash flesh in my mouth. I mouthed and tasted and cut and pushed the beautiful shapes around on the plate until he stopped me.

"Enough. Do you see what is happening here?"

I did not completely see, only that I was not hungry for dead vegetables and fermented plums. I only wished for the night to flow on, to still my growing restlessness, to combine with this man-god-demon.

I was still hungry. I merely could no longer eat ... food.

CHAPTER SIX

IT GETS COMPLICATED, VERY COMPLICATED

We looked at each other in both spoken and mind silence.

"Something is happening to me," I said. "I'm changing."

He sighed. It was the perfect exhale, as good as any diver. "It's become complicated," he said. "No. It began complicated. I should have seen ... I should have let you pass."

"Let me pass? I thought you plied your craft at the fair. That you took all comers." I was angry and wanted him to know it.

He waited to respond, weighing his words. "I work at what I do under contract. Somewhat like you in your work, I must conform. I cannot live without energy and I cannot live on squash either. So I present myself. I am paid handsomely. You probably didn't notice, but my services cost you half the credits you had at hand."

I winced.

He looked down at me angrily. "For some it is all they have and more. If they want final release, I do that. I take it all. But mostly, I just take what I need. They go on to live their lives remembering a pleasant afternoon that was strangely tiring—and not much else."

"But this is different, and I am not acting as I usually do. I never bring someone home. I never *fly* someone to my home. *They—*" we both knew to whom he referred, "have never come to my door. Oh, of course they know where I live—for now. They have never ... hauled a body away!" His eyes blazed. "I am a professional. I do what I do in the equivalent of an office at the fair. I come and I go. No one comes here!"

"I should have realized!" he said with what sounded like anguish. "I had never met—"

"You didn't realize that you were turning me into someone like you!" I interrupted.

I tried to hang onto my anger, but it felt unjustified somehow and I knew it.

"You are not turning into someone like me!" he said. "You *are* someone like me."

We stared at each other.

"You have the Blood, though not enough to be one or the other. Apparently you cannot be a human very well, although you've tried hard all your life."

I could not breathe. There was an overwhelming mixture of joy and validation, anger and confusion. *That is it. That is it!* The thought pounded in my mind.

"But you cannot become fully what you are. It is not allowed. You would be a danger to us. It takes great will and focus to live with humans, and yet we must. Or it ends in flames and rage." He touched his scarred chest briefly. "We have scattered ahead of human anger across the universe. Always our dealings with humans comes around to the chase and flames."

"Not *allowed*?"

"It is not my choice to make," he said sadly, "although I see the wisdom in it. You are a wild card. It is why we can read and hear and fully feel each other, you and I."

In spite of myself I smiled at that. But then, *"Not allowed?"*

"How long can we hold this balance?" I simply asked.

He shook his head. "The tipping point has passed. Your life will end one way or the other at the end of the contract. Things are out of my hands now. The people who came here are not the biggest problem. They will report this to … others." He snarled as he spoke.

I was still stuck back at the "how long" part. "How long is my contract?"

He looked at me sadly. "Two more days, little one. Maybe less, if other events occur."

"And if the result is my death, and the final clause is not signed, what happens to you?"

"Ahhh." He exhaled again. "I forfeit my holdings here and must leave immediately.

Or there could be other, ah, complications. Punishment. Or both."

I thought of the tapestry, the crystal bowls, the graceful house and garden. I thought of him jumping ships, working slowly to create another identity somewhere. *I am past a choice that I can see.* I thought. *Why take him down too? I have had the best few days of my life and I could have a few more days?*

"Give me the contract." I put out my hand…

"In the event that I find it appropriate for my total expression of pleasure, I hereby do surrender my physical life with no further claim against the company." I read aloud.

I signed *yes* and entered it. The pad went blank in my hand.

"What now?" I said.

He sighed. "Do you still wish to come to me?" he asked quietly.

I listened within. I expected fear and anger. But the anger had come and gone and left me strangely calm. I looked into his amber eyes and thought, *Perhaps we will both reach what we want tonight.*

He was the most beautiful being I had ever seen and I would have him. If he took my life, then he would. I walked over to him, as he stood motionless watching me.

"I want you, wherever that takes me," I said.

He drew me to him and our energies joined. First for me, he provided energy that I badly needed.

Soon I was floating in perfect balance, midway between body and my constant dreams of weightlessness. Unbodied. Taking and giving. We were dancing the energy dance of life and death. Waves of pleasure came and came until … he broke away; pulling back and making me focus suddenly.

"I have a request," he said. "I want to ask you out loud." (I almost laughed at his formality). "I once used the old, wild, ways, and to me they are still sweet and deeper, much deeper than mere energy transfer."

I waited.

"I want to taste your blood; to pull your living heart's energy into me. It will be a little different for you, some pain but … you will share my pleasure."

He waited for my answer but it surprised him when it came. "Do you remember when you said to me, 'be prepared to do whatever you ask me to do?'" I remembered my first awkward disrobing.

He stopped and then … he totally stopped, as if this request required his full attention. "Maybe that could be it!" he said.

I waited for an explanation but there was none.

"I will not say more at this time," he said.

"Yes," I said.

"Yes," he smiled. "The true surrender." He shivered.

I made an archetypal gesture from old movies I had seen, head to the side, heart pounding, making my blood offering to him.

He looked to see that I was watching, eyes open to his, and then sunk what felt like very sharp teeth into my shoulder, where the life force flows with a strong pulse, before going onward to the body's business.

Electric pain. I screamed.

He bent to the flow and watched me.

I gestured and felt his tongue moving slowly on me, heard a languid slow lap, and then swung out and over and away from my life and back, high, high over us and I heard a scream within me that was not my own.

The sound of a hawk, triumphant. The cry of having killed. That was from him—his ecstasy filled me, even as I faded.

I awoke to filtered morning light. I had an inconsequential almost healed wound above my shoulder blade. The cover on the bed was not the gory scene I expected. Nothing. Except—

I was still alive.

He had made his choice.

We settled briefly into what could only be called a strange routine. He left in the morning and I waited, my need growing as the day progressed. He introduced me to his library—computer access, of course, but also real books, books printed on paper. Books hand-lettered and bound in leather. Histories, genealogies … I studied them, drawn into a history and a story that, no matter what book or source I chose, no matter what middle page I might open—was the same. The story of The Blood. There were medieval manuscripts on vellum, meticulously preserved in enviro-envelopes. I looked down on loops and curlicue letters and block prints and elaborate illustrations of dark gods or demons. *His youth?* I shivered.

He had given me a low entry password and I researched in as many languages as I had—Pan Hispanic, some Amerindian, English, even Latin. There were unknown scripts in non-human languages as well, and related articles on shape shifting and witchcraft—an area that had interested me once. The screen would hold the indecipherable pages and then clear if there was no further enquiry on my part. Eventually I would return to the books and papers: magical treatises both modern and musty, alchemy and old maps.

I was bent over my studies when he returned. He seemed angry, almost fierce.

I was surprised. "Did you think I would not be interested? Am I not welcome to find what I may?"

He shook his head. "It isn't that. I have shared with you and this is part of it." He glanced at the materials I had gathered in front of me. "It was easier when all one needed was a fresh fast horse to successfully escape."

"Well, there are faster means now," I suggested. "And further to go."

He shook his head. "It always comes to this, the midnight flights … the torches. And before we learned to tolerate the light, the final torture by sun." He shuddered. "But I always escaped. Until now. I am not free to leave now although I should. I cannot leave with you. I cannot leave you to your fate."

"There is an agreement," he said. "And I have broken it. I fooled myself or perhaps you have more skills than either of us realized."

The flames were in his eyes again, although this time there was no reflecting light to cause them. "I cannot leave you to what will come. I do not wish to end what continues to grow between us. But others will. There is one faint chance and both of us must take it. If you fail, I fail also."

In spite of the terrible calm words that he was saying, I felt a rush of relief come over me. *I wasn't in this alone! He would stand with me, this Other. And were we distant kin? How could that be, and what would come of it?*

He wouldn't leave me—dead by his actions or alive but now unable to return to my old life. I thought I had won the lottery. All would be well. I was wrong and he knew it. And would he tell me what was to come? Would I, could I understand?

We studied each other. The panther in the tall man I saw before me had a terrible, controlled tension that threatened to uncoil into a leap, a spring for the door, but did not. But I also sensed gentleness.

"You never asked the questions; you let the truth unfold between us. It is why we are in the danger we are in. The Council of Five has met and will be here soon. All pleasure contracts are monitored. You have signed off on the lethal clause, and this is the last day."

I was uncomprehending. "I signed … I did what they asked me to do."

He looked grim. "I did not. There has been no 'removal.'" He narrowed his eyes at my confusion. "No body bag. No vaguely worded notification of kin. Nor are you returnable as-is."

A fierce grin came and went. "You, an untrained feral Blood on a long space flight? Anyone who pissed you off would be the first to go. But you would have to feed without being obvious. You do not understand your need or your power. They would dump you in deep space eventually…"

It was now my turn to deal with a rush of feelings and speculations. They did not fit into one answer. I did not have enough information, the information I needed.

"Soon," he said softly. "Tonight."

I missed the significance of this, my mind full of jumbled newly learned details from my studies. But this part I took in. *He could not take me away to somewhere else. It was not OK with someone—the Council—that I wasn't dead and that I had changed. Meanwhile I needed to float, to soar, to share and to feed. I needed him but I sensed that he had not arrived home sated tonight. Still, he could hold me. He had promised me his blood! He had said he would let me experience that. There was still time.*

"Ah, young one," he said. "I could but I must not. It would only prolong your ordeal. And mine. I have been suspended from the fair and I have been providing for both of us. The Council will soon be here. There is no bending of the law. There are few of us, very few here. This is not, as many are, an overpopulated world, but we predators have our use. He scowled. "The fair is one of our pleasurable duties, but there are others, for we will kill for those who cannot or will not, but want it done. As long as there is a contract and an informed decision."

He continued. "We live a long time and few die now of natural or self-chosen causes. But we have our own laws. We have learned by stake and fire to keep our numbers low."

He seemed at a loss to explain further. He stepped towards me, and I yearned for the connection that was so close. A step more …

Instead he stepped past me to his front door and let in three Shadakon. They were powerful; their psi overwhelmed me with an over-all message of indifference and malice.

There were three "people" standing before me. All stared at me unblinkingly. One man, two women. One of the women had a mane of grey hair and her green eyes surveyed me as if I was a something—not a someone—something that might have to be disposed of.

They did not bother with clear mind-speak, but most of the communications flashing between them were clear enough for me to follow.

"Fool. Soon you will pay for this!"

One hissed, *"I have waited for this day since the deserts of Africa!"*

"Look at her! A pathetic human. And I see that both of you are in need. Good! It begins now."

My fright was increasing and increasing until I felt the edges of the room darken and I feared that I was going into shock. My knees felt weak but I stiffened them.

This was no time to be useless to myself.

Reeling with their scorn, I felt thick-bodied, even though I knew my shape had changed recently. I was being lashed by their mind-speak. It rang in my mind ... *"Better that she dies, dies, dies... Yesss."*

Dagon gathered himself as if to leap at them. The unnamed man stepped back, well aware of his intentions. The lean, grey-haired woman made as to spit and stepped between her colleagues and us.

"Leave be. The trial will begin. You have all become as undisciplined as humans. Fools! No less than he," she said, pointing at Dagon.

"It seems no one is exempt," she said more softly to herself. "Do you have a suitable room?"

Dagon nodded and we followed him to a door. It had not moved under my earlier investigations but opened with his palm. Stairs led downwards; dull lights were activated as we moved forward. Unbelievably, this was an earthen floor basement. In front of me was a heavy door with a grillwork opening and heavy lock. It was cold here, and the sounds of our footfalls were silenced, absorbed by the thick walls and door. The air was heavy and smelled of rock and damp. To intentionally create such a frightening archaic place! Why?

"Too soon you will find out, as you learn more about your lover. And then you will decide whether the price is too high. Or if you can pay it."

I was unsure who mind-spoke me. There was fierceness but not the hatred I had felt earlier.

The grey woman, obviously their leader, watched me intently. She turned to Dagon. "Be brief. She is better finding her own way."

He stood before me and my fear of the others was eclipsed.

He was going to lock me up in a basement far below his house. No one would come here by chance. He had been playing with me; I was crazy to have trusted that anything between us was real. I thought he wanted me, I thought he cared about what happened to me. He wasn't even *human*!

"I hate you. I'll get through this to hate you! You are a monster!"

Nothing crossed his face or came from him. He seemed dispassionate. Worse than any of the demanding, predictable men in my life, perhaps *this* was his ultimate pleasure. Had others been here before me? I looked around wildly. My heart cried out to him, denying what I was thinking and saying and I fought with it. *Connection is a lie! Pleasure is a trap!*

He faced me without flinching but with no hint of satisfaction in his thoughts. He was shut down, refusing to let the others in on what might pass between us.

Dagon sighed. "Hold onto your hate. You have a lifetime of it. Use it."

Then he was gone.

They flung me into a small dark room covered with the finest sifting of dust. There was a bare cot, a bucket and the door. I paced and then curled up on the dusty cot to escape into a shocked withdrawal of sleep and dreams of floating, drinking, swimming, the cool water flowing through my gills, in and out, effortlessly.

I woke up shaky and thirsty. There was a plate with some protein bars and a water bottle next to me. Someone was outside the door. I paced, pushed on the walls, glared through the grill. The food, that I once had judged the most bland stuff imaginable, smelled stale and offensive. The water tasted flat and gave no relief. Like water one drinks in a dream, tips back and drinks until it runs down one's chest but with no relief. *No relief. No relief. No relief!*

It was beginning to get bad. I was hungry-thirsty.

I tried eating a food bar, gagged and threw up the bite in the bucket. I rinsed out my mouth with the dead water and eventually lost that too. Without realizing it, I had lost the bodily functions that were the consequence of eating and drinking. I had lost eating and drinking earlier. I tried and failed with the water one more time, and then yelled my frustration.

Not yelled. Howled. I was lying on the floor now, panting. My ribs rose and fell noisily. My fur was matted. *Gods!* I pulled myself to my feet and staggered to the door to snarl at the figure outside.

"I am a woman! I am a woman!" I was gasping, praying. My clothes hung on me; I was as thin as ever I had hoped to be. My hair now hung matted on my shoulders.

I didn't begin to call for Dagon until dawn. We were connected—we had to be. He had to help me. I knew he was there. *"Help me! Help me! Be with me! Feed me!"*

There was a faint connected feeling of sadness and regret for my suffering.

I came to on the floor where I had lain for who knows how long, legs pumping futilely, long muzzle stretched toward the door. I howled his name. "My mate, hear me. Dagon!"

More time passed. I no longer could sleep or dream. The agony was in me, every part crying out for the water of life. Energy ...

I was dying.

Dying was a slightly comforting thought, but as the hours wore on, madness seemed to be the companion that might stay with me. I was feeling in my body and mind—pain. Nothing but pain.

Eventually the door rattled open and my tormentors were in front of me, including a stricken looking Dagon.

I pulled myself up, the stretching of my tendons into human form causing more agony, to stand erect. The pain of transforming consuming me further, but I stood. I would not grovel on the floor if I had anything left in me. I picked out a wavering form that was the old woman and stumped towards her. Feet not paws, gaunt body and flapping clothes, not fur.

"*I will do this,*" I mind-spoke her. "*I will pay this too.*"

She nodded. "Pay you still may."

The others circled me. All had slim lethal needle guns. Outlawed on Earth but still popular, they could be filled with any number of substances that brought death sooner (if lucky) or later. The young woman was pointing hers at me. The man had idly put his in line with Dagon's chest.

Dagon looked like hell. I laughed, my unused voice ringing in my ears, my body reduced to bones and sinew. He didn't look as bad as I did. I laughed because I no longer cared about that or the silver toys they gestured with. *I was exempt. I was the walking dead.*

CHAPTER SEVEN

THE FINAL TEST

Somewhere within me I felt the pain and hunger that was burned into Dagon's face and knew that it mirrored my own. I knew then that he had been with me. That this was close to being over—for both of us. It was hard to think, to feel. I was still wolf bitch, uneasy with the closeness of the others, the open door tempting me to leap . . .

But I did not. I chose to stay and pay a little longer. A terrible curiosity, long my downfall, now kept me present. There was more to come. I had waited. I could wait a little longer.

"Good," said the older woman I had seen as a grey wolf. "You are with us."

It was then—oh, how could I have not sensed it before? —That I was aware of another presence. A human—food! I closed the distance between us. A young man, pale, tired and in pain — fearful, yes—but resigned as well.

The wolf within me tensed. Something was not right. *A trap! Beware!* I circled and circled him painfully. *Yes, a trap.* I turned back to Grey Woman.

Her gun was pointed at me. I pricked my ears forward. *I needed her permission, yes? She was the pack leader and she must give me permission?*

Her green eyes were on mine. "Yes. You must ask. You must have contract. You may take no more than what is allowed. No matter how great your hunger: it is the law. It is our only law."

She nodded towards the younger woman. "She has provided for you. You may take him—but not bring death."

I approached the man. Sick with hunger as I was, I was unsure how to proceed. He looked up at me, still a somebody. He deserved relief; if not pleasure, at least momentary attention and acknowledgement.

"What is your name?" I whispered.

"Daniel, Dan—look, I don't know what's going on here but I don't have much left to lose." He looked at me doubtfully. "I heard it was a high, and I don't get high anymore."

I took his hand and involuntarily took from him. He sagged against me. *So little!* Not enough. I needed more, the wolf within was wild but there was something ... wrong.

I stepped back. "He is almost dead already!" I sensed that he was a victim of one of the viral plagues, a dark energy within him that had already depleted his energy. And he was freshly taken to close to empty.

I spun around to my supposed benefactor. My tormentor—the young female Shadakon.

"Yesss. I have taken from him. Why not? Our kind rarely shares. I share with no one. But he is under lethal contract. Such as it is, you may have the rest. The plague is taking him; I merely hurried him along." She laughed.

I looked at the Grey Woman. She nodded. "You may have him. Your first kill, I would imagine."

But then I surprised them all. For I did not bend down to take the feeble life energy that I so badly needed. It was there, faintly flickering around him, as he lay quiet on the floor. It would help, would ease the scream within me, but I would not. I would take nothing from that young bitch Shadakon, now or ever. I would take on no debt with her. And so I stood before them, barely controlling my wasted body and waited for their next move.

There was an immediate jumble of psi and mind-speak, loudest of which was Dagon. *"You must take what is offered—I cannot stand your pain. Gods I had forgotten …"*

And from another, *"Would you refuse an order from the leader of the Council?"*

But from the woman who had provided him—nothing.

Just a seeping disclosure of hate and ill will. But Grey Woman smiled. *"I said she could have it. I didn't command her to take him. She declined your offer."* She smiled again. The younger woman's arrogance leaked away.

Dagon was the first to action. With a nod of approval from Grey Woman, he stepped over to Dan and matter-of-factly took what Dan did not wish to keep any longer. The stranger's colours flared briefly and then faded to ash.

I should have been more interested in this, should have had more feelings about watching my lover dispatching someone at my feet, but I did not. Pain and weariness had me and left room for nothing else. I dully wondered what the Council was and what relationships might be there. I realized that Dagon had been part of the test—that he might have destroyed me as readily as any other. *Had he too held a gun? Would he have killed me as ordered?*

He shook his head at me. *"No. Your failure would have been mine as well."*

He briefly closed his eyes. "The creation of a half-breed child is forbidden, but the Blood does flow in some family lines. It endangers us all—to have one such as yourself untried and unbound to us. We have all endured the hunt many times,"—there was a murmured assent from the others—"It has to be this way. They would not have spared me either."

His brother, kin, whatever, smiled in agreement and turned to go. "You of all of us," he said to Dagon. He looked at me with scorn, still on my feet but only through dwindling will. "Enjoy yourself," he said to Dagon.

Next to leave was the young provider. She smiled at Dagon and me, and I felt the energy of a mako shark, a tiger, or a great white. Her psi left a wake in the room of anger, disappointment, and malice. She slipped a tag on the body as she went by—a duplicate copy of the contract, listed as her kill. I briefly wondered who would ever willingly seek her out, and what she offered.

But not for long. The rest were leaving but I was wrapped in a thickening fog—cold, adrift, alone. I felt myself slipping under dark water, the unbreathable, undrinkable water taking me. I was in death, but now suspected that it would not end. That I might float here, suspended, unable to help myself. My last glimpse of the world was the green eyes of she who I had seen as a Grey Wolf. She observed me with what might have been admiration. She studied me and then turned to Dagon.

"You are both depleted and she needs much."

She held out her hands and took Dagon's and there was a brilliant flare of energy exchange. Then she left us. And I was carried up the stairs, my head on Dagon's shoulder, from that room and nightmare.

I drank deeply from the energy that had been shared. And then I slept.

CHAPTER EIGHT

SO, NOW WHAT?

I awoke to morning and Dagon still in the house—restless and waiting for me to come around. "This is where I wish I could have that cup of coffee," I grumbled. "Even ship coffee." I felt stiff and noticed that I was leaner than ever, not gaunt anymore, but long and lean like he was. It felt … right.

"We still have business with the fair and your ship." He jumped to full seriousness in mind-speaking me. "I still cannot work, and you are still missing from duty."

"I'm sorry … I totally forgot all that shit!" "Can't I just go tell them I'm fine, but that I am just too crazy to go back to work?

He surveyed me carefully. "You passed all the mandatory screening when you entered your term of service—full medical scans and body screening, etc. But now … I'm not so sure. I think you might be held long enough to go into true hunger again."

I shuddered. My mind could hardly take in the sharp fragments of memory I had of last night. They say that one doesn't remember pain, that if we did, women would never bear a second child. Of course, few humans now experienced pregnancy, labour and delivery. But that was the old way and price that women paid to bring forth life since the creation myths. And in some places they still did, accepting the pain of tissue stretching and sometimes tearing to accommodate the passage of the skull of their child. I would never do that, nor had I wanted to. But my pain may have been close if not the same. Are there shades of agony? Or, at some point, is one's whole body and mind in service of it?

What I remembered was that, for a little while, I had borne the unbearable.

We both fell silent.

I believed that he was considering things he would choose to share or not share with me. But now, again, my relentless curiosity drove me forward.

"How likely was it that I got through the trial?" I asked.

He just looked at me and shook his head.

"To my knowledge, it has never happened with someone who had not been given blood," he said flatly. "I felt your pain and the only thing I could do was not give you false hope—that I could rescue you or stop what was happening. You had to reach the point of being willing to endure—anything—and still remain conscious and able to make the crucial decision to follow our law. You had to show the understanding and discipline of contract. Had I attempted to intervene, the needle guns had charges of a poison, designed by and for my kind. They would have left me helpless in the basement of my house. Probably for a very long time."

He went very still.

"And I would not have died—and as you now realize—there are far worse things than death."

I looked at him in disbelief, the horror of it slowly forming a picture in my mind. I knew one could not imagine something or bring it closer without some contact with it. Feather of bird, a single strand of hair from a lover—this was the basis of magic. There had been a forever moment in which I realized that what I was enduring could go on and on. He already had understood that this was likely to be his fate. He had let me rail against him, accepted my misplaced hate …

For the first time since I had first taken his hand, I wept. "That was what you meant when you said, before they arrived, that there might be one way through. But we never did that!"

"Yes," he said. "But we will. I have made you mine.

Although you gave yourself as well, without being glamoured, without the sharp fear that so many bring to me. Now I wish you to make me yours."

He looked at me without looking away. He looked at me until I …

"None of that now," he laughed. "I need to ask the Council how to proceed with our immediate problems. You are not really," he smiled, "fit for human duty."

He went to the door and opened it and a small white envelope fluttered to the floor. Too small, with elegant cursive writing no less, to be an official missive. He opened it.

Consider this my gift to you both. She has been discharged from her position and all records deleted. She is no longer who she was. We will provide a new identification when a perfect match becomes available. Welcome to our people, Danu.

My chosen magical name! Fierce early goddess of Ireland. I had only spoken it to Dagon on a whim, before I had any idea of what path I was on, and where it might lead me.

Signed,

Grey Wolf (as you knew me)

Dagon and I studied the note in his hand. I felt such a rush of feelings that they piled up on each other until he shook his head at me.

"Even I can't read you right now. We'll take some time for this."

He closed the door, and gestured me to a safe distance away on a comfortable chair, while he sprawled on the couch.

"No distractions," he said, with a slight smile.

"I would think that you'd be happy," he said neutrally.

"I am," I said. "And … but now, I'm sort of dead to my life."

He raised an eyebrow.

"I mean, I didn't like my life; I always felt the outsider and as a child blamed myself for not fitting in."

I brought to my mind's eye a birthday party in my youth, a litter of wrapping paper and stupid, unwanted presents surrounding me; the guests leaving, clutching their small gift bags but not looking back. Me in tears, telling my mother that I didn't want any of it, that they didn't like me, nor I them. And then her crying, and later lecturing me about the effort she had made, the social strings she had pulled to get these particular popular children to the party. Their gifts, many pink, laid in unwanted heaps in my room until she removed them.

"Note to self," he said wryly, "no pink."

I threw a cushion at him that never reached its destination.

"But what did you want?" he asked, and I sensed that he did want to know.

"I didn't know!" I said. "Just not things and false connections. They were smirking at me. They had been made to attend, but would be busy later describing the awfulness of the party my mother had worked so hard on to get right. And my absolute indifference to them was obvious to them." I paused.

"Yeah well, that was childhood," I said, as if that could dismiss those times entirely.

He nodded. "Looking back now, what do you think you wanted?"

I stopped. I really just stopped trying to answer with the right answer. The one everyone expected of me. I freeze-framed the girl I had been, looking longingly out the window and wishing that she could just ...

"Fly away?" he asked. We both took a moment to review our flight together from the fair and later that night.

"Ummmm" ... I felt the wind against my face and my wild delight.

He smiled. "Then you have come to the right place for yourself.

It may be easier for you, born with the Blood. Many of us were turned, and remember simpler lives being human, sometimes with sadness. Some lost much." He read my confusion. "You do understand that you are not entirely human? And getting less so all the time?"

I knew that. I was aware that I did not look like my former self. That now I was lean and fast and more and more distanced from things I once tried to pretend were important.

"Like wearing clothes?" he ventured. Another pillow, but I put some energy into this one. It lightly grazed him. "And feeding on other sources such as your fellow man?" He smiled unhelpfully.

"But my parents?" By now I was trying to feel regretful, but finding it harder to hold that feeling convincingly.

"What did they think would happen to you, working in space?" he asked mildly.

"Oh ... that I would sooner or later die and they would be notified."

"This will be more mysterious and perhaps more satisfying for them," he said. "No record of you can mean many things. But generally, if they ask and there is no record, someone creates one. Because The Company doesn't like to do a search and discover that you don't exist. So you will have died in an accident, helping your crewmates, etc. Or perhaps you were working under deep cover and cannot connect with your old life anymore. It will be sufficient for your parents. You will have made them proud in death." He smiled. "These things happen."

I began to get a sense of how well the Shadakon controlled things from behind the scenes—their computer network and control that were behind many systems on many worlds.

"We learned to erase our tracks," he said dryly. "Yes. It is another skill we have gotten very good at. But only if we follow contract." He looked at me intensely and although I wanted to protest, "*I understand!*" I did not.

"Yes," he said. "You partially understand and you impressed some of those witnessing that last night. What you do not understand is that it was us who devised the contract. It is our strongest weapon against being turned against—again. Even out here, beyond your star and home planet, places to run are limited. We must be able to survive to arrive at the next town, so to speak. Ships arriving with dead or missing crew are sure to bring the wrath of those we need to live beside."

I tried to enlarge my thinking to bring into focus what he was saying.

It was not the Company who were protecting their crews as much as … it was the contract that protected the Shadakon. The contract was from them, for them, and they would punish any of their kind who broke it in such ways that would discourage others from doing so.

"Yes."

"Hunger nor rage cannot be a reason to break contract," I said. I did not say, but thought, "*Or love.*"

"Yes," he said.

"So … are you free?"

He looked at me with his own mixture of feelings.

"I have existed for a long, long time," he said. "There were times when we were '*free*' to do as we would. Some killed beyond need, for sport and bloodlust. Human wars covered those activities well. Taking blood is the ultimate pleasure for some of us."

I thought of him, holding back from me, telling me he must honour something that I might not. I remembered his anger at my inability to understand, to feel what he had struggled with. He had showed me something important. It would have been easier for me at that moment not to know.

"Yes. It is easier when dealing briefly with people. I glamour them; I excite them enough to take what I need. And then I often wash them with forgetfulness, as if I had not happened, as if they had never seen me, never felt the flare of excitement that I brought to them."

He stopped. I had never made a kill. He did not want to tell me more about this now.

"But you let me remember!" I said.

"Well, you saw me, invited me, with some inner understanding of what I was. You asked me my name! You gave me your most secret name! And within only minutes of meeting me." He smiled. "You flew fearlessly without me having to drag you along. And you wanted me and did not pull back after you glimpsed my true nature."

We both sat quietly across from each other, wordless, without mind-speaking. It was a peaceful moment, although I did note that we were both still depleted and needing energy.

"This doesn't happen to you often?"

He shook his head. "You don't understand yet. It doesn't happen to any of us '*often*'—or at all! I've lived for—" he shook his head, "… sometimes I feel, too long. Over and over to meet and woo and bed, if I chose to not just take and leave, but then leave sooner or later because the neighbours had noticed something 'otherly' about me. Or have my partner among those screaming for my death, driving me out into the sun if they could."

"To be hated and wished dead," he said. "Over and over."

"And when I screamed I hated you?" It had to be said.

"I knew you did not," he said. "But that was part of my trial as well. If you failed, I would have died the True Death in time—or been eventually revived out of my agony, if and when the Council saw fit. I would have accepted that fate, knowing that I had acted against my kind, endangered them, as well as you and me. That … I had been a fool."

I crossed over to him then. Our lean bodies fit together differently than I had ever experienced before. I felt both of our respective energies flare, like northern lights they flickered in the room around us. We blended and shared all of what we had. It was not a place of wild exhilaration.

But it was good; very, very good. And there was more to come.

CHAPTER NINE

SURPRISINGLY, LIFE GOES ON

In the afternoon, Dagon was notified that he was reinstated in his position at the fair and hurried off.

I spent the first day free of my space contract and old life trying to make a list of what I needed now. In no particular order: something to wear besides the provided robe. Wearing nothing was now pleasing to me, now that my body had assumed a honed look. It was doubtful that anyone would suspect that I was, or had been, the dumpy shorthaired spacer who had wandered around at the fair, drawing the attention of the company guide, but not really anyone else. I stopped at that thought.

Well, one "anyone else." The one person on this world or any other that I might have wished to meet, if I believed that such a thing was possible. But meanwhile Dagon had suggested that I stay inside until I had a watertight ID. Being a nobody in an advanced society meant you were up to no good. Which meant someone would certainly lock me up while they tried to figure out who I was. I had no interest in being confined ever again. But people might come to the door? His door?

I wasn't sure that it would be wise to order clothes delivered to his address and I could not go and shop in the boutiques around the fair. What they offered were more like costumes anyway. For the first time in my life I fancied something that swirled around me, something to go with my swirling dark-red hair. Hmmm. I might need clothes just so—I could shed them later. Or he could remove them slowly. And shoes—I didn't want to wear my company issue shoes. Onward then.

I needed the comfort of a weapon when I was outside.

I still had my service issue gun, but it would be incredibly unwise to draw and point it in anyone's sight. Much less shoot someone with it. Besides, did I want to wear a belt that accommodated a weapon of significant weight? Even the thought of it made me feel encumbered. But perhaps a blade? I went over and studied the tapestry and the familiar figure that sat beside the queen. He played his music for her alone and she bent closer to hear, to sense the strange draw that she had never before encountered, even though troubadours had intimate access to some of their patrons. Had she later yelled for his death while fearing for her own? Across his shoulder was a thin leather thong that dipped over one hip where a small sheath hung. The hilt of the blade was simply crafted with one rounded, red stone gleaming there.

Could I really be seeing this in the details of a tapestry? I shook my head and looked again. The details, although rich, dissolved into threads and colours. I saw no knife. I saw no stone.

OK. I would consider a small weapon. I wasn't sure if my newfound physical powers included fighting off more than one person at a time. There was a time that I had practised with throwing knives. It was a skill I had never really needed, but it pleased me to pull the blade out of the centre of the target, over and over.

I did not need gadgets or cooking utensils. I did not need groceries.

This line of thought brought me to the final item on my list: I needed a job. Everyone had one, even vampires. What was I going to do?

And would I continue to live here? Should I assume that Dagon wanted me as a permanent houseguest? He had said that he was glad to have met me, to share with me. He said that he wanted me to make him my own.

I had never wanted to have anyone of my "own." The shield that protected me from the indifference and casual cruelties of those around me also hid something from me.

I pretended at times to be upset over their lack of interest. But I had never wanted to come together with anyone for any length of time. Ever. Perhaps it would be me that chose to move on? The thought made me shiver. I wanted—this. I wanted—him. I wanted to find out what having the Blood would mean to me.

How had this happened? How had I happened? It had probably been an event that occurred rarely. A thought crossed my mind like a cold draft. Perhaps babies from fathers of the night were created and some even born, but seldom survived. It was likely that a woman accused of consorting with a demon or vampire who became pregnant was consigned to the flames with her child, born or unborn, by her neighbours or village priest. I had always assumed that at least one of the watching men knew the true parentage of that coming child. But maybe not.

Perhaps the twisted, crazed rambling of the Malleus Maleficarum, the Hammer of God, an official torture manual used by the witch finders to catalogue the most useful methods, also held an under-story of women burned and torn apart, to prevent them from preserving an unaccounted for and unholy child. But some far-ago mother somehow preserved herself and her demon child. Even if it cost her everything. She was my ancestor, I her progeny. I briefly gave thanks to her.

I was on the computer when Dagon came home. I could immediately sense that he had fed well. He also had several boxes under one arm, and a carefully wrapped sheath of flowers. He dumped them down and crossed the distance to me.

How could I wonder if he wanted me here? There was no hesitation in him and none in me. We used mind-speak more now, and could hear each other more clearly than before. He looked at me, then at the tapestry.

"You have been looking into things, which may not be timely for you to know. All people—ourselves included—may want to feel that the bond between them and their current lover does not admit past lovers. But you cannot hold me responsible for the many lives that

I've moved through … So, yes. I cared for her and she, perhaps more than was safe, for me. It was a long time ago but I will not forget her.

He stopped. *"And that has to be enough."*

He tipped my head back and looked directly into me. Past my eyes, past any impulse to block him. I felt the centre of him, a radiating mandala of energy. It drew me in, and I went gladly. We stood, rocking slightly, as if in a small boat on a calm, limitless sea.

"You are my now," he said, stepping back. "And I have brought something that you can choose if you wish to not to wear that robe." He gestured to the boxes.

I had never seen clothes like this before, and if I had, I would have assumed that I would look foolish wearing them, even if I secretly wanted to. One was an over tunic and wide pants made from gossamer in grey dusk with a hint of purple. It flowed out of the box and settled in my lap like a cat.

The next box held a garment suitable for … flying? It, too, was a dusky colour, once called ashes of roses. It swirled and floated to end just below my knees. *Silky. Could it be silk? A king's ransom!*

He had been busy taking the flowers out of their delicate wrapping and installing them in a tall vase. Blood red roses they were, almost black and giving off an intoxicating scent. When he turned back to me I was enveloped in twilight softness that swirled when I moved. I moved in a way I had seen others do the night before; much like observing someone under a strobe light, in which the person appears motionless, and yet moves from point to point in the blink of an eye.

I drifted across the floor, never seeming to move. He just watched me with silence within.

Finally he said, "You are a good observer and quick student. It would seem that you are discovering many talents." And then he said, "You are so beautiful …" and stopped as if he could not go on.

I twirled and arrived in a heartbeat in front of him.

"You must understand that I am as amazed as you. It began as a pleasant game that neither of us wished to stop. You were under contract, and I trusted that I could keep to it. I did until it came time to take you to the edge for the last time and return you to the fair, wiped of your experiences." He paused. "Or end you."

I remembered that night. I remembered that he had been deeply angry with me. Because it was easy for me—I was in bliss and not caring about tomorrow. And then I also remembered the night I offered to him that which he wanted above all else—to take my blood. And he took, but not more than was safe for me. I remembered his joy that I was a present and willing lover. I awoke in the morning, surprised somewhat to be alive. More alive than I had ever been.

"And now you will know more of that," he said calmly. "Because we will enact the old Blood Ritual tonight and I will share more than energy with you. I will give you of myself. It will change you, even more than the Trial did. I believe I know the answer, but I must ask, do you want this? You must say it."

We were no longer in the living room and I saw the flowers glowing like dark rubies beside the pelt we lay on. I no longer had my dancing outfit on and he was bare and smooth in the near darkness.

"Do you remember when I said to you, 'You must be prepared to do what you ask me to do?'" I asked huskily. He nodded.

"Do *you* want this? You must say it."

I heard "Yes" and I heard a moan that I knew was not pain.

"I do not know how to do this," I said honestly. "When we, when you ... you seemed to have sharp teeth. I do not know how to gain entry."

He offered me two ways. He could make a small wound in his own hand, or I could remember my wolf nature and the teeth that I had licked in frustration as I circled Dan, in the last and critical part of my trial. They had been long and sharp and I had wanted to turn and bite deeply into the young woman who had tried the last thing she could do to guarantee my failure. I nodded.

I evoked the wolf bitch; but tonight she was strong and healthy and knew what to do. I took his hand in mine, turned it palm up and drove those keen teeth into him. There was a welling of deep red blood that I stared at fascinated.

"Take!" he said huskily.

I pressed now-human lips to his hand. I wasn't sure that I could or would take, but it was like ...

It was like nothing else. It was like riding the hurricane, laughing, never coming down. I took and I knew him in a kaleidoscope of images and feelings that entered me.

I stopped before he stopped me, and he smiled. "Good! You are a good bride," he said. "This is our honeymoon and it can last ... forever. Or until the stars fall. Or one of us is incautious. Or ..."

I laid my slightly reddened finger against his lips. I fell into him and him into me, and we pulled and pushed the energy that was us into a great golden ball. It blazed and then glimmered until my eyes closed and I found the peace I hadn't believed in.

CHAPTER TEN

BUT WHO AM I NOW, AND WHAT MUST I DO?

I was afraid to open my eyes the next day. Where we had gone and my becoming one with Dagon could not be matched in day-to-day living. I still used the word "living" because my impression was that I was still alive.

Very, very much alive. I fed on living energies no less than a human does when eating starlight that some hardworking plant had gathered and encompassed into its seeds or flesh. There are a few beings on Earth—and probably out here—that did not feed on other beings. Those few lived as simple organisms in black smokers, volcanic vents deep under the sea. Or as bacteria that lived very slow lives in seemingly inhospitable pools and mud. But the rest of us must eat someone else; even plants require the nourishment of once-recycled organic nitrogen.

Just as the farmer is unwise if he doesn't allow his crop to go to seed and put some away for the next planting, so the Shadakon were in a life-death balance with humans. If they could use other alien races, I was not aware of it. But I understood their relationship with what I had thought of as "us"—us humans—better now.

Take too much, and the community starves. Be indifferent shepherds, and the humans would perish or scatter and the Shadakon would be forced to move on and on, often with scant reaping. To perhaps wander in the desert in harsh circumstances. A whisper of a memory rose up. *"Remember the sands of Africa."*

I wanted to know more about the clan that I had asked admission to, and who had claimed me. I wanted to know how I had come to be this way, with enough Old Blood to be able to transform, aided only by energy. Before, I had had little curiosity about my family line but now I did. Did I have far-removed reclusive cousins or unacknowledged loner family members?

How many humans carried the genes that hid behind the human facade? All babies were scanned before birth now of course, to assure that they carried no undesirable genes. But unexpected traits still showed up, perhaps hidden amoung the "junk genes."

The legacy of Shadakon, how did it persist? How far back in the history of humanity had it entered our human bloodline?

I was still on the computer when Dagon returned home. He looked weary, but was curious about what I was chasing now—family lineage charts, medieval accounts of dancing and sexing with the devil; shamans who could fly, or become and see through the eyes of an animal.

My mind was full of data that might be true, half-true, or merely malicious lies made up by the church so that they could appropriate the land of witches—usually women who had outlived their male protectors. Or the solitary witch living on the edge of the village, who people came to with their wishes to secure the attention of a lover, or get rid of a child he may have given them on a summer full moon night. Or be helped to deal with pain, or illness, or the wish for a peaceful death. They came by night and later said little of the help they had received.

But when the church was determined to rid an area of people who held and practiced older beliefs, the tide turned against them. They ran or died at the hands of their neighbours. The women, some no doubt of the Blood, were the wild cards, and could not be tolerated. The sons of the Shadakon might live long enough to blend into armies and groups of migrating humans.

Dagon turned me toward him and smiled. "There is no crash course in our history. Would you know it all now if you could? We are a selfish and fierce group and have shaped the history of Earth for a very long time. You cannot begin to guess how long. And how could you understand, you, who have yet to make a kill?"

He stopped then and looked directly at me. "You have learned to hone your control over your whole life, and that training saved your life and mine in your trial. You have joined me in as much abandon as was possible for you—and I have gloried in it. But you have never taken all of a person's life energy and felt it extinguish as you took the last drop, leaving a husk behind. I will not make you do that, although I thought you would cross that line in your extreme need. I partially understand why you turned away from accepting the young man dying at your feet—you did not want to be beholden—but that was not the only reason, I think."

We looked at each other. The silence grew. I did have questions but probably feared the answers.

He did not turn away from this topic, much as I would have wanted him to. He was well aware of the questions brought up by his own.

"Yes," he said. "You never asked me and I gave you many opportunities. You said, I believe, 'I will not judge you or myself.' It was a good answer, especially at the time. But is it a true answer now?"

"Do not answer hastily," he said. "Much may ride on this in our future. And not just between you and me. Were you alert enough to hear the mind-speak of the council members when you refused the kill?"

I nodded. I did remember, and felt that Grey Wolf had somehow protected me from that judgement.

"Yes, she did," he said. "She is head of the Council and can interpret the law. Had you failed to keep contract, she could not and would not have protected you from your fate. But others were not so happy. "You took on a very powerful woman," he said. "She and you are not over your animosities. You did not take what admittedly was a dangerous 'gift.'

You were an untested person seeking through the trial to join the clan. A person who had lived—thirty-five years? Forty? You stood her down in front of her peers.

She is thousands of years old. You are brave, but you are also a risk-taker." He smiled. "But we established that early on."

I stayed with this. "Yes, I did not take the residue of Dan's life. It was there for the taking. But I will have to do that," I said reluctantly. "I cannot be your mate if I expect you to feed me from others and not question the rightness of that."

"Yes," he said. "For now, I will provide. But what if one day I do not return? Or worse, what if one day you decide that you are not what you are, that you are a pacifist vampire?" He smiled coldly. "The clan would not accept such a person. We are hunters and humans are our source of life. You came to me, perhaps unknowingly, not treasuring your own life. I would have enjoyed all of it." He met my eyes. "I do not kill often, but never reluctantly. You were closer to death in my arms than any dangerous situation you have ever been in. You had signed the contract."

I knew all of this, or thought I did, but I let it sink in, without responding. I knew what I should say: that I would do what I must do. That the changes that I had asked for, had endured for, had brought me this far, but there was more that I must know and become skilled at.

"Yes," he said. "But you still have some time."

After our conversation I felt unsettled, unsure where I stood. I needed to sort out how I would handle killing. I had shot someone once, a man in a crowd who was randomly using his weapon on the strangers around him. There was a young woman, a girl, unmoving on the pavement. I shot him, and not so he would be available to be questioned later. There were no questions asked of me, I had status as a spacer. I never found out if she had lived.

I only know that he had not.

This was different. I thought it was different. *Was* death different under different circumstances?

I thought of Dagon and the incredible pleasure I had felt, even as he weighed whether or not to continue to my end. Once again I was awed by the fact that I had awoke in the morning. That he had chosen to leave me alive over—over what? That was what I could not know. I only knew that I doubted that I could or would give the gift of pleasure to strangers, even in a slight form, such as he did. He was a player, and played erotically with his prey. They asked for more, and with a no-kill contract he usually demurred. But when someone signed that lethality clause, then yes...

I shook my head, trying to dispel a feeling that I had never experienced about a human—jealousy?

I had never felt I had anything to lose or fight for in my comings and goings with them. This was different and deeply disturbing. *Did I want to keep my lover from actions that I might not like? Did I expect or want him to restrict his true nature?* I was not proud of these thoughts.

He was behind me before I knew it and he had heard my musings. I knew that too. I felt disloyal and mean-hearted. *What a terrible emotion to lug around!*

He turned me to face him, and smiled, and it was a gentle smile.

"This is all new for you," he said. You will come to understand what I cannot just tell you."

I thought of my trial and shivered."Yes," he said. "You had to act genuinely. You do now as well. I will just say this. I told you that we, Shadakon, rarely chose mates.

And I told you that we were a selfish and fierce people. I, perhaps, am kinder than some, but you have seen me and know me for the predator I am."

I remembered him over me, with the lithe body and eyes of a panther.

He nodded. "Just so," he said calmly. "And if you had begged for your life, it would have been easy to take it."

He looked within me to see how I reacted to that information. I knew it already. I had given myself to him without fear of death. But the togetherness was so powerful ...

"Just so, lusty wench," he said. "But now you know I went against my nature and my clan and put myself in jeopardy of a living death, poisoned and incapacitated in my basement. You didn't ask me to do that. You didn't know what my decision involved. That's how powerful our 'togetherness' was for me!"

I thought, yet again, of my railing against him. Of accusing him of being part of a horrible torture scenario that I could not understand. I brought to mind saying that I hated him.

"Yes. That was my dark time, although your pain eclipsed mine. But I will say it once more and then perhaps we can let it go: I knew you were angry and frightened, but I could feel your heart calling out to me even as you spoke. And that last morning, when you howled my name and begged me to come ..." He shook his head. "I have been betrayed and I have suffered from that. But I knew you ... loved me, even as you starved and moved towards your death. I never doubted you. I could not help you. That was the worst of everything so far. There are many reasons beyond our natures that we do not partner. One is that we might see the other helpless, as I saw and felt you. We set aside whatever love is, and walk alone in the world. We cannot hurt anyone that way, except our prey. And even that is different, as you will find out."

And then we set aside talking, and after awhile, thinking.

He came to me and I to him in a blaze of sex and energy that left us both spent on the floor of the living room.

It was at this moment, the doorbell rang.

I didn't expect for him to have a doorbell; it seemed like a politeness unnecessary for someone who could easily read who was outside the door. He threw me one of my pleasure outfits and nodded at the door. Hair hanging in a tangle, feeling incredibly unready for greeting anyone, I nevertheless went and opened it.

Grey Wolf Woman was standing patiently outside. I wondered how long she had been standing there. She smiled. She did not enter.

"Ah ... yes. Please enter if you wish," I said. I stepped aside and she came in.

"It is time for you to call me by another name, Danu," she said. "My name is Morag. I understand that you saw me in the form of a wolf at the time of your trial, and the image stuck in your mind. I saw you as a wolf as well."

I thought of what I remembered at the end. Muzzle to the door, howling, starving.

"Just so," she said. "But a survivor for all that. But I came to bring you something. Something that will open the door for you."

She smiled. "An ID, which will never be questioned and is, as much as can be, totally genuine. You are now Althea,"—she rattled off two more names—"I suggest you practice answering to it. As for you old name and old self, they are gone. You do know how your appearance has changed? And your presence in the world has as well?" She asked, referring to the activities that were going on when she arrived. "No one could possibly recognize you as the human you were. And if anyone who you cross paths with seems to have even a glimmer of recognition, you can glamour him and wipe away that thought with another."

She smiled again. "Sexual attraction is good for so many situations."

"Who was Althea? Before I became her I mean?" I asked.

"Oh, a spacer woman, much like you were, who died under deep cover. But of course, she was not in a reportable situation and so she did not have a reportable death. So the records show that she was unstable after her last assignment. It was once called a post-trauma reaction. They may have another name now. She suicided and we, ah, assumed custody of the body before it was allowed to be found. We made some adjustments to agree with your physical attributes—hair colour, etcetera. She was washed out of the service with no details to be given out to any surviving family. You are now truly free to walk under the sun and stars. Or perhaps fly." She smiled again.

I wondered what she did *not* know about me and us.

"I am Leader of the Council and the clan on this planet. I make it my business to know what all of you are doing. A lot of us noticed YOU, however." This was directed at Dagon. "We allowed you to make your decisions, no matter how unwise they seemed. I have lived long enough to know that one cannot predict whether a thing is good or bad. There were some that wanted to bring you both in earlier and force an end to your growing connection. I prevailed. You still had time remaining on the contract. It has turned out … interestingly. I am content with the outcome, even if others may not be." Here she mind-spoke to Dagon something that I could not hear. He grew very still. "But enough of all this. You, Danu, must be ready to go outside and see if there is work that you might do. I will pick you up tomorrow morning to show you a place where you might be useful and that would suit you."

"You are to come as well," she said, nodding at Dagon. "I think this will work."

I froze inside.

Was tomorrow the day that I would be confronted by the need to make a kill? I wasn't ready! I didn't know what it would take to get me ready. I heard Dagon, refraining from saying or obviously thinking anything. I had heard that silence before, when he said his last words to me before my trial. There were things he did not want to indicate to me now. And he did not.

Grey Woman—Morag—smiled again. "You hear and sense more than even I expect of you. Silence can be telling. But rest easy, there is nothing that will be forced on you tomorrow. I am taking you to a potential job site. You will be good at it, or not. I am counting on you being very good at it. But I do not predict as much as watch keenly."

"Enjoy yourselves," she said, still smiling. "May you have a long run together." And then she let herself out, and was gone.

CHAPTER ELEVEN

OFF TO WORK

The next morning found me wearing what might loosely pass as presentable to the world—hair pulled back and in the same loose white shirt and dark pants that Dagon wore. In fact, I found that I could wear one of his shirts and, with a double roll at the pants hem, his pants, as well. I had found a soft pair of slipper-like shoes of Dagon's too.

He studied me. "Note to self, different kinds of clothes. But now you can go shopping for your own clothes." He smiled. "Not that you ever loved shopping and accumulating things. But a well-chosen few are necessary. Today though, this will do."

I had burned my clothes and everything else I had used or carried. I had gone out with Dagon to an old fire pit in his backyard where I buried my gun deep in the ground and doused my uniform with some brandy I found in his house. It burned hot. I imagined all the pain of my ordeal and the drudgery of my old life, burning blue in the flames, returning to their basic units of carbon and such—free to recirculate into the world of the living again. I had done this instinctively as a troubled teen. I took the hurtful messages from my father (short notes left for me on the table before I left for school—*I am disappointed in your ...*) and the garments my mother gave me, hoping that I would relent and become more like the daughter she had hoped for. I had burned them surreptitiously and scattered the ashes. I thought then that perhaps my otherness had been that I was a witch. Or something like a witch.

I was beginning to realize that I had not been so wrong.

Morag arrived as the sun rose above the horizon and Dagon opened the door and invited her in. I noticed that he made a slight gesture that might have been a bow. She surveyed me, taking in the too-long pants and inappropriate footwear and sighed. "Good enough," she said.

"I could not have expected him to provide appropriate clothing."

Dagon smiled at the truth of that.

There was a small flitter, the equivalent of a flying taxi, waiting outside on the street, with a mind-silent driver who didn't turn to face us when we got in. I sensed him carefully and realized that I knew him. He had been the male who came to Dagon's house for my trial. He was a Council member then? Another part of this clan, I decided.

We went swiftly, just skimming above the tops of buildings and avoiding the spaceport and its traffic. For the first time I wondered, where were the people or beings that called this home? Who were "The People" before the humans came? There was greenness stretching away outside the city limits with no signs of buildings or farming. Perhaps still out there? I hoped that they could hold their own against us, the humans.

Identifying with humans now puzzled me. I was no longer one of them, but, I reminded myself, most of Morag's clan would not completely identify me as one of them either.

At that thought the driver turned and made brief eye contact and then allowed me to hear his under-thoughts. It confirmed my speculations: *I had been accepted and passed the trial, but I was ignorant and untried. He wondered if Dagon was tired of me yet.* At this Dagon stiffened almost imperceptibly, but said and thought nothing. I suspected that my translation of his thoughts had not been a complete one.

Morag put up her hand. "Civility, civility is required. Only that. But always that."

The car got very quiet after that.

Soon enough—too soon for me—we dropped out of the sky and into the back area of a building surrounded by trees and fragrant flowering bushes. It seemed to be a peaceful place, with the sounds of the small lives murmuring and trilling unseen around it.

I relaxed slightly.

We went forward and a human woman gowned in soft grey draped material met us at the door. She was welcoming and, seemingly, expecting us. Morag dismissed the driver, having made some unheard-by-me arrangements with him.

We entered. There were a handful of humans here, all suffering. Pain surrounded me from all sides as I walked behind our guide. Some of it was dull, blunted by strong painkillers. Some came in waves, allowing the host to feel almost normal again before he or she retched or stiffened again, and again.

"We will explain this to her now," Morag said, indicating me. "She may be what you seek—a healer and also one who can ease or end pain and inflict none doing so. She does not yet know if she is suited to this, or how skilled she may be."

The woman nodded. I sensed in her a deep quiet, rarely broken by speech. She did not carry the pain she walked through, but moved seemingly untouched by it. She was obviously a woman of some spiritual practise that allowed her to do this. I was impressed.

She looked at me for a long moment and asked, "Are you accepting, Althea? This is a final place, where people face what cannot be changed. They may experience healing—either temporarily through pain relief, or as a result of coming to peace with what is coming—or they may not. It is not ours to judge how another should face what is coming for them. We give what can be given. But sometimes their suffering is long and they eventually ask for relief from their lives. This we cannot do. This is why we have called you to work with us. We only ask that you do not step outside of our guidelines and attempt to tell another how to live or die."

Her blue eyes looked at me and although it was not the same as with the clan, I knew she saw me deeply. I was willing for her to do so.

After the moment passed I asked, "But surely there are doctors who would administer death? It's done all the time."

"Yes," she said. "But it is granted surrounded by the drama and intensities of a medical ward. A doctor who would not *be* with them"—she emphasized, "at the loneliest time of their lives. They come here instead, seeking final true peace. With someone who is with them to the end."

There were no judgements hidden in her statements, and, again, I was impressed. *A hospice with humans and those of the clan working together? Was this possible?* I wondered.

"It remains to be seen," said Morag.

"Give us a moment," she said, and the woman nodded silently and left us. Morag studied me carefully. "You dimly remember working as one who practised the Craft?"

I nodded. What I had was dreams of bonfires and gatherings in the woods. Of living alone and being sought out as the village wise woman. Perhaps dancing with a tall, dark winged one, as an energy cone rose and rose into the night sky. I had thought that I had those dreams because of the various books I had read, and information that I had sought—that they had entered into me and I had made them mine by appropriation. Now I was not so sure.

"Yes," said Morag, speaking her point aloud as Dagon often did. "You healed when you could." She paused.

I nodded.

"You gave relief when you could do no more. Even before you knew what you were, or what you were doing. People died at your hands." She said this matter-of-factly. "When the tide turned against you and all others like you, who would not enter the church and swear allegiance to the sky god and his son, you were separated from the protection of your village and kin.

Your neighbours and the clergy remembered what you did, and they imagined far worse than what you would do. During the burning times two million or more people died in a sparsely populated world. Most were women," she added. "Many were as you are."

"But that was not me!"

Morag shrugged. "The Blood carries its history with it," she said. "Here you will be protected. Here there is contract and it will have been arranged before you meet your ... client. Here you can find your own way to heal or ease pain with your own energy, or to take theirs."

She glanced at Dagon, who had been totally silent since we entered this place. "You will decide. The Mothers will monitor you. If you cannot do this, or if you inflict more suffering than the people here already must contend with, she will call us."

"We will then have to find something else for you. Because you cannot live off Dagon indefinitely." She looked at him briefly. "He is sometimes in deficit. You know this, but have not wanted to face that fact. He needs all his strength and wits about him!"

"The two of you," she continued softly, "will have to protect each other and yourselves. He could not do so at your trial, and he may not be able to do so later. I welcomed you, Danu, and I have trust in you. While I am present and in my power, I will stand by you. But I may not always to be able to do so."

We were all silent for a moment, thinking of what had been said. There was no argument to be made, no defences, no attempting to avoid what was and might come into being.

"Dagon will observe you today," said Morag. "He needs to know that you can do the work in your own way. No hot flirtations and raising the sex energy for you as a daily job. Perhaps you can teach us all ... compassion ... without refusing our true nature."

"Perhaps you have already begun that transformation?" She looked at Dagon.

"Whatever happens today will be sufficient. There is no direction to take life, even though the contract has been signed, as you well know." And now her gaze fell directly on and into me.

The Mother arrived almost as silently as we could.

"I want to introduce you to someone here," the grey-robed woman said.

CHAPTER TWELVE

WHEN DEATH CAN BE LOVE—OR SOMETHING ELSE AS TENDER

The Mother led me down an empty hall and into a room with one occupant. The window covering was pushed aside and a light breeze blew through the room. It was a pleasant space, and beyond the window were many colours of green and the scents of unknown flowers.

I was aware that Dagon was nearby, but I purposefully shut him out—if not entirely out. (*Could I ever shut out someone who was now part of me?*) But out at least to the point that he knew not to interact with me. I would need all my wits about me; I would need to find my own way, if there was a way for me …

By the time I focused on the person propped up in a bed strewn with pillows and a light blue cover, she was already taking note of me.

Momentarily I thought that this would be a pleasant place to nap, perhaps to read or write.

But the woman in the bed was neither napping nor any other activity that required her attention. She looked up at me with both hope and anger—a lot of anger—although it did not show on her face.

The Mother approached and took her thin hand. I noted a slight flinch from the woman, although the touch was light and brief. She introduced us. Her name was Lara and my name, oh yeah, it was Althea. Even though I came as what I was, the outside world was not to know my inner name for now. That pleased me.

Then the Mother left us, leaving the door ajar as it had been.

We looked at each other without speaking. I noted that she was guarding what she wanted me to know about her. A test then. But more than that, she did not trust me. Why should she? Everything should be carefully negotiated then.

She would let me know what, if anything, would occur between us.

A fleeting thought crossed my mind, while I honoured her silence. I saw in my mind's eye, Dagon at the fair, observing me before I approached him with the welter of feelings I had carried with me. Again I saw the patience that he held throughout the interaction that occurred before a word was spoken between us.

In the time it took me to recall that—instantaneously? between breaths?—she beckoned me closer.

"Yes." I smiled a genuine smile. It wasn't Dagon's, but he had taught me. It was my own. It acknowledged her curiosity and courage. It encouraged the beginning of … connection.

I could feel energy rising in my body and the aura that we all project around us. When I closed the distance to the bed, our energies merged slightly. I saw the widening of her eyes in acknowledgment. She was, perhaps, an empath, more so than most of our kind. *Her* kind.

"Tell me what you can tell is happening here. To me." She spoke in a whispery voice, although I could hear a husky contralto. She was a singer perhaps, or had been one.

I needed to find my place here. *She was everyone she had ever been. If I saw her as broken, I could not connect. Could not help her. Could not help myself.*

Again my thoughts went to Dagon. From the moment that I realized that I was drawn to him (and it was well after he realized that), I felt beautiful in his eyes. Worth smiling at, even if it turned out that I would insist on seeing it only as a mild flirtation or something fearful and move away.

But there had been no genuine flirtations in my life, and his had been the only one I wanted to respond to.

This was the key then, for Lara and I: I must find her beautiful.

A woman walking proudly to the end of her life. That I had time, that *we* had time to share something significant together.

"May I draw closer? I asked. I figured that covered some version of her welcoming me into her home. Because her home was now this room, this bed with a view of the rich life outside, going on without her.

I felt her anger flare again. That she might need something from a stranger. That she was helpless to say no.

"Your life is your own," I said. "I will sit quietly, or leave if you wish. This morning's visit can be as long as you wish it to be."

She really focused on me then. "They said you might take my pain away. Or perhaps take me from the pain …"

I did not acknowledge that immediately, nor did I answer her questions. I would, but now I actually didn't know what could be done, including the latter.

"Let me scan you," I said quietly. Again the flinch. "I will not touch your body." I smiled gently again.

So much was becoming clearer to me. The patience required, the tact, the quiet disarming while moving nearer. But most of all, that one can like and even love what one might take and use to one's own purposes, as well as meet the other's needs. So it is in love and sex for its many purposes.

I started at her feet. They were cold and twisted. The nerves that were designed to carry messages up and down, to coordinate walking, dancing, could no longer send their information uneventfully. The returning messages were a constant scream of alarm and pain. "*Something is wrong, something is wrong!*" I proceeded up.

Her legs were wasted and there was a fine almost continuous tremor. Pain here too. Her hands and arms—I had already observed her flinch from being touched. Her fingers moved almost imperceptibly, opening and closing as if she struggled to let go of what had her. It was not going to let go and she knew it. It had settled in, consuming her and what she had been.

I nodded. Then her torso. Her organs were shutting down, and the sounds and signs of life were slight. I doubted that she could eat and perhaps not even drink.

I nodded again. I was looking at her as I did what I did. Her grey-green eyes were locked on me as I learned what was happening within her body.

At last I went to her face and head. Again, those intense eyes; they refused to close even as I passed my hands over them. It occurred to me that perhaps she could no longer see. Or see much of this world anyway. I didn't ask. It didn't matter between us.

"I am finished," I said. "I do not have the words for what is happening to you, but great damage has occurred. Have you had medical attention?"

She laughed bitterly. "I did not get here in a week or even a year, Healer. They have done what they could."

"Yes." Once again I thanked Dagon in my mind for what I had learned from him.

"Can you help me?"

I sensed this was too big of a first step for her, and for me as well.

"I can perhaps dampen your pain, for a while. Let us start with that."

I quieted myself. I invoked Quan Yin, the Chinese goddess of healing and mercy. I had learned about her in my earlier life during the years I had holed up in my room. She was a healer, an ancient Chinese goddess. I had even ordered a small statuette.

She had arrived in a small box and as I lifted her out, her calm ceramic face looking up at me, I noticed that one of her hands was an empty socket. In the box, I found various hands, all holding a different tool, necessary for a specific task. I could no longer remember what the various hands held, but I was pretty sure that none of them held death.

I moved back to Lara's feet and legs. Using my own energy, I quieted the screaming nerves, moving up and then to her arms and the rest of her. I paused at her face and wide-open eyes.

"Do you wish to rest or sleep?" I asked.

She shook her head. "Every moment counts now," she whispered.

Then I knew that she did not want to let go of her life, that she was being forced to make a decision dependent on what she could continue to endure. She was in her own trial. I didn't know if there was a chance of her succeeding at it, or whether she would receive peace at the end. I hoped she would, although I had never given such thoughts much credence in my previous life. I had never asked Dagon, or found out in my studies, what the Shadakon believed, if anything, about an "after."

Perhaps, I thought, I should find out what she believed, what might continue to hold her in her increasing pain and helplessness.

"There are many answers to the question I am going to ask you," I said. "All of them may be right. But what do you see before you?"

She shook her head, and I saw one tear, sparkling and then sliding down her pale cheek.

"I don't believe in anything!" There was heat in this, and I suspected many had asked her this, and then tried to move her place of truth to their own.

I said nothing. As Morag had told me, there is a lot of information in what is not said.

We sat with her statement. A breeze entered the room, bringing green-scented air with it.

This might be all that happens today, I thought. I will not push her, as I well remember how that felt all my life.

"Yes," I said.

But then she surprised me, as humans must surprise themselves, each other, and us—when they set aside wants and hopes, and all the negative expectations gained over a life time, and then speak their truth.

"Sometimes I hear a song," she whispered. "I believe it is from Earth and now from this world. I have heard in my dreams, heard it on the high plains of fever and pain that plagued me since my youth. I cannot explain it, cannot hum it. It was sung to me, but it is not mine. They came to me,"—my senses prickled—"I begged to leave with them but they said they had to go. That I could not go with them."

There was a wistful feeling in her now that had replaced her anger.

"They said I could not go with them, because I was alive."

I thought of the myths of the faerie. Of people who were visited, seduced, invited to a night of revelling that lasted a hundred years. I thought of the stories of people who lived to tell the story of being lured out onto the moors or unexpected meetings in oak grove or on lonely highways. Of people and the songs and stories they wrote that suggested pleasures beyond bearing.

"I can still hear it sometimes," she said, slightly turning her head towards the window. "I hope ..."

She became silent.

Although I had not achieved the larger goal that I still faced, I was content.

"I will come again later," I said.

She smiled.

I walked out of the room and was joined by the Mother in the hall. She matched her steps with mine.

I was heading back to the room where I hoped Dagon and Morag still waited.

Saying only—"I'll be back in a little while"—she left me, as I had found the door unaided. My sense of direction worked in buildings as well as wider spaces. There is no moss growing on the north side of anything when one is underwater or outside in space. One had tools, of course, but they were not infallible.

They were standing and waved me in. Morag shut the door.

I could not hear anything from Dagon and that unnerved me. However, I was good with what I had done. Whether it was what anyone else wished of me ... that was a question that would soon be answered.

I felt depleted, though not much more than the slight hunger that I was used to have building during the day. I suspected that one has to go hungry frequently as Shadakon, and to allow it without panicking, as I had during my trial. I had no idea how long that had actually gone on, or if anyone else had replenished themselves. Dagon had looked drawn that day, but certainly not as bad as me!

I wasn't sure how much they had followed of my thoughts. I stopped and waited.

Morag spoke first. "It was just as long as you could endure without being totally broken," she said without emotion. "And, yes, hunger is part of our heritage. There are some who would obtain excess ... 'food' and consume too much every day. There are always gluttons in any group. If they can do it under contract, it is no business of ours.

But learning how much one can expend without putting oneself in deficit—this is something you will have to pay attention to carefully in this work."

I thought of the gift I had given as I eased Lara's pain.

Morag nodded. "You are an intuitive and you have healed, probably in many lives."

I pondered that. *Did one have many lives? Did the Shadakon?*

She shook her head. "The Blood allows us to live from one life span to the next. When it is over though, it is truly over. Humans live short lives and die between. You know the mythology of reincarnation. It is not as straightforward as it may seem, although it does suggest that one might carry memories of past lives. But when I see such as you, having some intact memories ..."

There was a question I did not think to ask; it was about Dagon and me. He had told me that he had already lived a long, long time, but would I? They said I had some Blood and I had been brought in for that reason. That I was partially of the Blood was proven by my fast transformation from human to other. *But now? Would I grow old while he did not?* That would be a question for later.

I waited. There was more to be said about what had transpired between Lara and me.

Morag continued unperturbed. "We monitored of course. Quietly." She looked at Dagon pointedly. "We would have intervened before any other had you gone amiss. It is a delicate thing, building the bond between humans and us. Many predators often fail to successfully close on their desired target. Many leap too soon and waste their efforts."

She looked at me.

"There is always an expenditure of effort," she said. "Even if all one does is to fly another home."

Dagon did the mental equivalent of shuffling his feet and looking vaguely guilty. Morag smiled.

"The proof is in how well things turn out. I did not expect you to get this as right as you did," she continued. "The Mother is pleased. She has checked in on Lara and is grateful that she is as easy as she is. Her relentless pain and clinging to her life have been difficult to witness even for those dedicated to this work."

"It was not expected that she would accept you in any capacity," she said. "That will sometimes be the case here, even though you have had an early success of connection. I am pleased that you honoured our requirements of seeking permission, as well as those of contract. One is larger and older than the other."

I remembered Dagon saying, "Do not pull back ... I have your contract and your inner permission."

Morag smiled again. "I hope there will come a time when not everything you refer to about the skills of our kind is solely a reference to Dagon—as good a teacher as it turned out that he has been to you. But there is another lesson that you might draw from his choosing you as his, and in mating with you."

I had never used the word "mating." I understood it, as a wolf would take a life partner.

"Yes," she said dryly, "and if the couple break pack rules, they are driven out. They may survive but often do not without the support of their kin. Dagon broke pack and clan rules in allowing you to live and to turn. It was taken into consideration that he was not fully aware of your Blood, or how rapidly you would transform. It was a serious problem for him when he could not make himself obey contract and either return you, your memories wiped, or take you. It was a close thing, I believe, for him. And for you ..."

I had known this; it had never been a secret between us. My life had been balanced between his hunger—with a lethal contract—and his wanting me for more than a one-time event.

"It is not allowed, however, to turn someone without permission of the Council. Exceptions can be made, and obviously have been," she said. "They are exceptionally rare, for good reasons. The punishment for him would have been severe."

I knew this too, and shuddered.

"Yes. But you must stay within the boundaries of this job. Many eyes are upon you. You must take life energy when it is offered and you have contract. You will have to square that with what humans call their "conscience." If you do not, another position will be found. But you do not have unlimited time to become proficient and willing to kill."

She looked at me fully. I knew we were both aware of the other levels of what had happened when I refused to kill at the end of my trial.

"Yes," she said. "It was noted. You are not yet accepted and you are still in jeopardy. You have been granted a gift of time, given that you arrived at what you are so recently, but that time will run out."

It dawned on me that Morag would not protect me indefinitely.

She just looked at me. "I could not and I will not. You either will become what you are, or you will fail to survive. I believe however that you will find your way here as well. In this, I agree with Dagon. I will leave the two of you here, as you have promised to return to your ... client and I have other things to do today. Dagon will be waiting for you when you are done. I know you both can find your own way home."

She smiled and started to leave.

"Oh. And one more thing." She looked at Dagon. "Do not feed her.

She must feel her part of this experience genuinely."

She left the room without looking back.

We looked at each other. So much hung on this day; not just for me, but for him, too.

"Not just for us, but for her as well," he said flatly. "You have no idea of the danger to her in supporting you. There are five Council leaders. Two are, to put it mildly, unimpressed with keeping you alive. Two are abstaining, and thus allowing a temporary go-ahead decision. Do the math," he said.

He stepped forward and gave me his arms and the closeness of his body.

Nothing else. I expected this and tried not to ask. Perhaps I was effective at that, or perhaps he was willing to let me think I was.

The Mother knocked softly on the door and came in.

"She is asking for you," she said simply.

CHAPTER THIRTEEN

THE TAKING OF A LIFE, GENTLY

Once again I followed the Mother down the hall. Pain, like tide, has its rhythms. Often it intensifies as one day passes into another unendurable night. Companions, even as committed as these seemed to be (I had seen at least three other women gowned like herself in the halls), might falter as the long nights wore on, involuntarily napping or losing attention while someone struggled to part with their body and life.

Early in my space career I had seen someone die of radiation poisoning after an explosion and serious breach. He was in a sealed and shielded room and visitors donned heavy leaded suits. In the daytime, his friends and co-workers took shifts with him. At night he faced his fate alone. I knew this, because I always worked night shifts.

One night he was alone and, looking in on my way by, I saw him wide-eyed with fear and pain. His hair was gone and, in many places, his skin, too. Drugs could not keep up with the pain of a body that was being dismantled from within. Even he must have realized that death would be his only available mercy. He saw me watching through the window of his med unit and turned away, having been one who had scorned and belittled me in the past.

I did not go in. He died that night, and I had often wondered if I should have overcome his anger and confusion at seeing me there instead of someone he wanted to see. Or not. I would say now—I did not have his permission. Now I would say that suffering alone is the most unbearable part of it. Unless one can find comfort in a belief in God or angels, or whatever. And even then ...

But I would neither nap nor lose attention. That I could guarantee.

Lara was a little more propped up in bed, and her breathing was falling unmistakeably into a pattern I recognized from my training as a medico. Her breaths came like sets of waves on a beach, falling away to nothing and then building for some brief minutes. Each set took her further and further out and away from her life.

She looked up and me and then looked at the chair beside her. Conserving breath. When she spoke it was a whisper.

"I didn't hurt for a little while," she mouthed and mind-spoke. *"I knew it would come back but ... I had hoped it would not."*

I nodded.

"How long will it go on like this?" She asked silently.

I thought of my own near-dying experience. My personal answer would have been "forever" or "until someone else stops it." I did not say these things. But reading her, I could tell that she had a long way yet to go. And it would not get easier, because as she became dehydrated her body would suffer further. She had asked for no medical interventions and I wondered why she would not avail herself to oblivion while she passed.

She answered my question as if she had heard it. *"I want to be present to the very edge. I want to witness my own death."*

I shivered, as I had almost made a similar choice not so long ago.

"But if you—" she stopped and various confused thoughts crossed her mind. "If you took my life? If you helped me across?"

I decided to tell the truth, or at least the truth as I could provide it.

"If I take your remaining life energy, you will die to this body. What happens then I do not know. But one's life energy does not die.

It will leave you soon at any rate and will drift away to join the energy of the universe. Energy is neither created nor destroyed." I smiled inwardly, thinking about how my old physics instructor might have felt about me applying the Great Equation to this situation.

"But," she whispered, "it could be of some use? To you?"

I laid my hand close but not upon her own. Her's twitched with the tremor of her dying nervous system. I felt her pain encircling her, and her calmness in the face of it was heroic. But was it necessary?

I sensed the Mother look in and withdraw again soundlessly.

"Your life is your own until you give it up. For me to use or for the universe to recycle. Both are the same, but there is something I can give you in return."

With great effort, she turned to face me. Those green eyes drew me and I realized how beautiful she was. That whether she had ever formally danced or not, she was a dancer. That whether she had sung in years or not, she was a singer. I showed her with the absolute certainty that it was true.

I could feel the bond growing between us, and I wanted to free her from her relentless pain. I wanted her energy, too, but I would not take what was not freely offered, even though I had final contract.

I stroked her thin hair without touching her. Under my mental fingers it was thick and glossy, the colour of ripe wheat. I showed her that as well, that she was not this ruined body.

She had one more question of me and it was not what I expected. I expected fear of pain or some further indignity. I should have known better, for as we had bonded I learned her strength and bravery.

"Will you be with me to the very end?" she mind-spoke.

"So many left me as I sickened." I got a glimpse of a handsome man who came and went but one day did not come again. She felt that he had already considered her dead, or close enough, that he would not have to return. A wisp of rage came up from her.

I looked at her deeply again, making sure she was taking in everything I would communicate with her.

"He was not inconvenienced." I mind-spoke. *"He feared death—yours and his own. He thought he could protect his heart."* I considered and then said, *"He was not brave enough for this."*

"But you?"

She was close enough to kiss and I wished I could gently kiss her cheek. I had never kissed a woman in true heart's fondness and was surprised at how strong this feeling could be.

"We will be together to the very end," I said truthfully. "We will be one and then you will leave to go wherever one goes. I will not forget you."

This I knew to be true.

She nodded. It could have been assent and probably was, but I wanted her to make her decision clear to both of us.

"You must say it," I said.

"Take it!" she said, with as much breath as she had left.

I bent over her, holding eye contact and gently took her hand. Her body was no longer going to hurt her. I pulled, taking her in like a long slow drink of sweet water. She felt the flare of my energy and hers combining and faintly smiled. The next drink was also deep but the vessel was growing empty. The last sweet dregs came into me and I felt the exhilaration I had felt second-hand from Dagon. But I was not prepared for the last moment of her life.

I heard the song, her song, and I knew that she did too. It echoed through the room, wild and sweet, and unearthly. It marked my heart as it had hers.

Her last exhale was in tune with the last note that lingered in the room and in the wind blowing softly in. Her hand was now as still as stone and I put it down.

I looked up to see the Mother smiling beside me.

"Thank Goddess," she said. "And thank you. We will be in touch again soon."

No one had told me how powerful the last of the life energy is. Now I understood Dagon's anger when I flirted with not caring if he took my life and yet trusting him to hold the line. I was so high I could barely pull myself together to walk sedately down the hall. There were sparkles and vortices in the air around me as I accommodated another person's entire life energy into mine.

I wondered if the Mother could see them. I wondered if she had been able to hear the song.

CHAPTER FOURTEEN

NOW I UNDERSTAND— A LITTLE MORE ABOUT MY LOVER AND MY NEW LIFE

I wanted to immediately merge with Dagon, but the Mother was with him. She was praising my gentleness. I hoped he wanted to praise me for fulfilling the expectations of the clan and Council.

And I wanted to share some of this exhilaration with him.

He stepped back slightly.

"*Not now*," he mind-spoke.

I was now accepted and "on call." I did not know how often I would be called, so I hardly had an assurance of being able to depend on this for my, ah, livelihood. But it had been a long day and I had done what myself and others hoped I could do. And I had done it gently. I think I had feared that the ravening wolf would arise. That I would howl over her body. Or something like that. My relief was immense and as strong as the pleasure of her energy coursing through me.

Once we got outside, we walked sedately over to the edge of the garden and took to the air. We flew home, rising up in the sky and then falling together in a wheeling helix of energy. We called out to the stars, to the moon. Slowly our energies equalized, as he replenished himself with what I now could share. Inside the house, we ended up very awake on the bearskin pelt. Our clothes lay scattered between the door and the bed.

We began what I thought would be a nightcap of land sex. I loved the shared endings that echoed through us both, and I knew, I could feel, that he liked it too.

He smiled. And then he ran one nail lightly down the centre-line of my body, stopping at my navel. I shivered. I still wanted him. "We have a lot of time," he said.

"Time has opened up for us being together."

I understood that he meant now that I had taken a life.

"Yes," he said. "I wasn't sure if you would live to get to know me better if you had not."

I had some reservations. I had not taken her in violence, nor lured her with false promises, nor kindled blazing sexual need. I was not sure I could negotiate a kill outside of certain conditions.

"Hmmm," he said. The nail was replaced with his hand, which grazed, but did not linger, on my breast.

I struggled to reach him, but he held me immobile with his will. This was a new experience and one I was not sure I liked. I could move, but not quite reach his body. He, however, could touch mine.

And he did. He touched and moved me into positions of his choosing. My breath was coming ragged, as I felt the bonfire built within me. It blazed until I begged him to come to me, to end this game.

He smiled, and the fire got hotter. I was, beside myself. I saw myself as from a distance, maddened with desire and with no control over that. I could not even be angry; I wanted him too much for any other feeling to intrude. I wept and howled, alternately, attempting to be silent but failing at that.

"There may come a time when you want to take this much," he spoke calmly. "You will be mad with it, sick with it. Hopefully you will have contract, but perhaps even if you do not, you will make a kill. That is our legacy. It is why we scatter ahead of punishment and death by humans. You did not get there in your trial. The situation was not right."

I took this in as best I could. I had never known this level of sexual hunger before.

I looked at him imploringly, with no other thought than: *Have mercy. Take me now!*

"*Exactly,*" he mind-spoke. "*Now you are in the position I was in a week ago. I did not believe that I had your inner permission. I wanted you like this.*" And here he did another something that made me shiver and look up into his eyes, pleading.

His eyes burned into mine.

"I have been around a long, long time," he said quietly. "And I have learned a few moves."

He laughed. "Be glad you are now my mate, and that I will never take you."

The barrier between us suddenly dissolved and I fell into him. When I grabbed for him, he was there. There was no more teasing, if one could call it that.

"Some have called it 'tantric sex,'" he said before he surrendered to my body and its needs, and those of his own.

The stars wheeled in the sky.

Life afterwards seemed to settle down for us. I went to the hospice a couple of times a week. I did not always take life and, after a few sessions where I spent more than I took, I learned to balance the energy flow between my patients and myself so that it did not cost me to do the work. I did pain control, after which the person slept a deep sleep before they saw me again—if they did see me again, I had some refusals too.

The Mothers were a charity of mercy without denomination. They allowed all beliefs or none; although they enforced the rules that one could not attempt to convert another to one's own beliefs or decisions about what to do with one's remaining life. I had been under close scrutiny, and I did not doubt that the Mother who waited outside the door of Lara's room had been listening to what we said aloud.

I was ushered into a room one day, where a wasted man lay with a huge crucifix of the Dead Son—as I thought of it—weighing down his weakening attempts to breathe. He had no contract and they doubted that he would agree to any care from me. They had appraised him correctly. I had barely entered the room when he realized somehow what I was and what I might offer him. Despite the gnawing pain that I knew lived within him, he pronounced me a demon and to be gone.

A demon! Part of me was perversely pleased. Did he sense that much power in me? I respectfully bowed to him and backed out of the door. And bumped into the head Mother.

She beckoned me to a small room and gestured for me to sit down.

I knew that she and others there did not talk much. I was not sure how much she picked up from mind-speak or the emotions below it.

She smiled, taking my hands in both of hers. I sensed the absolute calm confidence she had in touching me.

She spoke then, in a voice that was soft and under-used.

"I know what you are, and to some extent, who you are." She smiled encouragingly. "I have known of the Shadakon and their history. Things were not always as … civil … between them and us for most of our mingled histories. There were exceptions. The people of the fields"—I knew another word for them was "pagan," —"were more comfortable in joining with them under, ah, certain circumstances."

In my mind's eye I saw an old dream or memory. A bonfire with women— unclothed women—dancing around it. A tall dark figure with leathery wings accepting their energies and binding them into a cone of power that pulled from the earth and blazed upwards as wishes were made as it reached for the sky.

She waited for me to return from my flight of … fancy? Memory?

"The early people of Mesopotamia and later of the Old Testament, and then the ones who formed Christianity, provided blood sacrifices to their gods. Earlier groups on all continents did the same. Some sacrificed captured warriors. Some sacrificed their children and virginal women by flinging them into deep natural wells in desperate times. People have always understood the absolute power of giving blood or life to their God. Or gods. Or goddesses. Death is still the critical part of the Christian religion—death by public torture. Surrender. And then resurrection."

"Most people have not thought this out. They have a single piece of the puzzle and cannot or will not concede that it fits into a bigger picture—with other pieces held by many people different than they are. Some still kill for Jesus and Allah, whether those offerings are appreciated or not. Whole nations have fallen to the supposed sword of God." She paused.

"The Shadakon were there from the beginning. They could be seen as 'fallen,' as they came to earth and could not leave again. Or their offspring could not, at least."

My eyes widened.

"You are still learning who you are," she said gently.

"There is no good or bad power, only power," she said. "Its meaning only comes from the choices of those who wield it."

"He is a frightened man," she said, indicating the direction down the hall where she had found me. "He hopes that he will be saved, that his suffering is offered up to a good cause."

She can't know of my trial, I thought wildly, and that I thought the same.

"Many of us hope our suffering will serve us or others," she said. "This is his way of honouring his own path. He will allow neither pain medication nor your ministrations. He will die as a sacrifice of voluntary pain."

She looked at me deeply, and I felt her hands that were closed lightly on mine and read no fear, no avoidance of touch of me or anyone else.

"We are grateful to you," she said. "That you allow another choice."

She smiled.

"We will call you later," she said. "You are very welcome here."

CHAPTER FIFTEEN

THE TRUTH SHALL SET
YOU FREE. OR NOT

I carried my new information home and set myself to find validating information in Dagon's library and the documents he had accumulated. It was clear that he had blazed a trail through seemingly unrelated things. There were old books by Sitchin and Gardner and a host of others, some sensational, some dryly academic.

I was sure that he was aware of my studies, but made no comment. I found my way back through what I could read to the Sumerians, who arrived on the scene as hunter-gatherers and quickly developed civic government, public schooling, a money system, architecture with square buildings made of kiln-baked bricks—very quickly. Way too quickly.

There were myths of the Annunaki, an off-world race that had landed on Earth to re-provision the star ships with gold and radioactive minerals. They were tall and proud, and didn't like working in the mines. So they created a race of workers. A precise genetic adjustment was made by the addition of their own genetic material. The new miners were then smart enough to take orders, but not smart enough to disobey them. They were hearty and could do the required heavy work. They were short-lived but bred rapidly, filling the fertile valleys with their industry and offspring. The overlords, or some of them, grew weary of the worker race and of their incessant multiplying and wanting possessions. They may have caused a great flood in which most of the workers and their families died. Some, though, may have been spared by Visitors more sympathetic to them, and also the She who had provided her own genetic material to create them. In addition, some of the Visitors "… found the daughters of Earth comely and lay with them."

That bloodline concentrated in some individuals and families.

Eventually, the Visitors left. Or most of them did.

There may have been those who had slipped away to join with their simpler Earth offspring. They too procreated with the humans, gifting their children with larger amounts of the Old Blood than the original modified human workers had.

Sharing blood, the old rituals of sharing blood and genetic material; the words leaped off the page and screen at me.

As I left the library, Dagon was waiting for me.

I looked at him in shock. He looked back unperturbed.

"You know I am not human," he said.

"And you know you are no longer human enough to live as they do. We cannot live on … squash," he added "as pleasant as it may appear."

"It was not always energy without blood. And it is still the sweetest." He ran one finger lightly down my now healed shoulder. "It carries more of the full essence."

"You have had a taste of this knowledge," he went on, still lightly touching the place of my heartbeat. "It was gifted to you by me, and I was thrilled to do so. But I have only recently put aside the inevitable kill in which I take it all."

"Recently being a relative term," he added.

I attempted not to reveal what I was thinking—that he still was a lethal predator.

"I can hear you," he said calmly.

"Yes," I said, trying to buy time. "I didn't see. I didn't follow the history back far enough."

"I knew that you didn't. I knew that you would, although perhaps arriving after talking with the Mothers and going directly to the computer without mind-speaking me ... may have been a clue for me."

"I knew you would look at me differently after you found the information that you chose not to ask for. And then you would look at your bloodline differently."

"But first you would truly see the difference between me and your kind." He looked at me to assess his affect on me.

"Your kind. My human kind!" *I was not as he was. There was a reason, a deep reason for the scorn I heard from the others the night of my trial. I was no longer what I was, but neither was I what he and they were.*

"Yes," he said. "That is true." He spoke without false reassurances.

"How then is it that you can say we are mated?" I asked angrily. "Perhaps I am more of a pet? A companion animal."

He refused my attempts at angering him, although I had already done so in our short past. I sat and glared at him. Nevertheless, I had overstepped civility at very least. I had never asked about his lineage. I had known we were different. I knew that we were still different, *and yet ...*

"And yet," he said with deep seriousness, "I have pledged myself to you. I value the remaining humanity that you bring, although not all of it. You are reactive and lash out at me. I take it because I know it means you are feeling the difference and distance between us. You are at times uncomfortable with that. Others though, might not be so understanding ..."

"I cannot say what the original Visitors thought about their human workers. Yet some lay down with them, and gave Blood royalty to the children of those liaisons. Not that they were acknowledged by all the Visitors, who, by then, had problems away from Earth to occupy themselves with."

"Many of those children did not die," he said. "No matter what their fathers' or the villagers' intents may have been." He continued."

They found each other and amplified strands of the Blood strengthened in one place and died out in another."

"I am not one of the Visitors," he said. "Perhaps a great-great-great grandson of one. But probably later than that. And during that time the Blood, before we called ourselves Shadakon, were spreading and sometimes inducing the change in susceptible victims. Or lovers. Or both."

The quiet between us was absolute. I knew what his next question was, but dreaded it.

"Which are you?" he asked. "Lover? Or victim? Or both?"

His eyes held mine fiercely. I did not know whether I wanted to break free of his influence over me or not. I felt the longing for him rising within me.

"Not good enough," he said flatly. "I can induce that in anyone … susceptible."

I finally recovered enough to give my own answer. "We are mated. We will fight. That is part of it."

"And you are an expert at mating?" he asked.

I ignored my impulse to protect myself, to fight back at him. I set aside the heat that was generated when he was near me.

"I am what I am," I said, "as are you. I was always aware that you wielded more power than me. I have never falsely mated, nor wished for that. I know that you are mine and I am yours. Nothing can change that for me, no matter what might befall us, or what you do."

I thought of his trade in the pleasure pavilion. It meant nothing. His anger was frightening to me, even though he had never fully turned it on me. But in this, it too, meant nothing. If I could not be with him, then I would have to accept that.

But he was my mate. We were blood bonded. "I am sorry," I said. "I have been thoughtless in the face of your plan to let this information come to me in manageable parts.

It was there before, but I could not see it. Now I can, but I still do not know what it means to me. I do not know where I fit in. If you wish a break from me, I will do that. It is not what I want, and I don't know if I could survive without your protection that you provide to me every second of the day and night. I have my arrogance as well. But I cannot and will not undo the bonds between us."

I had not begged. I could add no more. To my surprise he grinned.

"Still betting on your unrevealed cards," he said. "You would die if I walked out and others knew that I had withdrawn my protection or, even more so, if you left me. But you know that."

"But you must say it," he continued. "I will not have this same conversation again. Are you victim, or lover, or both?"

I raised my head. "I am of the Blood. We are not victims although we may fall to enemies. We know as much as we can of who we were and are. To know our own weaknesses confers strength."

"I am your mate," I said calmly. "I am Danu of Dagon of the Shadakon."

He knelt at my feet and gathered me in his arms. He rose, and seemed very tall, taller than what I had remembered. He carried me to a comfortable place and made me howl with pleasure.

It had been the only answer I had. It must have been enough.

CHAPTER SIXTEEN

NO BUTS, ONLY ANDS

Eventually I had gone to the stores and bought my own better-fitting version of what Dagon wore. I was glad that we had benefited from half of my accumulated credits. The rest had been absorbed into the system, where they would sit until the allotted time ran out and they disappeared.

It appeared that money was not something that he—and now I—lacked. So he handed me a credit stick and away I went. I wanted little, but I wanted perfect fit when I chose to wear clothes, and I wanted real material. The shirts I chose were Camden and linen, Egyptian cotton—still the best in all the worlds. My pants were soft napped and felt as good inside as out.

Clothes had always been problematic to me, something I had solved by settling for uniforms. Uniforms didn't feel good to wear, but neither did they draw unwanted attention to me.

These clothes though … I moved around carefully that first morning, relating to this new pleasure. These clothes did not particularly give away to a casual observer how they felt as I wore them. But Dagon noticed immediately when I came back in my new outfit, and ran his hand down my side like one would stroke a glossy horse or the pelt of some wild thing.

I wondered if there would ever be a time that I would weary of him being in my head. It was a passing wisp of thought. But the thought of never surprising him—

He interjected in mind-speak. *"You wouldn't be here if you hadn't surprised me."*

How could I argue with that logic? But generally, I felt he held more cards than I did.

He stopped what he was doing and came and faced me. I knew we were going to have another version of "the talk." He was not one to mumble important messages from another room. The Shadakon had honed communication, of all sorts, to a fine edge.

A shake of the head did not mean "no." A nod did not mean, "yes." It might, but it could not be left there. And here he was, eye to eye with me, lounging in front of me with the grace that he had in all his moments. A cat, impossibly comfortable on an overhanging branch. A large cat.

He smiled. "I do hold more cards than you. I am old and I have walked on many worlds."

"I've walked on a fair few worlds," I protested, already knowing that my remark was not thought out.

"Yes, you have come as a brief visitor and spent time in spaceports. Perhaps I should have said 'I have spent lifetimes on many worlds.' And in many time periods of Earth. Power is cumulative. You are astounding in what you can do." He raised an eyebrow. "You did something at the hospice that was truly a gift to the rest of us. Morag is delighted, although she may never show you."

"There are few places where we can be truly appreciated for what we are," he continued, "much less be invited back." I was following him without questions or protest so he continued.

"I have one of those … careers …"—he did not smile but looked at me very carefully—"you have another. They are not so different."

I thought of his skills at creating fires within women who did not know what was within them.

He was still regarding me carefully, choosing his spoken words carefully.

"I start nothing. Sexual energy is within all of us. Whether one becomes acquainted with it or not, uses it respectfully with oneself or others or not, it is within. For those who do not know themselves, it can be a driving force that leads them to hurting others and themselves terribly. Those people who engage with me—I start nothing. Perhaps I blow on the embers," he added slightly smugly.

Here was part of a large almost-visible-to-me basket of feelings that I carried around, trying not to reveal them to him. I knew what he did first-hand.

"That is not accurate," he said calmly. "Mostly my dialogue is, 'Come, let us sit somewhere quiet. You are curious about me.' I do not fly them to my home."

He sighed then and continued. "We might as well have the rest of this conversation. It is not just women who come to me."

I was stopped, as they say, "dead in my tracks." I had always wondered what that statement might mean. I knew now. I literally could not go forward with that information. I had not guessed. I had not asked.

The moment stretched between us in silence. *What could I say? That this changed things?*

"Does it?"

I tried to block my thoughts. He took my hand and shook his head. His eyes were luminous but he was not influencing me. Nor was he letting me off the hook.

I remembered Morag's comment during my trial. "You are about to learn more about your lover." I had thought I understood her. I had, in a limited way.

"Yes, you understood more than most humans. But we both know that about you. Do not fall back into old prejudices and moralities forced on humans by punishing religions as a means of controlling their flocks. What if one day, no one came with offerings? Or chose 'no' to over-procreating to supply more Christian soldiers? Or Muslim warriors of Allah? Or …"

He let me catch up for a moment, and then returned to the more problematic issue we were discussing. "Is calling up the fire in a man any different than in a woman?

The sexual power—some have called it 'Kundalini'—waits at the base of one's body, waiting to ascend, to transcend into the energy of a soaring eagle. Men are even more locked down than women. Women have held onto the knowledge of their sexual energies. Some women," he amended. "In the right circumstances," he added. "Men are still claiming their own places. But usually they have to choose. This or that. He or she."

"But," I said. Without any idea what came after that …

"No 'buts,'" he said. "Only 'ands.'"

He sighed. "I followed you at your first assignment, whether you knew I was there or not. Why do you think Morag positioned me at your side? You do not shield your thoughts," he said without apology. "Especially when you are in your power and bliss."

I flashed back to the moment before my kill. I had wanted to brush Lara's cheek with my lips. I could see her beauty, her bravery. I had taken her hand. I hadn't needed to do that.

"Yes," he said. "At that moment you felt close to her. You gave her that, and she wanted that even more than her release. She was not alone, not even in the presence of a stranger. You knew her, although not in the biblical sense."

"What I do is no different. Sometimes I allow a man to retain the knowledge of what happened within him as he interacted with me. I know that it will confound his life, but we are not always protective of those who come to us. Maybe I think he needs to remember—that he was happier in one afternoon than he had ever been in his previous life."

He looked at me intently, the panther very up now. "Maybe I do it sometimes because I can."

I shook my head, as if I could clear out the thoughts that were clamouring for my attention. "We spoke of this before," I said. "About your work. What you do there …"

He nodded. "We spoke of it. It is not a finished topic between us. It is definitely not a shared experience between us. You know only what you learned about yourself, and me, in our first interactions."

I could not argue and didn't try.

He smiled. "I have gone with you to your work. I will not do so in the future. Perhaps you will come with me to mine." He stretched languidly and smiled some more.

"It would be, ah, personally informative. Whatever fears you hold will not hide from you—or me. But I warn you—" he gentled his tone, "you may find that you are very much like me. More than you could have imagined earlier."

Like a good musician, he held back the last beat ever so slightly. "You may learn to love it."

★ ★ ★ ★

I did not immediately accompany Dagon to his work at the fair. I let the idea sit with me, as I worked to soften my immediate reactions and fears that this information might change things between us. I thought I had rejected the dictated limitations of religion that were woven through my childhood. I had quietly investigated various alternatives of human sexuality throughout human history and suspected that there were critically important parts of our, of human history. that had been covered over or distorted into something ugly. I realized now that I did not know what I did not know.

But somehow I had brought in, unquestioningly, some limiting definitions of what was acceptable behaviour.

Oh, I had heard the scuttlebutt that sometimes circulated among the crew.

That I was a man-hater and thus, perhaps, a woman-lover. The chance to experience that had been available in most ports we set down in and I had considered it once or twice. But checking within, I found the same dreary lack of interest. I had not been looking in the wrong place. Nor was I was a different sex within. None of it did anything for me.

I thought of the fair that day, not so long ago. Heading—with very few detours—to where Dagon was standing in the sunlight, hanging out with others who shared at least one major characteristic with him.

They were all takers. Predators. Some took more than others.

He was in the latter category.

I had walked directly up to him, separated only by a symbolic fence which could be unlocked easily with one simple act: signing the contract. Then he was free to make full contact with me, and I was free to—well I was not sure what I truly had been free to do. I thought I had known. But one can only make a completely voluntary decision with the necessary information to make it. Or if one retains the will to pull out of a growing fire of desire, a fire I hadn't believed could burn in me at all.

I did this pondering when he was away, doing what he did. It was, of course, on the top of my mind when he came home, bearing energy and flowers. These were of two varieties, one a hot, reddish purple and another that was a glowing blue. They went well, blending across the colour wheel.

They had not been chosen randomly, I knew that. People used to use flowers to send messages. Messages like *"I love you"* or *"I miss you, be true."* But I did not know what these flower colours signified.

OK, I did know what they signified. That each held the other within it.

They both were lovely, but even better together.

He smiled and faced me. And then he said something I never expected to hear, nor would I have asked him to say. Because it was not natural to him, not part of the clan life that he had been in since before … well, I didn't know how far before.

He said in both words and mind-speak, "*If you remember only one thing about what has passed between us, and how I behold you, remember this: I love you.*"

"*It is exceptional in our kind and we haven't spoken of this. You may not have believed me before, or worse, seen it as a ruse to keep you in my power, so I did not say it.*"

He stopped for a moment, gathering himself, and then continued aloud. "I could not answer you as I heard you howling my name, knowing how desperately you waited for an answer. I could not tell you as you stood before us in your trial, almost broken. You could not take your attention off of what was happening—not for an instant. You were in terrible danger and could not think that I could help you."

I said nothing, lost in my recall. But I had felt a very faint answering call. It was perhaps only, "*I am here and you are there. I cannot come but I am here.*"

"Yes," he said. "We were connected. You can sometimes hear me even when we do not speak or mind-speak. You do not always listen as hard as you did that night."

And then he said it again. "I love you. Je t'amie. Ick liebe dich. Ana behibek. Volim te. S'agapo. Aishiteru. Doo . . . Set daaram. Tha gradh agam ort."

He went on and on, using languages I had never heard before. "I love you, Danu. I have given myself to you as you did to me. It is not a one-way thing between us."

He looked within and felt my relief and incredulity.

"I have shown and indicated this to you before.

I would defend you, would give over the rest of my existence for you. I faced shunning and even being hunted down by my own for this. What is between us will always be a source of danger for both of us, and makes preserving what you and I have difficult. This was not supposed to happen and it continues against heavy odds. But if words have power, and we know they do, then I will say it whenever you forget."

I went to him then. Like water when one is thirsty, I never tired of what happened between us. We gloried in our mutual energies first and then we lay down and connected as people who love and want each other have done since—forever. He had begun to teach me other avenues to pleasure other than my initial simple (but enthusiastic) ones. I could not hold him back from touching me. But I could hold myself back, dancing out of reach just as he reached for me with his mind and intention. I didn't say yes (of course I would say yes, but not just yet) and I didn't say no. I played with this until I wanted him too much to continue in this way.

Which wasn't very long. I was very easy lover, I thought.

"Ha!' he said. "We'll see about that." And then, seemingly casually, he said, "It's time for you to stop thinking about riding the horse, and just get on the horse."

I was momentarily confused, given that my mind had recently been overwhelmed by pleasure that allowed no thinking at all.

"Come to work with me tomorrow," he said.

CHAPTER SEVENTEEN

PASSION IS THE SAME
PASSION FOR ALL?

The next day dawned entirely too early. Dagon was already up and moving about. Although his kind had accommodated to daylight and to being active in it, bright midday was not his best time of day. He liked to travel in the dawn, and return in the dim light of dusk, if possible. I tolerated the light better than I had during my turning, but found the direct glare of sun unnerving.

He and I had both slept. In his case, perhaps he napped. Leaving my side so quietly that I did not sense his leaving, he often went to work on his computer and listened to music as he did whatever he did there.

I have not mentioned the music. We both had a wide range of music that we loved and remembered from various times in our lives. In his case, this was an unbelievably expansive collection. I listened to some of his more challenging music when he wasn't home. He sometimes listened to pieces that I could only call "space jazz" when he judged me asleep. As in everything, he did not force his choices on me or play music that made me feel … well, unsettled and uneasy. But I sensed that he went far out and away with strange blends of unknown-to-me instruments with strange tunings and vocals. Some were not written by or for humans, I believed. I wondered if I would ever know even a portion of the scope of his previous or even current experiences.

One song at a time, I guessed. Today, when he was quite sure that I was awake (although hiding out in our bed (and feigning sleep) he played Santana's "Turn Your Lights On." It seemed to do it for both of us and for the task at hand.

I got up and brushed and swished water over my teeth.

They looked small and ineffectively human. I brushed and tied back my hair. It was curling auburn, but had not grown past my shoulders. The length I wanted it to be, I realized.

We seemed ready to go out the door, but he indicated that he would like me to sit. He added *"Please"* in mind-speak.

I sat. I was in no hurry to find out how confused and emotional I might truly be in the coming hours.

"We need a bit of a game plan," he said. "I can easily get you into where I work. The company deludes itself in thinking that we are contained." He smiled a now familiar smile, an ever-so-slight indication of his superiority over humans.

"I have suggested that you attend with me. I want you to understand the boundaries that you must not cross while there. If you do, you will put me, and most importantly your new identity, in jeopardy. You cannot draw attention to yourself or me. You must stay close to me no matter what happens to you—in your mind or otherwise. I can glamour those around me. I cannot control the guides or others watching if you bolt out of my immediate vicinity. I am good, but I am not that good." He smiled to temper some of the seriousness of what he said.

"Do you, first of all, understand what I have said? There can be no falling back on feigned misunderstandings."

He waited and I knew what would always come next if I did not speak.

"Yes," I said aloud.

"Even if what you perceive contradicts or challenges what you have learned from your past?"

"Yes," I said again. I knew that I did not know what I was agreeing to, as often was the case while I was learning the intricacies of this new life.

"Yes," he also spoke. "But I believe you can imagine this at least. I will pay no obvious attention to you. I will not explain or hold your hand. You will be invisible to any who may visit me today. They will not sense nor see you. You will be my observer, as I was yours when you made your kill."

"You were not there," I said, suspecting that I was not speaking the truth.

He just shook his head. "I was there," he said. "And through me, so was Morag. But we left you room and free will to do what you would. You have to accord me the same courtesy."

I nodded and felt the sting of tears. I did not know I would cry, and wiped at them quickly.

"You will always be part human," he said. "Particularly since you still value part of that and draw strengths from your human experiences. You were not born yesterday," he grinned, "or even last week. Your Shadakon Blood has been recently actualized. Your humanity has not, and probably cannot, be removed. It is who you were and still are. Accept that, but do not accept the small-mindedness that comes with being human. That is what I ask and what I wish for you."

"But there is one thing I can do for you, and I will if you request it. It may be hard enough to watch what I do—" and his mind said, "*who I am*," "without your first experience being work I might do with a male. I can wipe those memories from you if that occurs, and bring you with me on another day."

I knew he could wipe away memories. My memories. But now confronted with a choice of what might be something difficult for me to remember, I wondered why he had not wiped out the worse of my recollections of my trial.

He shook his head. "You need to remember every part of that that you can," he said flatly. "Your continuing existence depends on it."

"Perhaps that is true of my experiences today," I said.

"Perhaps I have to pay attention to EVERYTHING as if my life depends on it. I will let the deck of fate decide. I will be silent and observant and not attempt to intrude in any fashion. I will not leave your side. Let whoever may come, come. Perhaps it is exactly what I should know."

"Betting the farm again," he said with a grin. "Too bad you never got good at poker. We could have enjoyed even more of those credits that you transferred to me."

"And the one thing that you must remember, no matter what?" he asked.

I quickly went through his directions. I finally looked up. "That you love me," I said.

"Yes," he said. "And no one else. And one more?"

I knew the answer to this one too. "That I love you," I said. "For as long and longer than I can imagine."

"Yes." He smiled.

When we arrived at the fair, there were few people present, and the ones who were there looked sleepy or inattentive.

I was still mulling over the idea that I had never seen Dagon vanish anyone, or wipe a memory either. But how would I have known? I locked that thought down. This was going to be exacting enough without bringing any additional material to it. I stayed close behind him.

The guard waved him into the compound and he headed purposefully to an area in the back that seemed to be a pavilion of tents. I stayed behind like a duckling behind its mother while navigating fast water. A few of his other co-workers watched him pass. One swung his head languidly, tracking slightly behind Dagon. I narrowly avoided those golden lion-like eyes and practised being nothing. Or better, the ground beneath my feet, the colours of the background. Dagon caught the interaction going on behind him and turned his own glinting eyes toward the other who started slightly, and then retreated with a slight growl.

I heard not one word or mind-speak from Dagon, but I meshed even closer to him.

We arrived at a pleasant, airy space that was approachable from the front, and could be closed at the back, presumably where his customers would be directed, after the contract was signed. It was decorated in crimson and blue. I thought of the flowers of last night.

"No one can come in here but me and my customer," he said in an under-mind whisper that I could faintly hear. "Sit here. Do not move and definitely do not leave."

He paused, "Unless someone is about to sit on you. Then by all means move! You will be able to see but perhaps not sense all the negotiations, if there are any. It is a light crowd today."

I sat.

I watched him glide along the fence, occasionally raising his head to sense what might be in the wind. The others, took similar actions. There was a very beautiful woman among the group today who I knew was not human. I sensed some variety of shape-shifter. I wondered briefly what lay beneath. When she turned slightly towards me, I thought about being a chair, and the matrix of material that formed the tent. She did not look again, and after a brief while Dagon sauntered, not appearing to move at all, over to her. They appeared to be exchanging pleasantries. I doubted it. She never looked in my direction again.

After a while, sitting in the chair became a minor trial of its own. Although undoubtedly comfortable enough in the short run, it began to dig in here, and not prove adequate support there. It was not an all-day chair. I wondered if Dagon knew that. I suspected that he did.

Time passed. Of necessity, I found a place "between" everyday reality and checking out to nap or enjoy daydreams. I drifted there, as if I was conserving air on a long dive.

I was alert for the shadow, the crisis that would undoubtedly come from any direction other than in front of me.

I wasn't disappointed. I had, in fact, missed something significant because the guide was ushering in a customer. Dagon sat on one end of a blanketed divan and indicated the other end. The person hesitated briefly, perhaps wanting a little more distance between him and this looming experience. He glanced at the chair. I tensed, ready to spring up if necessary. After a brief hesitation, he sat down on the divan as far away from Dagon as he could get.

He was a he. A young, pale, stoop-shouldered young man with blue circles under his eyes, and, I suspected, auto-inject marks on his arms and other less visible places.

I fought to stay distanced and not drawn into reading him or his energy.

But I had eyes and training as a medico, and I was familiar with the signs of addiction to Blue and its costs to the body. He was severely under-muscled, even for a spacer. He carried himself as someone in an old, weary body. I did not doubt that it was.

The high of Blue, I had been told, was a drifting and joining with the universe. One could hear the star songs and the flares of suns out of human vision. It was a space—a brief window into that reality—I had yearned for myself, but never the one provided by a drug. This drug, not unlike a visit to a Shadakon, extracted its price from one's life energy. And once one slept with, Blue and its brief bliss, there was seldom a return.

I put together a likely theory of why he might be here, sitting with a vampire who was manifesting as a panther at the moment (to me), although possibly being perceived by the young spacer as a calm man. His hands moved incessantly— picking, wringing, and changing positions. His whole body moved as if he was uncomfortable in his own skin.

It was going to get worse for him, I knew. He was in the early stages of withdrawal and there was much more to come. He probably had lost his supplier, or was behind in his payments, and he could not return to the ship like this. But Dagon did not offer charity here.

Credits must have been exchanged. Why hadn't he spent his remaining money on the drug? It could be found easily enough, although probably marked up to exactly everything he had, if he arrived in need.

Dagon had been sitting quietly for however long it had taken me to make my assessment. He had noticed the man's name during the signing of the contract, and now said it in the calmest and most respectful way that this hurting man, this human, may have ever heard, certainly not for a long time.

"Ian," he said, and made contact with those eyes of amber flames. "What is it you wish from me?"

Ian went momentarily quiet before the itch and pain of his withdrawal resumed again.

"I'm at the end of things," he said. He wiped at his nose and looked embarrassed.

"Do you wish to pass an afternoon during which you will not be in pain?" asked Dagon.

Ian looked up hopefully and then shook his head.

"I cannot possibly afford to continue as I am. I've spent my last credit that will be issued tomorrow. Guess I wouldn't have needed it then anyway," he said flatly.

Dagon was surprising me throughout this exchange. There was no perceivable heat that I could sense. He communicated that there was all the time in the universe between them. He had moved imperceptibly closer.

"You have been in pain for a long time," he said matter-of-factly. "You turned to Blue for relief and were caught, as most are. Let us speak a little of your pain, and then you will make a decision about how we will proceed."

He put up one hand and said, "If it is difficult to give words to the pains of your life, then show me.

Remember some moments when you lost hope in your own courage or faith in yourself and the universe."

Ian closed his eyes and a scrapbook of sadness spilled out. He did not look like his father and was punished for that for the entirety of his growing up. Maybe his mother had turned to a surrogate or even an available neighbour. Maybe, ironically, he was truly his father's biological son and that somehow had enraged his already angry father who saw him as not being the son he had hoped for. He was off balance on his first day of school and was easily singled out and tormented. He reported this to his parents and was beaten by his father for being a coward. He never spoke to them of what happened to him again.

Meanwhile Dagon had quietly managed to take his hand. The hand, and then his whole body stopped its tiny writhing movements.

"Yes, you learned to hide your pain at an early age."

The man quieted, looking down at his hand in Dagon's in seeming amazement.

"They said that you ..." He stopped in a fairly obvious place. "That men come to you ..." He finished on an out-breath.

"Yes," said Dagon. *How well I knew that yes.* "You have thought about this for quite a while. But let us speak about you for a little while longer."

The man boy, for he was barely a man in age, relaxed slightly.

"I got used to not telling people what I wanted," he said, "what I needed. I got into the space program at my first opportunity, before I even knew my own mind."

"Let us speak the truth here," said Dagon calmly. "I believe you did know your own mind at an early age. But when you moved towards what you wanted and needed, that may have been the worst of all." He waited.

I did a quick check of myself and could honestly say that I felt nothing but sadness at this story and a realization how it would end.

"There was a boy, two years older than me," Ian said. "He was everything that I was not. Smart, popular, handsome even at fifteen. He had the world and he didn't see me."

"But I saw him. I dreamed of him, thought of him, wished for him!" he sobbed. "I thought he didn't know. I thought it could be mine, the wanting him and feeling a secret bond with him."

He looked up finally and met Dagon's eyes without looking away.

"He and some of his friends had figured it out of course. It must have been obvious, but I didn't realize that. He invited me to go for a walk with them one night. We walked a long way, into a part of the city that I was not familiar with. He pulled me into the dark and we were as close as … as a kiss. I thought. I thought …"

"They hurt me," he said flatly, as if he was describing someone else's experience. "They buggered me, jeering at my pain. Then they beat me and left me there. He did that!"

Dagon sat silently for a while. "He may have been attractive and smart. But he was not courageous. One cannot really want another this way who does not have the answering flames of desire somewhere within him or herself."

Ian looked up, directly into Dagon's face.

"Yes," said Dagon. "I can be with you—for a little while. I will not be a lover or sex worker. I will be a true companion. I will stay with you … awhile."

"To the end?" asked Ian.

"If that is what you wish. But you now have a chance to restart your life, to seek a more genuine lover. I can give you relief here. Passion and then rest?" He paused.

"Or I can ensure that none of your troubles will find you anymore.

You will be one with the universe while you and I are together and then … you can stay out there, with no re-entry to this body. We are all just energy, and it is endlessly recycling. Some lives are a burden and perhaps should be laid down. But I will not answer for you. Your life is your own," Dagon continued. "To move forward, whatever the consequences, or surrender to me, and meet whatever fate awaits you. You have signed over to me, but I do not do what you have requested hastily."

He leaned closer. "I must have your inner permission. That you have decided to give over your remaining life's energy to me."

I waited, already knowing the outcome. I knew now that Ian had signed the lethal clause of the contract before he had even sat down with Dagon.

Dagon looked at him, waiting, while his power swirled around them both. "You could have been set up again," he said. "This could have been another very bad choice."

He paused, his timing always perfect. "But it is not. I will give you everything you ask of me and more. I think you can feel the truth of that."

He was very close now and dropped Ian's hand to run his own slowly down and down to where, in spite of his junk sickness, Ian was aroused. He then took Ian's hand and placed it on his own hardness.

"Bodies do not lie," he said. "They want what they want, whether we can deliver that to them or not. But you must decide now. You have signed lethal contract, but you must say it."

Ian's back straightened and he gathered his ragged pride around him.

He said: "I, Ian, being of fairly clear mind now, but having decided this a long time ago, give over my life energy to you."

Dagon slowly pulled him in and kissed him on the lips. He ran his hands gently down his marked arms and body, not judging, but joining with him to build as hot a fire as could be kindled in this sick man.

Then, although I had never bothered to watch anything explicit about men loving or sexing with other men, I watched as Dagon slowly brought him to white hot. Their bodies moved as one. Initially Ian was crying, but then his sounds turned to exclamations of joy.

"Now!" said Dagon. "Be free!"

There was a flare of energy that rocked me, even as I sat relatively unconnected to what was happening. He drained him in one take, never pausing until there was no longer an Ian present.

"*Thank you for practising fine discipline,*" he said in an under-mind whisper. "*Although perhaps it was not as difficult as you may have expected.*"

I found myself kindled by the energy transfer. I breathed levelly, willing myself to cool down to a neutral state. I had not directly partaken. There were no sparkles in the air around me, and I was grateful for that.

"*We should go home now,*" he mind-spoke. He spoke briefly to the guide on the way out who again, did not notice me.

We returned back to the house in a flitter. The driver never turned around and we rode in silence. Once in the door, Dagon strode back and forth, trailing streams of energy as he went. He had said that he infrequently made kills. I assumed that he was dealing with the excess energy.

On his second sweep by, I reached out and pulled him down to the couch I was on. He allowed me to pull him. We sat face to face.

"So? You left the choice to fate and it brought you to today. It was perhaps, the event you had feared?"

He waited. I carefully re-imagined the details of the day.

I searched my thoughts and feelings, hoping that I was not attempting to hide anything from him or me. I thought about the sexual connection I had witnessed between him and Ian. I saw again his deftness in taking the lead in the negotiations. I also saw myself as possibly being sensed by several of his co-workers.

"Yes. We'll take the easier part first. You are not silent when you think you are being so. When you began to think about, let's call him 'the lion' as you saw him, you did the equivalent of shouting, 'Hey, what do you do?' Same with the other. Most would respond to such a question, at least by noting where it had come from!"

"I admit I may have underestimated them," he said. "There were some perceptive hunters there today."

I took this in. It was useful information.

"What else?" he asked.

I turned back in my mind to the sex. How Dagon had kindled the energy in Ian that he had been asked for. I understood that.

"There are no different kinds of sexual passion," I said. "Only of intensity and length of time. I expected to feel differently about that. You are a very skilful … lover," I said carefully. I think he got fair value in his negotiation."

"That was not loving," said Dagon flatly. "You should find another word.

Love involves two. There was no two. He was frightened of his desire and ashamed of what he most wanted. There have been many Ians that have come to me," he said quietly. "Usually they come to ask me to ease their pain. They spend an hour so, adrift in vague pleasure that I don't have to work hard to induce. Or they are stripped of their pain for a while and then even of their memories. This was a rare day."

"The luck of the draw," I said wryly.

"Yes."

We sat quietly. I thought about how Dagon had awakened and fanned to life Ian's long shut-away sexuality; that he had done that for me as well. I was working on what, if any, the difference was, between his client and me.

"*You always see me in terms of yourself*," he said, with a touch of steely anger beneath his thoughts.

I did not expect this. I looked within again.

"Sometimes you do not ask the right questions," he said slowly. "Or any questions. What else did you observe?"

I was at a loss.

"Me? Did you take note of me? Do you wonder what my experience was, instead of the lost Ian?"

I returned to my line of thinking about how our early interactions had gone. How I had been naively inconsiderate of my effect on him, expecting him to hold a line, when I had no idea how hard that was. I remembered the night that he showed me that; that he was at the limit of what he could do and that my obliviousness and need for pleasure did not allow me to see that.

"Yes. You could have easily died that night." I thought of the timing of Ian's death.

I shivered.

"But you chose not to do that?"

"Yes," he said. "Lucky for us both that you were under a limited contract."

"But later I was not. I understood that you were in jeopardy. I turned without knowing what was happening. I began to understand about need."

"You began to begin to understand," he agreed.

"I signed over to you. I saw no reason for you to be punished for extending my life, since I could not return to my old one."

He looked at me, not bothering with the "*yes.*"

"I knew I was in mortal jeopardy. I knew that I felt so strongly about you that I would pay the price of having sought you out."

"I put your existence before mine," I said quietly. "I could do no less."

"Yes. And I knew you did not want to die. Far from it. And you were too far changed to return to your old life." He sighed.

"I knew that we were both in trouble. I knew you offered to die to and for me, although it was not what you wished to have happen—and neither did I." He looked at me with those eyes that drew me, and that I loved to fall into.

"You came knowing what I was, yet playful and open. I should have sensed that there was kinship, but even that might not have prepared me for the gifts you gave me," he said. "You gave me your heart's name, within minutes of meeting me. You wanted to fly! Your courage was a shining asset that you did not even realize you had."

"Few come to me awake and willing to know me," he said. "They have reason to fear me of course—as did you, if you had thought it through.

But you proceeded, expecting it all to come around right."

"The Fool," I said. I was referring to the tarot deck—a fortune-telling deck that was the predecessor of playing cards. I had studied this, too, in my quietly rebellious youth.

"The joker in the deck—that can change everything," he smiled. "Although you risked everything."

I thought of my trial. I thought of his trial that night.

"As did you, my mate," I said.

"Death or worse was close," he agreed. "Very close."

I was crying. I let the tears go and they made their way down my cheeks. I had never used to cry, but I was crying now. I now realized the unlikeliness of our continuing on together in those early days, and yet something between us held true.

He touched his fingertip to my face and picked off one drop. He put it to his lips as if to savour it.

"Few have cried for me," he said. "And I have existed for a long time. That something between us—I could not have said it then."

"But it is love," he smiled. "Apparently my activities in the pleasure tent were not enough to threaten that. And now?"

He stood before me, with the life energy of what had been Ian swirling about him. He looked within me and discovered what still surprised me, but not him.

I wanted him. I did not care who he had touched. I did not care who he had killed, although there was a gentleness about it that endeared him even more to me.

"We are more alike than you once realized. That, too, drew me to you," he said softly.

Drew him to me! I wondered when he had begun to see our connection like that."From the beginning," he said. "I just didn't know it for awhile."

"I will fill the tub," he said. "My parts have been in, ah, personal places. Not yours." He added helpfully.

I laughed at his diffidence in describing what I had witnessed.

"Join me," he said. "I know you can be another creature in the water. It is an old home for you."

I wanted him. I wanted him in the water, in the air. I wanted him outside under green trees I was not yet familiar with.

He nodded. "And I like that about you too."

CHAPTER EIGHTEEN

A WALK IN THE PARK

The days slid by, and I began to relax into what was now my new life. My body was no longer identifiable as the one the spacer techno once had. My short-cropped hair was now dark red curls that moved against my shoulders. When I went out walking or to the hospice, I was aware that men now looked at me in a different way. Human men. I could sometimes hear their thoughts and knew that they found me beautiful. None of them laughed at me now, or made unflattering comparisons between me and anything else.

I had learned something. After observing the change in how they perceived me, I realized that I was, for the first time in my life, in control of the situation.

But one evening, while passing a group of four men and sensing the bravado of alcohol in their thoughts and gait, I heard something that I had always been afraid of dealing with in my former life. I distinctly heard one man say, "Let's take her!" The others did not respond verbally but most agreed with the plan. One did not, but was silent. They turned as one and tailed me.

I was in an area of gardens and trees, in the lovely green space that ringed the hospice. I had just spent the day with various women who watched the empty chair beside their bed with hungry eyes. They wished and prayed for a son or daughter, long out of touch, to sit beside them for their last stretch. They wanted to see someone one more time—to make amends or just love them one more time. However, more often than not, it was only me that sat in that chair.

Perhaps I was distracted and not as attentive as I should have been this afternoon. And now I and these unknown men were moving to a single point.

It was hard to imagine any of them as having had a loving childhood.

They were hardhearted and bulked up with hard inflexible bodies. They had closed in a semi-circle, seemingly herding me towards denser cover.

I pretended that I had not noticed. I pretended that I was terrified and hoping this would all go away. However, neither of those states was within me. It was exactly where I wanted us all to be! As they finally circled me, I laughed.

A crowd rape rut was in the air. Except for one who stood slightly back and looked miserable. Very well, I would deal with him in a different fashion later. But keeping bad company should not be rewarded.

No stakes, no silver bullets, or fire. They had come unprepared.

They closed on me.

I moved without appearing to. First here. Then there. They bumped into each other, swearing.

I slipped between them, invisible.

I had been practising being background pattern. I could be within and then outside of their circle of violence in a heartbeat. Besides, they had a weak link. I knew that even if they did not.

I taunted them.

Dagon would later tell me that I went dangerously overboard with all of this, but after living as a bullied and disrespected woman for most of my life, I felt it was payback time.

I built a cone of energy around us and within it I was the Goddess. I surveyed them from my power while they fell back uneasily from me. They could not touch me.

But I could touch them. I touched here ... and here, dancing and flickering in front of them while they spun and then began to attempt to protect themselves.

I could have later identified them by their parts. Blindfolded.

Soon my touches became rougher, though not enough to cause lasting pain. Dagon and I had experimented with the interesting effects of slight pain while in a state of high arousal. He had told me more than once about being around a long time, and he had some interesting moves. I had not feared that he would lose control in our games.

These men had no such assurances from me. Sweating and painfully aroused, fear crept into their hearts, as I knew it would. Although I did not make it obvious, I spared the young man who had not joined in to what was to have become bloodlust.

I danced before them as an avenging goddess.

"Know that you are very lucky, that I choose not to turn you all into swine," I said.

They would not know that I referred to Circe, a powerful goddess who had stopped an boatload of horny Greek sailors with a single gesture. "You are already so close to being that," I said with my newfound arrogance.

I was so pleased to hold the balance of harassment without taking from them that I failed to notice my imminent death in the form of a slim needle gun in the hands of one of them.

"She's the friggin' Blood bitch!" he snarled, and turned it on me. "I'm loaded for that."

It was then that the abstainer found his courage and saved my life. He seemed to fall against the other's gun arm and it discharged harmlessly in the trunk of a tree. Its owner swore, as the charge of designer death was no doubt expensive. The group split into two factions, one side holding back the would-be shooter and the rest backing away from me. Considerably cooling from any ideas of further revenge on me, they attempted to walk away, looking as if nothing had happened.

I mind-spoke to the young man who had turned the tide by coming to my aid.

"*I will not forget you,*" I said to him alone. "*You have proven today that whether you know it or not, that you have a good heart.*"

Then I disappeared. I had conducted a very dangerous experiment without thinking of the possible consequences. The charge that was now trickling harmlessly down the trunk of a small tree would have sickened my body beyond repair. Or, if there was a repair, it might not be available to me.

I wondered where the needle gun, obviously expensive, had come from, and what instructions had been given to go with it. I remembered the last time I had seen some like it, in the Council members' hands that had attended my trial. I remembered Dagon saying that the Shadakon included those who would fight and kill each other to ascend in power. I knew that I was not wrong about who was behind the attack. I felt the faint shadow of the shark, seemingly swimming off without further interest in me. I knew that often they circled, coming in again from another quarter.

There was no blood in the water tonight. I went home to confess my part in what had occurred.

There was obviously a grapevine that I was not acquainted with. Dagon met the flitter that I arrived in and brought me inside. Morag was there, looking angry, but I was surprised that it was solely aimed at me.

"Show me!" Morag shouted in my mind.

I thought of that same direction that Dagon had given to Ian. This was not put to me as a request. Nor was there choice in what I would show. I knelt at her feet and she took control and knew everything that had happened this evening. I could feel her probes, looking to see, I thought, if I had broke contract.

"Who?"

First I showed her the men and their exact characteristics, some of which had been hiding under their clothes. She studied the group carefully.

"Is there more?"

I showed her to the needle gun and its charge trickling down the tree trunk. The liquid was thick and red.

She hissed.

"There is still more," I indicated. I considered what honorific term I should address her by. I decided on what felt more genuine. "There is more, my Leader," I said aloud. I bent my head slightly as I had seen wolves do before their alpha. I was immediately aware that this gesture left my neck defenceless. In old documentaries, I had seen a wolf leader seize another there and take him or her to the ground.

"Show me the rest."

I showed her the flick of the great shark's tail as she swam lazily away. I laid out my fear—that I knew that it might return from another direction. I had been a diver. I had lived through such encounters. I knew I wasn't wrong.

"You are not wrong," she said curtly. "You are foolish but we all know that. You didn't break contract. You did not take from them. You did reveal yourself as Shadakon, something some of us do every day."

She looked over at Dagon, who stopped pacing mid-stride at her words. "It is not against contract to tease humans, nor, I suppose, to bait them," she continued.

"It is, however, extremely unwise. There are many who actively hate us, and others who can easily be influenced by their fears." Here she pictured the fourth man, my saviour in this situation.

She surveyed me fiercely and I forced myself to briefly meet her eyes. "You do not like to be in debt to others? You are in debt to him, and it may come to pass that you will have to respond and repay that. It may put you into further jeopardy. Your adversary is very cunning and she is as skilled as your protector."

I again asked what her name was.

"It is better that you do not have her name at present," said Morag. "Having something or someone's name can bring it to us. We might whisper it in a dream." She paused. "Or call it out in fear. I believe, as you do, that she will return for you. She has lived a long time, and revenge is one of her enduring pleasures. That and un-contracted kills. But if she had managed your death …"

"We have no contract among ourselves," she said. "We expect the individual to protect his or her self."

"Your situation here, with Dagon, is unique," she explained. "You would not have survived as long as you have without him. And," she said while rising, "this has very little to do with you."

"We have long lives and often have complex relationships with each other." Morag was facing Dagon and I could not hear what passed between them. I knew that something did.

Then she was gone.

After Morag left, Dagon and I were left staring at each other.

"Wait a moment. Stay here," he said, and disappeared into the hot tub room. I heard water running and smelled a strong smell of astringent herbs. In a short while, he led me to the water. The surface was floating with dark green pungent herbs and flowers. The water swirled invitingly.

I stood where I was, without the energy to get out of my clothes. I shivered.

"I will help you if you wish," Dagon said softly, "but I am not entirely sure I can be near you without wanting you." He shrugged. "This is not a good time for more male energy, however welcome it may be to you later. Even my male energy."

He stopped speaking and sat, quietly, with his back to the door. The room was bright with indirect light, not candles. I looked around bemusedly.

"This is not a time for darkness," he said simply. "I am here to protect you. If you prefer, I will wait outside the closed door."

I shook my head. He was out of the range of unavoidable kindling and I did not want to be alone to feel as vulnerable as I had when I spotted the silver gleam of the needle gun.

"You have seen one before," he said quietly. "All three witnesses had them. One of them was pointed at me," he said, "by someone who badly wanted to use it." Dagon scanned me and my body. "You are in shock. You always bet that you will get the best cards."

"So far your luck has held." He looked at me as I eased out of my clothes and into the water. He retrieved them from the floor and put them in a heavy, dark bag. "The trauma hangs on these, much as it did on your old human clothes. They can be burned later."

I finally had achieved underwater status. I rose to breathe and then exhaled and sank down. I enjoyed the moment between breathing out and breathing in. It had always been a peaceful timeless time for me.

When I rose up again and glanced over at him, he was slumped against the door. He sobbed silently. I felt vast remorse and grief within him, where usually there was calmness and control. I knew then that we were in trouble. Not just passing trouble. I knew it had to do with something still running between Dagon and this woman I could barely picture in my mind. Dark hair.

Dark amber eyes where passion for cruelty flickered.

I was too tired to notice Dagon's stricken look as he followed my thinking. I was too tired to make the connections within my own thoughts.

Finally, I felt I had absorbed all the water and healing herbs I could tolerate. It was clear to me that I had unknowingly used more than my stored energy. I felt tired, so tired.

Dagon wrapped me in the robe that had been the subject of our amusement in our early time together. It was practical now, as I was shivering and it covered my body in warm softness. And it prevented him from directly touching my skin.

I looked at him questioningly. He looked down at me as he carried me to our bed. He laid me down and curved around me as if he cradled a precious instrument from harm. He smoothed my hair. I waited for the flare of energy that his touch evoked.

He leaned up on an elbow and continued to look at me. He was present. I expected to respond to his closeness. It did not come, but something else did. Not the post-peace after a great expenditure of energy. Rather, a slow golden cloud peacefully settled over me.

"*I know many ways of stoking connection. This one is challenging for me, given my appetites,*" he smiled. The peace of his comforting presence soaked into me. I looked at him with closing eyes.

"*It is an exercise of trust. I will bring you no male energy tonight. I will protect you. If I can, I will protect you.*"

I was almost too far under to perceive the last of this. Almost. I sank under the surface, feeling like I was drinking warm honeyed wine. His body was quiet against me. I swallowed gratefully, feeling a sense of quiet energy steal into me.

He leaned upon one elbow, looking down at me.

On my lips was a small droplet of ruby blood that I licked off without thinking. Then there was another.

It dripped precisely from his finger above me. I did not know this. Some part of me may have known, and thanked him. Some other part of me had heard and sensed some things tonight that I must remember later, but not now. Not now.

The moon sank past the window and the candles went out. I floated in space, the stars singing around me, the flares of distant suns passing through me. I smiled in my sleep.

CHAPTER NINETEEN

THE SHARK

I awoke in late morning light. I was still in the soft robe Dagon had wrapped me in the night before. I smiled as I took it off. On one cuff, there was a faint reddish brown mark. I went to the bathroom and studied my reflection in the mirror. My lips had the same reddish brown tinge. I licked them. They tasted like Dagon, or a faint essence of him. I understood.

There was a note on the table in the living room—

Your work at the hospice is temporarily suspended. They will be happy when you return, but it will not be for a while until some details are attended to—Morag

I knew that she liked written notes. It was not the first one I had received from her. She must have been here early, and Dagon laid it out for me to find. Or, she may have been here for any length of time. She, as Council Leader and, I was coming to believe, Dagon's friend, may have put it here herself. I faintly remembered the deep peace and safety I had drifted in last night. She may have been here all night.

I thought about the day before and things I could not quite focus on. I remembered an encounter I had had with a large shark, in a time when there were still large sharks. I entered the memory. It had appeared out of the deep blue on my right side, as I busied myself with repairing a fish enclosure. My heart hammered, while I fought to control my oxygen consumption. This was no time to be forced to ascend through the emptiness towards the bright surface.

In. Pause. Out. Pause.

My breathing became my inner mantra. I turned to face it. People rarely meet the eyes of sharks because they roll them back into their heads as they attack, protecting them from any final violent struggles of their prey. I saw the eye facing me. It was black and told nothing.

Teeth are replaceable for sharks. Eyes are not.

It had come closer, although its pectoral fins were in a neutral position. I had done a lot of research on sharks in the years I was a diver and knew this was a curiosity posture. It was assessing me. Some people, much more casual with their lives than me at that time, intentionally swam with sharks to learn their body language; some even lived long enough to make documentaries and live off their risk-taking. They touched them, temporarily quietening them with a light push to the nose. Some, even more intent on moving to the edge, rolled large females over and stroked a white belly that nothing else had ever touched gently. Like a cat, the shark lolled in a kind of stupor and seemed to enjoy it.

It was a mating reflex. The male forced the female over, and she stopped fighting so that they would both live through their encounter. I did not want to get close enough to attempt contact of this sort. A male seeking her would have to be very careful.

With a flick of its tail and ripple of its body, my shark disappeared in the direction it had come from. I knew it was still out there, just beyond my vision. I finished my work quickly and prepared to ascend.

When I was done it reappeared behind me; I felt its presence and turned. Its large pectoral fins were stiff and pointed down and away from its body. It began a tight circle around me.

I knew then that I might die that day. I had a stunner, but by the time I would be close enough to put that into use, my odds of actually benefitting from it were dismally low. The company I worked for cut everything to the bottom line. There were devices that divers could wear that generated a steady electric field, unpleasant to close-by sharks. I could have used such a device—if I could have found a charged one. And if I had trusted that the aging electronics had not already been compromised by the sea. I hadn't bothered.

Now I was here, and this magnificent predator was here, and it was seriously considering me as prey. I knew that the one in front of me was a female. Sharks wear their sex on the outside of their bodies; males have claspers, which they use to cling to the female shark's body to mate. However, he still had to be determined and stronger than she was, and she had to be somewhat willing.

I slowly headed for the surface and we began to dance her dance. I exhaled calm, taking energy from the sea. If I had to die somewhere, the sea would be my choice. I was here, suspended in her world, with my death-bringer in front of me. Again I saw her eyes. This time I could see both.

I focused and found my way past my state of fear. There is a mercy in some deaths, when the dying one realizes that there is no escape. He or she accepts and surrenders to death, which might be the only mercy available. I had felt that shift in my own prey at the hospice. It came suddenly, followed by the peace of no longer having to face pain or death or anything else.

I waited for her. Perhaps I communicated that I would be present and knew the fate that she brought, but that I would not fear her. She had turned away and disappeared as quickly as if she had never come to me.

I thought about my current situation. I knew the shark and more than that, I knew that Dagon knew her well. That he had learned how to quiet her and join with her, however briefly. I knew that they came from roughly the same time of the beginning of the Blood, and could even be related, albeit distantly. From a time and place where everyone had dark brown eyes, some with strange flickering lights within them.

I knew what had to happen. How we could end this somehow. She would return and return, drawn to me, no, drawn to him, to finish something that had begun a long time ago.

I had to ask him to do something and I had to do something as well, to best use the lesson of yesterday. I had spent a long time gathering courage to face what I had to do after my visitation by the great white. I had had to return to the sea, where the sharks were at home and I was not.

He must return to her. I did not know what that meant, but I knew it was true.

I curled up on the bed and felt my very being ache. I had to release him to do this. He could not be constrained by our conjoined energies; I had to let him go. He would always be my mate. Perhaps he would return.

I also had to go. I had to go somewhere safe, away from them both.

CHAPTER TWENTY

THE MAKING

Dagon arrived later than usual. He was completely shut down, but although he could hide his thoughts, he could not hide his silence.

By now I found his silence informative. We looked at each other. Perhaps he hoped for information from me before he revealed what he was holding back.

Poker then. I had learned to play poker and understood his references to the game in relation to me. I had, however, not learned to care if I played well. I had little interest in the stakes or the game then, or the people I played with.

I had everything that I valued in my life, piled in front of me. I was preparing to bet it all. The quietness that seldom was between us, though always significant, lengthened.

I had learned that I could not meet Morag's eyes indefinitely. They drew me in and away from myself and I always felt her true power over me. I knew that she would not, if the situation required it, hesitate for a moment in ending me. I had felt and seen it the night of my trial. I had had to submit to her, as my true leader, my Alpha. She knew I understood that, and yet she did not seem to enjoy making me feel lessened by this fact.

But Dagon? Although I knew that some of his powers far excelled mine, I had always felt, perhaps foolishly, that we were—on some level—the same. That I had given myself to him in all ways, but he could not have taken me without me willing it so. Could I have refused? Could he have let me walk by? I did not know where one ended and another began. I did not think that he knew either.

Which brought us to this place. I continued to look into his eyes, to sink into him. Finally, I spoke. "Let us not speak now of what must be said very soon." He relaxed slightly.

"I know we must. But once said it may come between us," I said softly.

I felt my inner fires catch and grow hotter. I felt him unshield his own, and I gasped before we even made contact—physical contact.

"Speak to me only of this moment if you must speak at all," I whispered.

He studied me carefully. He touched my lips where I had found traces of his blood from last night. I licked them. I put my hand upon the starburst scar on his chest after I removed his garments. I stood and looked at him.

The glory of him! He stood tall and lean, with thick dark hair accentuating his glimmering paleness. He was a male god, ready to consort with his goddess.

I never wanted to forget this, any of this, but especially him here, now—mine.

I did a different version of the dance I had danced last evening with the human men. I stayed just out of reach. I moved without the transitional movement one must make when walking or dancing in a usual fashion. Here ... now there ... and now somewhere else. I touched him. He allowed me to do so. Standing relaxed and following me easily, he waited.

I brushed up against him. Then away again. He was hot; I was hot. Soon our fires would join.

But not just yet.

I leaped into the air so I could be level with his mouth. I hung there easily and licked his lips before descending in front of him.

"What do you want?" I said aloud. "You must say it."

"I want you, Danu of Dagon of the Shadakon," he whispered. "I want you until the stars fall from our sky. And you?"

I knew that he knew, although what I would have to say later might cloud that truth.

I didn't hesitate. "I want you Dagon of the Shadakon. I want you for my mate and lover through whatever storms may come. I will be for you forever."

And then the distance between us collapsed. Two stars becoming one. We paced ourselves, giving and taking all that was offered.

"And today," I said eventually, "I want what you also want. I want us to exchange in the old ritual. I want us to share blood. To become one in matter as well as spirit."

I offered him my shoulder but instead he took my hand gently.

"It is easier this way," he explained. "We must do this at the same time."

He gave me his hand, palm up, calm and trusting in my own.

I sank my teeth into it. Satisfyingly sharp teeth. I pulled and his blood gushed into my mouth and instantly into every part of me. I took him. I took him deeply, sensing where the point of no return was, and moving towards it but not crossing it.

He did the same. I barely felt the momentary pain of it. He pulled in a great gulp as I had seen him do in the pleasure tent. I fell spiralling out of the sky.

A heart-struck bird.

I took again. I took as he had taken and sensed ... myself. I now tasted my own energy intertwined with his.

We did it, again and again. And then we fell into a swoon. We floated, our energies equalized, our appetites completely sated.

I wondered if our stars had already started falling from the sky. I knew I had this. That I had him within me and he had me the same way.

"This is the old way of Making," he said quietly. "Few are supposed to do so anymore.

I didn't think you would initiate it.

But in this, and many things, you surprise me. And it takes much," he added.

I smiled. I had heard what he said, "Few are allowed to do so." He and I had been allowed. We had previously been as one, as much as an ageless vampire and a partially human woman could be. I had turned spontaneously, or nearly so, aided only by his energy. I was different now. I could feel it.

"Nothing can break this bond. You will always be in contact with me, and I with you. Walls and distance do not affect this. What has been done now cannot be undone."

"So be it," I said.

"Yes. In sickness and in health … for better or for worse." He looked deeply within me. "Do you know what you have done?"

I nodded. "And so does Morag. I got just ahead of you both for once."

He laughed. "You are a deceptively fast learner. For someone who does not ask many questions."

"I am about to," I said. "We must talk now."

He nodded.

And so we began a conversation that neither of us wanted to be in.

I briefly touched the rapidly healing mark on my palm. Recalling what had occurred, I felt a faint flare of energy. Would I ever have enough of him? I shook my head. That might not be possible, given the situation we were in.

"You first," he said aloud.

"This is not about me," I said. "Oh, it is me that will probably meet my end at her hands. But mine will be a secondary death."

He didn't correct me.

"It is you that draws her. It is you she wants to take or claim or … whatever final thing that the old Shadakon do."

"We dissolve into nothingness," he said. "But at her hands, there would be a lot of pain first."

I continued looking at him. He gave nothing up.

"Lover?" I asked.

He looked surprised. "There are few of the Blood living together in little bungalows."

I winced.

"Truly you do not understand, Certainly we come together. We used to hunt and feast and run together."

He now held my eyes, not unlike Morag did when she chose to. "We used to band together and drive the humans from one village to the next. Across the moors. Into the deep forest …"

"For sport," he said flatly.

I refused to look down.

"There is a reason why the humankind and ours have treated each other as we have. We were among the sheep and some killed for the sheer joy of killing. As did the Visitors," he added dryly.

"But the sheep found their way," I said.

"Yes. Later we paid. But not all wolves slay the whole flock. Some stay their hand. Some become unlikely shepherds. And some of us moved away from our seemingly insatiable hunger for causing fear and death. It was happening from the beginning. The Visitors had some in their ranks who tried to protect the children that their favoured slaves produced, especially if those children were born of High Blood.

"Besides," he added drily, "it had become an interesting experiment for them. They let it run on uncontrolled. And then they left."

I thought of Morag and how she said she liked to see how things turned out. What I had taken for empathy was possibly just an ancient viewpoint—the long view.

He shook his head again. "You still have trouble sorting your enemies from those who can and will help you," he said. "But I forget how very young you are. You are, in fact, extraordinary in your strange timing and survival. She, who you think of as the shark, has waited because she assumed you would bring your own death down on yourself without anyone having to intervene."

"*The first pass,*" I thought.

"First she assumed that I would tire of you. Or realize my mistake and end you. You were under a signed lethal contract to me. But, ironically, that protected you. It bought us time; it bought you time to make a spontaneous change. Without blood!" he added.

"Then a Council vote forced your trial, with you as ignorant and barely turned as you were. Ending you would have been covered by our code of contract. I would not have been able to protest, had I chosen to." He paused.

"If I had tried to intervene, I would have died or been set aside to wait in hunger until someone came to free me. Or not."

"And then? I asked.

"She came in from an unexpected quarter, setting a brilliant trap for you. Your history of avoiding and being bullied by human men was open to her. She heard your early thoughts when you found yourself in my basement. She sent a small bumbling group of men as bait to distract you and end it."

"I thought that I was in control," I said. "I was enjoying myself."

"Prey often do, lulled into feelings of safety by the seeming absence of effective predators."

"The second pass," I thought. "Abandoned for unknown reasons."

"Not to me," he said. "As you said, this is not about you. She found an unlikely way to hurt me, and perhaps cause me to falter. I could soon be named to Council and even as Alpha. But to do so, I would have to bridge between Shadakon of many persuasions. My grieving or raging against the loss of a part-Blood mate would pit me against a group that she already has drawn around her. I would be deemed inadequate. Too much is at stake to take on those with weaknesses as leaders."

"Blood in the water draws others. So tell me, I see that you look somewhat alike. I think you may have come from a similar time and place. If not love, then, what is the bond between you?"

He did not answer that immediately. "I will tell this my way."

"There are few that work as closely as I do with humans. I think you have satisfied yourself that I do have concern for those who come to me. I well understand that few sign their contracts of entirely free will. Ian may have been an exception to that. I am careful how I proceed, and there are always several choices offered, especially if it may proceed to death. I require inner permission. It is deeper and more meaningful to me than the legal contract."

"You work a similar way," he added. "Even though your sole reference to taking is how I treated you, you take your time to find out what the person in front of you wants. Really wants. Although I thought I understood my continuing attraction to you, that you have the heat and appetite of my kind, I was underestimating you and me. You put me to my own trial. I knew you wanted life and more life, not an ending. I passed a test as well. I could not take you or turn you over to your fate with no memories to explain your hunger and despair. You would have died soon after at the hands of your own kind."

He stopped, wordless for a moment. "You signed away your life—for me. You endured—for me. You danced a healing dance of power for me and transformed yourself into a true goddess."

"To join with my god," I murmured.

"We are not in the clear yet, Danu of Dagon of the Shadakon. But we have come further than I would have thought possible."

There was a brief polite knock and then Morag appeared before us. She looked at us both and simply took my hand, and then his.

"Was there the slightest doubt that she wanted this?"

"She initiated it," Dagon said. "She evoked the full ritual. She took first blood."

She smiled.

"This may change everything," she said. "Again."

She kissed my hand and said, "Welcome, twice born Danu. And once more you continue to surprise me." She sat down with us and waved one hand slightly. "So have you two figured out what must happen here?"

I answered before Dagon did. I knew I spoke the only truth that would preserve us.

"Dagon must let her come to him. I must go away, to grow in my skills and not be a liability to him. I must trust that we will eventually return to each other."

I did not weep. I did not drop my eyes.

They both looked at me.

"It is decided then," said Morag. "Prepare to be moved to a place of relative safety in the morning."

Then she said to me. "You are not to know what Dagon will do next. But you will know if he is alive. You will know if he is not. You are his Maker, as unlikely as that is. Or perhaps you both simultaneously made this union." She shook her head. "What a wild card you are Danu!"

"Always the Fool," I said and shrugged.

She smiled and left us.

CHAPTER TWENTY-ONE

UNTIL THE DAWN

I cannot bear to remember much about the last night before we parted.

I had abandoned my curiosity in my surroundings and in others once Dagon and I had joined. I no longer had to take refuge in the vast sweep of space, my thoughts empty and my eyes seeking only to see as far away as I could. Out there was always more and still more. This reassured me, even though it was not a place I experienced with my body, trapped in a space can making a service run. I had thought many times after such solo reveries, *I will return, perhaps soon.*

But then I had come to this world, with absolutely no hope of any redemption from my fate of being alone until my death. And with death around me, holding me as I slept—I found life. And more than that, I found love.

I found love!

I had thought about what other people called love. It is often described as temporary setting oneself aside, while in the throes of (probably) short-lived passion. Oh, I had listened to old recordings of Leonard Cohen. I believed that he, at least, had lived his passion and loved deeply, even if fleetingly.

Time is not a measure of love then.

Sex was not a measure of love, either. But it was one tool we humans had to open doors past our usual preoccupations, though maybe not past our own beliefs that the story must come around round well for us, even if not for our partner. And that we were justified in transforming love to hate if it did not. I had gone beyond that. I could not un-love Dagon, even if I wished to.

We lay in each other's arms all through the night, having first built up the fire and warmed ourselves and then allowing it to die down as we waited until darkness turned to dawn.

I did not cry, nor did I give in to asking, or begging, that this must not be. It must be this way, if I had any chance of having a future with him without the patient shadow following us until the day that one or both of us had a moment of inattention. I had already proven that I was fallible. He had been awake and keenly alive for a long time and was more capable of protecting himself.

But he could not protect both of us all the time. Just as he could have been my death, now I could be made an agent in his.

So we held each other, long after the flaring energy we inevitably generated together had subsided. He brushed my lips with his and there was nothing but affection and longing to have things be other than they were.

For a fleeting moment I thought of Lara and the kiss that I did not bestow. It was somehow the same. I wondered silently, *"Are all farewells between people who love, however briefly, the same?"*

Dagon looked at me and was silent.

Morag arrived in late afternoon and looked at the small bag I had put together to take with me. It contained nothing of importance to me, but I knew one must not go crumpled, so as to not draw the attention of those who judged by such things. I would not stand out, but would fade into the distance with as much courage as I could muster. Those of the Blood might not understand what was between Dagon and me. But they might understand my fierce pride. I could do that.

Dagon disappeared briefly, and reappeared bearing a small package.

"I cannot keep you safe any longer," he said sadly, "not until this is finished.

But I am giving you something that you may use in the service of your protection. Only in close conflict," he added. "But it may also remind you of our pledges to live and return to each other"

He opened the package. Within was a slim sheath of leather and a thong that would, I was sure, fit exactly over my shoulder and hang to within easy reach of my left hand.

He drew a slender bladed bronze knife from its sheath. It was simply crafted, but for a single red stone that glowed on the hilt. I had seen it before. I started to touch the blade to my fingertip, but he shook his head.

"No, love," he warned. "Do not do that unless you must save yourself in the final way. We did not always use such things as needle guns. There is nothing of this that causes further pain ... but it will be final."

He looked at me with a terrible calm sadness. "It will take you, or any other of the Blood, into the final place one finds at death. For you, into the music of the universe and beyond."

We stood silently while I re-sheathed it and slipped it over my clothing. I made a slight readjustment of my clothes and it disappeared.

"You have to go now," Morag said, rising. "You will end up in a place of safety."

She looked from me to him and back to me. "You do both understand that you cannot communicate with each other?"

We nodded.

"Knowing that the other exists—that is all you can have." Then she smiled, "But it is more than will be known by the others you struggle against."

She turned back to me, saying, "Once again, you have somehow out-manoeuvred ones far older and battle-wise that you are, Danu. I have suspected this and now, as a slight gift of knowledge I will tell you this. You are of very old Blood.

You are not learning your new skills as much as rediscovering them. I could not have said this from the onset," she continued. "But now I think that both of you will persevere. I wish it so."

She walked me to the flitter and stepped back.

"Farewell, Danu of Dagon of the Shadakon." She touched my shoulder. "May we meet again in happier circumstances." I met her eyes fully, but then intentionally dropped mine.

In my memory she was looking at me with a look I could not identify.

CHAPTER TWENTY-TWO

JOURNEY INTO DARKNESS

I threw my bag in the back of the flitter and stood deciding whether to sit up in front or in the back where I could steep in my misery in slight privacy.

Morag had already turned away and Dagon had not accompanied me outside. I turned to check out the driver and let out an involuntary, though silent, yelp of anger and fear. The fear won out, and I felt it slowly crushing my breathing until I could barely draw a breath. It mattered not that I had kept my face in a semblance of normalcy; anyone with psi powers would have heard me from a block away.

The driver mockingly touched his finger to his forehead and smiled. It was the third member of the Council who had witnessed my trial. The same man who had stood ready with his needle gun as it unfolded. Also the same who had later made a sarcastic under-mind comment to Dagon, wondering if he was tired of me yet. His eyes and mind showed his scorn as he watched me sort out what had just happened to me.

I had been betrayed. Wherever he took me, if I got there at all, would not be safe.

There was no time to hone my skills. I had seen Dagon for the last time.

"I have my instructions as to where to take you, Danu."

I did not like the sound of my name coming from him. I wondered if I should attempt to bolt. I already knew that that was futile, but should I try? Anything but allow this freezing cold spreading to my limbs.

I faced him. "You seem to already have my name, but I do not know yours," I said with as much control as I could muster. "Other than second cur to she who hunts me."

I thought he would hurt me then. I didn't care. Let it happen here, in front of the home that I had been loved in. I drew in one adequate breath and leisurely exhaled. Then another. The cold slowly retreated and my fingers felt competent again.

He snarled at me and muttered in under-speech, *"I have been told to deliver you alive, and that I will do. What happens to you later is another matter."*

"Fine." (I had some time then.) But you have not answered my question. I am Danu of Dagon of the Shadakon. I request your name. Again."

I met his eyes and saw the slight surprise in them. Total mind silence grew between us as I assumed he weighed his options. Better to cover himself with Morag? I smiled and waited.

"My name is Gailan," he said finally.

I got in front with him. We were almost touching. I smiled.

"I like to see where I'm going," I said.

We quickly left the area surrounding the spaceport and flew into the setting sun. Beneath us was forest with nothing showing to indicate anyone living there. Again I wondered why. My driver handled the flitter competently, but I did not want to engage with him to ask him to fly lower. I saw glints of water in the slanting light. Then the sun, orange and dimmer than old Earth's sun, sank, and we were immediately in darkness.

There were no glint of lights—or was there? Sometimes I thought I saw a glimmer as we passed quickly overhead. The moon would rise later, as would the smaller one that orbited on the other side of this world. There was a high haze that obscured the unfamiliar stars.

I felt as alone and vulnerable as I ever had. I thought of dives in which I had turned suddenly, this way or that, expecting to see something loom out of the depths It did not materialize, but the feeling of being watched by something powerful continued.

Sometimes it had seemed to move with me, shrouded in the blackness, especially on deep dives. I did not argue with my sense of prickly awareness. If it was out there, just out of sight in the blackness, it was because I had dropped into its territory. I might not even see what brought my end if it came swiftly to do that.

Gailan smiled again, and it was not reassuring. I wondered if he could do deep-mind listening as easily as Dagon could. A wave of missing him passed through me and I hung on until it passed.

I had let him go. I had agreed to exile. And now?

And now I was skimming over unlit darkness in the company of a Blood who could not contain his own thoughts of malice towards me. I had met his eyes. I had dared to do that.

I wondered if I would live to learn to restrain my own growing arrogance. Perhaps this came with being Shadakon, this innate constant testing to improve the place one held in the clan. Always being alert to move up past another. In wolf packs, those unwilling to be betas, often the shunned once- alphas who would no longer hold with pack rules, were banished to their fate where they hunted and coped with their hunger alone.

I realized I was feeling the first wisps of my own hunger.

Unexpectedly, for I had been somewhat lulled by the lack of anything visible in any direction, we descended in a steep swoop and landed silently. I had seen nothing beneath us and knew he relied on instruments to find his landing place.

I got out fluidly and grabbed my bag. I felt the comforting slight weight on my left side of the small medieval dagger, given to me by my beloved, and well hidden in my clothes. Perhaps I would not make it easy for them when they decided to end me.

Meanwhile a slight woman met me with a shielded lantern. She turned away from Gailan's glance but reached out for my arm to lead me forward. Her arm landed lightly on my sleeve. She was shivering but not with cold.

I got a hopeless wash of fear from her. She knew what was going to happen and what had happened to her many times before.

Gailan grabbed her other arm roughly. He was going to take her, now, in front of me, although probably not to death. She, doubtlessly, had her other uses.

But she had chosen to touch me first. I knew, without knowing how, that I had first claim. I pulled her towards me, with Gailan still holding her other arm, poised to strike. In spite of it all, she hung onto the lantern whose circle of light wobbled on the ground around us.

"No," I mind-spoke. "*I claim first contact. Mine to take as I will.*"

He stood still in disbelief, then gave her another tug to wrest her from me. She could provide some sustenance for the flight home.

"No," I mind-spoke him feigning a calm temperament. "*I think not.*"

And then I did what I had learned to do with the dangerous men I had foolishly toyed with earlier. I momentarily stopped him in his tracks.

"Take me inside," I said to her. "I am weary. He can find his own way."

The unnamed young woman led me through the door of a solid wooden building, not unlike a reconstruction of an English country traveller's inn that I had once seen on Earth. Everywhere was bare but time-blackened timber. The floor was stone. There was a small, empty common room with an unlit fireplace in one wall. I wondered who had last taken a meal here, and what kind of meal it had been.

She led me up wooden stairs to a small room. My eyes darted to a shuttered window.

Perhaps I was in luck. Without looking at her again I strode over and opened the shutters.

Fresh air and the first starlight poured in. There were solid bars across the opening.

I moaned in disappointment, and then stood with my back to my guide, deeply breathing in air that smelled of trees and water and distance. At last I turned back to her. She stood resigned to what she knew would happen next. She had set the lantern on the small table beside a narrow bed.

Crossing the distance between us quickly, I sized her up. Young and hard used but still in her beauty, although tired and thin. I could well imagine what many of her duties were. I knew that Dagon was not the only Blood who used sex to stoke the maximum amount of energy in a body before taking it all away.

She looked at me as well through wary eyes. Steeling herself. I surprised her though.

"Have you had supper?" I asked.

She shrugged. I took that as either a "*no*" or that her meals were as she could get them.

"Have you been told to stay with me until I fed?" I asked bluntly.

She nodded.

"Well I am dissatisfied with a hungry source," I said. "I want you to go and gather up some food and drink for yourself and return to this room. Be discreet, but if you are challenged you may repeat what I just said. Repeat it back to me now."

"She wants me to eat before she feeds," she said flatly. "She directed me to gather some food and return to her room."

"Good enough," I said. "Hurry back. Take ample servings."

She feared me and I let her. She had to have her usual feeling about me so as to not draw attention to me. I smiled inwardly. *She would not have to feign her fear and anger.*

I paced around the room while she was gone.

One window, two stories up, no problem, but barred with iron. Solid wood all around. A reinforced door, no doubt with bars on the other side. Nothing for me to use on my side to hinder entrance.

I was imprisoned. Whatever was to happen to me could and would happen in this room, at their leisure. I held back a sob. I had no doubt that I would be monitored both as to my exact state of mind and physical condition. It was not hard for a Blood to do so, although possibly harder in my case than they might realize. The Making ritual that I had requested and received from Dagon had given me additional strengths and staying power. I would always feel his power and essence within me—until I did not. I touched my hand where no visible mark existed. I could feel that he was somewhere, and not in distress. That had to be enough.

I had tried not to think about the turn of events that brought me here. *Morag!* My anger rose, but not quite covering the grief of her betrayal. She had known and had walked away. She played both sides in her own game of power. Perhaps none of them were capable of loyalty.

The thought was so painful that my legs felt weak. I sat on the small bed. The panic and pain crowded in to have me. In spite of myself, I wept. I was undone. There was no one here for me but myself, and for the first time since I had landed on this world, I was not for me either.

I thought fleetingly of the dagger.

Had Dagon foreseen this all unfolding as it was now when he gave it to me? *"Not much good, except in close conflict,"* he had said. Perhaps my final conflict would be with myself. I had no reason to go on if my future was taken from me. My death would free him to live on and fight his battles, free of the burden of me.

I sat perfectly still and felt these thoughts move through me, tearing at my certainty that I was his beloved. Eventually I smiled a cold smile. I would wait awhile longer and see how this unfolded. I had time and the means to end my life. When it came to that.

The young woman returned with bread and various things I did not recognize. She put them on the table and backed away, her hands locked together. I noticed a mark on one cheek that was starting to bloom to red. She had paid to do my bidding then. My anger happily drove away my earlier feelings.

"Sit." I instructed. I indicated a chair by the bed. She sank into it.

"I want a few things of you," I said. "I will not hurt you." I wondered however if this was true.

There was no contract here, no leader to bestow permission. I had never taken outside of contract, although I knew it was completely possible. I had wanted to take the men who had followed me, to drain each one and taste their fear and their powerlessness to stop me as I did. I might have …

I shook my head. I had hidden this realization from myself. Had I done so, the dose in the needle gun would have been unnecessary, I would have been dispatched for breaking contract. This was the first thing that Morag had searched me for.

She who hunted me, Gailan's leader, had set an almost infallible trap that day. She would have been unseen and seemingly blameless in what came next. For a moment I admired the simplicity of her careful crafted plan. Her humans would have delivered me to her, even though they did not know that they were, in fact, disposable bait. I would have undone myself with my own old hate and need for revenge.

She had known that this was a liability to me as much as loving Dagon was.

Revenge could be a hindrance, I thought briefly. *Hate as well. And, yes, love.*

I turned back to the woman sitting motionless, waiting for the inevitable. I would not take what she would not give freely. There was no contract here and I could only rely on inner permission if there would be any. This was, as Dagon had taught me, deeper and older than contract. It was the first contract.

They would not turn me into themselves, not without a struggle anyway. I knew, as all of the Blood knew, that my need put me in endless jeopardy. I must feed, or fade into a living death. I remembered the ending of my trial when I turned aside from a kill. What if it had run another day?

"I want a few things that will be easy for you," I said. "I want your name, if you will give it to me. I want to know where I am, and what happens here—who comes and goes and what happens to those who are brought here. And while you tell me that, I want you to eat. You are hungry. We shouldn't both have to be."

She wolfed down some food and water. Then she raised her head and looked at me; her eyes were green and flecked with sunshine. She was fair, and the bruise darkening on her cheek stood out against her pale skin. Too pale.

She looked at me with her hatred still gathered tightly around her, only somewhat covered by her submissive posture. I nodded.

"You have reason to hate us," I said. "We come and take your life energy and hurt you. And you have no doubt been punished for what you cannot hide in your mind."

She shrank slightly away.

"I am Danu of Dagon of the Shadakon. Remember my name. You may not have met a Blood such as me. It is why I am here, in the hands of those who would enjoy stripping away all of me that they can. I will possibly die soon and it will not be easy." This was a partial lie, no reason to show my hand too soon.

"But you can help me—or not. I need to know, quickly, what this place is, and where. And who holds me here."

"My name is Lucia," she said.

Light, I thought sadly.

"I was turned over to the people here when I turned sixteen by my parents. I don't know where *this* is. It is surrounded by forest without roads. My parents receive money while I am … still here. If I complete a five year contract, they have said I will be free to leave."

"I no longer believe that," she said softly. "I do not believe that I will reach that day."

I did not correct her. It was not in my power to change her fate.

"I don't know who the masters are," she said. "Sometimes there are no arrivals for a long time. Recently some came and surveyed the place. They said it would do."

She shivered, as did I.

"You know more than you realize," I said quietly. "You can help me see what you know in your mind. I will not hurt you."

She just looked at me, and I remembered Dagon saying that many of his clients did not truly voluntarily sign the contract. It is very hard to not misuse power, to bend another to one's will and take what is needed.

I looked at Lucia and waited. She finally looked up, with agreement within.

"Come here," I said. I laid my hands lightly on her head, although it was not necessary. I saw flitters arriving in the night There were many people coming to this place. Others such as her were kept here to serve them. She showed me a place where contract did not exist. Where the old pleasures could be, and were, enacted. I heard, as she had heard, the screams that came through the heavy wooden doors.

I saw Gailan.

And I saw Her. They came and went amid the usual business of this place. They approved and availed themselves to what was freely available here.

"We used to run the humans into the forest," Dagon had told me. He had wanted to dispel my hopeful wish—that he had somehow been different. He had done that. It was in his past.

This was now.

I had experienced such changes that I could hardly believe who I was and what I could do. I was no longer who I had been. Unlike Dagon, I had not lived in those lawless centuries when the Blood hunted as they would. I hoped that his recent change of heart would hold in the fact of his re-entering his old world.

He was still alive. He was still alive. I was still alive.

I turned back to Lucia. She was sitting beside me on the bed. Dispassionately, I noted again how beautiful she was in a faded way. She still wanted to live and had a touch of innocence, in spite of all that had occurred to her. She could still hope that I would not hurt her.

I tried to imagine parents who would put a daughter in the hands of renegade Shadakon. I had never felt close to a child, or wanted to be. But I was sure that I would not have been able to harm a child—for any reason. I was sure that witches did not toss their own or anyone else's babies into the flames. They valued life and worked to preserve it, when possible.

The stories of ritually sacrificed children were mostly a distorted and ugly fabrication of the Christian clergy and witch hunters.

But children and young people had been sacrificed at various times to various gods. The meaning of Passover was, as I understood it, centered on leaving a blood sign outside the homes of those who trusted that their sons would be spared execution. By who? Avenging angels? I shivered.

And then there were the small skeletons of Mayan children, found in the bottom sediments of deep cenotes in Middle America, who had been tossed in alive, the glinting of their gold ornaments as they floated down through the dark water the last thing that would be seen of them.

Meanwhile the prostitution trade was still brisk on all worlds that humans frequented. It continued to be an easy source of money, though not for those used and discarded. Humans, had long had a taste for youth and innocence, and were no less bloodthirsty than the Shadakon.

I shook my head. I was unavoidably hungry and knew that I must use what was provided for me.

Lucia! My mind corrected. *Her name is Lucia.*

Still, she must come to a place to grant me what I needed. I hoped so anyway. *And if she did not?* I wondered. *Could I abide by my largely untested principles?*

This is the beginning of me being broken, I suddenly realized. It was not just casual hunger that caused Gailan to grab this woman, intending to take her in front of me. He knew that his actions would bring her fear and anger spilling out. And then she was presented to me to take as he had, sooner or later to death. Someone must have smiled when I sent her out for food and water. I had acted in a way that my trial would be further prolonged.

I remembered Dagon saying before my trial that he would not feed me. That it would only extend my pain. I was now locked in with a human who I might eventually see only as prey as I entered the Hunger. It would last as long as it took.

I remembered Dagon saying that there are worse things than being dead. He would not die easily. Now he was within me, our Maker bonds providing information that my mate was living. One would know if the other was dying. And dying and dying. I was the bait that would bring him, if he could find me, to the beacon of my despair. I might, I would, call for him at the end.

"Lie down and sleep, Lucia," I said gently. "For the moment, you and I are safe. I cannot protect you for long." *I cannot protect you from myself,* I thought.

I smoothed the wheat-coloured hair back from her bruised cheek. I suggested sleep, but she could resist. I would not overpower her for as long as I could manage to avoid it.

"I have to go," she looked embarrassed. "I have to go outside to empty myself."

I waved towards the closed door. "If it is open, then by all means go,"

Stay gone, I thought, but I knew she would be retrieved and returned to me. Probably in worse shape.

Later I heard her come quietly back into the room. I sensed a false hopefulness in her that somehow things could change. I did not share her optimism. I had no hidden cards to play that I knew of. I pulled the thin blanket over us, and stroked her back briefly. She fell into sleep without struggling against it.

I said one more thing before surrendering to my own uneasy sleep.

"I am sorry," I whispered. "If I cannot say it later … I am so very sorry."

I awoke in a dream. The room was full of green light that sparkled and blended with the moonlight that now came in through the barred window.

I heard something. It was faint, and came and went as if it was blowing in on the wind. It was wild and beautiful, and alien to me. I had never heard anything like it. Or I had heard something like it, but I could not quite remember. My mind was full of green light and music.

I felt joyful and did not question that. It was a dream; a small mercy perhaps, in light of what was to come. Lucia slept on beside me, trusting. I knew that at some point I would break and destroy that trust. Or use my knife. Perhaps I would take her with me on that last trip, out to the stars and beyond.

She did not want to die. There was no doubt that she would rebound if allowed to.

There was someone bending over me, his finger to his lips. It was a long tapering finger, held up to a face that was not human. *But beautiful, ah, yes.*

"*We are seeking someone,*" he mind-spoke. "*She was known to us, and us to her briefly, and we would repay a kindness that she did.*"

I floated in green energy. My growing need was gone. His eyes drew me in, but told me nothing except that this beautiful being was looking into me deeply. I opened to his inquiry. He was welcome to see who I had been and why I was here.

Soon I might not be this me, but another, reduced to need and pain and desperation that I could not control.

"*If I could grant you one wish,*" he mind-spoke, "*what would it be?*"

I thought of Dagon, struggling in his dark world of the Shadakon around him. He might return to careless violence and blood taking. There were Shadakon who would eliminate any of their kind who had learned to walk another way among humans. Eliminate compassion or even empathy between the Shadakon and humans—rekindling the old wars. I thought of myself and my desperate love for him and the fear that what awaited me would bring him to his doom as well as mine unless I took the one preventative action he had given me. I knew that if I waited too long I would think of it too loudly and it would be taken from me.

"*Well,*" the thought rose lightly up through my mind, "*we made our choices, not in what we were, but how we chose to act. We loved while we could.*"

"Love is not measured in time," I thought. *"I will always love you Dagon!"* I thought. I touched my palm and thought I felt a faint flare of energy there. And then I answered.

"Take Lucia away from here. Wipe her mind of the pain she has endured here if you have such powers. I am afraid I will hurt her in the end. I ask that betraying her trust is not the last act of my life."

"So be it." Another being like himself materialized from the moonlight and green leafy light and effortlessly picked up the sleeping young woman.

I felt emptiness creep into me. *I can do this,* I thought. *Only this.* I hoped that this was truly happening.

"You are the one we seek," mind-spoke the beautiful one.

I now knew that I was neither asleep nor dreaming.

"I must induce deep sleep now," he mind-spoke. *"You can have no awareness of where we are taking you."*

He bent over me and I surrendered, willingly, to what now seemed to be a song. It was louder now, and filled the room and me as well. It was wild and strange and joyful; it was not of either of my histories. But I knew it, and I remembered before I forgot everything, where I had heard it. It was Lara's song. She had sung the last note on her last outgoing breath.

CHAPTER TWENTY-THREE

IN BETWEEN

I awoke in the morning in dappled green light—somewhere. I guessed that I was hidden in the vast forest that had surrounded my prison. I assumed that Lucia was out as well, though I did not think she would know me if we met again.

I knew that we had been transported somehow, past the vigilant evil that had surrounded us. I felt remarkably OK. Good, even. Not hungry. I sat up and was relieved that my knife still hung at my side.

There was a man, or someone not human but somewhat like a man, sitting next to me, obviously waiting for me to wake up. He laughed.

"Had it been steel, it could not have come along," he said. "A pretty piece, for such a tool as it is. Very old. But you knew that."

I was stunned, unable to really focus on anything around me. The colours shifted and swirled slightly in my side vision. Things shimmered that did not usually do so—the leaves, some blowing grass nearby. I was struck by their beauty and fell silent.

He waited and I turned to look at him fully. For a moment, he looked very old and fierce but then his features softened into an attractive younger face with dark green eyes and almost foxy features. I could see why humans had accepted invitations to dance at faerie parties, no matter what the cost was later.

"Faerie glamour," I murmured, and he smiled again. I wondered what his real smile looked like.

He shrugged. "We prefer the name of Sidhe," he said. "It was a name chosen by our kind on Earth. There are few there now because we require a natural world.

We can live in gardens and small wild patches briefly. But we need—" he spread his arms, "the intact web."

I sat up, noting that I had a deep persisting tiredness.

"But no hunger," he said. He did not ask.

I shook my head. "How is that possible?"

He paused and looked at me again, more closely. "You have been granted the gift of the elixir of life. Among other benefits, humans who drink it extend their lives past their natural lifetimes. That might not be a problem for one of the Shadakon," he continued, shrugging. "I could not say, as it is not our practice to offer it to them. Or that we will do so again. But the request came down from high places."

He looked to the swaying top of a large tree close by.

"I do not understand," I said

"Yes," he said, and I startled.

"We inform ourselves of what is happening in the human population. They are an invasive species, and seed and survive wherever they go. Wherever they live, the life force of the planet sickens. They refuse to limit their numbers and spread their toxic material all around them.

"You have held this land safe," I said, looking around at the lush greenness that surrounded us.

I could not read him completely, but I felt an under-mind rush of anger and sadness.

"We did not get here before the humans did a preliminary scourging of this place. You have noticed no large animals and lasting fear in the little ones. The humans see a place of no humans or their activities as empty and wasted potential. They conquer under the principle of Terra Nullus."

I understood the term. The waves of European settlers who swept into what was later called "The Americas" made treaties with those they found there, and then infected and murdered them after enslaving them or corralling them in inhospitable areas. Eventually the original inhabitants were gone or nearly so. This was the justifying clause used, first coined in the 1500s Old Earth date: that it was *empty land.* So the invaders claimed the right to do what they would to it.

"Raped it," said my companion. "Poisoned it and covered it with concrete. Ended most of the life in the ocean. It will take a long time to recover if it does. And it will not be as it was before this man-made extinction."

"Yes ... that is why I left Old Earth for good." As I said it, I realized that it was true even before I had left the ship, supposedly for a short shore break. I had gone AWOL from my planet as well as my career as spacer.

"Yes," he said. "As did we."

I wondered at the similarity of his speech and Dagon's. His use of laconic and give-nothing-away "Yes's."

"We, too, are the children of visiting gods or space invaders—take your pick. We too retained the thread of our bloodline. Like the Shadakon, we have many skills, and forgot less perhaps. We can go ... between."

"It probably comes of age," he said, answering my original unspoken question. "From living long lives. So many words are unnecessary."

"I can bring you more of the elixir of life," he said. "Just know that it is very precious, distilled without harm from the Life Force. That is why it quenches your thirst for energy." I thought of living with no hunger. How it might be both wonderful and terrible.

The connection, the passion ... I thought of Dagon and my body momentarily kindled.

But I was not hungry. Not now.

"Thank you," I said, "Perhaps later. However I must leave here soon. I don't know where I am going next, or how I can do that. I think there is something important that I must do, but I don't know what that is."

"That is the way when our fate draws us and we surrender to it," he said quietly. "But you have already done many important things, Danu of Dagon of the Shadakon. It is why we are helping you."

"Which reminds me," he said, with precise timing. "There is someone here to see you."

I stood up, got my feet under me, and followed my host for a short distance. There was a blanket spread on top of a natural lawn of short growing flowers and the two blended into each other. Maybe they were actually were part of each other. I shook my head again. Everything seemed slightly … askew.

There was a grey-haired woman sitting there in the dappled light. I saw her from behind, but I knew who she was. I should have sensed her even before that. However I felt like I was swimming in heavy water, I could not focus or sense very far ahead of me.

Morag stood and turned to me. We locked eyes. My feelings, long held in check, spilled out.

"Betrayal!" I blazed. "How could you?"

I would not cry. I would not. But the tears streamed down my cheeks. I clenched my fists and willed myself not to sob.

Morag neither spoke nor mind-spoke. She accepted the waves of rage and grief that I projected onto her, my assumptions of her compliance in my kidnapping by the hateful Gailan. That I believed her actions or inactions had resulted in me being imprisoned with a young woman; a human that I might have taken without contract, without her inner permission, because I must. I had had only the ultimate plan I had clung to, to use the slender knife I had carried—that I still carried.

Her total silence, both verbal and mind-spoken, would have further enraged me if I hadn't sensed that she was listening to me, waiting for me to be calm enough to hear her. She was quiet, taking it all without reacting.

Time passed. I stopped and managed to draw a few free breaths. I gathered myself—better late than never. Now I waited.

When she did speak, I was ready to hear what she would say.

"I am sorry, Danu. This was part of a desperate plan that could not be explained to you. Not all of it was under our control."

"When the Council suggested taking you to safety, I knew you would not be safe at all. That anywhere you or I or anyone who cared for you could picture in their mind as a destination would be the place you perished—if you ever reached it at all."

"So we let She, whose name you did not know, and her minion, her 'cur' as you called him, whisk you away and hide you in a place we thought we could find. They felt briefly smug about that." She smiled. "Once again Danu, your conduct with others brought you to the attention of those you had no idea were watching over you."

"And your inexplicable talent for finding a way through seemingly impossible situations once again served you well." She smiled again. "You have not failed yourself or us in this."

I wondered who the "us" was she referred to but let it pass. "You had prior contact with faerie.

During your first assignment, the Mother and I knew that much hung on what happened on your first day. We had no idea how much."

"I also heard that song," said Morag. "I knew, then, that something larger than what was expected had happened. Sometimes fairies attend the deaths of those humans who lives have touched their own. This has confounded humans on deathwatches before. It is woven into the folk history of Earth."

"It would have been very hard for us to find you, but easy for these folk. They were aware of the base you were held in and saw the young woman come outside. They sensed that she somehow walked in hope, but there had been no hope in that place before you arrived."

"The Sidhe rarely interfere directly in the doings of humans," she added. "But that they sometimes do so is documented in stories that some now demean by calling them children's fairy tales. It has come to mean something silly that obviously could not have occurred."

"They hide in plain sight. And the slight manipulations or corrections they make in the fabric of the universe are not easy for others to perceive. In this struggle that you and I and Dagon are in, they are in accord with us. When the life force is endangered, there are usually humans present, and Shadakon who live out of contract. You may understand a little more today. The contract is not just something that serves us, although it does, or the humans, which it also does. It works in the service of life. We are the shepherds of the human flock."

Or the grey finned shepherds of the sea, I thought.

"Without the taking of life, life itself is threatened," she said quietly. "If not large predators, then the smaller ones of plague and pestilence must serve."

I remembered Dan who died at my feet with nothing left to lose.

"Plagues do not discriminate," she said, looking directly at me. "We can."

I looked at her with stricken eyes. "Did Dagon know?" I asked. I pictured him not accompanying me out the door and her sudden disappearance. I didn't know if I could bear to know that he had watched me walk out to an almost certain doom, to enter a flitter with a Blood who despised us both.

"He did not ask," said Morag. "Although I suspect he understood that there must be twists of strategy in this. He could not warn you."

I remembered her instructions to him at my trial as he stood helplessly in front of me. "She has to find her own way," Morag had said. He had encouraged me to hang on to my anger. And turned away.

"*Danu!*" Morag had shifted to mind-speak. "*Your choice to turn away every time you are presented with the opportunity to enter into bloodlust is changing the world of the*

Shadakon! We were sure we could not change, and most do not want to. It was a given that violence was part of us, and to not exhibit it indicated weakness, a quality to be weeded out."

"Many now have perhaps unwillingly had to acknowledge that you are not a woman of weakness. Dagon, too, had begun on his own path of gentleness towards his clients before you met him."

"Not that that guaranteed their continuing survival," she added aloud.

I looked back at our first encounter. I remembered flying with him. That in itself would have justified the cost of my life, but there was more. I briefly allowed myself to miss and want him. I burned with it—a fire that didn't ever go out.

"And what did you observe when you went to him to his work at the fair?" Morag asked neutrally. She had doubtlessly heard had had transpired.

"I thought I would become closed off to him. That I would close myself off.

I knew what he did of course; I knew what he offered to the afternoon pleasure-seekers. And he had told me shortly after I came to him that he did what he did with men as well. I did not know how I would perceive what was to happen! But I knew that my prejudices would come between us, if not that day, then later."

"But I couldn't see what was happening between them as anything other than a gift," I continued. "I watched a dead-eyed addict reach at last a passion he could not have imagined." In my mind I again heard his spiralling cries that ended on a single triumphant note.

"Dagon gave me that too," I whispered. "Except I kept waking up in the morning."

Morag reached her arms out to me and I went into them. "Then you understand why he and you must be preserved?"

"But what if it could be only one of us—then who should survive?"

Morag looked at me with deep sadness in her eyes.

"I think you and I would both agree on who that one should be," she said. "But he would not. And, because you invoked the Ritual, you two are truly one. Even those who have disapproved of his actions cannot deny that you are mated."

"I think that both of you must survive and thrive—or neither. And, once again, you have proven that you are a wild card of great value. But meanwhile," she said, "here you are in Between. None who would cause you harm can find you here. Rest awhile and enjoy the sanctuary offered from danger and from hunger. You have earned it."

But all I wanted was to re-join with Dagon. Again, I briefly flared with my longing for him.

Morag smiled. "And he for you," she said. "Unlikely as it once seemed, I know that this is true. You will know when it is time to go," she said.

And she walked what seemed a very short distance into the trees and simply disappeared.

CHAPTER TWENTY-FOUR

THE INVITATION

It is difficult for me to find words about what occurred while I recuperated and took refuge in Between. My hosts kept their distance except for the young-old one who had waited while I slept. He had slightly re-adjusted his presenting features so that he now appeared to me lithe and attractive, his blond hair bright gold, and his face unlined. His piercing green eyes were the same. He would come to me in the morning and bring me a small wooden cup of dark green liquid. Each mouthful diffused calm energy throughout me. It brought no desire for more than what I needed.

After draining the cup, I waited to enjoy the now expected dazzle of light and colours and the sense of the interweaving patterns of the life around us. I could now feel the tree elders as they leaned in over me.

I remembered him saying that the decision to allow me to partake in this life drink had come from higher up. He had looked up to the top of a tall tree.

I no longer doubted that. I did not touch plants here absentmindedly, but now asked permission. Some indicated *yes*, some *no*. I was standing beside a patch of exuberantly growing plants with fuzzy leaves when he happened upon me. I had asked one of the plants for permission to touch, and it was granted. I reached out and gently held its arrow-shaped leaf. I felt the richness and vitality in its soft furry under-leaf. I let go and stepped back.

He had come along at that moment, or perhaps he had been with me since I had begun my walk. They all had the ability to appear and disappear as they chose. He stood observing me, with a faint smile on his face. "This is similar to a plant called 'nettle' on Earth," he said.

"Its sting is worse here, and lingers long enough that few willingly touch it twice. Most call it '*Touch-me-not.*' I think you may have a different name between the two of you."

He had an incredibly kind smile, even when he was delivering information that might be disturbing. One evening, with a large moon rising, he came to me with something significant to say.

"We will dance to the midsummer's eve moon tonight," he said. "We too have our passions that we feed and enjoy together. I suggest that you move as close to the edge as you can."

He indicated one direction, but I had by now figured out that Between was a circle, and we were usually in the centre. As one moved further away, it felt like one had stepped back from a fire on a cold night. It was always a relief to return to the centre glow and energy. It was always obvious which way to return.

He was asking me to step back as far as I could.

"We have accommodated you here," he said unapologetically, "but some things cannot be set aside for your convenience." He waited to see if I would protest. I did not.

"Humans are sometimes drawn to our gatherings," he said. "This is our summer celebration, and we dance to the joy of full summer and her energies. Humans who blunder into our rituals are forever changed. At the very least, they learn of passion that they will never again find among their own kind. I think you experienced this when you joined with Dagon. You would have done anything to stay with him, but he had to make the choice to accept and preserve you." He stopped abruptly.

I heard his silence.

"We do not make that choice," he said flatly. "We admit no one to our ranks.

It is, perhaps, impossible. We know the effect we have on mortals, and perhaps also on Shadakon. It is why you have met few of us during your stay. They would have avoided you easily, but you did not attempt to step over the boundaries we kept between you and us."

He looked at me from what I suspected were ancient eyes. "You have never sought me out, but waited for me to appear. This has been duly noted," he said calmly, "and approved of. But, behold the underlying truth of what I say. If you do come forward tonight, at a certain point we will be too …" he searched for words, "… too engaged and impassioned to notice. Your decision might be your life-long grief. And although you now yearn for your distant lover, that could be forfeit as well."

He shrugged. "So it is with humans. Shadakon are not known to us as those who do more than run together. Not known for long bonding," he said simply. "Some fires consume others by depriving them of their fuel—since you sometimes think in fire metaphors."

"Do not come to us, Danu," he said gravely, "though you feel the invitation." He looked at me, assessing me. "Though you may want to, as strongly as any hunger you have experienced. It could lead you astray."

I did not ask, "Is there somewhere else I can go?" I did not ask, "Can you give me shelter, that I might barricade myself in?" I knew that anything I could devise would not hold me. And, obviously, returning to my world at this time was more dangerous than this.

"I cannot keep you away, but I can keep away any of us who might test you for their amusement."

He handed me a bag of some weight that he had kept well away from him as we walked.

"When I am gone, shake out what is inside and make a circle around yourself. We cannot, or perhaps, *choose* not to cross it," he said. "It will protect you well enough from any of us."

He looked at me without judgement, but I wondered how he thought the evening would go for me.

"It will keep us out, Danu," he said. "It will not keep you in. You must do that yourself if you choose."

And then he was gone.

I walked out in the direction of the edge until I could not take another step. There was less growing here, and the trees were stunted like those in an alpine meadow. Rocks pushed up through the soil; a cold wind spiralled in toward me.

"Home, sweet home." I shrugged. I shook out a finely woven rope of steel and arranged it into a circle.

I felt a little sorry for myself. The soft summer moon lit twilight was less attractive here. Could I have known that this circle would be the ring where I fought for my continuing love of Dagon? At present, there was no opponent.

"Easy enough." I lay down and sought refuge in sleep.

When the Call came, it came in my dreams. I know that while dreaming, one cannot move. This is not true once one wakes up, assuming one is still dreaming.

I felt the stirring of passion, a passion that I had more or less locked down for the duration of my separation from Dagon. But time has passed, and I yearned to feel his presence. I could imagine him approaching me, and how my body always knew and flamed to life. I luxuriated in feeling this again, as in the last days … weeks? I had felt nothing. Instead I had felt the emptiness that I once always carried in me claiming me again.

I wanted him. I needed him. The green energy that had sustained and calmed me was inadequate. I wanted to share the primal energy that we both could gather and use to drive each other to higher and higher states.

Every part of me yearned and begged to combine with him. He was out there, but did not come.

Then I must go to him.

I opened my eyes. I could hear drumming and music that was not exactly music coming from the centre of the glade. They were tuning up and up towards a crescendo that would likely be the death of my connection with Dagon.

I knew this to be true. In his world it had been he and I. Here there were many of the Sidhe, all intentionally raising a cone of energy to the moon. It invited, it demanded, attendance.

I laid down again, head pointed towards the Call, but now it was all around me. It danced as sparkles in the moonlight that landed on my body. The light touch of them left spots of desire where they settled. I was afire. I wanted. Not like the trial, in which I fought the extinction of my life energy. Now I struggled with energy that would make me many times more than I had even been, and never again who I was.

"I am Danu of Dagon of the Shadakon," I repeated stubbornly.

"Forget all that." The message flared in my mind. *"Forget everything. Tonight we dance and you can dance with us. It will be worth everything and more."*

Something came together in my mind and I was able to briefly gain my will and power to think. "*I do not give permission!*" I mind-spoke. "*There is no inner contract from me.*"

"*Ah, but you will, you must. The night is passing and with it the bliss we would bring to you.* I noted that the moon had almost reached its apex in the sky. I would hold on.

Easier decided than done.

I realized that I was treading the inside of my circle a scant distance from the moment of deftly stepping over. And then I suddenly realized that I could fly out. But the thought of the steel perimeter seemed to extend up into the sky. I could not fool myself and cross over in the air without knowing what I had chosen.

At one point I had shed my clothes, to let the full impact of the energy touch me everywhere. I wanted to open to it, to take it in.

"*Not here.*" I heard, no longer knowing if I heard spoken or unspoken words.

"*Come closer. There is still time.*"

"*Dagon!* I begged. "*Be with me. I am for you. I am only for you.*" I touched my palm and felt a different energy there. I felt him within me. But he joined with many others in sexual passion! Why could I not do the same, for one night, under the moon in a place that was between our worlds?

I answered myself. He gave little of himself to the ones he served at the fair. They only gave him energy and demands for pleasure. It was not love and he had corrected me about that.

This would demand my surrender and void any promises I had made to those I knew and loved.

And then . . . this was an unfair contest tonight. He was not here to stand with me against this. I must stand for both. This was the Sidhe's joy, but also weapon to undo humans.

"We ran together," Dagon had said about his early history. "We ran them from village to village, out onto the moors and into the forest. We feasted together."

The Sidhe and Shadakon were branches of the same tree. Or scions of older ones.

"*I do not give permission!*" I mind-spoke.

I heard a laugh then. "*Oh, how you will regret your choice this night, Shadakon.*

The night in your life when you could have felt the full energy of the life force, rather than just taking sips."

I howled then. I howled and shivered in my lust and loneliness.

There were some of the plants I had innocently touched earlier on a walk, growing just outside my circle. They had granted me permission to touch them before; I had another request of them now.

"I ask that you give me pain," I said. "I must hurt you to attain that, but I ask that you hurt me in full measure."

I got affirmation. Leaning out of the circle, I grabbed handfuls of the leaves, ripping them from their stalks. I rubbed them on my naked body.

The first strike of pain was like that of a snakebite, a deep jab that stopped my breath. Then the areas of agony spread to fill all other spaces, whether touched by the crushed leaves or not. I breathed pain out and then even more in with each breath. I howled again. And then I lay down, unable to stand. The pain took me out like a giant tide, far, far from the shores of my consciousness. I did not know myself anymore. I no longer heard any Call but that of my anguished body.

"*Thank you*," I mind-whispered, as I faded from the moonlight and my green smeared body. "*Thank you*."

When I awoke, or returned, the pain was a faint reminder. The crushed leaves, now dried, fell off as I surveyed myself in the morning light. I looked over at the planting and was relieved to see that I had done no serious damage. The untouched leaves turned to the light and new unfurling ones were ready to use the empty spaces.

I picked up the braided steel rope and slid it back into the bag.

"*Such a small barrier,*" I thought, "*but effective.*" I replaced my clothes, wincing only slightly.

I stepped over to the Touch-me-not, smiling at the appropriateness of its name. I would not willingly touch it again I thought, until I heard, quietly in my mind, "*Touch once again if you will. We never meant you harm. We only did what we do. And what you asked us to do.*"

I reached out and gravely held an undamaged leaf. There was, again, no pain between us.

I headed back. There was no sign of the gathering of the night before. I hadn't expected to see any.

My host was waiting with the cup of the elixir of life. My hands shook only slightly as I took it from him. He did not directly comment on the remaining bits of green that darkened my skin. Only to say, "You seem to be able to find and recognize your tools here as well as in your own world. It has been noted and we approve of your skills."

And then he said calmly, "You have another visitor. We have made another rare exception for you. But perhaps you earned this last night. Enjoy," he said. "He cannot stay long, but we will shelter you and him for a little while."

CHAPTER TWENTY-FIVE

DANU ENTERTAINS HER LOVE BENEATH A LARGE GREEN TREE

I turned and he was there.

I had slept on rocky ground and was smeared with the remains of the potent leaves I had applied. My skin still tingled slightly. There were probably sticks and leaves in my hair. I hadn't seen a mirror for—however long I had been here. But none of this even crossed my mind. If it had, I would have remembered that he had seen me in worse conditions, including being a depressed, desperate human and later a dying wolf bitch.

I looked into his beautiful dark eyes, with their shifting lights. They might have caught me once, but now I thought I could have turned away if I had wished to.

I did not want to. I wanted to fall into a personal fire with him.

"First things first," he said. He stood in the sun and was glorious to me. I asked no questions, he asked no questions. I don't think I could have spoken anyway.

I led him aside to a glade that may have grown up around us, sheltering us in a green room to use as we would chose.

"You said you wanted me under a green tree," he said huskily. "As usual, you were ahead of us all."

He drew me to him.

"Say it!" he said. "You have to say it aloud."

"I want you Dagon of the Shadakon," I breathed. "I have stayed alive for this moment. I could say more but will not now."

"No, you will not," he said, and promptly bent to my lips.

He looked momentarily startled and I wondered if traces of Touch-me-not clung there. He pulled my shirt off. The knife hung, exactly as hand's reach, at my side. He held it briefly after he carefully pulled the thong over my head.

I felt his sorrow come, and then he pushed it aside.

"Time enough for stories later," he said. "I am very relieved that you did not use it. Although I believe you were close at times."

Then my pants and last my moccasin-soft shoes were on the grass. I stood in the sunlight and I wanted him. I ached for him, not the impersonal passion I had fought off last night.

"Now you," I said. "You must also say it, Dagon of the Shadakon."

I waited. A silence fell between us. Like an eclipse of the sun, it chilled my heart and I stepped back in alarm.

"I want you Danu of Dagon, but I fear that my wanting you will bring your death. I have thought of this in your absence and I could not bear to be the reason for this. This is the dilemma of our loving."

"It was always so," I said. "I have always bet everything on the wager. It was always more than just the farm."

"I want thee, Dagon. From our first moment until our last."

"So be it," said Dagon quietly, but there was no laughter in him.

I quickly removed his clothing and looked at him. I could play no games of coyness with him now. I leaned up against a tall tree and he took me by storm. I felt like I was riding a thunderhead that rose up and up, taking us with it. Everything and everyone close by probably felt the rush of our energy, the breaking up of our individual loneliness into a long awaited, hard-driving rain, and then the short peace that followed.

We did it again. This time we lay on the grass beneath that tree and took our time.

He gave me some of his stored energy and I shared the green energy that I was living on while I was here.

It stopped him momentarily.

"Is this possible?" he asked in amazement. "I wondered how you kept yourself here but I never guessed. You are fed by the Sidhe? They give you the elixir of life? To a Blood who takes energy from others? How can this be?"

So we began to tell our respective stories.

I should say rather, we showed each other what had happened to both of us in our absence from each other. There were only occasional clarifying questions.

He saw me get into the flitter and discover whom the driver was. He hissed. He saw me watch Morag walk away and felt the fear and sense of betrayal close in around me. He sighed.

He stopped momentarily when he saw me challenge Gailan to formally reveal his name to me. He just shook his head. "You will either rise in our ranks, or die trying," he said. "Your surety of your place is not to be underestimated."

"Although they continue to make that same mistake," he said, smiling.

When I showed him me sitting beside the furious Gailan he grew quiet. "Are you always so willing to take on your enemies at such close quarters?"

I thought about that. I thought about the height we flew above the forest. We were both armed, and the outcome of any struggle would have been a stalemate at best. But he had already said he was delivering me alive. I did not believe he was brave or ambitious enough to go against his orders.

"Hmmm," said Dagon. "I will tell you about his possible outcome later."

He saw me step out the flitter and the scene that developed between Gailan, Lucia and I.

"Lucia?" he asked.

"That came later," I said. "But she touched me first, and I claimed her. Later I thought that it all had been staged by Gailan."

I showed him the small room with the barred window and Lucia lying by my side, trusting me to keep her safe.

"With no wish to die." he said.

"Yes. You taught me some of what I dealt with. But the eventual outcome would have been the end of her or me—or both." I shivered.

"Yes," he said. I smiled. Goddess, how I had missed that one syllable.

"But that was neither of your fates," he said quietly.

I showed him the green glinting moonlight. I showed him the question I had been asked—'If I had to choose one to save, who would it be?' I wondered how he would take my answer. From the first time since we had re-joined, I intentionally lowered my eyes from his.

He waited. Eventually I looked up as he was waiting for me to do.

"Any other choice would have led to your end," he said. "What a pretty trap you were in throughout all of this. She must have been there, enjoying your growing realization that you eventually would become a killer against your will. So the fairies took Lucia away. But why you?"

I showed him the song I had heard in the room. I replayed the words of he who took me—that he had needed to know that he had the right person. That it was me that they wanted. And then they brought me here. I didn't know what happened to Lucia. I asked that they wipe away the years of her memories of that evil place. "Indeed," he said.

"And you can say all this with the innocence of not knowing that none of us have been allowed to be here before."

"Well, now three of us have," I said. And I realized that I might have surprised him again though he quickly guessed who that was.

"Now it's your turn to talk," I said, trying not to think about the previous night and that story.

He looked at me and ran one finger lightly from my lips, between my breasts, and then down to where, incredibly, I still wanted him. He held my eyes. I had thought he could not, but found out differently.

"I am older and more powerful than you," he said levelly. "I will not act against your will. But you need to know this. There is coming a time when I will be Alpha of the clan. You will not also be Alpha. You will, however," he moved his long index finger ever so slightly down to rest lightly on me, "have many benefits. You will be the mate of the Alpha."

He looked at me innocently while all I could think about was—

"Or, perhaps, someday you will be Alpha," he said thoughtfully. He pulled back slightly to look at me as if that was a possible idea. "It is impossible, but you have proved time and time again that you have skills that are unpredictable. That even you do not know what you can do."

"That would take some adjustment," he mused. "I will think about that."

"But meanwhile, finish your story," he said. "We have but one night to account for. Even though you are even hotter than I remembered."

"It could be our absence," he said. "Or it could be a night under the full moon with the Sidhe."

So, with my body holding a heat that he would neither encourage nor let die, I showed him my night in the circle of steel. My body told him how I had yearned to jump that circle, and join in what for me might be oblivion. For us would be oblivion.

I let him feel the first bite of Touch-me-not, and the welcome agony it brought. He put his hand to his lips. He had felt the fading effects of what I had willingly smeared all over my body. And I had asked the plant to aid me in this, and thanked it, and again made peace with it later.

He was silent. The wind moved through the tree branches above. A leaf spun down and landed on my hair. Neither of us moved it. It felt like affirmation. Time passed, or perhaps it did not. Between was a time of an endless day. I had seemingly only spent one endless night of the many I must have been here for.

I thought I had seen all of him, naked by moonlight, candle gleam, and now sunlight. I thought I knew him to the core. I had bet my life on it.

I had not fully seen him. I could recall him suffering with me through my Trial. And the night before I left—but he had not allowed me to openly see this. Now he wept, tears coursing down his cheeks. They made tracks down his chest and disappeared below. He did not make a sound.

I did not make a sound. I did not wish to stop him or even comfort him. I watched in amazement.

He stopped on his own, and looked at me with lashes beaded with what could have been rain, but was not. We beheld each other.

He shook his head. "I thought when I spoke of being mate to you as my Alpha, I spoke of impossibilities. I didn't even think beforehand of what I was saying. The Sidhe are close to what we are," he said. "They take of the life energy. They have no interest in humans or Shadakon.

We are as dust in the wind to them. In the case of humans, they see them as a blight."

"When they summon, few can refuse." he continued. "Their passions are too large for the others they partially share worlds with. What is passion to them is madness to the rest of us."

"It is no accident that you were here on midsummer's eve," he said. "They do not allow accidents. You were given a tool that would absolve them of any responsibility for what followed after you crossed out of the circle. Likewise, the warning you received. It was as ineffectual as the words of the guide who tried to dissuade you from leaving with me."

"Permission is a complex issue," he added. "I'm not sure I agreed to you loving me as fiercely as you do."

"I have your inner permission," I said. "I touched you first. I claimed you."

He started at my words.

"I am yours, Danu of Dagon," he said. "I cannot always believe how it is between us."

He was silent. Time wrapped around us and we had all we needed.

"I don't always think I deserve you," he said.

"Dagon!" I pushed him down into the grass. "We deserve each other."

I straddled him and moved with the sounds of the trees, the sliding shadows, and little leaves brushing against each other softly. I heard these things now. The earth energy entered me and then I stopped. I held us both in a hiatus of heat without ending.

"It's called tantric sex," I said. A wise-ass vampire taught me.

He groaned.

And so we passed a very long afternoon. Eventually, we left our tree and walked around.

The Sidhe who I had been in contact with throughout my stay in Between showed up, looked at both of us and smiled. I realized that I might not know if this was truly the same individual who was in continuing contact with me. I sensed, however, that it was. In fairy tales, they were interested in lovers and the energy they generated.

I showed Dagon the Touch-me-not and he surveyed it from a safe distance.

It was time for him to tell his version of what had happened between our parting and now. He related it to me in mind-speak and visuals. His skill in this was faster than mine, and I felt like I was seeing a sped up time-lapse version, with details missing between one scene and the next. I followed as best I could.

He was used to being closed and giving away little as a habit of safety. Some version of don't-think-about-the-white-tiger. I had read that in a book of Zen koans, written by Japanese monks when the Europeans were still Stone Age farmers.

Self-knowledge had always come and then was lost again by the humans.

I wondered where the white tiger lurked today, but put that thought aside.

As we walked nowhere in particular (in circles, I knew), Dagon showed me walking out the door the day I left. Morag had stopped him before he made a move to accompany me to the street. She had revealed nothing to him.

Dagon was also was familiar with the meaning of silences. He had turned his back on my leaving, looking at the tapestry that captured an earlier dangerous time in his existence, and tried to hold on to the agreed upon plan to get me away. He had heard and felt my yelp and surge of anger and fear as I entered the flitter. Then there was nothing. Quickly out of easy range, I disappeared off the radar. We had both been told to not attempt to use our bond to communicate. It was to be our hidden card.

When Morag told him later that I was nowhere to be found, she offered no information other than she would tell him where I was when she could.

"That is a very ambivalent statement," I said. He merely raised an eyebrow.

Meanwhile he was gathering and storing energy. Without me to share with, he was topped up easily as he worked. Work was work—there were no details.

The behind scenes of the Council was rocked when it was announced that Gailan had died a violent death in which his body was destroyed in an explosion of a flitter in mid-air. Dagon's mate was presumed to have been in the same accident. Gailan had been taking her on a tour of the planet. Many knew how unlikely this story was, but most accepted it without questioning.

Dagon had said nothing and shut down. There were few condolences to him or to She who Gailan shadowed. There were those who might have been relieved to be rid of us both. And there were many Shadakon who may or may not have followed the story of my recent entry into their ranks. They were silent either for their own reasons or because they simply did not care.

The loss of Gailan left a position open on the Council. Morag put Dagon forward. He was accepted.

The nameless She knew that I was not dead, or not by her hand at any rate. The human witness who could have been used to get the necessary information about what happened that night had also disappeared. Her immediate tool to bring Dagon down had failed. Humans died around her to appease her immediate anger, but in the spaceport anyway, she continued to act under legal contract. Few of her prey could have given truly voluntary permission, of course.

I saw this unnamed powerful Shadakon in his mind, a young woman with a bruised beauty in another part of the city that the space company also monitored. Human men came here with no pretence of hiding whatever it was they wanted.

Here there were male and female humans and others of all ages, all available for a price, as well as alcohol and expensive drugs. In particular, there were pleasure sellers for those who sought to receive pain in their search for pleasure, or at least release. Some of the travellers came to Her, hoping the pleasure they eventually might experience at her hands would be worth the pain they had agreed to.

I doubted that many of them later felt that they had received a fair transaction—if they lived through it at all.

In his recounting of our time apart, Dagon and his nemesis were together frequently.

"Keep your friends close, and your enemies closer," I murmured.

"We have history, Danu," he said. "I don't want to go into that now. We had something."

"It wasn't being mated," he said. "She kept up with me in some very old and bloody times. We followed the migrations of humans, burying ourselves in the sands during the day and preying on the endless streams of humans on the move."

"Remember the sands of Africa," I said.

He looked at me. "Not now, Danu. There are more immediate things that need saying now."

"Three days ago Morag disappeared. There were some who searched for her very diligently. She was not to be found by any of our means. I understand why now. She reappeared later with no comment," he continued.

"I don't know if those Shadakon most determined to hold onto the old ways suspect that there is a Between. And I don't know if they could enter it even if they did know. But if the old forests of this planet burned …?" He spread his arms. "The Sidhe would leave. This would cease to be. There is more at stake than you and I, Danu. Or Morag.

This planet holds undamaged forests and a largely intact web of life. It is the only one of its kind that I know of. The humans are waiting for the opportunity to take it."

"The Shadakon are as unaware that they are tied to the life force as are the humans?" I asked.

"Not all of us," he said.

I took in what he had given me. According to the official story, I was presumed dead, unable to regenerate from shattered pieces of my body somewhere in the forest. As was Gailan. But I was far from dead. What about him?

"She would not forgive him for losing you and the human witness. If she was there and it happened on his watch, she would have killed him just to feel better. Or, at very least, made him suffer. If he still exists, it is by now a terrible state to be in. She may revive him later."

"And you are able to move freely about without appearing to be upset about my disappearance?"

"Of course," he said unemotionally. "I have set aside my foolishness and am back doing what is expected of me—scrabbling for power both overtly and covertly."

I was silent for a long time. I did not want to say this accusingly, but in the end he knew what I was thinking anyway. And I had no other way to say it—

"Have you?" I asked.

"Have I what?" he asked. As if he did not understand what I had asked him! As if he didn't know the state of my heart at this moment!

"For all intents and purposes, yes," he said. "I must."

We stared at each other. *"I don't remember giving you permission to love me so fiercely,"* he had said. *"Permission is complex,"* he had also said. He had cried.

I held his tender heart in my memories. I continued to stare at him. We walked aimlessly and ended up where we had begun. The same grove, or somewhere like it, was in front of me and I entered it without looking back. He stood at the entrance without moving.

"Don't do this," he said. "This is necessary now. It's the only way that you will remain safe. I am being watched and monitored every moment of the day and night. I must be who I was, without the distraction of a new part-human mate. I can fall easily into my old routines."

"I am very believable," he said, in some failed attempt at humour or reassurance.

"I have always known that," I said. I felt like I was suddenly in some crushing atmosphere after being in space for months. I struggled to breathe. It seemed almost like a minor detail to me now, but I asked my last question.

"And what happens to me? I cannot stay here indefinitely. I have no place in the spaceport. I am now a Blood with a dead ID. I wouldn't get far any direction that I went."

Not that I cared. Maybe I'd show up and just let fate decide what happened next.

"Danu! Please. Let me enter." He stood in the entrance of trees, suddenly needing my permission to come to me. He meant something deeper as well.

"Permission is a complex issue," I said. "You can come to me here. But I cannot come to you. I can't see that as a good situation," I said sadly. "Not a balance that will hold indefinitely."

I thought of the gathering that I had fought and successfully resisted the night before. The passion that would have been mine for one night. Nothing would have remained of it by morning. Or possibly only its effect of driving me out of my own life.

But I was already driven out of my life. All my lives. "The circle cannot hold," I said.

"Please, give me six months," he said.

"Please give us the rest of this afternoon," he whispered.

In fact, the afternoon seemed not to be progressing, although I had moved from joy and passion to suspicious sorrow.

"Where am I to go?" I asked again. He looked at me from across the distance that had suddenly grown between us.

"Morag has a plan, and she will let you know soon," he said, knowing that I might not like any more of Morag's plans.

"I can only speak for today," he said quietly. "I can only show you what is between us now. I can only promise that I will try to honour this place you have grown comfortable in and the life force of this planet. I will be your mate forever." He touched his palm. "You are within me and me in you. You know that. You know and forget and remember again and again."

"I will never forget," he said. "Until the stars fall from our sky."

I let him come to me then and reach out and draw me to him. My head reached his shoulder and it fit there. We stood unmoving, one being, at rest. If I could have rooted and remained here I would have. A tall, lean tree and a slightly smaller one, under the sun and moons.

Later? A lot later? My host came to the entrance of our bower. "It is time," he said to both of us.

One more gentle brush of my lips, and Dagon was gone.

CHAPTER TWENTY-SIX

OUT FROM BETWEEN

I did not turn around to watch him go. Maybe this was how my leaving had been for him.

I simply could not bear to watch him disappear into the green. Leaving me.

I sat down beneath the sheltering tree, putting my back to its trunk and tried to breathe smoothly.

In, Grief.

Out, Grief.

So we must move through what we cannot change. One way out and that is through. Through and through.

After some time I must have fallen asleep. Or perhaps I had been granted an island of respite while the green energy of the place entered me to cool the fires that Dagon and I had created and sustained. Perhaps I was just exhausted by a long hard night and harder day.

When I awoke, the day was dim. Haze swirled around the bases of the trees and the small night songs had begun. I waited for something—I hoped I would recognize when or if I saw it.

What now? What now?

To my surprise, the Sidhe who was my guide or keeper appeared before me. He bore something that glimmered faintly, and in his hand he had a cup of what I supposed was sustenance for me. He sank effortlessly to the ground in front of me. Something that might have been fireflies or what was similar on this world seemed to accompany him and gently lit the space between us.

He studied me for a while in silence.

I thought I had no more questions, but then realized that I did have one that had crossed my mind every day that I saw him, and then faded out of my thoughts. It was not about me, or Dagon. It was not about the future of us or of this planet and its intertwined web of life.

I was not sure that my future stretched much further before me. It seemed now that I had never believed that it did. Events had occurred since I arrived here that made me more hopeful than I had ever been, but also more despairing. However, I would wait awhile longer. I would see what happened next.

I faced the deep green eyes of the being before me. Although he was not trying, I thought, I felt the draw of his energy envelop me. I remembered the fierce, no, the impassive face I had briefly seen at our first meeting. One who was very old, and whose interests were truly not focused on me.

"Not on you, Danu," he said, without attempting to pretend that he had not been following my thoughts. "But what you do, and what seemingly just happens around you."

"Everyone has wanted to test you. And everyone, except perhaps your lover, has gravely underestimated you," he said. "In some cases, many times, without seeming to learn from it."

He smiled, "You slip through unscathed from situations that could take you down or end your usefulness. Over and over."

"My usefulness?"

"Do not take offence at that word, Danu. We all have our usefulness, although in the case of most humans, we cannot see it. The Shadakon have their purpose. They bring death in a time that is highly regulated and where a truly random death is ... hard to come by."

"I am talking about humans here," he said unperturbed by what he might have revealed. "There are too many humans. Everywhere," he said flatly.

"And yet our fates were woven together before history was recorded, or any that survived anyway."

Two races of Visitors, and the subsequent multiplying humans, I thought.

"Yes," he said. "And we have more in common with the Shadakon than with your people. You, however," he said carefully, "are an anomaly. We continue to study you."

"You resisted our midsummer's eve magic," he said. "You find resources where others would not."

I finally remembered what I had wanted to ask. It was something that had left my mind every time I tried to focus on it.

"You have my name," I said. "I would like to have yours, if you would give it to me."

He started slightly. Happily, I now could see these things.

"Do you realize what you ask, newly-turned Shadakon?" I heard the ancient haughty pride and distance in his voice and mind-speak.

"No," I said. "I only know that you know my name, and I do not call you by any name."

"Who has no name cannot be called," he said. "The caller has no claim to expect that one would listen, much less come as called."

I remembered the story of Rumpelstiltskin. I was sure it was a very degraded version of a truth. But still ...

"Yes," said the very powerful ancient one before me. "Your lover understood the power of that. You gave him your name and asked him for his. It was the beginning of your power over him."

I sat stunned. I hadn't known.

"We all wonder what in fact you do know, Danu. It is a topic of great interest.

I don't recall you making the acquaintance of every bush here. But you knew one well; had met it open-minded."

"And then you laid your protective circle within reach of it. Now if you were, ah, watching this from a distance, what would you make of that?"

I shook my head. I could not find any thought that would indicate that I knew what I was doing.

"No thought. No. You act in accord with a path that leads you forward. And that path is what interests us, and should interest anyone who you may affect."

"You chose Dagon at the fair. He was, and is, by Shadakon standards, an individual not destined to go particularly far. Yes, he had opened his awareness to allow for some gentleness in his dealings with his prey. Yet a scant few months since he met, since he was claimed by you, those are your words—he was on Council. The voice for violence and no-contract killing suddenly has less power. Morag is manoeuvring to bring a new balance to the Shadakon."

"What affects the Shadakon and humans affects us," he said quietly. "But more importantly, it affects the web of life here."

"Dagon explained some of that to me," I said, "today."

"Yes," he said. "Events are unfolding rapidly now. And through it all, you walk unharmed. We decided to help you any way we could. We brought you out of sure soul death when you were imprisoned with Lucia. We brought you to Between. We gave you something no human and few Shadakon's lips have ever touched."

I bowed my head. I had been arrogant. He had had opportunity to give me his name and had chosen not to. I had not noticed this. I had accepted his gifts without question.

"Forgive me for my ignorance," I said. "I have only been reborn as Shadakon recently.

And my recollections of things faerie are far away in childhood memories of stories I read then. I thank you for the many gifts you have bestowed on me. Including a night of passion that showed me at least, how intensely the fire can burn."

He smiled and seemed younger and kinder than he had a moment ago. "I believe that Dagon was quite surprised at what you brought to him today. And yes, there was faerie magic still present within you. You chose not to dance with us, Danu, perhaps for the best. But he will never forget this day he passed with you. That is what we can do both for and to humans and, it would seem, the Shadakon."

"But I have brought you some things you will need," he said. "At present you are still bearing the signs of crushed Touch-me-not and, ah, a vigorous afternoon." He smiled as at a pleasant thought.

"I have brought you some fresh clothing, much like what you wore before, and a comb for your tangled red hair. You will find a pool behind your favourite tree," he said. "Bathe and restore yourself in the water of this world, and dress yourself. When you are done, drink this cup I have brought you."

"It will taste different than before," he said. "You will fall into a deep sleep, and we will move you on to the next destination of your journey. Nothing is guaranteed to any of us, Danu," he said gently. "Especially lasting safety. But we believe you will be safe enough in the immediate future."

He continued to face me and I knew he was reading my thoughts. I opened to it. I suspected most was known already anyway. I regretted nothing. Especially loving Dagon. Perhaps it all circled around Dagon and the fact that after a lifetime of avoidance I had learned about my own passion and ability to love.

"He is far luckier than he could have imagined. You are the queen to his king. And I am speaking about chess here, not poker."

He smiled again and I saw his full beauty for the first time and gasped.

"We could have danced under the moonlight, you and I," he said lightly. "I would have enjoyed that. But I am glad you resisted—for now."

"You may call me Fiórcara, Danu," he said. "Call if you have great need."

The pool was sparkling with starlight. The water was cool and refreshing. The clothes fit perfectly, although they felt lighter and softer to my skin than my old ones.

The cup was waiting for me. I drank it down.

CHAPTER TWENTY-SEVEN

DANU COMES HOME TO THE SEA

When I awoke, I lay curled on my side and my small sling and knife were no longer beside me. But in springing up, I felt the soft leather and hardness within beneath the pillow my head had been on a moment before.

I fell back, momentarily relieved.

I remembered swallowing the contents of the cup that had been left for me by Fiórcara. I remembered the stars going out as I slumped to the ground. He had allowed me the memory of his name then—and of Between. I brought that with me on the next leg of my journey to … I had no recollection of this room, this sea breeze. I had never seen the large tranquil sea of this planet that must be close by. The two moons almost cancelled out each other's tidal effects, except the larger could raise small tides. The sea's edge was, I thought, largely unpopulated. By humans, I corrected. I now knew that the majority of this planet, Exterra, was held by those committed to keeping it intact from others who might have eagerly bought and used it, but curiously did not think to do so.

But for a few parts held by humans and Shadakon, the entire planet had been glamoured out of existence.

"Avalon!" I thought, before falling asleep again. I knew roughly where I was, and I also knew who I was a guest of—the Mothers.

When I awoke again, it was afternoon and golden motes of dust sparkled in the slanting rays of this planet's orange sun. I remembered other sparkles of energy at other times. I shivered. But these remained what they were. The woman standing beside my bed was so quiet of mind that for a moment I did not know she was there.

She spoke to me, although she mind-spoke me as well. The message was basically the same.

"Welcome back to us, Danu. We are pleased to offer you sanctuary here, although it must be a working holiday."

She smiled. We both knew what that meant: that eventually I must feed.

"This is an isolated hospice, as you would call it, on a small island. The sufferers of the incurable plagues and various contagious diseases of man can come here, to be kept apart from the general population and find what peace they may without living out their remaining days of their lives in isolation units. Now that you are here, that may be easier."

Again I was struck by the total acceptance within her of what I did. And of what I was. She walked in the fields of death, and yet could or would not offer an easier option. I knew that there were drugs that could bring a peaceful enough, or at least unconscious, ending.

She answered my thoughts. "Yes," she said. "And some of our guests choose those. But surprisingly, many do not. And no one here would force such a thing or trick them into such a choice. Many are waiting to see if what they have been told is true—that their bodies will die. Some cling to every remaining day."

I thought of Lara who had told me she wanted to be a witness to her own death.

"Yes," said the Mother. "Some would not sleep through such an undertaking until, perhaps, the pain becomes too great, or the weight of further living too heavy. And then you can offer a choice. An informed choice, consented to in full."

Inner permission, Dagon had named it. To be soothed or energized a little. Or to be taken to the end of life. Beyond contract.

"Consciousness," she said softly, "is all we have. And it is enough."

I could hear the murmur of the sea outside and yearned to see it. A living sea! I heard the calls of what might be gulls. I had seen few animals in my stay on this world.

After what Fiórcara had told me—that the planet had been scourged of higher life forms, I was not surprised. The few remaining animals seemed to have developed the power and will to not reveal themselves to humans—or Shadakon.

"*Wise!*" I thought. "*Good for them.*"

"You are free to explore outside," she said. "I'm sure you will return when you are ready to."

When I have to, I thought. I smiled.

"I am yours for as long as I can be." That, I thought, pretty well covered it. Once more I had been helped along on my invisible to me path.

"Let yourself be drawn by what you truly love," she said. "Rumi, a religious mystic, said that. A very long time ago."

I slipped out a side door and took a well-walked path to the beach. Here were the plants that made a stand between salt tides and the salt meadows of the back beach. They were not familiar, but did as all the members of the vegetable kingdom do. They caught the sunlight and drank from the rain. They availed themselves to the occasional offerings of what might come ashore by storm. They endured and flowered and fulfilled their destinies. They needed no answers. They arose from their seeds knowing what to do.

Unlike us, I thought. *Oh, we had the basics embedded—seek food, safety, and later territory and sex and procreation—but even those we did not achieve gracefully. Few plants killed each other.*

Although there had been exceptions in the forests of old Earth, such as adder and strangler fig; and the fruits of some discouraged any but their own seedlings to grow nearby. Nothing on the scale of what we humans had achieved in our drive for territory.

I saw nothing on the horizon. The world went on and on, seemingly intact and untouched by those of us who carried our aggressive form of sentience everywhere we went. And more than that, we carried an entitlement belief that we could have anything we wanted, at whatever cost. That we unconcernedly could bring death to those we consumed or replaced and all that died as a result of our actions and inactions. Humans and Shadakon were killers and users and largely unaware of their cost to the web of life. Sidhe walked more softly on the worlds they inhabited.

I had known this of course, on the planet I had once called home. I had stopped going down to the shore; plastics and acidification had been just the latest weapons against life there.

But now I sat on a beached log here and felt the sun shine upon me, and the small bright waves slap against the shore. I was allowed here, although I did not deserve to be. I was not a child of this place.

I sat in silence until the next thought came.

We were not full children of Earth either. What would our fate have been, if the Visitors had not chosen to leave a part of their own nature behind? They came as exploiters, seeking gold and radioactive minerals to get them back on their way. They turned us to their own purposes. Some of us were closer to our original parents than others. And then they left. Some humans thought a few still slipped under human surveillance and followed their experiment as it ran unchecked on Earth.

A home left to the humans, born to rapidly populate and follow orders from above. But also a home for the Shadakon.

"Cain slew Abel—the first documented murder to satisfy a need for power? Or possibly to sate a taste for the life force? And then eventually we all came here."

And now …?

We were on a planet where the surviving beings hid themselves from us. We were here much as our distant parents had come to us. Would we be as indifferent as they had been?

I thought I saw something large swimming in the shallows, parallel to shore. I hoped that what I thought I had glimpsed was really there. I did not walk down to disturb it.

I settled into my role with the Mothers. Although I never felt judged, I was not invited into whatever circle they might form to draw energy and solace from each other or the Goddess. There were occasional long nights of chanting and the smell of candles and soft footfalls in the hall outside my door. I did not search out information that they did not offer.

I had been given a corner room that faced the sea. I realized that it was a generous gift. I was offered long pale green gowns that, after consideration, I chose to wear. They were, I realized, a uniform and gave me some anonymity.

There was always a risk of contracting one of our guests' viral diseases that continued to sweep across the tightly inhabited parts of world and were spread by the ships, mutating as they went. The Mothers seemed to accept the likelihood that at some point they might fall to an illness. I, as Shadakon, was unlikely to be affected. Changing my gown between patients protected me from unknowingly spreading another form of death to the others here.

The days passed. The nights were longer and often found me sitting at the side of someone struggling through their final hard stretch. During those nights, when the pain and despair crept closer, I sometimes wondered if I felt as bad as they did. But I knew deep down that I did not.

I knew that I had what they did not: a longer stretch, perhaps, of life; a healthy body, and the hope that I would be reconnected with someone I loved.

That was the good and the worst parts of it. I was healthy and passion had dwelt in my body. Now it visited me only in dreams that I awoke from alone, with only the smell and sound of the sea around me.

There was only the suggestion of an ending for me to struggle towards; with whatever courage I could gather.

"Wait six months," Dagon had said.

This planet swung through space, orbiting a larger and slight dimmer sun than old Earth's sun. It spun more slowly, its day longer than an Earth day, twenty-eight hours instead of twenty-four. I had disregarded comparing this time to that of old Earth's. I became disinterested in time, I wore no reminder of it, and there were no visible time counters at the hospice. Time was now. The sun moved across the sky. Other days it did not, obscured by great storms. The waves moved up the beach, taking some things back to sea and leaving others in their place. As the season turned to fall, the storms grew more frequent and rain drove hard against the windows.

I walked in the salt spray and rain. I walked in the mornings and marvelled at the rich variety of life that had been left on the beach the night before—Long, beautiful fronds of lilac seaweed. Small stranded creatures.

I remembered the story of the old monk who was admonished for carefully carrying storm-stranded starfish back to deeper water. Someone pointed out to him the curve of the beach, littered with these unfortunate creatures.

"What you do doesn't matter."

But he had calmly continued, only saying, "It does to this one."

With this in mind, I did my work, one person at a time. I heard confessions of crimes and of love that had never been fully spoken. I sat in briefly for people's mothers, fathers, lost siblings and children.

I comforted myself with my assessment that I gave full measure for what I took. In the end, they needed their flickering life energy no more, but often did not gift it to me. There was often little to sustain me. Always Dagon had shared with me when I did this work. Now I was constantly hungry and felt empty and distant from myself.

The passion I had shared with Dagon seemed as if in a long-ago dream. Why, I wondered, would he bother to retrieve me? He was living as he had before. He had not entered into what we had as a solution to any sadness or loneliness of his own that he might have identified. My despair had been a challenge to him. My blazing sexuality was perhaps a pleasant surprise. But that too was his talent to call up.

I knew that these thoughts were at least partial lies, demons of doubts that I conjured up.

I walked calmly in sadness. Sometimes I stripped off my clothing and went into that chilling unknown sea. There may well have been dangers to me that I would not have recognized. There was life in the shallows that darted away from me. I thought of the large shape I had seen from the beach my first day here.

I found that I wished for neither death nor safety.

I did consider that perhaps I could be terribly injured and still live. I had not asked questions about what could hurt or kill me, or the question of the likely length of my life. I had assumed that Dagon could tell me these things when I had a need to know them.

Now I accepted my state of not knowing. I no longer chased information about my ancestors. Instead I read Rumi and Zen koans.

I pondered the circuitous language of poetry throughout the history of humans. What was it that could be loosely caught in words, but could not be said directly? I spoke almost as little as the Mothers did now.

Meanwhile the flitters came and went. I usually stepped into a building while they were off-loading their cargo. I had no idea who piloted them to this remote island, but did not want my problems to follow me to this peaceful place.

So it was with slight surprise, but no expectations, that I attended a summons after the latest flitter had left. I did not foresee who was there and entered without guarding myself.

It was Morag, although if I had not known her within, I might not have recognized her.

She was ... frail. Without thinking I crossed the room to her and took her hands. I gave her energy and felt it fade even as she received it. Her green wolf eyes look directly into mine and she mind-spoke.

"*Yes, Danu. The enemies of the Shadakon, or perhaps those within our clan have devised a weapon that seems to work against us. No one knows if I can survive this. I have my doubts.*"

I met Morag's eyes and kept my mind open and quiet. I knew that deep within me, I begged to know if Dagon was well, if he remembered my exile. This was not the time, if there would be a time, to ask these questions. I waited and the sea sang faintly outside.

She smiled. "*You have learned much here, Danu,*" she mind-spoke.

I thought of my trial. I thought of Morag's instructions to Dagon— "She has to find her own way."

"*Yes,*" she mind-spoke. "*Just so.*"

We regarded each other. I saw her as before, strong and clear minded even as I saw her current state. I showed her that she was still my leader.

"Ah, Danu," she said. "Any debt you may have had to me has been more than repaid."

I remembered wondering while imprisoned with Lucia, if I could have survived a longer trial, if the outcome would have been different.

"Yes," Morag said. "Again you have seen the balancing actions behind the scenes. You have learned more about us already that many know after centuries of experiencing being Shadakon."

"But now I come to ask you a favour, if you can do it," she said. "My only hope now is to go Between and drink the elixir of life, if the Sidhe would grant that. I have never contracted them."

"*Never contacted them!*" I gathered the separate strands of my memories and found that they were forming an unbelievable pattern. I had assumed that Morag had somehow set up my rescue by the Sidhe.

She shook her head. "No one can direct the Sidhe. Certainly not us."

"But you told them of my predicament?" I asked.

She dropped her eyes away from mine. "Not exactly. Although I was sure that they were aware of you and likely knew where you had been taken."

I fought for calm and perhaps I pulled it off. She had seen me kidnapped then. And by whom.

"Technically you weren't kidnapped. I expected that you would be taken to a questionable place of safety and we would have to rescue you. Or that the Sidhe might."

"But—"

"You were flown directly into the forest area. It is forbidden territory. It is a zone of no communication."

She looked at me to see exactly how I would take the next bit of information. "We lost you."

"I thought you would protect me!" Finally my calmness had melted away. "You left me in the hands of She who wanted, more than anything, to get rid of me and separate Dagon and I."

"Yes."

I breathed smoothly and waited for the next part. I forced myself to go to the calm distant place I had lived in for months here.

"She did not care what happened to you, or how it occurred. She wanted to stand beside him if and when he became Alpha," said Morag. "Or overcome him and become the Alpha herself."

"You think she wouldn't have particularly enjoyed hurting me?" I glared at her. I said nothing else, but finally I consented to speak. "You have come to ask something of me, in spite of telling me that you abandoned me and placed me in the hands of a certain enemy."

"I hoped your timing would hold. I believed that the Sidhe would assist you."

"Why would they?" I asked.

"Lara was your contact with them. I, too, heard the song that surrounded her when she died. They were there with her and for her, and they met you that night. Lucia was another of your seemingly endless wild cards," she said. "When she went outside to urinate, they were there, all around that bleak place. They read her hope and knew that, unlikely as it was, she had gained hope somehow recently. They knew you had given it to her—much as you gift all those you assist, bringing up joyous memories or simply true companionship. They knew that the person they were seeking was within."

I folded my hands. I listened to the sea roll and roll against the beach.

"Tell me what you want me to do for you, Morag," I said quietly.

She sighed and moved slightly as if even sitting was an effort. I could feel pain in her, but she did not ask me for assistance.

"Can you contact them, Danu?" she asked. "It is not a good time for me to disappear forever from the scene. Much is at stake here and it is not only my life that I would cling to."

I waited and thought before speaking. I had an answer that might surprise her.

"I will call he who gave me his name," I said. "He told me I could call if I had great need of his help. Perhaps he will come for one I love, and because I cannot see the fragile balance holding without you."

She sighed in relief. "There is one more thing," she said, and this time she managed to smile. "I think you are ready to hear this. Dagon needs you by his side now. You must go to him."

CHAPTER TWENTY-EIGHT

THE NEGOTIATIONS

We moved Morag into my room. I hoped that the open window would make it easier for what might happen later. I gave her all the energy I could spare. I had gotten used to hunger, and it no longer frightened me as it once had.

I lit a shielded candle, sat beside the bed and took her cool dry hand. I thought of my time in Between. I envisioned the Touch-me-not and my cold circle with me burning inside of it on midsummer's eve. I unabashedly remembered the passion I had shared with Dagon in Between, which brought with it some of the high summer magic of the Sidhe.

I let the floodgates of memory open that I had kept intentionally closed during my stay here. I let it all wash over me. I felt my heat rise.

And then I called his name.

"*Fiórcara, I call you. I would ask a boon, but not for me alone. Not for only Shadakon, human, or even Sidhe. I also call for this beautiful world.*" I showed how I had swum unafraid in the shallows, how I walked and watched the sun set in orange and lavender.

"*I call you in the name of love,*" I mind-spoke. "*Love for this place that you are a guardian of.*"

I paused before I added the next thing.

"*I will accept any debt that must be repaid for your services.*" I showed him Morag, already drifting towards an edge that she would not return from. "*We're in trouble here. I would ask that you take her to Between and, if possible, heal her from this new threat to the Shadakon, and protect the delicate balance of this world.*"

Suddenly he was there, facing me, looking grave. "You ask much, Danu," he said.

"Well you know that we do not give the elixir of life to outsiders. Morag has been in Between as a brief visitor. It is not our way to befriend the Shadakon, nor to sustain them," he added.

I heard the highborn ancient dismissal behind his pronouncement. Perhaps all was lost then. I bowed my head. I imagined the Council falling, the renegade Shadakon drawing down the wrath of the humans as they took from them with abandon. I envisioned, because I believed that it was a possible future line, the forest burning to the edge of the sea.

I looked into his green eyes that could so easily hold mine. "I promise to fulfil whatever you ask of me," I said. "My name is my word. If I still have life, I will honour it."

He was very still. He knew I did not know what he might ask, but that I had pledged to accept whatever his conditions were. His green eyes grew brighter and his beauty wrapped around me.

"Very well, Danu of Dagon of the Shadakon," he smiled as he spoke. "Come next midsummer's eve, you will fly with me for a night under the moon. With no Touch-me-not or steel between us. I need not tell you that to break a commitment to the Sidhe is unwise," he said quietly. "Do you still agree?"

I felt the life leaving Morag as I held her hand. I hoped that others had not fallen prey to what was killing her. I looked out of the window to see the little moon over the unmarred sea.

I knew that I could willingly surrender to him, even though there would be no way to undo what might be done that night.

"*So mote it be,*" I mind-spoke.

The last thing I saw were eyes the colour of fall touched leaves and a smile that teased even in my memory of it. I awoke at dawn. The candle was out. Morag was gone.

I flew out later that day. Once again, the Mothers thanked me for my service, assuring me that there was a place for me here, or wherever they were. There were no last minute gifts given before I left except for those I carried within me.

One was a calmness that I had never felt before. I could now walk in the world, neither excited by, nor trying to avoid whatever emotional state was upon me. I had learned to accept.

I accepted that I had made an agreement with the Sidhe that would take me far outside of who I thought I was and who I had been. That might make everything in my current world unbearably less.

They, and the elixir of life, and the very fabric of Between was a charged world, full of primal energies and one's relationship to the those who lived there was not that of user and used. Or perhaps, one must consent to be the used as well as being the user. One was invited to sit (or love) under a tree—or not. By the tree. I no longer doubted that I had had to secure permission to remain there, not just from the Sidhe, but also from the place or state of being that was Between. And even so, I would have a limited permission to stay. Maybe only one more night—to be remembered if I could remember anything, for the rest of my days. But much could happen between now and later.

I hoped that Morag would find health and a way to stop what she was stricken with from spreading to us all. Or, at least, find peace. I had no idea what or if she thought about her imminent death, if that was her fate.

I accepted that I had done what I could for her, and more.

I flew home.

I flew back to Dagon.

I assumed that he had known that Morag had gone to me with the message to return to him.

What I did not know was whether that had been his choice, or if he had accomplished, at least in part what he had hoped. I did not know if he and I had a future together.

These musings did not hurt me as much as they might have before my training in being apart from him. I thought dispassionately that if I no longer had a home with him, I would return to the island and the Mothers and spend what time I had being useful there.

"Everyone must be useful," the Sidhe had said, before he had given me a name to call him with.

It would be determined in the coming days where I would be most useful. I did not bother to guess at the unfolding of my fate. The flitter touched down outside the house that I had been brought to less than a year ago.

The door was closed. I stood outside, calling to Dagon in mind-speak.

I waited.

As a last attempt, before going—but where? —I put my palm on the door palm lock. It opened. I went in and all was as before except ... there were no flowers live or dead, or the scent of recently extinguished candles. Our bed was as before, but felt long unoccupied. I curled up in it, trying to sense him around me. It offered me faint comfort.

I could not move forward from this spot. Hunger would drive me on at some point. But for now, I laid still, trying not to brush up against the edges of a terrible hurt and fear that I had fallen into, no, that I had laid down in. It felt like the walls I was trying to maintain to contain the pain around me could cave in on me at any moment.

I breathed and my breathing slowed and my feelings calmed while I wondered dispassionately if I should choose a means to die and, if so, how?

It was a quiet thought that took up little room.

No one, even a Shadakon, could or should live forever. Why would I want to?

I could somehow trick my way onto an outgoing ship. When they discovered what I was, perhaps they would jettison me—out into that velvety black place of burning stars. I hoped that if that were to be my fate, I could see, even briefly the glory of it. Perhaps I could take a suit and jettison myself. Then I would be free to see death coming, free from rescue and later of regret, if regret would come at all. I would fall into a final airless sleep, to float and eventually burn up. If I returned to this world, it would be as a brief glow, bright dust falling into the sunset, my elements drifting back down to the sea.

It was a solid plan B. I had totally forgotten about the dagger. It was a long time since I had thought I might use it. Of course someone would find it and take it from me.

I went to soak in the tub, expecting when I opened my eyes that Dagon would be there, but each time he was not. The water grew cold and I finally noticed a note I'd missed lying on the table. It had been written two days before and read:

I am away and can't say when I will return. This is not how I wished your homecoming to be. If you are here reading this, then you know you are welcome in my house—your home. Dagon.

I wrapped in the soft robe as I had before. There was still a faint reddish brown stain on one sleeve. That was what undid me.

That was when I finally began to cry.

It was then that Dagon entered the room. He read me in a heartbeat, curled up in our bed, tear-streaked—although I had hung on for a long time. It was not how I had wanted him to first perceive me. I fought for my hard-won calm, but it was elusive.

He folded his long legs up neatly, and knelt beside me, not touching me, or mind-speaking. His eyes had changed. They still drew me in and, if anything, the shifting sparks of light were brighter now. His beauty had been changed by something. He carried himself with more confidence, with more power than he had had before.

"Yes, Danu," he said formally. "I am now Alpha. If Morag returns we will have to decide how to handle that fact."

"What would you have me do now, Dagon?" I rose and drew the robe around me and he too stood. I sensed his tallness over me along with his newfound sense of power. He had always been someone who should be feared by humans; now, I knew, this extended to the Shadakon as well.

"I do not know the necessary ritual here," I said. "Do I somehow formally acknowledge you? Does this change everything that has passed between us?"

"Yes," he said. "And no—unless the change comes from within you."

We both waited as I sorted out what he had said, what he had meant.

I bent my head to him. "I acknowledge you as my Alpha," I said. "I will follow your directions, unless they conflict with those of my heart. Then I will step back if allowed, to live alone."

He looked at me and smiled. "You continue to get very skilled in contract, Danu. This is and is not an oath of complete loyalty. But it is the only one I will ask of you."

He continued to observe me. I wished I was not unclothed, I wished we could replay this meeting after all the time that had passed between us and in the new version he would not find me sobbing on our bed.

"I will leave you to dress, if that is your wish," he said softly.

I felt the carefully banked fires of my hope and wanting him flash into flames. I just shook my head.

It had been a long time. I had found refuge from my unsatisfied passion in a state previously unknown to me. A calmness that held me steady and protected me from dreary depression.

I had waited. I waited now. I did not know for what, except that there was something else to be acknowledged between us. I looked up at him. I held his eyes. "And ..." I said.

He seemed to take a long time to find exactly what he wanted to say to me. "I acknowledge you, Danu, mate of Dagon, Alpha of the Shadakon whose loyalty I command. I will present you as such and you will share in my power. I will teach you what you need to know. However," and here he smiled, "as always you will continue to find your own way."

I was almost afraid to touch him—not because of his new status, for I had already deduced that would happen from what Morag had said, but because I feared the awakening of the need and longing for him that I had set aside.

I wondered if he had missed me as much as I had him. I remembered our last union. I had been under the influence of faerie and of Between. What had occurred between us was like a fast-building thunderhead, that carried us both up on the energy generated between and around us. And then stayed until we finally grounded that energy and became a part of Between for a little while.

Since then, I had walked in soft rain along the shore for a long time. I felt like I did not know where to begin.

"Let's start here," he mind-spoke me calmly. "The beginning is always a good place to start." He kissed me and I remembered how to kiss him back.

It went on like that, slowly spiralling up in intensity.

I remembered the first day we stood before each other, looking across at each other from either side of the room. I had suddenly noticed that the distance had closed between us. I did not know which of us had done so.

It could have been me; it could have been me now.

I felt our hearts beat on time with each other. Our bodies decided when the moment we waited for had arrived—for each to come to the decision of full connection and permission. Then I gave over to my sexual wanting of my lover, my Alpha. And he to me.

We became, for this time, as one.

CHAPTER TWENTY-NINE

MORE QUESTIONS AND SOME DIFFICULT ANSWERS

I didn't leave the house for two days.

Dagon left for the fair every morning and returned as early as possible. I protested that I was not getting on with earning my keep, not being useful. He merely raised an eyebrow. In truth we had moved well beyond what might have been called our shyness of each other after a long parting. There still existed between us a wanting that I was not sure many had known, human or Shadakon. We took our pleasures in the pool, in the various spaces of the house, and the air one night, swooping like mating bats under a bright moon.

He, I was sure, was certain of me and my abiding desire to be with him. I, knowing his appetites and the larger world he moved in, was perhaps less certain of him. But perhaps also because I harboured a secret. I believe he knew there was something, although I held it close. I just could not bear to threaten what we had so recently re-established.

Finally though, we had to talk. If I was to stand by his side, I had to know the situation I walked into.

The same was true for him.

I knew that no one on the Council would know of the deal I had struck with the Sidhe except Morag. But there was silence across all the ways Dagon had of communicating with her. All he could deduce was that she was still alive.

We lay together one afternoon, the late fall sun briefly appearing and entering the house through our bedroom window. Again I wondered why light was no longer a problem for the Shadakon, however, I knew that he preferred the early and late sun over the midday.

Relaxed (as I'm sure he intended me to be) he simply turned me to face him.

I felt the draw of him and his new power. I knew what was coming next, yet still I hesitated.

"Do not make me do this, Danu," he said almost too quietly. "You are holding something back from me and have given me few details of Morag's passing to Between. I can only assume the story starts there."

I looked into his brown eyes with their shifting flames. I would have simply fallen into him and let him take what he sought there.

He shook his head. "No, Danu. I will not take what you struggle so hard to keep hidden. But it is time to tell me of your own free will. I cannot wait much longer." He leaned above me.

And so I showed him the images of bearing Morag into my room. The sea air swirling in through an intentionally left open window. I showed him her frailty and how her energy, even when augmented by mine, was draining away.

He continued to watch me closely. "And somehow you trusted that you could contact the Sidhe—and that they would respond?" This was not a question and I didn't answer.

"I summoned Fiórcara." I finally said.

"Fiórcara! True friend! That is the name given to you by the Sidhe who was in contact with you in Between? He just gave you that name?"

I realized that this story had taken a twist he had not expected.

"Are you unaware that the Sidhe guard their names, even a name such as this?"

I showed him the conversation that had passed between the ageless Sidhe and me. That he had rebuked me for asking, but then had given me the name Fiórcara, and promised to respond if I was in dire need.

Dagon continued to look at me, as if he would find some other answer than this, but this was the truth. The information seemed to affect Dagon, and I grew concerned. A faint but discernible distance now existed between us, and there was still more challenging information to come.

There was nothing to be done but continue.

"Initially he answered me but seemed very displeased to be called," I said hesitantly. "I told him simply that I believed that not only the fates of the Shadakon and Sidhe were at great risk, but also this planet which I have grown to love."

I showed him great fires burning the forests of this world. It was a future line I believed could yet come into being.

Dagon shook his head and continued to look at me, his eyes growing sad. "You have placed yourself in a place of great danger," he said. "The Sidhe do not do things for others without some bargain being struck."

"I said I would promise anything. To save Morag and you, and to not bring in another time of the hunting and being hunted of the Shadakon. And also to give even a little more time to this world and all that live upon her," I said, with my strength of conviction growing. "I regret nothing of the deal I struck. Though I fear it. I have said that I would die for you. Perhaps I may come to that place in the future."

"What did your true friend ask of you, Danu?" He spoke so quietly that I almost didn't hear it. Almost. It must all be told now.

"He warned me to reconsider my open offer to him but I declined. I felt that all must be wagered."

"And?"

"He asked me to attend next midsummer's eve gathering and spend the night with him. Without, as he said, Touch-me-not or steel between us. I must come of my own free will."

"I expect not to survive the night," I said calmly. "Certainly not as I am now. Madness came to me on the hill. I heard the Call and it took all my will to not join. Now I must set aside my will to resist," I said. "I have given consent, no matter the cost to me. For I know that when the next morning dawns I will leave Between forever."

"Even if I am driven beyond what can be borne," I said. I suddenly thought of his green eyes even as I looked into Dagon's brown ones. "He had said, 'I do not care who you are pledged to in your world, on this night you will dance with me.' That's what he said. And asked me again if I would accept his terms."

"That is what you must now know," I said. "The date is in the future and I know that I have no guarantee of living long enough to keep it. But this is so."

"It is perhaps not entirely unlike what you do," I suggested unwisely. "To use and be used. Because I do not think I am of more than a passing interest to him, a small challenge in a very long life. You yourself told me that love was not the word to be used for such transactions. Even though I seem to have more vulnerability of heart ..."

I saw his anger then, and knew that he could have taken me to the ground for what I had just said. He stood perfectly still, only just controlled. He stood over me and I wished I had stayed alone on the island and not had to bring this to him.

He next questions surprised me though. "You resisted his Call, and it was his Call to you the night before I was brought to you. Did you regret not answering? Did you wish to be even briefly in faerie arms?"

I shook my head. Tears long fought against rolled down my cheeks.

"I expected only madness or even true death from such an encounter," I said.

"You expected no less for me," Dagon said. "You spoke of giving me your life even though I knew you wanted nothing more than to live on."

We faced each other. This then was the cost that I had not taken into account. That Dagon would see me yearning for a Sidhe king, or whatever he was. That perhaps he had come to me in Between to assure himself that I still honoured our bond.

How had Dagon come to Between?

He heard me and dropped his eyes. "He made me an offer I couldn't refuse. That I could come to you for an afternoon. I asked no questions."

So my mate, too, had made a deal with no understanding of what he might be required to pay later!

I shook my head, as if to clear away the off-kilter feeling of Between.

"I promised to possibly die or be destroyed for you and yours," I said. "He had already told me how much he hated humans. Humans, newly-made Shadakon, I think it matters little to him."

"I can return to the island," I continued. "I will do that if you request it. I will continue to serve there in what might be a very dark time for the Shadakon and everyone else on this planet. But you have gifted me with a clean exit. There may come a time that I will use it. However I cannot do so until after next midsummer's eve. Not until then."

He ran his thumbnail down my cheek, following the dried tracks of tears and then down and lingered where my heartbeat announced itself. He paused there, as if reading my life's vigour. Or perhaps some darker impulse came upon him. It was a line of fire on my skin and I wanted him again as if for the first time.

"No Sidhe has ever negotiated with a Shadakon," he said thoughtfully.

"We failed you and you were in danger beyond your imagination in the house in the forest. They saved you—not me. They took you to safety in Between and gave you the elixir of life to drink. He gave it to you, by his own hand."

He continued. "And then he set a test for you, bringing you steel, sure that although he would not cross, he would not have to. You would come to him—as everyone he has ever called has come. You did not, although you heard and were affected by the Call. You lay in agony instead as the party wound down."

"He told me that I was not important, but what I did was. That I found a true path somehow. They had been observing me," I said. "They had the house surrounded and were sure they had the right Shadakon when Lucia came out, showing faint hope. Even though I was aware that I could not have protected her from myself indefinitely."

"Yes. In this he and I are in agreement. You are unique. In our case, we are mated and have shared blood. You have taught me to love you," he said. "Perhaps he is interested in that aspect of you as well."

"I am being forced to his side," I said. "Perhaps he thought to cause difficulty to you. For I have given my word to betray you and, even worse, to want to with every fibre of my being. That is not love. I must find another word."

"Yes," said Dagon. "You are correct. And so must I. The Sidhe, like the Shadakon, seldom have more than fleeting connections with each other. I will ask you no more about this or your feelings arising from it. I do remember your loyalty oath to me yesterday. You promised that you would follow me as a leader unless what I asked of you was in conflict with your heart. Did you think ahead to this conversation when you offered me that?"

"I do not think about most of what I do," I said. "I see what must be done and do it.

I never meant to hurt you, only to protect you. Please forgive me."

He shook his head and my heart sank. "There is nothing to be forgiven for, Danu," he said, and again touched me lightly when I turned to him. "I believe I have your attention here, with me."

"As you have mine," I said. "Please keep me close."

He smiled. "This close," he said, moving in on me until our shadows merged into one.

CHAPTER THIRTY

DANU'S TRUST IN DAGON IS THREATENED

Very soon we would have to make an official appearance. Many had probably guessed that I was back and now we had to show our mutual intention to continue on together with me as a mate of the Alpha.

We began what was to be a conversation to catch me up on events that had happened in my absence, but I felt anger rising in me from the moment it started.

Dagon mentioned my newfound calmness.

"I'm a little better with calmness now, "I said. "But not ignorant calmness. Not just get-in-the-flitter-and-assume-everything-is-handled calmness."

Dagon winced. "I think you have not seen how loose the allegiances are within the Council, and Morag and my limited resources. But yes, it is time for you to start asking questions."

I looked at him with what I hoped passed his scrutiny as a neutral mind state to begin a necessary conversation between us. But in fact, I was reviewing thoughts that had troubled me, and did so even more when put together.

"I'll go first then," I said. "You sensed that I withheld information and wanted disclosure. We are living with the aftermath of that now. You, however …"

"You have told me nothing of what has happened since I walked out of that door four months or so ago."

"I still have an enemy without a name."

"You recently moved onto the Council—and are now suddenly Alpha."

"Someone tried to kill Morag, and may have succeeded. I was supposed to stay gone.

But now I am back."

"None of those are questions," said Dagon, predictably.

"Correct." I said. "There are many things I need to know about those statements. But I don't know what those things are. So, no good questions. But I want answers, even answers to things I don't even know what to ask you. Things not on the list—"

He waited me out.

"Tell me what I need to know now, Dagon."

"Where do we start," he asked.

"Now, Alpha, are you are hoping to hide things I have no knowledge of? Doing this is and was dangerous to me—such that I had to be rescued by the Sidhe."

Once again I saw his anger rise and his necessary control of it. Why did I do such things? This was not the way to meet this proud and powerful man in the middle. Why did I struggle against him? I shrugged. Perhaps I was continuing to transform to Shadakon. Maybe, like Dagon, I must be what I was.

He was quiet but I felt his coiled anger. "We are arguing, not talking," he said. "You are inviting my anger. It is a dangerous game, Danu."

"It is no game," I said. "Or if it is a game, then it is winner takes all." I stopped, horrified by what I had revealed to myself, and to Dagon.

We looked at each other very carefully. I suddenly felt the seriousness of this moment. What, what to do now? Not to apologize. But not continue on in this fashion. My calm fled.

"I'm going out," he said after a moment. "I will return. Please be here."

He covered the distance to the door between one breath and the next. The door closed and he was gone.

I paced, trying to place necessary pieces in the riddle of how he and I fit together. Lovers? Hopefully still yes. Mates? Yes forever. Mate of an Alpha? Who now walked and thought as an Alpha everywhere that he was and in everything he did?

"There cannot be two Alphas," he had said.

For a moment I pictured Morag, fading painfully in my bed. I was shocked about my suspicions about her as well, but they bore thinking about. I was not feeling better after bringing this all to mind.

She who I didn't know her name? Even Morag had not let slip this information. Dagon spoke of her neutrally, seemingly dismissing any connections that they had brought along from their distant past together.

He and Morag had let me get into a flitter piloted by her cur Gailan. Was he in fact dead?

A fear swept through me greater than any I had known. What pattern was I caught up in? I knew nothing of the political fierceness of the Shadakon. Was I a sacrifice or, at least, a diversion? A distracting sleight of hand?

I shivered as if I was very cold, though I did not feel the cold as much as I once had. I wished for a cup of tea. That had ceased to be a possible comfort. I wanted to feed or be fed today. I had no means of providing for myself in the immediate future. I would not force consent on anyone who might easily fall prey to me today. Tomorrow though, I must act.

That also shocked me. I had lived in a sheltered reality, provided for by Dagon and then by the Mothers and for whatever period of time I had been and for whatever period of time I had been with the Sidhe. I was not an experienced hunter. I honoured contract and often went without.

I was not realistically able to stand up to Dagon in the way I had been doing. I had nothing to fund a struggle or possibly even survive to reach the Mothers.

I moved into a state of calm, or perhaps numb shock. If he answered my questions fully and honestly, perhaps we could never go back.

If he did not answer or refused to tell me what I needed to know, we could not go forward.

I lay on the couch and watched the closed door. I knew he was alive. I had been told not to contact him. I did not.

The room darkened. My eyes adjusted to the darkness easily now. Time slowed. I waited.

I heard the door open and I immediately knew it was not Dagon. I was very quiet, as I now knew how to be. It would give me a split second edge, if that would make a difference.

"Put on some lights," a familiar voice said. It was Morag. I did as I was bidden.

"I have just returned from Between," she said. "You do know that you cannot refer to this?"

I nodded.

"Are you well?" I asked. I could see that she was. I remembered the feeling of the calm elixir of life. I had a momentary burst of desire to taste it again. Another thing I had taken for granted. I sighed.

Morag had followed my thought of course. She was stronger than even Dagon. And she was my Alpha. Or was she?

She shook her head. "I will let him go ahead in his new position. He has many hard lessons ahead of him though."

"Come here, Danu," she said suddenly. I knelt in front of her.

"Why can you not do this for Dagon?" she asked quietly. "It is the response he requires now, especially when you appear together. It is a part of old pack rules.

You may not have any memories of your lineage, but we remember a time of more structured clan life. One cannot be an Alpha with a mate who doesn't accept you as one," she said. "He came and found me and sent me to you."

I blinked back tears. "I don't know why I challenge him. Perhaps underneath I still fear what my part actually is in his world, in the world of the Shadakon."

"And perhaps something else as well?"

I looked into her green eyes. She had been my Alpha and requested no less than the full truth from me.

"Yes, Danu," she answered my unspoken thoughts. "You are finding accepting his authority over you difficult. You began your relationship with him and the Shadakon accepting it. But it is harder now that he must show his position overtly. And meanwhile, you have grown in your own strength."

"To remain as Alpha, I never allowed anyone too close to me. Dagon has allowed you dangerously close. You both have bonded in a way that is unlikely and also probably distrusted or at least misunderstood by our kind. You are a danger to him just by existing. Your attitude could now be the end of him. Especially now, as he comes forward as a new Alpha. He will be tested and tested again. You must have his back, if need be."

She waited to let me take in what she had said. I heard the truth in it.

"If you cannot do this," she added quietly, "you must honour the loyalty oath you swore to him. You must leave, and soon."

I searched myself to see if I could do that. I thought briefly about the small knife with the red-gemmed hilt. I then remembered the promise I had made to Fiórcara. I must live through whatever came. Until midsummer's day.

The idea of withdrawing from Dagon was so painful that I could no longer even think. I stayed kneeling, facing Morag, who had returned from a place of almost certain no return. She looked deeply within me and sighed.

"He is your life right now, Danu. Enjoy your time together. Don't be overly eager to try out all your own strengths. The time may come for that, but if I were you, I would not wish for it to come too soon." She indicated that I should sit beside her. "Take my gift of intervention between you two tonight to heart. I know I owe you my life, and I thank you. But one more thing ..."

She drew a small bag out of her pocket. She shook into her hand a smooth rounded gem. It was bright green, the colour—

I pulled back my hand. "I cannot take this," I said. "It is from he who aided us."

"Yes, Danu. I know that and a lot more about it. But you must. He will still come to your assistance if you have your back to the wall. He is impressed with you, as many of us are. Do not use it unless you must," she said. "But if you must, there are worse fates than spending time in Between."

"Not for Dagon though," she said thoughtfully. "I know that you have saved us by pledging to go to him later of your own free will. But this is a very heavy burden for Dagon to carry without bringing it up again and again. He knows you are a woman of your word, as does your Sidhe."

I put the wrapped gem in the sheath of the knife and put both away.

"I think you need to offer Dagon your word in how you will carry yourself with him. He needs to know that you are with him. This testing and quarrelling must stop."

She stood up. "I still tire easily. There may be a vaccine developed from my blood.

If so, you will receive some. That is all I will say tonight." She stood up and walked calmly to the door. She opened it and Dagon walked in.

He stood in the centre of the room and looked uncertain as to what reception he would receive. I felt a fierce rush of relief at seeing him return. He finally sat beside me, still silent in word and thought.

I sank to my knees before him as I had with Morag. I did not meet his eyes. Mine were filled with tears.

"I did not understand, my mate. I did not think through my behaviour that, although done while we were alone, could become a danger to us both. I accept you as my Alpha first, and my mate and lover second. It must be this way. I cannot guarantee that I will not get angry with you, but I will be more respectful to you."

I drew up courage for what I next had to say.

"I will leave if you direct me to," I said softly. "It will break my heart but I will do so. Events are unfolding that are more important than any one of us. You lead your own now."

I waited. I was truly calm. I knew that I had done all I could do. I surrendered, as an ancient Chinese sage had said, "to the will of heaven."

I didn't believe in heaven, I believed in Dagon.

Dagon sighed and put his hand lightly on my head. "I accept your new addition to your loyalty oath, Danu. You still leave yourself room," he said with a smile, "but I would expect no less."

He pulled me up to him and kissed me hard.

I caught his lower lip in my teeth. He grew totally still beneath me.

"What is it you wish, Danu?"

"I wish to renew our blood vows," I mind-spoke.

"I want you within me such that I will have no trouble remembering that at all times."

His eyes were almost luminous. Watching me up to the last moment he entered my mind and I felt his new strength and vitality. Then he bit down on the spot where he often touched me, the pulse-point. He took me fast and I felt myself spinning and spinning out and out. He bit his own lip and kissed me again, and I drank deeply.

I felt the lines between us blur. I felt his strength within me. When we pulled back from each other, I saw myself in his mind. I saw a beautiful woman. I saw a warrior who could walk proudly as a Shadakon.

I would have stopped time here forever. For a little while, perhaps we did.

But I still needed some information. I slowly returned to something close to my usual state of being. While the connection between us was even more strengthened, I decided to try again. To find out what I needed to know.

But he beat me to this plan with one of his own. Laying one finger lightly to my lips, he took me by the hand and to a table. There, still in silence, he lit many candles in a semi-circle in front of us. He asked me to place my dagger, the one that was once his, on the table unsheathed. I did so with shaking hands. I placed it pointing between us, its blade glittering in the candlelight. He traced a few invisible markings on the table.

His solemn actions were not accompanied by thoughts. I could read nothing— not anger and certainly not fear. I felt no threat but still …

I forced myself to breathe—out and out and out. In would take care of itself until the one day it could not.

"Now, Danu," Dagon began. "You want answers and fear you will not receive the truth from me. I will give you what you ask for. I swear by this blade, that is a death bringer.

If you find out I have withheld what you seek, or distorted the truth to my own purposes, you may visit me with it. In this matter, I am not your Alpha."

I looked at him with fear, but there was no fear in him. We were entering a place of no return. I had had my turn. Now it was his time to say what must be said.

"Let us start with, what I think is, the hardest part for you," he said.

"Her name in this time is Lorelei, she goes by Lore. I have known her since we were savage hunters. She had a fierce joy for the hunt, and loved running her prey to the ground—or to the edge of sheer drops where they faced her or certain death on the rocks below. She wasted more than she took."

I tried to take this in. The horror of a chase that offered no mercy, no turning aside by the hunter. So too had humans hunted down and killed the buffalo and other large herd animals as it pleased us; shot the passenger pigeons that had blanketed the evening skies until not a single one was left. I nodded. Bloody pasts were not unique to the Shadakon.

"She and I knew of each other and at times we knew each other more closely. Do you want to hear the details of that?"

I shook my head.

He smiled. "I will later grant you the same courtesy," he said.

"There was no overall organization of the Blood. We ran in packs that fought for territory with each other over the centuries. As our numbers grew and the humans realized what we were, we were the ones that ran before the stakes and flames. We were still bound to the night. Neighbours watched and reported neighbours who did not leave their houses until dark. Among the ones that died, certainly there were those of the Blood. We had no count of our living or dead members."

"Many of us died of the light, whether caught outside with no shelter, or caged in squares to wait for the deadly dawn—for the entertainment of the townspeople."

"Those were brutal times. But we all had slightly different skills or powers. Some survived light exposure, if only barely, and healed from that. Other developed an immunity gained by gradual exposure. Still others, like you, had less Blood and could move about freely under the sun—although you felt the primal response in your first day of turning."

"We found individual solutions to passing in the world of humans both on Earth and elsewhere. Most of all we learned to feed without taking blood. We left no marks. There are so many things that can quietly and quickly kill a human," he said calmly, "including us."

"Now we govern ourselves. If we do not, the humans will find ways of curtailing our numbers, if not eliminating us completely. The red substance in the needle gun you dodged may not have entirely killed you." He looked at me, assessing my understanding of what he was saying.

"Those of us who enjoy hunting down their own generally prefer to give endless pain, not death."

"The craft that resulted in what is on my knife comes from knowledge now lost in our many dark ages. To my knowledge, we have not recently developed a means of a final death, other than arranging for the total destruction of the body."

"Like a flitter accident," I said thoughtfully. He looked at me.

"As far as I know, none of us took the action that resulted in Morag's near death," he said. "And I have made enquiries."

He read something then, in my eyes or under-mind, although I was attempting to shield from him; it brought him out of his calm recital.

"You cannot think that I could do such a thing!"

I did not give voice to what I thought—that it might be possible. That I also had thought that my own death, alone in the hands of enemies, might have been an expedient plan.

He sat and stared at me. "That was under your anger and distrust of me as your Alpha," he finally said. "That my desire for leadership was stronger than my bond to her or you. How long have you held these questions within you? How could you have kept them without my knowing?"

"They only recently rose up in my mind," I said. "I had hidden them well from myself as well."

"And yet again, you requested to strengthen the bond between us with the blood ritual!" He stood before me. "Why would you welcome me into your being as you have, if you believed that my intent was to sooner or later rid myself of you?"

I could not answer. The very air in the room stopped moving, undisturbed by even the slightest movement of either of us.

"Have you never entertained such a thought?" I asked. "Ever? In the beginning? After I was either delivered to or fell into the hands of my enemy? While I was safely out of sight, and walking on a small island and wishing only to return? We both know that I threaten what you and Morag have worked so hard for."

Silence.

"This is where the balance shifts and there is no going back," I said sadly. "Because you pledged that you would tell the truth here. I would hold you to that now."

"Truth is as complex as consent," he said slowly. "Are you asking if I ever acted to bring harm to you?"

"That is one of my questions." I said. My lips felt numb.

"No, Danu. I have never knowingly taken action or inaction that would lead to harm or death to you."

I heard and felt him mind-speak this, and it was as he said. I believed him.

"Have you ever allowed thoughts that my permanent disappearance, or death, would be an advantage to you to enter your mind?"

He turned his dark amber eyes on me. I saw the ever-flickering points of flame move. This is how he could perhaps have erased these recent words between us.

Perhaps not though. We had shared his strength between us. So too had he received of me—my connection to the life force, strengthened by my months of solitude.

"And by your time in Between," he added.

"Yes," I agreed. "I was watching Old Earth die as a living being before I left. I had never encountered a healthy life web."

"I will answer you now," he said. "But I would ask a question of you on this subject as well."

We faced each other, our eyes putting us in synch, our hearts beating the same tempo together.

"I did contemplate it. It would have and still would simplify things. I allowed myself to experience uncomplicated time when you were gone. I returned somewhat to who I had been. I took more people in lethal contract. I fed and I ran with those I had neglected when with you. I imagined how easy it would be, to keep living as I was, as a superb predator, with little real concern for humans or for this world."

"I tried it on," he said. "In the end, I realized that I did not fit into my old life anymore.

My old life without you. But now—what about you? You have had many close calls. Yet you did not once call me through our shared Making."

"I was told not to!" I protested.

"Yes. But there are times when need overrides reason. You knew I would hear you, and yet you never called."

"I thought you would come," I whispered. "I thought I was the living goat, tethered out to draw you. I have told you before, and meant it then and now, that I would die for you."

He sighed.

"And on the hill? You did not give permission—but did you want to? So much that you turned to the agony of Touch-me-not to drown out your longing for what awaited you?"

"Did you not … consider it? And somehow, now you have an invitation back—that you have already accepted."

We looked at each other and incredibly, we began to smile.

It is the way of this love, I suddenly realized. One must know what one is missing to make an informed choice to stay. Only that is true consent.

"A few more answers then. Morag was going to turn over leadership to me; she had been grooming me for years. It was part of her shocked disbelief when I presented the Council with the dilemma of you, a spontaneously turned person of the Blood. Yet she was more than fair to you."

"You have more than repaid your debt to me," Morag had said to me recently. I nodded.

"And yes, Danu, I ran with Lore in your absence, and took her once under the moon. And whatever it meant to her, it meant only one thing to me: she had no power over me. I tried to read how she had pulled off your kidnapping. She would not have easily revealed that to me.

I could have easily taken her then, dragged her to my basement and left her. But I didn't bother. I think that in the end it will be you that takes her. I have no idea how, but I feel this to be true." He continued. "And as for Gailan? He betrayed her with his incompetence. I do not think he will rise any time soon to return to us."

"I am now Alpha and I will not bring death in its immediate or endless version of it to those of my clan unless they challenge me. You are my mate. If you are further threatened, I will make an exception."

I was suddenly done with questions for now.

"So, Danu," he said. "What might you want to do now?"

"I want to fly! There is a full moon and we are together and have this night to do so."

He laughed and just opened the door. Something large and dark launched silently from it, followed by a slightly smaller one. No more words were needed or possible.

CHAPTER THIRTY-ONE

FLYING

Oh, flying!

I never lost my awe and gratitude that I could fly now, or perhaps simply that now I knew that I *could*. Technically I had done so, with a mental assist from Dagon, at our first meeting. There was a certain risk to it, flying over populations of humans. I had never seen anyone else in the air when we were out.

For someone who has never flown, there's nothing I can say to catch the joy of it.

As a child, I had felt the lift one gets when the roller coaster gains momentum just past the apex of its climb. I felt like I had risen up then, my body straining against the safety belt to go higher.

In hindsight, I believe that it knew it could, that my body knew even then.

I also believed that the many dreams I had had and remembered throughout my life were practice for my activities now. At first in my dreams, I couldn't go very high; it took concentration to fly up to the tops of trees. In fact, the trees were a source of energy that drew me up to their tops. In the beginning, I went tree-top to tree-top, dropping low in between them.

I thought of my stay in Between. I thought of my time spent with a large tree participating, I have no doubt, in our activities at its base. I had drawn up that green energy and shared it with my mate.

In my dreams, I had practised barrel rolls and spins, banking turns and long distance flying.

In my child's dream eyes, I had seen the flat roof of our house from above with a forgotten ball laying up there. I had told myself that it was just a dream. But this was real, and my practice had paid off.

I had also had dreams of being in a building, unable to fly away because the windows were closed or barred. I wondered if this fate line had been present then, even in my childhood dreaming. I saw the bars on the window in the room I had shared with Lucia and shivered.

Tonight I climbed and dove, swerving easily out of reach of Dagon who settled in to chasing me. At first it was easy and I out-manoeuvred him without effort. But, gradually, I wearied and had to work to stay aloft, and to stay ahead.

And then he closed on me. He fell on me from above, out of the darkness like a falcon on a sparrow. We plummeted towards earth together, me with any conscious thought I might have had knocked out of my head, and only the joy of our speed and my surrender to him in my mind.

"*Yes!*" I mind-spoke, moments before we landed with a thump. He smiled fiercely in my mind.

And then he took me. He was above me, looking down with his dark eyes locked on mine. It was not tender, nor long. There were two cries that went out into the night.

We walked home, still without words.

CHAPTER THIRTY-TWO

SURRENDER

At dawn I heard Dagon open the door and let someone in. I knew it was Morag. I heard nothing and caught only fragments of deep mind-speak as both were very strongly shielded. They were not intending for me to hear them, so I decided against intruding.

There was no coffee to be served, no small talk to serve as a social bridge. Morag came and left from Dagon's house, and no one else came at all. This was a business meeting.

I dressed and did what passed as the minimal tidying that I did. It helped that we did not spill food or leave crumbs or any of the usual human things I had once cleaned up in my own quarters. I sat in the library and scanned the books to see if there was one that covered vampire etiquette in meetings—not that I would recognize any helpful bits even if I saw them. Still, I found pictures of gatherings.

A circle of people of the night, with a leader standing slightly elevated above them. No one standing beside him then. That did not surprise me.

Another gathering where everyone was smeared in blood. Hopefully that would not be my first experience.

I knew that Dagon and Morag were discussing a coming meeting of Council. Dagon would have to present me and I ... I would have to be accepted as suitable. There was no plan B.

I was summoned into the living room where Dagon and Morag had been talking. I felt the formality of it and came immediately. I made brief eye contact with Dagon—what did he want me to do? He looked down. I sunk down before him and lowered my eyes. He put his hand on my head momentarily and I stood again, slightly to the side of him.

I looked at Morag and lowered my eyes. I did not kneel to her. I waited.

"Good," Morag said. "Now you will scan the group quickly without being caught by anyone's eyes."

I nodded and remained silent.

"Good," she continued, looking at me carefully. "Your form is good Danu. But what conclusion have you come to about being the Alpha's mate—to letting him lead?"

I looked up. "I do not let him lead," I said with a half-smile. "He is faster than I am."

I briefly touched on the memory of our flight. Of him waiting until I tired and then falling out of the sky from above me. Of our rush to earth. Of wanting him as he was—strong, able to out-manoeuvre and outlast me. And then take me because it was what I wanted with my whole being.

Morag smiled, "Yes. You are now mated to an Alpha. And you want him as one. This is better than I had hoped for."

She turned back to Dagon, who had kept his face expressionless but was obviously following my disclosure to her. He looked at me appraisingly with a faint smile.

"You two just may make it," she said. "Once again, Danu arrives at where she needs to be by her own ways."

"Not completely true," he said calmly.

Later that day we three travelled by flitter to a stone building at the outer reaches of the city. I could sense faerie faintly and wondered if the others did, too. It comforted me.

I wore my dagger beneath a short tunic, with a loose shirt and pants. I was dressed in rich browns with soft shoes on my feet. I felt at one with the fall that was manifesting outside in the nearly bare trees. I had the green stone secreted away where I would not accidentally touch it.

I could feel it come slightly alive in the area we were in. The Sidhe were present, interested perhaps in what would unfold.

I wondered, briefly, if Morag had orchestrated this. I had come to the conclusion that I had been allowed to fall into Gailan's hands because there had been an under-plan that Dagon had not been aware of. The Sidhe had been watching the house and expecting me; they came, as planned, after being alerted somehow.

I dropped it all from my mind. "*Showtime!*"

Dagon went in without looking back. We followed slightly behind, making no claim on him.

There was a collective hiss.

Without appearing to, Morag fell slightly behind me. "*He may need you to have his back,*" she had said to me earlier. Now she had mine.

I lifted my eyes and saw over a hundred Shadakon in an open room. They said nothing aloud, but the mind-speak flew back and forth.

"*Newly turned human! It should have ended before it began.*"

"*He is mad to bring her here. We will drain her blood before the night is over.*"

But occasionally also, "*Let's see how she handles this.*"

Dagon ascended onto a platform and overlooked his clan. I saw the power on him and also saw that they felt and saw it too. He waited until silence fell on the gathering. His timing, always good, was very good tonight.

"*It is well that we are gathered here tonight,*" he said and mind-spoke as well. A slight restlessness could still be felt in those assembled. He waited them out.

"I have someone to bring forward," he said with an icy calm.

"As most of you know, I am mated. My partner is here and you will see her and perhaps come to learn why I made the choice I did."

"Come forward, Danu of Dagon of the Shadakon," he said formally.

I had waited through the Trial. I had chosen to live in calmness for many months. I felt my breathing deepen, without me willing it so. I had swum with the creatures large and small on this planet without fear. I was doing what I could do. All that I could do.

I walked forward.

I lowered my eyes and sunk to my knees in front of Dagon. I felt his hand on my head and sensed that I needed to follow his lead carefully in what happened next.

For what may or may not have been a very long time I paused there. I was patient. My mind was clear. This was my choice. I had given my full consent. Our future would unfold from this moment.

"Rise," he mind-spoke me. "Return to Morag."

Silence held for the time it took me to return to her side. I made brief eye contact and then lowered my eyes. And then raised them again to note that everyone in the room was looking at me.

I raised my head ever so slightly and scanned those who eyed me. I sensed outrage and disbelief. I also sensed the awakened curiosity of the predator. Morag slipped slightly behind me again. I balanced on the balls of my feet.

I smiled slightly. From my left (always the unexpected comes from the left?) Lore appeared suddenly, like the shark I had seen her as. She circled me slowly; I pivoted on the balls of my feet. I was relaxed.

Suddenly she spat at my feet. There was great interest in our interaction now.

I stepped over it lightly and came very fast and very close to her. I met her eyes but did not engage hers.

"Is that it?" I asked. "Spit in the dust?"

I shook my head and drew yet closer to be inside her reach. I had taken some martial arts courses, a skill set you never forget. Especially if you think you might die momentarily.

I breathed in and out, pausing in the sacred space of no-movement between the top and the bottom of my breaths.

I waited.

I had gotten so much better at waiting. I did not want or not want her to make her next move. All of them, warriors and predators that they were, understood that I was not bluffing.

Dagon intervened, saying, "There will be no fighting in this gathering."

In this I knew he meant there would be no further fighting. I had already won this fight. Lore stepped back and melted back into the crowd.

The rest of the Council meeting seemed to be passing uneventfully. Not everyone had taken in my interaction with Lore. I had accounted for myself well enough, but what lay between she and I was far from finished. She may have chosen to pull back, sensing that she did not have a clear chance yet.

Dagon had showed her her place with him earlier. Humiliating me in front of the clan would have been very satisfying to her. Having him as an enemy might stay her hand, at least in a situation in which it was obvious that she was the main agent of my pain.

Bite and circle while the prey bleeds out. This is what shark attack survivors describe: the catastrophic first bite and then … a slight chance to reach shore.

Shore and protection were very close, but our interaction could have weakened me for later. She had missed. No blood was shed. She was invisible again, somewhere out in the dark deep water. Perhaps this had merely been a sizing up.

I stood facing Dagon from the middle of the room, attempting no contact and getting none. Morag, too, was running stealth, saying and mind-speaking nothing to me.

For a while, nothing extraordinaire occurred and I let my attention move over the gathered crowd. Briefly I counted those against me. Then I realized that my accounting was faulty. I began noting only those who were neutral or accepting.

It was a small group. I memorized each face and how I might recognize them from mind-speak or recognition. Having finished this, I resumed keeping my eyes roving easily over the gathering as a whole.

Something had changed. I felt Morag stiffen behind me in anticipation. I deepened my breathing again, letting my fear come and go as it would without bracing against it.

A question was put to Dagon in under-mind-speak and I saw that he grew very quiet, whether in anger … or fear? Probably most would not have heard or noticed anything.

I had learned to listen for the silences and I saw the stillness in his body.

The statement was now spoken aloud with icy scorn.

"You have presented this woman as your mate. All we see is that she is willing to kneel before you. Perhaps she is more of a pet than a mate. We have no time or interest in seeing how she eventually proves herself, if she can."

Dagon did not say anything right away. After a pause he calmly responded, "That is not a question."

How well I knew him!

But then, "We invoke old pack rules. If she is yours, show us now."

Dagon was silent again. Then he said with studied calm, "Would you have me take her sexually before you all? I often do that as my living," he said unsmilingly. "With humans. It hardly proves anything. Afterwards they generally do not remember."

He paused briefly.

"Alive or dead." He shrugged. "If you confuse surrender to sex with having a mate, then it explains why I am here," indicating his position above them, "and you are not."

There was momentary silence. But a brewing undercurrent of challenge was growing in the room.

Morag spoke but once to me in mind-speak. *"You must now do whatever Dagon commands you to do."*

"Take her then. Take her to the edge of her life before us all. Let us see if she obeys without fear or withdraws her consent as she nears the edge of her death. Will she give it all to you as her Alpha? You may revive her, if you choose, afterwards. Or we will lock her away in the long sleep."

The mental picture that flashed across this speaker's mind was like the shock of icy water. The challenger smiled, less of a smile, but more a showing of his teeth.

The clan clamoured for this. I stood relaxed.

So Dagon and I had begun. I had offered to die for him even though I wished only for life. He had taken me close in our first days, but could not make himself end me, or what was growing between us.

And I had told him only two days ago that my decisions involved putting him first, even to the point of my dying, or even worse. I was not confused about this. I hoped that he was not.

Because I knew that this would be the last day that he would stand as Alpha before them if I had regrets or fear before them. Or if he did.

Interestingly, before I was summoned, as I must soon be, my mind touched briefly on the tree-green eyes of Fiórcara. What would he have demanded of me?

But I was shocked by a simple answer, from close at hand. "*I will ask only what you will freely give me, Danu.*"

"*Surrender.*"

I heard Dagon's summons from far away. "I summon you to come forward, Danu of Dagon of the Shadakon." His words reached the back of the hall easily.

Did he trust me fully? I had struggled against him recently.

But neither of us any longer had another choice. I came forward and after greeting him briefly, he raised me to my feet and up to where he stood, and gently but firmly turned me to the crowd that was drawing closer. I did not lean against him, or seek reassurance in any way. I already knew what I knew.

"What is your wish in this, Danu?" he asked in his carrying voice.

I, too, appreciate timing. I faced the crowd with my head up. I let time pass. Then I spoke and mind-spoke clearly. "*I will die for you here, my Alpha,*" I said.

"Blood!" someone shouted. "To the last heart beat!"

We stood together, an island of calm in a growing ancient bloodlust. *Did they not know that I would emerge from this stronger than ever?* I smiled.

"So be it," I said to the crowd and to my lover.

I turned slightly to him and moved aside my shirt, baring the place where we had last done this in joy. I felt my heart pounding there. I stood steady.

"*Look at me. Do not lose me.*"

I looked into his eyes, down into the flames that burned there. He then sank his teeth into me and took me hard, down and down. I floated in his arms as I lost the ability to stand. I felt grey fog creep over my extremities. Not cold. I smiled. One more time, I think, and then my body was spent. I felt from far away, my heart shudder to a stop. I was able to wait, in the timeless moment between breaths before I would have to go. I felt the pull of the stars and quiet of space.

He held my now drained body over his head, smeared with my heart's blood. Morag told me of this later. The crowd roared, some in approval and some in disappointment. No one doubted that I had willingly surrendered my life to him. He then bit his own wrist and drizzled the free-flowing blood into my mouth.

"*Drink*!" He mind-spoke to me from far away.

After a while, I did. Once again, I was reinforced by his blood and strength. I returned to him as I always would, as long as I had the ability to do so. When he kissed me, my blood and his were on my mouth. I licked my lips. I looked around the room. I did not drop my eyes. Dagon's strength flowed through me.

"This is my true mate, Danu of Dagon of the Shadakon," Dagon announced. There was a roar of approval.

CHAPTER THIRTY-THREE

COMING BACK

The Council meeting broke up after Dagon claimed me by Blood Trial. We quietly made our way back to the flitter and waiting driver.

I felt … outside my life. I felt green faerie energy around us and smiled a little woozily. My feet felt like they did not quite touch the earth. I felt the flare of the stone in my pocket and, without thinking, I touched it. I asked for nothing, but felt a surge of calm energy from it and cradled it in my fingers.

Morag looked directly at me and I knew that she was aware of the connection I had made, however inadvertently. She shook her head. I let the stone drop and felt the energy I had briefly received recede.

"Not now." I heard faintly. It was not mind-spoken by anyone here.

I put my hand on Dagon's arm and felt a faint flinch. He was shut down. Morag got out before we arrived home and we entered without speaking.

He went to the library and firmly shut the door. I stood before it in disbelief. He had never barred me from entering anywhere—except the basement—by shutting or locking a door. I still felt his energy circulating within me even as I dispassionately noted that I was no longer standing completely upright. It seemed that I floated sideways to the floor and perhaps I did.

Or time slowed as I moved slowly but inevitably down and down. Finally though, I lay silently with no will or energy to stand or do anything else. Something had gone horribly awry. Dagon should have been glorying in his victory tonight—both of our victories! I needed him!

I struggled to my feet. I approached the door and mind-spoke him.

"I request entrance Dagon. I am ill and frightened by how you are now acting."

I waited. My heart began to form some serious questions. I struggled to stay on my feet.

He opened the door, but stood in the entrance, not coming forward to reach me. He did not meet my eyes. I searched for what I might say next, to not make a bad situation worse, and settled on a course of action.

"You are my Alpha and I am in need. I feel ill and strange. I require you to care for me."

He still said nothing, lost in whatever he had wrapped about him.

"You do not have to tell me until you are ready what you are going through. Though I expect that soon."

"What do you need of me?" he asked hoarsely.

"I need you to remind me why I almost died for you," I said simply. "If I can die. Or whatever would have come next. It was coming very fast."

"Not with words," I continued. "I need you to hold me to this planet tonight. I need to feel part of you—not sexually because I don't think that is possible right now," I said. "That in itself frightens me."

"Don't lose me," I whispered, as he had said before he, well, took me to death.

I reached out my palm and took his. Palm to palm, Maker to Maker. He and I had been forced to re-enact that in front of a pack of aggressive Shadakon. It had gone further than I had expected.

He dropped his eyes.

"No, Dagon," I said. "I need you with me. I need you."

He suddenly caught me as I swayed on my feet. He carried me to the pool and filled it with warm fragrant water. He undressed me. He touched the healing spot on my shoulder.

He looked from me to the water.

"You will be with me and keep me safe," I said sleepily.

He stripped off his clothes and mine and carried me in. I floated above his chest, rising and falling slightly in the water with my breaths. I felt his breaths slow and join my rhythm and some ease creep into his body.

"I am still far away," I said. "Do not leave me here alone. Find me and bring us back together."

He turned me to face him. He met my eyes and I saw great sorrow in them. I held them then, not letting him go. "I thought I needed you in every way possible. Tonight I needed you to bring me back from the edge of my body's physical dying. You did so. I need to know whether I would have died, and, if so, if I would have continued on somehow. No one has explained these things to me. But for now, I need only to be part of you."

"I did not take you to the edge," he said flatly. He continued to look into my eyes because I compelled him to. "I took you over the edge. You died in my arms."

I smiled. "Not so easy for a Shadakon," I said.

"You are still detached from your body," he said. "Only your will brought you back."

"No, you gave me your blood. We stood together."

"Danu," he said. "I have lived as the predator that I am for endless years. I know where the edge is, as do you. I took you beyond. I lost my control as the clan was shouting for your death."

"I delivered you dead to them!"

"I returned then," I said simply. "I think they will not forget that."

I released him from my gaze but he continued to look deep within me. I fell into the flickering amber lights and felt a faint stirring of desire in my body. He laughed.

He stroked me like a cat. I could feel wherever he touched me become warm and answering to his touch.

"Time to get you out of the tub," he said, carrying me out.

Later we lay together. He combed his fingers through my hair and it awoke to his touch. He massaged my hands, my feet, and then gradually worked to the middle. He stopped.

"It would be so easy to continue, I can feel your desire rising. But I need to say a few things first if we are to continue."

"If you are to continue," I corrected, "I have already started and am continuing with or without you."

"Ah, Danu," he sighed. "I know you are back now. But listen, I had no idea what would happen tonight. Oh, I knew that Lore would not be able to resist attempting to humiliate you. Incidentally, she now hates you more than ever. Once again you have stood her down in front of her peers."

I nodded.

"There was no reason for what happened next," he said.

"Oh I don't know. I think seventy-five of the hundred or so Shadakon there wanted me dead or worse. Twenty-five more were only somewhat indifferent. As a group, they saw me as an outsider to be run off or destroyed."

"Even you, my Alpha, are not invulnerable to group pressure—especially mind-spoken pressure. If you were bent to what you did, then remember next time to avoid this possibility. Do not allow everyone to synch together. But I do not think that is what happened," I said.

He looked at me quizzically.

"You have good timing. I have trusted it before, and will continue to bet my life on it.

Very, very good," I continued. "But then you have been a musician in your back lives. You took me to death. Just to there. I felt it and I also felt that there was the moment beyond that in which I was still present and who I am."

"You were cutting it fine. I trusted you. This has continued to work for us," I said, adjusting myself slightly under his hand to present parts he had not yet touched.

He looked at me and then let it go. I saw and felt the self-doubt and fear leave his body.

"Lie still," he said. "Do not move until you can no longer bear staying still."

Then he awakened me slowly and skilfully until I finally moved without further thought.

CHAPTER THIRTY-FOUR

KNOWLEDGE IS POWER?

When we had finished lolling about and the light was strengthening, Morag made her appearance. Dagon opened the door for her before she announced her presence.

First she came to me, and to my astonishment kneeled briefly before me. I drew her up, shaking my head, puzzled at her action. She scanned me carefully. I noted her smile as she completed this, I could feel her relief grow.

She briefly bent her head to Dagon, but subjected him to a similar scrutiny.

We both sat calmly with her. My ability to find calm quickly, strengthened by my solo time on the island, was something I did not have to search for under most circumstances.

"Perfect trust," she murmured. "Once again I am amazed by you Danu. Not the least being that you helped Dagon back from his darkness."

I remembered a fragment of something I had once read that Aleister Crowley, an Earthman of formidable and frightening magical talents had said, "*Love is the law. Love under will.*"

They both looked at me.

"That's it then," said Morag. "This was your return route, Danu, that and your knife's edge timing," she added to Dagon.

"I hope I never see anything happen like this to you two again," she said. "But it was something that has now put both of you beyond reproach from the clan and the Council. No one will harm you or let anyone else do so now," she said. "Lore's manipulations have crumbled."

"Perhaps," said Dagon. "For now."

We all sat with that thought but it did not rob me of my joy today.

I placed my palm briefly to his, and the energy shared between us flared. I asked Morag, "What Dagon and I had done before—was it known to the others?"

She shook her head. "Sharing is rare among us, Danu. And our sexual connections are usually brief and fierce." She looked at Dagon.

"She knows Morag," said Dagon. We have come to an agreement about what has and may pass between ourselves and others."

She looked at me and said nothing either aloud or in mind-speak. Nevertheless I knew what was beneath her silence.

"*He knows but he does not understand. You will go to Fiórcara and it will be in repayment for my life, and perhaps the beginning of cooperation between our kinds. The Sidhe has chosen to let you live your life as you will until next summer. But he is aware of you. He would have intervened and carried you away yesterday had it come to that. A bond grows between you.*"

I thought briefly of touching the green stone I carried and his message to me, *"Not now."*

Morag nodded slightly, then changed directions to draw us away from this unspoken topic.

"I understand from Dagon that you have questions about the life span of those of the Blood.

He thought I could lay this information out simply to you," she said, "but I cannot do so. Too many things have intervened, not the least being that you have shared blood many times, and also drank from the elixir of life."

"However, I will say what I know to be truth. Some of it might be frightening information," she said quietly, "but it is time for you to know what lies before you."

"First let me offer a brief history of what I know.

Dagon may add his own experiences to what I say."

"In the beginning of our kind—a very long-ago beginning—there were hunter-gatherers in a region on Earth that was generous in its supplies of wild game and good water. They gathered fruits and wild seeds but made no attempt to stay and tend to any future source of food. Life was short and simple."

"So it was for a long time," she mused. "Whatever fate they may have found on their own, we cannot say. But then the Visitors came to Earth. The early humans served as labourers for them and, in some cases, their daughters were taken and impregnated. Most of these offspring died, but a few did not."

I had pieced together most of this on my own in Dagon's library, but neither he nor I interrupted her.

"The workers were short-lived and of short attention spans. Slaves cannot do more than is possible for them, no matter how frightened or mistreated they are. So the Visitors enhanced them with their own bloods."

"Bloods!" My attention caught; here was the part I most wanted to know about.

"There were two main groups of Outsiders who came to old Earth," she said. One wanted manual labourers. And a food source," she said flatly. "They took from those early humans, drinking energy as we do, along with tapping the resources of the planet."

"The others we did not know about for a very long time. But in the deep unbroken forests of Earth there were other bases and other Visitors who had their own plans for those they found there. They were enhanced with different skills. One was creating and moving in and out of Between. Those Visitors also found their enhanced charges comely. They lived very long lives and gifted their offspring with the same." She looked at me briefly.

"When their masters left and did not return, they remained in the forests.

They bonded with the life force and took no lives to live as they did."

"The humans had been gifted with rapid procreation and hardiness. They spread quickly out of the valleys where they had sheltered. Some of them carried a richer version of the Blood. Those sometimes found each other and enforced that bloodline. The bible is full of such stories," she said.

I looked at her questioningly. "Check out the story of the bloodline of the House of David," she answered.

"The humans and their sometimes strange children went to the four corners of the Earth. The Shadakon were hidden among the humans; their numbers increased by birth and by Making, and the old fierceness persisted."

"The children of the night turned on their parents and all of humanity," she said. "And then the humans retaliated and our numbers were decimated."

"Meanwhile, those that call themselves the Sidhe remained in the wild places. They had passing interactions with humans. Some were cruel or indifferent. Some were merely curious."

She stopped. "Some, perhaps driven by the loneliness of their long lives, took humans as brief lovers." She paused again and I heard her silence. "Some of those children also lived."

A silence spread over all of us. The obvious question hung unasked between us.

"Could one carry both lines of ancestry?" I finally asked.

"It would appear that this may be true," she replied.

We sat, and I heard outside noises of the city and the sound of the wind whirling and passing by. "Tell me, Morag," I said at last. "I thought I had found my kind here with the Shadakon. With Dagon." I shivered.

Morag reached out and touched my cheek.

"You found your way to him and to us," she said. "And you turned spontaneously. You had an inner understanding of permission and consent, of contract." She smiled. "As unlikely as it may seem to others, Dagon taught you that early and well. However, you have a reluctance to kill or even to hurt. Happily there is a place for one such as you. But most of us carry a darker streak. Bloodlust," she said simply.

She caught my eyes to bring home her next point.

"Dagon does," she said. "You know this and this knowledge helps you understand what he sacrificed for you in your first days together."

I remembered. I remembered his rising anger when I wished for bliss from him, but denied him his own. And so he showed me his frustration and anger at my ignorance. I remembered waking up the next morning and being surprised. I remembered signing lethal contract.

"Yes," said Morag. "But by then he was unable to part from you. Your passion exceeds that of our people and of humans, Danu. The two of you continue to want each other and to return to continue on together in spite of your partings."

Was she educating Dagon as well as me? I wondered.... Was there reassurance in this story that he would later return to?

"But as to the length of your life and what happens when your body is damaged badly—the Shadakon go into a state of suspension if their bodies are injured and they cannot feed themselves, or no one else will. In these cases they're often placed in a place of no escape by their own kind."

I shuddered.

"That can last a very long time," she continued. "Sometimes they are redis-
covered and revived.

Or the jailor continues to come and feeds them just enough to remain conscious
of their continuous Hunger."

I thought of Dagon's basement. *"Who, besides me, had spent time there?"* I felt
him freeze beside me.

"Most of us have basements, Danu," Morag said. "They are useful for ... ah,
interrogations and short terms of interment. Our innate savagery does not usually
stretch to torture. You can ask him more about this later, but you are not mated
with a cruel Alpha. May it always be so."

She stopped without adding further details on the matter.

"Being drained of blood kills the body," she added matter-of-factly. It is not
something that can be healed from. Certainly not without being immediately
revived with blood. Perhaps, as you explained earlier, will enters into the possibility
of being restored. Perhaps love as well."

She looked at both of us.

"I was dying," she said unemotionally. "Perhaps love and will entered into
my being saved."

"With no lethal incidents, we can live a long, long time, Danu. And you have
drunk the elixir of life. You and Dagon have had many exchanges of energy and
blood. Yet you have remained yourself, in spite of these ... experiments ... between
the two of you. You, Danu, are walking a path no one else I know has walked."

"We are not interested in who you are, but what you do." Fiórcara had said to me.

CHAPTER THIRTY-FIVE

THE QUICKENING

★ ★ ★ ★

And so we settled into what might have been called, in hindsight, a peaceful stretch of time.

Dagon went to the fair daily. He came home looking like, well, a well-fed, pleased-with-himself predator. His Alpha status was obviously attractive to his clientele. If one wants to die, it's good to come to someone who can calmly plan that with you and make your wish come true. And probably make you happier than you had ever been in your life.

Briefly.

I worked at the hospice with the Mothers. I was glad to spend long days with them, often sitting beside someone sleeping (sometimes because I had induced it). I took what was offered and some lives ended quietly at the end of a dream.

When I was in their quiet surroundings, I felt more able to find my still centre and work without thinking too much about anything.

About Dagon. OK, about Dagon.

And Fiórcara.

So, not thinking was a bit of a lie. OK, a large lie. I struggled with the order of importance of my thoughts: to Dagon, to me, to Morag . . . I rearranged those names over and over.

It was now the middle of winter on Exterra. Storms blew in and slammed rain and snow against the windows. Walks outside were likely to whip my breath away but I took them anyway. I would return soaked and grateful to be inside.

But restlessness soon drove me out again.

The Mothers would just hand me a dry robe. I had gotten used to wearing such a garment while on the island, working with those who carried many kinds of deaths. No one had asked me to, but after awhile it had been soothing have my bare skin away from the breeze. To not feel every moment the different quality of sunlight as the sun transited across the sky.

I didn't remember ever feeling like this before. I wondered if the Shadakon felt these sensitivities. I knew that they and I had the focus to hear anything that moved. To hear anything that breathed without moving and even the sound of a beating heart. These other senses, though, were growing. They were pleasant but intense, and sometimes distracting. So I shut them away when I worked.

When I was home, even if Dagon and I were in different rooms, I sensed him. I felt his energy that eventually drew me to his side. He would look up as if he was surprised, as if he didn't know that I had been resisting coming to him until I gave up. I could play, I could fly high, I could hide in the bottom of the pool practising deep breath control. He would sit on the edge, dabbling one hand languidly in the water, like a cat waiting for a goldfish to rise. Once he looked at me, he had me. He did not make me look or keep looking, but I spiralled into his energy. Flames circled my body. Desire stopped my breath. He knew this and never wondered if I had anything—or anyone—else on my mind.

Why should he? He was my mate and my Alpha. We had gone through the trials together and returned to each other again and again. Our heat had stayed constant.

I harboured a small but growing concern, however. I felt a shift within myself; it was at its strongest when I was outside. Sometimes I sought the company of an old tree that grew nearby. I would put my cheek against its rough bark and lean into it, wishing for …*ah, what indeed was I wishing for these days?*

Spring would come after winter; and after spring, summer, bringing the closing of a deal struck in desperation. But had I been so innocent of what I might agree to? I had been counselled not to offer so generously, not to offer myself, as it turned out. Yet I kept making my deals: my life for Lucia's life; my life for Morag's life. The Sidhe were apparently interested in just how important a thing that a human, or Shadakon, might offer them.

Had I been informed, before I consented—to anything?

Consent is complex, as Dagon had said. I could say, no, I had no idea what might be asked of me.

I would be lying to myself, however. I was hardly the confused maiden, lost on the edge of the forest, confronted with something that she could not imagine.

I could imagine. I had spent hours imagining before I applied the agony of Touch-me-not to my body. I had felt the speckled moonlight hit my skin and glow each place it touched. I had removed my clothes, the better to feel just that.

"*I will take what you offer me freely,*" Fiórcara had mind-spoke calmly. "*Your surrender.*"

I realized how similar my lover and mate was to the Sidhe. They both required the same from me, no more but no less. They were both powerful and ancient and not to be lied to, or deceived in more subtle ways.

Dagon had realized the peril we were in before I did. He had felt it in me when he visited me in Between. And who had invited him to keep company with me there? Who knew that I could not help but pass on the energy I had absorbed there on the night of midsummer's eve? Did Dagon realize what state I was in and what I brought to him? I knew that he did afterwards. I now realized that Fiórcara wanted him to know just that, and to know what he might lose …

"I don't care who you are pledged to in your world," Fiórcara had said.

"On midsummer's eve you will dance with me without steel or Touch-me-not between us."

I walked in the rain and wondered and feared and hoped that I would live to see that night. I no longer lied to myself about that. I realized that I now moved in two worlds. They required different actions from me. I hoped that I could continue to keep them separate in my mind.

Almost accidentally, I brushed my fingers against the green stone in my pocket. It flared briefly. I'd started to carry it with me ever since the night of the Council meeting; I let myself pretend that I had chosen to do so.

One afternoon I returned from my hospice work early. Dagon was away doing Council work and I was not needed to attend with him; we both thought that it was wiser if I stayed in the background.

There was a loud mind-speak request for entrance at Dagon's front door that I recognized as Morag. She sounded urgent and I immediately feared for Dagon. He was still new to his role and, although no one was in a position to challenge him, I still wondered if he should have let Lore off the hook when he had her in hand. But he had left that unfinished—as he probably had done previously over the millennium.

Morag sat down and immediately called me to her. Although not my Alpha, she had been, and I saw her as having elder status. I knelt before her. She did not invite me to rise, but instead tipped my head back and looked into my eyes.

"I am going to ask you for permission, but if you do not give it, Danu, I will do it anyway. I need to know what you are drawing around you. I need to gain this information while Dagon is away. You may tell him later, or I will," she finished flatly. There was no pleasant sensation when falling into Morag's green wolf eyes; they looked in without giving anything away.

I had never been read deeply by anyone but Dagon, and possibly Fiórcara—both I had freely opened to.

Mentally, I reeled back from her. There was no holding back, no shelter. I allowed and allowed but wondered how far she would search. And what she might find.

After awhile—however long that was—she let me go. I felt … used. I was surprised at the pain of it. In spite of myself, tears fell.

"I am sorry, Danu," she said softly. "I am so sorry that you have been caught up by the bargain you struck for my life."

"It happened before that," I said. I decided then to say what I might never have said to her if we had not begun our conversation this way. "It happened when you set me up to be picked up by the Sidhe from where I was conveniently imprisoned."

I went another step. "It was something I finally realized months after I saw you in Between. You had free passage there; you had been there before. And then you passed on to me a talisman that I could neither refuse nor ignore."

We looked at each other without words.

"You would not be here now, if I had not made my own deal with the Sidhe," she said. "You would have discovered first-hand what happens when one of the Blood is locked away, neither living nor dying cleanly."

I knew this was true, but for the rest?

"You and, through you, Dagon, have been moving in a course of actions that were forced on you by others," she said at last. "Just as what happened in your first Council meeting was a set up—and not by me!

So too your connection to the Sidhe was strengthened by proximity to them— spending time there, drinking the elixir of life."

"Spending midsummer's eve on the hill with them? With him intent on me," I said.

She nodded. "Some of it was happenstance. But I, too, have made my bargains with the Sidhe. I have decided, like you, that the good of this planet and of my kind is more important than I am. Than you are …"

She sighed. "If you had fallen to the Call that night, no one would have blamed you. Your '*friend*' would have had his curiosity satisfied. You would have been returned to Dagon in whatever shape you were in, blameless in everything but not resisting faerie power."

"Which few can do," she added. "Maybe none but you. Ah, but you fascinated him, clinging to your refusal to not step over that link of steel," she said. "And your choice to counter the Call with pain—I don't believe that's ever happened to him before."

"If you had failed in your will, whatever happened to you that night would now be over. Instead it builds within you. And what of Dagon? Will all my work, and his, go for naught because he loses what he has struggled so hard to keep?"

"We have spoken of this," I said defensively.

"He thinks like a male!" she cried angrily. "He thinks that one night spent with someone, unwilling but fulfilling an obligation, is a minor thing." She glared at me. "Is it a minor thing, Danu? Will you be able to retain yourself and come back as before to Dagon?"

I dropped my eyes. I took out the green stone that lay innocently in my hand. It did not glow.

"Throw it away," said Morag wearily.

I shook my head and tears again spilled down my cheeks. "I have tried and I cannot."

We looked at each other.

"What, then, is your plan?" she asked.

"If I cannot leave, or my love for Dagon is extinguished, I will use the small tool that he gave me," I said sadly. "I must somehow experience this without holding back. But if I am shattered, then I am."

"Ah, Danu," Morag said softly. "That option will not be available to you. He will not allow it. You will come to him with no tools, no possible escape."

"You will do this willingly," she said. "Meanwhile, even your slight contact with the Sidhe is changing you."

We looked at each other. In spite of the interrogation she had forced on me, I did not sense ill will. But there were many pieces of this puzzle that continued to be missing.

I decided to fill in some of these, knowing that I could not go back from this moment. Earlier there had seemed to be safety in not knowing, if for no other reason, that Dagon could not sense it in me.

The thought of hurting him, or turning him back to an earlier hard-hearted state, was painful. I felt it swirl through me, but continued on my inquiry.

"Where did the poison come from, Morag?"

She startled.

"Do you truly want to know this, Danu?" She looked at me sadly.

"I already know," I said. "It did not come from the humans, as you would not have been the only victim. It did not come from the Shadakon, or it would have been for me or Dagon, administered by a predictable hand."

"The Sidhe undoubtedly would like to rid this world of humans.

However they know that more would just keep coming. Would or could they exterminate them all? Perhaps this is being pondered," I said. "Likewise eliminating the Shadakon, the wolves that arose from those sheep. We are useful here to keep numbers down, and away from the untouched parts of this planet. Loosing a plague on the Shadakon would not serve the Sidhe."

"It was not done in anger, or as a hasty impulse. It was passed to you as a friend might pass a cup," I said, now beyond bitterness. "There was some pain—there had to be some pain. And it could not act too rapidly." I continued to look at Morag. "You began this conversation," I said.

"I am not the first Shadakon that Fiórcara has had claim on." I said sadly. "You speak wisely about what is likely to befall me; you speak from first-hand knowledge. When you awoke restored in Between, you knew that he had succeeded in his plan."

"Morag," I said, and leaned into the usually reserved empty space between people. "I have faced jealousy and struggles for possession. I live and love someone who uses his sexual skills intentionally both on his clients and me. I cannot resist him, and do not want to. Passion means everything. Passion means nothing! It is what we do, the allure to draw others to us. It is nature's best trick to ensure procreation, and thus survival. The Shadakon and Sidhe now seem to be outside of that mandate now. Ironically both use passion as a finely honed tool, to draw humans away from their supposed safety—to more easily use. In unlikely situations to love, although I am not sure that is always the right word. To kill ..." I shrugged.

"We simply must work together to stem the plague that is humanity. We cannot afford to distract each other through old enmities. I am pledged to the life of this planet," I said.

"Perhaps that too was enhanced in me, but I had it within me for as far back as I can remember as I watched my own world sicken. As a child, I sensed the faerie nearby.

They came to me in what might or might not have been dreams, when I lay sick and alone with fever in the night. I wanted to go with them then but they would not take me."

Time stilled between the two of us and I continued, "You, too, have danced with he who allows me to call him Fiórcara as well as having many other names. You returned, retaining a connection of some sort. You did not go mad nor lose your way back. Neither will I."

"*I was not mated to an Alpha,*" she mind-spoke. "*And as an Alpha, I never again connected with one of my kind.*"

"*In this I am not like you,*" I responded. "*If it is possible I will surrender to both, and return to he who is my life. Fiórcara does not want anything more than what he asks for. He witnessed Dagon and me as we lay together in the grove in Between. He knows that Dagon is capable of reclaiming me if he will.*"

"*He asks for everything,*" Morag mind-spoke.

"*So does Dagon. And I have been awakened to be a self I could never have dreamed possible. I am beyond joy at how my life has progressed since I came here seeking death. The Sidhe used you almost to death, and afterwards he came to you with the elixir of life and restored you. I hope you found kindness, if not love, in that.*"

"*I hope I find that as well.*"

We looked at each other deeply. "Perhaps neither of us will report this conversation to Dagon," I said. "Certainly I will not."

She rose then, and left silently.

CHAPTER THIRTY-SIX

A SMALL BOUQUET OF SPRING FLOWERS

Dagon arrived one afternoon, bearing a small bouquet of spring flowers. As he busied himself in finding a vase, he seemed to miss the surge of feelings that came over me. Or perhaps he did not; perhaps he had chosen his gift very intentionally.

Spring! Spring flowers. I had felt this spring quickening on the land and in me. I started to see the small beings that peered out at me from among the leaves at the edge of the wilderness. I sensed their quick eyes. They flew or moved off immediately unless I remained very still; I did so. I was sad they feared me as much as they did, but appreciated their necessary response.

Humans hurt and kill their fellow beings; Shadakon look like humans, so they might be dangerous as well. I knew this was why they withdrew from me whenever I encountered them.

I had seen flowers growing in the wild places that touched the city's edges. I had smelled them at night, carried on the breeze that entered our room. Still cold, it brought a clean green smell of renewal and the musky notes of early blooming night flowers. I heard the night moth that flew under the moon, drawn to a mate who waited patiently while she scented the air downwind of her.

I had never felt these feelings before, or at least never so strongly. Spring was surely rising in me.

I looked up to see Dagon assessing me quietly.

"*Danu*," he mind-spoke, but there was no command in it. I moved towards him, hoping for the distraction and no-thinking that he would kindle in me.

"No, Danu. Stay apart from me for a while.

You are troubled and the solace of passion will not remove that from you. Not that we haven't both tried," he said.

I looked at him, hoping that we would not speak of what was happening to me.

"Could you believe that I don't know? He said sadly. I told you that bargains with the Sidhe are incredibly dangerous," he continued. "I knew you had been drawn in when I was allowed to join you in Between. If I had not immediately known, you quickly showed me."

He smiled. "You are the most attracting being I have ever met."

He reached out and ran one finger idly from cheek to neck to where he had taken my heart's blood in ultimate pleasure for both of us. He stopped then.

"Do you see how fast this is for both of us?" he asked. "Can you see that I could not end what I continue to want and want more and more of?"

I looked at him and willed myself to pull back from the effect he had on me.

He laughed, stepping back from me slightly. "Even though I could walk away now," he said, "I would never choose to. Ever."

"You are now entering into that feeling. If you are of the faerie as well as our blood, you will feel the same about who calls you now, softly but incessantly. When summer arrives you will go to him willingly, no longer to pay a debt. But you will pay, my mate," he said sadly. "That has already been established."

"I do not want to want this!" I said. "I only did what I felt I had to do. For Morag. For you. For the Shadakon—although most of them would not understand that—and for this planet and its vibrant life."

"You are already going," Dagon said without anger. "As the summer's energy floods you, you will be completely gone. This is already so," he said.

"Morag may feel that my preoccupation with my Alpha role and your gift to me at the Council meeting has made me oblivious to what is happening to you. That I assume all is well and we three have somehow come through unscathed."

He shook his head. "The only way that I can let you go is if you choose to go. I do not have the power to order that myself. I should have known that from the moment you touched my hand. I suspected something, after thinking I might thrill you with a little fear, in preparation for the larger one ..."

"I lifted us both up above the glamoured people's heads and we flew here. But I did not hold you up. And you were not afraid—far from it. Even in your depleted, angry human state, you came into your glory."

"I worked to fan those flames of course," he said with a slight smile. "The flames of my own undoing."

We looked at each other. I felt his passion as well as my own. This was not just about me, I realized; this was changing my lover as well.

"And now what?" I sighed.

"Exactly. The only way through is through," he said eventually. "You feel the changes in yourself and know that you have a set day when you will face whatever will occur, but until the day comes, please do not shut me out. Stay with me until the moment that you have to leave," he added in a whisper.

"I do not think I will get angry about this, although I may," he said. "It goes against what has been true throughout my long lives. We of the Shadakon do not share often. I heard his pride of being the Alpha of a long-lived clan."

"I do not think that the Sidhe want to bring you to your knees," I said. "I could be wrong. I suppose it might be part of an old blood feud." I looked at him questioningly.

"No," he said ruefully. "We never carried off each other's mates and we cannot live in the forest without human prey. They held us in disdain. That is my fear for you, when I am not considering myself at the moment—that you will feel their ancient scorn and dismissal after having made good on your promise. That you will return to me feeling used and abandoned by he who was so significant to you. That might be worse than some of the alternatives that I sometimes can't help thinking about."

"Those being?"

"That you will chose faerie and Fiócara over me. That you will give up everything to him—including me."

"I have already given up everything—to you. Over and over. And here we are, together and moving forward towards a common future."

I looked at him and caught his eyes. "I will return, Dagon. I always will return. The only question for us is: will you have me?"

"A simple answer then, milady," he said. "It will have to do for now. Yes, I will have you. I will have you over and over, now and now and now."

He divested me of my clothes and then his own. The smell of the flowers seemed to fill the room. "Come to me, Danu."

We had stood apart until he drew me towards him and turned me away from him such that I faced an empty wall. In my mind, I suddenly could hear the howls of a crowded clan meeting room of Shadakon.

"*Take her!*" There was enthusiasm and excitement in that but no hatred.

I remembered how he had earlier spared me from a public mating.

"*They wouldn't have understood what they saw,*" he mind-spoke me. "*You would have, but we needed more than that on that night. Let us finish this part. I will enjoy it and I believe that you will also.*"

I smelled the open flames of a fire burning long ago. I saw all eyes on me, as I stood naked before them. I heard the pack howl to see their Alpha take his mate in front of them. So it had once been.

I wanted it. I wanted him. Every cue I could give was, "Yes!"

And then he did. And he did and he did.

CHAPTER THIRTY-SEVEN

AND THEN IT WAS SUMMER

Spring unfolded in green leaves and freshened creeks. The wind seemed to touch every inch of my skin when I walked outside.

And I had to be outside.

One night I prowled the house restlessly, knowing that Dagon lay quiet but unsleeping. We actually needed little sleep, but it was a pleasure to lie down and stretch out beside him. I was used to him leaving me after I dozed. If I awakened, I expected to find him in the library, as he had renewed his interest in things faerie.

I had not. I didn't want to know more than I already knew from the old stories of Earth—of people invited to go with them who came back years or even centuries later to be judged as mad while they looked frantically for their wives and children, long dead and buried behind the church. I didn't want to know any more than I did about the effects of connecting with beings so lovely that the human's everyday reality turned to ashes even if he or she did return. In my teenaged years I had read about the Seelie Court, those who chose at times to help humans. And also about the Unseelie Court that included others not so lovely—whose interactions were indifferent or malevolent to their human neighbours.

I doubted that these divisions were more than the hopeful wishes of the villagers trying to make sense of the early interactions that occurred between them and the Sidhe. Meanwhile the humans continued to trespass into the forests, felling the great trees and ploughing their land even as they foolishly hoped for good luck or easy fortune from those they took from. I was sure that my Sidhe contact had lived on both ends of the spectrum of good to bad and all between.

He had lived through what I had only caught the last chapters of before I had fled Earth's ruin. People who sought them rarely found them, and they certainly did not find what they thought they wanted. Somehow the part where faerie gold brought them true joy in their lives never quite worked out. The love and passion of moon madness failed to help them to live happier within their own human lives.

I felt that I would be better off hoping for nothing; asking for nothing except what came and holding to my calmness if possible, or if not, regaining my lost calm eventually. Just that. All or any of that.

I went out the back door into the wild space in the back of his—our—house. The moon was a small crescent that rode high in the sky. It was silent outside, so incredibly silent. I would just sit in the moonlight for a moment, breathing in the spring air and breathing out my fears for the future. Breathing out the feeling of slowly spiralling out of control. I breathed out, out, out. In would come if there was further need of it; in would take care of itself.

Until one day it would not. But I had already faced that day, and I remembered that it had not hurt much, and that there were stars.

I lay on the dew damp cool grass, just for a moment, so that I could better see the sky. I felt peace soaking up into me, from the soil, from the planet that humans had named Exterra. *I wondered what the Sidhe called her. Did they converse with her? Ask her for shelter and life? Thank her? Or was that a given for them?*

The stars whirled overhead as I watched. I felt safe, lying on the ground, with nowhere to fall. I awoke in the morning, damp but strangely calmer than before.

I did not know that Dagon had sat apart from me out there, quietly watching over me until the sun rose.

I did not know that he, the Alpha, the strong leader of his clan and of me, had quietly wept. Later, after he and I had both ventured out seeking sustenance and being useful, in the day now lit by the slanting sun of the late afternoon, he led me outside to the same small wild space. It was glowing golden and peaceful.

I, however, was not peaceful. I could read nothing of his thoughts. His body was seemingly calm. I saw intention in his relaxed posture, that of an attentive predator. Things could go any way from the coming moment.

He indicated that I sit down and after a moment or so, so did he. It was quiet here in this untended garden, but I could hear and feel the slight breeze and the leaves that rubbed together when it touched them. I could sense the small quick little animals that were observing us from the shadows.

I refused to ask why he had brought us here.. My fear grew until my calm breathing was a lie. I waited.

"Ah, Danu," he finally said and mind-spoke. "*You would make me do this?*"

He turned his beautiful dark amber eyes on me and there was not an immediate invitation there. "We cannot pretend that you are totally here anymore." He indicated the surroundings and then put his hand on his chest lightly. "This was a place of once great pain for me. And now it is again."

"I realize now that I cannot bear for you to be here when the summons comes. Would he take you from beside me as I slept? Would I open the door and watch you walk away to join him?" He shook his head in pain. "I cannot be effective as an Alpha and watch this unfold to the end." "*It is still ten days to midsummer,*" I mind-spoke, alarmed. "*I have no other place to be. No place to feed. Are you turning me out?*"

"No, Danu," he mind-spoke and spoke as gently as I had ever heard him speak. "*You know better than that.*" He looked at me as from a distance. "*But I ask you to consent to leave and wait out the remaining time with the Mothers on the island. They will give you work and shelter. I think you should return to the seaside if you will. Your connection to the sea strengthens you. I will watch you leave as my strong mate, going on an unimaginable adventure. That would be the best way for me, and, I think, for you also.*"

"Please!" It left my lips without warning. "Please don't withdraw from me until it is time!"

"I am not withdrawing, Danu," he said, and again I heard gentled grief. "You are my mate. We must both trust in your abilities to find a clear path back."

"Not now," I breathed. "Not this now."

He looked at me and I felt him with me again. I touched his leg lightly and felt the muscles tightened under the skin. He looked at me but made no move towards or away from me. I took off my shirt and pants and shook my hair to free it. I asked with my eyes if I could undress him. He stood and I pulled off his shirt and pants, and I saw him gleaming in the last of the golden day.

"Here?" he asked.

"If faerie draws near me, I want them to know who my mate and lover is. That you are the one I desire. I will join with you here, in the sunshine and encircling trees. Let them bear witness."

He bent to me and our eyes met and held. I shivered. He commenced to drawing up my energy until I could not breathe. I could not think, I could not wait but he made me do so. He was tuning me, taking me up and up and then … taking me, then giving back, and taking me again. We shared our combined energies in slowly quieting waves of pleasure.

I melded with him, making one thing of two. We lay in the now twilight, observed by we cared not who.

"I will hold you here, in my mind's eye," he said. "Wanting only me and waiting for me."

"But on this next part of your journey," he added, "It is I who will wait." He sighed. "Please forgive me for anticipating this. I have already asked Morag to accompany you to the island tomorrow."

And then he said something that allowed me to know that there were few secrets around him that he could not sense, whether he gave that away or not.

"She will best understand how you feel," he said. "There will be no judgements from her."

Morag was at the door at dawn. Dagon and I had not slept, but lay cocooned in the comfort we had generated in each other. As dawn had arrived, he shared more energy with me.

"Something for the road," he said as he transferred it to me. I knew it left him in deficit but did not refuse. He could give me this.

"I had given him my word. But I had also given it to someone else."

He shook his head. "The time is past for wondering if you could have avoided this," he said. "Remember as I do that you sat at the side of a dying ally."

"It is who you are," he said gently. "And all of us who know you, know this about you. I love you, Danu of Dagon of the Shadakon," he said.

"I love you as you are and for who you are." He smiled. "And this too,"—his finger touched me in mock innocence and I flared under his touch—"this that is between us as well."

In the morning I had arose and donned the clothes I would wear. They were the ones that Fiórcara had presented to me before I left Between and I had not worn them since then. I put the cord that held the dagger in its sheath over my head before donning my shirt. The material was soft on my body.

Dagon observed me without openly watching. He saw me adjust the knife sheath, so that it hung on my left side and in perfect reach. He said nothing. I put the green stone I did not think he had seen in one pocket. He said nothing.

There were no longer further questions that could be answered between us.

He let Morag in at the door and accepted her gesture of respect to him. He looked at me and I sank to his feet before him, even though he had not required me to. He put his hand lightly on my head.

"Yes, mate," he said. "I require you to return to me."

I arose and we walked out the door. He did not watch me go.

The flitter was piloted by a Blood that I had recognized at the Council meeting. I was certain he was one of the few who had born no animosity towards me as the night unfolded, of which there was only a handful. He averted his eyes briefly to Morag and longer to me.

A different trip then.

The forest we travelled over was unbroken except by small glades and edges of waterways. There were unnumbered and unnamed colours of green and I let myself feel them as we glided overhead.

The silence in the flitter was complete. Morag was locked down and I did as well. Our driver was almost invisible to being sensed. *"A very fine predator,"* I thought briefly. He touched his head lightly with his finger and smiled.

A Mother was waiting when the flitter landed. She watched me alight and looked questioningly at Morag, perhaps remembering her from her brief stay here. Or, perhaps, they were well known to each other—the Mothers gave little away.

"Please!" I asked of Morag. She shrugged ever so slightly and instructed the pilot of the flitter to wait as we walked away.

I headed directly down the small path that led to the dunes and beach. The small waves were working the rounded pebbles back and forth, and they made a chiming that was soothing.

We sat on a log, and I looked as far as I could see out to the horizon. This world was slightly larger than Old Earth and appeared flat and unchanging; it seemed that one could see forever.

I knew this was not true. It was never true, but even more so now.

I asked Morag a question without any previous warning to her. Although she was shielded, I knew it struck home.

"Do you feel each spring and summer like I do now?" I looked at her directly, not challenging, but waiting for her to answer.

She smiled. "You've grown stronger, Danu, who so recently joined us. But I foresaw this."

But then she added, "I do not feel what you feel. I long ago made peace with the fact that I would never again feel the Call from the Sidhe."

I felt quiet sadness in her.

"It took me a long time, and it will be a major task for you. We can only hope that that will be achievable for you when you return. But if you are, in fact, of their lineage as well ..." She shrugged.

We sat and faced the water.

I breathed in the salt air and exhaled the city and confusion surrounding me there. I had gotten better at appearing calm when I was not and I spaced my breathing evenly. It would have to do.

"Do you have any other questions of me, Danu?" Morag finally asked.

I shook my head.

"That is best. Once again you go forward as the Fool."

I smiled at her reference. It was what I had called myself. It was the only unnumbered card in the old tarot deck, appearing at the beginning or the end. One of the oldest versions showed a person dressed gaily, stepping off a precipice. A little dog barks alongside—whether in alarm or joy of a coming adventure—one cannot determine. Perhaps that is the choice then: not whether one might have to step off and away from one's seemingly safe reality, but whether one goes in fear with their mind yapping in futility. Or, with some strong trust that one's path will continue on, accompanied by one's own animal joy and faith in oneself.

"Our wild card," she said, with great kindness in her voice and mind. "I will be glad to greet you later."

And then she surprised me, as her gesture was, as far as I knew, not used by the Shadakon as an act of fondness. She stood, bending slightly, and kissed me. It was a sister kiss and as tender as that.

Then she was walking quickly away and I was left with myself. I did not return to the Mothers until twilight fell.

I returned to my routine of witnessing some of the people at the hospice in their last days and hours, and helping and taking what I could. I fit in as if I had never left. When I was gone, did another take my role? I asked the Mother who was in daily touch with me.

She shook her head. "There is no other like you that we know of.

No one who honours the inner wishes as fully as you do."

I thought of who had taught me, and letting Dagon even briefly into my thoughts washed me with longing. He had taught me about inner permission. He had shown me my own place of indecision and honoured it. What he did not take from me once without it, he now had while I lived. I shivered.

"We know you will not be with us long, Danu," she said in her soft voice. "Do what you can while you are here."

Three days passed. I had had no direct contact from the Sidhe although I felt the sun building towards midsummer.

I swam in the sea, sometimes among long trailing fronds of iridescent purple seaweed. It slipped easily past my skin and I gloried in it. Dagon had been right; the sea strengthened me.

I allowed myself to lose my sense of time as I had intentionally done during my last stay here. Morning came, morning passed; as did the whole stretch of the day and the slow arrival of nightfall when, finally, the stars were revealed, shining through the rest of it out there. The mysteries ...

It must have been a day or two before the date I was waiting to arrive. I sat on the beach, allowing my hunger to grow rather than returning to the building. I had grown to appreciate the emptiness before true need set in. I felt light on my feet; I felt the moonshine of the waxing moon. I was, I think, calm and content. I supposed waiting for an eminent birth might be like this. I waited as mothers-to-be waited, who knew that soon they would be taken to the edge of their lives, but looked forward to it nonetheless. Suddenly I was not alone. First I felt the swirling energy of faerie; it was visible in the fading light as sparking luminescent vortices. I took out the green stone I now always carried; it glowed with a mesmerizing emerald green light.

I looked up to see Fiórcara before me.

He stood between me and the sea that I heard but could no longer see. He looked at the talisman and smiled. He came to me in all his ageless beauty and knew his effect on me.

"You have kept your word to me," he said quietly. "I expected no less of course. You would have done so in the end. But I sense no fear in you tonight."

"Tonight is not midsummer's eve," I said calmly. "I can afford to be brave tonight."

He stood and studied me in silence. "I came only to remind you of the small points of your promise to me. That you come of your own will, with nothing between us."

I thought of the small dagger that I had laid aside when I got here. I knew that I would not, could not use it in Between; I did not want to. Time enough for that later if it came to that.

"I have only my love and bond to my mate," I said.

"Ah, Danu," he said. "You may return to him later if you chose. But I will not dance with him and you." He looked at me and perhaps within as well. "I will take that from you if I must. You offered me a bargain with no conditions."

"I counselled you not to," he continued. "I knew, however, what your offer would be, or I would never have answered a call to what is not my only name."

I thought of Morag, her life energy leaving her in spite of my stopgap attempts to support her. I thought of the mysterious illness that took her. I looked at him with that knowledge up and available for him to read.

"The Sidhe work deeply beneath the surfaces of human and Shadakon affairs," I said. "It has always been so." There was no bitterness in me as I sat in the warm moonlight.

"We are trying a more, ah, straightforward course here," he said. "There is now so much to lose. But I am glad that you understand how you came to be here. I too will come to you in truth.

I will not come to Danu of Dagon, however. I care little for that except that it has been noted that you have tamed the heart of a particularly predatory Shadakon." He paused. "And that you died for him."

"You are a woman of many other powers though. I will come for you and you alone. You will come alone and be glad to do so. I want no dazed or glamoured partner for this dance."

I looked at him, radiant in the fading sunset. He had a lean strength and moved with ease faster than I could follow. He melted into the surroundings when I was not directly looking at him. I looked into his green eyes and felt the magic that humans had tried to describe in the old stories—and failed.

I felt the truth that I had never spoken or even framed in my own mind rise within me.

"*I will dance with you. I will come of my own free will, irrespective of any bargain that I struck. You tricked what you could have had freely.*"

He just shook his head. "You could have fooled me, Danu, smeared with Touch-me-not and howling on your side hill."

"Timing is everything," I said. "The time for us has almost come. I would not turn away from it even if I could." I smiled sadly. "I will come to you of my own free will and bring no impediments as I join you on midsummer's eve."

"Yes." He came closer and the air between us shimmered. "This is not glamour, my Queen. You generate it as well as me." He looked at me questioningly. "Did you ever wonder why we were part of your world? When you were a sick child, begging to leave with us?"

"We played for you then," he said. "Now we will again. I will come for you in two days, Danu. Lay your world and its expectations aside."

And he was gone.

CHAPTER THIRTY-EIGHT

PREPARATIONS FOR THE DANCE

I worked through the two remaining nights after my meeting with Fiórcara. I was particularly attentive, not wanting to compromise my ability to stay focused on the person before me. Each was an individual, with a unique life story. Each was missing someone, perhaps on another world, who would not arrive for this last leave-taking.

"Tell me more about your son," I would say, settling into a practised place of calm, communicating that we had until the end of time for the story to be finished.

In truth the time before their ending was brief. As it drew closer they often deeded the last of their energy over to me. I acquired some lethal contracts, yet often felt unsatisfied. The rest of my work was providing measured amounts of energy to people as I worked to keep the pain away as much as could be done.

There continued to be those who turned their faces away from me. I dropped my eyes briefly to them. They were playing out a hard exit that was hopefully significant to them.

I sometimes heard the words "demon" and "vampire." It was not my job to correct others' perceptions of me, but I did ask the Mother how she viewed me. She smiled and sat down with me in what was, for now, my room again. Her clear blue eyes met mine easily.

"Questioning who we are and what we do," she explained calmly, "allows us to correct our course if need be. The Shadakon feel that they are a force accountable only to themselves. Humans, of course, believe that as well."

She shook her head slightly. "Here we hold a peaceful place for people to enter into what has been called a state of grace.

There are many paths to it and one may not be better than another. This is the last place and time where these people will have an opportunity to open their hearts, to let go of their lives without undue grief and anger."

"Not all here wish to avail themselves to this of course. Sometimes we wonder why they came to us instead of staying on a high-tech medical unit. Cost, of course, must be factored in." She spread her hands gracefully. "We take everyone here."

"Sometimes you are the only one who gets paid here," she said. "But I know that you often walk in hunger, as do we. We are pledged to serving, as our way of being useful."

I heard the word "*useful*"; the Sidhe had told me when I was in Between that we all must find a way to be useful. I wondered if Morag had volunteered to be useful to the Sidhe. I was coming to see that I might have as well.

The Mother sensed my distraction and waited. When I had returned to attending our conversation, she continued. "You are more like us than you may see now," she said. "Right now passion is your path." She smiled. "You might be surprised to know the roles that we have held in various times in our lives; perhaps not as demons or vampires, but enacting some of their qualities."

She studied me. "You have never asked what we do hold as true. There are no crosses of the sacrificed son here, or regalia of other beliefs. We hold ourselves apart from looking at the world in one way or another. Division of reality into exclusive parts does violence to the truth; that might be the closest way I can say it simply."

"Preserve the mysteries," I said without over-thinking it and she smiled.

I wondered if she would attend to me in the days after my return. I could imagine lying in this room as I struggled to reintegrate with—whatever lay ahead.

"You, as everyone, are welcome here, Danu. There is the matter of sustenance to be considered, of course, but perhaps Morag could arrange that." And then she left me to my thoughts.

I decided that I had some preparations to make. I tidied my empty and already clean room then went for a walk—first against the wind, and then turning and putting it at my back. I felt my body move smoothly and quickly across the sand.

When I got back to my usual seat, I took my clothes off carefully and laid the green stone on top of them. It gleamed in the sun, but not in an unusual way. I walked into the water, entering the small waves of summer with pleasure. I dove under and glided, waiting until I must return to the surface. Things touched me in the water but they were weed and small bits of flotsam that drifted, waiting their turn to rest on the tide line.

Feeling immune to minor dangers today, I swam out deeper. I could no longer see the bottom. I floated. Hold, quick release, in. Repeat. I drifted outside of the wave line, waiting my turn to reach the beach, too. For a passing moment, I felt like I was being observed. It was a large calm mind that briefly touched mine and then swam on.

It was turning to twilight when I returned to my clothes. I knew before I saw it that the stone was glowing. I knew before I saw him that Fiórcara was there for me.

He was again clad in green but nevertheless blended perfectly into the background of the beach wrack. We faced each other, and I was glad that I had the energy of the ocean still on and in me.

I indicated my neatly piled clothes, my shoes, and the stone and gave him a questioning look. I would not have to fear when this part would come in the evening, as I was sure it would. I stood bare in the light wind that had come up with the tide change; it stirred my red hair about.

He smiled, not exactly reassuringly. "Bring them along," he said. "You may want them later." He reached out for my hand. I realized that he had never attempted to touch me while I was awake before this moment. I reached forward with my left, the hand that would have been comforted by the small dagger than sometimes hung within reach but was now in my room.

When our hands met, I knew that I was, as promised, leaving this place. As we touched he took me to Between. I was not asleep and I was not glamoured. I had a flash of the dark velvet, the draped dark material that holds the stuff of the galaxies in place. I felt deep cold, but then became instantly aware I was in a warm meadow.

There were many Sidhe there. I saw them shifting and moving like green shadows against the background of trees; some came closer and looked at me curiously. They moved and shifted, taking to the air and settling again. It was somewhat like being in the middle of a flock of uneasy birds.

I did what I did whenever I had encountered the wild life of this planet. I stood perfectly still, something which my Shadakon gifts had allowed me to become very good at. I had practised with the small creatures. I stood as a tree, breathing slowly and evenly. There was a trilling that rose and fell in waves and I knew to be their language.

Fiórcara stood by my side, his hand still on my arm. "Please bring some gossamer for my queen," he said. I was reminded of my first silky clothes after discarding my uniform. How I wore and did not wear them as it pleased me in my early days with Dagon.

He turned to me with a quiet hiss. "I told you the conditions of this night. I told you to set aside your world, your life there, and any you are or were connected to."

I looked at him with tears that I held back with effort. I nodded. "I have been warned, my king," I said. "I meant no disrespect to you."

Although I had not done so before, I dropped my eyes to him.

"I could take it all from you," he said calmly. "I will have no one but you with me for this one night. It will be enough for you." He smiled again.

I was led away to be dressed like a night-blooming flower. I felt their cool hands upon me, and their curiosity. I knew without understanding their language or even mind-speak that they speculated and joked about my fate.

I would have no impediments to what was to come.

CHAPTER THIRTY-NINE

MIDSUMMER'S NIGHT EVE

I tried to stay present to all and everything that was happening. I felt energy, rising from the earth and glowing in the trees that surrounded us. Fiórcara led the making of a large circle that was joined by increasing numbers of the Sidhe. My free hand was taken and I could feel the energy circling through us. The circle became a spiral that led in and in. We could not have all fit within the meadow's circumference. Tighter and tighter and faster and faster we turned until my feet left the ground.

There were the sounds of drums and the haunting song I had heard before, but now it did not sound strange or alien to me. I had known it. I had felt it within me and did again.

We spiralled higher, up into the sky and above the trees. It was exhilarating and I opened to the bliss of it. The moon whirled overhead and the singing and songs entered me. I saw female Sidhe whose beauty struck my heart. The males were all also beautiful, quick and, I imagined, deceptively strong. They too made my breath catch in my throat. Sly green and blue eyes caught mine briefly and then whirled off.

We flew until I felt that I had stopped and it was the universe that whirled around me. The sound and movement were peaking into a cone of energy. My Sidhe sang and his song was picked up by all present, shaped into an intentional force that I knew with certainty was an offering to the life force of this planet and was their name for her. I added my voice and will.

The spiral collapsed slowly, and by the time we alighted, the grass was full of couples taking their pleasures with each other.

"And now it is our turn, my queen," said Fiórcara. We walked to a glade that looked very familiar. I greeted the trees there as friends, keeping the inevitable memories at bay as best I could. I turned to him, "Please bring me what you intend to bring to me. I stand willing and open to you. I would have only this," I said, "and you. But you know ..." I struggled. I saw that he knew what was in my mind. "To bring me to this place could not have been an accident!"

"There are few accidents," he said drily. "Surely you understand that. Nor are coincidences accidental. This is where I will be sure that you will fully uphold your promise to me. That you will have no one in your mind but me. For if you are my queen tonight, then surely you understand that I am your king."

He stood, dazzling in the moonlight, still holding my hand. He turned me to face him and I fell into those ancient green eyes. I did not know my own name and knew I didn't really know his. I stood in the flooding moonlight and wanted him. It grew in intensity as he merely held my hand. My skin glistened, the light sticking to me and spreading as an awareness of energy and of passion that I wondered if I could bear.

"Please," I whispered in mind-speak. *"Please."*

He smiled and watched me. I met his eyes fully then and opened to him and there was no one there but he and I. I felt him search deeply within me.

"No impediments then. What do you want from this night, Danu?"

I was beyond considering anything but what was now. *"I want all that you would bring to me."*

"That is probably an unwise request, Danu. But you are not a queen who would be backed into a corner and helplessly watch your fate come to you. Come to me then. Let down your red hair over me. The night is young."

He pulled me gently down and I settled upon his maleness. It was as if the moonlight had entered my body, burning bright, and lit me from within. I knew, as much as I could know anything, that the old stories could not begin to describe what happened when a Sidhe came to a human lover.

But I was no longer human. I wanted it as much as he did. We moved as one in the glade and later, we flew again, he joined with me high above the dark trees. Anywhere and everywhere he touched me was almost unbearable yet I reached out to him to continue and continue.

As the stars dimmed, I was still in his arms as we lay in the leafy glade and still I wished to be nowhere else. He looked at me and said, "Morag was right," he said. "You carry our blood."

He ran his hand down the centre line of my body and I shuddered in pleasure. He smiled. "I have had many human lovers, Danu. Some came in fear and I took that. Some came unwisely in innocence and burned with fire they did not understand. Some later came undone," he said and shrugged.

"You gave me fair measure. You were worth the wait." He pulled back and stopped touching me reluctantly. "And now what, Danu?"

"Do I have choices now?" I asked. My will had been stilled and it was almost painful to call it up again.

"Oh yes, my Midsummer's Eve Queen. Since you gave me yourself so generously, it is only fair that I return with a gift of my own. I will let you choose."

"I can take the memory of this night away from you, I would remember, of course, but you do not have to. That would be the easier course for you." He looked at me with a smile that suggested he already knew my mind and what I would choose.

"Or I will send you back to your world as you are now. But you have read the old stories. You know that your previous life"—he smiled again—"may suffer in comparison."

"Passion is passion," I repeated, quoting something I had said earlier. "It is no different except in duration and intensity. I surrendered to you. I wanted you last midsummer's eve. I lived with that memory and still forged becoming the mate of an Alpha Shadakon. I surrendered to him first."

"I would forget nothing," I said. "Even if I pay by remembering and yearning for this for the rest of my life. A small price to pay."

He took my hand then and raised it to his lips, "It will be as you have decided. But one's life can be a long time. We will meet again, my queen. If you can still see to call me by this name, please call me as Fiórcara. Such as a Sidhe can be, I will be your true friend." He smiled. "Certainly now a well-known friend. Sleep now, Danu."

The last thing I remembered was his smiling face above me.

CHAPTER FORTY

THE LONG WAY HOME

I awoke in the small bed in my room with the Mothers. The sun was high and I was hungry. I began to sit up and the room shifted around me. I achieved sitting only briefly before slipping back to a comforting horizontal position.

There was someone in the room. For a moment I was afraid that it was Dagon. I was still not shut down from my experiences and feared hurting him with what might be uppermost in my mind.

It was, however, Morag. She sat very still, not imposing any connection with me while I struggled to fully return.

"You are hungry," she said. "Although you have obviously been sustained since you left."

She smiled but her eyes held something I could not immediately sort out—sadness, pride, concern?

"I knew what you would choose, Danu. I would have expected no less."

In saying this, she confirmed what I had already known—that she too had spent time in that glade or elsewhere with the Sidhe. I looked at her with a question that I truly did not want answered. "Will I ever experience what had occurred in Between again?"

"I cannot say what will remain of your connection with him," she said flatly. "He may have use of you later, and you will choose what he offers then, too."

That statement hung between us. *How was this any different that any deal any male had ever offered me? That to be one with them, I must surrender everything?* I thought of my parents' union, their passion, if it had ever been there, long burned out.

My mother had tried to maintain a piece of her own power in the world by trying to force me to enact what she had failed to achieve. I thought of Dagon then and mixed with the slowly rebuilding yearning for him, I saw him holding my lifeless body above a crowd of shouting Shadakon. Was it always so?

"You have observed other unions. You accompanied Dagon to his work. I know that the day that you observed, his client under lethal contract was a young man. You saw them combine and what it cost the human to come to his full passion."

I remembered that I had watched intently, not pulling back from witnessing what was in front of me. The man had surrendered to passion and to Dagon at last. He had burned white hot and then faded to ash.

"You have surrendered to the most powerful evoker of passion that is known in the universe," Morag said. "Their roots are not of the Earth, although she and all places of life are now their mission to protect. They underestimated humans earlier and lived to see the consequences of their mistake. Frightening and glamouring humans were not enough to stem the tide. Slowly, but inexorably, the roads, the shopping malls and later the slums cut through and covered over the sacred spaces."

"They still have a taste for humans though," she said, "Much as do we."

"But enough talk. I have found someone and brought him along for you. You are going to have to make it outside if you can. The Mothers are not fond of witnessing taking when it is not in the service of bringing peace."

"It can always be so," I said, "of one sort or another."

She smiled without comment of speech or mind-speak.

I hobbled outside; my perceived horizon at odds with what was so. Standing beside the flitter was a fit young man. I remembered him—he was the one who stood aside of the planned attack on me and who had intervened between me and a needle gun of death or worse. I was surprised that Lore had spared him. Perhaps in the confusion, the others had not realized what he had actually done.

I had told him I would remember him.

"He understands your need," Morag said simply. "He is not under lethal contract."

He faced me with bravado but fear was in him. I looked at him deeply and said, "I will not hurt you or take what you have not agreed to. What do you agree to?"

"She found me," he said, indicating Morag. "She said I could repay you for my part in what happened that afternoon."

"It is I who owes you. I'm glad you survived your decision. But you can help me again now. What is your name?"

He said his name was John. I smiled and sat down on the grass (in truth I could no longer stand).

"Have you ever been in love, John?" I asked.

He shook his head.

"Well someday you may be. If you chose to be truly present with your partner, and come openly offering yourself, this is what you might discover." I gave him a slight taste of what I carried from my midsummer's eve. He gasped in pleasure. I took him then until he lay napping in the sun.

"I think I can go now," I told Morag.

"Let me only return and thank the Mothers for their care.

I returned to my room and gathered what was mine there. As I hefted the small dagger, I noted that its weight was wrong. I unsheathed it and shook out a familiar green stone. It had a faint glimmer within it. I smiled and briefly held it to my heart.

Also within the sheath was a coin that was undoubtedly gold. It still was one of the most precious materials in the universe, much more valuable than it had been when there were still easy amounts to be gathered on Earth. It was now commercially extracted from seawater and mined from asteroids.

I doubted that this had been recovered that way. I knew who had put it there. I wondered briefly it this was some sort of payment, but I discarded that thought. I knew it was not. I knew what I would do with it.

As I walked down the hall with the Mother, after briefly thanking her, I reached out and put out my hand dropping the coin into hers.

"I know you will use this for the good," I said. "Even though both of us are clear that good is an elusive concept. I trust you."

I walked outside and entered the flitter. Morag sat with the pilot, who again greeted me with briefly lowered eyes. I sat and watched from the window as the forest below fell back and away from me. I was returning home. I held onto that thought even as I replayed what had occurred between me and the Sidhe I still called Fiórcara.

John slept the sleep of the almost dead beside me.

It was an uneventful journey. Morag and I were quiet on the way back. She and the pilot offloaded John, who was sleepy and confused about why he was sleepy and confused. I had attempted to haze over his last twenty-four hours.

If he were curious and determined enough, he would uncover at least parts of it. Having been offered to have something significantly more permanent done to me, I had no desire to do it to anyone else. I had pondered as we flew away from my island sanctuary that I might have benefited from a few days to return fully to this world. I would have swam in the sea and walked in the wind and cleared the faerie from me.

Because I still felt somewhat "away" I learned accidentally (and here I heard Fiórcara telling me that there are few accidents) that I had not been gone overnight. Not by our usual way of accounting for time anyway. I had lay in the arms of Fiórcara as his Midsummer's Queen for two weeks.

"Enough time," he had promised me. The information quietly pleased me. Not a one-night stand then with the faerie king. Although for the Sidhe, who knew?

Morag dropped me off, still in silence. It did not occur to me until later how completely silent she had been on our trip back.

With no real considerations except a growing wish to reconnect with Dagon, I approached the door. I still felt slightly out of synch with this world and yearned to sink into the tub and come back to myself.

The door opened before I touched it, and that should have informed me that Dagon had been forewarned of my homecoming. He stood in the door and all thoughts of my stay in Between dropped from my mind. He was as I remembered him, lean and powerful with his dark eyes that I had fallen into many times.

I said only, "I have returned, Dagon."

He continued to stand and read me—not a taking of deep information, but it occurred to me that that might follow. I met his eyes.

I waited in the total body silence as I had learned to do so well. I slowly allowed in the realization that he might not allow me access—to him and to this place I considered my home. "A long midsummer's eve, my mate," he said, too calmly. "I believe the bargain that was struck was for that time."

"For me, in Between, a single night passed. I did not realize until I got back that time there and here is not necessarily in agreement. I was provided with a meal by Morag this morning, but I am weary."

Still he stood, neither shutting the door nor admitting me. Belatedly my anger was building. Somehow I had just never anticipated this reaction.

"Would you have rather greeted me here battered and despairing? Broken by what happened to me?" I shook out my hair that had not seen a comb in, well, two weeks. "I will tell or show you anything you ask. I will not deny that I joined with the Sidhe without 'impediments,' as he required. That I understood before the evening began that this was the bargain I had struck. I honoured that in spirit as well as the words I spoke."

"But in truth, it would have mattered little. He might have enjoyed it at least as much if I had attempted to resist him. I walked the only path that was open to me. I believed you understood that too." I felt him continuing to withhold his connection to me.

"I request the shelter of your back garden," I said then. "I cannot go any further and have nowhere else to be. I well understand, even if you do not, that I will not be rescued from the aftermath of the collision of my world and theirs."

"I chose to remember it all!" I said defiantly. "I'm now glad that I did."

I saw his anger rise up then. *"You may shelter in the garden, Danu,"* he mind-spoke. *"Perhaps tomorrow will bring us to a different set of actions."*

It was then that I recalled the small dagger that hung at my side again. I felt a detached frightening calm steal over me. I had thought I might make the choice to use it before or immediately after I had fulfilled my bargain. When I realized that Fiórcara, my "true friend" would not allow me that escape, I left it behind on the island. But telling the truth to myself now at this crossing point seemed very essential. I had not protested our evening, nor had I wanted to. But more—and this hit me like a slap—the Sidhe King had foreseen what the effect of detaining me for two weeks would have on my mate. This was possibly just another one of the under actions of the Sidhe. I saw in my mind's eye the vast forests of the planet in flames as a side effect of the wars that could start up between the humans and the rest of us here. Would it be worth it to the Sidhe to have to regenerate a burnt out world?

It was then that I cried, but by then Dagon had shut the door.

The garden, although left completely to its own devices, provided a sheltered growing place to many plants, some of which were blooming as the high summer day moved towards dusk. I would wait until the moon rose. I retreated to a far corner. I laid out my knife, hoping the moon would touch it before I felt compelled to use it. I glanced briefly at the green stone that was dark and cool in my hand. I returned it to the sheath. Let him find that then. A very brief explanation.

Perhaps I slept. I awoke to bright moonlight and dark shadows. I lay my arm across a stone and picked up the dagger. I was satisfied that my hand was not shaking. I could do this then. I hoped that Dagon had not lied about the lack of pain. But in truth, even that mattered little. I raised the blade to catch the moon and then—

My arm was immobilized.

Dagon had come out of deep shadow and moved as he could to close the distance in a heartbeat. I struggled briefly but knew that this would be taken from me as well. I bent my head in despair.

"*Wait but a moment,*" he mind-spoke, so softly that it was a whisper in my mind. He linked his fingers in mine and both of our arms lay side by side in the moonlight on the cold stone. "*Please do not go without me,*" he spoke. And handed me the dagger.

Still caught in my progress towards death, I brought the blade close. I felt the calm acceptance in him. That his long life would end today, here behind his house. That he would be my mate to the edge of whatever awaited us—if anything. We had pledged each other that.

The world stopped. He did not move. I felt a vast sadness within him matching my own.

I put the knife down carefully.

I faced him and finally could feel his presence. Our hands were still clasped together as if they would not be parted.

"I want to try this again, Dagon." I knelt before him. "I have returned, Dagon, my mate and Alpha."

He raised me to my feet and we melded for the lengths of our bodies, my head resting on his heart. Without saying anything further, he scooped me up and brought me inside.

"Some warm water first," I suggested.

He shook his head. "Later perhaps."

I looked into his amber eyes and saw what I had hoped to see.

"You may be a royal Fool," he said. "I am a more ordinary one."

"We will not be parted from each other," he said. "Even through the passionate skills of the Sidhe. He recognized in you what I already knew well. You are intoxicating and alluring. In this the bloods of two old races have joined to make you a formidable lover. I can understand why it took him two weeks to part from you."

He then smiled at me genuinely. "I, however, have a very, very long time to enjoy you and intend to do just that." He caught my eyes and I felt myself sinking and sinking into the flames of his energy.

With the last of my will, I asked because I thought he deserved the choice, "Do you wish to look within? I have not lied to you, but the truth might be difficult to see."

He shook his head. And then he laid his hands on me. It was not unbearable as Fiórcara's touch had sometimes been—but just short of that. He stroked my limbs, sweeping away the other's touch. He kissed and touched every inch of my body. I cried out for him.

And not long after, I cried out with him.

CHAPTER FORTY-ONE

THE CALM BEFORE THE STORM?

In the dawn, I awoke to see Dagon watching me. He appeared calm and satisfied. He looked to me then like a large sleepy cat. He rolled and casually pinned me with one paw. He was totally relaxed but when I tried to move he applied just enough force to keep me where I was. I felt the strength of him and also that he had intent beneath his play.

I could be still, and so I was, but I was not relaxed. After a short while he sighed and let me up. I still did not move, but now for a different reason.

"So it is with us," he said. "I cannot hold you down for my own comfort. To try to do so keeps me from my work. And yet ..."

He sighed and I stroked him, still seeing the big cat, almost hearing a deep purr in his chest.

"It was not easy when you were gone," he admitted. "Others noticed and I would have preferred that they had not."

I thought then of the clean cutting of the water's calm surface by a shark fin that dipped below, but then reappeared, still moving purposefully forward. I shivered.

I wondered if this planet had something that filled the ecological niche of the sharks of Earth. I knew of one, however, who I would meet again, but not in this world's ocean.

"There is another Council meeting soon. The Shadakon who do not value keeping contract have been busy. This is a somewhat boring world for a predator," he said. "Especially for a predator who would prefer to hunt freely, without having to account to someone about the outcome."

I remembered him telling me of Lore's early days chasing the terrified humans to the edge of high cliffs and facing her or death. Death—or death.

"This will always be a place of disagreement between our two factions."

He looked at me, intensely awake now and asked, "Do you think the Sidhe have some part in solving or making this situation worse?"

I thought carefully of what I had heard and been told (they were not always the same).

"I do not think they would want to appear to be," I said. "And I don't know what course they might choose." But it came to me and I spoke without knowing how I knew, "It has something to do with me I think. They knew this even though I don't."

I stopped, knowing I went into untested territory after Dagon's reaction to me yesterday. "I think that you are part of it as well. That I somehow tie you to the Sidhe."

Dagon lay as if calm now, but he was not. I felt no anger rise in him. He watched me with his dark eyes half closed. I thought we were done talking but then he turned to fully face me. I saw the look in his eyes change and I know before he asked me what was coming.

"I had said I would not ask, and you freely offered me to see into your mind's eye of what occurred. But I did not want to see you do this or him do that. I can imagine it well enough without making it more real. I do think you had access to his deep-mind in moments of abandon. As he undoubted did of you."

You were gone a long time and it is possible that you know more than you might guess, and also that he knows more about me that I might guess. About the Shadakon ..."

"Unimpeded information," he said quietly.

I lay still, shocked by how the puzzle pieces might fit together.

How I had put myself into his hands? How Morag had put me into his hands!

"Yes. I want to do this before I see her again. Which I am guessing will be soon. I'm not unaware that nothing conclusive was discovered about her fatal condition."

"You are not a queen who would be backed into a corner to wait for your fate to come." Fiórcara had told me that before I set my will aside and surrendered to him.

"I'm sorry, Danu," Dagon said with great gentleness. "But I have never done this to you to the extent that I will today."

"Today then," I thought of his arm casually pinning me beside him.

"Now, Danu," he mind-spoke. *"Waiting will not make it easier."*

"I will not cry," I thought. He stroked my hair briefly and only said, "You may indeed cry, Danu of Dagon of the Shadakon. I may bring you pain." He sighed. "I will bring you pain. Lay still my love," he said quietly. "Do not attempt to avoid this."

He looked down at me and for a moment he was Dagon and I was willingly falling into his eyes. But I could feel him continue and dispassionately see me as I was in Between. He saw me set him aside with my free will in the grove. And he went further and still further. Woven through all was the controlling hand of the Sidhe, who had also gone where he would in my mind, as I hung on the edge of pain-pleasure.

And then deeper and I felt that I was no longer who I was and might never be again. I lapsed into the merciful dark of the space that surrounded Between, and hung there under the burning stars. I heard my name being called from far away and knew somehow that I had a choice not to return.

"Love," he said. "Return to me, my love. I am so sorry, Danu, to have caused you pain."

I returned. I was shaken and sick.

The feeling of disorientation I had felt when I returned from Between was upon me. I turned away from his eyes and he winced.

"Let me say briefly what I found," he said. "I went nowhere that your true friend had not gone. If I had been more skilled, perhaps I could have hidden this from you in passion at pain's edge as he did. Yet you rode that storm out alone in Between. As queen to your king. Had you tried to pull away from him..." He stopped.

"Please look at me, Danu," he said.

I was lost and sick. I returned his gaze and gradually felt grounded in his presence.

"I found what I sought, just as he did," Dagon said. "He expected no less from me. We have to meet in the future. You will be between us on that day," he said. "You will perhaps be ... a translator."

I shivered.

We lay still and beheld each other. I now recalled Fiórcara's last touch and his smiling to know that I was still completely with him.

I had stayed open to him to the very end. Now I looked into the eyes of my mate who could and had taken me in the same way. I had agreed to both, though neither had truly asked.

They were not so very different. And there was the other thing: I had chosen to return to Dagon. But there had never been any other choice. I had been dismissed from Between. What Fiórcara wanted from me—and it was becoming obvious now that I had never guessed what that might completely be—he had obtained. In a pleasurable enough way for him I thought.

I would not have used the word pleasurable for all that I had experienced as his queen. One can withdraw from or stop activities that cease to be pleasurable. That had not been an option, for me. For him, perhaps the whole enterprise could have been concluded in one night.

And why did I only remember one moonrise and later dawn?

Dagon shook his head. "I told you that bargains with the faerie have always been dangerous and in their favour. Why would this one be different?"

My mind went to Morag and her dealing with the Sidhe and subsequent illness. "Many would have let her die," he simply said. There was no accompanying mind-speak and I wondered if he was including himself.

"It matters not what I would have done. You are on a path of heart and passion. You seldom used either in your previous life. Now they are your high cards." He looked amused. "Isn't life interesting? It has kept me alive and curious for a very long time."

"I think it's time to talk to Morag now," he said. He walked over and opened the door.

Morag stood there quietly. She looked at both of us and lowered her eyes to him. He stood aside and she entered, seemingly reluctantly.

"Sit," he said quietly. It was not a request. She looked at me carefully. We three sat in silence.

"I have figured out a lot and Danu has filled in more. She did not want to, but she did anyway. She is my mate. Although we might not be having this talk if I had not come to my senses last night."

She looked at me and sighed. "Things were put in motion before I realized how deeply I cared for her," she said to Dagon. "She had been delivered to the Sidhe earlier but avoided his Call. He realized her importance then and knew that although she was susceptible to him, she kept her will wrapped about her."

"He seldom is refused," she said, and smiled.

"And then, Dagon, he brought you to her on his turf, supposedly for altruistic purposes? She came to you with the faerie energy that had infused into her on midsummer's eve. Even through the effects of Touch-me-not. Did you not wonder why you were there, a guest in his grove?" She shook her head.

"Neither of you did. Danu is somewhat loud and open in mind-speak when she is being …" Morag hesitated, trying to find another word to say, but I heard it in her mind-speech and flinched. "And he was able to appraise how serious an obstruction you might prove to be to him. And of course, see her vulnerabilities."

"Why me?" I had unwanted tears in my eyes. I was being discussed in third person. Both turned towards me.

Morag took a breath and then laid it out. "You came here as a human and spontaneously turned and claimed your Blood. You were thrown into a trial before your unexpecting lover had even explained consent and contract. You had observed it, however, and learned much from him in your short time together."

She took another breath. "Let's all take a step back in looking at this. I had dealings with them before becoming Clan Alpha and leader. They did not have any preference as to whom I might choose to mentor. I chose you, Dagon, for your leadership abilities and your desire for it, my ability to influence you, and your adherence to contract. Things were unfolding predictably. I had established contract as an agreement between the Shadakon and humans on this planet. This fit with their needs, but ours also."

"The Sidhe watched without interference. Time passed. A ship landed midweek, you, Danu, came as prey to the fair; I was not paying attention to that. Dagon had proven himself as more than capable at dispatching humans such as you seemed to be.

Whether you got back on your ship or your body was returned to the Company was of no consequence to me, or to the Sidhe—or to Dagon."

"But he who you call Fiórcara, Danu, realized that you had an uncanny ability to avoid predictable consequences. Events seemingly arrange themselves around you to allow you passage through difficulties. Over and over."

"Should I say you 'glamoured' Dagon? Perhaps. He has had his pick of women going far back into his history. He has honed his charms. He never questioned why he took you from the fair and to his house. You were a dumpy, depressed human," she said flatly. "But you were more, much more than that. Again, no one was paying attention, certainly not him."

"You had somehow shielded the fact of your Blood from yourself and others. You hid in your room and took nights shifts on your ships. And within the small amount of time that the two of you spent together, you turned!"

"We got to the two of you then and some assumed that you would fail the test—certainly Dagon feared you would—and the fact of your sudden intrusion into our life here could be corrected." Again she smiled that half-smile. "I did not. I granted you a slight chance, but Lore out-manoeuvred me. Everyone could see that Dagon was unwilling to let you go. Lore saw her opportunity. With Dagon gone, she would assume leadership. Instead she was humiliated by her failed attempt and your standing up to her."

"To refuse food when one is starving, after but a small taste—I saw the will in you and the intricate course you took. I also knew that you were not using reason to find your way. You had no facts, you seemingly had no options, yet you found open water and a way past."

I remembered Fiórcara asking me, if I had observed myself from a distance, befriending the one plant that could help me here, and then making my circle within reach of it—what would I think?

"You were still in constant peril, of course. Dagon could not protect you everywhere. So Lore sent a posse and you were baited by your hate of them, so that in a distracted moment you would have either taken without contract or been killed. Once again you danced away from danger."

"The Sidhe contacted me. I agreed to send you to them." Dagon stared at her, but she avoided his eyes and shrugged, "We can talk about my part in this later if you wish."

"Your first midsummer's eve, although not going as he had expected, taught him much about you, Danu. About your pride and strength and also your bond with Dagon. The Sidhe, like us, enjoy each other's company, but seldom pair. There is usually a new queen every midsummer's eve, and they take lovers whenever they choose."

"Fiórcara did not suspect your faerie blood. He saw you as an unusually desirable human, turned Shadakon, who could be used as needed. He had not known many Shadakon and so he saw you as representative of us. Once again you eluded careful scrutiny. It was I who concluded what other gifts you had."

"The Fool is not of the deck," I said. "It can turn up anywhere. Even though she does not know what her value will be."

They both looked at me.

Morag sighed, "I am almost done, my Alpha.

I believe that you have already discovered that the Sidhe can work around will and compel others to set theirs' aside. Getting to Danu was already obvious; she is faithful to those she loves." She finally looked at me and I saw grief in her mind and eyes."

"He handed me that cup and I drank it without hesitation," Morag said. "Please see the lesson in that, Danu. I waited, knowing that if his effort failed, it would matter little to the Sidhe. I would like to think it would have, but I truly don't believe that. We are all expendable. They have the long view …"

"Both he and I knew what Danu would offer—it is what she always offers—to trust and act with love, and that her word is truth. It delivered her to him."

We sat pondering all that we had heard. Moving pieces together that had previously seemed unrelated.

Dagon shook his head. "So what is the long view? What is the plan we must bring into being?"

"The Sidhe want an alliance with the Shadakon. With you. Please hear everything I have told you. Your mate—and I see that she is still your mate—will not turn away from her *true friend* if tested. He has tied her to him with high summer sex magic that no other has ever undone. She will not try to elude him even if she could. He may summon her later as he did me, and she may do something similar to what I did. Or, maybe not. She is our, or your, wild card."

"But what does he want?" Dagon asked.

I answered for Morag. I could feel the heat of those fires, burning across this green planet; I saw the fires, lit in rage and indifference burn without stopping until they reached the sea.

"To save this planet," I whispered. "If I love others unwisely, then I do. But I would do anything to prevent this world from turning into a version of old Earth."

I thought of the trees that had comforted me when I quickened as the spring energy rose in me. I thought of holding onto the base of the one in Between, when the energy of faerie and Dagon and I combined into a power that we grounded into that tree, into that living Earth.

"So here we are," said Dagon, "now what?"

Both Morag and I looked at Dagon. So much of this depended on him. I thought of his pride and his desire to have me as his mate, available and not overly distracted by life outside our door. I wondered how long he had watched from the shadows of his garden, and if he would have had a change of heart towards me if I had not taken it to a place of my final decision.

I had not been bluffing. This was no place to bluff or attempt to deceive each other. The stakes were high for us, but far, far higher for the world we were on, one that humans had called Exterra, but the Sidhe, who monitored and preserved it, called by another name, unspeakable by the human tongue.

A different kind of silence fell as we each pondered the roles we might have to take in making possible a meeting between Dagon, leader of the Shadakon, and the Sidhe.

I looked at Dagon and he met my eyes. I heard the unspoken question that he could not shield from me. *"Will I lose you?"* I felt the terrible grief behind this. He, whose fate had been to lose everyone he had cared for and often by eventual betrayal, faced me with this question that he did not want an answer to, or at least the answer I could give him. I felt my tears gather. I faced him, as if no one in the world was present but the two of us.

"I have told you and showed you that I will always return, if it is within my ability to do so. But how and when I return, and who I return as, is changing."

I thought in a brief lightning strike of memory of my midsummer's eve contact with Fiórcara in the grove in Between, how I instantly had felt his power and my desire rose, sweeping everything else aside. Even remembering now, it swept through me again and I knew that Dagon felt this.

"Yes, that too," I said, although I did not and would not call it love. "He has offered to continue to be my 'well-known friend.' What that means, to the Sidhe, I do not know. Morag has spoken about what she, also his friend, was asked to do for him."

"I do not expect this to be easy, for none of us can go back to who we were and how we viewed this world. Even though we might desperately want to," I added. "I think our honeymoon is over," I said to Dagon. "I can at times see past your eyes. That does not make me love you less. Anyone can trust in a relationship before the storm comes, it is afterwards that one appraises what has withstood the fury, discovering what is gone, never to be found again." Another memory came unbidden. I was holding aloft a slim dagger that had just caught a moonbeam that it reflected as a small cold flare of light.

"We cannot do this if we are not truly together and committed to rebuilding as we must, over and over." I remembered him carrying me inside and brushing away all but my need and desire to connect with him.

I turned to Morag. "I knew your part in this and how I came to make the bargain I made with Fiórcara before I went to him," I said simply. "I told him that your sacrifice and my forced acceptance of what was asked of me had probably been unnecessary because I would eventually have found my way back to him. But there is a timeline that we are all working against now.

If we do not choose to work together against what is coming, what always comes when humans arrive ..." I shivered. "I have been mind-touched by something in the sea. It was large and sentient, and hopeful that I would not prove to be what I appeared to be: another ruthless predator. We do not have the trust of the remaining beings of this planet. But I wish for a different future, in which we are not hid from fearfully."

"How this will affect the Shadakon —I do not know. But they have found their way to stay with the human flock, in spite of everything done to them. If nothing else, there will be other worlds to hunt on, and probably a lot of mop up work on this one, enough to keep everyone satisfied for the foreseeable future."

They sat silently.

"We should make contact now." I thought of what Dagon had said to me earlier; that waiting would not make it easier. He looked at me.

I said what had to be said: "It is time for you and the Sidhe to talk, as respective leaders of your clans. And for other reasons."

"I will accompany you," I continued. "I have no idea if you will be offered sustenance, or if he will bend time such that you have enough time"—I shivered—"to complete your conversation. Morag, it might be well that you stay and monitor the situation here. *And to resume control if we do not return,*" I added in under-thought.

A part of my mind was very aware that I was telling my mate and leader and my elder and previous clan leader what they should do. I continued on anyway.

"Take my hand, Dagon," I said. "I would not make contact with the Sidhe without you."

He raised an eyebrow. I rephrased my comment.

"I would speak to Fióracara now with you present."

He took my hand. I went to where Fiórcara resided in my mind, I recalled his energy as we flew up and up into the sky, calling a name that I believed was the true name of this place. I felt the building energy of the flight in my body.

"I call you Fiórcara, my true friend, my well-known friend. It is time for you and Dagon to meet and talk together. He has received the message that you left in my mind, and knows that I provided much information to you. It is now time for you both to meet face to face."

I waited. I knew that he was there. I sat in mental silence, then …

"Well-met, my Midsummmer Eve's Queen," he mind-spoke coolly. *"I see you have regained he who you might have easily lost."*

"I have no time for this," I replied fiercely. I showed him the forests burning all the way to the edge of the sea, an image that continued to haunt me by night and day. And on Old Earth of the mounds of garbage and fouled waterways; of the gaping holes of mineral extraction, torn into the hearts of hills and mountains. I showed him the humans who would come and come, drawn to the very thing they would destroy.

"I flew in your rising cone of energy. I called a name that I could not later hold in my mind. But I knew it was her name, the name of this world. The Shadakon could help in stopping this future from coming into being."

"It is why you drew me to you," I continued quietly. *"You were assessing the power you could bring to bear upon the invading humans and their life hatred. Or indifference. I have secured the attention of the Alpha leader of the Shadakon. He comes willingly to exchange information with you, without having to use me as a means for this."*

Dagon had sat in silence, following our mind-spoken dialogue.

The Sidhe mind-spoke to Dagon then. *"Do you wish to have this meeting with me Shadakon? Would you risk bringing Danu with you? For I will require that. You and I must come to a clear understanding about many things—including Danu."*

My breath stopped and I saw Morag look at me in alarm. What had I done?

I searched Dagon for the anger I expected to be uncoiling. He was the Alpha leader of the Shadakon. I was his mate. What was the Sidhe asking of him?

He looked at me then. I saw calmness and sadness in him, not anger.

"She will come if she consents to that. She will do what she does, with or without my consent but I give it anyway. It is the only way that I can truly have her."

"Once again I have underestimated Danu," the Sidhe replied. *"And I may have made the same mistake with you. Feed well Shadakon. I will meet you both in your back garden tomorrow morning—a place of recent significant events."*

And he was gone.

CHAPTER FORTY-TWO

AND SO DANU RETURNS TO BETWEEN WITH DAGON

Dagon had heard enough from Morag and she left without saying more. I assumed she expected to answer more questions about her actions later.

"We must feed, Danu," Dagon said. "You do not presently have a day job and I do not work at night, but I believe I can make do." I heard an edge to his voice and he was shielded from me. He went out the door.

I went out into the garden and retrieved the knife and sheath that still lay outside. I shook the green stone out into my hand. It was dark under the pale waning moonlight. I replaced both it and the knife into the sheath and placed it neatly on the pile of clothes that I intended to wear in the morning. Without thinking, I chose faerie garments. I ran my hand across what seemed to be a plain shirt and felt the softness of moss, of cobwebs or gossamer. I sighed.

I drew a full pool of water and, on impulse, returned to the garden and picked two of the white moonflowers growing there. I put them in a vase in the corner, but soon their scent was everywhere.

I slipped under the water. I wished to not think. I was not sure I could trust my intuition about what I had heard and the pattern that the information had taken. I had moved ahead to broker a meeting with my mate with those he considered, with good reason, to be dangerous in their dealings with those not of their kind. The two species had known of each other from the beginning, though they had not had a reason or inclination to cooperate with each other. They had both fled old Earth, although some of both of their own kind had stayed behind.

The over-populated Old Earth in its last days was doubtlessly a bountiful killing ground for the Shadakon still there. Some Sidhe still stayed in the more remote areas.

Still thinking too much then. I breathed, sinking slightly on the exhale and then holding while I floated easily, almost in a gravity-free space, almost peaceful.

I realized I was hungry. Once focused on, it became a force in my body. I was used to being hungry from my stays with the Mothers. I pushed it aside.

What was I about? The thought would not be ignored nor soothed away by warm water. I had just returned from Between. Did I want to return so badly? I had sensed the distance in Fiórcara when I left, even though I had been a long-awaited goal.

But the goal had been reached. I was not unaware how the energy between two people changed after one was done with the other. I had seen the drama and tears of these futile negotiations that I personally had successfully avoided while passing as human.

If Fiórcara wanted me present, it was to have an effect on Dagon—he was not done with him. I had delivered him to the Sidhe as surely as Morag had delivered me. And I would watch as she had watched me falling unawares under the spell of faerie.

I thought about consent. About consenting to something when one had no idea what one was committing to. I thought of Morag, accepting a poisoned cup from a one-time lover. I thought about me choosing Dagon and he choosing me, and of my choice to return to the Sidhe. Had any of us consented to anything more than a beginning?

I regretted nothing. That I could say, and know I was not lying to myself. Even if others had created the situations that I now found myself entangled in, or we had created together. These thoughts brought some comfort.

I emptied the pool and threw the moonflowers outside in a weedy corner of the garden. I emptied the vase and opened the windows to clear my head of the scent of them. I lay on our bed and curled up, hugging the emptiness in the centre of me.

This, too, was the cost of faerie and what they offered. In the old stories did people not continue to search for the rest of their lives for the grove they never found again? Led on by faint laughter deeper and deeper into the woods, or out onto the desolate moors, where they might die by the natural causes of a fall or meeting with a predator, or simply from a broken heart.

It was not my heart that ached. How could Dagon and I continue on with me yearning for another's touch?

I must have slept. I awoke and Dagon was not present. I noted green swirling motes in the moonlight. Dreaming then, I thought, and closed my dream eyes. I had a deep weariness not unlike the early days when Dagon took deeply from me, deciding anew each time to not quite take it all—this time. And then he would revive me and I would willingly receive what he offered. And each time, I exchanged more of my unwanted humanity for the sleeping Shadakon patterns within me.

I dreamed that I was offered a cup of cold spring water, with reflected moonlight dancing on its surface. I drank and my growing ache of yearning, of wanting, eased. I uncurled and relaxed, feeling soothed and replete.

"I told you that you should have chosen forgetfulness," a familiar voice said. He lightly touched my forehead and whispered, "Sleep."

Dagon entered the house in the darkness of predawn. He came and stared down at me and we observed each other in the darkness, me seeing better than I could have as a human. He had fed. Had he obeyed contract, hunting outside of his allowed work?

I had never questioned this before. He lit a candle and continued to look at me. "The manner of my hunting is not your business, Danu," he said drily.

I heard the full Alpha stance of his rebuke and said nothing further. I clung to silence, feeling a coldness that he seldom revealed to me.

"I could ask you the same thing," he said finally. "You are not as hungry as you should be my mate, by my reckoning."

I sat up and realized that the constant hunger I had taken into my sleep was gone. I did not have the high energy of another's life energy, but I felt a stillness in my body.

"I felt sick," I said. "Some aftereffect of faerie. I dreamed ..." I stopped.

"You dreamed that you drank the elixir of life," he said flatly. "It eased the faerie need that was established in you during your two week stay in Between."

"What a useful dream," he said. He sat on the edge of the bed, being careful not to touch me.

"I lay in our bed and awaited you!" I protested. "I was hungry and fell into a dream. Now you are here, and I am here." I looked into his eyes and implored him not to shut me out. I felt his resistance finally melt, and he smoothed my hair gently.

"Ah, Danu, we are set on an unknown course. Your time with Fiórcara is seemingly not at an end. I am Alpha leader of the clan of Shadakon. You are my mate, proven by trial to death in front of the Council. And yet, you are no longer fully mine."

"Please make me yours Dagon. Over and over. Please do that."

He sighed and then he came to me. He did not bring pain-pleasure. I felt the swirling energy of him and hoped he would share with me. He began and held back and then gave again and again. My body slowly caught fire and he came to me amid the building flames.

His energy entered me and claimed me. All was forgiven? My eyes were wide open and he was laughing down at me at how much I wanted this, wanted him. He hesitated once more and then brought it all to me.

That was how the morning found us.

CHAPTER FORTY-THREE

A RETURN TO THE GROVE

In the early morning, we stepped into the wild garden behind Dagon's house. Spider webs festooned with dew sparkled in the sun and two wilted moonflowers lay in the corner. I saw them and knew that Dagon did as well.

He just took my hand. "What now, my mate?"

The air shimmered with golden green motes that swirled in the rising sun.

"Over the precipice," I murmured. I felt the electric jolt when Fiórcara, took my arm. Then we were elsewhere.

We stood together in Between. Fiórcara, always more solid here than in the world we walked in, studied us carefully. Dagon stood balanced and seemingly calm. They took each other's measure. I felt the energy between them build. I stood between them, still holding and being held.

Fiórcara then turned his attention to me and dropped my arm. "Did you sleep well, Danu?"

He would not wound Dagon with me, if I could help it.

"We chose otherwise," I said. "And yourself?"

He smiled then. It almost undid me. Almost. I raised my chin slightly.

Both of them were watching me carefully. *I regret nothing,* I reminded myself. *I am here for something larger than two males in a pissing contest.* I smiled back.

"Let us get down to business then," said the Sidhe, addressing what I had not said or seemingly mind-spoke. "Shall we walk a little?"

We walked and I reached out and touched those who grew here and allowed it when I asked. Fiórcara smiled. "Do you see, Dagon?" he asked. "She is becoming part of this world. It has her allegiance beyond even what she grants you or me."

We stood in front of the dark green stand of Touch-me-not. It had fully recovered from my actions on the first midsummer's eve. Green and perfect, each branch held flowers and those already setting seed.

I smiled. *"Thanks be to you."* I got curiosity, for few thanked this being, and then recognition.

The Sidhe asked me, "Could you stand among it?"

"I could," I said. "Although the agony of it would take me. Would you require this of me?"

"Would it permit you with no pain?" he asked.

I shrugged. I approached without touching. I pictured myself carefully placing myself in the centre of the stand, acknowledging that I would undoubtedly cause damage to it.

There was no immediate response. it stood in full flower, fulfilling its destiny of seed and renewal.

I waited.

"Why would you ask to do this?"

"I am being considered to be an ambassador to your world." It mattered not whether it would understand the word I used; intent would be translated.

"The Sidhe already fill that role."

"Yes. But I am of the other clan that could help hold this world safe from human destruction. It is not certain. Your sacrifice might be in vain."

There was silence, then. *"Would you enter in, not knowing our answer?"*

I gently placed one foot and then the other among the branches.

I took a deep breath and let it out. Would the next be a scream? I had howled on this hill before. I felt the soft brush of its furry leaves. Leaves that bore great pain as the plant's defence.

"I am doing what I can," I thought. "Only that, and all of that."

A breeze blew and the leaves moved against me. I saw the muted purple of the small flowers and smiled. I stood in no-pain and looked at the two who watched me. Dagon let out his own breath.

Fiórcara looked at me and smiled. "I expected nothing less of both you and your plant ally," he said. "Earning trust can be a difficult trial. But you are now familiar to us in this world."

"I could do this," he continued. "You, Dagon could not. Can you see why she is valuable to us, no matter what contact may continue between she and I?"

Dagon was silent. Finally he said, "She is of faerie blood as well as Shadakon." He shook his head. "I was told, but didn't understand."

"You were not alone in this," said Fiórcara. "The Touch-me-not was the first to know for sure." He bowed to it. "It did not see her as we do, but rather felt the truth of her when she requested to touch it a year ago." He gave me a steadying hand as I gently extracted myself with as little damage to the tall stems as possible; afterwards a few tiny purple petals clung to me.

"Thank you for your trust," I said gratefully to it.

The leaves moved gently in the morning breeze.

"Now we should talk," said the Sidhe I called Fiórcara.

We sat in the grove, with me between the two of them.

Both extended their energy to me and met in the middle of my ... mind? My heart? My passion that cared little what words might be used? All of these?

I held my calm. I breathed in the calm energy of this place, this sacred space.

"What do you think that we, the Shadakon, can do to bring about the plan of saving this planet?" Dagon jumped to the core of it. "We are predators of the human flock. We go where they go."

The Sidhe smiled. "I think I have a proposition that will appeal to your followers," he said. "This world needs enforcers. We will close all but a few areas where humans would be allowed and then only under surveillance. Right now it is passively held by the unbroken forests, but you know that will not stop the humans. You and your clan will enforce the boundaries that we set. You will have free hunting of those who accidentally or intentionally stray." He smiled. "They will not believe this at first. But they will as time goes by."

"There must be no survivors to tell tales of what happened to the foolishly brave," he said with a cold smile. "You will be paid and have safe access, of course. And all the prey you can … eat, but we will allow no buildings or clearings inside the forests."

"We will grant continuing limited use by the Mothers," he added.

I sat in the warm sunlight and shivered and thought, *the Shadakon are being offering a paying job to be the wolves that they are. Who of them would not accept this bargain?*

"There must continue to be a spaceport. It will bring income to your people and mine. But the communication black out of most of this planet will be tightened. Those who fly must do by skill alone."

"And the costs to us?" Dagon asked.

"You expect me to lay out the unseen costs?" The Sidhe smiled.

"You already know that my answer might not be the truth, or perhaps, not all the truth.

We can see further ahead than you can, and outcomes change—as I think you realize today. You should wait to ask me questions later that have not yet occurred to you before you commit yourself and your clan to this plan."

I remembered them both asking me at various times if I had any questions. I had known then that I did not have any that mattered—any that would cause me to turn aside from the fate before me. Dagon said he would send a return answer; I didn't have the slightest doubt of what it would be.

"But now is the time to speak of another important part of our meeting," Fiórcara said. They both looked at me. "We are both takers," he said calmly to Dagon. "We Sidhe do not, strictly speaking, need prey as you do, but we keenly enjoy taking. Not daily," he added. "But I, too, am the leader of my people and I do not let go of what has been offered to me and I find desirable. Offered in full consent—as much as anyone can truly consent to us. Or refuse." He smiled again.

Dagon said nothing. He would be thinking, no question had yet been asked.

The Sidhe looked him fully in the eyes and they stayed that way for … I do not know how long—time outside of time.

"There can be no questions, Dagon, and no argument nor agreement from you will matter to me. It is only between Danu and me. You and she will settle this as you can in your own world. If and when she wishes my company and I am available, she is welcome here. There is no guarantee to her how long that offer will hold. I, like you Dagon, have lived a very long time. Like you, many have come and gone from me. Also like you, I realize how special she is. And finally, like you, I know that she desires me.

That is how it is now, for me. But perhaps we should check out what I have said with Danu. Danu who, while she is here, is not your mate.

Morag had said that when she accepted the cup from the Sidhe that she hoped her death would matter if it had come to that, but she doubted it. She told me that I was caught in an evoked state of desire that none resisted nor wanted to. But then she had said that, due to my faerie blood, the outcome for me was not clear."

I wanted to lessen the pain of my answer that I believed would rock Dagon. But I had promised myself to both tell and show both my lovers my truths. Fiórcara held a high card. It was I who had no will to end it, but neither did I wish to lose Dagon.

I thought of my dagger then, and Dagon took my arm gently but firmly. He shook his head.

"No, Danu. I will open the door when you have to go, I will open it again when you return. I could not bear to lose you permanently. You know this. I would follow you to true death without further concern for anyone or anything including this world and its fate."

Then I knew who truly loved me, and I wished with my whole being that would be enough. But when I searched within, I knew that I did not wish to choose him alone.

"I want both. I will have both if I can." I had no answer other than that.

Fiórcara had touched me only briefly since we three transited to Between. Nevertheless, I felt his absolute confidence. None escaped him. Like Dagon, it was only a matter of contract, and that could be adjusted as the attraction deepened.

"I will accept your offer, Dagon," I said, ignoring the Sidhe. "I know that you have never made one such as this before. I love you and I am your mate. But at times, I will not be at your side. That is the truth for now."

"Well," said the Sidhe.

"I think we have covered the immediately important parts of our meeting today. There may be some clarification of the details later." Here he looked at me.

"For the immediate future, do not call me unless you are in danger that you cannot extract yourself from. Otherwise, expect an invitation to return to me when the leaves fall. We love the high points of the season, as you now know. We are uniquely energized then."

"I have known few Shadakon. None were such as either of you. I am impressed by the love-bond between you. We do not forge such unions, but then, neither do those of the Blood. We have both lived long lives," he said to Dagon. "And neither of us has met one like Danu before."

"I will now take you both home," he said and stood.

CHAPTER FORTY-FOUR

WHAT IS GOOD FOR ONE, IS NOT NECESSARILY GOOD FOR THE OTHER

We arrived home and for once we seemed to have a mutual agreement to not talk about what had happened in Between. Dagon was often on his computer and some nights the door was shut. Some nights I heard the strange music he sometimes played. I did not attempt to intrude.

The energy between us was good enough. I worked frequently with the Mothers. Whoever had the most surplus energy shared with each other, usually during the sex that we both enjoyed.

I noticed I now used the word sex, not making love. Was making love an exclusive act between two lovers? Dagon had told me that his skills he used at the fair should not be called love.

What about what I offered him now? I felt myself getting quieter and less sure of myself. Once again, I did not feel good about the invitation that I had accepted in front of him for a fall visit in Between. What if he would treat me similarly?

I got to find out a few days later.

He had gone to the fair in the early morning and I expected him by dusk. Dusk came and went and the stars brightened in the sky. It was late summer and everything was setting seed and fruit. The plants in the back garden had put on their summer show and now had occasional second blooms that were smaller and faded quickly. Their energy was beginning to sink into the earth, no longer feeding leaves or last attempts at flowering.

At high moon I began lighting candles. The living room gleamed and flickered. I did not enter the library or dispel the darkness of our sleeping room. I did not pace, but only because if I had started, I would not have stopped.

I was not worried about Dagon, but I was very worried about my state of mind.

I had no right to complain about any absences he might choose to take from me. We had not spoke of what Fiórcara had stated was a given—that I would return to him. I had not attempted to disagree with what he said.

I heard a soft thud of a landing near the front door and I heard laughter fading off into the distance. My heart sank. A Blood companion then, a flying partner. Oh …

He entered, took in the room and my state of mind and simply said, "I will not speak of this now."

He was full of energy, both his and another's. I continued to sit seemingly calm even though I breathed as if I was on my last quarter tank of air. I willed that I would find a way to the surface before I ran out.

Listening through the door, it didn't sound like he was doing anything. I sensed him sitting behind the closed door, angry, but not choosing to reveal what was in his mind. So we both sat with a small closed door between us. The candles slowly burned down and extinguished themselves. I felt like something was extinguishing itself within me as well. My heart actually ached, I noted.

I have no right. I have no right. The thought rang in my mind.

I knew it was Lore who had laughed as she saw him to his door. *What one could do, the other had the right to do as well?*

I felt my air run out. There was simply not enough in the room. I tried to stay on the top of the fear that I now rode. Of all the situations I had been in on this planet, I had never felt the terror that I felt now. I was caught up in a web that was not of my making; I did not see a free channel to move forward to safely from the moment I was in.

Dagon came out and looked at me; he managed to look offhand. "Are you going to lay with me tonight?" he asked neutrally.

I went to him and knelt. I could say nothing. So there we were—he standing and looking down at me, me curled in pain as if I had received a mortal blow.

At last I felt his hand on my head. He drew me up and looked into my eyes. He saw and felt the pain in me, and my fear and knowledge of who had left laughing from our, from his, door. He sighed.

"I didn't think I would say this, Danu," he said softly. "But I am sorry. I wanted to hurt you. She always wants to hurt you. For what it's worth, she sought me out. She is fast and hot."

I looked at him in shock. I tried to activate some self-preserving energy. Anger. Denial. Nothing useful came. Unwanted tears slipped down my cheeks.

"Look at me, Danu," he said. It was not a request. I stood swaying, as he looked deeply within me. "Will we continue to do this to each other? Will you be compelled to act such that I am tempted to hurt and endanger you?"

"What would you have me do, my Alpha?" I asked. "What would you ask me to do my mate?" I could no longer stand. The last of my air was gone; I felt darkness arrive for me.

From a very long way away, I felt him easily pick me up and carry me to our bed. He sat beside me, quiet in his thoughts. I hovered between consciousness and darkness. I opened my eyes to see him and felt a wave of despair. He was keeping himself apart from touching me. He just didn't want me cluttering up his living room.

"No, Danu. I just assumed you didn't want me to touch you with another Blood's energy upon me." He sighed. "She is fast and hot and I felt nothing. It was a revenge fuck."—He used the word that we had never used between us. "Being Lore, she didn't care.

It has always been that way between us. Fast and hot and over with, until the next time."

"I wanted you to feel as I feel," he said simply. "I see I have achieved that. "I don't feel what I thought I would feel—that you deserved it, that I would enjoy hurting you."

"I am so sorry my love," he said quietly. "What would you have me do now?"

"I always expected you to stay within boundaries, even as I did as I chose," I said. "I have hurt you by assuming you would accept the dictates of the Sidhe and that it could be the same between us."

"I am also sorry my love," I said. "What I experience at the hands of Fiórcara strips me of my will. I go to him knowing that he cares little about me. I am part of the manipulations that he is busy with. I do not want to be used to hurt you. But I have been used that way. And I am still used that way."

We looked at each other and I felt a softening in the knot that had clenched around my heart.

"Should I stay apart for awhile?" he asked.

I shook my head. I felt my body begin to come alive from the state it had been in.

"All passion is just passion," I said again. "It only varies in intensity and duration. I would have you as you are. I beg you to bring yourself to me. Now."

He lit several candles from our much-diminished stocks. "I want to see exactly who I am with," he said. "As if I didn't know. As if I ever would forget."

He stripped me of my clothes and then his own. I saw that he had not depleted his passion. He laughed at the thought and skilfully kindled the fire hotter and hotter in me.

I'm putting a large log on the fire," he said laughing.

"You are in for a long and warm night. "Hot night," he said a moment or so later. He traced the sweat that ran down my chest. He tasted it. "Almost like blood," he said, "salty." He expertly kept me from avoiding any of his touches that grew in intensity.

"Dagon!" I said. He then helped himself to me and allowed me now to do what I would.

It was not fast. It was, however, very hot.

CHAPTER FORTY-FIVE

FALL

We were truly together again. We were as together as ever we had been. I attended Council meetings. He had not yet broken the news of the offer the Shadakon had received from the Sidhe. I was glad that it did not have to be done today or tomorrow. I had thought of some long-range questions and had sat and discussed them with him.

Would the Shadakon clan of this planet be the exclusive patrollers of this world? Or would Shadakon and Bloods arrive from all corners? Would there be a war to maintain a favoured position such as this?

What effects would occur if the Shadakon (and here I thought first, Dagon) were able to live a simpler and more bloodthirsty lifestyle? Would they become feral, no longer able or willing to re-join other civilizations if they chose to later?

I could offer no answers.

Morag had gone to ground, possibly still healing from her induced near fatal illness. She was not aware of what was being deliberated, at least that I knew about.

The first leaves turned to yellow and still hung on, but their destiny was soon to lie at the feet of the trees and give back their nutrients. The annual plants were stripped down to the stems of their dried leaves. Their last few unscattered seeds rattled in the pods.

The air changed. No longer carrying the scents of flowers, it now smelled like distance and of sea winds making their ways through the tops of the great trees.

Small creatures came closer to me now. After observing me as I sat quietly—like a rock, like the ground itself, some ventured out. I did not bait them to me.

It was not safe to trust food from strangers. I did not want to teach them differently.

One day I looked down at the soft touch of a brown creature that looked, I suppose, like a mouse. Its whiskers tasted and assessed me. Its quick heart beat even faster. After considering bolting but returning several times, it settled against my ankle.

I wept. My transformation was progressing; I had no doubt. I told it that it was quick and beautiful. I wished it enough offspring to replenish the seasonal losses of its clan. Good luck in finding tasty seeds. Its touch was so light that it had left before I noticed.

Dagon and I lay together, eye to eye in the near darkness. He would often stay totally still and I would do what I would. I loved the charge that met my fingertips when I touched him. I never awakened without seeing him looking at me with love and sadness. I wondered if he slept.

One morning I awoke to see drifts of red leaves on the ground. I asked Dagon if I should go to the island but he just shook his head.

"I too am part of your bargain now. I would not act like some animal mate of yours, or a human. He can come to the door; he can look me in the eye."

I wept again. I felt the last of the seasonal energy concentrate within me. Soon life would take its rest in the roots. Not yet, not quite yet.

One day a storm blew all afternoon and died just as darkness fell. Our lesser moon rose, giving ghostly light to shine on the water everywhere; it glinted off dripping branches and puddles. I knew, had known for days. Dagon crossed the room and kissed me. He offered comfort without judgment. He went to the back door and opened it. The garden was shining with green light. He took my hand and walked me to the door.

The Sidhe stood there. He smiled at Dagon. I did not think it was a cruel smile.

"I assume you are still puzzling over my offer to you, leader of the Shadakon. You still have time to come to a satisfactory agreement between us, but not unlimited time." He looked past Dagon to me. I stepped forward, and he took me to Between from my own doorstep.

The place we came to was empty of others. He read my question and said, "Sometimes we honour this time in more private ways. The task of this season is the grounding of the energies of the life web. You will find this visit different, Danu. The planet has spun and tilted from its sun. This is the beginning of our dreaming time."

"I have prepared a place of comfort for you. Although you can and have slept on stony ground, I assumed that you would enjoy a place more comfortable for tonight." He took my hand and led me to a low dwelling. My mind recalled something from what I had read as a child. *A faerie mound? An earthen hall?*

"Yes, Danu. But before you would enter such a place, we must refresh our agreements. I would not have you blame me for any misunderstanding on your part."

He turned me towards him and caught my eyes with his green ones that now were flecked with golden highlights. His beauty once again took my breath away.

"Do you come to me of your own free will, Danu?"

I wanted to be able to say no. But now, standing in the pale moonlight with him, there was only one answer.

"Yes," I said, and he smiled.

"And will you set aside the connections and expectations of your world?"

"Yes," I said again.

"You, being Shadakon, are aware of formal consent and inner consent. I will return you tonight if I do not have the latter."

I shook my head.

"You must say it," he said.

"I wish only to be here with you this night, without impediments."

"Nights spent with the Sidhe are sometimes long, Danu. Especially in the fall. The earth energy is strong and we partake deeply of it."

"Please," I said. "He who waits in my other life suffers my absence. Please don't keep me here overly long just to bring him pain."

The Sidhe I called Fiórcara looked at me coldly. "I told you last time I could wipe your other life away. You would live here with us until you outwore your welcome. Do you test me, Danu?"

I shook my head and tears flowed down my cheeks. "I ask you as a true friend. So you identified yourself to me."

He stepped back from me and said nothing. Then he smiled. "You have gotten better at bargaining, Danu. And you have caught some of the subtleties of giving another one's name. I agree to your requirement regarding time. We will have time enough."

He took my hand and led me to a low door, framed in roots. "Enter if you truly wish to, Danu."

I bent my head and entered. It was spacious and had a low platform strewn with blankets and throws that looked like they might have been made of fine woven grass and perhaps … spider silk? There was a small table that held a small pitcher and one earthen cup.

"Sit down, my fall queen," he said. I looked up surprised. "I will have you as nothing less than my seasonal queen, Danu."

I sat and wished my clothes would fall off, that I would feel all over my body what I now felt on my arm where he had lightly touched me.

"Ah, but we have barely begun. I am glad to sense your enthusiasm for me."

He poured me a half a cup of what was in the pitcher. "This is a variation of the elixir of life," he said. "I would cool the energy that you taken from others."

I looked at the cup with a moment of dread. I thought of Morag and the state she had fallen into. He followed that of course, and shook his head. "I never lied to her and I will not lie to you. If ever I offer that cup to you, you will know beforehand, as she did."

"But I will caution you about this offering. I wish to take a very long time with you and I want you with me every moment of that time. I will play many songs on your body, saving perhaps the best for last. We will be undisturbed. I want you calm under my hands. You will feel"—and he smiled here—"*languid*. Perhaps you will see through windows usually unavailable to you. I ask you to agree to this, Danu, in the service of our mutual pleasure."

There was only one cup. I asked with my eyes and mind.

"No, Danu. This is for you, however much you might want of it. I need no alternation of my being."

He handed me the cup. It was slightly warm and tasted of honey and something else covered by—a bitter herb? It was refreshing and soothed the slight hunger I carried.

228

"Once more over the precipice," I murmured.

I saw his luminous eyes above me. My clothing was gone and I lay without wanting to move. Warmth suffused out and out from my centre, lighting up all that it encountered. I sighed of it, of pure pleasure. The feeling continued to intensify to become the beginning of a deep need. Still he waited. "A little longer," he said. I looked up at him as he studied me calmly.

Now my body felt sensitive to everything—my hair lying on my shoulders, the blanket beneath me. I felt my need for him as an overriding whole body ache.

He smiled. "Now it begins."

He touched me with various things: the stem of a fallen leaf, a blade of grass. Each contact made a spreading circle of intense pleasure that made me gasp. He stroked my hair and ran his finger lightly down my cheek and then continued on leisurely down. I could move slightly but did all I could to encourage that touch. The heat of wanting him washed over me and I thought no more. It was a minute or an hour or a day before he entered me and did nothing further.

"So, Danu, my queen of the season, you are now fully in the hands of faerie. But I want to reassure myself that you are still with me and willing. What say you now, Danu?"

"*Please*," I whispered and mind-spoke.

"No conditions then?"

"*There never were conditions, I asked you to bring it all to me.*"

"So you did. I am glad that you have remembered that."

And he began. My pleasure bordered on pain and sometimes crossed over. But each time a cry was wrung from me, it was immediately followed by a wash of stronger desire. At one point, the cup was refilled and I drank deeply. Then neither of us was what we had been, although I could not say afterwards what that meant. I can only say that as I got higher and wilder he took me up and up until I lost my contact with everything but him. He was my guiding star and I followed his lead. I questioned nothing, following, following …At some point I must have lost my connection even with him. I floated in the darkness, feeling the light of stars on my naked skin. I wanted nothing; I did not want to leave where I was.

I returned to his touch, which must have stopped at some point.

I looked and saw him lying beside me, glimmering faintly in the darkness. He was smiling and even deeper when he saw my own smile.

"Ah, Danu, you are so fine." He ran his hand along my arm and I glowed briefly.

I generally do not ask questions like this, my queen," he said. "But I got lost with and in you. Can you tell me even a word of how this was for you?"

I spoke without thinking. "I have touched and been touched by the mysteries," I said. "I will not be afraid to die."

He grew still and looked at me and I had cause to recall what I had just said.

"There are far worse fates, my lover," I said, to which he raised a questioning eyebrow.

"One can pass one's life dead inside. I have first-hand experience in that. I regret nothing. I also will come if you call me by my name." I thought then of Morag and wondered at the bargains she had struck—and fulfilled.

"Another offer you should consider before making," he said softly.

I just shook my head. "I died for Dagon. It was not a day for staying dead." I smiled. "A different day will come for me, for all the long-lived ones here, but a planet—a planet should a have a long, long joyful life; to come into being and shelter its life and only then slowly fade."

He did something then that surprised me. On this brightening morning with no moonlight to add to the magic, he kissed me softly on the lips. Instead of the instant sting of desire, I felt something more illusive. Kinder.

"You are unlike anyone I have met in a very long life," he said. "Be well, my queen. He handed me another cup and I drank it without question as he watched.

"I'll take you back now," he said. And once again I left Between.

CHAPTER FORTY-SIX

EVERYONE DIES, EVENTUALLY

I was standing alone in the frost-browned, drawn-down energy of the garden behind Dagon's house. I shivered. It was late afternoon and the neighbourhood was quiet. I had walked out of the house earlier wearing minimal clothing and I realized I didn't know how long I had been gone. The Sidhe had promised that he would not keep me overly long. I was aware of one night passing, but I knew that time was more fluid in Between.

I scanned the house. It was completely quiet.

No! It was not silent. Someone was within, but their energy was very low and hard to read and, I guessed, muffled by the thick walls of the basement. I sprang back, instantly aware of my peril. I now caught the damped down traces of others' presences. The whole situation screamed, "Trap!"

I flew up and out of the garden area, for it was too confined a space to want to meet more than one attacker in, or perhaps even just one with a needle gun. I heard familiar laughter in my mind and it struck fear deep within me. The shark had appeared out of the dark deep water. She watched me now with interest. Perhaps it was time for her full attack.

I knew it was Dagon whose life energy flickered weakly somewhere in his house, that he was in the hunger and prevented from leaving. He was unable to help himself.

I took the most difficult action that I had ever done since our first meeting. I left without doing anything. I considered trying to contact him, but I refused to rouse him to an energy expenditure that he could ill afford, and, of course, I would only be announcing my presence to whoever held him. I rushed to Morag's house, but it had an "almost" silence, too. Both of them then!

It was a Council meeting night, I had deduced, once I got back within the range of the spaceport and its circle of electronic functioning. The Sidhe blanketed the wilderness and Between with silence, with no transmission there except psi. The Council meeting of the Shadakon would be called to order in two hours. I could well imagine who thought she would stand as leader before them.

I smiled. Today might be the day I died—or worse. I wondered if Fiórcara would come and give me a merciful cup if I called him. I hoped I would not have to ask, but I knew that if I was captured that at some point I would implore anyone to help me. He might be the only one who could come.

My dagger, with its offer of quick escape, was in the house that was no doubt being guarded against any who might come to free him. I had left it there, knowing that there would be no one to fight and nothing to fight against in Between. That had been a serious error of judgement. I had no delusions that I could take on a hall full of Bloods, no matter what weapon I might carry. Unless I could quickly win them to my side, I would join my mate tonight in relentless pain if not outright final death.

He had faced this reality as he watched me going into the trial—that his path would end in the basement of his house; now both of us might face that fate.

I breathed in. I felt the strength of the elixir of life that I had drank copious quantities of last night, and I was grateful for it. I briefly pondered my statement to Fiórcara: that I was not afraid of dying. Had I seen this future line opening in front of me? Had he seen it as well? I remembered his gentle kiss of parting.

I did not have the green stone that had been in the sheath of my knife. I breathed out.

And out. And out. I practised various things I might say in front of the gathered crowd before my voice was drowned out. I decided that a direct approach would be best. I smiled and the calm that I had learned to generate settled like a cloak around me. I felt my true surrender to what would be. I found the place beyond fear; I would face what was coming as best I could. That would have to be enough.

I went to the hall early, but concealed myself in the trees on one side of the building. I became ground and faded from sight and psi vigilance. I leaned against a tree and felt for its energy. I followed it down, winding and twisting through the dark earth to its roots reservoir. I greeted it and asked a boon. That if I did not return to this spot tonight, to let Fiórcara know, if it could. I imagined another tree that I had spent happier times with in Between. I hoped that my message could somehow be passed on. For a moment, I allowed myself to feel my grief of Dagon and Morag's predicament, and that I might die or worse, join them.

But I would not attempt to summon Fiórcara. Although he may have intervened on my part, I didn't know if that offer might extend to my mate or Morag. I had nothing left to bargain with and I could not bear to be refused now. I would need all my focus and energy.

The hall was filling. People who didn't know about the event taking place in our home looked about for Dagon and Morag. The clan did not particularly notice my absence.

Timing was everything. I entered at the back. I noted that a few of those who had been neutral or even friendly to me still seemed to be so. I caught the eye of he who had been serving as our pilot. I lifted my head and said only in mind-speak, *"I could use you now if you would be of assistance."*

Nothing more.

I saw Lore stride in, heading for the platform where she would spin some story and attempt to take the position of Alpha. She looked confident. She must have been reassured by the presence of many supporters here.

I made my move then. I flew directly to the dais and was standing above her before she was quite ready to act. I faced the crowd and paused in the precious moment before the chaos might begin.

"I call the meeting of this clan of Shadakon to order on behalf of my mate and your Alpha leader, Dagon," I said, and my voice carried easily to the back of the hall. This was the exact moment from which everything that might happen would come into being. It felt spacious and I allowed my ringing pronouncement to hang in the air.

I had time to wonder if the potion that I drank still worked within me to lengthen time.

I smiled. "I expect no less than the respect that your leader well deserves. He would be here tonight, but unfortunately he is in the hands of Lore and her supporters, suffering the hunger. As is Morag," I added calmly. "But I am here and I am calling to enforce clan law. As leader, my mate could and would punish any who would threaten the strength of this clan. I will now take his place in this."

There was a din of voices and mind-speak. I purposefully did not pay heed to any in particular, but took in the general tone. Excitement. Anger. Confusion. I would take that as a good sign.

I looked down at Lore. "Have you come to acknowledge me as your leader?" I laced scorn into my tone. "Soon, very soon, you will be standing before me to face judgement as this moment unfolds."

She shrieked. I saw the eyes of the shark roll up as she readied for the killing charge.

I smiled. "No? Then we will settle this now."

I dropped lightly in front of her. Her first rush toward me, I stepped inside and close, to avoid the killing zone of whatever she might carry. She wasted a precious moment attempting to free a small needle gun from her waist.

I broke that arm. The gun dropped and skidded across the floor. I saw my ally stop it with his foot and pick it up. He held it calmly and efficiently as others stepped back from him. A good predator takes all advantages offered.

Lore might have quit then, but she knew what she now faced. Dagon's interrupted fate could be her own tonight.

I had ducked under her wounded arm and she drove the other elbow into my ribs. I felt bones break. I corrected my position, rotating on the balls of my feet. I would do no more flying tonight. I felt agony and laughed. I felt closer to the burning stars and perfect blackness. This would end tonight, one way or another.

"I would ask that others check out what I have told you," I said. "But be prepared to meet some of her curs there."

I saw Bloods leaving the hall.

This was going well enough. I thought of the deep earth energy that I had interacted with while in the arms of Fiórcara. I felt it within me. I suffered my pain, as a tree would endure a lightening blasted limb that was a safe distance from the heart of things...

It was then that I saw the dagger jump into her hand and realized that the odds had changed. I had not broken her knife arm, and it was my dagger that she held. Others might not have seen it as a defining fact of our struggle but I knew differently. She would know of its special property as she had known Dagon for a long time.

I had one, possibly two moves and then this would end at best, for me, in stalemate. I bared my teeth and felt my centre of gravity sink as I moved in again. It would take little to end this. A major wound would be overkill with that knife.

"I have died for my mate and your Alpha, here, before all of you," I said to the crowd in a seeming mild tone. "This one will now die for him as well."

I never took my eyes off of her. She feinted but it was obvious and I stepped back—*agony, agony*—looking off balance. I then faked a stumble forward and brushed her knife arm down. She would have recovered in an instant but she had few instants left. The little knife sliced slightly into her thigh, a minor wound.

I stepped back. I saw the realization in her face. She dropped slowly to one knee and her breathing changed to begin a death rhythm I knew well.

"I accept your acknowledgement," I said. Her head drooped, and all could see that she would not rise again. A warrior to the end, she attempted to throw the knife at me, but she was spent and it skipped across the floor. My man with the needle gun scooped that up as well.

"Be careful with the blade," I said offhandedly. I continued to breathe evenly, although I felt bone grate on bone, and the trickling of my blood somewhere, running like a diverted stream.

The groups who had gone to investigate my claim returned. They carried in Dagon and Morag and put them on the dais. They dragged Gailan and another Blood unknown to me behind them and flung them at my feet.

"Send a cur to do a wolf's job, ..." I said. "I do not think you want any such as these to have your back, if ever you require that. I care not what you do with them, but I don't want to see them again. Ever." They were dragged away.

Shadakon were lining up, waiting to contribute to the revival of Dagon and Morag.

When they were somewhat conscious, they were offered blood. There were a lot of volunteers.

I walked over to Dagon and his eyes opened and there was no madness there. "I started the meeting without you, my mate," I said. I knelt beside him and bent my head. Then I lost the ability to rise.

A cold, deep weariness came upon me and I knew I was bleeding out. I was picked up by the strong young Blood who had had my back. He walked with me to the back of the hall and outside and laid me on the grass. He looked down at me with clear amber eyes. "I am yours," he said, then he bit deeply into his wrist and put it to my lips.

"Take whatever you need, Danu, mate of my Alpha leader." He had sheathed the knife and placed it at my side.

I was just able to touch the tree that I lay beside.

"*I am well,*" I messaged through it. "*All is well. Tonight was not my time to die.*"

I availed myself to his rich red blood that flowed freely. I pulled deeply and stopped well before the line that cannot be crossed. The pain in my side was no longer hot agony, and I sensed that my life tide had turned and was returning.

I lay outside on the grass and recovered as my Blood protector stood nearby. I heard a whisper in my mind, "*I am glad you are still with me, Danu. Be well, my queen.*"

I woke in the morning on my own bed, with my mate beside me. I sensed that Morag rested in the living room. Opening my eyes, I saw Dagon's eyes looking into mine. The flames were low, like banked fires. He laughed at me and shook his head. He was still gaunt, and his hair did not have its full gloss. He reached out and touched my side. There was still pain there and the swollen area indicated where bones were knitting on their own. "I suppose that you would have me in this condition if you could," he said smiling.

"But both of us must heal, my love. You were preserved by one who still guards us." A figure rose lithely from the floor at the back door. He had golden amber eyes that I remembered well. He put a finger briefly to his head and smiled at us.

"I owe my life to him," I said. "Or something close to that. I no longer know what is and is not death for me. It would seem that I am harder to kill than some might expect."

Dagon went totally quiet. "You fought hand-to-hand with someone with two deadly weapons and long accumulated skills. She had battle experience, honed over the centuries."

"You had told me earlier that I would take her out," I said. "I hoped that you spoke from some future sense."

"You found one of the few Bloods there who would come to your assistance."

"Yes. That is not a question."

He continued to look at me. "Please, Danu, allow me to see through your eyes what occurred."

I looked at him without answering. There was no "*yes*" and no "*no.*"

He sighed. "You saved me and Morag, and also saved my place as leader and Alpha. If our relationship was the simple one of Alpha and his mate, this would not be a difficult request, but you recently spent time in Between and arrived … slightly altered. It saved your life and saved Morag and me from"—he shuddered—"the living death. I have no right to ask you anything that you do not wish to offer."

Still I looked at him without replying. "Still no question, Dagon," I finally said. "Can you limit your search to what happened after I returned from Between?"

It was his turn not to answer. "I'd like to guarantee you that, Danu. But much like a computer, our memories have links and those have still more links.

The fight might be the most significant immediate memory and certainly I could see that easily.""But …" he sighed. "I sense that something occurred in Between, in your stay with the Sidhe you call true friend. You came back with something that gave you an edge—another wild card from your deck, Danu. I also believe that it is now harder for you to be either here or in Between. You are now in both places."

"Lore could not easily close on you," he said thoughtfully, "because you were slightly shifting. And you were able, perhaps, to play with time. I asked your rescuer, one of the very few who would have agreed to your request in the hall, what happened during the fight. He said you walked into her space like you were sauntering and brushed the knife down to her leg. He appreciates that you think he's a good predator, but he is in awe of you."

He looked deeply into me without pushing. "Something happened on this visit, but it had begun from your first contact with the Sidhe. You have been given, ah, exceptional consideration in Between." He sighed. "You are being trained and shaped by them. Morag was too, but her ultimate task was to deliver you to them.

"We are all being changed, Danu. After tonight, the clan could easily have been ruled by a group that would set aside contract and do what they would. But I have been asked to bring the Shadakon into an agreement with the Sidhe—to act as protectors of this planet. Do you think Lore and her renegade group would have abided by Sidhe contract, even though they might give us permission and even wages to take and kill without recourse on their land?"

"They want trustworthy wolves to keep the humans out of their territory, the wild lands. We will be in contract with them. Or we will leave ... fleeing the consequences of breaking that agreement. We know now that they have a substance that kills us quickly without undo suffering. I doubt that it affects any other life form on this world," he added. We looked at each other.

I attempted to sit up and managed on my second try. The room spun and I felt slightly out of synch. I remembered feeling this way on my last return from Between. I also remembered what had brought me relief in a dream that was no dream. For a moment I craved the elixir of life.

"Dagon!" I wanted to kneel at his feet, to feel his hand on my head and rise again in my right place. He slowly shook his head and gently pulled me back down beside him.

I wanted to disbelieve what he had just told me but I could not. I remembered wanting to say I was not with Fiórcara by my free will, but I knew then and now that that wasn't true. The bargain was now forged by a bond stronger than what mere will could intervene in. I had nothing left to bargain with because I had already put everything on the table. I had delivered Dagon and I and everyone else who would continue to live here on this planet to the Sidhe. I was betting on the planet. The rest of us might eventually all be collateral damage.

"I will tell you the truth," Fiórcara had said. "If ever I offer that cup to you, you will know beforehand."

"Yes, Danu," said Dagon. "I will discuss the offer with the clan and they will accept it. This planet is a peaceful and lovely place, and touches my heart as Old Earth once did. We will see how this unfolds. Perhaps in this, our two ancient races will finally cooperate. Meanwhile I am the only one called to do so. My mate is indisputably of faerie blood. She who was the weary life-hating spacer has vanished, much like the empty cocoon is left behind so that a butterfly can fly away. Once she was in my hands, and I could have ended her life and this fate line. But more likely, I could not have," he said, "any more than Lore could have."

"We both tried," he said softly.

"*Please!*" I mind-spoke. "*Don't set me aside. Don't leave me Dagon!*"

He stroked my hair gently and again I remembered another's touch.

"Danu," he said, and his words were gentle and sad. "It is you who will leave me, in the end. Not in the near future my love. We have some time and we will use it as well as we can. Believing that one can live forever, or that one's world or loves will remain the same is a false hope and a liability. Fate turns on a fine balance point, as Lore discovered at your hands last night."

"Please! Make me yours again, Dagon. In whatever small way you can. I will take a promise of more vigorous pleasures for later."

He carefully drew me to him then. I lay close and felt his beating heart and mine find one rhythm. He touched me, and it was like a warm afternoon breeze. I relaxed under his fingers. No pain for me here, no pain for this proud Blood that I loved. I had never been a praying woman, but this was my only and most sincere prayer.

CHAPTER FORTY-SEVEN

WINTER: THE CONTRACT IS SIGNED AND DANU STAYS FOR AWHILE

Time passed and we were restored in all but the fact that we would carry within ourselves the events that had happened. We could no longer pretend that we could be restored to an earlier point in time. Nathaniel, my second in my fight with Lore, had naturally become our personal pilot and sometimes protector if the need arose. Dagon no longer assumed that he was invulnerable. I never asked him how he had come to be trapped and imprisoned by Lore. He had had ample time to ponder that as he wasted down to the event horizon of his living death. She had been, as he once said, fast and hot, and I could see that her wild energy had drawn him back to her many times in his long life. No doubt he had enjoyed the simple transaction of what she had to offer him. She had died as she had lived.

Morag became Dagon's second at clan meetings. I did not want to appear to expect any special treatment other than what was afforded to me as his mate. There were those within the clan who had fervently wanted Lore to survive her challenge to Dagon and Morag and me. They had had time to rethink those thoughts in the aftermath of what had unfolded.

In due time, Morag, Dagon and I requested a second meeting with the Sidhe. In the dead of winter, the world shining with frost crystals in the winter sunlight, we once again went to Between. He who I called Fiórcara transported us and then formally greeted us there, and announced us to the many Sidhe were present. Some were visible to me, but many more I sensed as movement and shifting shades of green under the trees. The energy of winter was harder to shape and use to manifest to those who were not Sidhe.

It was fully the time of their dreaming but they attended as they could. A contract was signed. There was a collective sigh that rose up from the glade and beyond.

We three were presented with a cup of the elixir of life. I saw Morag accept hers with an almost imperceptible hesitation. She looked at the Sidhe king and something passed between them that was not for us to know. We all drank and the deal was done, signed and witnessed by all in Between.

Now the wild lands would be posted. Later, some of those who thought to set aside the fact that the planet was now off limits for business came anyway. Their communication systems, after unavoidably synching for a landing at the spaceport, ceased to work. No messages were sent out. The humans who walked off those ships, if any did, either got off planet by other means or simply disappeared.

The Sidhe obviously had means of interfacing with the larger universe, and the new status of the planet was gradually accepted. In time, perhaps the whole planet would cease to exist in others' perceptions.

But on this day, we four stood under a clear blue winter sky. I had not discussed with Dagon before leaving for this meeting about my growing wish to remain for a visit after our business was concluded, and he had not asked.

When it was time to leave, I felt my reluctance to return with him, and I felt equally my profound wish not to hurt or disempower this discerning one who loved me against all odds. Morag looked at us both, understanding without hearing what passed between us. So did the Sidhe.

But Dagon was the one who knew my heart as well as I knew it myself. He simply took my hand and kissed it saying, "I will see you when you return, my mate. We will have time to make up for what you might miss of me." I felt the flare of his energy and looked into the flames behind his eyes. I wanted him. I wanted to step to his side.

But I did not. I could not say or do what was not true for me now. I stood, surrounded by the lightly materialized Sidhe and watched Fiórcara take Dagon and Morag's arms and wink out of existence. Then he reappeared at my side.

I realized that I had not considered what might be his will in this. I looked at him, his now silver hair blowing lightly in a cold breeze. The realization that I had assumed anything regarding his wish for me to be here struck me, although I stood quiet and calm. There was nothing else that I could do.

"Always betting it all, Danu," he said and smiled enigmatically. "Are you again sure of your hand?"

I shook my head. "I must play the cards I have, and only hope that the uncovered ones turn out well for me." I was silent again.

"Perhaps I might ask for a small time of sanctuary here," I finally said. "I have given what I had to preserve this place and beyond. I have delivered it all."

He smiled then and reached out to take my hand. I felt the icy burning of deep winter that felt inexplicably hot and powerful. I felt my own response to him and almost went to my knees. Ice and fire. At the interface was ecstasy. Could he bring this to me without being swept up by it himself as well?

He smiled again, and his eyes swept around the circle of those who watched.

"My Midsummer's Eve Queen has returned to us," he mind-spoke.

"Through a very unlikely fate line and many trials. She will now walk here as well as with those outside Between."

"As she chooses," he added. "Let us revisit our vows then," he spoke aloud to me. "Where do you wish to be on this day, Danu?"

I thought to ask for clarification—how long a day? But I did not. I asked nothing. I looked into his winter blue eyes and thought and said only, *"With you, my king."*

He nodded. "And what do you wish of me?"

I smiled at the assembled Sidhe, "I want what you would bring to me. Only that and all of that."

He looked at me. "Few other than Sidhe lovers have asked that of me more than once. Some regretted it before the first night had barely begun. Others fled back to their usual and tried very hard to forget. They later fought to disregard the dreams that came later in other springs. Our passion is, ah … transformative. Do you accept being changed as we lie together, my queen?"

Again I felt the presence of many, interestedly leaning forward for my answer. Could I answer this without giving up my contact with Dagon and his world? I searched within.

"I would choose not to get lost here. I wish to be able to continue to move freely between my worlds—and loves. But when I am here, I am yours and will willingly take all you offer. I ask but cannot demand that I am free to do so—to leave and to return again."

He smiled, "I am as impressed with your growing skills as negotiator as I am with your offer. This will suit us both, I think."

He looked at me fully then. I felt his energy of full winter, holding the mysteries of seeds of spring deep within. I saw the life force within him and it called to me. I waited without fear.

"I accept your offer, my summer queen." There was a murmur from all around us.

"We will take our leave of you all then." He and I now stood before a snow covered hill. The door was open and there was light and warmth within. "Enter as you wish, Danu," he simply said.

There were soft white coverings on the sleeping platform.

"Pleasure platform," he corrected. "Although this visit we will sleep and dream together."

I came to him then. He held me lightly and I felt his burning cold and my own heat flare. I looked into his winter blue eyes and wished only to go with him wherever he could take me. He was intent on me and did not hurry as the stars spun down in the winter sky, and only later did we come to a peaceful resting place. I curled up beside him at last and felt him draw me close.

And then I dreamed. I dreamed of being a sick lonely child, calling out to the faeries that came, but then left me to live my life and later come to this time and place. I dreamed that once I had walked in sadness and anger, unable to imagine wanting to combine, as I now combined with my lovers. I dreamed of living as a solo, unhappy and alone. I slightly awoke to another dream. I was wrapped in bliss in the arms of a faerie lover whose energy covered me even as we both slept. At this point, the dream had a very happy pausing place.

I returned to sleep in the arms of Fiórcara. I did not see, but felt him smile in the darkness.

BOOK TWO

Exterra Saved

CHAPTER ONE

BEGINNING IN THE MIDDLE

I awoke beside Fiórcara, my Sidhe lover, in his snow-covered hill hall. His energy covered me like warm ocean water. It was the Dreaming Time, when the life energies go to root and rest. We were actually sleeping (often we were not) when I sensed the flare of swirling colours shining through my dreams to touch me in his underground home. I went to the entrance, unconcerned with the fact of being unclothed and without shoes. The aurora borealis was flaring in the sky, reflected back by the white snow; I felt it sing in my body. The sky was an icy black invitation, with pinpoint stars and strange, swirling fire.

I wanted to fly.

Fiórcara joined me at the doorway and I launched up and away. I had flown with him on midsummer's eve, and knew that it was effortless for him. It was less easy for me—but always euphoric. I could feel the flicker of the different colours upon my bare skin. I could taste the tang of the electric energy of the planet in the cold air.

I flew. He flew. Eventually a game evolved to include even more interesting activities. He transited and was suddenly gone from my vision and also my immediate perception of him. I searched for him, feeling for his energy and then did what I had never done: I covered time and space instantaneously to arrive at his side, a skill the Sidhe have, but one I hadn't known I had before that moment. We were still in Between, which I had always sensed was not a large space.

I wanted to go further. I concentrated—this time not on him, but instead on the seashore outside Between where I had walked many times and knew firsthand from spending several periods of time there when I took refuge from conflict between Dagon and myself.

I knew the exact curve of the beach and the sounds of small waves raised by the little moon. I landed successfully from my first solo transit, and laughed in the midnight darkness with the aurora flaring across the sky and reflecting on the sea and snow that covered everything up to the tide line.

I was kindled by the sky, entrained to the light and power of the planet's magnetic field dancing above me. I danced to being alive and one with the light and night.

Fiórcara found me easily and began to do what he did with me without effort, smiling and confident of the effect his touches had. When he landed and took my arm briefly, I swayed, all thoughts but of him driven out of my mind.

I wanted him—lit by the sky, outside of Between. He surveyed me calmly; it was always he who appeared calm and I who came to him with a need that seemingly could not be slaked. It was how we began and how it was this night.

I saw nothing in his eyes but the bright colours of the sky. I wanted nothing more than for him to close the distance between us and take me to an edge that surely few would approach and even fewer could cross. I had crossed over with him many times. Physical connection with him was intoxicating and pleasurable beyond description; neither of us easily tired of each other.

Still he studied me without moving. Had I had at that moment the ability to think, to compare, or come to a conclusion, I might not have been so surprised by how things unfolded for me and those I loved soon afterwards.

However, I did not and could not think any thoughts or come to any useful conclusions. He knew this. He continued to smile and took his time to build the fire between us until I burned brightly. Tonight I also burned with sky fire. It and I flickered blue, green and red, with plumes of arcing yellow across my skin.

I wanted. I wanted. He did not bother to ask me what I wanted. He knew. I followed his lead and in due time we joined and I could feel those sky fires within me, for he was a manifestation of this world, and her energy flowed through him.

At one point there was intensity that crossed into pain. This was sometimes part of our coupling, but it was so fused with desire and building heat that I never turned from it or he who brought it. I became dimly aware of two stinging stripes down my back and when I rose I noticed two thin bright lines of scarlet in the snow where I had lain.

I laughed. I had brought it all and he had taken me to a surrender in which he was the only one, the centre of my universe. He could have dropped me in the sea or done almost anything else; and, as long as I was in his strong arms, the passion of otherworldly sex driving me on. I would have not protested.

This was always the way it was with me when I was with him. It was this way for any human or part human who joined a Sidhe partner under the moon. Later I was to learn that they had this effect on each other.

I could only consent to the starting, the surrender.

Eventually (and time with my Sidhe King was a very variable quantity), he disappeared—knowing that I could and would follow him. I returned to where we had started, in his hill hall in Between. He had arrived before me and, although my transit seemingly took no time, it seemed that I had been gone for longer than I could account for.

I knew that Between keeps its own time. A night in Between could last weeks outside. I had discovered that I could not keep my promises to Dagon of when I would return to him. The unexpected lengthened time of Between had been a serious problem between us.

Now there was soft light illuminating the snow outside the entrance to the Sidhe's hill hall, and the sound of murmuring voices within. This had never happened before. Previously I had been the only guest in his bed or wherever we took our pleasures; I had always held his full attention until the dawn, or until I awoke and it was time to leave for my other home and reality.

He had never brought others into what we shared. Still, I was more confused than apprehensive as I stooped and entered. This was his home and these were his subjects and, presumably, friends. His clan had smiled slyly at me on my first flight with him, but had never been unkind. In fact, I saw few of the Sidhe under usual circumstances in Between, even though, at times, I had sensed them, both in their world and mine.

There were two beautiful beings in his home: a female who, as they all are, was heart-achingly attracting and beautiful. She was fairer than Fiórcara, although his winter manifestation was one of frosted hair and icy winter eyes. Come spring, his eyes would be emerald green, and his hair golden.

Her hair was spun silver and gold and framed a pixie face with slightly slanted aquamarine eyes. She was ageless; she could have passed as a teenager or any other age of human. She was curved into Fiórcara's arms, held lightly but surely, and she looked content there.

On her other side was a male Sidhe, dark in comparison to their usual presentation, with pale skin and dark curling hair. His eyes held a laugh even when his lips did not; he, too, was entrancing. Fiórcara, a name the Sidhe king had given me to call him which means "Dear Friend," had kept me apart from his kind, as they all had the same effect on humans that he did—of being irresistibly attracting and therefore, at very least, distracting to me.

I was, after all, still part human; and although my other bloodlines had been activated by exposure to both him and the Shadakon, I still carried the vulnerabilities of being human—of being unable to shield myself from their effects on me and my answering desire. Early on, this had come between Dagon and I, and I now faced it here, in the stronghold of my Sidhe lover. I arrived at his door naked and barefoot with two bloody marks that he had made still stinging on my back. I felt socially vulnerable. I felt that I held no power, having arrived expecting to be alone in his company, and discovering that a gathering had started without me.

Immediately I froze, realizing that I had not asked or waited for an invitation to enter. I felt awkward and off balance and stood in the place of my first step across the threshold, my face burning with shame. Underneath was anger. Nothing had been indicated while we lay under the flaming sky that I should expect anything other than his continuing intoxicating attention. I wasn't sure that I trusted my impulse to feel the way I did.

"*What now?*" I mind-spoke to him. "*Should I leave now?*"

In truth I was weary from the night's activities and uncertain that I could transit to Dagon's home. Even if I could, how would he receive me, arriving unexpectedly in the middle of the night and bearing fresh marks of faerie sex upon me? I had not recently drunk of the elixir of life. This drink the Sidhe distilled from the life web, and I used while here to replenish myself and stave off my energy requirements. I needed human energy or the elixir every day to survive, otherwise I would enter into hunger. Having been in an enforced state of that during a trial forced on me by the Shadakon Council, I had no interest in experiencing serious hunger again. But now did not seem to be the time to admit my need and ask this favour of Fiórcara.

In fact, when I was first attempting to understand why I was in his world and falling under his influence, Fiórcara had told me there were no accidents in Between.

So, here I stood, naked and needy, and facing what appeared to be an exclusive gathering of his.

There have been many times in my life, when I have needed to be brave, or appear to be brave (a different thing altogether). And I knew appearing to be brave and confident, if not backed by inner strength, is doomed. I took one breath and exhaled and then another, attempting to find a calm centre for myself in the midst of what I felt to be a complex and unwanted situation. I searched for my calm centre, breath after breath.

Calm did not arrive for me.

Fiórcara did not respond to me, and this, too, I took in as information. In my early weeks with Dagon, I had learned that what he did not reveal or say was as important as what he did. Fiórcara usually revealed little except his pleasure with me, and how deeply he could affect me. He also valued my connection with the natural world of this planet and specific plants in Between.

But I was in unknown territory here. I stood without moving, awaiting some additional information from him. And he let me stand there while all three viewed me in my predicament.

Eventually he beckoned me over and indicated that I should sit at the side of the dark-haired Sidhe. This one faced me easily and I could feel the pull of his energy, although he was not initially focusing on me. This was how it was for me: I knew I would be increasingly affected by his presence. I also knew that I did not want to respond to him, even though my body was already warming to his energy. Fiórcara was King of the Sidhe and had described himself as such to me. He also had referred to me as his queen. We had flown in the Sidhe's great midsummer's eve ritual of energy building one season before.

Now I felt like an interloper, or perhaps a humiliated past queen, forced to witness something I could not prevent from happening. I saw Fiórcara return to his attentions to the female beside him, and my body responded as if he was touching me. It was no doubt evident to everyone present, and I could do nothing to block it out.

I stood stiffly, reviewing my options. I could attempt to get back to Dagon's side, and pay for whatever anger he might have over my predicament and state of being. He had told me in the beginning that I would be hurt by my dealings with the Sidhe and I had set aside his advice, feeling that I could manage any situation that might arise.

He knew then, if I did not, that I could not; so did Fiórcara.

"Ah, Danu," mind-spoke my unwanted companion. *"Do you not find me attractive?"* He, of course, knew I did. He knew all humans he had ever crossed paths with—young, old, male, female—found him irresistibly desirable. It was his gift and power over humans.

"Have you been given the duty of entertaining me?" I asked with a touch of my unraveling pride.

He made full contact then, and lightly looked within me, as Fiórcara had done so many times. I fought his contact and he frowned slightly.

"Perhaps a duty," he mind-spoke and shrugged. *"But a pleasant one. To be offered a queen to pleasure, and one such as you. It will be a night for you to remember."* He smiled.

There was no unkindness in his mind, no gloating over the obvious power imbalance between the two of us, but my business now was with Fiórcara. I turned to him.*"I know, because you have taught me, that there are few accidents here in Between. So surely you know that this proposed partner looks much like Dagon!"* I no longer bothered to disbelieve or hide my anger, although I knew even at that moment that it put me in jeopardy.

I had been warned to not make reference to Dagon and my other life while here. I had been told, not warned, that Fiórcara could and would wipe the memories of my other existence from my mind. That would leave me trapped in Between, until he tired of me or I took a desperate action. I knew this, and he knew I understood this. Tonight would not be a good time to see if he would follow up on his pronouncement.

He hissed at me then.

"Yes, Danu," he stated. *"We both know this, even if your proposed partner does not. But how else would I know if you truly surrendered to my will in this? That you surrendered to my and his will to pleasure you in my presence. I would see you from yet another viewpoint. Perhaps before dawn we will all come to you and see what the effects of that might be. I think, if you set aside thinking, you will enjoy wherever this evening takes you."*

Then I knew that I was lost. I could barely return to myself after a night—or span of whatever passed as a night here—with Fiórcara. The Sidhe beside me had been given permission to do what he did best, and soon he would have my permission, too. I might briefly protest, but I knew I would eventually surrender to it all. Would my love and other life with Dagon be forfeit?

I felt total despair replace my earlier anticipation of further joy. I stood while I still could, and bowed briefly to Fiórcara, the Sidhe whom, in my own mind, I had called my lover.

"I must decline your offer, my King," I said and mind-spoke. *"I am going home now."*

I ducked out the door and transited. Perhaps I meant to arrive at Dagon's garden and back door, naked and flaming with faerie desire, with two fading marks of pain and passion on my back, but at an early critical moment, I made another decision.

Surprisingly, I was still strong enough to navigate accurately. I arrived, as I wished to, just outside the atmosphere of this planet I had begun to call my home. I could see the glow of the aurora borealis below me. I watched as the love and sadness for all I was turning aside from, welled up in my heart. Then there was pain and more pain as I had known there would be, and I surrendered to it. I had exhaled the moment of my arrival and there would no inhale. There would be no reprieve. And then, there were no thoughts ...

CHAPTER TWO

A DESPERATE INTERVENTION

Blackness quickly took me away from the pain of my body. I hung dying in space, my last memories of my eyesight dimming and the terrible need to breathe what could not be breathed.

Previously, Dagon and I had enacted a ancient Making Ceremony, in which we both had exchanged blood and took within the essence of the other. Although the act of dying for one of the Blood is difficult, I had been told that I would know if Dagon died. It had not occurred to me this night that my death would announce itself to him before he found out any other way.

Or maybe it did. But I had nothing to say except, "I am sorry." At the moment I made my choice, I was, in my own way, choosing him over faerie. But very soon, I thought nothing as the planet wheeled beneath me.

Fiórcara knew me well and could easily read my thoughts. He had known the moment I set my target of arrival, and now he transited towards me, into the death zone I had chosen for my destination. Humans have nine to eleven seconds of some degree of consciousness when exposed to outer space; they do not explode, although the last breath and contents of one's body might rush out. I had exhaled. I had no food or even liquid within me. I floated, my skin beginning to frost, the small blood vessels in my eyes and under my skin breaking, my lungs accumulating small bubbles of gas escaping out towards the void. None of this would trouble me for long.

This is how Fiórcara found me. And returned us in time to spare us both, although I had not asked him to, and, even in my terminal pain, I had not called out to either of my so-called lovers. Space and its comforting darkness and depths had been my home, not a space ship and not old Earth. I had simply returned to it—and to a last look at the planet I loved.

Fiórcara laid me down in his now empty hill house. He attempted to put a cup of the elixir of life to my lips. I do not know if I refused or was simply more dead than alive with no will to return. My skin was dusky and cold, and small bubbles of red were in the corners of my mouth; I laboured with each breath, and moaned as I did so.

I do not know what his feelings were, or if he felt in any way responsible or remorseful. I knew he was capable of providing death, but until later I did not know that he was also capable of providing me with life. He bit down into his own hand and held his welling Sidhe blood to my lips. There are not even rumours about the effect of such a thing—a faerie giving blood, but one can surmise that if their presence is overwhelming, that their life's blood would be such that the recipient would never forget. Somewhere within me I tasted blood, and perhaps I hoped it was Dagon's. Somewhere deeper, I knew it was not. I took from him weakly and then slid under into a state beyond sleeping.

He left me there, curled around a place of just surviving, with pain still ruling my body. He called Dagon by mind-speak and met him in the garden of Dagon's home, saying little but betraying much.

They returned together. Dagon came to me and read my body, frowning as he did so. He felt the chill of me and saw the red froth that indicated damage within. He rolled me slightly to my side to ease my breathing and found the parallel scratches on my back that had not had time to close and now might never do so. He covered me and turned to Fiórcara. Although the Sidhe could have avoided him by transiting or possibly even killed him, Fiórcara remained silent, facing Dagon's rage and pain and unspoken question: *"How could this happen?"*

Fiórcara sighed and only mind-spoke. *"First do anything you can to aid her survival. I did what I could. Then I will tell you what you want to know."*

Dagon returned to me, noting the untouched cup of elixir of life beside me. He scanned me, frowning, and turned back to Fiórcara.

The Sidhe simply held up his still injured hand. Dagon looked at him incredulously.

"This is my fault," said the ageless Sidhe. "I pushed her towards something she would not accept." Matter-of-factly, he mentally showed Dagon the last scene that ended with me stepping out the door.

"Danu said she was going home," he said. "It took me a little while to realize and sense what and where she meant."

It is a measure of many things that the two did not enter into direct hostility at that point. Perhaps Dagon realized the vulnerability we were both in. I would not survive much more and needed the elixir of life as well as what Dagon could provide to me. He had arrived somewhat depleted and was dependent on the Sidhe to get him and, perhaps me, back to his world. He was silent as he studied the Sidhe.

However, it is also possible that he sensed the Sidhe's uncharacteristic sadness in admitting his error and my likely fate.

"She is a woman who will not be forced," Dagon said finally, "even into a surrender to that which she desires above all else. I knew that already. You should have known this as well. You do now ..."

Dagon sat next to me and gave me what energy he could spare. The Sidhe king handed him the cup of elixir of life that I could not drink and then poured more. *"You will need it,"* he mind-spoke. Dagon downed it without comment.

And then they talked—because they were more like than unlike each other.

Both used attraction to bring others to them, and enjoyed partaking in the energy that was built up in their prey. Dagon could and would take it all. What and how the Sidhe took was less clear, but after driving a human to an unforgettable state of longing and sexual heat, take they did. Neither felt bad about what they did. They were what they were.

Dagon had chosen not to take my life when we first met, even though I had eventually signed it over to him. He fought his own nature and the disapproval of his clan to refuse lethally taking me or abandoning me. He had been put to his own trial by loving me. However, even now, he had short liaisons with other Bloods. Some I knew about, but there may have been others that I did not. The Sidhe sighed. "I have accommodated her. She has come when she chose to and generally that was workable. I enjoy her—" he looked at Dagon to see if he was reacting angrily to this.

Dagon just shook his head. "I cannot deny her. I have never experienced anything like her in all my years of living, of sexing and even of my rare times of loving. I could not leave her to her fate within three days of meeting her. I faced my own living death if she failed her trial of hunger. It was close. She called out for me for two days before it was over." He looked at the Sidhe.

The Sidhe smiled. "I chose her twice for my Midsummer's Eve Queen. She came to me the second year. I lusted after her before the first shoots of that second spring came into the light."

"During the fall equinox she came to me again, and we went beyond... I followed her spirit out into space. She hung amidst the stars and gloried in their streaming energies. I have never had anyone remotely like her. She told that night that she was not afraid to die."

"And later the next day she almost did," said Dagon.

They regarded each other.

I think, although I have no memories, that this is when I decided to return to life. I had been strengthened by the Sidhe blood and Dagon's energy, but the missing piece was my will to return to these two, the two whom I wanted above all else. I did not hear Fiórcara's admission of at least shared responsibility, but perhaps I sensed it.

When I awoke later, I felt like I had been out of my body. I felt disconnected and unsure how to make my limbs work. Happily this state spared me some of the pain of healing.

Dagon did not ask the Sidhe why he had set me up for a perhaps typical faerie interaction, but one that I did not wish to partake in. It was one that we had never discussed, and that I had never agreed to. In turn, Fiórcara did not ask Dagon why I had had to kill his occasional Shadakon sexual partner and would-be murderer. Or perhaps they allowed each other some knowledge of these things. They did agree to a certain basic realization, at least for this night: they did not want to lose me.

I half awoke in the arms of Dagon, who lay curled around me, radiating heat. He fed me twice during the night although I dreamed I had fed earlier on blood and had felt that energy radiating out from my centre. I awoke again and felt the warmth of Fiórcara's energy. He propped me up and gave me the elixir of life, which I now drank eagerly. Then I slid under again.

My eyes, which had been bright red, faded to their usual hazel. My skin lost the dusky colour of bruising, and the aches in my joints disappeared such that on one brief awakening I dazedly stood up beside where I slept—and promptly collapsed. One of them picked me up and soothed me.

"*Soon, Danu. Soon.*"

I believe they spelled each other off.

On a day not much past my first awakening, I awoke clear-headed to see both of them looking down at me. I sat, while things spun around me before settling. I swung my legs over the side and tentatively tested taking weight.

Then I realized where I was, and who was with me and why. This was a dive into icy water. I came to what memories I had, which included deciding to leave for a final destination. I even remembered arriving there, and the brief glory of it before the pain came. My last recollection was of a rush and grab and then blackness.

They did not speak or mind-speak to me immediately. In that moment, they seemed to be easy with each other. Then they took turns telling me what I could not remember but now wanted to know.

Fiórcara had found and retrieved me. Then he had sustained me with his own blood. I had a faint memory of that. Of glowing ... it reminded me of a night that we had spent in autumn: the inner glow. I briefly wondered ...

At this time, I sensed no obvious tension or anger from Dagon. He had been summoned and brought to my side, and they had both worked to keep me alive long enough to heal. He had been provided with the elixir of life to be able to feed me and maintain him. He had even fed me in Fiórcara's home!

I looked at them both in amazement.

"*There is more,*" Fiórcara mind-spoke. He looked at Dagon and they under-spoke such that I was aware of this, but not the content of what was said.

Dagon walked outside.

I was dumbfounded. Fiórcara waited until he had my full attention. Sustained thinking was still difficult. Then he knelt and bowed his head to me. I was alarmed.

"*Please.*" I said. "*Don't.*"

He looked at me but did not stand.

"*Please allow me this, Danu. I was toying with you and with your connection with me. The sky energy was high in me, but I will not use that as an excuse. I wondered if you would, in fact, take another partner and accept me doing the same for the remainder of the evening. It is how we are. We often pleasure each other in various combinations. But I did not secure your permission in this ahead of time or allow you to refuse. And perhaps I tested you, by providing someone who would remind you of Dagon.*"

I was amazed that he mentioned Dagon in relation to what had happened between he and I. I was silent.

He sighed. "*There was no 'perhaps' in this. I tested you. You chose to leave rather than accept what I had planned for you. You should not have sent yourself to your death. I don't even know how you managed to get as far as you did. In this, I greatly underestimated you.*"

I still said nothing. I was shocked, but perhaps I was also holding out. Sometimes I don't know why I do the things I do; sometimes I do. He continued to stay where he was, on his knees beside me.

He took a breath and exhaled simply saying, *"You are going to now hear something that one who is not a Sidhe has ever heard from me."* He paused. *"And only a few Sidhe have ever heard. Let this stand on record and do not use it to hurt me, Danu."*

I was still silent but now completely attentive.

"I am sorry, Danu. I am sorry I hurt you and that you felt driven to take your desperate solution. I will not do such a thing in our future. And I very much want you in my future."

"I accept your apology," I said aloud. "I thank you for saving my life and also giving me the gift that preserved my life.

I believe it was above and beyond what any would expect you to do for me—or anyone."

We both understood that I referred to his gift of his faerie blood that had kept me from slipping over the edge, away from survival. If a Shadakon's body is past healing, he or she dies. I was not full Blood, my survival had been far from guaranteed.

"And I wish to return to your side in the future."—*"Of course,"* I added in mind-speak, and he smiled.

"Later then," he said. He smiled at me and rose.

Dagon returned to me moments after Fiórcara got up and moved away.

"Let's go home."

Fiórcara accompanied us to our garden but let me guide the transit. It was uneventful, the only part of what had happened that was.

CHAPTER THREE

LIVING ON

We arrived at the house I sometimes called ours and sometimes identified as Dagon's. It had been solely Dagon's and in truth I had changed nothing in it, feeling comfortable and nurtured in its spaciousness and sparse but beautiful decor. In my heart, I thought of it as "*ours*." I wanted to lie down on the red fur pelt that lay across the bed. To spread out on it, warm after a soak in a tub that I had to submerge in to find the bottom. I wanted Dagon to shut the door—shutting out Between and all the other issues that were piling up outside the door.

He did so.

Neither of us were hungry, thanks to Fiórcara generously supplying us with elixir of life; that eliminated one major necessity, at least for the present. We eyed each other carefully.

Then he did something he had done before when I had returned from Between with Fiórcara's touch and effect upon me. He slowly brushed away that energy with his hands, replacing it with his own. As always, I did not feel crazed or overwhelmed by the states he induced in me. I did not fear Dagon as I believe I feared Fiórcara beneath my attraction to him. I had never feared Dagon, not even in the beginning. Rightly or wrongly, I felt secure and safe with him.

I did not, however, feel complacent. He was capable and willing to take many different roles in how he brought himself to me and me to the blaze of energy that we both created.

Tonight he drew a hot bath and encouraged me to spend time there, soaking until I was almost dozing. I eventually got out—finally warm—and made my way to our shared bed and space.

I spread out, wanting only to relax into the induced comfort of warmth and freedom of no-hunger. He came to join me and removed his clothing beside the bed without ceremony. He didn't touch me immediately and didn't respond to my sleepy enquiry of him.

"*What now, my love?*"

His silence was complete. I opened my eyes to see him gazing at me slowly as if he was memorizing me. He touched lightly down from my lips, down to the pulse point where he had taken me and tasted my heart's blood. He lingered there as if he could still see it fresh in his mind. I shuddered but not in fear, I wanted him in that way too.

He continued on, breast to belly, belly to lightly touch my now-aching places of pleasure. One finger settled precisely and I moaned.

He was not close to done with me, however. Having revealed that he knew very well what I wanted, he continued on, sliding down the inside of my thighs as I trembled under his touch like a barely tamed wild thing.

"Roll over."

It was not a request but rather the first Alpha action he had taken with me since our return. I rolled over and then shuddered as he traced the now-faint marks Fiórcara had left down my back.

"We have both marked you," he mind-spoke to me, revealing no emotion in his statement. *"Others will not be able to see it, but the Shadakon can see my mark on you, and I will see his on you as well."* I felt some fear creep in then and attempted to roll back over but he restrained me effectively. Then he resumed touching me, kindling me into a great wanting that he did not quench.

"Do you require more pain from me?" he asked quietly.

"I found pain in your memories from the first of your meetings with the Sidhe. You did not allow me to seek information from your second meeting. And here you are, marked where you bled as he took you. Perhaps I am missing something … do I not bring you enough fear or pain to our pleasure sharing?"

Again I tried very hard to roll over, to look into his eyes, but he held me back.

"I lose myself when we look at each other. You might rather to leave this question unanswered, but I require you to tell me. I am your Alpha. I am also a centuries-old predator. I once gloried in my prey's fear and pain. I have not brought you that, but it could be available if you wish it."

By now I was crying, but he disregarded my tears. He let me sit up and looked straight into me. I saw the panther then and his look was one of a calm predator. He had told me once that if I had feared him in the beginning, he would have enjoyed taking me to death. He studied me to see if I understood his state of mind.

"I am still waiting, Danu. Do you require me to show you my power over you? Power equal to what the Sidhe holds? Do you want to wonder whether you will wake in the morning?"

He had once told me that the most dangerous thing I had ever done in my life was to lie in his arms those first few days that we spent together. He had shown me the intensity of desire that he had for my life energy—all of it. And I had been under lethal contract to him. I had signed willingly because I had realized that I could not return to my old life aboard my ship. I had turned spontaneously. I knew I was doomed and offered to simplify things for him by ending my life in a way enjoyable to us both; I knew he could and would do that.

But he had not done it. He had held back, knowing that he did not have my inner permission—knowing that I did not truly wish to give away my life. I had wanted more of *him*.

He had disobeyed both the legal time-limited lethal contract and the more serious rules of his own clan. In doing so, his feelings for me had drawn him into terrible danger that we had both only narrowly survived.

He let me stand and I shook before him. I lowered my eyes but he tilted my chin up again. He didn't ask; he accessed all that I had experienced. It was not gentle, and I tried to turn aside from his probing. As surely as if he had pinned my arms, he continued on. I saw myself then, dying in Fiórcara's winter hall. He lingered on this memory.

"I promised you that I would die with you if you chose to die by your own hand," he said with horrible calmness. "You left me to go die alone because you were forced into a situation that Fiórcara found interesting to inflict upon you. You said nothing to me, your Maker. You sent me no farewell. I came to find you dying, sustained only by his Sidhe blood. I had to make peace with the one who watched you leave on your way to die and knew the exact moment you chose that, and then later be the one who retrieved you, more dead than alive."

"You have certainly brought me pain," he said quietly. "Now you would like me to restore you; to bring you to pleasure after you have returned, marked by him."

"To not ask these questions ..." he added, "to treat you gently ... perhaps I have taken a wrong course with you?"

I wept. The pain of even the idea of us entering into a way of being that allowed for cruelty or indifference on his part hurt as much as airlessness had. I slipped to the floor and went to my knees. I bowed my head and said nothing. I could not say or think anything for a long time.

"Do what you will, Dagon, my mate," I said. "Punish me if you wish. I will accept it. But I do not want pain as part of what we have together. Give it to me now, if that is what you have to bring to me tonight. Bring whatever you wish to me. Just do not abandon me now."

I remained still while I felt him study me. I still ached for him. I feared only one thing: that he would walk away from me or send me away. Anything else, including death at his hands, I would accept.

"I surrender to your wishes, my Alpha," I said. "Do what you will."

He lifted me onto the bed then and his gaze was what I had hoped. I watched the flames flare in his eyes. I felt his heat rise. He drew me down to him and continued watching me as I moved to meet his own movements. When he knew how close I was, he abruptly put me beneath him and took me hard until I cried out. And cried out. And we both cried out.

We did not discuss pain again for a fairly long time.

To casual inspection, after a few more days I had healed well from my short journey to the Great Beyond, but I was still healing within. At times I cried out in my sleep. Other times, while awake, I would feel far away and cold. Whatever was before me receded in importance to me. I stood frozen until I could regain myself in this time and place. I feared that I would hurt Dagon's feelings if I disappeared at some critical moment with him.

I also feared that it would continue or even grow worse. Like looking through the wrong end of a scope, suddenly everything became small and far away. In fact, it did happen sometimes at inopportune times. I once returned to feel Dagon rocking me, still within me and doubtlessly hoping I would return. But meanwhile he just rocked slowly, and I felt like I was in a small boat, riding safely at anchor in a protected bay. I knew he was with me, and waiting for me to regain myself. Without the added fear of this making it worse, it slowly became a rarer occurrence. I never noticed when it stopped.

At the end of my first week home, Dagon asked me if I would speak to Morag.

He had informed her briefly of why he had been away for days and she had been waiting for a time when I would be recovered enough to speak of what had happened to me, if I would.

I just nodded. In truth, I did not wish to speak of what had happened, or what I had chosen to do. I felt shame now—not the relatively minor shame of standing confused and naked before a group of Sidhe. Instead I had had time to think of what I had done—again—to Dagon! If Fiórcara had tested me, I had tested Dagon and forced him to make an alliance he would never otherwise have agreed to. I had coldly gone to my death without a farewell to my mate and Maker. Dagon was the one who truly loved me and he had had to accommodate himself to the repercussions of my choice.

I arose early but Morag was at the door immediately. She had been the Leader of the Shadakon and of me and again, I wondered how closely she could still monitor me. I let her in and dropped my eyes. She stood looking at me and I dropped without thought at her feet. She remained silent and still and finally put her hand on my head.

"*Rise, Danu,*" she mind-spoke. She sat and gestured for me to sit but not so close such that she could not observe me clearly. She exhaled in a sigh and looked at me deeply, holding my eyes.

"You may see within," I said quietly. I knew, of course, that she could make that happen anyway and felt that it was coming, but she shook her head.

"*You have shown the one who most needed to know. I do not want to see Fiórcara driving you to ecstasy anymore than you wanted to see him giving and receiving that from another.*"

I looked at her with questions.

I had once asked her if she, a one-time companion of Fiórcara—*Perhaps more,* my heart whispered—still yearned in the spring.

She had attempted to indicate to me the costs I would pay but I had gone forward as the Fool, stepping happily off the edge of all safety and familiar reality.

I hoped that Fiórcara had saved me for similar reasons that he had healed Morag. But he had told me, that a person's usefulness to him decided their fate.

Apparently we were both still useful.

"*I hope you remember that you promised yourself to Dagon—as his mate and then as mate to him as Alpha and Leader of his clan. I told you a long time ago that if you could not respect him, you must leave.*"

I shivered. There was only one thing that I had had in my mind before launching to my death, that was: if I stayed I would never leave Between again unless I was forced out. I would no longer be able to move between my two worlds and between Dagon and the Sidhe.

And I did not believe that I could show up again at Dagon's door love-wounded and undone.

"*You chose wrongly,*" she mind-spoke sadly. "*Once again you have unwittingly set up lines of connection that may not have come to pass without your seemingly random choices.*"

"*It would have been easier for Dagon if you had died out there, or if the Sidhe had allowed that. But I told you before, he who you call Fiórcara will not allow you an easy exit. He continues to have use for you. He may continue to even want you as you want him to. But even that is changing now, is it not, Danu?*"

"*You may have your own faerie inclinations and passions, carrying their blood. But you are not fully one as he is, and you will never have the power and will that he wields. He is their king, Danu, and that is a hereditary title. He is very old and very alien and sees you more differently than you might wish to know.*"

I wanted to tell her that he had apologized to me, that he regretted pushing me out his door as my only real option, but he had specifically asked me not to do so. I had given my word on this. And I had also pledged not to speak about the other thing: the gift he gave me that kept me from my appointed death, as my body continued to die.

She continued to look at me. "*You do know that Dagon knows it all? That he had to watch his mate lie down in pain, surrendering to anything the Sidhe might choose to do—to you, Danu. Including Fiórcara laughing at your shock and painful realizations when you returned from what had been a glorious night for you?*"

"We spoke of that," I murmured.

"*Yes,*" she mind-spoke. "*You spoke of it and bowed your head. Dagon would have had to send you away as you knelt before him. It is not within his power to do so. What Fiórcara can and does to you, you do to your mate—a Shadakon Alpha Leader who constantly endangers himself by standing beside you.*"

She snarled at me.

"*Now I wish that we had somehow stopped this before it started. I wish that Dagon had done what he does so well—charmed you, flew you, enjoyed you, and then took you once he had lethal contract!*"

I said nothing. I let the pain rage through me. *She had set this into play! She had delivered me to the Sidhe.*

"*Yes,*" sighed Morag. "*I am one of the few who can understand and possibly forgive you, Danu. Dagon and I. Only us.*"

"But let me speak clearly now about the situation he is now in," she said aloud.

"He has shared blood with you many times. You are within him and he in you. And now you and a Sidhe king are joined by blood! Will you bring that to Dagon? Have you already done so?"

I stiffened in shock. "*I had not ... I had not indicated ...*"

"*Danu,*" Morag answered matter-of-factly in mind-speak again. "*You are not a secure place to leave secrets. I had guessed as much already and Dagon confirmed my fears.*"

For what it's worth—the night that you and your Sidhe went outside your usual realities and you drank deeply from his cup ... I suspect it began then. He had claimed you that way as well and Dagon realized it recently. Because you saved your own and his and my life the night of your return, he did not push you for more information. But he did see that you had been capable of putting down a seasoned warrior who held your own poisoned knife—Dagon's knife, in fact. She would have enjoyed the irony of killing you with that, but you were in possession of powers that you had not had before. Besides those—you were unarmed. She, of course, underestimated you."

"You have many of our traits, Danu," Morag continued less fiercely. *"You are attentive and able to establish the bond necessary to take from others. You can move as we do. But now you can transit as they do. You do not necessarily like taking someone to death—although you feel the euphoria of it. You would prefer it given to you second-hand. Make no mistake: Fiórcara has taken from you that which feeds his own needs. The elixir of life is not all that he requires, and he is very old and very accomplished at getting what he wants. Unlike them, we must approach our prey and work to establish an intimacy between us and them. The Sidhe's prey comes to them, begging to surrender and be taken. Do you think your confusion and sadness and half-hidden anger at him were not up for him to take, even as you stood shivering before him in Between? Have you hidden from yourself the fact that he knew, before you stepped outside the door, where you were going? Your life had a tipping point at that moment.*

Longer than ten seconds and the damage might have been enough to kill you, retrieved or not."

"Less than that, and you could have probably survived on your own, albeit painfully. How long do you think you hung dying over the curve of this planet you love? How long did he leave you out there?"

"He, too, left you on the edge, Danu, and perhaps past the edge. Now you have died and been revived by him as well. And Dagon lay beside you in the Sidhe's hall. He lay on your faerie lover's bed that had been prepared for you and the Sidhe's activities with you! Dagon is a predator; he could smell the lingering passion you exude. Dagon held you there and kept you from a death that had been orchestrated by a clan that the Shadakon has never had connection with before. What do you think his critics would do with this information?"

I wept. She did not comfort me.

"And one more thing, Danu," she finished, as I stopped and fell into a deep silence. *"You have promised to return to him. As always."*

I looked up into her green wolf eyes. *"What am I to do, Morag?"* I asked simply.

"This is the thing with you, Danu. I don't know. None of us know, and we know that you don't either. Dagon and I both know that you do not act out of malice or covert wishes for power. If I thought that was true I would do my best to kill you right now.

At very least you would be locked away to suffer and consider your actions for a very long time. We do use our basements at times."

I returned to my knees before her and bent my neck. I think then that I almost hoped that she would do what she threatened me with and I surrendered to whatever fate she might bring to me.

Time stopped for a very long time.

"Oh no, Danu. You would tempt me to further undo Dagon? He barely passes as a confident Alpha now. He would find you and hate me, and all would be lost."

Then I knew that I was not the only one who felt fiercely protective of my dark and powerful Alpha mate. Once again Morag and I were sistered in an eerie constellation of those we wanted, those we loved.

She brought me to a standing position. Once again she kissed me briefly on the cheek.

And then she let herself out, and was gone.

CHAPTER FOUR

BACK TO WORK, BACK TO NORMAL?

★★★★

Dagon now went regularly to the fair and plied his trade while I pondered my status in Between. Was I merely convenient prey, who delivered herself regularly to be useful or interesting as the Sidhe king chose? I vowed that I would not ask to come to him. I did not know what I would do if he requested my presence, I had to be content to leave it at that.

I cannot say that I did not wonder what his activities were when I was not in Between. I had never thought to do so before. I had allowed myself to feel that I was overly significant to him, or, at least, that I had his full attention. But I now knew that I should question these beliefs.

Now I knew I had been wrong.

But why would a powerful being such as himself not avail himself to pleasure as he wished? I had been content not to know. But when I thought of him now, I saw the beautiful ones close by him, stoking each other's pleasure and, of course, his own. I could see this as a mutually pleasurable way to pass the winter. Why had I been so sure that joining them would result in my downfall? Was my intuition about this merely a long-held, unquestioned prejudice, instilled on Old Earth where the churches still attempted to outlaw all pleasures but those that they sanctioned?

As much as I had softened around the fact the Dagon could and did kindle and pleasure anyone who came to him (and who paid him and signed contract), I hadn't fully understood until I witnessed it.

I now went back to view the memory of my brief interaction with the male Sidhe who was seemingly willing to do to me what his kind did best, and do so unselfconsciously in the presence of his king and lover, who would have been busy with her own interactions with Fiórcara.

"Well-known if not best friend," Fiórcara had said of himself after our first encounter. Would I be merely better known after such a night?

And now I suspected, no I knew, that Fiórcara had observed and sensed what occurred the day he brought Dagon to Between and we joined in the glade there.

Occasionally I took out the small green stone that Fiórcara had given me before I came to him the first time. It glowed when he was present. But today, it only reflected the sun and I put it away again, vowing not to repeat what I was doing. It only proved that I craved contact with him. I hoped I could withstand his attraction.

I decided that every time I put it away again.

Mornings were still frosty, but in the afternoon sun, water ran, finding its path on it its journey down and around and past those who would drink of it on its way to the sea. Spring was underway.

Again I worked at the nearby House of the Mothers, a hospice for any who would come to die as they chose. When I was there, I provided several more choices: inducing sleep that did not leave a drugged grogginess later, pain control and companionship, and, of course, a peaceful and quick death if they signed a contract for that. I sat and listened to their last wistful wishes: that those who they still loved—lovers, children, parents—would come and see them out of their lives. Instead, they had my company, if they wanted it. The Mothers monitored me, of course, but were pleased that I took my time to present their choices and did not influence my patients in the one they eventually made.

I wore the long robes that they wore, and kept my red hair tied back; sometimes I covered it as well. I could not, however, cover what I was, and what I offered. I was paid in small amounts of energy, with the occasional bigger pay off of a human's entire life energy. I took from them gently but quickly, much as Dagon had taught me. I did not regret my actions, having carefully checked beforehand for inner permission, as well as having a signed legal contract. Often I had to wait a little longer for the former.

Often they suddenly yearned to die and I would calmly see them across that line. At these times I would come home bearing extra energy and, since Dagon still fed me regularly, I was happy to provide for him when I could.

Dagon and I fell into a routine. We were present and attentive to each other. Our pleasure was there to be called up and yet, increasingly, we did not.

I struggled alone, wondering if I was solely to blame for the lessened bond between us. When he was not home, I wondered if he found other, newer pleasures apart from me. He had not shown his anger to me since our first reconnection and truly little even then. He had not asked what Morag and I had spoken of. He did not ask me to attend clan meetings with him. He walked as ... a solo Alpha. I wanted to believe he was posturing to throw off any questions that might arise about he and I, and my ties to Between and the Sidhe. I did not doubt that some information moved from our private sphere to the wider one of the Shadakon. Being a clan able to read both mind-speak and under-mind made this almost inevitable. Morag had once refused to give me the name of my nemesis (Dagon's sometimes Blood lover); she had said thinking it or whispering it in my sleep would draw her closer to me. I understood both the magical and practical logic of this. Morag had also told me repeatedly that I was easy to access, so, I understood why I could not attend clan meetings with him.

As Morag had said, I was "... not a good place to leave secrets." It was not the first time she had commented on the fact that I did not shield my thoughts well.

I would have liked to see Dagon in front of the Shadakon, a confident and proud Alpha leader. But I knew I would not be contributing to that with my presence. It saddened me; the whole unspoken process between us saddened me.

I grew quieter and quieter, both in speech and mind-speak. I attempted to remain calm, but in truth I was not.

And, of course, Dagon knew, if not why, at least that I felt the distance between us. He now shut doors and stayed behind them. Where once I had felt his passion for me and confidently appeared when I could not deny my own, I now looked sadly at the closed door to his library. If I had knocked or called out to him he would have probably politely engaged with me in some fashion, but only because I asked.

We did not fly together anymore. On one full moon I sat and watched it through the window and ached. I was sure that he heard my thoughts. The moon set hours later and I was still huddled in front of the window. When I went to our bed he was seemingly not in the house; he was certainly not in our bed.

I slipped out before dawn and stood alone in the still frosty morning. Dispassionately, I noted that the first green shoots were coming up along the line where the snow melted.

I was the proud mate of an Alpha and had fought for him successfully against long odds. I had died for him and, most recently, he had called me back from my own death, floating high in the evening sky, above the glowing atmosphere of this planet.

I walked and wept.

The green stone stayed dark.

Both of them then were ignoring me then. Human women had always been punished for loving or sexing outside of the expectations of their society. I hadn't been able to move past this, despite my transformation away from my humanness. A distance continued to grow between me and both of my lovers.

I considered a final leaving, but would not do so without speaking with Dagon, and I could not bear to think how that talk would go. So I delayed and waited and the days grew longer.

It might have been the same week, or one soon after. I stood outside his closed door and called him to come to me. There was silence within—total silence. He was shut down so as not to provide any information. This was not an I'm-thinking-how-to-say-this silence.

I persisted. My emotions were there for any and all to perceive, especially him. When I could no longer stand, I sat on the floor and waited. There was no window in that room so he would have to come out eventually. I would wait.

He must have understood that this would be a long or short standoff, but eventually we must come into each other's presence. He opened the door and stood in it, not stepping out to me. He looked very calm. *Indifferent?*

I felt pain radiate throughout my body. I was glad I was sitting but brought myself to kneel at his feet. There we stayed.

He reluctantly touched my hair, but even this touch seemed merely ritual and distant. He sighed finally and said, "Rise, Danu." I fought for every calm breath. He did not give me his eyes, but stared off, thinking his own silent thoughts.

"You would make me do this then, my mate," I simply said. "But I have been unable to until now. Please look at me, Dagon."

He shook his head. "You will have me if I do.

I do not wish to fall under your influence tonight. Whether you cry or swoon or demonstrate any other show of emotion—I do not want to be drawn in. Say what you would say, Danu."

The shock and pain of his pronouncement rocked me. I had felt broken bones move in my chest and felt the river of my blood draining away, I had hung in space and felt death wrap around me, bringing fierce but hopefully short pain. But this was like no other. I did not try to show him this, but it was there for him to feel and see.

"I pledged to stay beside you as your mate and obey your commands. Up until a time that you deny me as your mate, I will do what you require of me; including leaving, including dying. I was sworn not to do that without you, but I give you my permission now to change your decision. However, I would not die now without informing you. I was very wrong to do so when I fled Between without attempting contact with you."

I took one more breath of what felt like my very limited supply of oxygen. "I have had time to revisit that hasty decision. I had never allowed other humans to reduce me to feeling ashamed of who I was, but now I hold great shame and sorrow about what I did to you. I often act without thinking and, in this case, I know now that I deeply hurt you. The fact was, I thought arriving here, half-wild with faerie longing, bloody from my earlier encounter with the Sidhe and reeling from my last one, would be unbearable to you."

"I would have hurt you no matter which course I took," I continued. The companion for the night provided to me by Fiórcara looked enough like you that I could not have gone to him, until I would have had to. That, of course, was no accident.

Nor, perhaps, was my decision unexpected. Nor was the degree of my dying a random thing either. The Sidhe transit instantly. The damage that happened while I hung dying was probably done over many seconds—maybe right up to the edge of no return.

I was the bait to bring you in."

"And you came to my side," I said, beyond sadness now. "You accepted his hospitality, such as it was, drinking elixir and holding me in the very place that he had taken me as he chose. And you, of course, knew that, as he knew you would."

He met my eyes then, but there was no engagement. I hung on, for I was almost done. "You both brought me back to life. I thought somehow that we could continue on as before. I was wrong. I have lost both of you. I will not beg

EXTERRA

nor request anything further from either of you. I only ask that you free me to do what is still left to me."

The silence lengthened between us.

"I simply cannot and do not wish to live without you, my mate and Maker, my Alpha, and, yes, my lover. I simply love you more than I love anything else. Morag wanted to kill me during our talk. She stayed her hand only because it would have been confusing to you and would have broken the bonds between you and her. She is your Second in your leadership and you need her."

I stopped. There was nothing left to say.

Dagon suddenly swore an oath in a language I had never heard; it sounded bleak and black. He paced before me.

"Come here, Danu!" I shakily found my balance and crossed over to stand before him. He suddenly laid hands on me then and twisted my arm until I felt the bone flex slightly. The pain blazed up into a fiery haze.

"You profess to like pain, Danu, or, at least, you do not protest it when brought to it by your 'Best Friend.'"

I did not cry out, although the corners of my vision grew dark. I prayed—to any and all gods I did not believe in—to allow me to pass out. But Dagon knew his business in this.

He held me there, easily and seemingly calmly. I was engulfed in pain but darkness did not come.

"Now I will speak, Danu. And you will answer my questions. I will break your bones one at a time and I will be sure that you are conscious for all of it." He let go of the one he had and it hung in spasm at my side.

For a moment he did not have his hands on me and I could have transited then, or even taken him with me to Between. He read that thought and grabbed the other one.

"I will not flee from you, Dagon. I have nowhere to go. There is nowhere I want to go, even now. This has been long in coming and I could have accepted it better on the day of my arrival, but I accept my fate at your hands now."

"Clever, Danu," he said icily. He began wrenching the other arm to a sickening point of pain.

I stood as still as I could, for each shudder stirred up additional agony. *Where was the merciful shock?*

"I am good at what I know how to do here," Dagon said. He was now staring into my eyes, taking in my pain as it came off of me in waves.

"How often have you transited to Between since we came home? Tell me the truth and I will offer you some mercy in the end."

I gasped as he ever so slightly increased the pressure.

"Never."

I heard the slight inner sound of my bones breaking.

"Look if you will," I whispered. "I cannot lie to you, I never have and will not now."

He threw me to the floor then and I could not break my fall, for my arms were no longer useful. He straddled me and held my head steady and looked within. I could see and feel him through the flames of pain. I did not beg yet. I hoped it would be he who took me to my death. Perhaps I would beg him for that soon.

He did not find what he was searching for. He saw me shaking a small green stone out into my hand and then putting it away. He did not hear me calling Fiórcara. He did not find him as an active part of my now. I had not even considered returning to Between, unless he summoned me. Even then I had hoped I could refuse if that came.

I looked up at Dagon. I kept looking up at him. I was undone, the pain of his cruelty and doubt in me surpassing that in my arms. I hung onto one thought as I approached the edge of consciousness. Something he had told me once, the day I had accompanied him to his work at the fair. He had said that two things were essential for me to remember: that I loved him, and that he loved me. Nothing else. I was still sure of my part of this truth.

I heard and felt his grief strike then, although I couldn't clearly see him through the red haze of pain. I felt his sadness and shame at his actions spill over me, I heard him sob. But I knew we were still in great danger.

"Do not leave me now, Dagon. Kill me if we have arrived at that place, but stay with me through that, as I have learned from you to do with those I take. The last thing I want to see is your eyes." And then I lost my grip on awareness. Perhaps he induced brief sleep as he did what he did next. He set one of my broken arms; the other was stressed but would heal straight.

Then he called Morag. She came straight away or perhaps she was already on her way before he formally called her. She found us both on the floor and took it all in.

"Oh, Dagon. Oh, Danu." She lowered herself down to where I lay and he crouched beside me. I had partially returned. Someone was crying; it was not me. I was beyond tears. She did not touch him, as he was an Alpha, even in his grief. She did take partial control from him by setting him to a task that might, at least temporarily, give him something to focus on.

"You have set this well," she said. "Study the natural shape of her arm and go find a branch that best approximates it. We might as well bind it while she heals."

While he was gone she took away my pain—at least the pain in my broken arm. She quietly noticed the other arm and looked at me. "You were not aware of his power," she said quietly. "He hid it from you. He believed you hid things as well—and you did," she added matter-of-factly, "but not what he thought. The Sidhe king has dwelt in his fears since you returned. The situation took him too far from his centre. He did what he had to do, but meanwhile he raged to be in the situation you put him in."

She stroked my hair. "Not that I am excusing what he did to you today, but for once you got the answers you did not ask for. Today you know what Dagon has carried since you returned from Between."

"You are both in terrible jeopardy again. I will only give you one piece of advice now: do not go back to Fiórcara. Even if you have to go to the island, or the basement, or anywhere he can't get to you or you to him. If there is such a place," she said sadly. "Your death at this time is not an acceptable solution," she added. "Dagon may need some time to realize what he has done and what you did not do. Give him that time. Keep your heart open a little longer," she said. There were tears in her eyes.

Then she induced deep sleep and I slid under, free of pain.

CHAPTER FIVE

NOW WHAT, MY LOVE?

I woke up in relative comfort but immobilized by two injured arms. I took that in for a moment before the rest of what had happened crashed in on me and I moaned. I sensed Dagon nearby and at first I was reassured, then a new terrible fear washed over me. He had calmly and intentionally broken my bones and promised me he would continue on and keep me conscious while he did so. He had looked at me without any feeling as I sank deeper into the pain he was causing. I could not breathe when I thought of it.

The room was dim. I was on our bed, terribly weary and hungry. *Had he given me permission to die and leave him without further affecting him as Alpha?* I couldn't remember. How I wished that Fiórcara had allowed me my escape! Trying to rearrange the past was a futile exercise. I had, as I saw it, no future. Finally, I wept.

Morag and Dagon approached the bed where I lay. She stepped forward first.

"You are with us then," she said to me. "Good." I dimly remembered her saying that to me when I entered the last phase of my trial by hunger.

"Am I still on trial?" I mind-spoke her.

"No. Dagon is."

I turned my face away.

"Is that truly how you want to continue, Danu? Do you not want to retain what you hung onto throughout what he put you through—that he loves you and you love him? Do you want to even try to see if your faith in each other can be restored?

I looked within. I found pain that surpassed anything he had done to my body. I saw his calm attentiveness to his task of breaking me—in truth breaking my bones—but worse, showing his indifference to me. Taking in my pain as information only. *How could we continue on from that moment?* But, as I was still alive, I needed to settle the question of gaining his permission to die. I thought of the knife then, and wondered if I could somehow reach it.

Dagon stepped forward. He did not sit nor try to touch me in any way, but knelt beside me with his head bent. I felt his sorrow and confusion about what might come next.

"Oh, Danu!" Dagon mind spoke. He then continued to stay by my side without speaking or mind-speaking.

"I want to finish our conversation," I said, "but I beg you not to inflict more pain on me. I thought I could handle whatever you needed to say or do, but I was wrong. If I can gain permission from both of you—I want to leave now. Leave permanently. Not find myself restored yet again."

I shook and my body subtly attempted to move away from his, from he who had, with so much skill, given me pain. The same he who had once brought me to my first taste of bliss.

So we stayed for a long while.

"I do not give you permission to die," he said softly. "Not yet. I ask only for a little time from you. If you still feel this way later, I will ask that I can travel on that road with you. But for now, neither of us will be allowed to use the easy out. Morag has the knife. She will return it to us in ten days. Whatever solutions or forgiveness we might achieve by then will either hold or will not."

"I beg you to look at me," he said. "Just that. I will not touch you again unless you want me to. I know I do not have your inner permission to do so now, and I know I might never have that again." He went silent, but it was not a silence of shutting me out.

The pain in him was as severe as any I had felt at his hands. There was just nothing more to say. "Why did you do this?" I asked finally. "Because you could? Because I had accepted slight pain at the hands of the Sidhe in the service of greater passion? How could you have done this to me?"

At first he remained silent but finally he spoke. "What I say next is in no way an excuse for what I chose to do to you. But please know this: I have been many, many different Dagons in my long life. One of the reasons that I stopped trying to love humans is that they have all eventually betrayed me. I walked in jealousy and pain until I learned not to feel love anymore. I thought I had triumphed over my rage that came specifically from seeing lovers who I had trusted screaming for my death. Or became indifferent to my pain."

He was silent again.

"You came in under my radar," he said. "You came in as a kindred spirit and I felt your full acceptance of me. Eventually, I felt safe to love you, as you did about me." He sighed. "I think that has changed between us."

We were both silent.

"At one time in my long life, I was an interrogator. I had the job of extracting information. Pain shortens that process considerably, as does the threat of continuing the pain indefinitely. And I was very good at what I did," he said simply. "Now you know firsthand."

I shuddered.

My mind lingered, however, on his statement of extracting information. He had told me that Fiórcara had gone into my mind while I was experiencing the pain and ecstasy in our first union and I recalled Fiórcara's surprise that I continued to want him after a long night of this. I had thought he brought me pleasure—and he had—but it came at a cost.

I looked at and into Dagon. It was a brave act but I knew that we would have to reach it at some point or we would fail each other and ourselves.

"Lie beside me."

He did not immediately move to do so.

"Do not avoid this. If you can give pain, then you must now receive it. Not from me, but from the part of you that wishes that this day, this moment, had never happened. I have lived with my version of it since I returned from Between with you. I allowed myself not to see or acknowledge your feelings because, as you have accused me of before, I often think of things only in relation to me and what I want. I wanted all to be well, when it fact it was not, my mate. You continued to use your professional skills to keep our sexual connection intact—until you could not even do that. You treated me as prey, and our connection as a necessary duty. I went to my death outside of this world because the one in front of me would have done the same, while Fiórcara watched and sensed all with interest."

"We will be together and thrive, or I, and perhaps you, will not exist. I can wait ten days for that, but let us not waste any more time."

He edged up on the bed beside then. I dispassionately noted that my body, which he had held at the edge of agony, wanted his. It surprised me, but I did not give in to it. I looked within him; I felt his sadness and pain, I felt his hopelessness that we could somehow get past this. I felt his love, reaching out to me even as he attempted to shut that door. I continued on. *"All we have to remember,"* I mind-spoke softly, *"is that I love you and you love me."*

He sobbed then, and tears slipped down both of our cheeks. One of us touched the other. In this case, I am sure it was me who touched him. I used my least injured arm to reach him briefly and I felt him receive my touch. I knew then that I had not lost him.

Relief rushed through me and drove out most of my fear—but not all of it. That would not be banished in a single moment.

"I might as well get this said as well," I said sadly. "I drank the Sidhe's blood. I was not in a position to refuse or even know what I was doing. For what it is worth, I thought I took from you, until I realized later how it had affected me."

He looked at me questioningly.

"It is as attracting as the rest of them is," I said wearily, "but I have not wanted to repeat that. And I will ask now, even if the answer may not be what I want to know, does this mean that you will not wish to enjoy me in that way anymore? Because faerie is now part of me."

I braced myself for his answer—I had to know.

"You would even think of deep sharing with me at this time?" he asked in amazement. "You would have a concern about that—now?"

"Look and see," I mind-spoke. "Put aside your sadness and remorse for a moment and see what is."

He did so.

"I would have you as you are, whoever you are, now and forever," he mind-spoke. *"It was always there—your Otherness, from humans, from the Shadakon. I felt and saw it from the beginning, but even more strongly when I came to you in Between. When you came to me there, it was as he must come to you: as a force of nature, greater than merely who you are. The struggle I had to resist you over the last weeks fuelled my anger—the anger that*

you had that much power over me. I once suggested that you might be my Alpha; I jested then, but there is truth in it."

"I did not break you, my mate, even as I inflicted your pain with my own two hands, *your will held firm. I was the one who journeyed into what I now understand as hell.*

I know that I would have rather burned under the sun."

"Love under will," he whispered. "You taught me that ... again."

"One more thing then," I said. "Please don't interrupt me in this. When you snapped the bones in my arm, for one heartbeat I remembered Lore. She was a fine warrior. Our contest was thrown by Sidhe intervention. I never asked how you came to be in the long hunger in your own basement, but in the end she betrayed you as well."

He said nothing, but was following along with me.

"I never asked or indicated that I thought you might need to grieve her, to grieve what was once between you and her. She had been part of you for centuries, and I killed her, with your knife."

Still he was silent—and not breathing.

"I am sorry, my mate, for my part in that. I did what I had to do. I did not enjoy the outcome, although I was relieved. I never thought to ask or even listen to what you carried in your heart about this."

We looked into one another. Tears glistened in his eyes and in mine. How could two be so close and yet avoid knowledge of each other's places of pain? I felt him come close to me, as close as sharing. I wanted him, wanted us to find the ease we had had at our beginning. I wanted him to want me to be part of him.

"What do you wish from me now, Danu?" he asked huskily. "I would do anything. I want to do anything in my power to help us put this behind us."

"No, I do not want to forget this, and I don't want you to either." I remembered once holding an empty wine glass in my hand. It seemed so fragile and I curiously bore down on its fragile stem until it snapped in my hand. *"That much force then,"* I had thought.

"Just that much. There will not be a second time," I said. "Or, if there is, you will either kill me or I will make you do so. Or I will drag us both to some shameful place of reckoning in front of others. I did not transit today because, in part, I believed I deserved at least some of what you brought to me. And I believed that I had nowhere to go. But I will not endure more from you like this; it would be no favour to you or me. I do not want to meet that earlier Dagon again. Hell has a way of growing on one ..."

We lay in silence.

"And now is the time that you must speak of the complications that I bring due to being part of the Sidhe. You have the right to know what you need to know. You have seen within what happened to me there—at least some of what happened. You have seen the changes in me with the seasons."

Dagon did not speak or mind-speak.

"I will answer whatever you want or need to know. If there are things you still do not know, it is because I felt they would further hurt you."

He sighed. "Will you return to Between, in spite of the pain that is in store for you there?"

I searched within. "I have not contacted Fiórcara since I left. I wanted to. You saw that. He is letting me experience distance from him. He is waiting to see if I will set aside my pride and request his company. If I do not make contact, he may let me go." I shook my head. "But I do not truly believe that; and you should not overly hope for that outcome. He has used me to get to you, and I assume he will continue to do so. He knows his effect on me, as do you."

"And?" Dagon mind-spoke. "If you had to choose?"

I sighed, wishing I could give him the answer he wanted.

"That was the choice recently put to me as I saw it. I chose a third option: final death.

I did not expect to be retrieved from my desperate action. I cannot choose to refuse go to him if he summons me. In that he has done something far worse to me than what you did. I can heal from your worst acts against me, but it seems that I cannot heal from my bond to him."

"It is that way with you and I," Dagon mind-spoke. "I cannot leave you or send you away. I will take you back again and again, in whatever state you may arrive in. I will not appreciate that, but I will never raise my hand against you again. He cannot make that happen. And if you did not flee to Between in your time in my hands, I do not think you will have the need to use that way out in the future."

"Well," I said. "May that be true, for now, anyway." I added," We don't need ten days then. I am hungry and wondering how I can possibly have you with no arms at present. I will not speak of all this again unless I feel we have drifted back into dangerous waters."

He was with me; he was right there! He edged closer and bit down into his palm and offered it to me. I drank deeply, watching him and feeling his energy enter me. I shifted slightly, baring the place where he most wanted to take me when he wanted to take me in the old way.

He did not hesitate. Whoever and whatever I was now, he relished me; he took without concern. I felt our energies pool and burn together. Our silence, then, was that of bliss.

And that is how Morag found us later, both of us looking up with sated eyes and one reality between the two of us.

She shook her head and left quietly.

CHAPTER SIX

BUT IT IS SPRING AGAIN

Spring came closer. The first flowers appeared and there were furled leaves of every colour of green waiting for their cues to come out.

I felt it. As I had last year, I felt the season arriving before it manifested. The wind tasted different and the air felt different upon my skin. The sun moved across me as a touch that I could feel. I walked outside more—into driving spring rain and moments of breakthroughs of bright sunlight. I loved it.

I hated it. I could feel it within me. I was surprised that I didn't look different than my winter self. I wouldn't have been surprised to find myself looking back from the small mirror I sometimes consulted with bright green eyes.

I did not look at the stone. I knew if I looked and it was shining that I would not be able to stop myself from attempting contact. I walked with a mantra of: "*I-will-not.*"

I was hot with the spring energy rising up in me. I came to Dagon and he simply put down whatever he was doing and drew me to him. I wanted him. I wanted him. I wanted …

He knew. But he also knew I fought with all my will. I wore the gowns of the Mothers and stayed inside, until I could not. I sat patiently with those faced with their dying—until the day I could not.

The Mother summoned me into her small office and indicated that I sit. She faced me and smiled kindly.

I did not feel judged, or if judged, only in a realistic way. I knew what was coming.

"You are restless, Danu," she said.

"Your work is still good but I don't want to have to talk to you if one night it is not. You are more distracted. You bring the energy of spring in with you. Our patients do not look forward to new growth and vigour. Instead, they search for calm endings."

She stopped and watched me for my response.

She was right. But if not working …

She smiled. "I have been in contact with the Mothers on the island. You were able to be there and working right up until last midsummer's eve. You can walk and swim and take yourself apart from others there. I will not tell you what to do. But your position there is open if that is helpful. Later, we will be glad to have you with us again."

The Mothers spoke little and this had been a long conversation. She stood and I stood. And I left the gown behind as I walked out of the building.

Later at home, I simply told Dagon that I had been laid off. And then, because I was working very hard to be transparent to him, I told him why.

Once again, if I stayed, I would be dependent on his hard-earned energy every day. No one succeeds daily at our way of living, of hunting. My daily need would put him in deficit. He didn't bother to argue this point with me. The Shadakon were dependent on energy that cannot be funded and that is their major vulnerability. A Blood could go a day or more, or be under-fed for a few days, but it showed.

Dagon was an Alpha, and he needed to show strength at all times. Having a hungry Alpha was not a concept that the clan would accept.

Meanwhile the Sidhe had been moving quietly to secure the wild land and forests of this planet. Announcements had been made, and warning signs and electric barriers were going up with clear information of what awaited any trespassers.

It was time to ready the patrols of Shadakon who would willingly hunt down and take anyone who disregarded those warnings. All contracts would be lethal ones in the protected zone. This would require meetings to discuss details and expectations, and meant that Dagon would be contacted soon. Both of us waited, not willing to make connection for our own very real reasons, but finding the inevitable day something that we could not forget for very long.

Once again, I had to go. If the Sidhe did reach out to us in two days, I would have to attempt to transit to the island. I needed to see if I could still do it. I didn't want to be dependent on flitter travel.

This required Dagon to let me go. To trust me to, if not be true, at least return. It required me to trust him not to fall back into the dark thoughts and anger that had almost ruined us.

I found myself absent-mindedly rubbing the once-broken arm that was now fully healed. There was a ghostly pain in it. Whenever I saw Dagon looking at me, I immediately stopped. The first time he noticed he went still and quiet. I went to him and stood in his arms.

"It will pass, my love." But perhaps both of us wondered if the horror of it would ever totally leave us.

Would leave me.

I could not delay my decision and he already knew what was coming. It was the cost of living a long time—but only on others' energy. It would be that or the elixir of life and I had no reason to believe that I would be granted elixir by the Sidhe. I had to work. Dagon had to work.

We slept lightly that night. I did not want to be apart from him for any length of time, but did not want him remembering me as needy.

I was needy. I wanted to stay with him. I wanted him to kindle me and come to me; to wrap me in his arms and keep me safe. He came and found me and we lay together until dawn

As the sun rose, I had a certainty that I had not had in a long time: Fiórcara was close by. I didn't bother to shake out the small green stone; I knew it would be glowing. We stepped into the gone-wild garden behind Dagon's house. Fiórcara was standing in a beam of morning sunlight.

"Well met," he said somewhat formally to Dagon. "We have some upcoming business to conduct, Leader of the Shadakon." Everything he said was courteous, but it had a faint twist of something cold underneath.

Then he turned to me. I stood in the early morning sun and begged any old gods and goddesses whose names I still remembered to assist me in not wanting him.

He just shook his head. "And, Danu, you are going to the seashore to renew yourself. Will you be taking a flitter or …?" He smiled his faintly mocking smile, "… or trying out your new skills? I would have thought that you might have taken a few more practice runs by now."

"I will attempt the trip," I said. "I wish to be inconspicuous in my travel."

He turned back to Dagon. "I have a proposition for you both. Let us all go to the beach. Danu can get us there, and I will merely be a back-up plan. Dagon, I will bring you back in time for … lunch."

It seemed reasonable and I was secretly relieved. I had gone once on my own, but the night had been charged and I had been at full energy. I was not absolutely sure of myself, but I felt the entanglement of the situation for both Dagon and I.

Dagon had not gained and held Alpha status without learning a lot about choosing the best path among limited choices. He also was capable of appearing satisfied with what he must then do. He smiled.

"Both of us must feed today, Sidhe. But I would like to see Danu settled into her new position."

And so, we stood together, with Dagon in the middle, and I pictured the beach and heard the waves. I smelled the salt in the wind and … launched.

My first breath assured me that I was where I wished to be. We three stood in front of the log where I often sat, where Fiórcara had first found me, where he had taken me to Between on our first midsummer's eve.

Fiórcara smiled. We sat, and after a few pleasantries, Dagon and he talked numbers regarding the patrolling Shadakon, wages (they were not assured prey) and contract. All the time that they talked rationally and logically, I felt Fiórcara's energy extend well into my space although his actions gave nothing away. If Dagon felt it, he did not comment or show it.

I briefly took and held Dagon's hand and then gently let it go. I did not want to bid an emotional farewell to Dagon in Fiórcara's presence; nor I did want Dagon to witness or sense what was happening to me. I excused myself to go inside and check in with the Mothers. They had known, of course, why I was coming. Had they looked out the window, they would have witnessed us and drawn their own conclusions, but even if they did, I knew they would never ask me or refer to it.

When I looked at the log it was empty and as there was no one inside immediately needing my attention, I returned to it and sat down, letting my eyes go as far as I could to the horizon. I tried to ignore my need and achieve calm; I came close.

"A picnic then?" asked Fiórcara, appearing suddenly beside me. "Since it is a lovely day here and you have no work to attend to." He handed me a cup. Elixir of life. I knew that he could and did read me closely, and that he knew I was in need. I too chose my best and only choice.

Longing forced me to drop my eyes to him.

I felt my body disregard any plan I might come up with to deny it; it called out to him.

He smiled. "Ah, Danu, so passionate. I am always happy to feel your desire for me. In spite of everything ..."

I took the cup. I looked at the faerie lover who had left me hanging, dying, in the night sky of this planet and who was part of what I had endured at the hands of Dagon. I asked with my eyes as I took it from his hand.

"No, Danu. I have never wanted your death and do not now. This is a courtesy to you as I sense you are hungry and that enquiries at the hospice were not immediately promising. You and I must renew ourselves every day."

"Walk with me, Danu, in this favourite place of yours."

He extended his hand, and when our hands met I knew that I had made no progress in resisting him. He smiled then and drew me along with him down the beach. We stopped around a bend in the shoreline, in the small cove we had laid down in on a night when the sky flared above us. He removed my clothes and ran his hands down from face to arms; he lingered on my arms and frowned. He touched my back lightly where no sign of his own marks on me showed to others. I shuddered. Then he lay me down in the sunshine and sand and looked down at me, pausing as I waited breathless.

"Contract, Danu, or at least a renewing of our friendly agreement. We parted under difficult circumstances. I was not careful in securing your agreement for pleasure last time, and I will not make that mistake again. But now, Danu, what do you want from me?"

"*I want you.*" I mind-spoke, for I had no breath to speak. "*I want what you would bring to me today.*"

"Yes," he said and smiled. "I generally would like that spoken aloud.

But I see that you are beyond that at this moment. Perhaps we should have negotiated before I ... or you ... began."

"*Please.*"

"Ah, Danu. We will have this dance and many more. I feel spring quickening in you like a freshening tide. It will, of course, carry you along as the season builds to midsummer."

And then he brought sun and spring and the life of this planet to me. If I was the shoreline, he was air and the life web's song that sang through it. The sun moved across the sky and still we continued until I wept. He knew I was not making a complaint and continued until I lost all sense where he or I or anything else was separate. Finally, I closed my eyes and sank into the earth.

When I opened my eyes he was gone.

Dagon had been gone for less than an hour before I had totally surrendered to the Sidhe.

CHAPTER SIX

BACK WHERE 1 STARTED FROM?

I slipped into the cold water, allowing the chill to cool me from my activities and hopefully remove the more obvious traces of how I had spent my day. While walking back to the hospice I tried to piece together the facts of my life now.

I was here—Dagon there. Once again, my vulnerability to spring and to Fiórcara kept us apart. Once again I would attempt to find and build on the calm that was more accessible to me here than anywhere else.

Except when Fiórcara showed up. But I sensed that he had had his fill of me for a while and, in truth, my underlying relentless thinking of him had been eased. He had wanted me and treated me with care; I was still useful to him in that way. More and more, I sensed that what I struggled against was not only him, but also the life force that was carried within the Sidhe … the life magic that would assure that any and all capable of procreation would find each other this way, and pay whatever dues necessary to complete their part in producing new life. Ironically, Fiórcara and his clan and the Shadakon had stepped outside of renewing their numbers.

Or had they? I existed, an individual who carried both bloods. Perhaps not fitting into the human herd put the outsiders at higher likelihood of finding each other … of creating new life together and having the survival skills to keep such a child alive.

Did Dagon have children? Had any of them survived to this time? Did Fiórcara? The Sidhe seemed less likely to combine with humans. I tried to imagine a child who faded in winter and who was beautiful in an unearthly way. Was it possible?

Obviously it was. I could not be the only one.

I arrived at the door and put these thoughts away. A Mother (the same who I had connected with during my other stays here) met me and ushered me to the corner room where I had slept while with them. It was a kindness that made my eyes sting with tears.

She smiled. "I will not say that your previous contribution guaranteed you this. But we are happy that we can accommodate you here." We both remembered me gifting the Mothers a coin of faerie gold on my previous visit.

She was silent and observed me carefully. I had come to assume that, although I could not perceive it, she could and did read me: my mind-speak and under-mind and body as well as any Shadakon or Sidhe could. But I had never felt invaded by her gentle direct contact. I waited. I could hear the sea outside the window and it was soothing to me.

"We were informed that you were in a state that perhaps excluded you from the work we do here. Since our patients are more ill, it seemed possible that your state of … excitement … would not be as obvious to them, but I sense that you have somehow corrected that." She smiled.

From my window I could clearly see the log where we three had sat earlier today. And later I had sat with the Sidhe king and drank the elixir of life before taking a long walk with him.

Early on in my life, I had vowed not to take on false shame or embarrassment that others might strive to put on me. Earlier on in my life, I had not been she who would walk down a beach in full daylight and willingly lie on the ground, begging to be pleasured by a faerie. Apparently it was now my life task to come into my own acceptance of this. I met her eyes.

"I do feel more grounded, or perhaps, more oceaned. I feel that I can do the work and to be honest, I have to do something somewhere. My mate cannot support my needs." I took a measured breath and let it go easily. I paused.

"I am under the influence of faerie," I said matter-of-factly. "I am faerie," I added suddenly, surprising myself, and possibly her as well. "I didn't know until recently that although I am more human than simply Shadakon or Sidhe, the bloods are joined in me."

She and I looked at each other and she smiled. "Our patients do not usually disappear from their beds," she said. I knew she was referring to Morag, who had previously arrived dying. Her urgent state had me negotiate a deal with Fiórcara to take her to Between to heal, and left an empty bed in the hospice in the morning.

I would not tell her the rest of that story—that Morag had been asked by the Sidhe I called Fiórcara to drink a cup that caused her to begin slowly dying. That the Sidhe had rightly assumed that I would bargain for her life with what I still had and what he wanted: my surrender to him on midsummer's eve. That knowing them and being part of them was not always a thing of dancing and joyful gatherings. I sat with these thoughts. If she took note of them she did not react in any way.

"I am confident that you are ready to work," she said. "I will introduce you to some patients if you are ready."

I put on the long pale robe of the Mothers. She got up and we walked down the hall together.

CHAPTER SEVEN

WHO WILL COME, WILL COME

My first few days with the Mothers and their patients passed uneventfully. I relieved pain temporarily, presenting myself as someone who would take the time the patient might need to trust me, if they would. And hopefully eventually trust me to deliver a painless death and grant me their life energy. Or not.

I did not short those who I knew would not sign over to me. I was often in deficit. I swam and attempted to renew myself in the water. Perhaps I was partially successful. I meditated on emptiness and not requiring anything but what was now before me. I was partially successful at that as well, but it was high spring and I knew that soon, very soon, it would be summer. I had been pleasured and put temporarily at peace by my interaction with Fiórcara, but I had not been given an invitation to join him, although he had mentioned summer in passing. One thing I did know: it was not an oversight on his part.

I would be most vulnerable then to the Call to join the Sidhe in their cone of power and celebration of the planet's life force. *Could I fly and return alone? Would it be possible to remain alone in Between on that night? What would be acceptable to Fiórcara? Or did he expect me to come and accept whatever might happen? Or might be arranged by him? Was there some small part of me that wanted to do just that?*

I would run through these questions and then put them temporarily aside. I had no information and no true indication through intuition of what path I would walk.

I was quietly attending someone who was still unaccepting of his death, still hoping that he could avoid the path he was on, when I heard a flitter land and the murmurs and sounds of transporting someone into the building. The Mothers would eventually let me know the status of the new patient. Meanwhile I sat with the man who wished only that his daughter was sitting beside him. He called her name, but I did not falsely represent myself.

"I am here," I would say. "I am not she whom you are calling for, but I will sit with you, and do what I can to ease your pain. If you so choose, I will be with you until the end."

And he would open his faded blue eyes and scowl, but then after ascertaining that I was the only one present, he would present his hand to me. Holding it and dulling his pain was slowly but steadily putting me in deficit. I felt my hunger grow. So it was; I accepted that, and distanced myself as much as possible from my own pain.

Finally he slept and I disengaged from him and stood to stretch out my back. It was the dark small hours of the morning.

The Mother met me in the hall. She looked at me with a look that I could not decipher, although it raised apprehension in me. "We must talk before you attend to the next patient," she said carefully. I had learned their habit of saying no more than what was necessary. It was not unlike Dagon's refusal to be drawn in if no question was posed. I waited.

"This patient knows you. She came here seeking you. Since few know you are here, this indicates to me that she was told by someone."

We looked at each other.

"She knows your name, Danu."

"No one knows of my work here except Morag, Dagon, and ..." And then my heart stopped.

If the Sidhe gave her the information she sought, I knew who she was, even though the likelihood of it was ... incomprehensible to me. "Her name is Lucia. She has already signed lethal contract," The mother said quietly. I felt frozen in time. I had last seen her as the Sidhe carried her out of the prison she had lived and suffered in as a bondservant. The inn, hidden in the deep forest, was run by renegade Shadakon, who enjoyed acting as they would without contract. I had been diverted there and locked up with a pale, weary young woman. She had been hard used there after her parents had sold her to the owners. She had been taken all the ways one can be. She knew when she met me that night that she would never leave except in death.

And yet, she had been young and still beautiful. She had wanted to live. Locked in a room with her, I had well understood what was coming for both of us. Sooner or later, I would eventually bring on her death. I felt despair beyond my individual situation.

I had asked the Sidhe to take her away, to wipe the memories of her ordeals from her mind, and I watched as they carried her away. I had not thought of her since. I assumed she would not know me, hopefully would not remember what she had endured.

I looked at the Mother with tears in my eyes. *If Lucia was here, she was going to die with or without me present. But how could she have retained my name?*

"Would you rather let this one pass?" the Mother asked gently.

I shook my head. I had given Lucia my true name and she had somehow retained it. She knew who and what she had come here for. I had given my name. My name was my word. I would attend to her.

She was propped up, thin and pale, with the characteristic skin markings of one of the more horrible viral plagues. Swirls of lavender twined up and down her arms and highlighted her now sharp cheekbones.

"Danu! It is you!" She barely breathed those words, but I could hear her soft mind-speak.

"Lucia—I can hear you without you talking."

"Yes," she thought simply. *"The faeries can too. And I can hear them sometimes."*

I sat silently for a moment. I had many questions, but satisfying them might not be important to her.

"May I scan your body for pain and to let me know what is happening to you?"

She shrugged. *"I am dying, Danu. You already know that."* She indicated her arms bearing the characteristic violet swirls indicating a lethal virus. *"The pain is not yet so bad. I fear what is coming though."*

I nodded. I would not diminish her bravery by lying to her.

"I was curious as to what happened to you," I said. *"The faeries rescued you and me. I assumed you would not remember the place I met you. Or me."*

I looked down and saw her as I had that night—still young and somehow still having an intact heart. I remembered gently covering her with the thin blanket we shared as she curled up beside me.

I remembered my relief when she was picked up and taken away in a swirl of green moonlight.

That relief had been greater than my despair. Only later did I realize that I would be rescued too.

She sighed, obviously recalling that night as well. *"The beautiful one—the faerie king—gave me a choice: I could forget everything, or I could remember. They left me with a family who had lost a daughter and who were kind to me. I became their daughter in a way.*

"I was very lucky, Danu.

And the faeries came and checked on me, even after I moved away and worked for real wages. I didn't want to forget you, Danu. I wanted to grow up to be someone like you. We sat with her last statement. I was stopped by it, held in the present with her. *I had been important to her? She had been allowed to remember? The Sidhe, who distained humans, had found her a foster family? Fiórcara, "the faerie king" had continued to check on her?* This challenged much of what I thought I had understood, about the Sidhe and about myself.

"How can I help you now, Lucia?" I mind-spoke. *"If there is pain, I can move it aside, if not remove it. Do you wish to sleep for a little while?"*

She looked at me with her green eyes still flecked with sunshine. She smiled.

"I have never seen the sea, and I have always wanted to. It is close by, I think, because I can smell something that must be a sea." She took a slightly bigger breath and I could almost see her float slightly above the bed. She was of the water then, and would easily go out with the tide when it came her time.

"It will have to be soon," she said.

I knew that too.

It was a mild night with a clear starry sky. The water was still rising but soon it would reach slack tide and the breeze would die. Then it would slowly but inexorably go out. I wrapped Lucia in blankets. The Mother watched me carry her to the log where I so often sat. Lucia had one arm around my neck; she tilted back her head to look at the sky then looked towards the water again. I heard her unspoken request. I carried her to the edge of the small waves, where the beach pebbles made musical sounds as they tumbled against each other. I felt the waves lessen.

Slack tide soon.

She was breathing quietly and I wondered if she would or could speak again. I didn't care. I was willing to stand there with her until the sun came up or until she was cold in my arms. She surprised me, though. She mind-spoke clearly. *"I never said this to anyone in that house, and they wouldn't have cared if I did or didn't, but you can take me now, Danu. It will be good for both of us."*

I felt the same trust from her I had felt almost three years ago. When I had told her I was different. When I had given her my name and told her to remember it. She leaned her head against my heart. I saw small bits of seaweed moving out with the turning tide. I took her in two breaths and she never stirred in my arms. Except …

I felt her lighten in my arms. I truly sensed her moving out, into the Great Mysteries. I sat on the log with her body and wept. Then I returned to the Mothers and handed her body over to them.

CHAPTER EIGHT

BUT FIRST WE MUST TALK

The following morning I excused myself for the day, finally having enough energy to have relief from my constant hunger. I walked to the log. There was a beautiful empty spiral shell there. I did not think the Mothers had gone beach combing and left it for me. I sat beside it and closed my eyes briefly. Fiórcara was beside me when I opened them.

He indicated the shell. "*She had a strong beautiful heart. As do you, Danu. If all humans or part humans were as you two, we would not have to take the measures we now must put in place.*"

I knew this was the truth. I said nothing, waiting to see what else he might say to me.

"*Do you have no questions of me, Danu? I would think that you would.*"

I intentionally turned to face him fully. He had again changed with the season, his eyes bright emerald green, his hair golden in the sunlight. Early summer was within him. I let myself feel the full impact of him. I did not fall off the log, though I felt dizzy with it. I stayed present. This was my opportunity and I would not let it pass by.

"*I may not know enough to ask the right questions. I think you have read what I am pondering. I long to go to midsummer's eve but have heard you not invite me.*"

Here he raised an eyebrow and smiled. "*Well trained by the Shadakon.*"

"*I have been revisiting and thinking about the night when you presented me with the chance to experience a willing Sidhe lover, or whatever I might call him. I assumed that I would lose my way and not be able to return to this life and my lover and mate here.*"

He waited.

"*I am no longer sure that I am so fragile, or that I get lost so easily.*" He said and thought nothing audible.

"*But could I answer the Call and remain solo? Am I even allowed to enter Between on that night?*"

"*Your thoughts are growing more interesting. Let me have the rest of them.*"

"*I know that it was my choice to attempt to end my life by transiting out beyond. I didn't expect to be retrieved. But ... I think you knew what I was going to do well before I did it. Did you leave me out there at the point of death when you could have gathered me sooner?*"

He said nothing. He continued to look at me. "*Do not disappoint me, Danu, and tell yourself simple stories in which others shape your life while you are powerless. Every interaction we have had has served to provide you a chance to learn. If it served me as well, so much the better.*"

"But consider: I told you that the Sidhe do not chose permanent or exclusive partners. Yet you continued to want that kind of connection from me. You also forced it on Dagon, and he struggles with your expectations of him."

"Dagon awakened your sexuality and passion. I commend him for his part in your progress. I have shown you another part of how far that can go. You have been an excellent student. I have relished my role. I still relish my role ..."

"There is more for you to discover. Your decision to die did not suit me, as you would have ceased to be useful. However, almost dying made you very valuable. Your proud Shadakon mate and Alpha lay on my rumpled bed. He set his pride aside to do so. I left you out there long enough for you and those around you to experience the full consequences of your choice."

I sat still. Not just my body, but also my mind. I had already come to these thoughts.

Here were more answers that, until now, I hadn't been brave enough to ask for. Answers that I might not want, but needed to know.

"Good, Danu! We are almost through then, although the last might be the hardest part. You are, of course, invited to midsummer's eve, and I hope you attend. You understood what was being done there and contributed to that—This was noted by others besides me. The Sidhe heard me claim you for my seasonal queen, but they know what that term means. It is a title of respect but not exclusivity, and it would be expected that both of us would take other partners as we choose. I don't know if anyone will come forward for you, and I think that flying and returning to ground alone would be another hard lesson for you. Being passionate is not an unusual trait for the Sidhe, and it may not gain you special attention."

I thought of the beautiful Sidhe who had sat by my side. Just as Fiórcara had taken in the energy Dagon and I generated while in Between, so he could or would have chosen to be present when I surrendered to the one who offered himself for my pleasure. And as I would react to Fiórcara's caresses to his partner, as well as those I was receiving, I might have been moved beyond what ever I had experienced.

I feared that, but there was truly only one way that I could discover the truth.

"Yes, Danu. You are still limited in what you allow yourself, although, as I have said, you are a quick student. But you fear losing Dagon. He fears that as well, obviously; it is why he intentionally hurt you." Fiórcara shrugged. *"Perhaps there was a lesson in that as well—not unlike suffering your pain of the failed attempt at taking your own life."*

I allowed the information to fully enter me. I noticed a long-held deep sadness, but could not attribute that to Fiórcara.

Having been alone most of my life—and having fought to remain so—I now did not want to let go of those whose company I craved, whose effects on me I craved. Only at this beach did I manage to retain my sense of self.

"Barring accidents, suicide and murder, you have been gifted with a long life," Fiórcara responded. *"You can take time to combine with others and then to come back to yourself. The stronger the experience, the more time and solitude you might need to recover."*

"And so ..." I said.

"Yes," he said. "Like the day you entered into the stand of Touch-me-not, not knowing the outcome, I invite you to attend midsummer's eve. But you must give me your word that you will not do anything dramatic to take away from that night. No flights to the stars, no weeping, no assigning blame to anyone, including yourself. If you are offered pleasure and you want it, please know that I approve. If you can withstand and enjoy my considerable charms, you will not be undone by another Sidhe. Or multiple Sidhe."

I checked myself and was surprised to find that the information Fiórcara had given me had not wounded me. There was a part of me that was deeply disappointed but there was another part that had known that I had not been attending to the truth—to what was.

And then there was the curiosity …

He smiled at me and it was like looking into the sun. "Not so hard then, Danu," he said. "And there are compensations for insisting on the truth from yourself. You will suffer less and, perhaps, be more grateful for what is."

"When a walk down the beach might merely mean a walk down the beach, there will be less disappointment if that is all it is. On the other hand …" He took my hand and we transited to the cove we had spent pleasurable time in previously.

We stood in the morning sun but I did not fall to the ground. Instead I had a different thought.

"Let me start this, this time," I said. "Before my state of body clouds my thinking."

He smiled.

"What do you want from me Fiórcara, King of the Sidhe, on this day on the edge of the sea?"

"Good!" he said. "I want what you would bring to me, Danu."

I smiled.

I took off his clothes as he helpfully raised his arms, etc. I saw him in his glory. I then took off my own.

I came close to him. I reached out but did not quite touch him. I saw that he wanted me, but this time it was he who waited.

"When?" I asked.

He smiled again. "I am completely at your service now, my Queen."

And very soon, he was.

CHAPTER NINE

VISITORS

I had managed to find a middle ground at the hospice in which I took enough energy to live. People I attended to slept a little deeper, a little longer. I left the sides of those who continued to demand more than I could give. When I talked to the Mother about this she had shrugged and said, "You need to maintain yourself, Danu. You are no use to us, or yourself, if you are giving away more than you need to live." Still, I suffered some days. My commitment to remain patient and attentive in spite of my body's circumstances grew stronger.

Full summer was upon me, and although often hungry, I burned with energy from within. I walked and swam every day. One morning, I felt the fleeting tentative touch of a large calm mind again, and half-saw a large shape moving parallel with me in deeper water. I swam out, expecting it to be long gone. The water beneath me was deep blue, clear, and alive with small shimmering shoals of fish.

It was this world's version of a whale. It rose up and up from the depths and sounded near me. I was so amazed to be approached, that it would honour me this way, that it was a moment before I realized that there was not one being beside me. There were two.

A calf not much longer than I was swam in the shadow of its mother. I hung in the water and opened myself to the wonder of this encounter. The mother, who could have easily slapped and broken me with her giant pectoral fins or tail, sculled calmly beside me. I felt time expand around us while the slight wind, the small waves on the water's surface, stilled—it was just we three in the universe. It felt like experiences I had had in Between, afternoons that lasted forever, nights of loving that lasted weeks.

Perhaps it was not the Sidhe that created this; perhaps this was as it was. The Sidhe only sensed and allowed the different times to run their courses.

I spread my arms slowly out from my body, treading water now. I mind-spoke a blessing and thanks for the gift of their presence. I promised that I would do what I could to keep their world safe for them.

The large mother came very close. I saw her great eye looking into mine. She was mind-silent and then conveyed in some way that was very clear to me, "*We welcome you here.*"

I gave her my name. "*My name is Danu. I am honoured to meet you.*"

There was a long pause. She and her calf were now moving leisurely off. But I heard, "Our clan name is … and here I felt rather than heard a deep rumbling sound. It sounded, or perhaps felt, like the open ocean, of deep dives and sleeping on the surface under the light of the moons. Of making songs that carried for hundreds of miles ...

And then they were gone.

I swam in, tired and joyful. I tried to approximate the sound I had heard. My throat was incapable of recreating it, but I remembered the feel of it in my body. It was peaceful and powerful.

I walked to the House of the Mothers. A flitter had just arrived and people were stepping down to the ground. It was Dagon and Morag.

I was wet with salt water, and my hair sleeked down with it. I felt very alive as I walked over to meet them.

I was suddenly not sure if I wanted them in my world here, but I tucked that thought away uneasily and prayed I would not touch on it in their presence. I went to Dagon and stood before him and then sunk to the ground at his feet. I said nothing aloud or in mind-speak.

He, too, was silent and did not immediately bid me rise. I might have entered into fear then, but my experience with the whales had widened my perspective and I was still in their slow time.

I waited.

"Rise, Danu."

This was an Alpha request, not an informal or friendly greeting. I rose and bent my head to him, and then to Morag. I still felt the calm of the sea within me.

He studied me. I met his eyes with no fear, no challenge; I stood as a tree, a rock surrounded by the sea; these do not have passion as we understand it. I stood waiting to discover what had brought them to me.

The silence continued. Finally I addressed him. "*You have come a long way, my mate and Alpha. I believe there is something you have come to ask me or tell me. I am interested in hearing that. Also, I will willingly let you see what you might see of how I have passed my time here since we parted.*"

The whale time was still gathered around me.

Dagon looked closed and stood stiffly beside me. "*It is four days until midsummer's eve. I wondered if you were still my mate, and what condition I would find you in.*"

"*Let us sit or walk then. Do you require Morag to be part of our conversation?*"

He shook his head. He looked weary. We walked to the log, my outside room where I lived when I was not working or resting. I felt no desire in him for me, and that saddened me. I hoped we would get to what he had come to tell me soon, and yet I dreaded it as well.

"*Danu ...*"

"*Wait just a moment more, my mate, my Love. Let me be that for a few moments more.*" We sat silently for several heartbeats.

The pain was now sweeping across the beachhead of my calm. I felt myself falling in, deeper and deeper, to the old sadness of being alone and unwanted. I struggled to hold steady, but my will was like sandbags against the hurricane surge. I took his hand in mine; the hands of our Making were palm to palm but I felt no answering thrill of energy.

"I would share what little I have with you," I mind-spoke. *"You are tired and depleted. It is a long journey to make in this condition."*

He shrugged.

"Then say what you have come to say."

He looked at me more carefully now. *"You are different. I expected tears and perhaps begging."*

It was my time to shrug. *"Tears will come later, although not begging. I will not ask for what is not freely offered. You are distant, Dagon. You continue to hide something from me. I would know your thoughts now."*

Still he remained silent.

"Would it have been simpler for you if you found me half-maddened, begging another for his attention? Or with the energy of the Sidhe on me? Or once again, fearing you?"

He was silent.

"I don't believe this is about me, as we have not been together in over a month. If you have questions, ask them, but I have little to report. I am not invited as the Sidhe's queen, although I can attend midsummer's eve if I choose. The energy raised then is fed back into the web of life of this planet—it is a powerful and beautiful night."

"Perhaps less so if alone," I said quietly. "I have not yet decided whether I will attend or not." He truly looked at me then. I had not given him the lead in that he had counted on.

"Could you go and not be with him?"

"I do not have a choice of being with him. This summer it is not as you think," I said. "And, unless I am wrong, I believe my loss will double today. You have come to announce that you wish to set me aside as your mate. Morag has encouraged you to do so. Perhaps there is a Shadakon partner who is more suitable. I was always a handicap to your and her ambitions."

"These are just guesses," I said. "I would prefer to hear it directly from you. But I felt dread when I saw the flitter. You and her are well enough I think. But you came quickly, without feeding. There is a tight timeline you adhere to today."

He was silent.

"Have you come to kill me then?" I asked with surprising calm. "Must I disappear from your world with no threat of reappearing?"

He was still terribly silent.

I stood in the light wind. My hair was drying now and fanned out around my face. It had grown longer because I wished it so. I knew I was beautiful and lean, trimmed by my frequent fasting and swimming and walking. I also knew, or thought I knew, that none of this was touching him.

Inside me, my heart was quietly breaking. *"Just remember that I love you and that you love me,"* I mind-whispered. *"I signed lethal contract with you within days of meeting you. It is, as far as I'm concerned, still valid. But I request that it be you. Only that."*

He looked away then. *"I thought this would be easy. That you would act in a way to justify what I came to do."*

I felt Morag attempting to get a read on us. I turned my head in her direction and hissed at her.

"I will accept this fate from you, Dagon, but not from her. If she would attempt to make this happen, it will be a different event."

I looked into his eyes then and saw the flames beneath the dark amber. I opened myself to him and fell, as if from a high cliff, with no thought of spreading my wings. I felt him take me hard and knew I had but one breath left. I thought of the whale and her calf. I thought of the flaring sky. *"Goodbye, goodbye ..."*

I felt a rush of feeling from him. He took me again. The stars were burning in the sky. And I was—

"NO!"

I was pulled back from my final moment with a violence that brought pain. He hurriedly spilled energy back into me. We had deeply exchanged energy many times as a loving act, but this was not like that. I stepped back from him, shaking and sickened. He stood before me, seemingly unable to move, unable to do what he had set himself to do.

"I told you before that I would not endure violence from you again, Dagon. You were given choices then. Why are we here again?" I saw the pain in his eyes and felt it hit me like a storm.

I spoke clearly and coldly, although my heart ached like a fresh injury. "You are no longer my mate Shadakon. I release you from all vows. I do not know if Making can be undone, but I will not respond if you call me in that way."

Out of the corner of my eye I saw the blur that was Morag, and I felt, more than saw, a small silver object in her hand. I transited to Between.

CHAPTER TEN

THE RECKONING

I arrived in the grove in Between and sat down shakily. I had Dagon's energy within me—and for the first time since we had joined, I felt … raped. I placed my palms on the bark of the tree that was so familiar to me, the one that had held me as Dagon and I had made … Love? Sex?

I tried not to think further than right now.

It was here that Fiórcara found me and knelt before me. He raised my chin and looked within. I felt, for the first time, his terrible anger.

"Stay here, Danu. I will send someone to attend to you." He disappeared.

Another Sidhe, the one who had been offered to me, immediately approached me. His hair was now chestnut brown with golden highlights and his eyes were hazel—the colour of ferns and moss. He handed me a cup of elixir.

I did not take it immediately.

He watched me for a moment and then said, "The human part of you is overwhelmed and in shock. You have endured much in the last few minutes. Please drink."

I took it and held it.

"Do not complicate this, Danu. You have acted strongly and spoken your own truth. You sought sanctuary instead of death."

I looked at him without will to continue, wondering why I would want to go forward from this moment.

"I do not think the whales would approve," he said then.

I drank the cup down. It was perhaps more than the usual elixir. "Yes," he said.

"You are greatly favoured by he you call Fiórcara. He would preserve you. I suggest you accept his gift and stay present for there is more to come." He left quickly.

Fiórcara arrived with Dagon. They appeared before me, Fiórcara looking older and fiercer than I had ever seen him look. Dagon looked … undone.

Fiórcara stood and looked at both of us. Dagon stared bleakly at the ground. For a moment my heart went out to him. He was no longer the proud Alpha Leader. There was no comparison between him earlier and now.

"You would hand out more pain then, Dagon? Breaking bones was not enough? You would kill her for your own ambitions?" Fiórcara hissed as he conveyed that.

Dagon remained silent.

"No … not just that. Your possessiveness regarding she and I has poisoned you. She is of the Sidhe. She is my queen although you also do not know what that means. I am not

hers—she is not mine. We have flown together in the great summer ritual of midsummer's eve. She brought that energy to me, as she did to you when you were last here." He indicated the grove around us. "*That means unless one of us chooses differently, she will always be one of my many queens, although we may never lie together again.*"

He drew close to Dagon and looked at him fiercely. "*I do not allow the Shadakon or anyone else to kill my subjects. Depending on what you tell or show me very soon, you may not live to finish the day. Do you doubt my ability to make this happen?*"

Dagon mind-spoke, "*No*," in a whisper.

I turned away from seeing him brought down this way.

"*You must stay focused, Danu!*" Fiórcara turned on me as well. "*You encouraged him to take you instead of protecting yourself. That may have been appropriate at your first meeting. You did come to him knowing what he was, what he could do, but that is last season's rain.*" He looked at me and I sensed that he did not want me to defer to him or Dagon. I felt the elixir and whatever else burning in me.

"You are Sidhe," he said flatly. "It is time to start acting like one. You are making progress but your time to claim those gifts almost ran out today. What a waste this would have been! A Shadakon leader who I have worked for years to form an alliance with. A queen who brought me joy"—he hissed at Dagon again—"both in my arms and watching her learn who and what she is."

"*You two have a little time here to talk and then I will come and determine your fate, Dagon. There is someone else I need to have a talk with as well.*" He disappeared.

Dagon looked over to me and lowered his eyes. We sat, very alone together. I listened to the wind in the top of the trees and felt the earth beneath me. Although my heart was still breaking and breaking again and again, I felt grounded and safe now. *How long had it been since I felt that way with Dagon? Would he have hated me every spring, as the life force flooded back into the land and me?*

"*You have changed, Danu. If I hadn't been driving myself forward to do what I had decided to do, I would have known that.*"

"*Yes.*" He had taught me that answer.

He looked up. "*Do you want to know how this came to be?*"

I looked within. "*Maybe later. Maybe not. Suffice to say you saw me as your enemy, or at very least an unacceptable liability, rather than your mate and lover, in spite of all that has passed between us.*"

I was crying and didn't care. The pain had finally hit, as some of my shock wore off.

"*I brought to you everything I had to bring Dagon. I thought it was enough. I thought after you hurt me that you had changed. That you had chosen to set aside your old rage and distrust.*"

"*Why did you bother to work so hard to keep me alive?*" I pictured him curled around me in Fiórcara's hill hall. I remembered his grief and longing for me there.

"*But the anger was there too,*" I sighed. "*The situation required you to set that aside as well as your pride. I did not intend to bring that to you, Dagon. I only thought to leave, a solution I have chosen again and again in my life. But now, I am not going anywhere. I will live out my span of life. If I am not safe from you, and cannot protect myself, Fiórcara will end you today. Or later. I cannot protect you from that."*

"I am learning from my mistakes," I added. *"You have built on yours. And I think even Morag is now facing Fiórcara's wrath."*

I felt the sun on my face. I breathed deep breaths of summer.

"Would you take me back, reverse your pronouncement of undoing our Making and your place as my mate?"

My heart begged me to accept this offer. I wanted to erase the whole afternoon and the sadness that filled me.

"It would be unsafe to do so, Dagon—for you and for me. You told me earlier that you had tried on your old life and found it didn't suit you. But you returned to your dark curse."

In my mind I saw him in the moment before he began hurting me. I shuddered. *"I don't know if Shadakon leaders often drive off or kill their discarded mates, but I will not allow that to happen to me. You have had your final chance to take me out. I gave it to you, not expecting that you would relent. It is to your credit and my good fortune that you did. For that I thank you, Dagon."*

He looked at me then. We shared a moment of mutual pain. *"However I will not give you a another chance,"* I mind-spoke sadly.

Very shortly Fiórcara escorted Morag into the grove. Her green eyes blazed but she would not meet mine. I wanted to walk away from them all. I knew that it was no accident that he had brought them to me. *"Show me,"* I thought to her. *"Show me what was more important that my life. More important than my love for both of you."* I sat and listened to the little sounds. Everything was connected to everything else here. I was still connected to these two. I knew this was true. I also knew that our connection was coming to an end. I felt my pain as if it was someone else's. Even so, it made my breathing tight. I practiced the out breath. And then another. It was a gift to be alive and I felt that as well.

"Danu!" Dagon mind-spoke. *"I will be head of the entire coalition of clans of Shadakon, both here and on nearby worlds."*

I did not respond.

"There is a witness who recently saw you lying beneath your Sidhe on the beach, naked in the sunlight for anyone to see."

I did not respond.

"Is this true? Do you now flaunt yourself now outside of Between with him, my mate?

"I am no longer your mate Shadakon. But yes, I was your mate and yes, I lay down in pleasure on the beach with Fiórcara."

"Twice," I added. I wondered then which patient or Mother had passed on that information. But it didn't matter now.

"Not unlike you flying Lore when she took precedence at that moment." I wept when I realized that was true. *"But we did not lose our bond.*

I did not make plans to kill you because of your choice to turn to her, Dagon. In fact, I saved you from her. She frequented the inn in the woods where I was first taken. She and her crew used it as a base—to take as they would, outside of contract. But to rape and injure first. This should have been a concern to you and Morag. She was clan leader and she sent me there."

"It would seem that there are double standards for how you chose to act in the sky above our home, and a similar act by me, on a remote island, far from the clan."

"And Morag—why did you allow that house of pain and no contact killing and taking to continue?

I sat quietly again.

Morag neither spoke nor thought anything audible to me.

"You both had my love," I added slowly. *"You both were secure in that. I cannot stop loving either of you, not now anyway, but I will not allow you to treat me as you have. It is over. I will never again be your prey."*

I pictured Dagon over me; his dark golden eyes those of a sleepy large cat and my thrill of him in this form. I hung my head in pain.

"So, Danu," said Fiórcara, appearing suddenly before us. "What have you learned from your enquiries? Apparently possessiveness of one's previous partners is not only your failing. Morag harbours much anger in her heart towards you; she sees you as doing what she cannot. She brought you to me initially because she hoped to ingratiate herself to me.

"I was grateful that she achieved that," he said thoughtfully, "but it did not gain her what she truly wanted."

I sat and waited for what might come next. The numbness that had encircled me when I came here was upon me again.

"Stay present, Danu!" Fiórcara said. "You have one more important task today, before you can rest from your experience. If left to me, I would dispose of these two. They have angered me by threatening what I desire—my former midsummer's eve queen. As you all know, I care not of your relationships outside of my kingdom. I have repeatedly told you two this." He looked at Dagon and I. "Danu left the entrance to my home and my happy gathering to inflict the drama of her death on me and my guests. This was apparently because she feared returning home—to you, Dagon."

"Dagon did, however, help restore you, Danu—also in my own home. He was not so secretly angry that I also took action to preserve your life. And he later broke your arm with his own hands, and threatened you with worse. Today he took you with the intent to end you or at least secure you helpless, to be put into the little death."

"Was that your fantasy, Shadakon? To rouse her again and again and feed her enough that she would be awake to her agony—and your power over her?"

I looked at Dagon in horror. I remembered the needle gun in Morag's hand. She had told me that they did not bring full death. *Who had shouted "No" so loudly in my mind? Even if it had been, as I assumed, Dagon—was he aware that she was coming to do what he could not?*

"Look at me!" I thundered. Dagon raised his eyes and I gasped in pain. He was so beautiful, standing before what was likely his own death. I went closer to him and looked into his eyes. We stood that way, for a long, long moment of whale time, of tree time.

The moment was broken by Morag's laugh. "Foolish, Danu," she said scornfully. "Would his skills still catch you?"

I ignored her and only reached out and took his hand, the hand we had used to do the old ceremony of Making, tying him to me and me to him.

I felt the energy between us flare although I had willed to break our bond.

"I have done only what you yourself had done, Dagon. I took another lover, although he was far more than just fast and hot." I smiled sadly. "Although he is that too."

I dropped his hand and stepped over to Morag. I saw her energy coiled to spring at me. I shook my head. I immobilized her and leaned in, and then placed one soft kiss on her cheek.

When I released her, she stood silent.

"I always knew you yearned for him," I said softly. "It does not excuse you for hating me. I do not think you always did so. But perhaps believing in the goodness in others is a weakness in me."

I stood quietly and then turned to Fiórcara.

"Well, Danu, I once gave you a choice and will again today. Will you save one? For you can only save one."

I had expected this. I shook my head. I went and stood between the two of them. "I do not kill people I love," I said calmly. Unless they request that of me wholeheartedly. In this I am apparently not Shadakon. Perhaps not Sidhe either. I suspect it is my heart," I said. I pictured the delicate spiralling mystery of the shell I found on the log after Lucia died. "Everyone who knows me already knows this."

"Do what you will with all of us," I said to the Sidhe king. "I will not choose." I took a long last look at Between, a place I wondered if I would ever see again. I heard the leaves rustle about me and felt the grass pushing up into the sun. I looked up to see Fiórcara looking at me. Then the glade grew silent, as if time was stopped.

"For the second time, my queen, I find that I must apologize to you. I did know that I would not have been able to secure your permission in asking you to choose. Yes, I knew that.

I am glad that you now know that as well. Once again, you are not broken. But then you told me several seasons ago that you were not afraid to die. I am again glad that today you did not have to find out the final truth of that."

He took my hand then and I trembled. He moved me to his side. I wondered dispassionately how long I would be able to continue to stand.

"Take them to their flitter on the island," he said to someone outside of my field of vision. "They deserve each other's company."

CHAPTER ELEVEN

BEYOND BETWEEN

I was laid down in a warm soft place after being offered and drinking another cup of the elixir of life. This one had an unusual taste, cinnamon-like with some underlying heat. I had looked up after my first sip.

"Yes, Danu," mind-spoke Fiórcara. "You need reviving, not sleep. Will you trust me in this?"

Trust seemed a tricky concept for me today; nevertheless, I nodded.

"I'm going to begin this, and then I will step out for awhile. I will leave you in capable hands. I will return to you later tonight. Will you consent to this?"

I paused. I did not pretend that I did not know what was being offered to me. "Who?" I asked.

"Ah, Danu, you like to have the names of us. If he will give you a name then he will. Perhaps you will find one for him that he enjoys."

He took off my tunic, stiff with dried saltwater. My pants had stayed behind on the beach in my hurry to greet Dagon and Morag.

"Never mind that, my queen. Never mind." He combed out my auburn curls with his long fingers, teasing apart the tangles and laughing when he found a piece of seaweed in one.

He slowly moved his hands down my arms. He slipped his fingers behind me; tracing the invisible marks of the two lines that had ran down my back. I heard him make a slight sound.

I caught fire and he laughed. "Slower than usual, Danu, after your long day, but always satisfying. Now listen to me for a moment. You desire me. You desire. Summer is in you.

You once said to me, Danu, 'Passion is passion.' You are right. Please enjoy what is brought to you tonight. It is a gift, as all passion is. Do you consent to this, my queen?"

Glowing warmth was taking over my body. I wondered if I was actually glowing.

"Yes," I mind-whispered. "May I ask him the same question, my king?"

He smiled. Where he had stood was now the hazel-eyed Sidhe who had offered to come to me on a previous sad winter's night, and who knew that I had met the whales today. Who had came to me and counselled me to take the cup of elixir I was offered when I arrived in Between today. Who had encouraged me to stay strong ...

I looked up into forest-coloured eyes and they looked calmly back at mine. His hair hung slightly down around his face. I felt his beauty strike me and I opened to that.

"*Do you consent to this beautiful Sidhe?*"

He smiled. "*It will be my pleasure and yours beautiful, Danu, Queen among us.*"

I reached out and laid my hands on him. He was sun-warmed rock. He was, he was...

What I wanted. All that I wanted and more.

He came to me then and I finally cried but not from sadness.

And then I was silent as I was carried along in a current of sexual pleasure that I had no wish to withdraw from. At one point he took my hand and said only, "Let us practice together, Danu."

We launched into the sky from Fiórcara's door. I flew in joy and joined with him in the darkening air. Eventually we spun down onto the green and continued there, as he took me and the life force of the earth and then gave back and gave back ...

He looked down at me, my body green from the grass and smiled.

"*I heard that you asked for my name, Danu. Would you call me then, rather than your king?*"

I pondered that. "*I truly do not know the Sidhe way with names. I do not wish to offend or suggest a tie where there is not one. But I will remember you, with or without a name, beautiful one.*"

"*I will give you further reason to, if you let me,*" he responded.

We walked back to Fiórcara's dwelling. "I was told to return you," he said with a sly look in his eyes. "Your king feared you might tire of me. Have you tired of me yet, Danu?"

"No." I said clearly.

He led me inside then. There were others there. He lay me down unselfconsciously among them and brought himself to me again. There were caresses up and down my body and a very beautiful and familiar female Sidhe kissed me deeply.

Time did what it sometimes does in Between, and later I did not know myself from the others. I tasted and touched and peaked with the summer sex magic that I had been warned was the most potent in the universe. It flowed around and through me. I was not undone. I was not in danger of becoming so. At one point my king came to me and smiled down on me.

"Danu was a goddess of Eire," he said. "A fitting name for you here. Hers was a lovely green world."

I awoke later in the arms of Fiórcara with my night's companion alongside. The king's beautiful Sidhe lover slept on his other side. His new queen of this midsummer's eve. I smiled and my body smiled. Morning came.

CHAPTER TWELVE

WHO DO YOU LOVE?
HOW DO YOU LOVE THEM?

★★★★

Would it surprise you to know who flew with me in the great cone of power of midsummer's eve? Or what happened afterwards? Suffice it to say that I flew in joy with, as I now called him, the Beautiful One, content in knowing that I would not be alone later.

In this summer's dance, I could begin to feel the other sentient ones who joined us in spirit or perhaps in mind-touch. I felt the deep rumble of the whale clan when we called Her name ... the name of this planet. Everyone called her name in his or her own language. I joined the Sidhe in their word of power, then whispered, "Gaia." There had been a time when humans knew the sacred names, when we were not apart from the others we shared our world with.

I felt connected with these other beings here, most of which I had not met.

"*We will come to you, Danu. Have patience. We learned our fear of those who appear like you at their hands. It was a hard lesson, but we continue on.*"

I understood firsthand the darkness in those who chose not to set it aside or successfully fight against it. For humans on their own Earth, it had become normal to bring pain and death to the other sentient beings and eliminate whole ecosystems. The engineers were indifferent to the suffering their machines brought to those living in those places. Thousands of miles of land in the northlands had been torn asunder to provide access to oil tar, before that source, too, ran out. Gaping holes remained in many places, where toxic ores had been extracted all over the planet. The silvery rivers that ran through these lands still brought slow death to any who would slake their thirst from them hundreds and hundreds of years later.

The humans brought that same indifference and violence to their own—their neighbours, their lovers and even their own children.

It might surprise you that the interactions with those of the living planet Exterra were as important to me as what I thirsted for from my lovers. I had danced my own dance of fulfillment just days before the energy peaked. I no longer feared pleasure. Or endlessly sought it.

After the season turned, I sought out Fiórcara by picturing him and he appeared to me minutes later.

"Not a summons then," he smiled. "More of an invitation to chat. You are learning the subtleties, Danu. You continue to actualize that which is within you." He sat beside me and briefly stroked my arm, perhaps to assure us both that passion for each other still encircled us.

"But talk to me. Or mind-speak. *I love your bright mind as well.*"

"*I am wondering where I can be useful, Fiórcara. I have skills of gentleness and healing. But I am not sure I wish to sustain myself with the energy I took in that work any more. However ...*"

He looked deeply within me. "*You are still Shadakon, Danu, although how you can be so and not pledge some allegiance to their leader is not clear to you or me. You may have been reported as dead. There may be another standing beside him now. However, I would guess that he may put off further lessons in that for now.*"

Fiórcara smiled but not with his eyes. "*But there is more than this, is there not, beautiful Danu? Your heart is not done with him. In spite of everything he has revealed to you.*"

I thought of my impetuous escape from Fiórcara's door—out into the stars to die alone. I thought of what I might have missed ...

Fiórcara smiled again. "*Yes. You were gifted with being able to return to a path you rejected. Few are, Danu. You would have lost what you would now describe as unimaginably pleasurable.*"

I briefly savoured the moment when I completely surrendered and breathed in the building energies of all those who pleasured me and each other in Fiórcara's house. I felt the deep kiss of the most beautiful female I had every seen. The intoxicating honey of it. I knew then—*had always known?* —That he had joined with us all and took it and us all in.

"*Yes.*"

"This, then, had been what Morag had fearfully alluded to. That he, as the Shadakon, fed off of others."

"*Yes, Danu. Yes. We all do, you as well. And do you not think it is a joy for all?*"

I nodded.

"*And—?*"

"*I need more information. I need to look into the eyes of Dagon again. Into his ... spirit. No matter what I might find there, I need to know.*"

He did not speak, nor reveal his thoughts immediately.

"*I am not at all sure he deserves to see you again, or that he should be given the possibility of hurting you again. I am sure that I do not want to lose you to your violent Shadakon lover—again.*"

"*Still you have claimed his life, Danu, and that of Morag. I will tell you, however, that she is no longer on the planet. Whether that will be useful to you, or me or not, I do not know. If it took both of them to bring him to what in fact he still could not quite do—perhaps his mind has somewhat cleared. But do not forget the decision he made and brought to you.*

And that you were willing to accept from him. As you know, I do not have to give you permission to leave—or to return again. This is your home, Danu. You are of us. You will discover that after you have stayed away awhile. Perhaps this will be the necessary information that you need to gather."

He stood up then, and pulled me to him. Once again he kissed me gently on the lips.

I shivered, remembering the last time he had done so: when I had returned to almost die in the Council Hall of the Shadakon.

I set my course and transited.

CHAPTER THIRTEEN

THE REJOINING

It was midday, outside the fair. I knew he was there immediately, as he knew I was near. I touched the palm of my hand. I felt the flare of energy, and I knew he felt it too.

"*Danu!*" I felt his pain and longing. "*You would come to me—here?*"

"*Would I have come to your home? To your home and its basement?*" I shuddered.

"*I would sit with you, Dagon, in a safe-enough place. I, of course, have no money to secure your time. And perhaps it would be wise of me to sign a non-lethal contract, given the nature of our interactions recently.*"

"*Yes,*" he mind-spoke quietly, although the pain in him was almost more than I could bear.

Almost.

"*I will bear the necessary costs.*"

Soon I was offered the tablet that I remembered signing three years ago all too well. I signed as Althea, an alias that had been arranged by Morag in my first weeks after I had turned. I hoped it still existed in the system. I would soon find out. Transiting made this a minor problem if it did not.

Soon I was ushered into Dagon's "office"— a room that was airy and bright and could be closed off with hangings that were insubstantial, but provided the illusion of privacy. I sat on the divan—noting it had a different covering since my last visit—when I had once watched my mate take a man to his first true sexual passion, and then to death. I had learned many things about Dagon and myself that day, and I was still grateful for the lessons I took from it.

I sat as far from him as I could. He smiled sadly. "But not the uncomfortable chair?

I continued to smile though my heart was pounding. We looked at each other. I felt him wanting me, and beyond that, sensing and—even though I knew he might not realize this—wanting the wild faerie energy that was now within me. He was no longer my Alpha or my mate. I did not lower my eyes to him in deference or because he could make me do so.

Time passed. Whale time. Sidhe time. Perhaps longer than starport time.

"*Why have you come to me, Danu? What do you want from me?*"

I continued to look within to his under-mind thoughts. I did not see the dark Dagon, but he had hidden from me before.

"*I want to know,*" I simply mind-spoke, "*I want to know if you still love me.*"

I didn't ask if he ever had, or when he had decided to stop, or why he had been able to come to take me to death or almost-death, or what had been planned for me later. I did not think that Morag would have trusted him to keep me in the pain of endless hunger in his basement. It would have to have been in her basement then ...

I thought this all in under-mind, which he accessed, of course. We had been, and perhaps still were, one.

"I would show you," he simply thought. I felt his energies flare around us.

I shook my head. *"This is what you are best at. I am learning how to be better at sex energy and power too, Dagon. I am now probably as good at it as you are."*

"Better," he said quietly. *"Always better."*

"It didn't protect me from you. In fact, it brought up your ... what? Anger? Hatred?"

"Fear," he said simply. *"Fear of losing myself, of not being willing to face what was within me or what you wanted from me."*

I remembered the fear that had driven me stumbling and angry out of Fiórcara's door and out beyond air and life. How I had believed it was a right and necessary decision and then learned that it was me who would have lost the most from my decision, although Dagon was next in line.

"I would lay these old pains aside for a moment. I have no foresight of the future. I don't know where I will be or whom I might love later. But for now, Dagon, for now ..."

He did not touch me then, although he wanted to. I knew what we had to do next. I had signed a form, designed and implemented by humans. In some near future, they would no longer regulate the actions of the Shadakon— at least on this planet.

"Inner permission then, Dagon. Do you choose to put yourself in my hands?"

Perhaps he feared me then. In his world, he might be agreeing to whatever I chose to do to him—desired or not. "Yes," he just said.

"And, Danu—or maybe Althea. Would you come to me, knowing what and who I am, and what you have suffered at my hands? Do you knowingly come to me of your own free will?"

I thought of him pulling back from the ecstasy of taking me to death, more than once. His *"No!"* I remembered the pain I had suffered at his hands and his own afterwards. I remembered being one with him through many trials.

I knew he followed these thoughts. *"Yes, Dagon,"* I said. *"I promise briefly to be with you if you so chose. It may bring you more pain. But for now, my love, for now ..."*

We came together then. Later we left and flew wildly in the darkness. When we arrived at his house and he opened the door, I walked ahead of him into what I had once thought was my home. The small moon hung outside the bedroom window and threw bars of light across our pale bodies until it set. Later, we could still see each other in the darkness. I could be there for three days. I was protected by contract as well as the bond between our hearts.

How things could change in three summers.

It was the second day before he caught me up on what he had dedicated himself to bringing into being: Nathaniel was now his second. I had smiled at that;

Nathaniel was a strong and loyal Blood. Later, perhaps, he would take Dagon on, but for now he would learn from him. It was the way of the Shadakon.

Dagon had given Morag twenty-four hours to leave the planet. Because he had been depleted when he arrived at the beach, and he had spilled extra energy into me in his reaction to almost taking me, he simply took from her what he needed. She knew then that she no longer had a place beside him.

The Sidhe's energy barriers were up and functioning. The Shadakon patrols were keeping watch on the borders. Humans had disappeared, and there were signs that made clear that trespassing (an Old Earth biblical word) was punishable by death. Perhaps some thought that might mean some court process and a fine or bribe, but there was neither court nor process and no one accepted bribes.

The Sidhe refused to account for anything or to anyone about what happened in the wild territories they held. I thought about the so-called Indians of old Earth, the many First Nations that could not hold their lands against the better-armed invaders. And I thought about the old Sidhe in the old forests of Europe, who fell back and back from the invading humans who continued to cut their way into the woodlands, retaliating for any inconvenience they perceived came from their faerie neighbours.

It was not going to replay itself here. Soon there might be larger assaults.

The fact that the Sidhe could control, stop and distort any communication or navigation system in the vicinity of their planet was known by some, but it would become more apparent if necessary.

I wanted to know who had reported my actions on the beach back to Morag and Dagon. Dagon had not asked in that last black day with Morag; she had taken that information with her when she left.

It was the night of the second day. Dagon had been feeding me and at first I was overly affected by the life energy of humans that he brought. The elixir of life could be served with many additives, as I had learned, but human energy had a harsh edge to it that I no longer craved.

He had brought me beautiful flowers in a bowl, but they were cut off from their cycle of life. They would not set seed; they would not feed their own roots and those of their offspring. He saw me touching one with slight sadness.

I knew I did not have a place anywhere here but lying against Dagon's heart, I knew that my home here was now, only briefly, in his arms.

He knew that too.

He had arrived home the second afternoon of the contract, carrying energy but no flowers.

"Only matters of the heart tonight," he mind-spoke quietly. *"Let us talk of practical things in the morning if we must, Danu,"* he continued. *"Oh, my love. You have gifted me with knowing that it was not just a dream—a dream that ended as a nightmare. You are here. And you are here."* He indicated his heart. *"My joy and my necessary consequence are to carry you here. I would not change that."*

He wept. The tears fell on my face as he leaned above me and joined my own.

I wanted to relent, to promise him that I could change, that I could quiet my Sidhe blood in the spring and summer. That I would pass on loving or sexing with those who would bring me into the streaming energy of this planet. That I would somehow feel that this was the right action for me to take—to please him.

I wanted to say I loved him enough to make myself believe that myself.

And I wanted to believe him when he told me (and meant it when he said it) that he could change. I wanted to forget the Dagon who looked at me with cold eyes and brought me pain —and a barely averted death. Or worse, much worse, who might have delivered me to the little death of enforced hunger; to lie somewhere, helpless, given just enough energy to stay conscious of the pain, for the foreseeable future ...

I had seen him recovering from that fate, placed there by someone he had felt connected to for a long time, though I do not think either of them would have used the word "love" for what they shared.

Unlike the fact that he had told me he loved me, before I used that word.

The little death and hunger may have been brought to him many times in his long existence. He knew the horror and helplessness of it—and he had chosen that fate for me. He had known that Morag carried the slim, silver needle gun as either a back up plan or even primary objective. They had discussed my fate before setting out.

I still loved him fiercely, but I loved myself every bit as much. I would make no false promises. I would accept none.

He followed these thoughts and hung his head. *"Do you want to know?"* he mind-whispered.

"I am ready to hear some of it now.

I do not want you to assign blame to Morag in your story. She may some day tell me her version, although I doubt that now. I want you to tell me how you and I arrived here tonight, me by your side and at least partially protected by a contract that runs out tomorrow. My safety is perhaps still owing to fact that my disappearance would be a great inconvenience to you and how you provide for yourself."

"Unlike ending me on an island outside of enforced contract. Perhaps bundling my still living body into your flitter and simply leaving again, although I do not think our interactions went unobserved by the Mothers."

"I want to know how you made that come around to right or right-enough in your mind. In your heart."

He was silent. I sank into the quiet I so enjoyed to be in now. I waited without waiting.

"I asked you these same questions in Between," I said calmly. "You had no answers then. It was you who asked me this night if I wanted to hear your story that justified the reality that unfolded around us three. I saved your and Morag's life that afternoon, a decision I made with no information except ..." I touched on the deep sorrow I still felt, "... except that somehow I still loved you both. And I could not turn you over to your probably deserved fate from Fiórcara."

I met his eyes and did not look away. *"Mind-speak me, Dagon. Let us not blame inadequate words for any confusion between us."*

He shook his head. *"I wanted power. Power over you. I wanted you to be a submissive Beta to me. Except ... I also did not want that. I never even started with that, but fell further and further behind as you gained your own strength. And yet I raged within at your actions. With you leaving my side when we went to Between, stepping over to the side of a Sidhe king I was negotiating with, when I was doing all of it for you, more than anything.*

"Further and further behind?"

"You have to know that you have always had me. Morag saw it early—as you went to trial. She was amused that night, but not so much later. And you were unstoppable. So many times when you might have miss-stepped and I would have gone on as she and I had planned."

"I didn't sense that until after I was forced to stay in Between. And even then we recovered—we renewed our faith in each other." I briefly touched my palm. *"But this is your story, Dagon."*

"I wanted you as much as you wanted me. I loved to bring up your energy until you begged me to begin." He looked at me sadly.

I said nothing, as he had taught me.

He sighed. *"I could imagine you begging to surrender to the Sidhe. I smelled your scent, your scent that you only have when you are hot and ready, I smelled it in his bed as I held you there!"*

I nodded. *"My action that night was a poor choice and aimed at hurting others, I now realize—certainly hurting myself. But I have already confessed my shame and sorrow about that to you; I did not, however, ask you to forgive me."*

"You tortured me before we got to that part."

"Why did you keep returning to me?" he mind-spoke. *"Why didn't you just stay in Between and claim your new clan?"*

"I was not invited to. I was a guest only, and by the time you came to end my life, I wasn't sure if I would or could return. Interestingly, you drove me into their arms. But not Fiórcara's arms. He enjoys me occasionally, but has a new queen who has much of his attention these days. And he was weary of my drama and insistence on being special to him

I had to accept hospitality on his floor, and passion that I could not refuse ... that I did not choose to refuse."

I looked at Dagon and thought clearly, *"However I have learned not to confuse passion with love, or either with possession. I can have the first two—I can keep none."*

"Perhaps I needed to be in love with you to allow myself to open to you as I did. But sadly, I did, and still do love you. I will not recant that, even in the light of hearing what I am hearing—that you were from the beginning silently struggling against me. That you were often angry at me yet did not speak your mind, but rather built a toxic story about me. That I came and captured you at the fair and. that I had plans, even then, to somehow lessen you. That my plan was to stand in front of you—rather than beside you."

"About how I was enjoying how my behaviour while with the Sidhe was affecting you. That my transit out beyond life was aimed at you—to hurt you only, and saving me was some evil design of Fiórcara's."

"I will do this one more time, Dagon. It seems appropriate in that many of the injuries that you suffered due to my actions were done after I swore my loyalty to you as my Alpha. And before I renounced my role."

I sank to the floor beside him. I bent my head, my tears streaming down silently.

"I beg your forgiveness, Dagon, for not being able to be an appropriate mate to you. If I had been braver, and less desperate about being alone ... if I had not wanted you and loved you as much as I did, I would have left. But I chose death by my and your own hand again and again over the choice of leaving and standing on my own. I wanted you to be the one who protected me, who sheltered me, and who took me back no matter how far I strayed."

There was more, but I stopped there. I waited. I passed into whale time. Tree time.

Dagon knelt beside me. He did not put his hand on my head, or tell me to rise. He just put his arms around me. If a heart can speak directly, I heard his speak to mine.

His under-mind was begging me to reconsider, to give him another chance; to give us both another chance together.

He looked me in the eyes. *"I am sorry, Danu. I have been angry with people who broke my faith in such things as loyalty and so-called love many times in my life. My own recourse was to quietly vow to live beyond them. Even to eventually kill them if I could."*

"I achieved that. However, I succeeded in becoming them. It was a dark curse. I thought you had broken faith with me and I ceased to believe that I could be who I was and still have someone like you by my side and in my bed, guarding my back, as it turned out."

"Life and fate sent me you as my mate, a self-turned Shadakon with faerie blood. Shadakon and Sidhe—impossible! We have been, at best, guarded and avoiding each other in all of our long histories. How could this have happened?"

"Like us," I thought sadly. *"Just like us."*

Later I sat up, took his hand and gave him my own, saying only, "I understand now that the bonds of Making cannot be broken. I denied them earlier, but I was wrong. I would renew now with you, Dagon of the Shadakon. In some ways, no matter where our paths take us, we will not be separated. At least not by will."

Wordlessly and without mind-talk, Dagon turned up his palm.

I evoked the calmness of the waves and the large and peaceful curiosity of the whales who had joined me. I drew up the still powerful summer energy that resided in me and I felt the earth and rocks beneath his house—the bones of this planet. I was not sure if I had sharp teeth to call on anymore, but I was still able to do this.

I drove them deep into his palm and waited until he did the same, and I drank his heart's blood as he did mine. He drank faerie that spun him out and away to bliss. I took in his sadness and a calmer power that I had ever experienced from him. He was not posturing as an Alpha anymore—he was one, and would be one until his death.

I took in his strong and exclusive energy that I had learned to love beyond anything else in my life.

All night we lay enfolded, a precious ball of energy between us. A golden bridge spanned briefly between our hearts.

In the morning there was nothing more to say or do. I simply rose, kissed him and went back to the fair.

I signed out with the slightly puzzled agent. My name and identity might have not synched perfectly with the company's system anymore, but since I had signed out, it would not provide undue difficulty. I mind-wiped his slight curiosity and concern and went on my way. What had I looked like? Just another spacer. More than that he would not be able to say. Dagon's record was clear, and it was not his concern if their records had occasional glitches.

I next went to the Mothers on the island. I was waiting in the Mother's office when she joined me.

She sighed. "I am so sorry, Danu."

I waited.

"One of our newer members was more and less than she seemed. I realized that a Mother must have been involved when I saw the flitter land and you disappeared. Soon the Sidhe came and gathered them. A grave disservice has been done to you.

You thought you were safe here."

I looked into her clear blue eyes. "There is no truly safe place," I said. "One should not relax into expectations of ongoing safety.

I am well," I said. "Dagon is also. We are not together, although …" I paused wondering how much to say to this friendly stranger, "I have faith that we will not lose each other. That we cannot lose each other," I added softly. "Even if one or both might wish it so. It is the gift and the—I used Dagon's word—"consequence."

"I would work here again if you have use of me, if you would have me. I yearn only to swim in the sea and watch the moon rise and fall. However, I cannot guarantee that I might not frolic on the beach on occasion. I told you that I was faerie, and it is in our nature." I smiled.

She led me back to my empty corner room, once again causing me to wonder what and how she knew the things she knew. The beautiful spiral shell still sat on the window ledge.

CHAPTER FOURTEEN

THE IN-GATHERING

★ ★ ★ ★

Fall brought high tides and storms. Fewer flitters arrived, and the day came when I had to admit that I could no longer nourish myself adequately here. I had walked in undeniable hunger for days. Still I hesitated returning to Between. It was colder and the light tide was pulling out and out. I did not know how or where the other Sidhe rested in these months, or if they required warmth. I knew that I needed those things. I did not assume that I would spend the time with Fiórcara in his winter hall.

I was also lonely. It was not the panicky feeling of being airless or the fear of not knowing what, if any, choices I had. I knew I had choices, even if I did not know at present what they were. The night I went to my room and saw shutters on the outside of the windows I knew I would not be wintering here.

Lead with your strongest card, I thought, remembering something that someone who had once attempted to teach me some tedious card game had said. The game and the players had been boring, but the intricate strategy had held my attention for the evening.

I don't believe that the deck for that game included the Joker. The Fool. I was still she.

I would return to Between. I had nothing to take, having only the clothes I wore and the soft shoes I wore every day. They were all faerie-made and had not noticeably worn. I would leave in the morning. Meanwhile, I walked outside in spite of the evening's chill and saw the green swirling energy that announced the Sidhe to me. I heard voices and laughter. Two figures were dancing in and out of the small waves on the shore. The moon's light lit up one's bright hair. The other was darker, the shadow of the moon. I would have known them even in a dream.

Seeing them touched me ... I hesitated and then joined them. They caught me up in the circle of their arms. *"Are you ready to come home, Danu? We will keep you warm and make you even warmer."*

It was Fiórcara's new queen and my beautiful one. I felt them enfold me into their energy and joy of the night, of the moon. We transited in a heartbeat and landed in the centre of Fiórcara's hill hall. "Two queens for one evening," said Fiórcara. "May they burn brightly together."

He did not seem surprised that I had arrived. Perhaps he had sent them. Or he had merely known that they intended to go and retrieve me this night, or that I was now ready to be retrieved.

He stood in front of me. *"Once more I will offer you a fall cup, Danu. Once again it will give you another way to perceive us and this world. You will be, ah, altered. You will be in all our keeping tonight, rather than just mine. Would you take this cup from me? Would you join us in what follows?"*

I heard the pause between breaths, the silences between in Between. I smiled. *"Yes, my king and queen and beautiful one. I would join with you all for this night, however long it may be."*

Fiórcara smiled at my naming of my previous companion. *"It would be hard to ignore such a name."*

"It may get easier and easier for you to find bliss, Danu." He poured a cup and put it in my hand. I tasted the bitter taste beneath, and the spiced honey that brought sweet balance to that. I fell into something like a dream.

It was so unlike even my unusual life that it could have been one, but was not. Fiórcara's beautiful queen took my hand and led me to a comfortable place. I began to glow and felt my passion rise and entwine about us. She laughed then and leaned over me, her long fall hair slightly darker now, her blue eyes sparkling with a touch of frost. Together with Fiórcara, she removed my clothes. She gently stroked my body, and her touches grew more and more intense to me.

Fiórcara watched intently as I crossed from pleasure to the ache of desire that took me over. She kissed me and I kissed back, not unlike the night that I had learned what kissing Dagon was like so long ago: that I liked it, and that I wanted nothing else. However, I did not think those thoughts this night, as thinking in the usual sense had been suspended.

I entered fully into what was. I followed her lead in returning the pleasure she gave me. I gasped when her fingers came to calmly claim what no woman had ever touched before.

I begged her then as I had often begged her king. *"Please …"*

"What is your wish now, Danu?" I also felt Fiórcara and the other male Sidhe in my mind. I wanted them all—I wanted it all.

My experience of wanting both my Sidhe and Shadakon lover and refusing to choose was that punishment followed. And although my human crewmates had endlessly searched for sexual access, they sneered and belittled those who gave them what they wanted too easily or too soon. I had always known, in a smaller and larger way, that the women would pay both for asking for and giving what both wanted.

"We worship through pleasure. We see you as glowing and beautiful. Two beautiful queens. Why should anyone be excluded?"

I let that idea enter into me although I was past speaking my mind.

Everything was swept away except wanting to receive—and to give.

We four combined throughout the night as we would, with no possibilities left unvisited. My Sidhe companions were as energized as I was. At one moment that I could remember later, I heard Fiórcara mind-speak, *"Did I not say from the onset that she is fine? Did her slow start with you fool you?"* I knew he spoke to he who I had once refused earlier, he who I would have made a reason to go to my death.

Later, I drank another cup of fall elixir and spun up and out in a moonlit flight, and they followed me. We had long before ceased to be four. I floated in the now familiar place of stars and space. I was not dying and it did not hurt. I felt the invisible energies enter me and pass through me. I knew much, but could not speak of it later.

The Great Mysteries of creation and chaos—I said yes to that also.

CHAPTER FIFTEEN

'I CAN SEE MORE CLEARLY NOW...

When I awoke, it was dawn, but a dawn that had taken Between time to arrive. My king slept with his new queen beside him. I was on his other side, and beside me, the beautiful one. When I opened my eyes he was looking at me calmly. He had waited for me to awaken, much as Fiórcara had on my first day in Between. I had known that then and I knew the same now.

His eyes had darkened to the colour of winter evergreens. I knew what his lips and other parts tasted like, and retained most of the memories of him and what he had brought me during the long night.

"Do you still want me then, Danu? Even now that you can directly compare me with your king?"

"Yes."

"One of fewer and fewer words now. But do you still want a name for me?"

"What would that mean to you? What would be the consequence of that?"

He shrugged. *"We will know that when we will. We all carry many names that we take and are given to us over our long lives. But "beautiful one" is perhaps a little vague. We are, as you are beginning to realize, all beautiful ones. Or so those of human blood perceive us. And how we perceive ourselves and each other."*

I remembered when I first saw the Sidhe king bending over me that he looked … alien, and for a moment, old and aloof. I knew he had changed his appearance to become more desirable to me in my first stay in Between.

"Yes. As did I."

I then realized that he no longer reminded me of Dagon. *"Perhaps your way of perceiving me has changed, rather than my appearance, but you are partially correct. When you arrived in Between, in shock and heartsick, I saw no reason to remind you of him. You were having a hard enough day."*

"Danu. You may call me Céadar. So you have thought when you looked into my eyes."

I continued to look into those eyes and smiled. *"Thank you."*

Cedar had been a sacred tree to the First Nations of the Pacific Northwest of old Earth. They built their Big Houses from it and, fashioned it into canoes. It had safely carried them to hunt in the open sea. It had kept away confusion and sadness when burned as a smudge and the fresh green branches were used to sweep away grief or fear and restore balance. It was part of their Winter Dances of reclaiming their spirits.

I knew he had heard my description.

"*You honour me in gifting me with this name for me to use. You have been all of these to me. Except the canoe part—although we travelled across dark seas together last night.*"

"*And flew together,*" he added. "*That must count.*"

"*I feel much the same as our king does about bringing human or Shadakon affairs to Between, but because you have visited us with them since you began coming here, I would only ask you this: is your heart peaceful now about your connection with the Shadakon?*"

Briefly, I touched my Maker hand and felt a flare of energy there. "*He is well, and working to continue the plan of protection of this planet. I would know if he was not alive. That is enough for now. Perhaps ...*" I sighed.

"*But?*"

"*When I revisited him recently, his heart was calm. I loved him and I believe he loved me. But I have no place beside him anymore, and he has turned me into the Other and fought against me for what I am more than once. Each time has been worse for both of us; I will not allow that to happen again.*"

Céadar touched my lips lightly. "So mote it be," he simply said aloud.

"*But, as for what I will do now to be useful and earn my elixir of life, I do not know. I will join in pleasure, but all the Sidhe provide that for each other. My job on the island with the Mothers has concluded for the winter. In time, I believe, they will shut down that house of healing. There is another near the spaceport that will last longer, but that places me too close to the Shadakon clan and to Dagon ...*"

"I cannot see it now," I said, "but paths tend to open before me."

We had been talking quietly and mind-speaking but I should have realized that Fiórcara was taking in everything. Leaving his queen to sleep, he sat beside us.

"*No one is undone this morning?*" He looked within at me and found contentment and calm. "*No unfinished passion that needs to be dispatched? I no longer have to feel diminished by you calling another Sidhe 'Beautiful One?'*" There was no sting in this, and it occurred to me that I had missed what might be humour in him.

We all smiled then.

"Take a walk with me this morning, Danu," Fiórcara said and took my hand. As usual, his touch woke me, no matter what had passed the night before. I let it be, as we walked in the circles of Between.

"You are right, Danu," he spoke almost formally. "You need a purpose and job, and I have one for you, if you want it."

I remembered how frightened and unsure of myself I had been when I was presented to the Mothers.

"Yes, yes," Fiórcara said somewhat shortly. "But you have done some things very well in your life. However, you did not advance or get to feel the appreciation of others for your work. This work will also challenge you and allow you to feel your confidence and competence grow."

I waited.

He smiled.

"So many skills you don't know you have, Danu. You will be our interface between the Sidhe and the humans who will eventually come here. We do not like many humans except ..." He looked at me directly, "... when they willingly surrender to us, obey us, and survive our attentions. You did not like them either, but gained compassion for them in your work. You also have the means to control them and read them skilfully. Few spies or information of whatever type will slip past you, I think. You will be our ... ambassador."

I immediately remembered telling the Touch-me-not that I was being considered to be an ambassador for this world. It had let me enter among its leaves, and stand amidst it without pain.

"Yes," said the Sidhe king. "So many times I've wondered what you know. How far you perceive into the future. In this you show your Sidhe nature to be at least equal to mine. I did not take you as queen to impress you Danu. I have never flown with a part human before in the midsummer's eve cone of power. Nor has, as you now call him, Céadar. I would never have invited a human to the beginning of our high ritual of midsummer's eve. Those that arrive inadvertently are not necessarily ... enriched ... by their experiences there."

I remembered him telling me that he was pleased that I surrendered to him with no fear, and that I had an understanding of the ritual's energy gathering, and had participated in that.

"Yes. I have tended to ... toy with human partners. There is a short pleasure in that, not unlike how your Shadakon lover might treat them."

I looked at Fiórcara in amazement. In the past he had threatened me with removing all memories of my life with Shadakon if I didn't stop thinking of him and referring to him while in Between.

"Yes. You could think of nothing else. You would have thought of him even as I came to you! But I did not hear his name last night. And he was not lying between you and Céadar this morning. My queen did not feel him shielding you from her love-making."

I was further surprised. I had attempted not to call what was between Fiórcara and me and now between the four of us as "love." I did not use the word lover, but had no other word to use in its place. We had had sex, yes, and consensual touches of mind and body, and perhaps spirit. But we had promised each other nothing. *Did "love" imply obligation? Could it arise in an evening of passion?"*

"Once again, Danu, you like to capture things in words. What are many things and different for each involved, you would use one word for. But we touched more than each other's bodies last night—I think you would agree."

I nodded. The feelings came up and I felt, again, how at no time did I feel alone or not-enough; the gift of it brought tears.

"Yes, Danu. What we shared was deep and genuine. But as long as you realize that it puts no demands on those you shared with, you may call it love. I believe you returned to Dagon recently to teach him this same lesson. We teach what we need to learn."

I looked at this old and wise Sidhe beside me and sighed. It was ... a complex sigh.

He laughed at me then. "I am curious, Danu, and think I know the answer to this but …"

He reached out and held me lightly by both arms. He ran his hands lightly up to mine and turned over my palms. He touched the hand of my recent Making and lingered for a moment, then continued on to run one finger lightly down the mid-line of my body. I sighed again. It was a simpler sigh. My desire flared for him and I shivered in the sunlight.

"So you have not transferred your old wish of having an exclusive lover to Céadar?"

I simply shook my head, my tangled red hair catching in the breeze. I was open to him. My heart was open to him.

"Soon again then," he said. "We may visit you together or separately. I know my queen enjoyed giving and receiving your attentions. That was another victory for you—in throwing off the hateful constraints that were laid upon you earlier by your fellow humans."

I thought of the sick shame that a young man estranged from his desires for other men, had brought to Dagon as I witnessed what passed between them. *Had I harboured the same within myself?*

"Ah, Danu," Fiórcara said gently. You are as pleasing a student as you are a lover. We must find you a job so that any of us can continue with our work." He drew me in and kissed me again, and the passion turned into a gentleness that was as undoing as the other. He held me briefly. "So little passion, so little tenderness in your past life … so much time to make that up!"

He laughed.

"I will tell you the details of your assignment soon, Danu. For now, relax here and sleep in my hill hall if you will. It will be quiet there now. We are in the in-gathering. We will … sleep more." He smiled. "But you have one more question that you haven't quite prepared yourself to ask me yet?"

I thought of his revealed tenderness to me. I saw myself standing in the small waves, holding Lucia, letting her be with the sea before I took her and set her spirit adrift on the outgoing tide. She had told me that the faerie king had placed her in a loving home. Checked on her, spoke with her. Allowed her to retain my name.

I looked at Fiórcara with tears in my eyes and my question, although unformed, was in my mind.

"You offered your life for her, Danu. I knew then that she was important and deserving of our help. She had, as I said before, a strong and beautiful heart. She had trusted you and she trusted me without reservation. In her own way, she surrendered to faerie without needing to question it or fear it. How could one not care for such a bright spirit?"

"I told you this as well—if all humans were as she, we would not be in the situation we are here, and earth might not be dying. Not all humans carry the life-hate. We sometimes seek those special ones out; Lara was another. You had an affinity with both of these people."

"You loved both of these humans," he said with certainty. "I don't know if many humans can ever rise above their arrogant claims on everything they want. It is partially what you struggle against as you learn that love is not possession. Sexual passion is not possession. Saying goodbye, over and over and keeping your heart open to that has strengthened you. Refusing to be owned in spite of her circumstances strengthened Lucia."

"*Thank you.*" I mind-spoke. "*Learning at the end that she had had loving contact gave me ease.*"

"*My pleasure, Danu,*" said the one I knew had held my life in his hands more than once, who had retrieved me and began anew to show me what I could not or would not see in myself.

"*My pleasure, Danu,*" he said again. "*Just one of the many rewards I receive from you. Rest. In that you harm none, do what you will here.*" He smiled to see that I recognized the quote passed down from Wiccan lore.

He walked away, leaving me calm and pleasantly anticipating my future.

"*New clothes first,*" was the last thing I heard him say that day.

CHAPTER SIXTEEN

FURTHER INTO THE FLOW

Later—that day? Another day? I went to the pool in the grove that Fiórcara had directed me to years ago. Shucking my clothes, I took a breath and quickly entered, sinking as deep as I could, willing myself to stay relaxed in the cold water. Looking up was like looking up through clear ice, and I saw the wavering face of the Midsummer's Eve Queen looking down at me.

I exited the water in one fast glide up onto the bank, not unlike an otter I had once seen, in an animal preserve on old Earth.

She laughed and swirled her hand in the chilly water. *"There are warmer ways to do this, Danu."* She laughed.

I shook off in the cool wind. She continued to be beautiful and alluring to me.

"In our home on old Earth," she said somewhat sadly, "there were many sacred pools used by us. Some of them were warm," she added, smiling. "We enjoy water, as do you, Danu. Would you come with me to the Queen's Bath? Today it will be empty. And warm," she added.

I remembered the warm pool in Dagon's house and sighed, I had so enjoyed spending time there. On the island, when I was troubled I had cleansed my body and spirit in the sea. This water, however, would soon freeze and be unavailable to me.

I looked at her, and once again I was entranced. The Sidhe were slim, with a strength not immediately apparent until one came into closer connection with them. The queen was beautiful in a different way than me, although I could now see the faerie influence on my own body. I was now lean and strong and it pleased me. My hair, however, was dark auburn, a colour I had not seen among the Sidhe.

"Do you still wish to accompany me, Danu, without the efforts of the fall elixir on you?"

I only looked at her in amazement. *"How could I not?"*

She smiled again then, and took my cold hand. I shivered but not from the air. Her touch and its effects on me were so unlike that of Fiórcara or Céadar, but were somehow familiar beyond our recent connections.

"Lara," she mind-spoke. *"You loved your first woman that day."*

Lara had been my first client and I had been surprised to find her beautiful to me. I had reflected that back to her. I remembered my strong desire to kiss her cheek. I had seen her in that moment young and untouched by the disease that later claimed her. But I had not done so.

"There are kisses and kisses. As I recall it—you did. Her body was a place of pain and a physical kiss may have brought more. You have grown braver, Danu. Or perhaps you have merely come closer to your true nature by coming to us."

She took my hand then and we walked in another spiral in Between that brought us to a series of pools that bubbled from the rocks around them. Steam rose. I gasped in the pleasure that only water could bring to me.

Leaving my clothes on the edge, I entered the lower pool but quickly choose a warmer one, and then—a still warmer one. My hair spread out in a halo around me, and I floated happily. For a moment I truly forgot the one who had brought me here. When I brought her to mind again and looked for her, she was sitting on the edge of my pool, bare and shining against the grey stone. Her hair hung to her waist and the water reflected the sky into her eyes, or perhaps her eyes shone on their own.

Once again I fell into her calm and confident energy. I rose from the warmth to come to her. "Wait a bit, Danu. Soak and warm yourself. When you are ready, join me in the lower pool."

She shimmered, as Fiórcara did.

"When you are ready," she mind-spoke and slipped away.

I floated and felt the heat steal in to replace the chill of the pool in the grove. I felt the warmth grow and knew it was not coming from the water alone. I felt my body indicate that my arms wanted to hold her, my lips wanted ...

Waves of pleasure and longing radiated from my centre. When I could not stand it any longer (and it was not long), I came to her. She drew me in and her dark blonde hair hung on my shoulders and brushed against my breasts as we kissed. For a moment I felt like I was floating in space again, but the pleasure built and built until I gasped. Her hands went where they would and at last I knew that it was time to leave the water and attend to her fully without fear of inadvertently drowning.

We lay on the side of the pool and, although I did not drown, I went deep and deeper into her loving. I cried out, as did she at various times. She tasted like sweet grass, like the flowers that I used to pull off their stems as a child in my parents' small garden and savour the small drop of nectar I found at each flower's base.

There was no beginning or finishing to this. We continued on together until we lay, temporarily spent, our hands entwined.

I could feel Fiórcara present. Perhaps he had been there for a long time, but had not intruded or brought his energy to us. Now he sat beside us and reached down and stroked his queen's thigh. She shuddered, as I always did, at his touch.

"Too much for just one to love," he mind-spoke me. *"And this she does not bring to a male—even me."*

He smiled. *"Except that I can attend to her pleasure from afar, to both of my queens' pleasure.*

"Now do you know why I was angry at you for taking to the sky and your death Danu? I knew this lay within you even if you did not. I wanted to see you truly happy; I knew you were close to discovering it."

There was no argument for what he said. He smiled at my thought.

He reached down and ran his long fingers through my red hair; he always seemed drawn to it. "No seaweed today," he said, smiling. He looked at us both fondly and then walked away.

CHAPTER SEVENTEEN

ΛΜ 1 TRUSTWORTHY?

"It's time you got a look behind the scenes," Céadar said to me, coming up behind me as I walked the spiralling paths of Between. The winter solstice was more than a month away and true cold had not yet set in. I was beginning to wonder what the Sidhe did as the planet's energy went to ground.

"We'd like to lay around in our hill halls and, well, you know, Danu, but in truth we have ongoing business with the outside world, now more than ever. There are questions and complaints coming in as the outside meta-corporations realize that they have lost their chance for this lucrative piece of property. They are more distressed when they discover that the contracts are truly legally binding. We hold full deed, having claimed it first and paid in full. There are no extenuating conditions on that."

"Of course many believe that they will be able to bend or break or buy into that contract. Or bully us out of it. It may come to a limited war in which we will have to disable their ships before they get into striking range. The sky may be on fire, Danu. Hopefully it will remain safe enough on the planet's surface."

I was totally stopped by what I just heard. Again, I had not questioned—what Dagon tracked in his nights on the computer, who he may have talked to, or what alliances the Shadakon or the Sidhe had off planet.

"Yes, Danu. However, your area of expertise required a calm mind and healing skills that have changed little in the history of your kind. After all the substances were tried ... only at the end, for a lucky few, was there a chance for them to strengthen and calm their spirits.

Your clients had exhausted medical science before they came to you. You practice the old arts; however, you are not unfamiliar with the new ones. You did work on ships as a techno and we could use those skills here."

"Now, I am going to show you something that was hidden in plain sight from you, and from everyone else who has no need to have knowledge of it. It is time for you to be useful in other ways." He stopped in front of another hill hall that I had never found in my wandering around Between and palmed open the door.

The space inside was much bigger than could be accounted for from the outside. There was steady lighting and smooth curved surfaces. Sidhe sat at monitors, studying incoming information and inputting it, moving it on to where it could form a useable pattern to them.

It was a Sidhe communication centre. Those working were all dressed in soft brown clothing. There was a calm purposeful air and only a few looked up at us before looking down at their work again.

"First the brown uniform," Céadar said to me, leading me towards a door. Inside he stripped off his clothes and indicated that I do the same. There was no element of sexual purpose in this. He handed me a loose shirt and pants and soft indoor shoes and he donned a similar outfit. He clipped a small pin or device onto the shirt I was wearing and then turned me to look at him.

"Listen carefully, Danu, for I do not want you to believe that you can claim a misunderstanding about this later."

"I and others will know exactly where you are while you wear this. If you take it off for any reason while you are in here, or if you are where you aren't authorized to be, you will be seen as an unacceptable security risk."

For a moment I saw the old fierceness that I had seen in Fiórcara in the beginning, before he hid it from me. I did not think it was accidental that my carefree Sidhe lover had now showed me this.

"Yes," I said.

"Yes," he said. "This is an unusual situation, because you could have had no informed consent before entering here. This space and what we do here must be invisible. But I will grant you the courtesy of asking if you are willing to work with us here, on the front line of preserving this planet."

He waited.

I did not ask what the alternative would be if I said no. I did not think that the Sidhe would trust in memory removal to preserve the safety of this operation.

Had I been them, I would not have either.

So, another path opens up suddenly, I thought. *The old ones now cease to exist?*

The Sidhe I called Céadar stood quietly, awaiting my answer. It occurred to me that I might have been frolicking with a galaxy-level communications expert. In this facility there were Sidhe who were savvy with the outside world and able to manipulate it. I felt slightly giddy with that thought and brought myself back and down, breathing smoothly.

All this is for two whales—and hopefully more—swimming in a safe sea, I reminded myself. *For all that live in the great forests.* I felt the undisturbed lovely rock bones beneath the building. Old magic had not been enough to hold the wild living spaces on old Earth. Underestimating the drive of humans to possess all things resulted in old Earth's fatal illness.

"It would not happen here. I would do what I could," I stated to myself. I knew he had followed me in my thoughts.

"I do agree to be of service here, and accept the consequences of the job," I said.

"But?" asked Céadar.

"Dagon and I are each other's Makers. Each of us will know if and when the other dies. And if I am in contact with him again, he has proven that he can read me deeply."

Céadar kept looking at me, waiting for me to come to the inevitable conclusion of this information.

I looked back at him in alarm, and he returned the look with an unusual blend of sadness and irritation.

"Your king and I will have to talk, but you told me earlier that you had no place beside your Shadakon lover, and had to stay apart for your own safety. Now you will have to stay apart for all of our safety. You will have no unmonitored contact with him for the foreseeable future."

I wondered how long the foreseeable future was for a Sidhe.

He just shook his head.

"Give me a moment to process this," I said.

He shrugged, walked out the door, and it shut behind him.

I sat on the floor, knees drawn up to my chest. I had, not long ago, announced that I had no further ties to Dagon. I felt strong and right in that decision. Then I went to spend two days and nights with him, and, for reasons that also seemed right at the time, I renewed our Making vows. He had told me that he would carry me in his heart and I knew that I would remain connected to him in the same way.

Would I now disappear, indicating only by our Maker's bond that I was alive? For the foreseeable future and beyond?

Did I have any claim to be angry about this?

I was now dependent on the Sidhe for sustenance and shelter The place where I had worked outside of Between, where I was safest, did not have enough clients for me to survive the winter. Working near Dagon's home and the star-port would unavoidably place me in the path of Shadakon who would recognize me and who would question Dagon about my status. They might kill me because they could. It would put Dagon in a bad light, defending someone who was, in truth, no longer his to protect. And he also would have to supplement my energy requirements. It was too much to ask, whether he would accept the burden or not.

No path there then. We were lucky to have had a kind goodbye. Perhaps we had both known. I tried to calmly accept these facts and could not do so. "*Let it hurt then,*" I thought sadly.

I opened the door again to find Céadar leaning against the wall outside.

"I am ready," I said. "I accept the restrictions and responsibilities of the work without exception."

"I am sorry to seem distrustful, Danu. But the responsibility for our safety also lies on me. I must now read you deeply as well. There is no choice for you, but I would ask you to accept this."

It seemed obvious to me that this question had only one acceptable answer as well. I looked into his tree green eyes and attempted not to be drawn into his energies, to react to him—inappropriately.

"Yes," I said.

He laughed. "There is little that is inappropriate between two Sidhe who enjoy each other. We do what we have to do here. But we would not chose to act humanly about it."

The room contained little useful furniture for our purposes. He shrugged and indicated the floor, then walked over and locked the door. He provided cushioning for under my head and I lay down, facing up into his eyes as he sat beside me. He stroked my cheek for a moment and then engaged.

Like a clip of time played backwards, he looked within. He saw my pleasure with the queen and earlier with him and Fiórcara and his queen and he smiled. He went back and back and down and down. After a while, I could no longer perceive what he saw. I stayed quiet and open, breathing calmly as I did when I had once dived to great depths. I hung weightless in the dark blue, awaiting my return to the surface, intentionally relaxed.

Time passed, time of some length or other. I heard him calling me back. When I saw him over me I had a rush of wanting him. I looked at him with some confusion. *"I do not understand the social rules of the Sidhe. Wanting someone in the middle of a job interview ..."*

He laughed and helped me up. *"Soon perhaps, Danu. I must stay focused when I am here—as do you."*

Then he stopped smiling. "You have provided me deep access without the discomfort that might have occurred had you resisted. I am glad we could accomplish that. But that in itself tells me you have been trained to open to and allow such probing from others."

I had always opened to my lovers; it had been part of the taking between Dagon and I, and myself and Fiórcara. When I had returned after my first stay with Fiórcara on midsummer's eve, Dagon had insisted on accessing my memories and said that he did not go anywhere that Fiórcara had not already gone. It resulted in us visiting in Between and beginning the negotiations between Dagon and the Sidhe king.

I felt that I had bridged the two together. Later I was not so sure that that was a safe position for me to be in. Céadar listened to my thoughts without interrupting.

"I need to bring our king in for this one," he said. "Perhaps I should not have brought you here—that would be my error, but a serious one for you."

"I want you to stay here, in this room. Go nowhere else. Do not open the door. Stay centred where you are. Don't see this is a 'test.' It is a serious situation and you need to do what I have asked you to do—*exactly.*"

He left and I heard the door click behind him.

I stood and stretched. I was in a bare room with shelves of folded uniforms and bales of things I would not examine further, a supply room, perhaps. It was a strange way to begin my first day of work.

I lay back down on the floor of the room exactly where I had been before. Slowly the chill of the stone soaked into me. Céadar had placed a spare shirt under my head when I had lay down; now I shook it out and lay on top of it. I could faintly hear the others outside who were working and talking. I could probably have mind-spoken to them or listened in on them but I did not. Nor did I get up to check the door.

I was afraid but it was not yet an unmanageable fear. I fell into an uneasy sleep.

I awoke to the door being opened and slightly stiffly arose to my feet, re-folding the shirt that had provided some comfort to me.

Céadar and Fiórcara stood before me with the light behind them.

I had not moved, and I had neither listened to nor attempted to communicate with anyone outside the door.

Céadar responded to these thoughts.

"*We know that, Danu, it bodes well. I think, though, that we three have to talk.*" I looked about the room I had been in for … I had no idea how long. I was unmistakably hungry. I shrugged. However I did hope for some additional comfort; it had been a long day (or whatever) on the floor.

They waited while I dressed in my own clothes. The device was removed from the brown shirt and put somewhere—my attention didn't catch where. They ushered me out of the door and outside.

"*I would not involve my queen in this,*" Fiórcara mind-spoke to Céadar.

"*Elsewhere then. We will go to my dwelling.*"

Once again, I found myself in a part of Between I had not seen. I began to conceive of this reality as not just one place, but a series of them, folded into the greater Between. Between might in fact be much bigger than I had originally imagined.

Fiórcara smiled at me then in his mind. "*Good, Danu.*"

Céadar stood at the entrance to another hill hall. With quiet formality he asked me, "Would you enter my home, Danu?"

I said, "Yes." However, I had a growing fear that I could not shake off. I believed I knew where this would go. I prayed (an action I still attempted at times when in extreme circumstances) that I was wrong, and I felt some tears gathering that I hoped would not fall.

We three sat on a low platform, much like the one in Fiórcara's home. It was warm enough, but I shivered and pressed my palms together. I felt my connection to Dagon—he was well.

"First, sustenance," said Céadar.

"Would you tell me if that cup would obliviate memories of my lover?" I looked at both of them sadly. I remembered a cup handed to Morag not so long ago; one she drank willingly.

I, too, might drink such a cup today—this one bringing a different kind of death. Fiórcara sighed. "I told you, Danu, that I could erase your other life if you persisted in bringing it with you to us, to me. I know you believed me then and did what you could to avoid that. Yet you still had slips, in spite of additional warnings."

I looked at him and the pain took me. My honeymoon with the Sidhe was now over. Fiórcara could and might today take she who I had been, and how I had come to be who I was now. He would take my lover from me in a way that Dagon himself could not do, even through his violence towards me.

I remembered dying for Dagon in front of the Council Hall full of Shadakon. I remembered him promising to die with me in his back garden, a small poisoned knife in my hand poised over both of our moonlit arms. I brought to mind our first connection, and our last.

"I cannot do this," I said. "I do not give you permission. Perhaps you must make another decision about me. I will not consent to this."

Once again I said something that I thought I would never again have to say.

"I would rather die, the final death. That, at least, would be understandable to him—a clean ending. I will not betray him this way, to pass him on the street and not know him. I will not betray myself or my heart this way."

I faced the two who, even now, I yearned for. I thought of transiting. In a flash, Céadar put his hand on my arm.

"No, Danu."

I knew that if I went he would go too. I remembered Morag saying to me, "He will not allow you an easy exit."

We three looked at each other. Fiórcara sighed and mind-spoke to the other Sidhe.

"We have made a grave error. Would we make it worse?"

"A different cup then," said Céadar. "One that will ease your hunger only."

I looked at him with suspicion up in my mind.

Fiórcara mind-spoke to me with intensity. *"I promised you that if I handed you that cup that you would know it, and agree to it."*

I knew he referred to Morag's cup and her acceptance of it, hoping, still, that she would gain favour with him. I knew that he understood that I saw what they were considering (would do anyway?) as a death, a death that, perhaps, could not be undone. The death of who I had been, my history …

Time passed. I felt the dizzy and the disorienting headache of hunger; I pushed it aside. Would I go into the Hunger for the second time in my life—here? I shivered. I did not feel brave or believe that I could indefinitely last without breaking. The Sidhe had saved me from that fate in our beginnings together; would they bring it to me now?

"Danu, I will not do this," Fiórcara finally spoke. "Neither will Céadar. You have my word on this. But there is a cost that you will pay. However I think you will choose that path."

I listened.

"From this day, you will not be able to transit from Between. I cannot tell you now for how long. I can and will do this tonight. No flights to the beach or to the stars, or back to Dagon's arms. This is my only other offer. There will be no further ones."

I pondered this. "Will you allow me to remember *why* I will not be able to do so? Or that I once could—joyfully?"

"I have always before offered you the choice of retaining or surrendering your memories. That choice is and was available as a way of freeing you from your past and protecting us from it.

I think choosing to remember may bring you sadness and anger towards us, and that could make your stay here difficult. But I will allow you that choice."

I shook my head. "Dagon told me in our last meeting that he will always remember and love me, in spite of the fact that it is not safe for us to be together. He called it his 'consequence.' If he can carry that without blaming me, then surely I can too. Fate has brought me to you." *With help,*" I thought. "There are no accidents. You taught me that, Fiórcara. This, then, is my consequence."

Things were wavering and off kilter to me. I felt seasick. I wondered how long I had been in the small bare room. That had not been an accident either.

Dagon was not the only lover who was skilled in interrogation and manipulation, in taking his subject to the place of agreeing to the lesser of two horrible realities: to comply ... or to continue to suffer.

I knew they heard my thoughts. No one was smiling any more and the yearning I had for them now felt like terrible irony.

Céadar poured me a cup. After studying it and feeling my growing pain, I drank it down.

"Would you be awake for this?" Fiórcara asked me with a terrible gentleness.

I just nodded. A few of the tears I had pushed aside slid down my cheeks. *"Crying in happy Between!"*

He sighed. He touched my head briefly and I felt my thoughts being blanketed in a thick haze. Some seemingly small realization was removed—that I could travel at will, under the stars or sun. I would remember that I had once done so. I could touch on the joy and terror that I learned about that on the night that he taught me, but now, I could not. I did not doubt the reality of that.

Like a bird with a broken wing, I thought. *Still a bird and perhaps still living a useful life. Coming to the hand of who had done this thing. Still remembering the sky beyond ...*

I was satisfied to read sadness in both of my companions. They would carry the effects of this, I thought. This was a decision with consequences for them as well.

I felt a deep weariness wash over me. The two spoke in under-mind that I could only partially take in. *"She should be with someone ..."*

I felt Céadar move me further onto the place where I lay and cover me with a blanket. I looked at him then, other questions in my mind.

"Will you hold this day against me, Céadar? Knowing what you had to do, what you both did, will you turn away from me? If so, I would rather be in true loneliness somewhere else. This is your home, and what was done was business necessary for the well being of the Sidhe and who and what you hold safe. But perhaps it is asking too much of you to ask for comfort from you."

I felt my old pain of being abandoned and alone arise. It was like hearing the pack baying on the hill, or the shark circling above me as I sat on the bottom knowing my air was running out, with no tender above to even witness my demise.

Let it come. I thought wearily. *Bring it on. I will accept nothing not freely given.*

"Danu." He looked down on me. *"You are a warrior equal to any of the Sidhe. You drove a bargain today that I did not think was possible from your king."*

"I feel no hate from you," he continued. *"No blame. I have witnessed another victory for you tonight. You guard your heart and those you are connected to in that way with a ferocity that is unfamiliar to me, but I honour it in you."*

I then remembered Dagon saying, "I do not remember giving you permission to love me so fiercely."

Céadar smiled then. *"Let me test this out then, Danu. Would you take comfort from me now? Would you still accept me as one who can and wants to bring you pleasure?*

"See what is," I mind-spoke him. I remembered saying the same thing to Dagon, not that long ago. I was glad that I could still remember.

He brushed my lips with his, and then slowly but surely drove all further thoughts from me. I did not have to ask, for he brought it all. At one point, I cried, the tears that had waited until it was safe to cry. He brushed them from my cheeks and neither of us was concerned about them.

CHAPTER EIGHTEEN

WORKING ON MY JOB DESCRIPTION

I shouldn't have been surprised when Fiórcara showed up in the morning. He looked at both of us carefully.

"Danu falls in what she calls love quickly and deeply. It is entrancing to the other, even if he or she was not looking for this sort of ... entanglement. Are you—" he looked at Céadar, —"growing ... entangled?"

In fact we had just been physically entangled. I pushed the hair out of my face and sat up, unclothed, my body still cooling from our last joining.

"No," said he who I knew as Céadar. "But I can feel the draw of it."

"Yes," I said to Fiórcara. "But no less than to you or your queen. Who, after learning her most intimate desires, I still call, your queen, or the Queen."

Fiórcara smiled. "Good answers," he said. "Honest ones."

"You, Danu, may be called upon to use your powers of 'love' to charm and side-track those who might come as friends but turn out not to be. It would be what humans once called a 'last ditch' effort. I hope it is not necessary, but it is a skill in waiting that you have. As you know from lying with me, Danu, high arousal opens many doors."

"What you might ask of me goes well beyond lying," I said. "I'm not good at that either."

"Therein lies the beauty of it," said Fiórcara. "With any luck at all, you would fall into your love with such a person, and he with you."

I could not believe the instant pain of what he had casually said brought to me. I said nothing. I thought nothing.

I even damped down feeling to nothing. I began putting on my clothes. I could not transit. I would fly then. Even though I knew I wouldn't get anywhere.

"No, Danu," said Fiórcara again. "I am speaking about possibilities only. But surely you must see how it is with you. You wisely stayed apart from your human crewmates because they would not have seen you as a desirable enough object of their affections. You want it all. In this perhaps you are like a siren or other luring one. We are all predatory, Danu, you as much as I. Your net is gossamer surrender. What could be less dangerous than that? My queen is currently teaching you some lessons about her own wiles. She is fond of you, Danu, be glad of that. But nevertheless, she could and would have dealt with you differently than I did yesterday."

I remembered him saying to Céadar, "I would not involve my queen in this." I looked at him now in shocked curiosity.

"I cannot speak for her of course, Danu, nor would I if I could. But my best guess is that she would have pressed me to wipe out your past or end you. She is as old as I am, and perhaps wiser. She is studying you under conditions of her choosing."

"*Why do you tell me this?*" I mind-whispered.

"*You have always been reluctant to ask questions when you sense you will not like the answers.*"

He turned to me and for a moment his eyes were as fierce as Dagon's ever had been. "*I chose you for a Midsummer's Eve Queen, Danu. I sated my wanting you with a Sidhe that first summer, while you lay cozied up in the Touch-me-not. And then I gifted you with choosing you as my acknowledged queen the second summer.*"

"*Does that tell you something? I who can have anyone, contacted you, keep the communication between us open. Stoked you even as you slept beside your vampire lover.*

I confessed this to him later, while you lay deep within your battle to heal from what would have been your first and last flight."

"Why did you set up Céadar then?" I asked. I felt him grow still beside me.

Fiórcara laughed. "He volunteered willingly. Most would now very willingly volunteer to come to you, Danu."

"But if you knew what he did not, if your view of me is true ...?" I tried to keep moving through the pain of being accused of being ... what? I had no word for what I was being branded as.

"There would be a problem using you this way though," he said thoughtfully. "You fight fiercely for those that you have claimed—in love. Even those who had proven more than once that they were ready to kill you or let someone else do so."

I briefly got a flash of Morag's green wolf eyes.

"Yes," he said. "And ..."

I bowed my head to the pain then. I was once one who would or could not love. Now I was one who loved too much. As much as I enjoyed the Sidhe and how they brought me to pleasure, I was not of them. Nor, since I refused to stay put with Dagon and play my role as his obedient mate, was I of the Shadakon.

"Now what?" I said simply. The path I thought I was on had narrowed to a crumbling ledge that perhaps would not lead me further forward. My lodestone— my heart—my feelings of being connected meaningfully to another? *All* was *perhaps something I just did, to get what I wanted from the Universe?*

"And in that you honour both your bloodlines." said Fiórcara.

"And now, how does it play out, Danu?" Somehow there was no pain intended in his question. "I feel alone and abandoned. I seek my own ending in various creative ways."

"Yes, and then?"

"I am comforted by someone who would provide for me in my distress."

"Good, Danu! And where does that lead to?"

"I fall in love with him."

"And the net is cast again," said Fiórcara. "How are you feeling right now, my Sidhe knight in white armour?"

He who I called Céadar looked at me and his king carefully. "I can see what you are talking about. But Danu does not do this out of malice. She is, in fact, a warrior. I saw that she would offer up her own ending rather than give up her memories and love for her Shadakon mate. Even knowing what little I do about the Shadakon I was surprised. But I do not doubt that she follows her own truth."

Fiórcara smiled at him and simply said, "You are in good company. I also care for her differently than I do my own. And I, a Sidhe king, have passing thoughts even now, wondering if she has left my side—where she badly wanted to be a very short time ago—to be content to be with you."

"What was your first thought when you realized that she would continue to serve as a conduit to the Shadakon, if we allowed it?" Fiórcara asked Céadar.

He who I called Céadar looked at me and then looked away. "I hoped she would violate the strict rules I set down for her. I hoped she would deliver herself to some necessary course of action that I would not have to take responsibility for ... the inevitable consequence."

"Ah ... but Danu sidesteps better laid plans than yours," said Fiórcara.

"I may have treated her callously at our first meet, but no ... she avoided me creatively. And then the new Shadakon leader, Dagon, was challenged to take her to the edge of death, which he did. And over that edge. But she made her way back to her dying body. I waited outside their hall that night, to ascertain for myself that she had not died."

"As she recently almost did in my own bed," he added. "Her lover was incensed that he later lay where she and I had enjoyed each other, but I was the one who brought her back and kept her alive—AND retrieved him and brought him to her."

"And I did not sleep alone in my own bed for quite a while. It certainly broke up the festive fall atmosphere," he said. "But then you were there ... for some of it."

They looked at each other.

I think it is correct to say that at that moment, I felt as bad as I had usually felt before I reached this planet. I could hear the truth in what had been said. But that couldn't be all that I was: a predatory female who secured what she wanted from her "lovers." I clung to the hope that I could continue to believe differently.

"I used to go to the island," I said. "That is no longer possible. And I would not be of use there. I need somewhere to live or at least curl up and sleep." I felt weariness beyond anything I had experienced. I wrapped my arms around my legs, curling to protect my centre, which felt endangered. I was hungry. I refused to think about how badly I wanted to be held. And that, apparently, was the problem.

"Accommodation is more difficult to arrange in the dark months," said Fiórcara. "And I will not ask you to curl up under the roots somewhere outside."

"I could not," he corrected.

"I will sleep in the locked bare room," I said, my anger rising.

"I will shelter there like some captured and tagged dangerous human animal. I believe you have eliminated continuing hospitality from this Sidhe who recently willingly gave me a name to call him by."

"I will not call you again, Sidhe," I said to him.

"Nor you," I said to the Sidhe king. "You have trapped me here, but in truth it is as good a place as any. I now see that I am in the ranks of the foolish humans who have thought they had a faerie lover. I will be of use as I can be, because of the whale and her child," I said. "Because of the sea of trees."

The pain finally came and claimed me and I went within to where it was dark and calm.

When I awoke I was warm and held. Someone held a cup to my lips that I drank without thought. It allowed me to fall back into sleep.

When I awoke more fully I realized that both sides of me were warm. I reached out with tentative fingers and discovered the chest of who could only be Fiórcara. The other side then? I knew by his feel that it was Céadar.

How could this be?

Fiórcara reached out and pulled me closer. He began kindling me in an unavoidable fashion. I soon gasped and arched under his touch; there was no thought of not-wanting.

"What is my name, Danu?"

"My King."

"And would you set aside a way to personally call me, Danu? Give away a way to secure my attention?"

"No, my king. I would again call you Fiórcara—my friend. I call you now … I beg for your continued attentions." My body trembled on the edge of a lonely finish.

I heard him mind-speak to the Sidhe I had called Céadar. He took over then, pushing me up and almost over. Stopping and starting again.

"And me, Danu? Am I not even to be your Beautiful One? Just a Sidhe? You and I flew in this midsummer eve ritual. Are you as uncaring as the most fickle faerie, Danu?"

I wept. As both brought me to what I had once both feared and wanted, I begged them both and called them both by the names they had given me. I knew I had spoken earlier in anger and could have given away something precious that had been gifted to me. At some point one of them, perhaps Fiórcara first, brought me slight pain. Not such that I wished to avoid it, but previously it had been between he and I and no one else, and now it was between us three. Dagon had asked me if he had erred in not bringing me pain. And he finally had brought me agony.

Perhaps he had been somewhat right. Though he eventually used it not in the service of passion, but rather as cruel punishment.

Perhaps this, too, was a flaw or weakness that I carried, along with wanting to love unwisely. Because I wanted, I wanted … it all. There were new marks now, and both had made them. I soared on the energy they raised in me. I could not refuse permission.

Or I chose not to.

Dagon had told me that consent is complex.

"What do you want now Danu?" One had asked me. Or perhaps mind-spoke me. Or maybe both did.

"Bring it all." I answered. *"I would take everything you both bring me."*

And that is how we passed a long night.

In the morning I returned to the hidden hall.

I was given a seat at a console and a low-level password. Céadar stood behind me, both of us looking professional even though my back still stung slightly and I knew he sensed it. I also knew how it affected him. By the end of the day, I discovered that the Sidhe had imported experts to help them set up and train them in the network they now accessed. Information was coming in at an amazing rate, sorted into what must be dealt with immediately, and what was the usual flow of activity of commerce in the vicinity of their planet. Since I had worked on a ship, I knew what would likely be unimportant; others however, would check my assessments about this.

I also knew where messages might be hidden in seemingly unimportant details and searched for those as well.

And I found some. Lading lists might contain objects whose weight could be accounted for but were unlikely to be legitimate cargo, ships that might have too many crewmembers, or too few. This was information I had absorbed without thinking about it in my years in space.

There were several high-priority issues. One was that no agent could be allowed to launch or leave a death star or satellite in the orbit of this planet, or use a ship for this purpose.

The Sidhe looked into the space around their world. One such object had been almost positioned when its final adjustments seemingly caused it to veer out past a useful orbit, moving slowly but inevitably towards the sun of this planet. I knew that an investment beyond what I could imagine had gone with it.

I understood much without being told, as well, while other things I observed as anomalies but could not put into a great picture.

At the end of the day, Céadar debriefed me. There was now a more comfortable place for me to rest while he looked within my mind, specifically for what I had seen that day.

He was perhaps seen as my handler, although my Sidhe co-workers, being easy telepaths and curious about each other's activities (and particularly interested in their frequent combinations that they formed together), soon realized that both of us relished the idea of leaving together at the end of the day.

And yet ... I did not feel what I had before called *love* for him. I did not see him as a solution or protector. I did not fantasize or think about him much while working. I wanted him often, but did not always act on that, nor did he. Often on arriving at his home, we slept. Sometimes he was not there—and I slept easily. We drifted toward winter and the Dreaming Time.

I knew I did not have Céadar, even though I knew both what he needed and wanted. On occasion I made him wait, but I did this in the service of the eventual satisfaction for us both. Sometimes as we continued to raise the energy between us, I could pull away, at least briefly. I had learned how to do this with Dagon, knowing that it was to both of our benefit to play this game. He and Fiórcara had acted in unison to achieve the same effort on me. So too I played with Céadar. He certainly did not complain.

I had no doubt that Fiórcara could monitor us, and did firsthand when they met together so he could see for himself the state of affairs between Céadar and I.

I was a high security risk for the Sidhe now. Monitoring was not optional. But, for the time being, I was content with my work and connections here.

CHAPTER NINETEEN

CLOSE ENCOUNTER

We entered full winter. Both Fiórcara and Céadar were in their winter appearances. I had not seen the Queen since our last encounter at the pools. I wondered if Fiórcara was trying to keep us separate and cover the fact that I continued to live and work here; separate and out-of-the-way. And with an intact memory of my past.

I should have known she would find me, but I did not immediately recognize her in plain brown garb when she entered the command centre. She stood behind me, with no tell tale mind-speak, not even under-mind. Yet I sensed someone powerful behind me and turned.

"My Queen, I must log off," I said.

"I am interesting in what you are doing," she merely said.

I thought that covered a lot of ground.

"I would not be distracted and make an error or omission. Please let me transfer what I am doing now to another."

I did so and turned around. She was in her winter beauty; her hair silver, her bright eyes now the colour of pale blue sapphires. Even in drab brown, I saw her surrounded in silver light.

For the first time since I met her, I felt the urge to kneel to her. It was at that moment that I realized that she was not Fiórcara's Midsummer's Eve Queen. She was the Sidhe's Queen. And she had been so for a very long time. I thought of the casual time she and I had spent in the pools. I shivered, both because my body remembered her touch—and because I had taken our experience for granted. No one had revealed this to me, but I could have known earlier, had I thought it out.

"What may I do for you, my Queen?"

She, of course, had taken in my thoughts. She continued to study me, and no doubt read me.

There were a few pieces I would have liked to withhold. I knew with certainty that she would know the significance of that—if she didn't already.

"Let us walk, Danu." It was not a request and I did not take it so.

"Should I change to outside clothes?"

"No. There are places here that will do. That will provide privacy for our ... conversation."

I knew then that her king did not know she had visited me and that he would not expect her to be here.

Everyone around us kept their head down and pointedly showed no overt interest in our conversation. I hoped they would remember it later.

"You fear me, Danu? I had hoped to delay your realization of who I am. But I suppose now that doesn't matter."

We walked down a long hall that might not have been visible earlier. There was a door and a room with two chairs and a table—an interrogation room. I shivered again.

"You have generated a lot of ... excitement around you, Danu. Part of this, of course, is that you are beautiful in a way we are not." She gestured to my hair. "Ah, and also able to participate at a Sidhe level of passion."

I said nothing. Once again Dagon was briefly with me. There was no question and I volunteered no additional information.

"My king, in particular, has been taken with you for longer than I have seen him act with others that he fancied. However, he no longer brings you home for me."

At this point she looked me fully in the eyes and I felt her power swirl around us both. "And you have not called for me or sought me out."

I said nothing.

She leaned forward and my breath stopped. The energy that came from her was both arousing and frightening.

"*Frightening,*" she murmured in mind-speak. "*But you like that edge, Danu, do you not?*"

"*Yes,*" I answered her. "*Sometimes. It is something within me that I only recently could see. I still do not understand it. Or know whether I should yield to it.*"

"*Or if I can avoid doing so,*" I added. "*I haven't succeeded at that in my past.*"

"Hence the vampire," she said dismissively.

"*No. I came to him for pleasure and he delivered that without pain or fear. In fact he delivered energy and bliss to me and I spontaneously turned. The rest came later.*"

She looked at me a little more carefully, and then shrugged.

"*I am only interested in your past and connections with the Shadakon in one way,*" she mind-spoke me.

I picked up the ancient indifference that I had once sensed in Fiórcara. I guessed what she was referring to, but refused to acknowledge it. I did not feel like being helpful in this process.

I prayed that her action upon me would be interrupted before she did what she had come to do.

"*My king, who allows you to call him Fiórcara, seeks to protect you. Suddenly you are not present in our hall, although I know he still wants you, and then he is gone. And I know he has been with you—somewhere else.*"

I said nothing. I met her eyes briefly and then intentionally dropped mine.

"*I cannot allow this situation to continue.*"

"I am useful," I said. "Your king explained to me a long time ago that being useful was what he found interesting about me."

"We will muddle through," she said.

There was the sound of running in the hall. It would not happen soon enough. She glided to my side of the table and placed her hand on my head. I remembered the joy I had received at her hands.

She paused momentarily. It was enough.

I had to try whatever I could do. I imagined Dagon's back garden and the frosted leaves. I saw him inside and alone in his library. I launched myself like a bird with a broken wing.

And transited to his back garden.

The king would be in even more trouble now with his queen. Perhaps his own foresight had caused him to make the decision he did.

Apparently I had not been blocked from transiting outside of Between. I stood shivering in the cold, wearing only my inside brown working garb. *"Better the devil you know ..."*

I called out to Dagon. *"I seek shelter, Dagon, only that."*

CHAPTER TWENTY

ONE MORE NIGHT

Dagon opened his door and stood in it. Seeing him again overwhelmed me. I touched my Maker hand and stood in the watery moonlight. And then, without further thought, I sank to my knees before him.

There was nothing more I could do. Perhaps I had jumped, as the old saying went, from the frying pan to the fire, but I had not let her take my past with him from me. I would live or die intact.

He raised me then and looked deeply into my eyes. *"You arrive at my back door by moonlight. I take it you are not under contract then."*

I shook my head.

"No, Danu. You must speak your intent before I may choose to admit you. Why are you here? Specifically, what do you want from me?"

I tried to gather myself. I didn't know what I wanted except to live remembering who and what I had been. Except to not hand over the love that I carried for him, love that was seen as an aberration by the Sidhe. But what could I ask for from Dagon?

There was nowhere on this planet that I would be safe anymore.

I looked at him without looking away. "I would ask from you what you once granted me at our first meeting: one night. Only that."

"You were under contract then," he mind-spoke to me impassively. *"You paid a lot for my attentions then."*

"I will give you all I have," I said simply. *"As I have always been willing to do. I only beg you treat me gently, my love."*

He drew me up then. The transit had cost me more than I had experienced before. I tried, I really tried to remain strong and upright, but the last thing I saw were the flickering lights in his dark eyes.

I revived on what had once been our bed. There was no great pelt and there had been other small changes in the room. My brown clothes had been removed; the small device that I wore every day was still clipped to my shirt collar. Dagon had turned on lighting that I didn't know existed. He was tapping the monitor carefully with one finger.

"I know you are weary, Danu, but we must talk, and maybe more than that. Were you sent here so that we might have this talk?" He looked at the device under his fingertips.

I looked at it in horror. Why hadn't I ripped it off? I was already dead according to their security rules, but had I been used again? Was my flight expected?

"I was tagged so that I would not go beyond my approved security clearance area," I said.

He looked at me a long time, and then seemed to accept this explanation.

"Well. This gets more and more interesting. I have been following some of the communications of the Sidhe. I had recently noticed a slightly different, ahh, hand on some of the information stream. Someone who might be more skilled than the average Sidhe at knowing what stood out as unusual about the coming and goings of freight ships. And, of course, their cargo. It never occurred to me that it might be you. But why not? I knew you survived." He briefly turned up his palm.

"Can you get in from outside the system?" he asked.

"I don't think so. Someone else logs on for me. I am limited in what I know and do."

"So ... you didn't get the raise you wanted? Inadequate working conditions?"

I felt his sarcasm and seeming indifference, yet his under-mind was intense. I felt his attraction to me, but I knew that would not necessarily save me from his anger.

"The Sidhe king I have called Fiórcara flew a Midsummer's Eve Queen this summer and later she stayed by his side. I did not realize until today that I had misunderstood her title. She is his all time Queen and has been for ...?" I shrugged.

"It was revealed in my security interview that I was disciplined in my acceptance of deep mind probes. This brought you up as a subject of concern. The solution to the Sidhe was simple: they—he—would wipe out my past. He chose not to. His Queen sought to correct that error today."

"That seems like it would have been a good solution for you as well. There is no place here for you, Danu."

It was then that the path before me disappeared. I stood where a rock-fall had taken out every possibility of moving forward. None of us can go back. I could not go on. I did not want to die; I did not want to lose my past, my memories. Perhaps Fiórcara had allowed me the small mercy of going where I chose, to experience this final truth. My old life no longer led to a future from this moment. I hung my head.

My love had been an aberration to this Shadakon too.

I had been allowed by fate or luck, or whatever guided me to find love within that I could give another. But nothing can last forever. Fervent wishes couldn't change that.

"Perhaps you can trade me and the monitor for something you value," I whispered. "There are those that want to tie up remaining loose ends, the queen being the first in line."

"I can only imagine how she feels about you, Danu. You have kept her king totally preoccupied for years. I would suppose that her patience has run out with him and you."

I said nothing. The ache in my heart was slowly pulling me in like the centre of a dark star.

I wondered if I might simply die of sadness; there were those who seemingly had achieved that—medieval maidens mostly. I thought of the woman in the tapestry.

I heard his hiss and expected instant pain but I didn't flinch. Where he had briefly grabbed my arm I felt the sad response of my kindling to him.

Dagon paced. He left me standing in his now well-lit bedroom, naked and cold. "Can you call him?"

I nodded. "Would you ask me to do this now?" I tried with all my remaining strength to put my yearning, my wanting him aside. I kept my eyes down.

"Hmmm. I could read you first. He would expect me to anyway." And then he indicated the bed. "Lay down, Danu."

I lay down where I would never again lie surrounded by joyful shared energy. He sat beside me and bent over me. I did not attempt to block him or contact the part of him that I longed for. However my grief could not be damped down. The tears slid slowly down my cheeks and I blinked to clear his access to my eyes. I saw the dancing flames in his eyes and the pain blazed through me. Then I finally knew, after all my experiences, what it was to be undone, to be lost with nowhere to go. I lay still and looked at him and went down into the pain of it. Here we were. *Farewell my love.*

I heard a sound that would have come from my own heart if it had had any hope of being heard. The keening of the hawk whose mate is heart shot while beside him in flight. He fell across me and I felt his heart beating against my own. I could not move; I did not want to move.

He gathered me up. We lay face-to-face, heart-to-heart. "Ah, Danu ... I cannot do this. I promised myself and you that I would never raise my hand to you. But later I went to you with the intent to taking you to your death, or little death, and still you returned to me again and again.

You bring with you the wrath of the Sidhe, no matter what I do. My clan depends on the work that they provide."

"Please let us have this night," I said. "Just this night. I have no future line. Return me and their device in the morning. Decline to search my mind. There is much there that would unavoidably hurt you. And little that would be of use to you. Dagon ... I do not want to cause you further hurt or pain."

He grew still. And then, as he had in our past, he slowly and carefully brushed my body, ritually sweeping away the faerie energy on me. I shivered under his touch. How could I have let this life go?

"No, Danu. We are going to use our time tonight for one thing only. No doubts. No regrets. Just remember one thing."

And then I wept as he mind-whispered. *"Just remember that I love you, and that you love me."*

It was a cold night of silver moonlight. I was hot and so was he. I knew I had brought more and more faerie each time we had reunited. This night, our "one more" night, he pleaded for me as I did for him. We did not sleep. We did not doze nor drift. One or the other of us would stir up the fire and add more energy to it. We burned it all in one night.

There would not be another for us ever again, I believed.

In the morning I donned my brown clothes and walked into the garden. I had barely pictured Fiórcara. much less summoned him, and he was beside me.

Dagon had come outside with me, and the two of them walked apart and I could hear nothing that passed between them––two leaders of their people. I stood as a tree, as a stone, and waited. I felt the energy meridians of the planet that ran through the frozen soil beneath my thin shoes. I felt the cold wind that eddied into this space and found easy access to my body through my thin inside garments. I did not wonder what would happen to me. I saw nothing before me. I had stopped at the edge of my life and lit a great fire last night. The cold was now seeping in, but it didn't matter.

When Fiórcara grabbed my arm, I barely noticed.

And then we were in Between.

CHAPTER TWENTY-ONE

THE TRIAL:
WHAT SHOULD I SAY?

We landed outside the control centre hill hall. I momentarily stopped and turned to Fiórcara, who had not said a word, or looked at me since we had met in Dagon's garden.

"I just want to thank you, my king."

He looked at me without responding.

"For not taking away my one escape. For giving me last night."

He just shook his head. "I did not do that, Danu, you did that yourself. It is now very clear that you are powerfully Sidhe. I cannot mind-force another Sidhe. You can, however, be killed. If that happens today, know that it is not my wish."

We were both silent. We entered the hall, him behind me but not touching me.

Céadar met us at the door. He unclipped the monitor on my collar and carried it with him down a familiar hall that I had been in only yesterday.

We entered the small room. There were more chairs now, and a few Sidhe in the chairs. There was a mind-quiet and frosty grey Sidhe who seemed to convey great age was presiding over what was to happen. He did not look at me and I didn't remember seeing him before.

The queen was seated in front, no longer in brown. She looked glacial. She was dressed in many shades of blue shining through ice, and her sapphire eyes were icy as well. Her long slim fingers were clasped together. Her king seated himself beside her and, although I had not noticed in the garden, he also was dressed in shades of snow and snow shadow. He took her hand.

Then I knew I was lost.

I went to my knees before them both until she said dryly, "Enough. Go to your place."

A few of the Sidhe that I had worked beside were there as well. They looked like they wished they could be anywhere else—maybe sleeping under the root roofs of their own hill homes. No one made eye or mind contact.

The meeting—or trial, or official ritual of termination or whatever—was called to order by the presiding old Sidhe. He read an account that was correct in details but did not touch on the reality of what had happened yesterday.

I had left my assigned area and went to this place—in fact I may have gone anywhere. This was a serious offence with little latitude in sentence.

I had then transited out of Between, to the private home of the Alpha leader of the Shadakon. There I remained for the span of a night before Fiórcara retrieved me. I had taken all the information in my mind, and also the device I was wearing at the time. This had resulted in a serious security breach; there was no knowing what information had been transferred to him during that time.

In addition to the above, it was noted that I had kept continuous company with the communications expert I called Céadar while working in the Sidhe facility. As he was the one who had raised the issue of security before I was given access to the information flow, there were several concerns noted. One, that his ability to evaluate me might have been compromised at the onset. Secondly, that any evaluation of me now should be re-assigned to someone more suitable.

I remained like a tree. I heard, or maybe felt, the wind rising. I made no resistance to it. I breathed deeply and slowly, feeling the winter energy cool the spot fires of panic within me.

It didn't matter. It didn't matter. I knew what had happened, I even knew why. There was jealousy among the Sidhe and believing that they all were content with brief connections had been a wrong assumption. Easy to make, but wrong.

I was asked to stand.

I was proud, in a remote way that I still could.

He asked me if I had entered this wing of the building yesterday.

"Yes."

"And had you been instructed that you had limited access in this facility, and breaking the rules would result in being considered an unacceptable security risk?"

"Yes."

"And who instructed you about this protocol?"

I looked at Céadar who did not make eye contact with me. "This leader did," I said and indicated him.

"The Sidhe you refer to as Céadar?"

"Yes. He told me that he wanted no possibility of me later saying that I had misunderstood."

There was a faint murmur of mind-speak at this.

"Did you in any way misunderstand what he had told you?

"No." I noticed the queen smiled faintly.

I waited to see if I would be asked anything faintly helpful to my case, but it didn't happen.

"We now have to move to an even more serious issue. Did you transit out of Between yesterday, still in uniform, to the door of your previous Shadakon lover's door."

"Yes."

"Had you been told not to leave Between?"

"No."

The effect of that "no" sent more ripples into what was no longer a still pond.

"I'm sorry. Would you repeat that?"

"I was not told I could not leave Between."

"Explain this."

"I was told that due to the fact that I allowed my Shadakon lover deep access in times past, that I would not be allowed to retain my memories of my time with him that occurred prior to my taking my position here. In that way, the Sidhe would be safe from me returning to him. The chance of loss of any information he might gather from me would be eliminated."

"And you agreed to that?

"No."

Another larger ripple.

"I don't understand. Why was this not carried out?"

"You will have to ask your king," I said.

The room grew loud with mind-speak.

"I will return to that," he said, with perhaps less assurance than he had had earlier.

"Why do you think it was not carried out?"

I sensed the far-reaching net that could catch whoever it could. I was grateful for how Dagon had modeled his way of dealing with questioning. He had taught me well when not to add more, and perhaps dangerous, information.

"I cannot speak for my king," I said. "Nor would I do so even if I could. But I did state at that time that I would choose true death over losing who I was and therefore am. My memories and the love that I came to have and still bear for the Leader of the Shadakon continue to be precious to me."

There was a little more space that I could use and I took it.

"Your king, and mine, told me that I was useful to him and to the Sidhe. I assume that I would be of little use dead."

I sensed anger then in my questioner. He had assumed that he been well briefed by his queen but this information now put him between her and her king. Perhaps she had hoped that I would be silenced early on, and these facts would not come to light. Perhaps she hoped her long-time king would lie or twist the facts and leave me to my fate.

He turned back to me. "What then would prevent you from transiting off to visit with this Shadakon and passing on information?

"The ability to transit was taken from me by my king," I said. "I was effectively kept here in Between for the foreseeable future. I accepted this. At least I could remember who I had been. The path of my life ..."

"That apparently didn't work, because you did transit out yesterday."

"Yes."

"How then?"

"I felt that my memories and probably my life were going to momentarily come to an end yesterday. In this room," I added. "I had nothing to lose. I was not sure I could transit. I didn't care if I didn't arrive," I added dispassionately.

"Is there anyone who can substantiate this?"

There was a loud silence. Strange to say, but I heard every faint sound in the room. Breathing. A faint sigh. Sidhe moving in their seats restlessly.

"There is one reliable witness." I heard the clear voice of Céadar. He came forward with the device that I had worn clipped to my collar. Everyone, and especially the queen, looked at it with concern.

Technology had not come easily to the Sidhe, and most were not comfortable with it even now.

He pointed it at the smooth pale wall. He made some adjustments and then an image with sound brought us what had occurred yesterday. It showed the queen coming up behind me as I worked, and me politely asking to sign off before attending to her, and then her demanding that I accompany her down the hall that led to this room. It continued on to show what she had said to me, that she would correct the error that her king had not attended to, and then her quick movement to me and touching my head.

My disappearance.

Céadar stated that he had arrived, a moment later, to find only the queen in this room. The security breach had been complete.

"This enquiry is larger than first realized," said the moderator. "But does this device show anything useful further?"

"Yes," said Céadar.

I watched as I entreated Dagon for shelter—for the night. And then my monitoring device had sat, recording all as we spent our night together. I sat, reliving it all: his early decision not to access information after I asked him not to; the fact that he had already recognized my hand in the new information flow—without me having to tell him any details of that; my statement that I did not have clearance to provide further information. And lastly, he and The Sidhe King talking apart from me as I stood unresisting, waiting to return to Between.

"There are additional parts of their night together that I have edited for the sake of time. They document what Danu and the Shadakon did for the rest of the night. They are, of course, available to those who have need to see them."

"I will speak now," said the Sidhe king I called Fiórcara.

"I brought Danu to Between three years ago. It was clear to me from the onset that she would be useful to us. In the time that has passed since then, her Sidhe skills have strengthened, for she is Sidhe, as well as Shadakon. And human—although that is fading from her."

"Her first plant ally was Touch-me-not. She stood unafraid and communicating with and touching it with its permission on several occasions on her first visit to Between. She has touched minds with the whale clan."—Somehow, he pronounced their name. "She was my Midsummer's Eve Queen two summers ago, and although untrained, she sang and helped raise the cone of power and knew how to direct it."

"I have taken her to my bed and elsewhere and enjoyed her many times. I was not aware that this would cause distress to my queen. At any rate, she was not present in Between until recently. I, of course, made her my Midsummer's Eve Queen to honour her return."

"Early on, Danu brokered a deal between myself and the Leader of the Shadakon. Currently his clan is successfully holding the borders of the protected land. They do what we would rather not do and do it well. And inexpensively," he added. "He is also doing surveillance and co-coordinating their information with me and us even now. We reaffirmed this arrangement this morning."

"And finally ... I specifically promised Danu I would not take her memories from her. She had already proven to me earlier that she would die for her convictions and I had no reason to disbelieve her this time. As she spoke earlier, and accurately so, she would not be useful to me, or to us, dead. I did not disclose these matters to my queen. The information she received from other sources was possibly not complete or accurate. I take responsibility for that. It was my error in not confiding in her the fast-changing details of our activities here, and of our primary responsibility of preserving life and a place for us on this planet."

"I will correct this error as soon as possible. I believe she was acting in an attempt to protect all her subjects. The missing piece is that Danu is also a Sidhe, and subject of us both. And I continue to have use of her."

"Oh ..." he added, seeming casually. "I did, in fact, block the knowledge from Danu that she could transit and she never challenged that prior to yesterday. It is a proof of her focus and abilities that she overrode my inner command. But perhaps not so surprising, as she merely reclaimed her heritage. I could not prevent any of you here from transiting, or flying. Danu also flies very well."

"She is Sidhe," he said.

I tried very hard not to weep. No matter how this turned out, he had gifted me with a broader picture of myself than one who whose primary purpose was to ensnare others with my sexuality over and over again for my own use and pleasure.

The moderator seemed stunned by this defense of me. Nothing had turned out as he had been led to expect.

The Sidhe queen sat silent. She showed nothing. Her king had absolved her of any wrongdoing, while letting everyone know how the events had progressed. She was, at least now, boxed in as surely as when I lived in Between with no options. I suspected that this issue was not done between them and I hoped I would not be drawn in. I remembered how beautiful she was, floating in the water, and how much I had wanted to come to her. And that I had. I would hold that memory then.

I looked up briefly to see her looking at me. She had, of course, followed my thoughts. I could not read hers and dropped my eyes to her.

"Is there to be no consequence for Danu?" she finally asked quietly.

"Yes," said Fiórcara. "She has made a final goodbye with one she would have chosen to be with for a long time. There is no room or way in this world or his for that to manifest for her any more. I'm sure she will continue to feel the pain of that loss as time passes."

The queen responded coolly. "You speak of a Shadakon, my king, a foolish choice from beginning to end. Especially for a Sidhe."

"Her Shadakon blood awakened after two days in his arms. The Shadakon were, in their way, more welcoming that perhaps we have been; more forgiving, certainly."

The room fell silent. We were now definitely in Between time.

The moderator came to life belatedly. "This meeting is adjourned unless anyone else has something additional to bring up. There will be no further judgment against Danu.

There was more loud silence in the room; then everyone rushed out, and I was left standing with Céadar.

CHAPTER TWENTY-TWO

LIFE GOES ON ...

The room where I had almost died either to who I was or even to my true death emptied quickly.

I had been defended by my king. He and his queen left together, with no mind-speak to me. I did not attempt to thank him. Perhaps he had not done it for me. He had once told me, before I had accepted and surrendered to him, that he was interested in what I did, more than who I was. Perhaps that was still his primary interest in speaking up for me.

It was enough. I was still alive, and free to leave this room to go ... somewhere. I just did not know where.

Céadar waited until after the room had cleared.

"You have to leave this area," he said, and smiled at me. He read my deep weariness and hunger that I had blocked but that now was coming to claim me. "I would like to informally, ah, debrief with you what just occurred here today. I would ask that you accompany me to my home, Danu."

I looked at him but did not let my relief blind me to my circumstances.

"This is your chance to step back from me, Céadar. I have been a long-staying houseguest. I do not assume that our arrangement will continue. Is this still a duty that you are fulfilling?"

His green eyes were the dark green of the winter shadows of his namesake. He was, I could not help but notice, still the Beautiful One to me. More than the other Sidhe I noticed in my everyday contact. I excluded the king from the comparison. I had ties with him that caused me to see him as ... irresistible, and he would always be my Midsummer's Eve King.

But I had flown this summer with Céadar. "Does this continue to be a duty for you?" I asked again.

"Are my home and arms merely an expedience for you?" he asked.

I shook my head. "No, Céadar. But I come straight from the arms of the lover I have left in another life who is now inaccessible to me."

I thought for a moment. "I believe that way is closed now. I have been wrong before, but I carry no false hope that I have a place with him. For him to be useful, as well as I, we must both do what is in front of us. I wish him to have someone by his side, if he chooses that. I wish the same thing for myself."

I hadn't expected to say this. Perhaps the discipline of carefully holding my tongue earlier had made me less wary of what I would now say. I realized, however, that what I said was true: this was a part of love. I wished him well and content. I wished him safe. A mate could provide that to him if he so chose.

I knew that the Sidhe did not partner in such as fashion, although their king was obviously in a long-running agreement or partnership. I did not expect it for myself. I was tired and hungry. I wanted to leave this room, and I wanted Céadar.

"I would gladly accompany you, Céadar," I said simply. "If that is your wish."

He took my arm then and we walked down the long hall where I had believed all would end in me losing my history or my long gifted life. Also my hard-won realizations, my passionate connections, my time on the island. Who I had been and who I was becoming.

We walked past the roomful of Sidhe workers who now stared at me frankly and openly. Even those who had not been present at my trial mind-spoke to me with great kindness. I was surprised and grateful.

I had wondered how it would be when I worked with them again—if I worked with them again. Céadar smiled at me. "*There is more, Danu.*" As I removed my snow-stained brown garments and went to retrieve my own clothes from where I stowed them, I was surprised to find different clothes in my basket. They were the colour of snow over the sand and seaweed, a glinting of lavender and grey-green winter ocean. Tucked beneath there was a pair of soft, warm boots.

I stood in amazement.

"*They are a gift from your king, Danu. I believe he intended to give them to you himself at winter solstice, but you have clearly become threadbare while in our service and he may be absent from you for a while. He and his queen were joined when the history of Old Earth was still young. They have different interests, and as you have come to understand, somewhat different appetites. She will not stay here for long, I think. Or perhaps now she will. He will wait her out.*"

"*Does that information bring you pain, Danu? He may not be available to you.*"

"For the foreseeable future," I said.

"Yes."

"I believe that I should not make a comment about the choices of our king," I said.

"Yes," said Céadar again. "Once again you have deduced a truth about us that no one would have told you directly—we would not have thought to. Had you not acted as you did today, you might not be here now, putting on your winter finery."

"And they look wonderful on you," he added as I adjusted them on my body.

"I don't understand," I said.

"Somehow you do, Danu. There are some unspoken laws of faerie. We do not betray each other, and we do not blame another Sidhe to save ourselves.

As free as we are in making our sexual connections, we do not come to each other with an intent to undo or belittle each other." He continued. "Our queen was very vulnerable today. She greatly overplayed her hand, but both myself and our king were at risk as well. It all lay in your hands: how you presented yourself, what you said and left unsaid—what you even thought."

"Of course, our king absolved his queen of her questionable decisions yesterday—possibly decisions not based entirely on reason. I suppose that you now realize that jealousy is possible for us, but anger at losing one's position of power, or feeling that threatened, is even more likely."

"Our queen was preserved. And, you, as his previous midsummer's eve queen, were preserved as well, as you both should have been."

He looked at me deeply. "I have never seen him act this way towards a 'lover,' as you would say, before, and I have known him a long time."

I stood warm and ready to leave.

"Let us share a cup together, Danu, and possibly more. I was aroused by watching the information our device captured. I particularly liked the part when he pleaded for you. Perhaps we can continue to play our own version of that out this long cold winter."

I wondered if I should feel alarmed or insulted by what he had just said: that he had enjoyed watching Dagon and I on our long night. I checked within but could not seem to find any strong indignation.

"More and more like a Sidhe," he said. "And besides, it saved your life. And preserved our agreement with the Shadakon. His decision not to access you has been noted. Perhaps we can have more direct communication with each other now."

"And now," he said, opening the door to a swirling night of snow and cold, "it is time to return to our roots." And he led me to his home.

CHAPTER TWENTY-THREE

ANOTHER SIDHE SPRING

★ ★ ★ ★ ★

I will say little about how the rest of the winter passed. Céadar and I worked shifts that did not always correspond. He was often away while I slept. I never attempted to learn his schedule, nor see if his away time was always due to work. We were content with each other when we joined.

I could not imagine others not finding him intoxicatingly attractive. I had long ago learned every part of him. I spotted the lighter highlights in his hair as spring came to the land. His eyes were brighter, with dappled sunlight now part of the colour of them. He laughed at my delight in him. He saw himself as merely beautiful, but not exceptionally so, not like I did.

Sometimes I thought of the beautiful queen as well and when I brought to mind certain scenes, I felt the phantom pleasure of her touch. A part of me remembered with clarity the feel of her cool hands, However, I did not know her name. I could not call her.

I think I would not have if I could have, but I had fooled myself before.

I thought about Fiórcara. The silence between us had been absolute. Yet I wore the most beautiful piece of clothing I had ever imagined, a gift from him that he had not even been able to put into my hands.

I had thought about his actions on the night I transited to Dagon's house. I guessed at some of what had happened even though I would never know for sure. I believed now that he monitored me from the moment I landed at Dagon's door.

He was either present or confident that he could affect me from a distance, and if I had begun to disclose anything that the Sidhe could not afford to share with the Shadakon, I would have been silenced and the security breach would have been closed. He could have done no less. The device I inadvertently (?) wore saved him from disclosing that to the others and his queen.

He could also have demanded my return at any time that night. He could have humiliated the Shadakon leader by insisting I come with him then and there and taken me from his side. He was so close in the morning that I hadn't had to call him. I felt that he had been an unseen third to Dagon and my last evening together. He had done the same thing in Between, when he invited Dagon to spend an afternoon with me in the glade in Between on my first visit there; Dagon and I had been oblivious on both occasions. And later, he and Dagon had come close together with me as I slowly recovered from my transit beyond the atmosphere, and to death or very near death. Both alternated in nurturing me and wishing me to live. Both lay with me in the Sidhe king's bed.

Two leaders of their clans that had stayed apart throughout their histories were now cooperating with each other. Cooperating to save this precious world. Sharing and preserving me.

But both must continue acting in keeping with their positions. The social codes of the Sidhe and the Shadakon were accommodating of short-term dalliances, but if a leader took a mate or partner, she had to stay within expectations of the clan.

I had not been able to do so; my worlds conflicted with each other. I could not, or maybe would not, confine myself to what was required, and crossed from one world to the other. In the process I had put myself and those I loved in a dangerous balance that would not hold. I had endangered Dagon again and again. Dagon fought back. An ugly protector arose within him.

Fiórcara attempted to show me that I could not have, and he would not allow, an exclusive relationship with him. I fought him in this, but he did not harm me, nor even abandon me. Had his long-absent queen come in the timely fashion that she did by accident? Or did he summon her?

He brought me into sharing his circle of pleasure, and he had assigned me to Céadar, and Céadar to me. We both knew that. He had chosen well. We were, at present, content.

Fiórcara had saved my life more than once. And something had passed between he and Dagon on the morning that I returned to Between to face the consequences of my actions.

The queen was the Sidhe king's protector, and she would have simplified her job by ending me. I could see that I threatened the order of things she had lived by since my human ancestors were discovering the advantages of cooking meat. Kings and queens wandered. They did not set aside their duties to do so. Even Dagon had understood the problem I posed for her.

Dagon and Fiórcara had protected me and allowed me to become who I was now. I had visited sadness upon Dagon. I did not and might not know if Fiórcara missed me now; it wasn't an emotion I had seen or felt any Sidhe exhibit.

There was much that I still did not know or understand about the Sidhe. I did know, however, that both they and the Shadakon were old and proud races. They were children of the Visitors who were left behind when their ship mates left. I was of both, but could not be fully either of them.

The Sidhe king had claimed me as Sidhe. In front of his queen he had declared me to be so. I would be grateful and content with that. I had again arrived—somewhere, and it was enough.

And so spring slowly came to the land, unfolding leaf by leaf. The Sidhe began to take on their spring colouration; only I remained the same as always.

When I mentioned this to Céadar he smiled. He wrapped a strand of my red hair around one finger and simply asked, "Would you like some coppery sunshine here? Perhaps flames when St. Brigit's day arrives? To honour that goddess of her fiery forge and the tools and weapons she invented?

I must have looked puzzled. "We look the way we want to appear, Danu. You noticed when I changed my appearance slightly to not cause you sadness when you looked at me."

"Sadness was not exactly the effect I wanted," he added with a smile.

"Does anyone here actually look the way I perceive them?" I asked.

He looked deeply into my eyes. I felt the draw of the deep forest and the silent secrets there.

"Does anyone anywhere really look the way we perceive them?" He kept smiling and I got a glimpse of someone Otherly in his eyes. He lightly closed my eyes with his fingertips. "Look at me now." He put my hand on his heart.

I suddenly flashed on Dagon's heart. His scars of being staked there. I gasped.

"Danu." Céadar was calm and waiting for me to return. "My heart. This heart right here. This Sidhe heart. It doesn't want to be 'yours.' It does want you to be right here right now, with me."

"Other parts do as well," he laughed. I came to him then.

Later as we lay intertwined, I encouraged myself to imagine an early beam of spring sunlight touching my hair here and there. Céadar reached up and identified them among my curls and laughed.

"I hadn't realized that you didn't know how to do that. Or didn't know that you knew. I thought you just liked yourself exactly as you were.

Our work at the centre continued. Sometimes I intercepted information from planet-side. It was packets of information, gathered by another agency. I suspected it was from Dagon or those who he directed in this work. I looked at them and passed them up the line. One, however, seemed uncharacteristically short and I opened it curiously.

I sat without moving in my chair. I did not breathe.

Full spring moon. Joy to you, Danu.

I keyed back. *Received with gratitude.*

There goes my security clearance, was my first rational thought. *Oh well …* was my second.

I was home alone one night soon after this. Well, the word "home" meaning where I stayed, which was Céadar's home. It was comfortable and we were pleased with each other's company, when we kept company. Yet I could feel spring coming on again and knew that soon I would be more and more charged with spring energy, as would he.

It had occurred to me that he might like to have a bed—*his home and bed!*—without me in it every night. I had thought about whether I wanted the same benefit. There were only two male Sidhe who I wanted physically: the Sidhe king (who increasingly I did not think of as Fiórcara) and Céadar. I attempted not to focus solely on him but he was there and I was there and well … spring was flooding. He didn't seem to mind my extra attentions … OK, he seemed to enjoy my spring energy as I did his, but … and…

And then there was the queen. I had not seen her anywhere. I had not attempted to coincide with her. I did not picture her, or try to see where she might be. I did not take a seemingly random walk. But …I wanted to. I still feared her.

And remembered the deep bliss of her touches.

And perhaps … I envied her having what I could not have. Maybe that was the wrong word. I feared any further interactions with her if I managed to coincide with Fiórcara, her king. But I wanted him anyway.

But I did not speak of this to Céadar and I did not intentionally call Fiórcara to mind. If this contributed to his lack of strife with his queen, then it was something (really the only thing) that I could do.

I did dream of him more and more as spring filled the land with new energy. In oft repeated dreams we would return to the beach and then fall to the ground and move to the rhythm of the small waves.

I woke up restless and hot one night. There was a near full moon that would rise soon and Céadar was not there. I thought of flying, and then transiting, to the beach … no one had clarified whether I was allowed to do that now or not. My work at the centre had been uneventful for a long time.

I didn't want to draw attention to myself. It would be nice if I could live quietly, even if briefly, as an experiment. I went to the door and saw the moon rise copper-coloured over the forest. I launched into the air, not totally meaning to go further than Between. I flew over the dark trees and heard the calls of birds or animals that I had never seen. The wind in the trees reminded me of the night sounds of the small waves on the beach on the island. I transited.

I never reached the beach. Or not how I had intended to.

A powerful grey shape crashed into me and took me to the ground, pinning me beneath him. I saw fierce eyes staring down into mine in the moonlight.

"If I was not here, Danu, you would once again face an interrogation, and you would have no evidence to disprove wrongdoing. You have already communicated with Dagon through our system. It was seemingly trivial, but Sidhe are even now examining that to see if anything else had been hidden in either of your messages."

I decided not to play innocent about that or why I was here, but neither would I take full credit for lying under him on the sand, with what felt like talons in my side.

"Did you not invite me night after night in my dreams, Fiórcara? Was I mistaken in that? Were you not already in the air, waiting for me to make the decision I did?"

He did not let me up. He was mind-silent. Finally he sighed.

"I suppose I did, Danu. I did not summon you, or you me. I could feel you each time you chose to not-call my name. I even heard you think longingly of my queen at times. Perhaps she wanted you to come to her. It might not have been what you hoped for, however. You play with the slight edge of pain and it is an attractive addition to your many offerings. She would

not play with you in this, at least not in a way that you might enjoy. That is my opinion, but explore this further if you will. Like your Shadakon lover and his second, Morag, the Sidhe were once fierce and dealt with humans as they would. Some of us have tempered the old fierceness;, some have not. She is very old and powerful, Danu."

"Do what you will do," I mind-spoke, "or let me up."

"Which do you choose, Danu? If I let you up I will fly you down and catch you again. And we will merely have this conversation again. I would enjoy more of that."

Then I saw the fierceness in his eyes and the beautiful Sidhe disappeared.

"I surrender to you, my king," I said more carefully. *"I do so with no impediments, as I have always done. Bring me what you will."* I shuddered, but kept my eyes open and on his.

"Perhaps not a good choice at the moment, Danu, but your only one. I accept your terms and you will learn something about me that you may not have known."

He took the form of the large hawk again, and made a harsh cry over me. He calmly stripped off my clothes as he might have removed my skin, still holding me down and merely shifting his weight from one spot of pain to another to get them off.

He looked like frightening character in an old illustrated fairy story—a fierce winged being.

"I do not come as a mate, play flying with you, Danu, but as the Hawk of Achill. Do not think that because I saved you—and you do know I saved you do you not? —That I will tolerate your wilful nature."

I could feel the great flight feathers against my chest. He buffeted me with them and then stabbed down here and here, leaving hot spots of agony in each place.

I screamed and the wind took my scream out to sea. I screamed again and again and then he took me. I did not want to want him as badly as I did, amidst the pain and fear, but I did. I screamed again—a different scream.

He morphed into his usual form but there was still a wild fierceness on him.

"Are we finished here, Danu?"

I just shook my head. He smiled then, and then appeared to me approximately how I had perceived him in the years I had thought I knew him. My minor wounds bled and he touched his finger to one, and then to his lips.

"Once we, too, partook of humans, or our forebears did." He smiled. *"The elixir is calming. But this is …"*

He came to me again. I did not hear the waves. I saw nothing but his fierce eyes above me.

I pulled him to me again and again.

The moon set. At last we rose and I went to the edge of the water and washed my drying blood off in the sea. I dipped my hair and returned. I hoped my clothes would still pass as nearly normal when I arrived at Céadar's door. If he was there, and still awake he would know it all soon anyway.

"It is time for you to have your own dwelling," said my king, the Hawk of Achill—he did not seem to be only Fiórcara tonight.

"Consider yourself warned regarding transiting. I will find you, and in this guise I can and will kill you. I may take you first, but I will not spare you even so." He looked deeply into my eyes. "Are you confused about what I have just said to you, Danu?"

"No, my king."

"Yes. You saved Céadar with your clear answers. And made it easier for me to find a way to save you. And is there anything else you have neglected to say to me?"

"I thank you for the garments and boots. I have never put anything on my body so beautiful."

"Yes," he said. "I looked forward to gently taking them off you later."

"But this was good, too. I love seeing you just like this Danu, surrendered but still proud. Hot and seemingly never finished with me however I come to you. It is almost dawn. Transit back. You will work today, no matter how sore or tired you are. You will pass any messages from Dagon directly to me, and I will decide if you respond in any way."

He gestured to the sky. I transited to Céadar's door.

CHAPTER TWENTY-FOUR

THE NET TIGHTENS

Céadar was not at home when I arrived at dawn, but it took him less than a moment when he was next beside me to deduce that I had been intensely with someone else. And he knew well enough who that was.

He shook his head at me. "You play with fire, but I'm not surprised. This has been coming for a while. And now we must have the talk that we have avoided up until now. The king is preparing a hill hall for you. You may or may not need it much for the summer months but it will be ready for you soon and come fall, you will have your own warm shelter."

"We should step back from each other. Not completely, and not for 'the fore-seeable future.' But a few steps back. Some unaccounted for nights …"

He studied me quietly. His eyes had continued to brighten as had his hair and I felt his strong and gentle energy around us. He was beautiful to me. I looked back at him.

"Let us complete this, Céadar, while I still have the courage."

"I can't imagine you without courage, Danu."

It would have seemed hard to cry after someone said such a thing; however, I managed. If I had thought that having my humanity fade would take the tears with it—I was wrong. Or perhaps I had not changed so much after all.

He waited. This was another trait that I appreciated in this Sidhe who had taken me as a duty to his king and continued on with that, perhaps waiting without complaint to be discharged of his role. "It may have started that way, Danu," he answered my thoughts. "In fact, I felt that you so resented being handed off to me that you went out of this world."

He shrugged. "But things changed for you and for us. I have stood beside you as loyally as I could. You have another's claim on you, though I will not speak the name. I fear it will bring you … sadness. I am beginning to understand about that through you."

"We flew well together, Danu. We gloried in each other. Do not change that part of your story of me."

"But not this summer, Céadar."

"Is that a question or an answer, Danu?"

"Neither, Céadar. It is simply what is. You will stop my breath when I see you on that night. That I can promise you."

He just looked at me and smiled. "No struggle then. Manageable pain—sadness, you would call it. It has always been a pleasure, Danu. Please don't close the door, we may choose to bring pleasure to each other again."

He was smiling when he walked away.

I moved what little I had to my snug new hall. Céadar gifted me with a new soft blanket. I could now store my own supply of elixir of life. I was not given recipes for some of the variations that I had experienced, but I could not imagine wanting to bring on heightened consciousness while alone.

The better to miss you all, I thought, and then pushed that thought away.

Summer flooded in. There was laughter in the glade and elsewhere. Couples took to the air to practice their flight together, as we had last year.

I put myself into my work. I requested and was granted higher levels of clearance.

I was not merely concerned with the activities of freighters that came and went to the star-port.

I was now interested in why their routes now avoided specific quadrants of space or had radio contact out beyond where one might expect someone to be contacted. Radio contact that was scrambled.

I had a sense of a gathering out beyond easy surveillance: the sharks waiting for the flood tide to swim across the reef; the reckoning once they arrived in numbers too large to be dealt with individually. Or perhaps ships might leave things in decaying orbits that would eventually come to ground.

I put in extra hours, trying to ignore my growing inner summer. The more I formed a detailed a map of space around us—who came and went, whether they deviated from previous patterns—the more concerned I became. Finally I knew I had to speak with the Sidhe king about my observations. And Dagon.

It seemed to be unfortunate timing. I knew I shouldn't be around either of them; at the very least, it might distract me, at worst, I might go into some intense feeling-states that would disturb my fragile claim on calm.

I now lived alone. The energy in and around me grew. I had no idea how I would cope with midsummer's eve. Suffice to say I would be in Between, having my own version of it that might include flying alone.

I summoned Fiórcara. I told and showed him my fears—the now conspicuous blank spaces around this planet where before ships had passed through these areas on their way to and fro.

I feared that this planet, with its attractive forests and untapped minerals might soon be the target of ionizing radiation, an effective sterilization method that the gathering fleet of stealth warships could easily accomplish. This could and would wipe out existing animal life.

The forests might still stand, albeit damaged, but most animal life would sicken and die.

The web of life would be mortally damaged, and it had not yet fully recovered from the last event the humans had brought to it.

Life had been scourged off this planet long before by humans, and afterwards it had lain fallow to allow the effects to fade and dissipate. Later the off-planet inhabitants arrived and forgot or did not think about why the forests were empty. The next such event would take out the current residents of Sidhe and Shadakon as well as any humans present. It would take out the recovering animal life, or at least most of it. I did not think that Between would protect its inhabitants, but even if it did, the world outside would be forever changed.

It was to the Sidhe King's credit and mine that we both focused tightly on the matter at hand.

"And what do you recommend, Danu?"

"We need to pool our resources—Dagon has to see this. And if we are to create a psi barrier of confusion and malfunction, we have to extend it farther out. And keep it up long enough to disable the gathering fleet."

"Is that possible?"

I just shook my head. "I don't know, my king. But if there are other plans, put them in effect as well. I think we will be tested soon."

"Call him," was all he said.

And so we three met in the glade. They spoke alone and then we walked to the communications centre where the Sidhe king palmed open the door. We walked over to my work area and I showed Dagon what I had discovered.

"Seeing what isn't visible," he said at last. "Hearing what isn't said.

This has always been your talent, Danu. I can see the pattern. I have been in wars—although not leading large armies.

I can see the invisible strategy here as well."

He then turned to the Sidhe king. "How far can you and yours reach?"

"This has never been conceived of, or tried, but our midsummer's eve approaches. We will have maximum life energy drawn up then," said the king.

"We can ground all the crews and ships in the spaceport," said Dagon. Perhaps they will be less willing to kill their own."

"What else?" asked the Sidhe king, turning to me.

I found something in my mind that brought me hope. I knew that other beings honoured the raising of the energy on midsummer's eve; those that showed up were woven into the song of power.

This year we needed them all, and they needed to know that. They needed to set aside mating and eating and living their lives to join with the Sidhe

The circle energy would not go to ground this year; it would go out, past the atmosphere. It would fill the space around Exterra. All communications would be jammed, electronics would not work, and people in critical positions would forget launching sequences, passwords and fail-safes.

The death-bringers would be stopped by this, and many would probably die. *Could the life force be used that way? Should we do so?*

I saw no other way. I had seen a recently cleared planet once. We weren't allowed to leave the ship, but dropped off things that could eventually be useful to someone much, much later.

I shivered. "I will go bring this message to those inhabitants who dwell here in hiding."

I will start with the whales, who may be able to help spread the word. If there are other Sidhe who will spread the message, they should go as well."

"I need total freedom to do this," I said. "And to be able to fly and transit at will. The Mothers need to be told as well. They will no doubt choose to stay at least for a while, but they must be given the choice and a way to leave when it is time."

I pulled up a map of Exterra. There were small oceans and several large continents, all treed except for a few strips of desert and grasslands. Humans had not cut down the trees, nor squandered the water. The deserts were small. The vast deserts of Old Earth still had observable river systems under the now constantly shifting sand. This planet was intact—still mostly intact.

I will call a meeting tomorrow," said my king, "for all Sidhe. I suggest you do the same," he said to Dagon.

He turned to me. "There are, of this moment, no restrictions on your movements Danu. Dagon is an ally and if the two of you have some final things to discuss then you should."

I heard his under-mind. *"Take a little time if you would, Danu. This may be the true goodbye."*

He keyed in his commands from my workstation. The screens in the room all went red, announcing an emergency meeting tomorrow. The word was to be spread.

Midsummer's eve was five days away. I once again prayed to old gods and goddesses to grant us the time between to make our preparations.

CHAPTER TWENTY-FIVE

WE ALL DO WHAT WE HAVE TO DO

I turned to Dagon, "I will take you back now, if you wish."

He looked back at me with a look I could not immediately decipher. He shielded his thoughts.

Then I could not help but know that our timeline had ended.

"Never mind, Dagon. Never mind. We are all doing what we have to do. What we can do."

I took him to his back garden. I did not ask to be admitted to his house or to his arms. Although there was a fury of wanting him within me, I refused to either let it overwhelm me or to put it out to him. It just was. He knew of course, there was no way he didn't know. He had always known.

But to leave without more than holding his arm for the transit? I attempted to be a Sidhe warrior—whatever that was. A crying Sidhe warrior. I turned slightly to launch and return to Between.

"No, Danu. Not this way," he said. "You are right. Another stands beside me. I need her to do so, and I have been alone a long time."

We looked at and into each other. I saw the flickering flames and gasped. I attempted to drop my eyes then.

"No, Danu." He drew me closer. "You are still in my heart. The consequences of loving and being loved by you are still here." He put my hand on his heart. I shivered and wept.

"Now that you know what you must know, would you spend a small amount of time with me now? It is obviously growing more precious.

I have to first call a Council meeting—immediately. Meet me somewhere soon. Let us make best use of our small island of time."

I thought of the beach on the island then. The log where I had sat so often beside the hospice of the Mothers.

He winced. We had once come to what seemed like the end of our relationship there. He had come to dispose of me, to get rid of me for good.

"It is the closest thing to a home that I have outside of Between," I said. "I would invite you to my home."

I could feel my summer faerie energy flare around me. I could not damp it down; we both knew that from years earlier.

"One hour then," he said.

He would come to the space that had been my home—the log on the beach. While I was there and he was not, I went and talked to the Mother. I saw the alarm in her clear eyes.

I did not ask her what she or the others would do. I already knew they would stay if they had clients, and maybe even if they did not.

"Can you help with this?" I asked.

She shook her head. "You know the answer to that, Danu. I am only sorry that your spirit has been drawn into this struggle. I know you do not like to bring death—even to those who request it. Few of the people who will be affected will have given consent," she said. "They will die directly or indirectly at your hand."

I looked at her in horror. I hadn't thought this through. The Sidhe had already taken the action of commissioning uncontracted deaths, but at least the trespassers were warned. Some chose to ignore the clear warnings, and that could be seen as an informed choice on their part.

"They have to be given a choice," I said. "I had not seen that. Even if they come bearing death and intend to kill off everything on this planet—otherwise we are no better than they are."

"Yes," she calmly said.

I went to my knees before her. She had given me the missing piece.

She smiled and raised me to my feet. And then, briefly, she held me to her. "Ah, Danu. It has been a pleasure to watch you strengthen your heart."

When I went outside, Dagon was sitting on my log. He was looking out to sea—what one saw when sitting there. There was a small flitter parked beside the building and someone waited inside. I knew it was Nathaniel.

Dagon started the conversation, seemingly impassively.

"You know, Danu, that when this is finished, we Shadakon will have no way to live here. I doubt that many humans will come for a long time. We have to leave immediately."

This, of course, was the logical consequence of knocking out a billion credits or more assault on this planet. It would not be business as usual later, but I hadn't allowed myself to really understand that.

Fiórcara had known.

For a moment the pain of knowing that I would never, even in the far foreseeable future, see Dagon again in any capacity stopped everything. Certainly time. In slow motion I crumpled to sit beside him.

He put his arms around me. "I have known this for a long time, Danu. We have made preparations. We have ships and, ah, willing passengers, to travel with us to where we need to go next. I have been there and it also is a good world. Not like this one, but with more humans—not a bad thing for the Shadakon."

"I don't know what will happen between us here, Danu," he said gently. "But time is passing. Would you rather be somewhere more private?"

I took him to the cove with its small sparkling waves and soft sand. We said nothing further. We did not require permission of each other. He laid me down and I gave him my built up faerie energy. He gasped at times, and I did at others. In the end, we rocked together to the rhythm of the waves.

I placed my palm against his. I did not ask him to renew our Maker vows but the energy flared between us.

"Still Shadakon then, Danu," he said. "But Sidhe as well." He ran his finger down to the place where he had drank my heart's blood when I had wanted that as strongly as he had. He sighed. I shivered.

"Do you want this, Dagon? You know that I do. I am all yours for this final taking."

He then bent to me and took what was offered. He did not leave me in deficit, being impeccable in taking only what I could spare. He partook in who I was in my full faerie summer glory. He sighed.

"Beautiful Danu. Te amo. Para siempre."

Why Spanish? "Spanish is a loving tongue," someone had once sung. Perhaps he knew that as did I.

I said nothing. I could say nothing.

"I know, Danu. I know. I have known since I first laid eyes on you, and maybe before that. We are one. I did not gift you with my blood today. I hope you understand. Lately the ties between us have been painful to you, and I would not add to that in my final absence." "

Do not feed her," Morag had said, a long, long time ago. "It will just prolong this."

Her quote arose in my mind. "Yes," said Dagon. "You are still and always will be Shadakon. You understand then."

We stood for a moment, heart to heart, the energy of the life web flowing around and through us.

Then we brushed ourselves off, and he walked back up the beach, alone.

CHAPTER TWENTY-SIX

BATTLE PLANS

When I returned I summoned Fiórcara. He arrived shortly at my work centre. I repeated what the Mother had said to me, that taking action on the scale we were attempting would result in many lives being lost—that it was taking without contract.

He shrugged. "If what you think is true, and I believe that it is, then they are planning to annihilate us and most of the life on this planet. That would be a first and final act of war, Danu. Well beyond breaking contract."

"There was a time that countries declared war on other countries," I said. "No doubt they then felt excused in what they were planning to do anyway. You are proposing a pre-emptive strike."

He just looked at me.

"Contract is not required by the Sidhe. Permission is not asked."

I looked at him confused.

"I demanded your agreement to whatever I would do to you because I enjoyed your surrender to me and wanted you to understand what you agreed to, and I still do. It was significant to you to give away your protection and even your beliefs that I could not do this or that, or you could keep some part separate from me. I wanted you stripped of those pretences. I wanted all of you. More than your body, sweet as it is, I wanted you to give over everything to me."

"And you have," he simply said. "Again and again."

I thought of the hawk that had skinned me out of my clothes, as a real hawk would have divested its prey of feathers or fur.

I thought of the feel of its sharp beak, taking small tastes of my flesh.

"Yes, Danu, don't choose to forget that. Much as Dagon showed you a cruel interrogator who professionally broke your bones, so I can be the Hawk. It took great control not to cause you greater harm. I felt that you had begun to think you could disregard my rules for you."

"Or set your own rules."

"Do you still think that your energy and desire can tame me, Danu?" He looked into me and I sensed rather than saw the fierceness behind eyes.

"No, my king," I said. And I meant that fully.

He sighed. "Our energies are up, Danu, but we must set them aside now. If you do not approve in your Shadakon way of an effective first strike, what do you propose?"

"They are still far out and time will have to pass before they get here. We could make an announcement on every ship that continuing with their plan will result in their death. Since they haven't acted immediately, I suspect that there is already some debate going on—government versus business perhaps. I would like to say doves against hawks, but I am not sure there are any pacifists anymore. Everyone is just intent on surviving these days, trying to scrape together enough credits to buy whatever may bring them temporary pleasure, or what they think will bring them pleasure."

"Introducing the idea of informed consent to the hundreds of people on those ships might be a novel concept to them. They might want to at least briefly ponder if they want to die for their company or government or whether they want to have a last-chance choice in that decision."

I do not know how much energy we will have to work with, my king," I continued.

"But, if possible, I think we can immobilize—perhaps to unconsciousness—most of the crew members and certainly the decision-makers. Probably painfully," I added.

"Then they will take us seriously," I said. I thought of the hawk again. "It will be too late for most, but perhaps a few will escape to tell the story."

He smiled at me then. "Now, Danu, now you come to perhaps your ultimate use to me and the Sidhe. You are still recognizably human. You will not trigger, ah, species prejudice. You speak many Old Earth languages and you can think on your feet rather than adhering to a set script, which might become suddenly inappropriate."

"Go commune with the whales and whoever else will trust you enough to listen to you on this world. You have three days before midsummer's eve. You will make your announcement to the human fleet before we fly and we will use the energy of the cone of power to do whatever must be done. At very least to drive them away, and, perhaps, to annihilate them all."

"I care not how that goes for them," he said calmly. "I care for few humans. Very few," he said. "Perhaps I care for few of any others, save for my allegiance to the Sidhe. You have known a few that I did care for, as much as I could as a Sidhe." Briefly I saw Lucia, and my heart opened to that pain. "You are one, Danu. And I simply do not know what to do about that."

CHAPTER TWENTY-SEVEN

I PLEAD OUR CASE
AND AM TAKEN
BY THE LIFE CURRENT

"An ash I know, | Yggdrasil its name,
With water white | is the great tree wet;
Thence come the dews | that fall in the dales.
Green by Urth's well | does it ever grow."

—<u>Voluspo</u>, stanza 19
Translated from the Old Norse by Henry Adams Bellows, 1936

First I went to the whales. I stripped off my clothes and paused at the water's edge. I knew that their travels brought them past this beach shortly before midsummer's eve. I remembered the sound of their clan name and attempted to project that outward through the water. I summoned, if I could, she who had come to me last summer.

I swam out in the clear, clean water. I floated and waited. If she had heard me and chose to come, she would find me here, where we had last met.

A dark shape loomed up from the depths beside me. Her year-old calf still swam with her.

"Life has been good then, for you and your offspring," I thought. *"I apologize for summoning you, for we did not have that agreement. Please know that I do so out of great need."*

"And you, too, appear well," I heard. *"Too old for a calf—and yet the same as last we met. You are one of the long-lived ones then. Sidhe ... yet not exactly Sidhe."* She floated beside me.

"I need to communicate something that may be confusing. Then again, you may know far more than I suspect. I apologize in advance if it appears that I underestimate you.

"Continue."

"You know of the bottom of your sea, the mountains that do not show above the surface and the great depths. You know of the middle water, in its many shades of blue, and the life that swims there."

She floated in mind-silence.

"Above the surface of your water world are the air and winds. You know of the weather and storms that churn the waters below. And in the sky of that air are the sun and moons. They are farther away than the bottom of your ocean. They float in their own ocean—in space. You have felt the warmth of a sun too far away to perhaps imagine."

"The sun and the moons float in space, as you and I do now in the water. And also out there are ships with humans in them. I don't know if your kind has encountered boats—the Sidhe forbade their use a long time ago."

"Some of us remembered," she said with no emotion. *"The old ones told us in stories, so that we would not forget the first coming of the humans."* She shuddered and so did I.

"These are ships that can travel across the vast ocean of space. They are gathered in space around this planet. The Sidhe, the Shadakon and I believe they mean to kill off the life here again. We will warn these humans. If they do not respond quickly, we will sink their ships, if we can. Most of them will die then. Few will want to come to this planet again—at least for a while, while they still tell their stories," I said.

"You would make a good storyteller in the ways of our clan," she communicated. The calf swam over to me and nudged me like the curious child he was, except he was three times as long as I was and weighed over a thousand pounds. I ran my hand along his back and he rolled as a puppy would for more touching.

"What do you need from us, Danu?" she asked. I had given her my name last year and I was touched that she remembered it.

"The Sidhe fly to gather earth and life energy in two days," I answered. *"We need you there, however you can be, to contribute energy on that evening. And then we will do what we can do to preserve you and yours. I know some of you have attended before, I felt your energy last year, but we need everyone sentient in the seas—whatever and whoever that means."*

"The message will be passed on," she said. *"To everyone who will or can listen in the seas. Your task is finished here. We will carry it on."*

I floated while I tried to take in what I had just been told: that the beings on this planet were linked and communicated with each other. *Had they been so on old Earth?* I thought of the terrible acts visited on farmed animals. On the forests …

"All life is linked, Danu. All can communicate. Few humans attempt to do so. We support you in keeping us safe—if you can. Go with our blessing."

And then she slowly and carefully sculled close to me and I saw her great eye. I felt her read me and I received—I received sea knowledge. Sea stack and deep abyssal plains, strange beings the likes of which I could not have imagined; the joy of swimming along the coastline, covering hundreds of miles in a day, sleeping and dreaming on the surface under midnight moons.

I cried out at the joy of it. I, who had already felt pledged to the sea, now saw it unfold into the intricate dance of life beneath its surface. Her calf nudged me strongly again and she waved him back.

"We will meet again, Danu. Be well." And then they were gone.

I swam to shore, feeling over some edge in my mind.

The only response I could find to frame this experience was cosmic humour.

"Well, the seas and oceans are accounted for." I shook my head and headed back to Between to drink elixir and rest for the next leg of my journey.

At dawn I set out again. After pondering my interaction with the whale, I decided to divide my huge—*undoable?*—task into groups: birds, and the other mammals—predators and prey, others?

I landed in a small sunlit glade in the middle of the great forest. I sat as still as a stone for a long time, then I brought to mind the small mouse-like creature that had briefly visited me in an earlier summer. I remembered its smooth brown coat, its black attentive eyes and the feel of its whiskers on my foot.

I summoned the clan of … mouse? I apologized for not having any of their names. But maybe many animals were comfortable with no names. Had never had one. Much like the Sidhe perhaps. I simplified my story: fire. Pain. Nothing to eat; offspring sickening and dying; and finally my appeal for their help. Two more suns from now. Their energy needed. We would try to help them.

A few mouse-like creatures crept out of the grass and stood on their hind legs, studying me. I lay down on the ground at eye level with them. I felt some small understanding.

"Can you inform the others? The many, many others?"

A twitch of the nose, a small chittering voice in my mind. Then they were gone. If I received anything clear enough to be called a message it was this: *"We trust the Sidhe and you. We will do what we can."*

I moved to birds. I wasn't even sure there were birds, but I thought I had heard them trill both in Between and outside Lara's window. I spoke to empty air.

Perhaps something moved within the green, perhaps I received confirmation. Perhaps they heard me ask that they spread the information. I thought that the sounds of unseen small callers intensified.

I rose and carried on.

There didn't seem to be any predators or grazers. I called anyway. Perhaps there were unseen eyes on me.

At the end of the day I was far from home. And hungry. I had not paid attention to my own needs.

I sat and leaned against a deciduous tree that was in splendid new leaf. The trees! And the plants! *How could I have neglected them? How does one explain fire and sickness from the sky to a tree?* Nevertheless I pictured what I could: no insects coming to their flowers, silence throughout whatever would be left of the forests, and bitter rain.

I was tired. I wept thinking about these possibilities. I fell into a dream. I felt the web of life activating, integrating … in a widening circle around me. And the tree—I could drink from the tree—it was offering me sustenance.

I awoke parched and weary. Beside me there was a small break in the tree's bark and sap dripped slowly down its trunk. I tentatively tasted it and it tasted like life. It was wilder tasting and more concentrated than my usual elixir. I felt the spring energy as a sharp taste in my mouth and mind. I had some more, as it continued to trickle down slowly. The sap would not be of use where it was. I lapped until I was restored and sated.

I bowed to the tree, to all the trees. The sun was setting and I needed to make my way home. I noticed that the light still seemed very bright and the colours intense. I had felt this way when I had first tasted the elixir of life. I transited home—to what was my now home.

The early stars were out, and by this time tomorrow we would know if we had the means to do what we had to do. We would know if this had been our last midsummer's eve together.

I stood outside and briefly but deeply breathed the mild summer air. No one was in the sky tonight; the Sidhe had been put to work.

I knew I wouldn't sleep so I went to my computer at the centre. The room was full of people. Céadar intercepted me and drew me aside.

"They are moving forward," he said.

I saw the strain on him and I nodded. I also noticed that he was even more beautiful. In fact, he glowed around the edges.

He looked at me more carefully.

"Danu! What energy is within you?" He touched a faint smear of sap on my cheek and put it to his nose.

"You have taken directly from a tree. Did you injure it to do so?"

I shook my head. *"I leaned up against a tall tree in full leaf. I fell asleep and dreamed I was offered sustenance. When I awoke there was a small trickle of sap beside me. I was in need. I tasted it and it tasted like life. It continued to flow and I drank some. It was very strong. I took little. But still I feel ... connected, to all of them, to everyone I called to and spoke with today."*

I blinked in the overly bright artificial lights. He continued to look at me and I fell into his eyes. That's what it felt like ... like I had fallen into a refreshing pool of bright water that reflected the green trees and blue sky. *"With you as well, Céadar."* I paused then. *"It's all streaming in. Perhaps I need to lie down."*

"I will accompany you home," said Céadar. He came into my hill home and settled me on my sleeping platform. He looked down at me steadily.

"Even more beautiful, if that is possible," I mind-spoke. I saw the life force in him, and his male Sidhe energy. I tried to remember what our agreement had been. *"Not quite the foreseeable future?"* Or was that a gentle-let down?

I felt the ache of desire for him. I let it be. He had his own plans for tomorrow, and he was not required to pleasure me anymore.

He poured me a cup of my elixir. *"I think we need to dilute what you have taken in a little."* I drank thirstily for a moment, then set the cup down.

"Danu! You are goddess tonight. You have unknowingly accepted the gift of wild undiluted elixir of life. I am required to do nothing for or to you, but I want you. I want you as my own Midsummer's Eve Queen. If I could bestow that on you, I would come to you that way."

The walls had turned translucent and I felt the outside merging with within. Everywhere was full of the small chirping and chittering of little lives. I heard sea sounds and splashes in the shallows.

"*Never mind being a queen—that job is taken. But if I am goddess tonight, then come to me as my forest god, Céadar.*"

He did come to me then. We merged and I, at least, had no idea of where I began, where he began. Our sexual energies flared up and then held steady and bright. I heard him gasp and later heard myself call out, although if I actually made a sound I do not know. I felt the web of life weave around and within us. It was wide-awake and I could almost hear the song in it—as if I could hear it, but not commit it, even for a moment, to memory.

We would stop and I would have some more elixir of life. He declined, until the night was brightening. We would finish and lay still together, breathing as one. And then one would do something to the other and it would start again.

As the light slowly entered into my consciousness and the room, the walls were solid again. Céadar lay spent by my side. I simply lay quietly and looked at every part of him that I could see. His sun-touched hair, his strong slimness, the rise of his chest as he breathed peacefully. I was safe now. I could love him (as I did now) and he would not know; it would not trouble him and his Sidhe sensibilities.

He smiled in his sleep and threw an arm around me. "*We are still too close for me not to hear you, Danu.*"

He pulled me in and held me lightly. I could have moved away or gotten up without difficulty, but I did not want to.

"*Just like this, Danu. Just like this.*"

CHAPTER TWENTY-EIGHT

SOME THINGS CANNOT BE PREPARED FOR

When we arrived at the communications centre there was a hum like a disturbed hornet's nest. Fiórcara met us at the door, scanned both of us and then looked back to me. "Are you able to fulfill your work here today, Danu?"

I actually felt amazingly good, better than usual. I did not entirely attribute this to Céadar's attentions.

"I have been out for two days, doing what I could to communicate our need to raise as much energy as possible."

"And?"

"The whales promised to carry the message throughout the seas. Apparently they can do that."

He was totally silent at that information.

"The smaller animals pledged as well. I am less certain about the birds or any surviving predator or prey types.

"And?"

"The trees! I think I have the trees. At least on the continent I was on."

More total mind-silence.

"And the situation here?"

"Céadar briefed me when I stopped by last night. The stealth fleet is moving; they are now too close for another warp. They will not be here before we raise energy this evening. Shortly before we fly, I will address them, if you still want me to.

I was going to work on that right now, but the script must remain flexible to their response."

He continued to study me. "And why were you not here last night, Danu?"

I looked at him steadily. "I was gifted by a tree with wild elixir of life. I was hungry and thirsty and at the end of my energy. I had a brief sleep against a tree and it offered itself to me. When I awoke, there was a small trickle of sap near my face. I drank. And then things got … intense."

"I needed to be apart from this. I was part of the web of life last night. I don't mean as we all are, all the time. I mean I felt it and reverberated to it. Céadar noticed this and accompanied me to my home. I requested him to stay. By then, I was in a position of granted power and in need of a consort. He was god to my goddess."

Céadar looked somewhat horrified at what I was calmly telling his king, although I'd never seen a Sidhe look horrified before.

"Granted power?"

"I gave them my name so they will know where to direct their energy. I will fly it up into the cone of power. The wild elixir still lingers in me, but I believe I am very clear right now."

"And will Céadar fly with you?"

"You should ask him. I welcome him if that is his wish. However ..." I let time stretch slightly, "... if he does or does not, I will not be alone."

The Sidhe king just shook his head. "There is no time for another plan. This is your plan and, in truth, our only plan. We are betting it all with you today, Danu."

"When does it start?" he finally asked.

"It has already started, my king. The planet has awakened, the energy will be delivered." The day passed quickly.

I accessed all the translation programs I might need if I found myself talking to someone who refused to—or could not—speak common Old Earth English.

The afternoon had cooled. I remembered my first night of anticipation, wet from the sea when Fiórcara came for me on the beach. I shivered even from the memory of it.

When the sun dipped below the horizon I opened channels in every frequency that I was aware of, including military ones that I had found while pleasing myself at the radio controls alone on my night shifts.

There was a semi-circle of Sidhe behind me, as silent as I have ever heard so many minds in one place.

I opened all channels and began. "I am Danu of the Sidhe, keepers of the planet you call Exterra," I said. "I require your immediate attention. If you know of other channels this should be directed to, please do this now."

Silence.

"We are very aware of where you are and the human business you are hoping to conduct upon arriving near Exterra. This planet is closed to outside intervention. We have conducted our legal contracts impeccably and the planet has been posted for six months, but you, no doubt, already know that."

Far, far away, I faintly felt attention to what I was saying.

"We believe you bring death. If that is not true, you should speak up now, and make an immediate course change."

Finally someone jumped in, as I knew they eventually would. I was playing a game of strategy and somehow I could see the moves well ahead of where we were. I felt a calm confidence that may have been a result of the wild elixir of life.

Or it could have been the strange fate line that I had followed since I got here. The one that had led me to right here, right now.

"Danu of the Sidhe. What is your rank and authority to contact us?"

"The organization of the Sidhe is not of your concern. Who I am is not your concern. Your only concern should be that we will eliminate you from the space around our planet. We both know that there is no time for adequate demonstrations, although you may already be aware that systems of communication and navigation fail in our vicinity. The previous successful interruption of the launch of an unwanted satellite was only a courtesy reminder."

"I now speak to every crewmember who is able to hear this announcement. Your officers are likely to condemn you to a death in deep space very soon. No one will come for your life pods. You will live out the last moments of your lives glimpsing a planet that refuses the orders of man and mankind's business of destruction. I have no idea if you are capable of turning this around. If you can, I suggest you do so in the next fifteen minutes."

I repeated my message in several more Old Earth languages.

I listened to further threats and statements of arrogance. The Sidhe king behind me hissed.

"This is my final message. You have made this easy for me. I do not like killing those who had no choice in the matter, but I will do so this midsummer's eve—without regret."

"Oh. And since you have not chosen to leave immediately, any humans already on Exterra will not leave. Our ground crew will deal with them. Your time here is over."

I shut down the audio but watched the screen. Two ships pulled away and left the area, presumably heading for a launch to warp speed to somewhere else. No doubt they were very aware of the cargo of the other ships.

Approximately ten continued on towards us. "It's time to fly," I said.

We left from the door of the Centre for the glade. I could feel an intense energy, even before we started to pull the spiral up, and, although I put no importance in it, I flew at the apex of the cone of power. First we tightened the spiral, pulling more and more in. Then the centre of that spiral lifted up into the sky. Many voices sang the life song and I could remember it now. I felt the great clan of the whales and the many other creatures of the sea chime in, a tsunami of oceanic energy. The green energy of the forests and trees of the glades were there. Even the small timid ones contributed, taking time and energy out of their short lives.

We went up and up. And then I imagined the images on the screen. The dark no-shapes that defined themselves by the absence of stars.

"May the Goddess have mercy on them, if that is possible. May she preserve us here." And then the energy shot off over our heads and up into the stars.

Immediately, out beyond our planet in the dark ships, nothing that had worked was of use anymore. Circuits were jammed shut or open or alternated wildly until fail-safes were overridden. Human mental circuits suffered similar insults. People writhed with headaches that prevented them from doing anything useful, if there remained anything useful to do. The energy of the spiral was not available to the flyers. They drifted down, looking slightly dazed. However, all had heard the full song of the planet. It would not be a midsummer's eve to forget.

The Sidhe king, his queen and Céadar and I returned to the screens.

I opened various channels and heard the posturing and then the screaming for a while. As the ships' systems failed they came out of stealth. Some bloomed with horrible beauty and then winked out. Two more managed to streak out of the area. I had guessed ten in waiting. Four had left and seven more bloomed briefly as they returned the elements of ships and men back to the universe. Eleven ships then—not a bad guess by examining dark holes in space.

Finally there was nothing else on the screen except faint dots of debris.

I called Dagon without even checking with the Sidhe king.

"Use your own judgment on the remaining humans and their ships here. Get the Mothers out before you leave.

"Acknowledged."

"Be well, my love. May you have a safe journey and many new adventures."

In spite of my good intentions, I felt like I had been mortally injured. I was glad that he could not read this. We had done well together on our last day.

"Be well, Danu. Be happy."

Silence. I would have keyed off then, but my fingers were not working.

"Te amo, Danu. Te amo para siempre."

The connection was broken.

Midsummer's eve! A day of joyful communion with the life force, but I could not pretend to be happy. I looked at the Sidhe gathered around me. The queen clung to her king's arm. She looked paler than I would expect in her summer manifestation. She met my eyes. I actually saw grief that mirrored my own.

Céadar stood still, awaiting any cue from me.

I shook my head. "I don't know who I might be letting down tonight." I said. "I don't even know who flew with me. I apologize, but I must be alone."

I hoped that I could transit without being able to see well for the tears. I could not separate the joy of preserving this precious world and all of us here from the finality of the last message I had received. I was not undone. But, but …

I went to the beach, of course. The midsummer's eve full moon shone down on the dark water. I walked to the edge and then followed the moon path into the deeps, leaving my clothes in a pile where I dropped them. I could still feel the energy of those who had been connected to me and us to this night.

"What now, Danu? Did you accomplish what you hoped you would?" The deep-toned mind-speak of the great whale touched me.

"Yes!" I said. "I do not think the humans will return for a very long time. And in that time, perhaps they will forget about us and this lovely place. Or perhaps they will change."

"We will preserve the memory of this night. We will sing the Song of Danu that will cross hundreds of miles of ocean. We and our children and their children will remember you," she mind-spoke. "Call us anytime we can be of further assistance."

I saw the faint fluorescence that outlined her vast form. Her offspring stayed close to his mother in the dark water.

I swam back in and walked to where I had left my clothes. There were now further up the beach, folded neatly on a log. Céadar was sitting next to them. "The tide was coming in," he said. As if that answered anything.

"*I will go now again. I just wanted to see you ... safe.*" It was a mind-whisper. It was gentle as a leaf falling onto my hair. I turned to him in confusion. It was as if my vision had cleared slightly. He was next to me. He reached out and gently took my hand, and laid it upon his heart. "*I am here if you want me to be, Danu. You do not need to be happy tonight. Many died of their arrogance. It was your focus that made that happen.*"

"We all made that happen," I mind-whispered. "*Even the mice and those who I've never seen. Even the trees. And you as well, Céadar. And all the Sidhe.*"

"*Now we start over,*" he mind-spoke. And he put his arms around me.

CHAPTER TWENTY-NINE

NOW THERE IS A TOMORROW

Céadar and I transited back to Between without either of us knowing what would happen next. I stood and looked up at the clear sky. *"No fire. No death. Not down here anyway."*

"Was there another way to have done this? Had my whole life led me here? The lonely sad nights I sat and listened to other ships in our quadrant, never speaking. Listening. Learning. And being brought to the Sidhe ... and finally realizing that I and everyone else that lived was part of the web of life. This web of life, here on a planet that had risen from the fires of scourging"

"Never again. Or at least in the foreseeable future."

Céadar stood beside me, attentive and totally silent. I turned and looked at him standing in the moonlight in the glade.

There had been others who had joined me here. I had wanted them all. I had surrendered to whatever came next, with no guarantees, even though I might have wanted reassurances. In the end I wanted them with no conditions. In this time and place. Just that.

"Would you take off your clothes, Céadar?" I asked.

He did so with languid ease. I saw the moonlight play off the muscled curves of his arms, his chest. I could not clearly see his eyes but felt them locked on mine. As I had already foreseen, seeing him on this midsummer's eve, he took my breath away.

"What do you want of this night, Céadar? Would you spend the remainder of midsummer's eve with me?

He smiled easily, so confident of his beauty, but maybe more. "I want that. And I would ask you the same question, Danu of the Sidhe. What do you wish of me this night?

I took off my own clothes and drifted over to him in the way I had learned from the Shadakon. I touched him lightly—here—and there. Our bodies kindled. He was even more beautiful under the moonlight, with his desire showing clearly.

"I want everything you bring, Sidhe of the forest. I want to bring to you everything I am."

"I will take all that and more, Danu. I will be pleased to make you very happy that you are Sidhe tonight. And that I am as well ..."

The moonlight burned where it touched my skin. His touch left glowing tracks of sensation shivering down my arms. I wasn't sure I could stay on my feet much longer. As he continued, I knew I still carried extra energy from the spiral and that he did as well. I grabbed for support from a tree—the tree. I felt its rough bark and comforting energy. Then the wild energy of Céadar entered me and we spiralled up and up. When I thought it could get no better, he moved us both down to the ground and planted me into the earth. I called out in abandonment but far from abandoned. The moon moved across the sky and behind the trees before we shakily rose to our feet.

"Now what, Danu?"

"Please sleep beside me this morning, Céadar. Please be beside me when I wake up."

He smiled and gathered up our clothes. We walked to my hill house and entered. He scooped me up and placed me on the sleeping platform, then joined me.

"The thing about the Sidhe," he said straight faced, "is that they don't need much sleep. Especially in the summer."

A few days later I was summoned to the king and queen's hill hall. I went, not knowing what awaited me.

They were both present, the queen was dressed in sea green, her eyes deep aquamarine as they had been when I first meet her. I had decided to manifest a few coppery strands added into my hair, but I had nothing to wear that approached finery. I stood, lean and lightly clothed before them, then dropped to my knees. I stayed there, for a timeless Between moment.

In unison they told me to rise in mind-speak. I wondered, briefly, how I could not have recognized this powerful female Sidhe as the queen. *How had I blundered along? How I had dared to simply come to her?*

She laughed. "We were introduced informally, Danu. And I wanted nothing more or less of you. It was refreshing to meet you under more … intimate conditions."

Fiórcara smiled. He had, of course, watched this play out, waiting to see when I would come to understand the intricacies of the dance I danced with them both.

I waited before them. I could feel their personal spheres of energies as a united one. It affected me strongly. I bent my head. I wasn't sure if I could deal with their eyes. His eyes. Her eyes.

She spoke first. "I greatly underestimated you, Danu. I was willing to end you and your seemingly endless pre-occupation with your Shadakon lover. I was disdainful of his heritage and that you had claimed it as your own. I scorned you when you identified yourself as Shadakon—a vampire." I heard my mind-spoken thought then, that would not be stilled. *"I am Danu of Dagon of the Shadakon."* A shiver of pain ran through me. I waited.

"I didn't understand what my king already knew about you: the fierceness with which you protected your caring for Dagon, of being his proven mate. That you valued him enough to go to the edge of your life many times for him, and that you faced both of us down when offered oblivion of those memories."

"The fate of the planet hung on the fact that you were stronger and more resourceful than I was," she said thoughtfully. "When my king protected you before us all, I didn't understand that either—even though he provided me a place of no-blame."

"I am very old and I did not think I had further large lessons to learn. I was wrong. The sky is blue today, and the lives of this planet can continue on—raising their young, celebrating their short summers. I should have been out doing what you did—offering the little ones a chance to save their own planet."

"Once I realized our peril, I did not expect you to succeed."

I saw tears streak down her cheeks.

"Finally, and perhaps most importantly, I did not understand why he who you called Fiórcara, a name he gave you before you recognized his place in the Sidhe, continued to pay attention to you, a so-called Shadakon, that he seemingly could not part with ... can not part with." She smiled.

"His attention cost you much, although the rewards of being claimed as Sidhe ..." she smiled, "are significant. We have allowed no strangers into our ranks, Danu. Not in my memory anyway."

I dared to look up then. If she had thrown thunderbolts at me, I would not have been more surprised.

"A little more from me then, and then perhaps you can relax. I am sorry, Danu. I underestimated you and almost tipped the balance of this world's survival with my own arrogance. I cannot tell my king what to do, but I will step aside from impeding him from coming to you, if that is both your choice. I do strongly sense another's energy upon and in you now. It is good that you have someone close by in your daily life."

"And he is a very fine lover," she said. "As well I know."

I was supposed to say something useful now? I took several more long moments to gather myself. I took some long deep breaths of warm high-summer air and let them out again slowly. I could taste the life smells it carried.

In the end, I kept it simple. It is the easiest way to avoid complicating things. Dagon had taught me that well. I managed to smile at that thought.

"I accept your apology, but, more important to me, your understanding, my queen. I do not always know why I do what I do. I am often as amazed as any at the outcome. I regret nothing in regard to my own lessons at your hands and those of the Sidhe. And those of the Shadakon." The short stab of pain came again. "I am, as I can be, at your service."

I stood and waited again. She had caught my eye, and I felt the deep and powerful pull of her. I wondered ...

Fiórcara, my king, then spoke. "I have caused you both great pleasure and great pain, Danu. I already know that you accepted both in full surrender to me. When you calmly told me, in what might have been our last hours, that you had been 'granted power,' I never doubted it for a moment. You have never held back your truths, and I have learned to listen to them carefully.

Do you know, Danu of the Shadakon and of the Sidhe, that you led the spiral and forming of the cone of power on midsummer's eve? That by then, I never questioned your right to do so?

In the past I had said that Dagon received great gifts from you. I think in the end he realized that. I think he who you call Céadar is realizing your gifts to him as well. Perhaps that was my best move for you—although you went to outer space to avoid him initially!"

I flashed on that night, or bits of it I remembered as I lay between living and dying in Fiórcara's bed.

The two who kept me from passing over into oblivion stood watch: my proud Alpha leader and this Sidhe. I attempted not to remember Fiórcara's gift. (Unsuccessfully, obviously).

He laughed. "You are easily read, Danu, but that is a charm of yours as well. I have never doubted ..." He went silent.

"There is one more thing. I was charged to give back to you something that you value but lost. Dagon gave it to me, the last time I saw him. It is a curious gift, one that I wondered at when you first arrived with it in Between; old and finely made, but bearing death. I understand that you used it once against another, and it is as claimed: a death-bringer, at least to Shadakon."

"As I understand it, it will take you from your granted long-life if you are in a place of hopelessness. I am glad you never used it, although when we came to retrieve you from the prison in the forest, I believe you were very close."

"Consider today and what has passed since then and now. I hope you remain as curious and passionate as you are now as you live your long life. But it is an option, a dark protection of sorts. And I know that you know at least some of the history of it, and therefore some of the history of Dagon. I believe it is safe to say that he does not want you to totally forget him."

I let the grief his words brought wash over me. "Nor do I think that he will forget you, Danu. You tamed the heart of a great predator. He set aside much for you. Had I not brought you into reclaiming your Sidhe heritage, you might have been able to stay by his side."

I was undone at this. I was beyond weeping. I stood as a tree sensing the calm before an oncoming storm.

"Yet you, more than anyone, understand the pull of one's true fate. It brought you to this planet, to him, and then to me. You have surrendered to it all, and this planet is now still turning around and all is well here.

Whether you struggled against that fate or not, you know it was a true path."

He handled me a small, sheathed dagger. I did not take it out. I knew it by its feel. I had worn it for years. It felt like him. I touched the soft leather and, for an instant, I was back, remembering when he had given it to me. The morning I was taken to a prison in the forest where I would have lost all. Where the Sidhe, where this Sidhe king, had intervened and brought me to Between.

I sank to my knees and reached down and touched the ground. I felt the soil and beneath that, the stone bones of the planet. I placed it there on the earth. How far it had come from its making. How far we all had come.

"I thank you, Fiórcara, my friend, my king. I do not intend to use it for the foreseeable future."

He smiled at that.

"Is there anything further you want here today, Danu?"

I felt the invitation in that and allowed myself to be thrilled by it.

"I am again honoured to be in both of your presences. I do wonder, however, of what further use I will be of today." I left it like that, lovely and vague. A door left open ..."I would take both of your leaves then."

I felt Fiórcara direct some focused energy on me. I knew that if he called to me at some future point, that I would welcome him, and also the queen. I was not sure that I could handle them together, however, anytime soon.

The queen laughed. "Later then," she said.

I picked up the sheathed dagger and walked out into the sunlight, where Céadar waited, calm as always. He raised an eyebrow at the knife.

For the moment, I put it on and walked to the pool, now warm, beside the glade. He followed me without being asked.

That was the way it was between us now. I was happy.

CHAPTER THIRTY

THE GIFT

Summer ceded gracefully to fall. The Shadakon had left the planet, as had the Mothers and their charges. They had been placed in fast, modern ships—now empty and provisioned, thoughtfully provided to them by the Shadakon. A few humans had gone along with them; those useful and trustworthy to fly the ships to their next destination, and children who were not to be blamed for the choices of the adults. Some were memory-wiped to avoid the necessity of carrying the details of the last days.

Dagon had personally taken charge in the final days of occupation. He had a lot of credits accumulated after a long life of earning and investing on this planet and elsewhere, and I heard that he used them generously.

The star-port was deactivated. It would sit empty until someone might dare to land here—by design or invitation. The Sidhe would lose their benefits of access to off-world goods and return to an earlier way of life. However, they continued to monitor at their communications centre, interested in gleaning information about the fall out of their actions.

There was surprisingly little activity; which suggested that the giant companies rather than any one government or country had driven the entire invasion. Whoever they were, they had cut their losses. I doubted that they would forget, but at present there was silence. There were no more threats or even false promises.

The Shadakon ships had scattered. I did not know which one Dagon was on, or where he had landed. I knew he still lived. I knew that. As he did about me. It had to be enough.

Red and gold leaves whirled through the air.

Céadar and I split our time between our hill halls. We were entering Dreaming Time. I lay awake and alone one night, somewhat comforted by a flickering candle and the feel of the earth and roots around and over me. I had been changed by what I had put in action against the death fleet. I did not doubt that what had happened, had had to happen. Inviting—by allowing—the humans to do what they had intended, would have not have served them, and it certainly would not have served us and all those who called this planet home. I now realized that the planet had many, many names. And they were all ... home.

I had been gifted with a home. One where the streams and rivers ran clear and the ocean waves broke on clean sands.

Had I been able to remain standing beside Dagon, I would have traveled on, forever away from this. I doubted that he or any of the Blood had landed on another world as alive as this one.

I could think these things sometimes now without being overcome with yearning and grief.

But had I been given a choice? Dagon had taught me, *"Consent is complex."*

Would I have chosen him over my fierce protection of this world if I had known the cost of turning to the Sidhe? If I had accepted having my memory erased of my first midsummer's eve flight with Fiórcara?

I invoked the Goddess—a vague but comforting presence that I sometimes turned to. Gaia, Isis, Demeter ... I had always known that behind all the names was one presence, manifesting in infinite forms across time. I asked for a few things: a quiet heart—in that it harm none, joy, kindness and appreciation of what is, gratitude for my life.

I heard within, *"It is the night of dreaming, Danu. Do you choose to dream alone on this night?"*

I heard Her as if she was standing beside me. Perhaps she was at my door.

I arose and looked, but all I saw were the bright points of the stars in a moonless sky. Yet I felt her all around me. I stood outside and invoked the night and distance. The cold wind and the energy of root and conserved energy entered me.

"Would you come to me then ... Goddess?"

I heard a laugh. It seemed to come from all around me. This, I thought briefly, is why people had gone off onto the moors to be seen no more. They went willingly. They went hoping to find that which was not to be found in their everyday waking lives. In their everyday minds ...

I spun slowly in the darkness and danced the rustling leaves, the wind in the great trees that remained green throughout the seasons. I bared my skin to the cold.

"I am yours," I said to the darkness. "I surrender to you and what you bring me."

I saw the green swirling energy of faerie around me. I felt unseen touches. They burned coolly on my skin. I felt myself kindling alone in the darkness. I touched those places and wept for the loneliness of it, and yet I did not go in to comfort myself with warmth and candlelight. I stood and waited and shuddered, but not with cold.

He stood on the other side of my clearing, appearing as a large stag. I saw him test the air and then walk slowly and deliberately towards me. I saw the Sidhe king, and at the same time I saw a great stag whose back and antlers were frosted with white. They were one and the same. I felt the power of him and I wanted only that he would close the distance between us. Whatever happened after that ... I could not think further than just wanting to be in his presence.

Then he was close, standing taller than I, and I felt his warm breath on my chilled body.

"Do you know me?" His mind-speak rumbled within me.

"Some have called you Cernunnos, the horned god." I said.

"Will you call me that, Danu?"

"If you wish me to, here under the fall stars, my king."

"You might not like this any more than you enjoyed the Hawk of Achill."

And here he bent and delicately raked an antler point down the centre of my body. It left a thin, fiery wake of pain and I moaned but did not step back.

We looked at each other and slowly he materialized as the familiar form of the Sidhe king. I stood and wanted him in the cold and darkness, with his new mark on me. He finally reached out and took my hand; it blazed in his.

Lightly, he pushed me down into the fallen leaves and began with me there. The leaves clung to my hair and I felt like I was part of the forest. He took me, as stag takes his doe—surely and powerfully. I rose to stand afterwards and he took me down to the ground again.

"You have surrendered to the darkness and to your wanting. I will call the dance tonight, Danu. Do you agree with that, you who have summoned me?"

"Yes."

"Yes." He smiled. *"I would see where you sleep now. However, I do not believe that you are going to sleep tonight."*

I stood at the entrance of my home and bade him enter.

He kept me in the foothills of wanting. We went up and up, but still I was not set free. At last, however, we were both as high as we could be and as I felt that last moment coming I wheeled out and out, away from him and my world. I briefly saw different stars and smelled a different wind. *Where had I gone?* I spiralled down back into my life.

He was watching me when I returned fully.

"At least you did not get lost out in your search," he said quietly.

"I don't understand.

"Oh, I think a part of you understands. You are still seeking him, even though he is on another world and living another life. You would use both your own and my sex magic in the service of that search. Even though it took you from me tonight, and did not bring you any closer to he that you still yearn for. If this is love, it has a terrible consequence, Danu."

I sighed and did not protest what he had said. I briefly touched my Maker hand and received the faintest of spark of energy from it. Alive then, though very, very far away.

"I meant you no disrespect, my king," I said. "I left Dagon's side to come to you time and time again. I refused to choose between the two of you. My only solution to being divided, as I felt myself to be, was to end my own life.

I thought of the small, sheathed knife in the darkness nearby.

"That is still one solution, Danu. But not one I hope you choose."

"I have done what I was needed to do, perhaps I am not so useful now."

"Perhaps not, Danu. But one's later use is not always obvious."

There was no sympathy for me in his eyes, neither was there unkindness.

"I do not want to forget, but I am weary of the wanting, of the waiting that has no ending. It is a longing that will not leave me, that I cannot get free of—because I cannot make myself let go."

He looked at me fully now.

"Is it time now, Danu? To grant yourself and him freedom?"

I sighed. "I know it is, my king, my best friend. I need help with it, though. It is a pain that I return to again and again." I touched my chest and my fingertips came away slightly red.

"Yes. You have used pain that way. One pain to block another."

I looked at him.

"I never gave you anything you didn't ask for, Danu, even as the Hawk."

Then at midnight of a very dark night, I asked for something I did not believe that I would ever ask for, much less accept; that I had fought against to the edge of death.

"I would remember from a place further back, my king. Not entirely gone, but further back and with a sense of resolution, of gratitude instead of sorrow. I ask your help for that now."

He looked at me then and I fell into his turning-fall eyes. He stroked my face and put his hand on my forehead. "This can be undone by you, Danu," he said. "I will simply push it back. It can simply be recalled by you, if you feel the need to revisit this pain later. You are Sidhe. I cannot force on you what you do not choose. You already know this firsthand."

"Do you agree to this, Danu, my midsummer's eve queen? Would you make room for more simple gratitude? I will take away nothing. But will you cool those memories? Let them sleep?"

I looked deeply into his grey green eyes of fall. I felt his touch on my head.

"Yes."

There were tears sliding down my cheeks. I felt everything get dark and silent within. Then I slid into the deeps.

I awoke to gentle touches. They did not burn or drive me on. They did not demand or require me to surrender all. Céadar sat beside me. He looked down at me with affection. I did not ask how he had come to me, or if Fiórcara had suggested it to him, I accepted his gift gratefully: the simple gift of his presence.

"Please cover us both with your warmth, Céadar, if you wish."

"I do wish," he said. And then it was dark and warm and simple.

CHAPTER THIRTY-ONE

GATHERING THE GIFTS OF GOODBYE

I had to see if I had truly found a way to let go of Dagon. I waited until mid-spring. I needed to know if I embraced the fact that our parting was not, "for the foreseeable future," because even that statement had hope in it. I felt that I had to go for something more permanent—without false hope.

So, first, I transited out to the island. The hospice looked as always, the windows neatly shuttered, but it had a sense of total emptiness about it. My log, or maybe now just *a* log, still sat where it had been when I called it home—my only true home outside Between.

I went for a swim, knowing I would bother no one with my nakedness. The ocean felt alive and I felt the small darting ones briefly touch me, but no large mind was present today. I swam until I was tired, and no one met me on the beach.

I could see the on-lays of memories of what had happened here. I saw Fiórcara coming to me before our midsummer's eve flight and consummation. I shivered briefly. *How I had feared and wanted him!*

I saw Dagon and I and the Sidhe king together on the log. If Dagon knew it or not that day (and he had not lived as long as he had without seeing beneath the surfaces of things), I had already made my choice to be with the Sidhe even before he left my side. *Did he leave in pain? Resignation?* I could turn it over and over in my mind without losing myself totally to grief or blame. Likewise on the day that Dagon realized that he could not or would not end me. I was grateful for his choice. This island of calm, this planet, might have been unspeakably altered if I had not been present to fight for it.

His decision was a gift to many besides me; it benefitted a whole world.

I walked down to the small cove where I had joined my various lovers. It was lovely and quiet. I bent down and touched the sand where Dagon and I had made our final parting.

I knelt, and then I wept. It was as Fiórcara had promised: the grief was still accessible within me. I touched my hand and again felt the faint flare of energy. He lived then, he thrived; perhaps he loved.

I hoped that he would be open to that with someone else. *So be it*, I thought. I pictured him, a calm, confident Alpha leader. I had preserved him more than once so that he could follow that path. I had made significant contributions to his wellbeing. So, too, had I touched his heart. His power could be tempered by that if he so chose.

One more stop then.

I transited to his home and stood in confusion. There were no houses standing in any direction. The dark cedars of his garden enclosed a space of vines and native plants surrounded by blasted rock. The moonflower vine was still doing well.

I saw the gift in its disappearance. I could imagine transiting into the dusty bedroom, and to the dry tub where we had taken our pleasure—and wailing like the ghost I surely then would be. He had been very busy in the last days. This was a gift of time and energy—to the Sidhe and, specifically, to me.

Love was also about endings. I stood where I had once lived, now a circle of broken stone that was being reclaimed by the life force of the planet. He had known I would eventually return here. Love can be about making it easier for the other person—the one who might not so easily let go. I wept then, but there was no more anger or questioning fate in my mind.

I returned to Between. I was not surprised that Fiórcara was waiting for me. He looked at me and said, "Let us take a walk, Danu."

"So ... you have gone to see if you are free. Are you free?"

"I would show you, my friend, my king." I turned to him and he pulled me close and gently tipped up my chin. I felt him within my thoughts and there was nothing I wished to hide. I stood open to him, feeling his energy and being content to let it wrap around us both.

He gently touched the dried tracks of my previous tears. He saw that I had found the gifts that I had both given and received. He saw my last wish for Dagon, given freely in spite of the cost: that he continue to love and be loved wherever he might be.

"Ah, Danu. I almost envy this Shadakon. I don't believe that in my very long life anyone has fought for me like you did for him. Your passion for him was relentless. Perhaps that is the Shadakon within you. For you are Shadakon—with and now without Dagon. Even though you have lost your taste for the energy of humans, you could survive that way if you had to."

"And now do you want me to comfort you, Danu? Cover over your hard won realizations with passion?"

I stood in the sunlight and went within. I was not undone. I did not crave oblivion in his arms.

"What then?"

"It is high spring, my king. When last we came together, I lost you, or I lost myself—I did not stay present. I am ready to do that now. I want you to accompany me to the place of both of our surrendering to each other. I truly want it all—I want us both to bring it all."

"Ahhhh ..."

"If not now, then later if that is your wish, my king."

"And Céadar?"

I smiled. "This is not about Céadar. You brought me to Between and my Sidhe heritage, and there is a bond between us, as you well know. You gave me the chance to learn to enjoy Céadar and he to enjoy me. We are still doing so and not hurting each other, but my desire for you is the way it was when he and I first met. In accepting that, he seems to be totally Sidhe."

Fiórcara just smiled. *"No one is the way they were, once you have loved them, Danu."*

I looked at him. *An ancient Sidhe king who ruled a planet with a beautiful queen on his arm, how could he say that?*

He smiled. *"This is surely not about my queen and our very long rule together."* He paused for a moment.

"I saw the life force of this planet put itself in your hands—not mine—at least for a night. You were, in your own words on that fated night, granted power beyond mine, and you managed that with your heart. And that was why all of this ..." he swept out with both hands, *"granted you that power."*

"If you wish to have my company in loving, and I am not standing in for someone else or covering your pain, then I am at your service. Now ... later ... I will come to you in whatever form you want me to."

So we walked to the grove where he had once observed me and Dagon in my first visit to Between. And where he led me afterwards the night of our midsummer's night flight. The trees closed in around us and the outside was very far away.

We needed no agreements. He brought me full spring as I brought it to him. Our energies joined and we flew up and up and joined at the apex of our flight. We spiralled down and climbed again. So it went. And then at one point—There was only one in the grove.

CHAPTER THIRTY-TWO

MUCH, MUCH LATER

★ ★ ★ ★

I chose to go find out who still lived hidden in the depths of the forests. I spent many days sitting quietly in remote groves or grasslands. I waited quietly in the desert. I had been shown by the Sidhe king how to access the elixir of life. I was no longer bound to come home to Between every night and I felt that the whole planet was my home. I was fed by it and had its company wherever I traveled.

I began documenting those I found and I sketched them as they sat timidly around me.

One day I was sitting as a rock in the sunshine and I suddenly knew I was being observed—evaluated. I looked up into the eyes of a great cat. It was the colour of the dried grass and its eyes were golden. For a moment I thought of Dagon and the times that he had come to me as a large, seemingly sleepy cat with dark amber eyes, with flames that flickered within. I felt a rush of love and yearning before I had time to remind me myself—not now, not ... ever again.

This cat blinked, and looked puzzled. I had showed an unusual reaction to its presence. It, perhaps not unlike Dagon as the predator he had been when we met, stayed close and relaxed and studied me.

"*You are beautiful,*" I mind-spoke. "*I once loved one much like you.*"

"*Still love,*" I added. "*I am glad you are thriving and that there is prey for you to eat. And that they are thriving as well.*"

He—I was sure it was a he from his energy—sat in the sun with me. A slight breeze blew my scent to him and he learned about me from it: that I was not afraid, that I was no one to fear.

So Dagon and I had begun: with no fear—and then we entered into fear of each other.

Until at the end, we were back where we had begun. Free to be safe together no matter what our differences were.

Nothing to fear. I held that to my heart.

Although I thought I was paying attention, between one second and the next the great cat disappeared into the grass. There was not the slightest whisper of sound in his going.

I hoped that there were many more of his kind, and that those he and his clan depended on would be healthy and have the right amount of offspring to balance the dance between the takers and the providers.

When I returned, Between time had passed. It was cold and I went to my hill hall and found it tidy, with fresh blankets laid out. There were candles and tinder ready. I looked further. *Did someone else live here now?* A quick search revealed the small dagger still hanging on the back wall, in the darkness. I did not think about death these days, could not remember when I last had.

Céadar then? Céadar read and wrote Old Earth English? There was a handwritten note on the table. It simply said, *Call me when you return.* There was a symbol of a cedar tree beneath the words. Cedar, the tree of life, a grounding and calming influence used in many ancient cultures.

I called him by name. When he appeared at my door, I realized, once again, how beautiful he was. He smiled and brought himself to me. I knew, again, how fortunate I was, what a gift he was.

At the end now, I would like to finally say that somehow fate brought Dagon and I back together again, even briefly—but it did not.

Exterra now had a limited population of humans, brought in as contract workers and mostly working in the small star-port to set up and upgrade the necessary computer systems. They attended to the spacers who came and went.

There were no trespassers in the forbidden areas; the dancers of the web of life would report such a thing. It was kept safe by everyone who lived on the land and under the sea.

The Sidhe dealt in gold. As its value went up and up, they could afford to have what they wanted or needed of the outside world—and pass on the actual messy business of earning credits.

There was no pleasure fair.

If Shadakon came here, it was not on official business. If they did what they do, the Sidhe did not care—as long as they did not enter the closed areas or interfere with the Sidhe and their lives and what they protected.

On rare occasions I went to the star-port to attend to some detail or other. I will not deny that I looked for him among the crowd, but my Maker palm only registered the faintest pulse of energy. I believe now that he caught another and then another fast horse and is moving outward and outward with the Shadakon he may still lead.

Te amo para siempre, Dagon.

DANU'S WORLD

BOOK THREE

PROLOGUE

Once I was human, born on old Earth, after the tipping points had brought her and her beings into the great inevitable die off.

I arrived on this small earth-type planet as a space techno on a freighter star ship traveling from Old Earth to Exterra, a world on the edge of territory that was barely feasible to do business on. I took a needed break off the ship—and never returned. I went to try to find the answer once and for all: was it possible for me to want someone ... anyone? I had been unable to even imagine if someone might want me. Or love me. Or I might love another.

I had little hope in finding my answers.

I signed a short-term pleasure contract that protected me while I lay in the arms of a predator, a vampire named Dagon who availed himself to human energy and in return gave sexual pleasure to his customers. I was awakened to passion beyond what I could have imagined. I would have freely given up my life to him, but he understood, even if I did not, that I wanted to live, and more fully than I ever had. He did not follow up on my acceptance of what would have been a pleasant easy death for me and the full pay off of my life's energy for him.

I learned that everything that I thought was true about me was wrong or at least seen from a wrong perspective. I gained powers. Unknown to me earlier, I had been granted Shadakon (vampire) kinship from an ancient relative on old Earth. This accounted for my reluctance to join with other humans and my feeling of being separate from them. In my vampire lover's arms, I transformed. I learned what wanting someone meant, and how to use that in the service of great passion.

I was tested by the Council of the Shadakon after my spontaneously turning and, to almost everyone's surprise, I survived.

Soon lafterwards, the Sidhe, the Old Earth faeries, came for me and began training me for what appeared to be my most useful action: saving the planet.

CHAPTER ONE

MY STORY BEGINS AGAIN

I was sitting beside a large old tree who I had long perceived of as my friend. Most of the Sidhe and myself usually stayed in Between, a warded space—or perhaps another dimension hidden on this world—purposefully set apart from the everyday activities of the planet. The planet's animal inhabitants rarely connected directly with us except on midsummer's eve, when all living beings gathered psychically to celebrate the peaking of the life force. As the Sidhe and I carefully drew sustainable sustenance from that force, we were no threat, but we chose to live apart as a gift and proof that we did not consider ourselves to be keepers or above those who this planet sheltered.

I had leaned against this tree many times, with the high energy of spring and loving in me, and also sometimes to gain calmness and ground myself in times of turbulence. This day I napped, my back against its grey bark. The afternoon was long, as time in Between is not measured in human time, but that of tree and season and sun transit. Summer was upon us and the tree and all its companion flora were busy drawing up earth energy and storing water and transforming the light of this slightly dimmer than old Earth's sun into leaves and flowers. I dozed, feeling at home and peaceful.

I awoke easy and rested, and rubbed my hands together, noticing that my left hand stung slightly. I rubbed it lightly against the rough bark but the sensation persisted and if anything, intensified.

My breath stopped, time stopped. My hand now flared and it could only mean one thing. I then noticed Fiórcara king of the Sidhe and my ocassional lover, was squatting patiently beside me.

He took my left hand in his own and met my eyes. Fiórcara, a name he had given me to use between us, was an ancient Sidhe who was their king and leader. He took me away from my life with Dagon by binding me to him with the sex magic that the Sidhe wield. I later came to him willingly as a lover, although he had other interests and activities with others, as did I. It was no accident that he was in front of me, holding my Maker hand. He ran his fingers lightly across the now intensely flaring mark, as if thoughtfully.

"Yes, Dagon contacted me and apparently you as well." He watched me without and within to see what this news meant to me.

An intense feeling, that could be called pain but was more complex than that, suffused from the area of my heart throughout my entire body. I could still barely feel the calm energy of the tree and pulled it around me, in a failing attempt to help me balance myself.

I had once been a diver on Earth. Now I attempted to breathe as if I was at the bottom of the sea with an almost empty tank of air.

In. Pause.

Out. Pause.

I felt my body clamouring for more air, for action. The pattern of breaths I enforced was just that: calm forced over the reality of what was truly happening in my body. My Sidhe mentor and lover studied me as I tried to deal with the effects this new information was causing in me. When the tears slowly slipped down my cheeks I turned away, but he would have none of that. He turned my face to meet his eyes that were green with golden lights. He was, as always, even after all the years of knowing him, beautiful and entrancing to me. Here and now, he was my king.

"Ah, Danu. Would you set aside all your hard-won acceptance that he and you are no longer bonded?"

I just held out my palm, where the place of our joining was burning. "What am I expected to do? This is an intense need, a calling in of debt perhaps. I doubt this is about his needing a lover in this part of the galaxy."

Fiórcara smiled at me. "Yet that is the first thing you bring to mind."

We looked at each other. He knew the depth of connection that had been between Dagon and I. He had helped me regain myself after Dagon had left on a fast ship towards some destination he did not share with me.

In our last hours together, Dagon had told me that he had newly partnered with one of his kind. That had not stopped us from having a last passionate farewell, for by then I had set aside the expectations of singularity with a lover. Dagon had justified what we did that afternoon however he did. Our last act of intimacy was his availing himself to a taste of my faerie, high spring-enriched blood. It was, I knew, intoxicating and a farewell gift he would not soon forget.

But he had his own hungers and ways of filling them.

"*He is probably not regarding me at all,*" I finally thought.

"*And it took you a while to even consider that,*" thought Fiórcara calmly. We eyed each other and I knew to brace for more information. The Sidhe reluctantly used technological communication devices. But Fiórcara could have received information from him days or even weeks ago.

He smiled at me. "Dagon taught you the art of noticing what is not said. However that skill is more difficult if you do not ask the important questions."

"Tell me what you came to tell me," I sighed. "Tell me what you will, to help me prepare for being in his presence."

"Do you remember me telling you that you would be an excellent ambassador for us?"

I nodded.

"And what talent did I say would you bring to that job that would make you particularly useful, Danu?"

I well remembered the conversation and the effect it had had on me. Fiórcara had calmly told me that I fell in love easily. He predicted that I could fall in love with whoever the Sidhe were dealing with and could provide a good source of information about them—whether I wished to provide that service or not

I could serve as a conduit of information and also tie people to the Sidhe in whatever deal was being brokered. I could not hide information from Fiórcara. He had gone deeply into my mind, more deeply than I could recall later. Dagon would know that, though. He too had searched out what I might have kept hidden from him. But would he refuse contact with me because of his one-time vulnerability to me?

"That is the question," Fiórcara said.

"How long have you known that he was coming?" I asked. "And has he asked for me to be present, or not?"

"I have known for weeks," he said dismissively, as if this information was of little account. "And he specifically asked that you not be present, for the obvious reasons you just recalled."

"Weeks! So, he must be close," I muttered.

Fiórcara continued to study me.

"He is here now," I said with certainty, "but he does not want to be in my presence."

Fiórcara said nothing.

"You want me with you when you meet with him," I said, and lost my remaining breath as I finished that thought. "You would find it useful for me to be there. You would have me attend, heart-sick and compelled by you."

"Compelled ..." he said and smiled. "I compelled you to my side once, but then you had to decide if you would stay by your own choice."

"I will offer you the same condition today," he continued. "If you cannot bear to be in his presence, you may leave. But I would guess that you will not be able to leave his side, no matter how he presents himself you."

"But I am willing to be wrong," he said smiling. "That sometimes happens around you."

CHAPTER TWO

THE MEETING

Fiórcara offered me his hand and I put my stinging left hand in his. I did not pause to enhance myself. I wore simple clothes and my curling auburn hair remained at the length I wished. At times I ran my fingers through it, less frequently a comb. I swam in a fresh water pool or the sea; I was as I was, this day and all days.

"I require one thing to bring with me," I said to Fiórcara. We transited to my hill home and I lifted a small knife and its sheath and strap from a peg on the back wall. I had not touched it in years. It had been a gift from Dagon, a relic from his past. He had initially given it to me so that I could protect myself in a final way from any situation that I could no longer bear. Its blade carried a quick-acting poison, although some might have been wiped away by use. I had been ready to use it three times; the first two times I had been intent on killing myself. When it finally touched flesh, however, it took a female Shadakon that I was in mortal combat with to death, and it performed in a very satisfactory fashion.

Fiórcara took my arm and then we were in another place, Dagon standing before us.

I drew one breath and then another. On the second I looked up to his eyes; neither of us would drop our gaze nor look away. I saw only darkness in his, certainly no welcome or hint of fondness from times past. He had become an Alpha clan leader before we separated and I had observed the change that brought in him. It appeared to have amplified over the years. He was, I was sure, a very formidable leader.

Fiórcara, being the ironic host, gestured to us both. "You know each other of course," he said. "Or did in times past. But people change …"

I felt Dagon's energy circling me, feinting and working to make mind contact. I shuddered to feel even this part of him, however uncaring it might be.

"Fiórcara, I do not want her here," he said. "I told you that earlier."

"And I told you, in this same spot, many years ago, that any relationship you have with each other is not of interest to me. Including a renewed relationship of malice, or whatever Danu shivers from." Fiórcara stated this emphatically and turned to me.

"I told you the same thing," he said to me. "You might attempt to gather yourself to represent your kind today."

"So let us proceed," he said, returning to a lighter tone. "Do either of you require refreshment?" He was offering the elixir of life. Dagon had drank it in the Sidhe king's home while they both waited to see if I could survive a suicide attempt

I made in a transit to airless space. We had sealed a pact with it earlier, the day that Dagon pledged the Shadakon to protect the planet from marauding humans. But there was no plan agreed to today, and I knew Dagon would not accept it.

I also knew Dagon had the beginning of hunger riding him. I also was thirsty and hungry but could not accept if neither of them partook. I felt empty and slightly sick.

"A slight edge of hunger then," said Fiórcara. "To move things along."

He indicated that I should sit between them. I felt their differing energies overlap in me. I had felt this way before and had always chosen to come to Fiórcara's side. But now my heart ached to look at Dagon, to ask him how he had fared in the time we were apart. I wondered if he had missed me. I certainly had missed him. I had walked a long weary way to regain myself but would set aside that learning to feel a connection with him now, however fleeting.

I had gained no ground, I realized. I sat and willed calmness to arrive, but it did not.

I felt my heart beating at my pulse points and knew he heard it too. My body kindled, my desire rising and rising up from where it had quietly slept today. I felt ashamed that I wanted him this way while feeling nothing from him but aggressive attempts to read me.

Fiórcara smiled at me, and it was not in a helpful manner. My suffering was part of the advantage that he might have over Dagon, but only if Dagon cared. Otherwise my presence was merely a strategy that was not useful to the Sidhe at this time.

For the first time in many years I became aware of the significance of the small dagger that now hung under my clothes by my left side. Even as I brought it to mind, I saw Dagon stiffen, oh, so slightly. He had caught my thought. He had stopped me before, and at that time he had promised to go with me if I felt I must make that choice.

But that had been a long time ago, when we were one.

Dagon turned to Fiórcara and spoke only to him. "I came a long way to negotiate with you, King of the Sidhe. I did not expect the complication of Danu's presence. I mean her no harm. But I am content with my own arrangements for companionship and I cannot waste precious time dealing with her feelings."

Fiórcara shrugged. "I require her here at this meeting. If this becomes problematic I may make another arrangement. But tell me more about the nature of your visit. You have come a long way to speak to me in person. Obviously you need something—from me." He smiled.

"*Listen carefully, Danu,*" he mind-spoke me. He did not look at me and I wondered if Dagon had heard him.

I heard Dagon make the slight hiss a big cat might make. I had heard it in his under-mind. We were still connected then and he could read me as well.

I continued to breathe. I noted that my palm flared with pain. My Maker was here; our connection was pulling us to be together. I was glad that it hurt. I hoped the pain would clear my mind. I looked at Dagon.

"Our new planet has sickened from something," he said to the Sidhe king. "Birds are falling out of the sky, fish are washing ashore, dead. We wondered if you could tell us if it can be reversed, whether there is a cure."

"And the humans?" asked the Sidhe king.

"They seem unaffected. But it is only a matter of time before they will be unsupported by the failing life force."

"And you think we should or could go there and determine the cause? And put ourselves and this planet at risk?" Fiórcara spoke softly but I felt the anger rising in him. "Did you, in fact, bring this life plague with you? You once helped protect this planet. But then, you once loved Danu. Have you arrived for some long-awaited revenge?"

Dagon shook his head and looked weary and, unhopeful. "We went through an intense decontamination process prior to leaving. And you required a similar process when we landed. I bring nothing that I know of. I am a predator, but my hunting ground is fading. The flowers are not setting seed. Danu taught me to feel the cycle of life. We are watching the web unravel and it is sad. It is also very expensive. That is the best new home we have found since Exterra."

"You brought no evidence of what you speak of?" Fiórcara asked sharply.

Dagon shook his head. "I could show you ..." He put his hand lightly to his head.

"You would allow me to search your mind?" Fiórcara looked somewhat amused. "Somehow I would not have expected that."

Dagon froze. "I do not know what I thought could happen here.

I only knew that, like Danu years ago, I had to try."

The Sidhe and Shadakon. The Sidhe king and Alpha Shadakon had worked together with me serving as a fragile bridge between them. It was my plan to bring all the little lives together to protect this planet many years ago, and the Shadakon's contribution on the ground had tipped the balance. We fended off an attack of many stealth destroyers and the humans within them donated their physical material to the space around this planet. The Shadakon annihilated the planet-bound humans, sending only a few pilots, some children, and the members of a healing hospice guild to safety. Shortly after that, Dagon and the rest of his clan had left, seemingly forever.

Fiórcara gave away nothing. He was quiet within but I knew he was thinking, turning over possibilities. Seeing where the best advantage was.

"I must think about this," he said at last. "I assume you have, ah, provisions aboard your ship?"

Dagon nodded.

"Then Danu will take you back." He waved his hand and disappeared from our sight.

I heard Dagon mutter a curse in an ancient language.

"Do you have to touch me to take me back?" he asked with clenched teeth.

My anger finally rose in my defence. "I do not have to touch you. I do not have to take you back either. Right now, I really do not care how Fiórcara would sort that out with me. But it would be a lesser pain."

I turned and walked away, but I did not transit. So, already I was fooling myself, that I could abandon him in Between, without food and with both of us at the mercy, if he practiced mercy, of the Sidhe king. To Dagon's credit he did not make me reveal that I was bluffing. He called me in mind-speak and then covered the distance between us.

"You of all people must realize that my presence here affects more than me and you. I find myself pleading to the Sidhe for a way to undo what is happening on what has been my home for a long time now. And you know why I do not want you to touch me."

The dappled sunlight was shining on him. His kind had long ago lost their vulnerability to sunshine. He stood, careless of his own beauty and power. I knew that beneath the soft fabric of his shirt, he bore an old starburst scar on his chest where he had been staked—and barely lived. I ached to lay my hand on it once more. His black hair was glossy and reflected the light.

I looked away. The pain I had felt earlier claimed me. I wanted him. I wanted him. He did not want me. I was beyond words, beyond tears. I stayed on my feet by will alone. I wanted to sink to my knees, as I had learned to do when he was newly an Alpha and required me to do so ritually in front of the clan. I had also done so in times when we were alone. Often it was after I finally realized that I had wrongly challenged him and must make amends to this strong lover. I wanted to do so now, and feel his hand lightly on my head, bidding me rise.

I swayed slightly and I hoped, despite everything, that he did not know the state I was in.

He reached out and took my Maker hand in his own.

I gasped. I felt our energies synchronizing. I would have fallen then if he had not continued to support me.

"I should have known that the price required by the Sidhe would be more than I could bear," he mind-spoke. *"I should have realized that he would once again involve you—that you would once again be useful to him."* The Sidhe king had, time and time again, summoned me to his side—and away from Dagon's.

I knew that Dagon had loved me, more than his kind allowed, but still, I had left him for Fiórcara. The Sidhe had bound me to him with sex magic and something even deeper.

Being in Dagon's presence was reactivating what had been between us and could only cause us both further pain. I had carefully gone over the history of our relationship after he left, and realized that I had hurt him again and again. I knew that if we united, however briefly, we would both pay.

I felt his energy within me. My wanting him surged through me. My blood pounded in the base of my neck, the spot where he had taken from me many times to serve our mutual pleasure.

"I will do anything for you, Dagon. But I will not say that what is between us is not so. I want you now. You told me a long time ago that bargains made with the Sidhe always come out in their favour. You told me I would be hurt. I am hurting now, my love. The idea that you are here and yet not here for me is the most pain I have ever experienced."

Dagon had once, in the throes of jealousy and his powerlessness to stop my returning to the Sidhe king, broken my arm. He had threatened to break all my bones, with me fully conscious of the pain. I knew he felt the level of pain I experienced now.

"I did not want this," he whispered. "I did not come to bring you pain. We parted well, at the end."

"But?" I said sadly. "Now?"

"Whatever I do will make it worse," he said. "If I move toward you we will—you will—go through all of it again. If I hold myself back from you, you will suffer as you do when you feel abandoned. I will abandon you again."

"I will take you back to your ship," I said, sounding calm and resolved but feeling the approaching storm that would take me. Once again I thought with relief, of the knife and its promise of quick death. Once again I felt him grow momentarily still.

"Are you so selfish as to put an entire world at risk because you chose an easy death? Do you not know that we must follow the Sidhe's plan, no matter how much it changes our lives and affects us?" He looked fully at me and I saw the flickering lights of desire in him.

"Do you not know that I would risk all to be with you again, however briefly?" His mind-speak undid me. I stood as prey must finally stand and face their fate.

I shivered in the warm wind. I listened to hear what wisdom I might hear from the little lives of this planet. But they were busy promising each other true mating, to stay, to protect—if only for a little while.

"What now, Dagon?" I whispered.

"I have to return to the ship. Or, I have to feed." He looked at me appraisingly. "I would ask you for that. I cannot resist asking you for that." He looked away then.

"I am depleted now," I told him. "But I would take you to my home here and offer you elixir—or me. Or both."

I wondered quietly what punishment I might receive at the hand of my king. He had not told me to do anything other than to return Dagon to his ship, yet he knew the likelihood was that I would not be able to do just that, that I would not choose to refuse Dagon.

"He will be aware of this, of course," I said. "He may choose to interrupt or stop us at the last moment. But more likely, he will witness and partake in our passion as he has before." I thought back to our reunion in the glade in Between. Fiórcara had brought Dagon to me, the morning after I had refused his call to join him on midsummer's eve. Dagon had tasted the energy of that night still within me when we joined. The Sidhe king had taken in our passion as he did all passion in his kingdom, The Sidhe did not only live on the elixir of life.

"I put you at risk," said Dagon.

"There is no other path, my love," I said sadly. "Let us enjoy the time granted to us."

CHAPTER THREE

ĤOW 1 ĻOVE THEE

I took Dagon's hand, noting that my longing for him was now washing over me with only larger waves on the horizon.

I transited us to my small hill home. I invited him in, as was required for the Shadakon. I wondered if there was anything I could do to ensure us privacy. The Sidhe did not lock their doors and the king was welcome wherever he would go; he certainly was welcome in my home that he had had constructed for me. But now I did not want to call him in my mind to ask for this night. After pondering this, I took off my sheathed knife. Dagon watched me without revealing any thoughts. I shook out a small green stone. It sat quietly in my hand, with no glow to indicate Fiórcara's presence. I placed it outside in front of my door. It would keep any other Sidhe away, and Fiórcara would understand the message of it there.

I gestured to my sleeping platform that served as couch, bed, place of loving and dreaming. I unfolded some soft woven blankets. Once I had lain down on the red pelt of some great beast that was on Dagon's bed. Tonight he would lie with me on spider silk and the softest of grasses. He was in Between now.

He sat watching me. I filled my small pitcher with elixir of life, wondering if I would be forbidden to have my own supply after this night. I did know how to request it from the life force, but generally we Sidhe collected it ritually and infrequently, choosing not to make daily draws. I would find out later. At the moment I did not care.

I offered him the cup and he refused. I drank it to the bottom, feeling the calm energy replace my edgy hunger and thirst. I turned to him. "Take off your clothes, Danu."

Dagon's voice was husky and I doubted that we would be speaking aloud soon.

I let my clothes slip to the floor and stood before him. There were bright notes of copper in my auburn hair. It was high spring and the Sidhe often altered their appearances as they moved through the seasons. In truth, I now understood that I did not know their real appearance, if indeed they had only one.

I had seen Fiórcara differently the first night I met him. He had appeared ancient and stern. Later he was younger and entrancing beautiful to me. I had seen him assume other guises as well, however, including the silvery-backed stag, Cernunnos. He had come to me like that and I had thrilled to be in his presence.

Dagon, however, I had mostly seen as a large deadly cat who purred deep in his chest as he bent over me.

I shivered. "And you, Dagon. Be with me now."

He stepped out of his boots and stood while he took off what looked like a uniform. The filtered light in my room picked out the strong lines of his body. He was more solid now—muscled and clearly in his prime. He was Alpha. Without thinking, I slipped to my knees.

"Accept me now, Dagon, as I am." I bent my head and waited for what might have been a timeless time until I felt his hand fall lightly on my head. He raised me up and then his lips were on mine, his strong arms were around me and I wanted him with all my being.

"What I have is yours," I simply said. When his hand slid down from my cheek to my neck and paused I added, "That, too, Dagon. I am yours tonight."

We moved into passion and, as before, he was a master at building my desire for him. When I felt his fingers on me I cried out. When he entered me I cried out again.

But when he drank my faerie blood I was silent, lost in deep bliss

It was then that he called out my name, the name I had given him within minutes of meeting him. A name I had chosen for myself when I was an alienated teen on old Earth, living in my room with the door always closed, reading about magic and witchcraft. Reading about vampires and faeries.

Danu. Resident Goddess of Éire on old Earth.

It had taken me coming here to gain information about the history of various Visitors who had come to Old Earth for their own purposes and used the people they found there. They had shared their alien bloodlines with the human hunter-gatherers they found in Sumer and used them and their offspring as slaves.

Some human hybrids had lived and carried the wild gifts forward. Dagon was one, and I was sprung from both bloodlines: vampire and faerie. When I finally understood all this, my life made sense for the first time. He and I were not the same, but we shared a similar level of passion, although the Sidhe could take it further than anyone else so far discovered in the Universe.

My blood was intoxicating to Dagon. He could, and usually did feed on energy alone, but we had shared blood many times, and he had tasted me after my transformation to being—at least partially—Sidhe. Now he lay on my bed, totally relaxed and I curled up beside him, and when he put his arms around me I was wrapped in contentment. I wanted him again. Again and again, and I knew that before the night was through I would have that wish granted. Meanwhile, Dagon slipped his fangs into his favourite spot on my neck and sipped sparingly.

We could have this unless Fiórcara intervened. I listened without calling his name but heard nothing. I had no doubt that he knew what I was up to. So, I was being useful to him tonight. I would not, could not refuse to be in Dagon's presence in the future.

While I now questioned what love was, that desire to be with one lover until the stars fell washed over me, and some quiet tears slipped down onto Dagon's chest where the white starred scar was. He held me a little closer.

"I know, Danu. I know." He began with me again. It was a long satisfying night.

When we were ready to leave I stepped outside and discovered that the small green stone was gone. Fiórcara had been present outside my door sometime during the night then, and he had taken the calling stone with him. If I had been in a saner state of mind, I might have worried about that. But Dagon and I had set foot on a path and we would see where it took us.

CHAPTER FOUR

ꓘEGOTIATIONS

Dagon asked me to transit him to his ship in the early morning and I did so. I waited at a distance, not knowing if my presence would complicate things and not willing to find out. I had invited him into my home. He did not invite me into his.

So it was.

He returned in fresh clothing and topped up with energy. He raised an eyebrow at me. I looked like I had just, well, been awake with someone all night. Very awake. I shrugged. I had little extra clothing. Perhaps later I would go to the sea and swim. It was not as if the Sidhe king, or anyone else interested, would not have known what I was about. The Sidhe were curious and telepathic as well as exuberant and skilled lovers. My usual Sidhe companion, if he thought to observe me, would know immediately.

Fiórcara smiled at our arrival and made no indication that he noticed my state of being—much changed from yesterday. He knew, of course. He had known before it ever began to unfold. I would be his ambassador and spy. I would provide him with whatever information might be useful—now or later. After our success at diverting the death fleet that came to scourge this planet years ago, I had remarked that perhaps I was not useful anymore. The Sidhe king had merely smiled at that. I wondered how far his prescience extended into the future. He had wondered about that ability in me as well.

I had assumed I would never see Dagon again. His last words, keyed to me at my computer in the Sidhe communication centre were simply: *Te amo para siempre.* I had thought that my feelings for him would fade, but in truth, although I did not think of him every day, when I did bring him to mind it still stopped me.

I had continued to wonder, *Could I have continued to have him if I could have acted differently? Withstood Fiórcara's pull on me?* But I was on a path I seemingly had had no power to refuse. And now?

The Sidhe king smiled. "So, everyone is energized and well fed today?"

I had been told many times that I could not shield my thoughts, so trying to hide what I felt were the largest transgressions—that I had allowed Dagon to enjoy my faerie blood and that I hadn't taken him back until the morning—well, I knew that trying to block those thoughts from the Sidhe king just made everything more obvious. But I tried anyway.

"Yes," said the Sidhe king I informally called Fiórcara. Dagon sighed, knowing that all was known.

"I have thought about what might be done to intervene in the threatened death of your planet," said Fiórcara. "In truth, I cannot say that I am familiar with such a thing happening unless toxins or poisons are involved. I assume you did not bear the cost of consulting with me if the answer was that simple."

"I could read your thoughts and observations," said Fiórcara. Dagon grew very still. "Would you allow that Alpha Shadakon?"

And then Dagon surprised me more than he had in any of our previous time together. I knew his pride and inevitable anger at having to come to the Sidhe, and I thought I knew the obvious answer to this question.

Dagon bowed his head briefly and then looked up at the Sidhe king.

"I will allow that." And he said no more.

Our time in Between then stretched. Perhaps each leader was contemplating the possible outcomes of such a decision. I attempted to move back from my amazement and fear.

This was an unexpected turn of events, but then, Dagon's coming here was as well. He had not come for me, but had availed himself to what I offered. I had shared my home but I had not seen the inside of his ship. It was, for me, not a fair exchange; but now, for him, it was not either, and yet he agreed to it without bargaining.

The Sidhe turned to me. "Neither of you have anything to bargain with. You are both acting from your hearts. In that I am pledged to serve life, I cannot decline to help either. So we must arrange this to each other's mutual benefit, if possible. But I believe that we need another person to complete this task. I will call him now."

It was at this moment I fully realized how entangled I was and how much pressure Fiórcara could bring to bear on me. What I would not do willingly, I would do anyway. I stood up.

"No drama, Danu," said Fiórcara calmly. "Your Shadakon has offered something unique to the long history that our people have shared. You have always been the closest way that I could gain access to Dagon. He knows this already. And he has done the same thing, using you to see what I had learned. But this cannot be done through you acting as a middle man."

I flinched.

"I see that you understand, Danu. You know that he who I have summoned now is my second, someone very skilled at retrieving information. It was would be better to use a, ah, technician rather than for Dagon and I to enter into this. He would resist me in particular, even if he willed not to. Survival is stronger than will sometimes."

Dagon looked at me carefully. I had read surprise in him at what the Sidhe king had said. But now he studied me. "More surprises, Danu?" he asked coolly.

"He is bringing in another," I said. "He is very skilled."

"And you know this because?"

"He was part of my hiring process to join the Sidhe's struggle against the arriving human 'businessmen'," I said, involuntarily showing my teeth, a thing I had not learned from the Sidhe.

"And he did a deep reading of you?" asked Dagon.

"Yes. And he provided information that saved my life when I came back to be tried for breaking confidentiality the night I fled to you to preserve myself."

"Yes." Dagon half smiled. "And what else? No—I do not require you to say it because I already know. He is your lover too."

"No," I said, and at this the Sidhe king smiled. "He does not allow me to have him. We enjoy each other at times. He will not be concerned if he sees your recent activities."

I scowled at Fiórcara. "He was not, as far as I know, involved in the setup of this unfolding future line. But then, it is obvious again that I usually don't know the reality of what is really going on."

Céadar arrived and took in the three of us. He raised an eyebrow at me and turned to his king.

"How can I be of assistance?" he asked quietly.

And so Dagon lay down facing the sky with an incredible amount of calm. Perhaps revealing who he was in his personal life and how he took his pleasure was not a large concern to him. But revealing the organization of power on his world—that would be a larger amount of information to give away.

It grew quiet in the grove. Céadar leaned over Dagon and met his eyes. "You know how this works, Alpha Shadakon. If you resist it will be painful.

Everyone has something they do not want to reveal, but I wish to bring you no pain today. I will be as careful as I can be. Please choose not to resist me."

Céadar and the Sidhe king had already conferred in under-mind communication. He was clear about what he sought from Dagon's mind.

"Do what you must do," said Dagon with a great deal of grace, given his situation. And so it began.

I sat without moving. I felt Fiórcara regard me. I knew that Céadar had spoken the truth to Dagon. He was a gentle man, although quite able to do what he had to do. I hoped that the fact that he had my Shadakon lover in his power would not change anything, both now and later. Céadar paid no attention to me, though I hoped that in the foreseeable future he would not continue with that plan.

I heard Dagon moan and saw his fists were clenched. Then he was still and I knew that Céadar was in past his defences and outer consciousness.

Much time passed. I sat and attempted to merge with the life force and be aware of its level of awareness in every leaf and unseen creature. I thought briefly about the Touch-me-not that I had met and conquered my fear of during my first visit in Between. I felt a faint purple touch of its pollen on the breeze. "*We hurt others because we must. They bring themselves to us and threaten us,*" it had communicated to me. I remembered entering into a stand of it, after I had earlier asked it to bring me pain as I requested. It was then that Dagon, who had stood back and watched, realized that I was transforming. That I was more than Shadakon.

At long last Céadar moved back from Dagon who lay pale and still in the sunlight. I remembered how I had felt after being deeply read. I wanted to comfort him but he was an Alpha; I would not treat him as a weary, mind-invaded person. He was a Shadakon leader.

I sat quietly a small distance from him.

"I will now go and speak with Céadar about what he discovered," said Fiórcara. "Stay with Dagon. No one will enter the glade while you two are here. You won't need this to be alone," he said, casually handing the green stone back to me.

I took it without an inner or spoken comment. I felt tenderness towards Dagon that I was not sure he wanted to receive. I waited, perhaps as the Sidhe king had waited, the first day I had awakened in Between. I knew he had been sitting beside me, waiting, when I finally awoke. I would do the same.

The sun moved across the sky and at one point I wondered how much of Dagon's life memories had been harvested. I was woven into some of them. It seemed that the Sidhe king had spoken knowledgeably about Dagon in the past. I only knew this: I would wait until he revived and then do what seemed to have to happen next.

It was late afternoon when I realized that his eyes were open and on mine. He grimaced.

"More fun with the Sidhe," he scowled.

I tried not to flinch at his remark, but failed.

"I'm not referring to our night, Danu," he said more softly. "I would not call that 'fun' but it was very pleasurable."

"I had forgotten how desirable you are," he thought to me.

Again I tried not to flinch from the pain that brought. He had forgotten? I had not. Tears gathered that I willed not to fall. I was not able to stop them. They slipped down my cheeks even as I met his eyes.

He sighed. "Come here, Danu. Help me sit up. Help me get back to my ship."

CHAPTER FIVE

1 LEARN MORE THAN 1 WANT TO KNOW

Dagon sat leaning against me for a moment and then got to his feet. "I'm ready," he said.

I transited us to the ladder leading upwards into his ship. I wasn't sure if he could manage it but I assumed that he would find some funded strength to do so. I let go of his arm—maybe for the last time, my heart said quietly—and stepped back, turning to leave.

"Wait," said Dagon.

I waited.

"I sense that you are curious. Do you want to see my ship?"

"Would this cause you further complications?" I asked. I did not ask aloud what I thought. *Is your partner aboard? What will she think of me—and you bringing me here?*

I caught his initial thought response as he rapidly tried to extinguish it.

"Do you think I would be foolish enough …"

I hung my head. I was put in my place. I would not be introduced to anyone from his world—especially a mate. I was now in the role Lore had taken when Dagon and I were mated. She continued to come and make herself available to him, as she had for centuries. At times he took her on but dismissed her importance to him when I asked.

He had heard all of this of course and laughed.

"You, unlike Lore, would not wish to kill my partner. You are not ambitious or cruel. You would protect her because she is mine and you love me. I cannot say the same of her, however."

I stood in silence, the light breeze moving my hair around. So, she was safe from me but I was not safe from her.

Perhaps he had chosen another of his kind much like Lore: an arrogant warrior who would stand beside him but would take him out if and when she could; who might lock him in a basement to die the never ending little death of hunger and pain. He was fully Shadakon. I was not fully Shadakon or Sidhe.

"I would go swimming in the sea today," I mind-spoke to Dagon. *"I would see if the whale mother has reached the beach where I met her for the first time."*

Dagon's life was not my business. Even when I stood by his side he reminded me that he did not appreciate my judgements about his decisions. I turned to go again.

"I think the reality is not as bad as what you might imagine. Enter my ship and see—if you wish to, Danu." He had made it to the top of the ladder and palmed open the hatch. There was nothing playful in his expression.

I knew I should not go up the ladder. I felt a sense of déjà vu—or maybe simple familiarity. I, of course, had flown on many space freighters and thus was familiar with the general layout of a ship. This however was smaller, sleeker and no doubt much faster, than anything I had ever crewed on. The surfaces were polished metal with inlayed patterns. Once again I realized that I was in the presence of a formidable man, a very rich formidable man.

I listened without and within for a sense of other people. I sensed someone sleeping nearby but also the dim sense of other consciousnesses. I turned to Dagon with questions in my mind.

"You are here. You wanted to know; now you will. This ship requires a captain and back-up second. He is sleeping and will not wake until I summon him. He requires less sustenance that way."

I said nothing and, to the best of my abilities, I thought nothing. "He is Shadakon, of course. You knew him."

I searched my mind: Nathaniel! He had saved my life once. He was still in the company of Dagon then, continuing to learn from him. I looked around—there were recessed drawers along one wall. Body-sized drawers.

Dagon sighed and opened one. A pale young woman lay within, an IV tube running into her arm and no doubt a catheter for urine collection hidden under the light cover. I frowned and picked up her hand to read her life forces. She was balanced, neither energized nor dangerously depleted. She was too far under for dreams. She could last a long time like this, but would have to recuperate from a weakened body if and when she was revived.

There were eight such drawers, filled, I assumed, with the nearly dead sleeping inside. If Dagon and Nathaniel rotated who they fed from, all would be relatively unharmed by their trip.

He watched me carefully. I put her arm down gently, noting that she had a few faint healed marks on her neck.

"Nathaniel likes blood," Dagon said shrugging. "He is a young Shadakon warrior. He likes the payoff of living blood."

"Do ones such as these return to live a life of their choosing?" I asked.

"Who lives a life of their choosing?" Dagon responded. "We only select from the available choices before us. These have low status in their world. I am a fair man. They will receive generous wages on our return. They may, however, opt to continue on with us or on another ship where they may not be preserved as carefully as I do."

He watched me.

I recalled something he had told me about his past. How he and Lore had run the villagers into the forests, onto the moors, and—in Lore's case—off cliffs. They had little concern for their prey because the humans were plentiful and could not defend themselves effectively. This changed, however, as eventually the vampires were dragged out into the sunlight, staked, burned and pursued. This ship was the modern equivalent of a very fast getaway horse.

410

He had wanted me to know when he told me about how they treated humans long ago that he was indifferent to humans. He wanted me to know that he still felt that way.

"Thank you for showing me," I said carefully. I was sickened but realized that for Dagon, the humans in the drawers were necessary.

"Could you still take from humans?" he asked seemingly neutrally. "Could you pick up that limp arm and take what you needed and close her back into her drawer?"

I looked at him, alarmed. I had not fed from humans in decades. Even before he left and we had not quite concluded with one another, I had preferred drinking the elixir of life, an act that that did not harm the vast provider. Why was he asking me this?

He was silent, watching me work through the information. Then I knew, that he, like the Sidhe king, was ahead of me; had always been ahead of me. No Sidhe would travel to Dagon's blighted land. Yet they had an obligation to follow through.

They would send an ambassador. One who could survive on what was available. Fiórcara had said to me years before that I was still a Shadakon and could live like one if necessary. Perhaps Dagon had hoped to avoid this outcome, but I had put myself in his hands once again—in both of their hands. I would obey my king. I would do what I could do to help a sick world. I would stay by Dagon, effectively imprisoned by my love for him. I would not fail any of them if possible. I was in stalemate.

I would move in the limited patterns that I had left until another abandoned the game or I fell, moving no more. "This is hardly a romantic proposal," he said wryly. "Given the limited capacity of this ship, you, like Nathaniel, will have to spend some of your time asleep."

I thought of the faint marks on the neck of young woman in the drawer and shuddered. Would Dagon let Nathaniel feed on my faerie blood as a special treat? I saw his eyes darken dangerously.

"If you trust me that little, go back to Between. Face whatever fate Fiórcara, your 'true friend'" —the meaning of his name in Gaelic—"has lined up for you. He could, and probably will, compel you to come with me," Dagon added. "But I will not. If you are loaded aboard my ship against your will it will be done by your various Sidhe lovers."

The scorn in him was evident.

I breathed. In. Pause. Out. Pause. I forced myself to stay present. I was beyond tears and fantasies that he had come because he wanted me––that he had wanted to re-establish a connection with me. And Fiórcara, who had graciously nurtured me and gave me a forever home? He had been merely waiting for the next chance to put me in play.

"You think he will order me to return to your world with you?"

Dagon shrugged. "Even if there is an immediate cure, someone has to administer it. Someone who can read the life force as accurately as I can read the energy of the sleepers."

He indicated the drawers. "But I think our planet's dying is complicated and will require monitoring for the long haul."

"I will bring elixir of life with me," I said. "I will not take from someone who cannot grant me permission."

He continued to watch me.

"They have all signed lethal contracts. But it seldom comes to that and, as I said, they or their beneficiaries will be richly compensated. All knew my record as a Shadakon captain. But you will not drink the elixir of life while on my ship. You will withdraw from it while you have enough time to safely do so. You will eventually take from the humans or you will arrive in the Hunger."

"Those are your choices," said Dagon. "No doubt the Sidhe king will explain this to you soon. I can linger here another day or two. And then I will leave. And I suspect—no, I know—that you will be on this ship."

I backed away from him and he let me go. I stumbled to the door that he opened for me. I transited from the top step.

CHAPTER SIX

FAREWELLS

I did not transit back to Between. Let Fiórcara think what he would. I knew I would have to eventually return to him and agree to my part of the plans. But not yet, not now.

I went to the island beach, to the log where I had sat so many times when I worked with the Mothers in their hospice here. Now the building was empty; had been empty for many decades. The wind had worked some of the shutters off the windows and others hung and banged in the wind. A swallow type of bird seemed intent on nesting under the eaves, carrying straw and such in trips between her chosen spot and the nearby meadow. She was not worried about me and I watched her determination quietly.

Eventually her mate returned with a beak full of bugs. She appeared happy to see him, if such feelings could be used for one of the small lives. He provided her with security. He would stay beside her if he could, at least for the duration of the summer, and hopefully to see the successful hatching of their brood. They were fulfilling their destiny and it was beautiful to see.

Sighing, I took off my minimal faerie garment and headed to the edge of the ocean. I easily pushed through the small waves and, as always, delighted in the watery touch of the long fronds of purple seaweed. I wrapped and unwrapped myself in a long frilled piece, creating an ocean gown and then discarding it again.

There were no large minds nearby; no whales, no larger predatory fish. I swam until I was tired and finally headed for the beach as the sun sank into the water and one moon lit up the darkening sky.

"Farewell," I said softly. "Farewell to this time and place. I may or may not return."

"I wish you many healthy offspring over the course of yours lives," I said to the birds who had taken to perch by then. "Farewell to those who I danced with on midsummer's eve. I'm glad I could be of service to you. Thank you for your many gifts."

I let myself feel the waves of sadness that moved through me. Everything had a use. I had not earned being useless; in nature there was no position like that. One danced or died.

I looked up again and was not surprised to find Céadar beside me. He had found me here before when I was heartsick about my part in annihilating the many humans who had arrived to destroy us all. And here he was again.

He studied me and then touched my hair. His gentleness and beauty had always undone me, in spite my early efforts to avoid him. He had been assigned to me by his king, as I was to him. In spite of initially hating being told what to do, I had had to admit that it was a wise choice for both of us. I did not love him desperately; did not go into the all-encompassing painful pleasure that I seemed to generate within myself when around Dagon. I just wished we could sit together and that this day had never arrived.

"I am sorry, Danu," he said. "I am sorry that our king chose me to read Dagon. He is a proud, powerful man and to be read by another, and a male Sidhe who he knew was your lover, was very difficult for him. I was relieved when he surrendered to me."

I remained silent.

"Our king and I have consulted as to what has to happen next. But finding you here, saying goodbye makes my task easier. You have seen what has to happen. You do not want it to be so, but see the reason behind it. You will go with Dagon to his planet. You will observe and put into motion a few things we have come up with.

Then you may return—on his ship or another way. There will be further connection between us—or perhaps not. Our king cannot see how this fate line will unfold."

We sat together. He was Sidhe; I was Sidhe. I kindled in his presence as he did to me. Yet he did not move to close the distance between us. I saw the evidence of him wanting me and felt the answering heat within me. But …

"I would gladly lay with you, Céadar. I would stroke your body goodbye for the foreseeable future." I shivered. "But Dagon would know. He has always had to contend with the fact that I chose faerie over him. I will not do so this night."

Céadar kissed me and stood.

"It is time for you to return and talk to our king who you call Fiórcara when you are not angry at him."

He smiled and waited while I dressed. Then he took my hand and we transited back to the glade and sat on the soft dewy grass. The Sidhe king was already there.

It was dim and, like a night long ago, the space between us was lit by small glowing insects and the silvery moonlight. It was still warm but I shivered and held my knees against my chest.

"Don't make me do this," I thought.

Fiórcara looked at me without responding in any way. Finally he spoke aloud.

"You want him or you do not want him? You once tried to follow him— without a spaceship." I remembered using his and my built up sex energy to seek for Dagon. I had had a brief faint whiff of a strange breeze under alien stars. When I returned, the Sidhe king was just looking at me, our splendid evening undone. It was that night that I allowed him to help me push the memories back, so that I could attend to my life here and now.

He had told me I could undo what he had done, because I was a Sidhe.

"I remember my king," I only said.

"And when I confirmed what your bond had already alerted you to—that he was here, you could only think of re-forging your connection to him. You could have gone to the island then," he said as he continued to observe me.

"There is nowhere I could go where I wouldn't want him, my king. Except perhaps now I have seen such a place. He showed me his ship. I saw the drawers of the barely living … his sustenance," I said shuddering. "Some bore unmistakeable signs of being used for blood as well. Apparently that is something his co-pilot particularly enjoys. The hosts were alive, but all under lethal contract."

"And you were upset to have it proved to you again that he is a Shadakon, and enjoys taking what he needs to live? Did you not live the same way?"

I hung my head. "I did my king, but I do not wish to anymore. He told me I would live on human energy or go into the Hunger on his ship. He will not allow me to have access to the elixir of life while travelling and then have to go through the withdrawal at some later inopportune time."

"A wise choice," said the king. "I see that he has been sorting out the details on his end."

I looked at him balefully and he laughed. "You once relished the hard euphoria of human energy. You thought the elixir of life did not suit your passions."

He was right. I had thought exactly that. A long time ago.

"I have a few requirements before I appear to willingly walk away, perhaps forever, from this cherished home of mine," I said. He was silent, giving me his full attention.

"I want to know what you now see is happening on his world, and if there is anything I can do that will help. I wish to have what might appear to the Shadakon clan as a tool of power. Even if all I have is this." I gestured at my knife sheath that held a small dagger and a green stone.

"And …"

"And I want to arrive looking like a midsummer's night queen instead of wearing worn clothes more suited to the beach. I care nothing about clothes. But Dagon wears a uniform now. Unless he keeps me locked away somewhere, I am bound to be seen and introduced in some fashion. There will be scorn enough without the added amusement over my clothing."

"And these clothes would identify you as Sidhe?"

"Yes. As a true representative of the Sidhe."

"And you also have been thinking about the details you must attend to," he said and smiled. "Like clothing. And not rolling with Céadar before you returned to Dagon."

"What you require will be ready tomorrow afternoon. You and I and Céadar will have a session tomorrow morning and he will show you much of what he showed me of Dagon's memories. Not all though, Danu. There are things in Dagon's mind that he fought to hide. We would not betray his confidentiality merely to satisfy your curiosity. Do you understand me?"

I nodded. I knew that Dagon might expect that all would be revealed to me. But I was content to see how this played out. I bowed to my king, my sometimes lover.

He stood and briefly held me. I felt his energy swirl around me, and then, like Céadar, he kissed me gently and put me away from him. Rather than transit, I walked home as the moon rose and the night chorus began.

Perhaps for the last time, my heart whispered.

In the morning, Fiórcara was sitting on the foot of my bed. He had a cup of elixir of life that I guessed was not standard issue. He handed it to me. I no longer questioned his actions towards me.

I was aware that he had preserved me many times and that our time together as lovers had been … exceptional for him, as well as me. We had gone a long way past merely joining our bodies. I was, perhaps as Céadar was, his.

And yet I loved Dagon. I had always wanted both and that certainly complicated my and Dagon's lives. Whether it was problem for the Sidhe in my life—I did not know.

Well, I did know. I had left Fiórcara's home one winter's night and wilfully transited to my death above the atmosphere of the planet. I had wanted to die (in my own dramatic style) and the Sidhe king had followed me and brought me back, almost dead, and then contacted Dagon and the two of them nursed me back to health. Fiórcara offered me his blood, which I drank without knowing what I was doing. Later I hoped it might have been Dagon's, but somehow knew it was not. It burned with life and kept me alive until my body could regenerate. It was the blood of a powerful ancient Sidhe king.

This incident had been a source of anger and pain for Dagon. But the Sidhe king could have left me to my choice that night. Perhaps he retrieved me because I was still useful to him. But he had apologized to me and I believed that he was sorry for his part in my decision. That had been the night that earlier, he had offered me to Céadar—and Céadar to me. That Céadar and I later forged a friendship and became lovers was an unexpected pleasure. But then living with the Sidhe was not ordinary in any way. Everything in Between fit together in a shifting mosaic.

This morning was no different. I drank the cup of elixir of life, noting that it had bitter notes that I had noticed before in a cup he had given me.

So I was not surprised that soon I was unwilling or unable to move and that my king was on one side of me, and Céadar on the other. Each had a hand lightly on my head. There was no sexual energy. I felt myself straining to fly, even as my body lay limply on the bed.

"Join with me, Danu," Céadar said. "We'll have a bit of practice material and then I will show you some of things I saw in Dagon's mind."

"In order of most recent, I will choose a strong one," he murmured. Dagon and I lay intertwined in my hill house. He, on my invitation, drank my faerie blood and then surrendered to the pleasure of my gift to him. There were no word thoughts accompanying this.

"Beyond words," Fiórcara merely said.

Céadar went backwards and I could see Dagon going about his duties with the planet he lived on in the background. There were a strange feeling to the colours and smells outside. Even the dull green flora felt … doomed. It was as if a plague had arrived and there was no adequate response from the life force.

When he went to inspect the beach, my heart clenched. Much like old Earth, the shore was littered with dead birds and washed up bloated fish. Again, a smell or feel of doom hovered over the area.

"What is this?" I exclaimed, coming out of my dozy reverie. Both of my companions pushed me down softly.

I watched through Dagon's eyes as he went into the desert. He had been told that there had been a yellow rain. Indeed, the ground was speckled with a yellowish green power that clung to the tough stalks of the desert plants. Where the material was thickest, they were withering and limp.

I sat up, suddenly back in this reality and with a fast beating heart.

They were both silent, waiting for what I would say. So perhaps they were not surprised at my pronouncement.

"The life force of the planet is under attack. Whether by a simple life form that happened upon it or"—I did not want to voice my fears, but Fiórcara just nodded—"… or someone or thing has intentionally seeded this plague."

"I am ready to go, my king," I said. "I realize that I might not return. How can I communicate with you? How far does your communication system reach?"

He smiled and pointed to my dagger sheath where the small green stone was, without me having put it back. I shook the stone out into my hand. It blazed with light unlike anything I had ever seen. The faint glow that I expected from it was eclipsed by a blaze that I could not face directly.

I hurried to put it back in the sheath. *This was the stone that I had left lying on the ground outside my door?*

"I charged it for you," he simply said.

I wished at this time to go to my knees before my king. I had only done so a few times but had never truly understood who or what I knelt in front of before. I would have done so now, but he gently restrained me.

"I accept your fidelity to me, Danu. I have never doubted it. Your mind is uncomplicated although you have taken me with you out to the stars. But never have I found anything to make me believe that you were not exactly who you presented yourself to be."

"You are precious to me," the Sidhe king said. "Do not lose your way back home. But do not bring this plague home with you. If you become affected by it …" He stopped and was very quiet.

"If I am ill and no longer have the understanding to stay away, bring down any ship bearing me here before we hit the atmosphere."

He nodded. "I'm glad you understand. I told you that if I ever passed a cup bearing death to you that I would tell you first. But this might be a time that I could not do that in person. So I will say this in front of a witness: it would only be a last ditch effort to save the life force on this planet and maybe many others. If I would require such a sacrifice from you, I would enter it into the history of this world. The whales would sing your story as would everyone else who has met you."

He looked at me to be sure I was following him. "In as much as I could do, you would never be forgotten."

By now I felt the effects of the elixir fading and sat up on the edge of the bed.

"And there is one more thing."

He pointed to a pile of clothing beside me. "There are working grade pants and shirts of the style you seem to favour. And there is also this."

He shook out a garment that was a long tunic dress to be worn over flared pants. It was the colour of the seaweed that I had wrapped myself in at the beach. Shimmering deep lilac layers partially obscured my shape yet suggested that it would be well worth unwrapping me.

I smiled at Céadar and then my king.

"I'm going for a dip in the pool and then I will wear one of the simpler garments." I said nothing about what they could clearly read in me—my yearning to leave with Dagon, and my longing to stay on Exterra. I merely bowed my head. I swam and refreshed myself and put on some of my new clothing. And then I transited to Dagon's ship.

CHAPTER SEVEN

WE FLY AWAY

When I arrived, Dagon was at the door, watching for me. I came up and he once again asked me if I wished to enter. I met his eyes and he observed without comment that I had brought the package containing my new clothes. He held out his hand and I placed it there. He unpacked it and laid out everything within it. He examined the fine linen-like package covering and ran his hands appreciatively over my new work clothes and soft boots. When he unfolded my formal wear he went silent and did not move. He brushed his hand over it, perhaps remembering the silken garments he had brought home for me after I had burned my uniform and had nothing to wear in his world. They, too, had been shades of lilac and purple. I had flown with him wearing one later and he had dove on me from above and proved to us both that I now accepted him as my Alpha. I had shouted for joy as we hurtled towards earth and as we finished on the ground. Now I was very still. *Could we afford to remember those days?*

We were both silent. I noticed that Nathaniel was awake and watching our exchange. He nodded to me but did not intrude on whatever was happening between Dagon and me at that moment. Once again I thought that he was a very fine second and excellent predator. He smiled then.

"Nathaniel will take us into orbit," Dagon said matter-of-factly. "He needs the practice and I need to sleep." He looked at me then and it all came crashing in on me. There was the captain's chair and a single bed for the other sleeping crewmember. And there were the body-sized drawers.

I shrank away from Dagon who allowed me to do so temporarily.

But we both knew that I would soon have to be secured somewhere for take-off. Even if I had begged to stay on the floor, or tied to a wall or other contrived solution, it simply was not safe for the others or me.

Meanwhile the panic hit my body and I stood and trembled, trying and failing to breathe evenly. I had always feared sharks during my diving years, but even more I had feared running out of air, while a shark circled lazily and purposefully above me. Now it felt like I had no tender. No one would witness my ending if it came for me here.

I felt my death draw closer, circling …

Dagon would be asleep. Nathaniel would be in control of the ship, of the pale people in the drawers, and of me. I didn't want to reveal to him how much I feared it all, including his part in my situation. But he had to have heard my thoughts. He was a predator. He felt, and perhaps relished, my fear.

"Help me," I said softly to Dagon. "I cannot handle this and I must. I want only to flee now but I do not have that as a choice. Please."

He observed me, having never seen me in fear like this since my trial. At that time I was starved down for a few days and then offered a human's energy. If I had taken the host's energy without gaining permission from the old pack leader, I would have died that day. I had feared them all and feared Dagon the most. I had wondered if he was enjoying my growing realization of what I was facing.

He could not help me that day, but today?

"You can be out and about after we are in deep space," he said. "You will need to feed by then. Or at least, you will be feeling true hunger."

We both knew that his investigation of what I brought aboard was to ensure that I had brought no elixir of life. He would not let me put off what had to happen. I could not arrive on his planet and shortly afterwards go into a ravaged state of withdrawal from the elixir that I had now been living on for many decades. I could wait or I could surrender to my situation and feed. But eventually I would take from one of the humans in the drawers—unless I killed myself. If I had the energy to do so then.

I felt a whisper in my mind and knew it was Fiórcara. "*You are only useful to me and all of us alive, Danu. Do what you must do.*"

"Please put me into a deep sleep, Dagon. I know you can do this. Have mercy on me."

"Did you think that I would not?" he asked, watching me. "Did you think I would force you into a small dark space and leave you awake with your fears while I slept? When did you decide that I was a monster, Danu?"

I remembered an afternoon when he and Morag, his second then, had come to where I was staying on the island to kill me or put me into imprisonment and the never-ending pain of the Hunger. I shrugged.

"I thought we moved past that," he said, studying me.

"Is she who awaits you the same mate you would have killed me for, to replace me with her?"

Then it was he who winced. He shook his head. I didn't realize it then, but at that moment he knew that I hadn't been shown everything that Céadar had seen in his mind. But Dagon was not about to correct my assumptions.

He pulled out a drawer. It was empty and, I suppose, adequately comfortable. He suddenly picked me up and carried me over to it.

Bending, he positioned me and put his fingers lightly over my darting, panic-stricken eyes.

"*Shhh, my love,*" he mind-spoke softly. "*You will wake later.*" I felt the darkness coming for me and I welcomed it. I did not expect the kiss that he laid on my lips. It was the last sensation I had. I did not hear the drawer closing or the click of the latch. I did not hear the engine building to launch speed or Dagon lying down and strapping himself in to sleep while Nathaniel took over cheerfully, holding our lives in his hands.

I awoke to see Dagon bending over me, his hand resting on my head. For a moment I thought we had fallen asleep together and my heart opened to him. But then I felt the confining space of the drawer and the realization of my situation came back.

He looked … well fed, with energy swirling lightly about him. I felt off kilter. I knew I was on a spaceship and that the simulated gravity was low, but enough to provide a "down" and "up" and for things to remain where they were placed. But the metal angles were wrong. The artificial lighting was dead and wrong. And I needed to drink the calming elixir of life.

Dagon just shook his head. "No, Danu. No matter what it costs you to come to accept it, you will nourish yourself on human energy. I will not provide for you from what I have taken. I am sure that you will be able to tell which of the humans here"—he indicated the drawers—"can afford to give up some energy so that you will be strong enough to do what is necessary."

I didn't bother to try to sway his will. He lifted me out and my legs sagged under me. *How long had I laid in the dark without moving?*

Dagon continued to support me but there was only practicality in his grip on me. If he let go, I would fall.

"Let me go," I said wearily. He did so and I slid to the floor. He stood and looked down on me appraisingly.

"Do you take your … food out and exercise it on long journeys?"

He shook his head. "I seldom make long journeys. But, no, it is better not to, that way they remember as little as possible."

"But I am fit and a long-lived one, and I can barely stand."

Cannot stand at present, I thought.

"You will be stronger after you feed," he said calmly. "And even weaker if you do not. I will deliver you to my world on a stretcher if necessary. It would not, as you well know, be a good introduction to the clan awaiting my return."

His dark eyes held mine and I watched the familiar flames flicker in their depths. He bent over me and for a moment I felt like downed prey, with the predator pausing only to decide what he would enjoy first in the coming moments and meanwhile relishing the fear and powerlessness his presence evoked.

I heard a noise that might have been a purr or a growl deep in his throat.

"I have you now, Danu. You will not be rescued by the Sidhe today or anytime soon. You came to me by your own choice and, like your promises to Fiórcara, you will keep the ones made to me."

"My world is dying," he said flatly. "Because of you I can feel that more than the rest of the Shadakon. This is not merely a passing inconvenience. Whether it is random, or whether it is aimed directly at us, I do not know. You will help me decide whether we stay and fight—or leave."

I was silent.

"You know that it is likely that you will not return?" asked Dagon who still stood above me.

I nodded. I hugged my knees tightly into my chest and shut him out then. I awoke later from where I had sprawled on the floor to see Dagon sitting beside me on the floor. Nathaniel was piloting the ship.

"Is someone in a drawer going to pay for his extra energy requirements?"

Dagon did not answer. Then he said, "I should have known that forcing you would only strengthen your stubbornness. The 'drawer people' as you think of them, are safe enough. I do not travel with inadequate resources. So I will make this easier for you. You have not felt human energy within you for many years; I will bring some to you today. I will not force it upon you. But we will lie together and you will want me and what I would share with you. You will, in the end, beg me to bring it all to you. And I will, Danu. I will."

He picked me up and carried me to the small bed and pulled the curtain shut. Nathaniel had not looked up when we passed. I was sure he had been briefed.

"Pretend that we are in a glade, under a tall sentient tree," he said. "Pretend that we have all the time in the world. Which, I guess, in a Sidhe way of looking at things, we do."

He stood beside me and slowly stripped off his clothing and laid it aside. Boots, pants, and shirt—he would not spare me any possibility of not wanting him. He then slowly took off my clothing. I was shaking, both in reaction to him and due to my growing intense hunger.

In a replay of our first night together, he touched my cheek and slowly ran his hand down to my shoulder, lingering at the base of my neck, where he had recently received his ultimate pleasure from me. But today, now, whatever time in the universe it was, he continued to slide his hand down, in a tango of desire. Even in my state, I flared under his touch. When he reached the centre of my heat, he lingered and leaned over me and sniffed as the big cat that he was at times.

There was no scent of another on me other than his own.

He growled then and bent to taste me. I felt like I had been hit by lightning. My nervous system, already lit up by the need to feed and my subsequent withdrawal, flared and I wondered if I would survive his attentions. Seeming to know exactly how he affected me, he brought me higher and higher until at last I could bear no more.

But he did not let up, neither taking me over the edge to my release, nor letting up on his attentions. Patiently, calmly, he stroked and licked and watched me as I entered a place of no mind.

"Please!" I begged.

"Please what, Danu?"

"Please come to me. Please be part of me." I looked up into his eyes and shuddered. He was completely in control. He knew his effects on me and that soon I would agree to what I fought against.

"I would share energy with you, Danu," he said huskily. "It would be for both of us. You would have me and it—or nothing, Danu."

I felt like I was going into shock. I wanted him. I wanted him. He had come to me as an Alpha and there was only one way this would move forward. He wanted me too, of that I had no doubt.

I saw the muscles bunch in his shoulders, even as he delivered the lightest of touches. He would wait. Time was not on my side. Time in fact had not moved since he removed my clothes. We both were poised on the edge of surrender but neither moving towards the other.

I remembered loving him as an Alpha. My Alpha. I wanted him on his own terms. I wanted to obey him. I wanted … I wanted …

"Please!" I whispered. "I accept you as my Alpha and I will do what you wish."

My body burned, flaring with rushes of greater hunger. He entered me, even as the energy he held entered me. It was wild and fierce. His eyes stayed on mine as he brought me to my surrender to him. His own finish was as wild. He fell against me and our hearts beat time together.

I had found my old home. I felt him wrap around me and, for this moment, I felt safe.

CHAPTER EIGHT

WE HAVE ONLY THIS TIME, MAYBE NO MORE

There was a small observation window in the captain's area. I spent many hours there, gazing at the dark and its occasional light areas that whirled by. I could almost hear the sound of the no-sound outside the hull of the ship. Dagon sat at his communication centre, keying and talking in a low voice in a language I did not know. He shielded his thoughts from me.

I wondered if the situation on his planet was growing more desperate. I wondered if he spoke to his partner, telling her he was underway and that all would soon be well.

I wondered if she knew that he had gone to retrieve me. At random times he set aside what he was doing and focused on me, pulling me down onto him where he sat or casually holding my arms above my head against a nearby bulkhead and taking me until my knees went weak. I always wanted him and did not disappoint.

He had watched me the next day as I went to the drawers and, one by one, studied the occupants and read each one's energy level. After I selected one, I carefully took only what I needed to get through another day.

During what I still perceived as night on my planet, I paced; I watched the stars and sometimes I huddled on a small blanket on the floor. I practiced breathing. My constant low-grade relentless hunger reminded me to manage my body and my emotions moment by moment. I became very quiet, inside and outside. Dagon, too, was very quiet but this, I believed, hid an inner turmoil.

One night when I rolled over onto the small sheathed knife and was reminded of it, I took out the green stone. It flickered with some inner green fire, much like looking down into a tropical night sea. My Sidhe king was still in touch then.

I looked up to see Dagon looking at me intently.

Two can walk this path, I thought. I did not drop my eyes but moved the stone back to its resting place.

"I should have known that you would carry aboard something useful to you," he said dryly.

"You asked the Sidhe to see if anything that is in their power could be done. I was sent with a tool. It is more powerful than I had imagined earlier. It is charged with the life force of what you might still call 'Exterra.'" I looked at him calmly, breathing in a balanced strong pattern and staying as grounded as one can be in outer space.

"So you were when I came to you with my dark intent on the island," Dagon finally said. He sank down in front of my little claimed space. "I knew then that you would not break no matter what I might do to you."

"I have broken many times," I said. "My pain, when traced, always comes back down to you. Or my reaction to you."

He looked at me in inner and outer silence.

"I wanted what I wanted," I said. "I wanted you to change to suit me and to accept my changes. But I did not grant you that same gift of understanding and compromising. When you flew a lover, I wailed. When I did something similar, you broke my bones. We are not compromising people. And yet …"

He continued to watch me, his expression softening.

"Because I loved and love you, I still want you, Dagon. Even though my rational side tells me that I am once again setting myself up for pain, for another round of brokenness if you like. But please begin to tell me now, Dagon.

When I step off this ship, how, if at all, will you present me? Will I watch you join a beloved mate while I stand by, stared at by the Shadakon clan, some of whom may still remember me? Did you tell them decades ago that I was dead? Will my presentation be as a Sidhe? As a Shadakon? I have proven to you and to myself that I can take what I must of human energy. My powers have strengthened. I believe that my prey would willingly come to me now."

"I have avoided thinking about the answers to these questions," growled Dagon. "There can be no energy evident between us. Yes, you must stand and watch me greet my mate and not cry or do anything to draw attention to you. I don't know how we will pull this off. We will both be at incredible risk if we act unwisely. I thought I could get my fill of you—by using you indifferently while on my ship. But we both know that is not what is happening. As it once was between us, I crave you. I feel you in my dreams and I wait to catch your attention and bring up the blaze between us again and again. If this is what you call love, Danu, I am totally caught by it. And I know that you are too. If you were toying with me, or were sent to undo me I would know. I do know. I read you while you were under my command to sleep."

I just looked at him. Once again, I was in the place of the joker, the Fool in the tarot deck. I didn't know where I was going. I didn't know if help was available or if I was going to step out into the void and lose my life. But I was not afraid of what he might have seen in my mind. He may have seen me recently step back from a possibly final farewell with both my Sidhe king and his second, Céadar. I had wanted Céadar, on the same beach where a life and death decision had been made by both Dagon and myself. But this time, I was only for Dagon, even though I doubted I would be well treated by him. Dagon would have seen that I lived mostly alone, and that when I brought him to mind, I sometimes wept.

When he returned, but not for me, I burned for him and set self-preservation aside, as my king knew I would. The ancient Sidhe king also knew that Dagon could not be indifferent to me, no matter how he appeared. Fiórcara had told me that I was much like a predatory siren. I wanted it all from whoever I came to, or who came to me. He knew that the Alpha Shadakon leader would have to have me by his side somehow.

Dagon looked at me and it was his turn to be wordless.

"What can we do, Danu? We are two days out of port."

We looked at each other.

Only two days left then, I thought and shivered.

"No days left, Danu," said Dagon. "I must have time to gather myself and present myself as my people need me to be. I cannot have your scent on me or thoughts of your skilled passion uppermost in my mind."

I studied the inlaid pattern on the floor I sat on. There was no life energy to reach for. No ocean lapping beside me. The air was dead and had no smell of trees or sea. I was as quiet within as I could be, resolutely pushing one thought aside, over and over.

"When were you going to tell me?"

"I have been trying to for days," mind-spoke Dagon.

I looked at him then and he may have feared the calm resolution he saw there.

"You will have to talk to Nathaniel," I said. "He will be the answer to this problem. He has given me his blood. He kept me alive after I fought for you and Lore broke my ribs. He is still attracted to me, I think. I will stand by his side when it is time to present me to the clan. I will be his ..."—my mind skipped over various terms, none of which I liked—"I will be his trophy Sidhe, or something close.

Some might remember me as your mate, but you long ago passed me by. In the story we must enact, I caught his eye and since I was coming to this planet anyway—well, let's say that we have a possible alibi. But he must agree to it."

"And how far will you go to prove that you are with him and are interested in him?"

I just looked at Dagon. "You will greet your partner with the assurance that you are back, bringing a Sidhe who is the advisor to the Sidhe king. You will use your considerable skills to kindle the passion that is between the two of you."

He scowled.

I smiled. "I always appreciated Nathaniel. Not only because he saved my life. He is attractive to me and has a bright life energy. I will be totally convincing that I am, at the moment anyway, his."

Dagon was silent. I knew that he had not expected this. However, this was a plan and we needed one. But he didn't like it.

"How will you convince Nathaniel to provide you with the semblance of being his"—he scowled—"lover?"

"Is he mated?" I asked. I already suspected that he was not. Dagon shook his head.

"Dagon, he will not be the semblance of a lover. I will come to him. He will taste my faerie blood. He will be more than willing to pay for the inconvenience of covering for you, his Alpha."

"Danu!"

"You will speak with Nathaniel. He will agree to help you and me as he can. You will tell him that if I offer myself to him, that you approve of that. That you wish him at least temporary happiness. 'All passion is the same.'"

I had quoted a remark made by me after observing Dagon taking a young man up to his ultimate sexual passion and then to death. He wanted me to see how he worked. I had taken that lesson to heart.

Dagon dragged me to my feet. He kissed me hard and his hands held me tightly. I withheld for only a moment. I liked this part of his skills too. I melted into him, sighing into his mouth. He felt my heat, both in my mind and my body. He continued until I shivered and sought his eyes.

"Would you do this with Nathaniel?" he growled.

"Would you do this with your mate?" I countered.

"I have to greet her as befits her station. I have to be her Alpha mate before everyone."

"You will have to continue to convince her that you are her mate, my love," I said sadly. "Perhaps for a very long time. My time beside Nathaniel will be short. I will be able to help—or I will not. You or someone else will return me to Exterra—an expensive run for a small ship that carries no cargo—or I will be marooned on your sick planet. Even if I do make my way home, if there is any doubt that I, or the ship, is contaminated, the Sidhe will destroy it. If Fiórcara hears or senses from me that this is necessary, he has already told me he will end me. Reluctantly. But he protects the Sidhe and Exterra."

"I have already said goodbye forever," I said quietly. "I may not have had a true choice. 'Consent is complex,' as you have told me before. It came down to doing this with an open heart and accepting the consequences, or it unfolding as you said earlier, with me being unwillingly loaded onto your ship. I would not have forced any who I care for to have to do that because my courage failed."

Dagon continued to look at me, the flames in his eyes flaring, his energy up and merging with mine at our edges. This would have been when I asked him to, once again, refresh our Maker bond. I wanted to feel him inside me, an unseen-to-others strength and source of courage. But his partner would know, especially if she and he also shared a blood bond. He had refused to share blood with me when he left me for seemingly the last time. He said it would cause me more pain. This time it could result in our end.

He held my left hand, my Maker hand, and kissed it.

"We need no renewal of this, my love. Even when you denounced me years ago it stayed strong. I have known that you lived all these years."

There were tears in my strong Alpha's eyes.

"You need to invite some calm," I said. "I need to get into the box again. Nathaniel and you can speak freely without me present. If he will not agree to our plan, wake me. But it would make sense that you immobilized me on your ship. The Sidhe are a shifty bunch."

"If I cannot say this later, Dagon ... te amo para siempre."

He opened the empty drawer and I climbed in unaided. I felt his hand on my head and I heard his response as I drifted into darkness. "Te amo, Danu."

CHAPTER NINE

THE ARRIVAL

I awoke to Dagon calling my name. My drawer was open and there were new sounds outside the hull. We had landed. Dagon and Nathaniel had come to their agreement that would preserve both he and I.

Nathaniel, of course, now knew enough to destroy Dagon. But I did not sense high ambition in him. He seemed content to learn from Dagon and enjoy his own life as a free spirit. I wondered how the Shadakon accessed human energy on this planet. Nathaniel appeared to be a young man who would be too good to pass on for a young human woman. She would, as Dagon's customers had, get her fair value.

Dagon was dressed in a ritual dress uniform. Nathaniel wore a slightly toned down version. I shrugged and reached for my clothes. In front of them both, I slipped out of my everyday outfit and shook out my Sidhe purple garments. I shimmered, even in the artificial light. I transferred my dagger under my tunic and wrapped my other clothes in my woven packet. Dagon stopped my hand and I put it down.

"This will be retrieved for you," he said. He said nothing about my disrobing in front of Nathaniel.

Nathaniel, who had perhaps purposely not engaged with me before while I was on the ship, stood in amazement. Even I realized that the auburn of my hair was enhanced by the tunic dress. I also knew that Céadar had seen me twine myself around the shimmering purple seaweed as he watched me swim and had somehow turned that image into this dress. I felt, at least a little bit, at home. I had accepted over the years that I, too, was one of the beautiful ones—how I had perceived the Sidhe when I had first seen them. I could see awe in Nathaniel's eyes.

He was suddenly realizing that the duty he had agreed to was not going to be so difficult to fulfill.

I felt deep sadness in Dagon. I should have stood beside him in the breeze of his planet, with this dress drifting around us. I had been, and forever would be, a Midsummer's Eve Queen. Now I would stand beside Nathaniel as a … cheap trophy. When I was in Dagon's presence I would be a cool Sidhe female. After a while I would drop out of sight. If there was still time for the humans and Shadakon here, I would do whatever I could to gather information and, if possible, slow or stop what I had glimpsed in Dagon's thoughts: a killing plague that I already suspected was fungal.

I heard the murmur of many voices outside the now-open door. The traveling ladder had been replaced with a solid staircase that led down to a dais. This was a far cry from the clan meetings I had attended on Exterra. In front of us were at least five hundred Shadakon. They were dressed formally. I doubted that there would be any public sexual taking or blood-smeared mouths at this gathering.

There was a faint musty smell on the wind. I shivered. I didn't want to breathe it in—but I must. I would inevitably have to go and walk in areas that were heavily affected. I wondered if it was already multiplying in my lungs and sticking to my skin. I knew at that moment that it was unlikely that I could go home again. My heart ached for this world. Homesickness for my own world washed over me.

Dagon stepped to the front and faced the assembled crowd. A woman in a formal form-fitting black dress moved to be beside him. He put his arm around her and said a few private words to her. Then he moved into his speech.

"I have just returned from the planet that I, and some of you, lived on many decades ago. It still has a vibrant life force. There is no sign of the plague on their world. I consulted with the Sidhe king and he graciously sent along a, ah, specialist who could learn more from observing and sensing the situation here. She also has some experimental tools that might slow or stop the spread of what is happening."

"I would like to introduce her now. And also to explain that she is currently keeping company with my second in command. It was a long, tedious flight."

There was polite laughter. He waved Nathaniel and I briefly to his side, naming me as Danu of the Sidhe and, of course, acknowledging his second officer. Nathaniel smiled at the crowd and then confidently put an arm around my waist and pulled me closer. I moved to him as if this was a natural thing between us.

"*We will get through this*," I thought to Dagon.

The Shadakon, especially the males, looked at me appraisingly. There were two faint bite marks on my neck. They had not been left by Nathaniel, but rather Dagon who, after looking me up and down, suggested that the marks would complete my disguise. He had made them himself, but had not availed himself to more than a small lick as he induced them to close and begin to heal.

Nathaniel had looked on with great interest. Dagon had said that Nathaniel liked blood. He would love mine. I could feel his strong energy and knew that if I had to come to him (and I already knew that I would), I would be able to do so without actively resisting. But that didn't mean I desired him. I felt numb as I stood in my finery, being observed by what looked like a sea of Shadakon.

My first thought was, *What did they all eat?* Or, more exactly, *Where does all the energy for the humans come from? What do the humans do here besides feed the Shadakon?* What had been a scattered population of wolves on Exterra was now a large crowd. I suspected that I would not like the answers to my questions.

The gathering seemed to break up quickly, but perhaps I was absent from myself and did not notice the passing of time. Soon enough, Nathaniel and I were in a flitter (a newer model than what I had last flown in with him). I saw city and more city beneath us. There were people on the streets, human and Shadakon. The humans did not seem to be cowering in fear, but neither did they seem joyful. There was a dull tone, enhanced by the faint smell on the wind.

Nathaniel usually stayed in a group barracks for unmated Shadakon. Dagon had arranged, in deference to me, to house us in a small building close by. When we entered we were in a small space that had a sitting room, a small shower room, and two small bedrooms. I exhaled in relief at seeing the latter. There was a window overlooking a small lake or pond in the distance. The water looked inviting, but there was no one walking around its edges. I tried to open the window.

Nathaniel put his hand on my shoulder. "The windows do not open, Danu. No one flies from them and were you to manage to open one"—his mind-speak said, "*break*"—"we would soon have a lot of unwanted attention."

He sprawled at ease on the small couch.

"When do I go see what I need to see?" I said. "How does this planet work—how can there be so many Shadakon requiring nourishment in one place? Are you farming humans for your use?"

I did not mean to turn my fury on him but he winced.

"Dagon said you would not understand the setup here.

That I was to try to explain as best I could, but he will be able to better explain it to you later."

"But I imagine that you are hungry now," he said. "I know I am."

I stared at him not comprehending how quickly this was going wrong for me.

"I took the liberty of ordering two humans to our room," Nathaniel said. "They will arrive soon."

There was a tap at the door. Two young women stood without moving in the doorway. One of them had a compu-pad. She handed it to Nathaniel and waited while he scanned it quickly.

"*No lethal contract, no blood … hmmm … do either of you want to make some extra credits?*"

They looked at each other warily. He drew them in and then brushed the hair off the shoulder of one and inspected her for marks. Seeing none, he smiled.

"It won't hurt you know. Or … it will hurt for a moment, but will be healed by the time you leave."

After some consideration—and the private exchange of additional credits, the unmarked woman agreed to his offer.

Nathaniel took her by the hand and disappeared into one of the small bedrooms. There was the brief murmur of voices and then I heard a sharp stifled cry. I felt her fear and resignation and his pleasure mingling for me to take in.

The other woman stood looking at me. Perhaps she wondered why I, introduced as a Sidhe, would need her services. Or perhaps she had not heard Dagon's speech today and didn't recognize me as Sidhe. Or, most likely, she just didn't care. "Sit with me," I said. She sat. "What is your name?"

She said her name was Ker. Just Ker. She didn't ask or seem interested in my name.

"How often do you do this?" I asked.

She shrugged. "We are allowed to be on the registry three times a week. Blood service counts for two sessions but it is seldom entered that way."

She glanced at the closed door.

I sat quietly. Was this the business that kept Dagon supplied with fast spaceships? My mind was trying to take in information even as a part of me was backing away from the pattern taking shape in front of me. I was hungry. I was sick.

I took Ker's hand. It lay quietly in mine. I sensed no anger in her. No hope either. Unlike the young woman I had managed to save so many years ago, who was kept as a servant-slave to unprincipled Shadakon on Exterra, this woman seemed to accept her fate. But there was no curiosity. No strong emotion of any kind.

"I cannot do this," I said, dropping her hand.

She shrugged. "I need to fill my quota. I will ask your companion if he wants me as well."

I understood then that whatever I did, she would be used tonight before she went home.

"Wait," I said. "I will avail myself of you. I will sign you off as having provided. But I want something else from you. I want to look into your thoughts. I will induce light sleep, and, unlike what my companion said before, this truly will not hurt. I will take the energy I need first and then read you. Afterwards you can go or wait for your friend."

She looked at me blankly. "She is not my friend. I am not sure what it means. We sometimes are sent out together. I have been doing this longer than she has."

I continued to sit silently. I wanted her consent. I would not do this without it.

She faced away from me towards the window. "Why are you asking me to say yes or no? For me, there is no yes or no."

I continued to wait.

"There is always at least a small yes or no," I said. "I will not take you or read you without you agreeing. I realize that this seems strange to you. But I am a visitor here, and on my world we do not force our will on others."

I realized that this was only partially true. But it had more truth than falsehood.

She finally looked up and in her first movement towards me; she offered me her hand and bowed her head. I moved ahead quickly, not wanting to have to deal with Nathaniel when he re-emerged from taking his nourishment. First I gently took energy from her in one long, slow breath. I stopped well before I had to. Then I placed my hand on her head, although I did not have to touch her. We sat quietly like that for a moment, and then I read down into her memories.

She lived in a small room with many other people. There was bedding on the floor, and a grimy bathroom down the hall. There were people coughing and some just sitting apathetically. There were a few children and even fewer babies in the laps of older people. I saw no loving. I felt no hope.

I was viewing a depressed slave population. I saw outlying dilapidated farms and a few animals in the fields. It was moving to midsummer, at least on my world, but here there was a flatness and lack of life force. I saw no trees or forests in the distance.

I knew that some people would have judged the population of Old Earth to be in a similar situation by the time I left. Having children there was strictly monitored, with only one child possible and most families allowed none.

Most people had small repetitive jobs, some sold their body parts, others were murdered for theirs. Illegal sales were always more profitable, but the life expectancy of the sellers' was lower. To many, that would not have mattered overmuch.

I knew that the life force of Earth had been stagnated, poisoned and covered over with pipelines and concrete. I knew that birds fell from the skies there as well—though usually from having a belly full of plastic.

This planet was poisoned with despair and indifference. And something else as well.

I thanked Ker by name and she looked at me strangely. The other woman emerged, with Nathaniel behind her, looking rumpled and weary. I wondered how careful he was in what he took.

"I would talk to Dagon now," I just said.

CHAPTER TEN

ĦOW IT IS

Nathaniel did not say anything. His expression was complex and I passed on trying to read him at the moment.

"Dagon will be involved with his other obligations at least until tomorrow," he said finally.

I could see the truth of that. He was getting caught up on what had happened in his absence. *He is renewing his connection to his mate,* my under-mind said to me bleakly. I tried to put that thought to the side. He wasn't mine to miss or feel any connection to. What we had was a secret—not on my world but definitely on his. I could not change this and should not try. I was here to honour his request to the Sidhe to send help. His world had been sickening, I guessed, for years. It had just wearily slid over a tipping point recently. One day more or less would not change that.

I was here because I had allowed myself to love him again, and because the Sidhe king wanted me to be here. I had high, but certainly not highest, priority. I took myself to the other room to wait out the night.

The next day we were both up at dawn. "Take me out and show me, Nathaniel. I do not think we have to go far for me to begin to get a feel for what is happening here."

Nathaniel shook his head. "I was ordered not to let you leave this room until he comes to summon you. You have already learned more than he might have expected you to from the humans I brought here. In hindsight, I should have fed and then brought you sustenance without allowing you near the hosts. Besides, he has explained to me that you can transit to anywhere that you have been to physically.

He wants to bring you to the situation on this planet ... in his own way and time."

I remembered Dagon growling over me on the ship. *"I have you now, Danu. You will not be rescued by the Sidhe today or anytime soon. You came to me by your own choice and, like your promises to Fiórcara, you will keep the ones made to me."*

I sighed. I would not be forcing Dagon's hand in any way if he could help it. I would abide by his decisions; there was no other choice.

"Well, Nathaniel, both of us do not have to be in this lifeless space. I'm sure you can lock me in securely. Go take the day off. Do what you do—just not in front of me today."

434

He smiled. "I am not to leave your side. I am to observe you at all times, Danu. Dagon has explained that you have a … skill, in that you can find ways out and through that others have not thought of. He has entrusted you to me for the time being."

He smiled again but suddenly I felt cold.

I knew that Nathaniel, while not cruel by Shadakon standards, had high energy and enjoyed frequent impersonal sex and taking. Dagon had been much the same when I met him. Charming. Desirable. Unconcerned about the fate of his sources. He held to contract. Just that.

Nathaniel had been given the position of guarding me. Not so much from the outside world, as his world from me. He knew that I was capable of surprising the Shadakon with unexpected skills. Long ago, he had watched me kill Lore, Dagon's long-time lover and would-be assassin with the knife she carried. He had sustained me with his own blood while I lay dying from that fight. He valued me as Dagon's mate. But Dagon, on my suggestion, had given me to him. I had even suggested to Dagon that I bind Nathaniel to me with my Sidhe blood to ensure his loyalty and complicacy with his and my plan to pass as friendly strangers. I knew what was coming next.

This moment had been arriving since he pulled me confidently to his side as we stood in front of the Shadakon who had come to welcome Dagon home.

I looked into his golden eyes. I saw the immediate future there. I would let him take me as a … lover. But love was not really part of this. And I had to do more than merely let him do anything. I would bind him to me. Dagon knew as I did that I could do this and he knew what it involved. He had accused me of catching him at our first touch. Now that my Sidhe heritage was also fully activated, I had increased sexual powers. Few could resist me. Most would come willing, unaware of how that might change their fate. I was Sidhe. Those the Sidhe chose—for whatever reason—came to them willingly.

"Nathaniel, you should ponder whether you want to begin this." I already knew he would say yes, but I was looking for true, informed consent. I knew that he had already dreamed of this moment since he and Dagon talked on the ship, and maybe before that. He had heard and been aware of us as we combined, sometimes loudly and in prolonged sessions. And I had been given to him by his Alpha.

He shrugged. "Now, Danu. Or later. If not now, then I will feed again. And if you wish, I will feed you afterwards so that you do not have to lower yourself to take from a human."

There was, of course, scorn in his tone. He saw my reluctance as a weakness—one he could exploit.

I shivered.

"Feed," I said wearily. "I cannot take now. I will be in my bedroom."

He smiled as if that concept "my bedroom" amused him. It would not, of course, have a lock. And there was no "my" anything in his world. He was, by his usual standards of behaviour, being polite to me—but only to a point. And we had reached it now.

"Wait for it and me, Danu," he said confidently. "This need not be ... unpleasant ... for either of us." He paused. "And it was your plan, Sidhe queen."

I went into the second bedroom. The rest of my clothes had been delivered earlier and I was wearing an everyday set. My fine purple garment, fit for a queen, lay tossed aside. It saddened me and comforted me at the same time. I took off my clothes and loosely wrapped myself in the silken purple fabric. I tried to bring to mind swimming in the sea and the pleasure and calmness I took from that. For a little while, I succeeded.

I heard voices outside and knew that Nathaniel's energy sources, doubtlessly young and tired, had arrived. I heard no cry of pain. He was reserving his pleasure of taking blood for later.

I took out the green stone. Energy swirled in its depths. I felt how much more powerful it was than it had been when I carried it without thinking much about it.

"Help me Fiórcara, my best known friend. I have no cup of elixir to provide extra courage today. I have been given—no, I have suggested that I be given, to Dagon's second to ensure his silence. He will use me, as he will. He will avail himself to my high spring Sidhe blood. I do not want this."

I waited. I heard in my mind, a whisper in reply.

"I told you that if you wanted to avail yourself to passion in my world, I approved. Dagon has, perhaps reluctantly, told you the same thing. I sense within you that you can feel Nathaniel's attraction for you, and, if you are honest, you will feel some of your own for him." I heard a faint chuckle. "And you warned him, more than you have done with others you have beguiled."

I waited and thought about what he had said. There had been no judgement of me or my situation. He suggested, like a true Sidhe would, that I merely enjoy what was offered.

"Do what you must do to return to me, Danu. That is the only important thing for you to achieve." And then the stone went quiet.

I sensed Nathaniel outside the door. I unwrapped myself from the comfort of my queen's clothing and laid it carefully aside. I turned down the covers on the bed. We might as well start there. I opened the door to find him standing in front of it, filled with energy and assurance of what came next.

"Enter if you will, Nathaniel," I said calmly. I saw that he then realized that he could not have entered without my invitation. That if I was Sidhe, I was also Shadakon. He came in, leaving the door open and removed his clothing matter-of-factly. Boots, shirt, pants ... he stood before me proud and high on energy and eager for the feast before him.

I waited without saying anything. There was nothing to be said. I felt my effect on him and then observed it. There was no immediate answering heat in me. If he had taken me then, I could have called it something else. But he took his time, sweeping my body with his hands much like Dagon had done when I returned from Between. Everywhere he touched he left his own scent. He bent to my lips but did not touch mine until I realized that I wanted him to. He watched me, his eyes flickering with golden lights, while my body kindled to his. He then bent again and kissed me. First lightly, teasingly. I opened my lips to him and he promptly took my mouth hard and long.

"Food and sex, or my pleasure first?" he whispered. I shook.

"Ah, but a queen should be attended to first," he said.

I quivered under his touch, which was growing more intense. There was no uncertainty in him. He touched and tasted as he would and I wanted him to. I wanted him to.

"I believe you are willing now," he said with a laugh. "I know I am."

He pushed me down and began with me. It was wild and hard and I began the spiral up with him, wanting more, giving more. He was hot and fast and I remembered scorning that when Dagon once described his Shadakon lover that way. I scorned nothing now. I met his moves and moaned.

"And now you must ask for me and your nourishment," he said. He laughed, "No you must beg me."

That was when I know that he had listened when Dagon brought himself to me the same way the first day on the ship.

I lasted a little while. I lasted no time at all. I begged him. I called his name. He brought us both to our ecstasy then and gave over a large amount of energy such that I gasped.

"*To make up for the next part,*" he said in my mind. And then he drove his fangs into my neck and drew heavily from my sweet faerie blood. I felt his pleasure peak and heard him moan.

He lay beside me, dazed with pleasure.

"Well you may have ruined me for human blood," he said.

He hadn't bothered to lick the wounds he had made. I knew they would close and heal, but not as fast as they would have with the touch of his saliva. I decided he had done so on purpose. Nathaniel was quick and he obviously had paid attention to what had gone on between Dagon and me. I knew that one day he would try to stand Dagon down—kill or banish him to gain his own Alpha status.

He had heard my thoughts.

"Yes. I marked you. And I will do so again when I choose to. And you will let me. Dagon will then understand a little more about me. I am patient and I will be useful to him—for a while. But yes, my sun will rise."

I thought about the dreary sun outside the window. I shuddered. It might not be a desirable kingdom to take over.

"There are many planets within our reach, Danu. We can and will move on."

That was when I realized that the bloodline of the Visitors ran strongest in the veins of the Shadakon. Those space-traveling outsiders had plundered Old Earth and created human workers, elevating their intelligence and aggression to what they were now. And then they left, leaving behind some offspring bearing more than the original amount of the Visitor's genetic traits given to the workers. The Shadakon, even more than their human relatives, were takers. When there was a balance between the prey and predators, the populations balanced out and the life force could continue on. When humans or Shadakon exceeded the ideal proportion, whatever world they were on would slowly lose energy. Perhaps the kindest thing the original Visitors had done was to leave.

But by then, the damage was done.

Nathaniel had followed my thoughts but now he intruded with his own. He reached for me again. Still high on my blood he carried me to the living room where the door to the outside was. If Dagon had come, he would have unavoidably heard us from outside the door. I said nothing about this. He took me up again to wanting him, but this time, some part of my mind remained able to focus. This time, I took him. I wrung pleasure out of him until he cried out in both pain and pleasure.

Holding off my own body's desire to finish, I worked on him, neither letting him find his release or slacking my efforts. There was a moment that he looked up at me and there was fear in his eyes.

I laughed then. "There is an old saying that I learned a long time ago. Be careful what you wish for."

He was begging me now, though I doubted if he knew what he was begging for.

Dagon had taught me well, and the Sidhe had enlarged on what I had learned from him. I could and would do what I was doing all day. The Sidhe loved a prolonged level of abandon and surrender. Nathaniel looked as if he had crossed over the line of loving it. I eventually finished him and came with him. Then I got up and picked up my clothes on the way to the shower.

He would return to me, I had no doubt, but he would think twice before he did so.

CHAPTER ELEVEN

DAGON ARRIVES

I was renewed by the water that flowed over my body, washing away at least some of my body's evidence of our activities. It had not restored me to a neutral space. Once again, my belief that I had to protect Dagon had placed me in a place of diminished choices. I looked at the still visible marks on my neck and grimaced. I could have buttoned my shirt up higher. I started to and then stopped. If this was my sacrifice, why should it cause me shame? I returned to the living room to find Nathaniel still naked, staring out the window.

"I would suggest you do the same," I said, indicating the shower. "Although your Alpha agreed to this plan and saw it as reasonable, he may not still feel that way after observing you lolling about, scented with me."

It's just a suggestion," I said, and shrugged. "He has almost killed me for less."

Nathaniel looked shocked out of his post-sexual marathon state and shuffled off to gather his clothes and shower.

There was a small communication centre in the room. I had already tried to activate it earlier and gotten nowhere. When a green light lit up I sauntered over to it and tried again. Dagon's image came up in front of me and I felt his keen appraisal. His eyes narrowed at my wet hair. He saw the marks on my neck, the marks I had chosen to leave in full view.

"Danu!" I could not, of course, feel his energy through this connection but perhaps by more primitive ways. My Maker hand stung.

I shrugged and met his eyes. "It is as it is here. You surely aren't surprised."

He looked at me in silence. I saw him, well nourished and with power surrounding him. His Alpha status was secure. For now.

My continuing existence depended on him and his concern for me.

"Did you want this, Danu?"

I was suddenly angry in a way that Nathaniel had not managed to bring up in me.

"I wanted it for you, Dagon! For your continued well-being. I have secured Nathaniel's loyalty, at least for now. For you!" I stopped to take a breath.

"If it can be said of a Sidhe, I whored for you. Nathaniel is not the problem. Once again I have entangled myself with you and am paying the price. I will do so for a while. I already yearn to return to my home, and to my kind. You and the other Shadakon feed off slaves. They are too weary and used up to live meaningful lives—whether they are in a drawer or just waiting outside an officer's door. I imagine you did not give fair trade to whoever you took today. Credits do not compensate for an unlived life. I am sickened by what I have already learned."

I stopped. I had said too much, pushed too hard on this proud Alpha. I was on his world now. If he did not return me, or give the order for me to be taken back, I would die here. Yet again I thought of the small dagger. I saw Dagon grow still and knew he was following me somehow.

"Once again do you threaten me with your death?" He spoke softly but there was menace beneath the message.

"No, my love," I said sadly. "This is not a threat and I do not think of it to manipulate you. It is, at this moment, the most hopeful fate I can imagine for myself. Would you take even that from me?"

He was totally silent and I knew that he was gathering control over whatever emotions I had evoked. He studied me a moment more and then said, "Get Nathaniel over here.

We will discuss things that you do not need to hear." Nathaniel had come up quietly behind me, but not so quietly that I could not hear him. I stepped aside.

Dagon began speaking to him in a language unknown to me. It was not translated in Nathaniel's thoughts so I only "heard" the emotions that arose in him as they spoke. I read fear, some suppressed anger, and then more fear. I saw him sway slightly where he stood. He stole a glance at me, at my neck. I knew that he would pay for his arrogance. I looked at him calmly.

"*The arrival of a granted wish is often not as one might hope,*" I thought so he could hear.

Dagon had one more thing to tell us both. He spoke in standard english so I could understand.

"I will be there later this afternoon. I had intended to take a day to catch up with my business. I will rearrange my schedule."

Nathaniel went pale. So Shadakons can feel immense fear, I thought. I thought of Lore dying by my hand and how she was a warrior to the very end. I thought of Dagon, standing to receive the Sidhe's judgement after trying and failing to kill me, undone but not afraid of what came next.

I smiled.

"I will be ready for your arrival my Alpha," I said. "We await your coming." I was the now the cool Sidhe queen. I met his eyes but we could not lie to each other. He thought he could handle the agreement we had brokered with Nathaniel, but now …

Dagon did not announce himself or ask permission to enter. He arrived, I assumed, as fast as he could. Presumably this was his property and I was not the only one who could not refuse him entrance. The door crashed open and he was standing in front of us.

I knelt before him, my head bowed. He did not immediately acknowledge me and I remained, completely motionless, in Between time, scanning the sea for a hint of the great mother whale and her calf. I was as I had been the day I faced him when he arrived to kill or imprison me for enjoying Fiórcara on that distant beach. I had felt no guilt then, and I felt none now. He had planned to kill me then and he might now. I waited. It occurred to me now, as it had then, that I would accept that from him. I waited. I waited some more.

Dagon put his hand on my head.

"Rise, Danu," he said, and then continued past me to where Nathaniel awaited whatever would come. He seemed to gather himself to fight back against what he rightly assumed would be a condemnation of him. It was not a wise move. The predator in Dagon rose and I could sense the stalking quality as Dagon moved towards him. I saw the panther, large muscles bunching, bringing him without a whisper of sound to lethal distance between him and Nathaniel.

Part of me was pleased. But I also knew that Dagon's anger was misplaced. He had made a deal that he was finding hard to keep. He had promised Nathaniel something he could not now bring himself to honour.

I knew about desperate deals and how they brought one to unknown and sometimes unwanted consequences. I said nothing.

Dagon spoke quietly but the force beneath smoked with danger. Now it was Nathaniel who quaked.

"How did this happen?" he asked Nathaniel. "Did you force yourself on her?"

Nathaniel shook his head. "When we joined, she wanted me," he said.

"And did you ask her to allow you her blood?"

Nathaniel was a little slower to answer this one. "It was part of"— he licked his lips nervously—"the package."

"The package?"

"She was hungry but did not want to take from a human, although she did yesterday. But I think she shorted herself. Anyway, I withheld feeding her until…"

"Until?"

"Until she completely surrendered to me."

I did not know if Nathaniel realized that he was confessing to listening in on Dagon and my initial contact on the ship. That he had chosen to do exactly what Dagon had done.

Dagon said nothing but turned to me. "So he sexed you and fed you and drank from you. Is there more?"

"Yes," I said. Nathaniel stilled. "And then he thought to continue his morning's activities. I thought he deserved to know the true extent of what a Sidhe can bring to someone who is not also Sidhe." My lip curled.

"This time was more to my liking." I paused. "I took him down."

Dagon looked at me silently for a moment. And then he laughed. "All those sessions with Fiórcara," he said musingly. "I remember the pain you bore when you returned. I was angry that he had hurt you and that you let him. But this is another Sidhe skill that you have honed. I would expect no less."

He turned back to Nathaniel. "So you have had her and marked her—and marked her without healing it so that others beside me could see that. And she had you and, I think, marked you as well. You will never touch her again, even if she is standing a breath away. You will want to. Oh, you will want to Shadakon. You will want her for the rest of your life."

"I hope it was worth it," he said quietly. "It might have been if she had loved you." He came to me then and wrapped me in his arms, letting me lay my head on his heart. It beat strongly. I sensed no madness in him and truly, not much sorrow. "You asked me to accept you as you are, Danu. I am trying to do that."

He gently set me away from him then and merely said, "We are going out now."

CHAPTER TWELVE

DESOLATION

We flew by flitter over the dreary miles of city and then swerved out over what appeared to be a desert. I recognized the remains of bridges that now no longer spanned rivers. The crumbling structures now reached across steep dry gullies. Right next to any remaining water, or where it sometimes still flowed, there was a thin scraggly line of green. The desert plants looked like they worked hard for their meagre nourishment.

"I would touch the ground here, Dagon."

Without speaking he swooped down and landed on a flat landscape that offered no resistance to the wind. The ground was baked and the rocks had a polish that I assumed the relentless wind had produced over many long years.

I heard no creatures stirring. I saw nothing in the air. I knelt on the ground and Dagon pulled Nathaniel away out of my immediate space. I took a handful of dirt, compressed it, and then loosened my fingers. It flowed through my fingers like water. But there was no water here. I inspected the desert plants around me carefully. None bore buds in promise of blooms, however brief.

"Where did the water go?" I asked Dagon.

"You cannot hold us accountable for that," he said, sighing. "This was a semi-desert planet, but humans plundered what water there was. Much the same as old Earth," he added. "But Earth had more reliable water sources—oceans that funded water and returned it as clouds and rain. This planet has, or had, smaller scattered seas. I believe people held out here as long as they could. Had we arrived then, we could have pruned their ranks. I don't know if that would have made a difference. But all of this was done before we arrived.

The remaining humans were living in their grey cities. They sold goods to each other—what few crops they grew and craftwork. With no real export goods—did I say that they sold their water off planet for a pittance? —They turned to darker exports."

I looked at him.

"They sold, and still sell, their daughters and sons. There are few children but we have imposed no restrictions. But foetuses"— a look of disgust flashed across his face—"are valuable. More valuable than living children. Living, relatively healthy children are worth more than adults. The energy trade is what awaits those that manage to grow up. We did not set that up either. But we avail ourselves to it. The Shadakon have grown lazy and complacent." He scowled at Nathaniel. "We are affected by our life here."

A nightmare not unlike Earth. I had fled from that, willing to abandon the humans and all the little lives to their doom. Would I do so again? Could I, or even the Sidhe, do anything to undo this?

"That is the question, Danu," Dagon said. "But there are other things for you to see. Guard your heart—this will not be easy for you."

We continued on our journey into the sun. The haze in the sky was thicker here, a yellowish fog, and I wonder if we would be contaminated. Dagon shrugged. "If we can be, we already are. The humans are seemingly not affected. Nor are the Shadakon."

"You came to Exterra possibly bearing this?"

He was silent and then said; "I was in communication with the Sidhe king well before we entered the atmosphere. And he came to me and insisted on certain precautions before I opened my ship."

He stopped. So much had been revealed.

We looked at each other.

Always the two leaders had been in touch? Fiórcara had known where Dagon was? I could have spoken to him over the years?

I bowed my head. The tears, that were not present even while an unwelcome stranger took my heart's blood, spilled down my cheeks. I captured some with my hand and shook them ritually down towards this planet.

"I weep for us," I said, and then added numbly, "Land somewhere."

"It gets worse further along," he said sadly, whether referred to this planet or me and my pain, I did not know.

Shortly after this he landed. There was greenish yellow powder blowing along the ground, being picked up by the dry wind and whirled into the sky. This was the place that Céadar had showed me in Dagon's thoughts.

The dust, which seemed fuzzy on close inspection, clung to the clearly dying plants. Where it had accumulated on trees that had been dying for a long time, the bark was splitting and curling up, allowing the invader access to its inner layers. They would not live long—I hoped the life spirit had already left this area to its fate. I hoped no little life watched from a dusty den, hoping for one more meal; it would just prolong the inevitable.

I rubbed some of the powder into my palm. There was no sensation of pain. I attempted to touch its life force. It was very old and simple. It did, however, provide a service to the barely living. It was the last push to death, necessary for some caught in a long painful passing. And it would, thoroughly and finally, break down all the living molecules into their simpler parts. I dusted my hands and rose.

Dagon asked me in mind-speak, *"What is this, Danu? Can it be halted or reversed?"* I looked at him as such sorrow rose up in me that I would have fallen. He held me by the arm momentarily. I had no doubt that if I had fallen over next to Nathaniel, he would not have reached out to catch me. Dagon would enforce that he never touched me again.

I shrugged.

"This planet is in hunger," I said. "It has been starved down such that the life force can no longer sustain itself or correct injury or illness. The yellow dust is merely opportunistic, although it too has its place in this long story. It is mould on a corpse. Its job is to erase all traces of living life, and then die itself, or rest in a not-living state. It could have come from anywhere. It could have been seeded here—by a comet or meteorite, or by a drone ship that crashed unnoticed in an outer area."

We looked at each other.

"It could be that the off-world miners could more easily harvest what would otherwise be covered in deep humus. In trees and grass, and yes, in a population that might resist them. I sense that the humans are still relatively healthy in that they take nourishment near the top of the food chain. Whatever living energy this planet can produce is concentrated in grain and flesh. And, of course, the Shadakon partake of the humans' distilled energy. But the young humans look weary and dull beyond their years. The Shadakon will want more and more but eventually what the hosts can supply will not support them."

"Without the credits generated by providing to us, the humans will probably quickly starve."

"They are already starving. There is no curiosity, no spark to move forward.

I checked the compu-pad of one the human sources yesterday; she contributes life energy three times a week. That would not bring a healthy body to the point of the weariness that she walked in. Of course, the sources accept extra undocumented credits for blood contributions; these are supposed to be logged as double donor sessions but seldom are."

Dagon just looked at me. "And you know that because ...?"

"Did you not place me with Nathaniel that I might learn from him?"

"He was supposed to keep you away from the situation here. Until I could show you myself."

I smiled. "You should have known better, leader of the Shadakon. He was fresh from the space journey and had had to curb his appetites on that trip. Ordering two humans was the first thing he did."

"And then?"

"And then he bargained (in my presence) with one who had not provided blood before."

"And ..."

"And while he initiated her into her 'painless donation' I gathered a bit of information from the one left for me."

"Did you take from her?"

"I wasn't going to. But she explained that she would let him take her as well. I agreed to sign off her donor sheet. I took sparingly. It was clear in observing the one Nathaniel had used that he was not so careful in his taking."

"All this happened in a military secured barracks, with locked windows and no communication with the outside?" He studied me some more. "What was your human's name," he asked, surprising me.

"All she could remember was Ker. That was all she had left."

"And did you give her your name?"

"I would have. But I feared it would bring her no benefits. Perhaps it might even cause her further pain in her life." I looked at him. "She might have been seen as a security risk—holding information that could doom her."

"And who might have done that?" Dagon asked quietly.

"The same one who locked me up with a Shadakon who craved my blood." I was silent for a moment and then sighed.

"Nathaniel was more considerate than he had to be, given the circumstances. Like you, he enjoys most the energy raised by sex. He was good enough at that and took his time. As I did with him."

I laughed coldly and realized that I had once said I could not, would not, use my sexual passion simply to draw someone in to use them for the Sidhe.

"Fiórcara was wrong," I muttered. "I do not have to fall in love with my prey to be effective. I am however, saddened to realize that about myself." I stared out into the distance. The sun was sinking with no night sounds, no night birds calling. I bent my head and for many reasons, I wept.

CHAPTER THIRTEEN

EVENING COMES AND
LEAVES SOFTLY

We returned and walked silently to my small … prison. Once outside the door, Dagon turned to Nathaniel.

"You will stay in the hall outside this room tonight. You will not allow anyone in or out. If I find that you were delinquent in your duties I will replace you as my second."

Dagon continued to look at him.

"You may quickly take nourishment here," Dagon continued. "Do not become distracted while you do so. You will not have any sexual action while on duty. You will not avail yourself to blood, even if they are giving it away. I will come by and check on your compliance at some point. Do you understand everything I have said?"

Nathaniel nodded. I smiled. I knew that response would not be acceptable.

"You must say it," Dagon hissed. So he had once made me speak my mind clearly. I looked at Nathaniel knowingly.

Nathaniel muttered that he understood and would follow orders.

Dagon held me briefly and spoke to me in a whisper of under-speak. I could sometimes hear him even when he was not thinking loudly. *"May I come to you tonight Danu? I cannot ease all your pain. But perhaps I can share it with you."*

I looked into his eyes and found myself falling away into the flames there.

"You are always with me, Dagon. But yes please let us steal another sliver of time together. The moon is, I believe, ebbing, as is the life tide here. I would share my bright Sidhe energy with you."

I changed out of my clothes now stained a faint greenish yellow in places. I stood under the shower, regretful about the water that flowed over me and away. I hoped it was recycled. When I came out I started to put on at least a shirt. But at the last moment, I put on my queen's finery. I looked into the mirror and saw a beautiful woman, garbed in a true-life colour from my sea. It might have even been made from the seaweed I swam amidst. I wrapped a few strands of my hair around one finger and imagined deeper purple notes. I was pleased and added a few more. They glimmered softly amidst the rest of my dark curls. I twirled and then flew slightly in the small room. I slowly rolled in the air, letting the fabric slip around me. I felt, however briefly, happy. I could not have said why.

I heard a faint sound and saw that the door was open and Dagon was standing, watching me silently. Nathaniel was slumped against the wall outside. He shut the door softly and stood beneath me as I drifted down to him. The fabric flowed around us both, as I had imagined it doing before I arrived on this planet. He was shaking, as was I.

He moaned deep down in his throat, something like a sustained purr. With infinite care, he divested me of my clothes and then took off his own. He went to the window and hitting a few unobvious buttons, unarmed the lock and swung it open to the dry night breeze. It stirred my hair and the strands of purple waved languidly, not unlike the seaweed had in my swim in Exterra's sea. He put a hand up to one, almost disbelievingly, and stroked its length. My body, my heart's desire, was apparently attached to that strand and I immediately came to the place that only he could bring me. He was gentle but relentless. After he had touched every part of me he began to kiss me in those same places and when I could no longer stand he lowered me to the floor and leaned down towards me.

"How far do you want to go?" he asked quietly.

"If you want me, would you stand by me here?"

"And not return?" I only asked.

"Unlikely," he said, "Perhaps a visit now and then."

We looked at each other.

"I cannot answer that now," I said. "That is not 'yes' and not 'no.' But I am incapable of answering now. It has been a very long, sad day."

"And would you rather I leave?" he asked quietly.

"Dagon! Would you, could you do that now?" I burst into tears then, my proud cool Sidhe queen persona dissolving with them.

"What then, Danu?"

"Would you start over again? With the kissing and the joyful touching? Would you join with me, Dagon, tonight? Would you let me, if only for a little while, love you?"

And he did. He did. We were perhaps quieter than usual but the discipline of that was interesting. At times he simply placed his hand lightly over my mouth and then did something that drew a stifled moan from me. He then placed his lips over mine. I was happily and completely undone.

The air coming through the window was cool with whatever pre-dawn moisture might still ride it. He closed the window and pointed silently to the one-two buttons required to lock and arm it. He dressed. Then he picked me and my Sidhe finery up and carried me into the bedroom. He lay me down gently, with my hair spread around me on the pillow. He placed one hand over his heart and his other on mine and for a moment, forever, we were one. Then he was gone.

CHAPTER FOURTEEN

REVELATIONS

Later that morning, Dagon was back and I heard him outside speaking to Nathaniel. Apparently he had found him rumpled and seemingly tired from a night of standing up guarding me. In fact, both Dagon and I knew that Nathaniel had slept deeply and dreamlessly until the coming of the light, which was probably the signal to awake that Dagon had implanted in his mind.

I was dressed in my usual gear. Dagon came in and taking my hand, briefly transferred some energy to me. I did not protest.

"We will go to one of the shallow seas," Dagon said to both of us. "You will see what is occurring there."

We flew into the morning sun and soon I saw shining shallow flats of water—or was it something else? In fact it was something else. The shallows were briny pools encrusted in mineral crystals. They grew with their own eerie beauty over the bones of birds, some with bleached feathers still attached. There were skeletons of fish or perhaps something more like gar or eels of old Earth. They used to be able to withstand high mineral content and warm water there. Here, apparently even their tolerances had been exceeded. There were no fresh bodies and no tracks of predators around the old ones.

"We'll fly a little further," Dagon said. "I think you will find this the hardest to witness."

The beach had once been a steep drop off to very deep water. The shallow bottom was now visible and glimmered with bones. A carcass, very much like a small whale, bobbed, bloated and faintly stinking in the shallows. I turned away.

Yellow strands, undoubtedly spawned by the dust were quietly consuming the flesh.

Again, it seemed to be limiting itself to that which was dead or dying. A simple, opportunistic taker.

"Do the humans realize what is happening here? I asked.

Dagon shrugged.

Nathaniel said in under-mind, "*Strong drugs.*" No one responded and he closed his eyes and laid his head back on his seat.

Dagon looked at me to see if I was ready for his next question. I knew it would not be a casual one.

"How many humans do you think could live on this planet without stressing it further? Is there water beneath somewhere that has not been tapped?"

I knew that the individual lives of many might hang on my answer. Would or could the Shadakon kill off or somehow transport away the excess humans? Who actually owned this planet, if anyone? Could it be bought up, as say, a bankruptcy sale? Who would want to own it—for what purpose?

"I cannot begin to answer that, my Alpha," I said. "I would have to be on the land. I have a tool … it would require deep trance work. And also up-to-date geo-maps with underground water sources marked, if possible. That I could do on the computer before I set out. I would need to take the relevant material with me out into the field, of course," I said. I was aware that living as a Sidhe had left me out of the loop of technology.

"Technology is always being tweaked," said Dagon. "I can catch you up on what you need to know. However I am currently investing a lot of time in this project. Many of my followers have little interest in the fate of this planet or its humans. They will move on."

I grimaced.

"Just as you did when you left old Earth," he said, "and the life-loving Sidhe did as well. If it involved sparing or saving the humans, they found another planet and cut their losses."

"We Shadakon are honest about our indifference to humans. They have been our prey since we split off from the human genetic tree. Since they began killing us in imaginative and gruesome ways. There are worse things than having one's throat torn out."

I shuddered but could make no counter argument. Humans were ingeniously cruel and indifferent to their own kind as well as to all their animal and plant relations. A differing religion, a different skin tone could and had been reason enough for death sentences—many times over on old Earth. Humans seemed to be fascinated in causing pain, but few profited from that. Or perhaps they had. Property confiscated from Jews, from witches, from Christians—sometimes Catholic, sometimes Protestant—from the Indians and the blacks … the profits of those acquisitions ended up in someone's pockets. Most humans, however, did not excel at or enjoy torture. Most were merely indifferent to the effects of their actions and the pain and death that resulted.

"I appreciate that you do not endlessly stick up for humans," said Dagon. "But then, you were not a very good one and are not much of one at all anymore."

He smiled. "We both knew that few Shadakons and no humans could have endured, much less enjoyed, the night we had."

Nathaniel, I noted, seemed to be walking a little gingerly today.

"*Something to remember me by,*" I thought.

"What drugs?" I suddenly asked Nathaniel. He winced, either because I had heard him, or because he had rethought about divulging this information. He went very still.

Dagon turned to face him. "Once again, I find that the Sidhe I brought here to look into the health of this planet is turning up all kinds of information.

Information that I don't have." Nathaniel shrugged, possibly hoping that the topic would drop.

Dagon put the flitter in a tight dive and landed near a circle of stones. He got out, and pulled Nathaniel out of the backseat, throwing him on the ground. He immobilized him physically and then locked on his eyes and began what was doubtlessly a deep probe.

I heard Nathaniel make a small sound and I knew that his defences had been breached. He thrashed a few times and Dagon kept him pinned down matter-of-factly and continued. I had never attempted to resist the deep readings that had been done on me—by Dagon, the Sidhe king, Morag or Céadar. I knew that even with relaxation, and my permission, they were disorienting and painful, and that one recovered feeling nauseated and confused. I did not exactly feel sorry for Nathaniel—he had before and still continued to underestimate the power that Dagon wielded. Perhaps he had thought he could blackmail him now, by providing a colourful accounting of what had happened between Dagon and me on the trip. But Dagon could and would wipe his memories if he needed to; he might do so today.

I wandered over to the circle of stones. Once among them, their arrangement seemed purposeful. A calm lingered in their centre, as if many people (or others) had come here to focus and commune—perhaps with the life force. I drew a small circle in the dust, looking for four small items to mark the quadrants. Nothing presented itself so I drew four Old Earth runes in the "corners" in the dust.

First in what was North on this planet: Berkana our mother.

Then East: Dagaz, the dawning of light without and within.

South: Kaunaz, fire, passion, will.

West: Elwaz, the oceans of the worlds, the water of birth, but also—death.

And finally, in the centre: Algiz, sanctuary and protection.

I pondered my work and added an outer spiral leading into the circle's centre. I wanted to invite the powers of this place in, not exclude them. When I was done a small dry wind seemed to blow in around me. I drew out the stone I always carried from its sheath and put it in the dust over the rune for protection. I would not channel this energy through myself.

The stone glowed but not brightly. Rather it pulsed, as if in waiting mode. I realized that I hadn't formulated a question yet. But ever the Fool of the deck, I merely spoke what came to mind.

"Does this planet even want to be revived? It could go into a deep long sleep where only mineral time, wind and falling stars would mark events here. Perhaps it would recover by its own efforts ... But should I, or anyone else, work to restore it to supporting life again?"

I sat for a moment and then shut my eyes involuntarily. Green light penetrated my eyelids and seemed to sear into me. There was pain, but I allowed it. Around me the light was bouncing off the nearby stones, which seemed translucent to my altered vision. I could see, with my eyes closed, a lake of fresh water ringed in trees and plants. I saw beings come down to the water—feathered and furred, scaled and Otherly to drink and conduct their lives. They didn't seem to see me—they were perhaps holographic images of what had been and could be again.

There were two words in my mind as the light abruptly faded. *Sidhe* ... and *Australia.*

I picked up the now dark green stone. It was slightly warm. I touched it to my heart before returning it to the sheath.

When I finally turned to see what was happening at the flitter, I found Dagon and Nathaniel sitting next to each other on a rock. Nathaniel looked like he had lost the round, but Dagon was not one to use his power more than he had to. As I approached, he helped Nathaniel up. Both were looking at me. Dagon raised an eyebrow slightly.

"I thought you needed to study and plan to find the place you needed to be," he said.

I shrugged. "As usual, I arrive where I need to be."

Nathaniel looked at me with what was probably fear. He was replaying our earlier afternoon, and realizing now how far he had overstepped himself with someone who wielded the power I did. He had grown used to passive human females who came to be used by him and all the other Shadakon. I had come to this planet and been left with him, but whatever conclusions he had made about my position, continued to change.

He dropped his eyes to me and said clearly in mind-speak, "*I'm sorry queen of the Sidhe and once mate of my Alpha. I used you casually.*" He flinched, no doubt expecting a response from Dagon. "*I know that Dagon has said that I was never touch you again, but I pledge that as well, without his enforcement. I will attempt to prove my trustworthiness to you, as I did once before.*"

I smiled then and responded aloud, "I accept your apology. I can understand why you moved toward what you wanted. After all, it had been given to you by your Alpha."

Dagon looked at me.

"We all struck a deal," I said calmly. "This is about more than us as individuals. What was done is done. What is more important are what actions we now take to shape the future."

"But now I would like to hear about the drugs," I said. "Dagon can no doubt tell me, but I would prefer to hear it from you."

Nathaniel sighed. "The drugs ...the humans use various versions of one substance to alter their consciousness, to numb themselves mostly.

Often the sources are under the influence when they come to provide energy. Energy is energy and we are not affected by what they eat or use. You once took energy from humans dying of frightening diseases, yet you could do so without danger to yourself."

He paused and looked like he wished he did not have to go on. "But I enjoy their blood and avail myself to it frequently. And when I take that into my body, the drugs affect me as well." He sighed. "Generally it is subtle. The humans on the registry cannot be noticeably altered, or they will not be sent out. Those who manage the trade that the Shadakon here use for nourishment do not want any complaints about their providers that would interfere with receiving payments. The human woman I bargained with and took while you obviously observed me had never provided blood before. She should have been more frightened"—in under-mind he added, *"I would have enjoyed it more if she was."*—"But the human sources often numb themselves before they arrive and then, I suppose, afterwards, to bring themselves to some kind of peace when they return to wherever they live." He shrugged.

"Like most prostitutes," I murmured.

"So this is why the humans are not more frightened about the condition of their world," I said. "They are numb as well as helpless."

"They have no futures," said Nathaniel. "Many of them long for death, although they do not always understand that."

"And they can sign up for that," I said. "They can agree to serve as unconscious nourishment—on spaceships or whatever—deep under, where they would not have to be present for their own deaths."

"They can agree to be present to the edge of their deaths as fully as they think they can bear," said Nathaniel. "That is also available to us, for a higher fee of course."

I had agreed to that once. I had signed a contract of lethality so that I could remain with Dagon in our first days together.

I studied Nathaniel, trying to keep in mind that he was a predator like Dagon and that the death of his prey used to be always assured and even now was often inevitable. I shivered.

So close, I thought, remembering my close calls while in Dagon's hands. *One heart beat or less away.* I did not want to imagine Nathaniel or Dagon playing with a downed prey, inflicting pain and then temporarily stopping to perhaps induce hope and another attempt to negotiate or flee. I tried not to imagine that, but I could and did.

I tried to keep focused. "But the humans have barely enough credits to keep themselves nourished. They do not seem to have the energy to grow a crop that takes months to complete its life cycle. Where is this drug coming from?"

Nathaniel was silent. I thought I might have to turn to Dagon but then I looked at the faintly yellow wind and realized … the fungus consumed dying beings, beings that were no longer attached to the life force. I tried to put myself in the consciousness of the dying tree I had seen yesterday, whose bark had curled back to receive the fungus even more deeply into its core, bringing death on a little faster. Perhaps it was not a painful process at the end.

Perhaps the whole planet was being drugged in preparation for death and that, in fact, was a small mercy.

Both of them looked at me silently. Nathaniel perhaps seemed surprised that I was not angry with him for what he had revealed, and both had unavoidably heard or seen my images of possible death-play of a Shadakon with a prey human.

I had been told—and knew it to be true—that I did not shield my thoughts well. But Dagon knew that I had come to understand long ago the Shadakon's relationship with their prey.

I had narrowly achieved being an exception to how Dagon's encounters usually played out in our first days. And Dagon and I had revisited the possibility that I might still find myself there on more than one occasion.

Dagon let the silence grow and I was more comfortable with it than thinking. I knew the question that he would require me to answer. We knew each other so well now, even after the gap of intervening time.

"And so, Danu. I suppose that was your tool, although I wasn't watching you use it and doubt that it has only one purpose ..."

I didn't answer. He hadn't asked me a question. He smiled. He had taught me that response.

"Tell me what you discovered, Danu. I have had to go into one mind today to see what Nathaniel had chosen not to tell me. I would that you told me of your own free will."

"*Surrender now, surrender later,*" I growled in under-mind.

"This was and still is a holy place. A place of life and water," I said aloud, looking towards the dip in the hills where the shining lake had been. "I asked one question only—did this planet want to be restored to life? Because it could rest here, as is, in deep slow mineral time. But I was shown what it could be once restored. And I was given two words ..."

Dagon raised his hand to stop me.

"I do not think we will should burden Nathaniel with more secrets," he smiled. It was then I knew he had not wiped out Nathaniel's memories of being aboard the ship and how we conducted ourselves there.

"Silence, but also missing time and memories, as you well know, is informative," he smiled again. "It occurred to me later, with your reminders, Danu, that Nathaniel might not have understood what might be significant to me. And thus he thought to spare me from reports of what I might already be aware of. In doing so, perhaps details of importance were missed. I have gone over this with him today. If he is in any doubt of what I might consider important, I have no doubts that he will come to me now."

Dagon said this offhandedly, but I heard the steel beneath his words. From the look on Nathaniel's face, and his shut down thoughts, I knew he did too. Dagon might know that he was training Nathaniel to be his eventual replacement, but Nathaniel would put in his time and pay his dues. He would be loyal to his Alpha. If he did not, he would not live to see himself come to power.

"Well then," said Dagon easily, "the sun is high and I, for one, have other matters to attend to. Let us go back. Nathaniel, you have put in overtime on this assignment. I will take Danu to my home. I have many guards handy, and you can get a well-needed break.

I practiced breathing and not-thinking on the way back; I hoped I was at least partially successful. Although I had not noticed it immediately, the use of the stone had drawn heavily from my energy. I craved a cup of elixir of life, but knew I would have to accept life energy from a human instead. I sighed. The opportunity to see, much less touch, Dagon seemed to recede into the future. I would be in his home. No doubt his mate would be present—and curious. If not overtly hostile and deadly.

CHAPTER FIFTEEN

SAFETY?

We stopped to let Nathaniel out; he hadn't said a word on the return trip. I went to gather my clothes but Dagon stopped me.

"You will not arrive at my home carrying your possessions in a bag," he said. "In fact, I have arranged for additional clothing for you. You may like it—I hope you do. But it will also grant you anonymity while in my hospitality. Much like the robes of the Mothers that you chose to wear … Or somewhat like them."

I imagined bulky and to the floor. I sighed. He laughed. I put my head back on the seat of the flitter and surrendered for a moment to my increasing weariness and need for energy. I was too tired and unfocused to ask what I no doubt needed to know.

"I can provide some energy that you might consider more acceptable to you," Dagon eventually said. "It will not be taken from a numb slave. But you may find that it has a cost as well. Although," he added, "you are fully a Sidhe now."

I knew I did not know what I was being asked to agree to.

He laughed, "Indeed, Danu, you do not. But you are going to begin to see into my world here. It is perhaps not so much unlike how you dance with the Sidhe. There are many women here, human women, who want me—even beyond my wealth and position. I am in my power and, as you know, I have well-honed skills as a lover. As you also know, consent given in return for sexual bliss is perhaps not full consent, but it is the closest that most humans have with us. I am generous and, in my own way, caring."

He stopped and observed me.

"I do not kill my human providers, even when I tire of them. Nor do I turn them out to work on the service. They later work in my household continuing to be useful in other ways. It is a desired position for a host who provides for me. I delivered you some of that energy this morning, gathered in sexual passion from willing humans who I do not quite call lovers."

"Concubines?" I asked, with less interest than I would have expected. Dagon had not been monogamous with me when I was his mate. His variation of that was probably that while in a partnership, he did not have sex with anyone else he cared much about.

"I know that your prospective of what should and should not happen while enjoying others has broadened during your time with the Sidhe," he said mildly. "I too have learned to enjoy other variations of bringing myself to others and the pleasures that they offer me."

He had parked beside a large outbuilding in a walled compound. On his arrival a young, beautiful human woman came out to greet him. She was dressed in what looked like bright silks and her black hair hung thick and lustrous down her back. Her whole attention was focused on Dagon and she did not do more than briefly notice me.

There was a second, equally beautiful woman behind her, waiting her turn to greet him. He wrapped his arms around both and kissed them, first lightly and then with more intensity.

I quietly moaned. I felt his and their and my own desire rise.

I am in no shape for this! I attempted to climb out of the flitter and at the last moment lost my footing. It was the beautiful woman closest to me that reached out to steady me. She held my arm for a moment longer than might have been necessary and then turned to Dagon with a question in her mind.

"This is a Sidhe advisor I have brought to address the problems of this planet," Dagon said. "She is weary and needing energy. She is saddened by taking energy from those who are not in any position to grant her permission to do so.

I would like you to offer her every courtesy. Please bathe and dress her. Then we will all take some mutual pleasure."

I wanted to stop, to refuse to go forward another step. I had had no warning of what was now happening around me but my choices were limited; staying with Nathaniel seemed unwise even if that was on the table. Dagon was my only safety here, such as it was.

But more deeply—I was a Sidhe. Loving or sexing with many, even if I craved one more than the others, had been part of my life in Between. My king had brought me to his world of multiple pleasures—as had his eons-old queen. I had come to accept, and then open to her pleasuring me, also in his presence. I had not had to pretend; in fact I could not have pretended that I wasn't thrilled and willing as the night wore on. This afternoon, I had felt the energy of the human who held me briefly when I stumbled. She was hot and young and available to me as well as to Dagon.

His humans carried me away to the inner rooms of their ... home? Harem? One left to keep company with Dagon, while my immediate contact ran a bath and dropped fragrant dried leaves onto the surface. They smelled like the leaves Dagon had often put in his hot pool in his home on Exterra for me and I sighed with pleasure. She took off my clothes; I raised my arms to assist in that and quickly stood naked before her.

She smiled. "I would start with you here Sidhe queen but that would disappoint Dagon. So, let me merely attend to your bath."

She lathered my auburn hair with fragrant soap and exclaimed at its colour and the strands of purple in it. She rinsed me, grazing and then lightly caressing my body with her small quick hands. I sighed. I kindled, my nipples puckering even in the warm water. She laughed, seemingly delightedly. Her mind was shut to me except for her own growing desire.

I reached out and touched her arm. Just that. She made a slight sound of pleasure. Soon she had me out of the water, dried and wrapped loosely in a brightly coloured robe. She led me back to Dagon.

Dagon and his partner of the moment had already shed their clothes and were engaged in a deepening kiss. He paused, putting his finger lightly on her lips, and drew me to him. He calmly shucked me from the robe and approvingly ran his fingers over my taut nipples. I was already panting slightly, my weariness pushed aside. He made room for me on a large divan, placing the woman he was engaging with on his far side, me beside him, and she who had bathed me on my other side.

"See if this seems familiar," he said to me. He then assuredly and competently brought the woman beside him into full sexual desire.

"I knew then that he was not unfamiliar with my activities in Between when my king, my best friend Fiórcara, had done the same thing: pleasuring his queen while I watched and accepted the attentions of another Sidhe—Céadar. I know Dagon might have seen it in my mind, but I had another theory in the midst of what was building here. *He had visited and been pleasured by the Sidhe. But when?*

I did not have long to hold onto this thought. The woman beside me had laid hands on me and pushed me back into the pillows around us. She looked me in the eye (was this asking my permission?) and continued, kissing me until I was breathless and then caressed me until I moaned. My desire was building and building until I was powerless to even lift my head to see what Dagon was doing. I felt the mutual energy all of us rising. He had chosen them well. They truly liked sex, liked him, liked females as well as males. When I thought I was as close and high to surrender as I could get, Dagon rolled and turned his attentions on me. I looked into his dark flaring eyes even as the unnamed woman gently readied me for him. He leaned over me then, and I fell into his eyes..

I begged him. I begged them. All I could think was … *"Please!"* He left me in that state however, shivering and wanting while he finished with first one and then the other, taking them hard and fast and taking their energy as well.

As they sank down into their well-earned relaxed bliss, he returned to me. He was encircled with high sex energy and he paused just briefly to raise an eyebrow at me. "Still with me, my Sidhe lover?

I begged with my eyes and with my body.

He did not disappoint. He shared out the gathered energy and I gasped, feeling like I once had in Fiórcara's presence. I was undone. I surrendered to Dagon, my complex Shadakon lover. I wanted nothing more than what he gave me.

After a moment or two of drifting alongside each other, finally released and at peace and replenished, he rose easily and kissed his companions. He watched me for a moment, lying inert and satisfied, then leaned down and kissed me as well.

"You will stay here with them, Danu. You will be safe with them because they want and need me and you are mine. They will protect and care for you very attentively. There is a computer terminal here and I will send what you need over soon. After your nap," he said, and smiled. "'All passion is the same,'" he said, quoting me. Then he was gone.

CHAPTER SIXTEEN

I ALMOST GROW COMFORTABLE HERE

In due time I learned the everyday details of the house and the women who lived here. My companions were named Ka and Io. I gave them my name and they shrugged. Which made me wonder if many had come and gone here, to eventually be forgotten as time passed.

The humans were like bright-coloured butterflies. They listened to music and took time to catch up with their interests on the computer. They chattered to each other in a language unknown to me. I could make out some ideas by lightly reading them. Often they spoke of their expectations of when they would see Dagon again. They ate sparingly of expensive imported fruits and danced to maintain their lithe bodies. I often saw them pour a glass of water and hold it to the light before drinking it. It looked like; it felt like, a prayer of thanks to me.

I spent hours poring over geologic maps, tracing out deep aquifers and the basins of the shallow seas. The maps were decades old. At the bottom they were often marked with the words *"Study cancelled."* I also searched for and found old cave systems. Some of these corresponded with the places of known water. Many of these would be dry but some …

Dagon often showed up just after dawn. He would gather up his human almost-lovers, and stroke them gently, as one might stroke a cat. When they were willing and open to him, he would take them quickly in a breath or two. He was careful but he was taking for me as well. They would have allowed me—and often had asked me if they could serve me—but I always found a reason not to accept at the moment. I believed that they were sincere about their willingness, but, although they could stir my desire, I sensed that they held back their own, awaiting Dagon.

I wondered what would happen to these beautiful, pampered human women if one day, he did not come back. How long would their expensive food be delivered? Who would eventually come, to end them or drag them off to a much worse fate?

These were harsh thoughts, even if realistic. Dagon told me once, early in my time with him on Exterra, that if he had walked out of his house and withdrew his protection, or if I had foolishly left him, I would have been dead by nightfall. It was one reason that I carried my small dagger with me everywhere.

Nevertheless, I was lulled into thinking that this could hold—that Dagon and I could take time now and then to come to each other, with or without his human companions. I forgot, for a little while, that he commanded a population of Shadakon who were indifferent to the problems of this planet and might be wondering why he wasn't applying himself more to searching for another, more pleasant one. And I particularly managed to not-think about the fact that Dagon had an official mate and partner, living a short distance away. She may have forgiven or overlooked his pet human sources; she may have had some of her own—young, handsome human men who she could treat as she would. But I doubted that she would overlook or forgive him his time with me.

I did not think enough about this. We had been out all day in the flitter, searching the baked surface of this planet for clues of what I saw on the maps. Exact locations now yielded only desert. I felt that the planet's remaining life force was moving ever more quickly into its death spiral. When we returned, there were no lovely women awaiting him outside. There was a deep and dangerous silence around where they, and now I, lived.

Dagon was in the midst of landing the flitter when I shouted at him to take to the air again. He might have still been able to, until a skilful or lucky shot damaged one wing.

We landed heavily and I know it would fly no more. We sat silently for a moment before it all began. He turned to me then and said, "I am sorry, Danu."

I had time for my part of our last peaceful moment as well. "I regret nothing, Dagon. I am sorry for nothing."

He smiled, and once again I felt as one with him. And then we walked towards our pain.

Some armed Shadakon stood around us as we exited the downed flitter. Dagon stood at attention, furious but controlled. I stood as I imagined a cool Sidhe queen might stand: well apart from him and frowning slightly, but I knew the other Shadakon could hear my heart beating and smell my fear. Nothing could be done about that.

Our captors were not military. In the midst of my terror I was somewhat relieved that Nathaniel was not part of the group. It was not a coup then—rather a more personal accounting by someone who had passed her limit of tolerance for what Dagon did here.

I sensed no living presences in the small building. The humans were dead or not there. I wondered if the constant shutdown quality I had noticed in their minds earlier was in the service of protecting themselves from their constant fear of this very event happening. I could not help them. I could not help myself.

I could transit. But where? I had been to a small room next to the barracks. I imagined that Nathaniel had moved back into his usual housing. I had been to a few places on this planet, but I did not think my life would be extended very far in any of those locations.

We were led to the main building of the compound, escorted to whatever fate awaited us. We might have to witness each other's pain—no, we would have to witness each other's pain. I knew this with certainty. I began my deep water-diving breathing—conserving air and energy for the long return to the freedom of the surface, if there could be a return.

I strove to be tree or stone. I reached for the faltering energy of the planet and was surprised to feel some even here. It was dry and quiet and offered endurance.

We were seated in a small room and I could not avoid remembering a similar dangerous time when the Sidhe queen sat with me in an unadorned room. The queen had been moments away from killing me or, at very least, thoroughly wiping my mind. I had escaped by transiting to Dagon, who, against his better judgement, took me in and faced the Sidhe king the next day.

The Sidhe king had intervened for me the day of my judgement, but he was far away on another planet now. Our only link was that of a small green stone that might be taken from me at any moment. I put my hand feigning nonchalance over where it hung under my clothing against my skin; it was in a sheath with the small dagger that Dagon had gifted to me. I felt the energy of the stone come to life under my fingers.

He would at least know my fate then. I was, in a small way, comforted.

Dagon looked quickly at me and then away. He had grown better at sensing Sidhe energy, and I didn't know what contact he had maintained with the Sidhe king over the years since he left Exterra.

After what was probably a long time—certainly enough to ensure that I and perhaps Dagon were entering into full despair over our situation—a small, beautiful, dark-haired woman entered. Her eyes swept the room, quickly finding me. I had few choices left today, and perhaps none for the days that followed.

I slipped off the chair gracefully and sank to my knees. I lowered my eyes. I stayed down, head bent as she stood in front of me. I was no longer afraid. I would choose to be no further liability to Dagon. I could do that.

Eventually she grabbed my hair and pulled me upright.

I rose smoothly and ever so slightly shifted to maintain my footing.

She noticed and studied me, reaching out abruptly to make a mind connection with me.

I did not allow her easy access. There was little in my mind that I had done that I cared if she saw. But I would not give up memories that included Dagon if I could help it. I knew I was not a good secret keeper. The Shadakon and the Sidhe had told me so many times. I remembered how quickly Dagon had broken through the defences of Nathaniel.

"Why would you kneel before me, Sidhe?"

I felt only coldness, and perhaps satisfaction.

Had this been the pattern of Dagon's partnering since the dawning of the Shadakon? Mates who wanted to dispose of him—painfully?

Suddenly, she hit me. Dagon flinched ever so slightly, but I did not. I knew well ahead of time that this was coming. I noted, dispassionately, that my collarbone was now broken. My right arm hung limply at my side.

"Answer me!" she demanded.

"You are the mate of Dagon, Alpha of the Shadakon, both here and elsewhere. I offer you the respect required by your position."

She laughed, but there was no warmth in it. "And how do you know that, Sidhe, or Shadakon or human or whatever you are?"

I raised my eyes. "I feel your power but also that it is intermingled with his. You are blood-bonded to each other. You could be no one else, although we have not met. I do not remember you from my time on Exterra."

"What would you know of any partner of Dagon?" she hissed.

And then I realized that she was missing a lot of information.

I smiled through the hot, aching throb of my shoulder. "I feel the bond between you and him because I, too, was once the mate of Dagon, Alpha of the Shadakon."

I did not add that we were still each other's Maker. I did not tell her that he had fully intended to kill me to bring another mate to his side. I did not think it had been her.

I waited for additional pain and I was not disappointed. She left me to walk over to Dagon. There was now a small lethal looking needle gun in her hand. She trailed her hand along his shoulder and I shuddered, knowing there was no comfort in that touch.

"As deaths go, this will be a short one, my mate. Three or four days, amplified of course by the hunger." She stood very close to him and I sensed energy swirl between them.

She turned back to me. "You, once mate of Dagon, will have the honour of watching him die slowly. Of course, you will be well on your way as well. I wonder if you will still want each other at the end. I wonder who will, in the end, finish off whom. And whether it will be in mercy—or hunger."

She smiled a terrible smile and bade us stand. As I turned to go wherever we must go next, she reached out as fast as a striking snake and ripped the leather thong off my shoulder.

I knew I had only moments then. I had touched the stone earlier and it was still awaiting more information.

"*Help me my Sidhe king! Fiórcara! My life is ending soon. Dagon and I have been brought to face the wrath of his mate.*"

"*You have a strange predictable pattern of taking up with powerful partners with angry mates!*" Unbelievingly, I heard a chuckle.

"*I have loved powerful ones in complex relationships with their mates,*" I responded in what I thought might be my last thought statement. I heard his silence.

"Behold!" said the Sidhe king. The sound of his voice rolled through the room.

The stone flared as it had when I had consulted it earlier in the desert. We were all suddenly blind and silenced. Dagon's mate slumped to floor, dropping the sheathed dagger and stone. I scooped both up, and locked my good arm around Dagon. And then I transited with him into the dry desert of the standing stones.

CHAPTER SEVENTEEN

REDEMPTION

Heat. Dryness. Pain. We sat quietly.

"So, if this is your plan, are there more parts?" Dagon asked with a hint of some dark humour.

"Do you have some cavalry behind the next hill?" I asked back.

He shook his head. "Her action will be invisible to my troops. But as you know, a vacuum is filled quickly. She can plead innocence of my absence. Perhaps the flitter will be found, heavily damaged in the desert. By that time, that detail will not be important to us."

"Did she use the needle gun on you?"

He shook his head. "I might come to the place of wishing that she did. But, then your stage magic got us out … somewhere …"

I sat and breathed. I was sitting on the dusty soil of this planet. It was desiccated, its life force only faintly holding on; soon we would be in the same condition. In spite of knowing that, I felt a deep peace fall over me.

Even as the first wisps of hunger arrived, I sat, my back to a stone, feeling my bone knit slowly—knowing it might never completely heal, but appreciating that the sharp pain was gone.

"Make love to me, Dagon," I said after both of us had sat in long silence. "If this is where our path leads us and no further, then let us offer our living energy to this place. Let us join while we are not yet in desperate pain. And then perhaps we can choose to do what we have considered on more than one occasion." I indicated the poisoned dagger that lay on the ground beside me. "This is as good a place to die as any other I suppose."

"Do you wish to try and return to the building where you stayed, or the barracks?"

I shook my head. "I want no one to enjoy my final pain," I said. "Whatever there is left of me later I would surrender to this planet."

We sat quietly for another unmeasured space of time. The alien stars rose and moved slowly overhead and the air was dry and cold. I did not ask again, nor did I initiate contact with Dagon. I did not ask any questions about his mate. When Fiórcara told me that Céadar would not show me everything in Dagon's mind, I knew there was content that would be a surprise to me or hurt me. For his own reasons, the Sidhe king chose to let me go unknowing into the coming situation.

I had sensed today that Dagon did not love his mate—nor did she love him. They had forged a powerful alliance, probably to bring together different factions of the Shadakon. She had allowed him his human pets to sex with and feed off. They were of no consequence to her. But she did not allow him deeper happiness. In fact she might particularly enjoy taking that away from him. Therefore she had allowed us enough time that he and I had bonded, or re-forged our previous bonds, before making her move—to inflict maximum pain.

I thought of his previous Shadakon lover on Exterra, the lovely, ruthless Lore.

Dagon followed my thoughts and sighed. I had not asked any questions and he chose not to respond to any of the conclusions I came to.

He turned my face gently towards his and laid the softest possible kiss on my lips. I sighed into his mouth. The next one was a claiming and I opened to him, as I had always done. I wanted him. I wanted him on the edge of my death. He was concerned that he would bring pain to my injured shoulder but I just shook my head.

"There will be some pain, my love. But I will not notice.

Or if I do it will be part of the intensity that we bring each other."

Then there were only the small sounds of movement and sighs. He slowly took me up and up and I was present for every moment of wanting him, wanting him beyond my own safety, as I had done from the very beginning of our connection. As we drew near the final destination of our release, he asked a question with his body. With his eyes.

"*Take me that way too, Dagon. Drink my heart's blood. I am yours. I have chosen to be yours again and again.*"

I felt the welcome stab of pain and the accompanying bliss that this sharing brought, and even as I was swept away into mindless pleasure, I grabbed the stone.

"*We are here Fiórcara, my heart's friend and lover. We are loving each other, even as we proceed to the edge of our deaths.*"

"*How I loved you all!*" I said, as I let go of all further thoughts. Our finish included being suddenly enclosed in a pillar of green light that shot up to the stars. Then all was quiet, and we drifted together in peace.

I felt Dagon sit up beside me and sharpen his attention on something—a sound. Soon I heard it as well. A flitter was flying in circles near us, shining a light down onto the almost featureless desert. When the beam touched on the standing stone circle around us, the flitter abruptly swooped down and landed.

Initially I wondered if Dagon's mate had arranged that she would not be denied her pleasure in watching us die together, but immediately I knew that this was not her or her private guard.

Nathaniel stood in front of us, light in hand.

"Luckily I could access the coordinates from the system," he said.

"Everyone who was watching saw the green flare, but I knew exactly where you would be."

He studied us and handed down one of Dagon's human sources from the flitter. Io, I thought. She looked worse for the wear but her relief at seeing Dagon was touching.

"A moment then," said Dagon. He took me by the hand and led her and me into the circle.

"Another willing sacrifice," he said to me. "We might just wake this place up."

He smoothed his hands down her body and she shuddered. He read her energy level and then turned to Nathaniel. "You did not take from her?"

Nathaniel shook his head. "I bought her and the other one today. They had been left untouched so that they could be sampled by many others later. I knew they were yours and that you had treated them gently. It cost me two months wages," he added. I got their story and began to plan a rescue."

"I have changed my opinion about you quite a bit in the last few minutes," said Dagon thoughtfully. "You truly are my second and I will not forget this day."

Dagon moved closer to his human, soothed her and kissed her, and when she opened herself willingly he drew from her and then indicated that I should as well.

"Do not pass on this gift," he said.

I touched her cheek and she opened her eyes, fear still lurking in their depths. She had had a very bad day.

"I thank thee," I said. I kissed her and took what I needed of the energy she offered. Dagon smiled. I walked over to Nathaniel. He did not shrink back as I neared, but stood very still. "Again I am in your debt, Nathaniel of the Shadakon." He shivered slightly. I kissed him fully on the lips and I heard him moan in my mind.

CHAPTER EIGHTEEN

A DESERT RETREAT

Dagon needed to go back, gather his troops and dispel any rumours that he was in difficulty. Flying with four people in the flitter was close to its limits, but Nathaniel was a good pilot and took us neatly up into the air and away in the opposite direction than he had come from. Diminutive Io sat in Dagon's lap, her head against his chest. If Nathaniel had not rescued them from what was ahead of them—working at a much lower level of their trade—they would have suffered for being beautiful and young and they would not have remained that way for very long.

I broke the silence. "Dagon. If you want to preserve this one and her companion and me, we need to be safe somewhere. I cannot take us to a Between. I do not think we can live anywhere near you. But where?"

"Let me think about this," he said. "I am going to require my mate to attend a formal presentation with me tomorrow. There are several possibilities that could branch off from that event, most of them involving her dying or going into the Hunger. I am pondering the most satisfying ones."

I shivered.

So Dagon must have pondered my death prior to coming to the island where I was working at the hospice and awaiting my full summer reunion with the Sidhe so long ago. He had preserved my life at the last moment, however he had forced me into taking permanent refuge with the Sidhe They celebrated my arrival, but I yearned for Dagon and our life and had returned to his side briefly over and over. I refused to believe that I had lost him, but as the years went by, I had had to acknowledge what was.

I'd recently realized that he and the Sidhe king had been in contact with each other at least part of that time, and yet Dagon had never sent word to me, and Fiórcara had let me work through the loss of him without comment.

I was silent as we flew on in the darkness, though I knew that Dagon and probably Nathaniel had heard much of what I thought.

"*I would have died for you,*" I thought to Dagon sadly. "*I did die for you.*"

Dagon was silent. Io slept, momentarily without care, against his chest. I envied her innocence.

It was Nathaniel who added an additional unknown into what we were all pondering. He had said nothing since we entered the flitter and now he turned to me where I sat beside him and said, "I have a suggestion of where you might go for awhile. I do not think any will find you there—at least for the time being. By then Dagon will have regained his footing, or he will never do so."

"And would you seize control then, Nathaniel?" I asked quietly.

"I would try to do so," he said. "One day I will. I am patient and have a loyalty to my Alpha. But one day he will stand aside or ..." He went silent.

"I would expect no less," said Dagon without anger. "He is a Shadakon. We struggle to gain and maintain power and influence. That inevitably results in winners and losers. I believed that I had lost all today, and to be given a second chance is unusual in our world. But I am old, and value well-trained supporters. I allow mistakes as teaching moments. I certainly had one today."

I was not sure what distance a flitter could cover without recharging, but we had been flying for a long time.

Nathaniel suddenly put us in a steep swoop down out of the moonless sky and then continued to drop below the level of the hills.

I said nothing. Dagon said nothing. The ground rushed up at us but then an opening appeared and we entered it, into solid darkness.

He landed on what once was the mouth of a river that ran out of a large cave. The river was mostly white sand now, except for a tiny trickle of water that meandered towards the desert.

"*It will be close to get us back,*" Dagon thought to Nathaniel.

Nathaniel didn't say or think anything. It had not been a question. I smiled.

"You calculated exactly," Dagon said aloud. "There was no way to bring both humans. But where is she who is called Ka?"

Nathaniel looked at Dagon directly. "I saved her life, or at least a semblance of a pleasant one. I paid everything I had to secure both. She is in my accommodation with someone I trust guarding her. I would have her—at least for a while. We can discuss this again later. I thought this would be in her and my best interests. Perhaps she can decide who she wishes to be with in a few days."

Dagon was perfectly mind quiet. He looked relaxed and calm, perhaps he was. Probably he was considering his limited choices.

"All of this was well-planned, Nathaniel. I am assuming now that you were not part of the beginning of our day."

Nathaniel shook his head.

"Her name is Ka," Dagon said. "She enjoys sex and her energy is sweet when she is high with it. Enjoy her. You have earned her."

Io was awake and took in the information. She was very quiet.

I thought I saw a tear slide down her cheek. Nathaniel handed me a flashlight as we clambered out of the flitter, our feet sinking into the soft sand. Io and I looked at each other, and then she picked her way further under the overhang of the cave mouth.

"We must find a safe place to sleep," she said to me. "Not visible from the sky."

"Do you know if creatures live in the cave?" I asked. I imagined that they might welcome the unexpected meal of protein we brought.

"They are now mostly small and blind," she said. "Few leave the water or moist places. I would not, however, bathe in the pools."

"And can you drink the water?" I asked.

"I will have to," she said. Then I remembered her holding up a full glass of water to the light and drinking in the sparkling clarity of it.

She had been here before, but not with Dagon. He seemed relieved that there was anywhere she and I could go and not be immediately hunted. Where we could hold off our dying. I thought of the soft yellow-green powdery fungus and shuddered.

I needed to know what she knew, but the sky was faintly purple now and the stars were washing out. It was dawn and we had both had a difficult day and night.

I found a smooth indentation on the side of a large water worn rock inside the cave entrance. I sat and then lay down, shifting the sand under my head to find a comfortable position. She stood, looking forlorn, her beautiful but inadequate clothes fluttering slightly around her. I hesitated briefly. This was Dagon's pet. He had treated her kindly, not hurting her or insisting on what she could not or did not want to do. He took her carefully. *What did she think of their arrangement? Did she care for him? Did she call that feeling love?*

I put my arms out in invitation.

She curled up against me, although I felt guarded pain in her. I put a finger on her cheek and invited her to look at me.

"Nathaniel is skilled at sex. He will not mistreat your companion Ka. He will use her but, as things go with the Shadakon, he is a fair man."

"She is my younger sister," said Io.

She lay silently for a moment—and then she was asleep.

When I awoke, our sleeping place was still in shadow but the light was advancing and Io was no longer next to me. I found her further back in the cave, drinking water from her hands from a small pool. Two small translucent creatures flopped weakly on the rocks beside her. They appeared to be eyeless and I could see their pale hearts beating within.

I looked at her questioningly.

"Dagon told me to preserve and serve you. I cannot do so without eating and drinking. I do not want to do this," she said, even as she picked up a rock in her small soft hands and brought it down hard on the two creatures. She shuddered. She separated their heads and scraped their entrails carefully away from their now flattened and still bodies. She returned these bits back into the pool. Before they had sunk to the bottom, many more pale beings rushed out from their hiding places to fight over and eat her offerings. I wondered what she had used for her bait, and then noticed a few small bite marks on her fingers.

"I do not want to do this either," she said, and then as I watched she calmly choked down the two soft bodies. "I do it for Dagon. And therefore I do it for you. Give me a moment or two, then you can take from me."

I looked at her with growing respect. She had resilience and practical survival skills that I had not guessed at. She looked at me wryly.

"Yesterday I had fruit and fresh baked bread. Today, raw cave creatures. My sister and I knew that we had landed in an unbelievably generous life." She paused and looked sad. "We also knew that it could end at any time. I guess we did not allow ourselves the truth that it would.

Of what we discovered, the most useful thing was that he enjoyed us both and he knew that we never lied about the wanting that he raised in us." She wrapped her arms around herself and her dubious meal. "I miss him more than any of the pleasurable things he gave us."

She came to me then, ready to sustain me with her energy. I stroked her glossy black hair, and took both her hands in mine.

"I accept this on behalf of Dagon," I said, looking into her eyes. "I will take only what I need to keep from going into the Hunger."

She was silent and calm during the taking. "Can you really say that the Shadakon who now has Ka will not harm her?"

I sighed. "What female can speak for any male?" I said. "Shadakon or other? But I was in his protection, with permission given by Dagon that he could use me." Her eyes widened. "It is a complicated story and not one I'll burden you with. Suffice to say, I am Sidhe as well as Shadakon. I am desirable well beyond the expected. Nathaniel did Dagon a large favour and I, in part, secured that. When he came to me, I did not want him but I was fulfilling a bargain. But he was patient and in the end I freely gave him what he wanted."

More than he wanted, I thought quietly.

"I only tell you this to quiet your fears for your sister. We are all being protected by Nathaniel at present, although I hope to hear soon that Dagon no longer has to fear further actions of his official mate."

"But now we both have nourished ourselves, such as it was.

Show me and tell me about this cave and how you came to be familiar with it."

CHAPTER NINETEEN

SKY DANCER

Io took my hand and we strolled away from the light. As we moved deeper into the cave, there was a faint greenish glimmer that shone from the rock walls and stone structures that hung down from the ceiling. On Old Earth I knew them as stalactites, and the matching ones rising from the floor of the cave as stalagmites. When they joined they formed massive pillars. There had once been a lot of water on this planet. It had been very earth-like. A difference though, was there were three moons in differing orbits such that they moved together and apart from each other in complex patterns.

I stopped us and put my finger to her lips. The sound of water and air moving was around us; there was still running water here then. And moving water meant it was being replenished somehow to feed this stream. I got a sense of immensity and distance. I was ready to return to the light, not wanting to spend our flashlight unnecessarily but Io pulled me forward and I followed.

She took us deeper into the deepening darkness, although the footing remained safe enough and she seemed confident in her destination. Finally she stopped, dropped my hand and stepped away, and spreading her arms, moved in a slow circle. She pointed halfway up the wall.

"Shine your light there."

I obeyed.

In a niche in the wall there was obviously a resting place for someone of importance. There was a beautiful pottery bowl and a long, staff-like weapon, obviously carefully shaped and carved. The bones of the deceased were arranged in a seemingly comfortable seated position, supported by rocks. I perceived her to be a she, and she seemed to look towards the entrance.

There were shreds of fabric around her, but I imagined her regal and naked, with a cloak of honour over her shoulders.

I sunk to my knees. Io looked surprised, but did as well.

"I greet thee, Guardian," I said. "I ask your forgiveness that I did not ask permission before coming this far into this sacred place. My companion knew to honour you in her own way."

I neither heard nor sensed anything. I continued.

"I am of the Sidhe, from a planet a short distance from here, as distances between things in space go. Before that I lived on old Earth. I was a human but moved into being Shadakon and then Sidhe. I would show you a token of that now if you wish."

"I wish…" The answer was a whisper, an echo of my words. Yet I knew they were not my own words that I heard. I took the green stone from its sheath and lay it on the floor of the cave in a tiny clear pool of water. I gentled rolled it until it was wet all over. Dancing waves of green appeared on the walls and floor of the cave. The light lit up the Guardian, replacing her empty eye sockets with bright greenness. She seemed to come alive at this moment.

"Fiórcara, my Sidhe king, meet she who guards the cave of the waters of this world," I said.

I heard a laugh (did he think my emergencies were so funny?). "Well done, Danu of the Sidhe. And greetings, Sky Dancer."

I heard nothing further and stayed on my knees. The stone flared in time with what might have been a conversation between the two. At last it held steady.

"I have vouched for you and this human who brought you here. You were wise to pay this one homage. The reasons why your companion brought you to her may bear revisiting later.

I will answer your unasked questions, Danu, now if you wish. Do you want to know what I have learned here?"

"As much as I can handle," I said.

The Sidhe king laughed in my mind. "Well played, Danu! But I expect no less from you."

"You have found adequate water to begin to revive this planet. But this is the last treasure trove of it and it cannot be wasted. More must be added to this fund—much more. But the humans … and the excess Shadakon … must be dealt with. And the fact that you are a long way away from me, and I find that I am missing you …"

A wave of yearning passed through me and I moaned.

"Are you summoning me back, my king?" In my mind's eye, I was again facing him in the grove as I had promised long ago. The high summer energy was on me as was his own and therefore that of the planet. I had set aside everything including self-preservation and only wished that he would touch me …

I heard him laugh again. "Yes, Danu, yes, I certainly will later. But do you not have more questions? Like … 'Did I stay in touch with Dagon without either of us telling you?' Or, 'Did I invite him to be pleasured by Sidhe other than yourself?'"

"I know that the answer to both of these is 'Yes,'" I said calmly. I don't think I can handle those details now, however. Something has healed the possessive jealousy in him. Perhaps we are now at a place that we cannot afford to be concerned with things of lesser consequence."

"Good, Danu! You are continuing to learn and you are my favourite student. Stay well, my lover," he said. And then the stone went dark and the shadows again covered the Guardian in her niche.

We walked back towards the entrance of the cave. Io was silent but finally asked, "What is she?"

I smiled. "Ah, we have given them many names. My Sidhe king called her a 'sky dancer.' Some have used the word '*devida*.' She is a goddess, a guardian and, sometimes, a punisher—as most Otherly beings have been described at various times in their history with humans."

I stopped beside Io's fishing pond and lowered my finger towards the bottom, waggling them suggestively. Several pale, I suppose maybe fish, lunged out and bit into me. I closed my hand over them and pulled them out of the water and left them flapping on the edge of the pool. I had a slight wound that bled but stopped immediately and closed over. Io looked at me carefully, but didn't say a word.

"I will catch them for you, as it doesn't cost me as much as you to be bitten. But I don't want to watch the rest of it."

I sat in the twilight between the slowly sinking bright desert sun and the progressive darkness of the cave. I watched the sky and listened. I heard the wind. I saw a slight translucent cloud pass.

Good! There is still moisture in the air.

CHAPTER TWENTY

ANTICIPATION

I dozed throughout the night and woke early to a cloudless dawn. The rest of the day passed with me growing more and more hungry, and knowing I would soon have to put Io further into her own depletion if I took from her now. I reached down deep with my mind into the sand I sat on, and imagined water energy, in dark deep pools. I imagined that I might take a sip of that elixir, as I had once learned to take from a tree. I fell into a dream that was green and blue and alive and there was a celebration and I—I awoke to the sound of a flitter coming directly in for a landing.

When the engine was silent, Io stood before it, in anticipation of a joyful reunion. A slight figure darted from the flitter and rushed to hug her. Io clung to her sister, Ka, for a moment and then looked expectantly to where the pilot was getting out.

I already had sensed that it was not Dagon but Nathaniel. My Maker hand was active, so Dagon was not dead or dying. Nathaniel eyed me appraisingly and my heart sunk.

Was I now his prize of war in the endless struggles of the Shadakon?

He shook his head. *"Dagon is restored to his place of power. Unfortunately, his mate fell suddenly ill. A short and seemingly not painful death. All in all, unusual for us Shadakon."*

My hand went to my sheath and discovered only the lump of the small stone. *How could I not have noticed?*

"You know that Dagon is capable of making ah, corrections, in another's reality. Like making someone believe that he stood at attention for hours, when in fact that someone was probably slumped in induced sleep. Why would it be acceptable to you to observe him doing this to others, but object when it was done to you?"

I smiled at Nathaniel. "What have you come to tell me besides the timely demise of Dagon's mate?"

He smiled back. "He is planning the funeral. No expense or ritual will be spared. It would be better if you were not there, Danu. Or his delicious human pets." He licked his lips and I scowled.

He waved at Ka. "She is well. Her sister was at more risk with you. Although I sense that you have shorted yourself and are in deficit."

I looked into his bright amber eyes. Nathaniel was smart, and he was a strategist. I once again owed my life to him, as did the two humans. And Dagon.

"Io taught me today that a human can live on a squirming, eyeless bit of protein," I said. "That she caught with her own fingers and bore the pain of being bitten to do so. I have been surprised and terrified for days. You are right ... I am hungry and wondering if I will go to sleep in a cave again tonight in that condition."

Nathaniel took his time in answering me and I knew he enjoyed every moment of it.

"Ka, Io! I have brought food and drink for you both, take it out of the flitter and enjoy..."

They soon were exclaiming over baskets of fresh bread, fruit, and some pale dried material that I couldn't identify.

"Quick energy," he said. "Dried meat, but sweetened and spiced. Io will be replenished in no time. You, however ..." Nathaniel leaned back against the flitter and waited for me to catch up to his next negotiation with me. "I was told not to touch you and I told you myself that I would abide by that. But clearly Dagon did not give you a similar restriction. Or you would not have gotten away with kissing me afterwards, and leaving me hard, with a long difficult night flight in front of me.

I do not care for you, Danu; it might be after our last session that I don't even like you. I want you ... ah, yes. But you know that. Do you not think that an act of kindness might be acceptable to you? I have done what I could to preserve he who you love and also his pets and you. My hands are ... tied so to speak. Yours are not ..."

I checked within to see how what he had said sat with me. I expected indignation or anger. But Dagon had given me to Nathaniel, to protect me. Nathaniel had been promised my Sidhe blood, but when he took it Dagon couldn't handle his feelings about it. Seeing me with the mark of another Shadakon on my skin was much like seeing me marked after having been in the throes of hot sex with my Sidhe king, Fiórcara.

"So no marks this time," whispered Nathaniel. I felt his desire for me encircle us.

"Walk with me," I just said. We walked out into the desert. The sky was covered in stars and one low crescent moon.

"Take off your clothes," I said, much as I had said to my Sidhe lover Céadar on a strange midsummer's eve we had shared. Nathaniel took off his flight suit, eyeing me carefully. He had a strong, well-muscled body and his large cock stood at attention.

He looked at it and smiled. "Just for you, Danu."

I may have surprised him then. I could have relieved him while remaining dressed and let it be an insignificant event, but I have my dramatic flair. I took off my clothes and moved as I had learned to move as a Shadakon—close to him but not quite touching. He shivered and wanted me. He was not an overly violent or unkind Shadakon. He meant me no harm. I would treat him gently. But first, I drove him up and up until he moaned.

"Lay down, Shadakon," I said. He lay down on his back on the desert sand and I stood above him, my legs spread on either side of his, knowing he could see and smell and want me.

His head thrashed but he was silent. I did not sense fear or anger in him. Desire drove out every other feeling. He was beyond thinking, a state I was well familiar with. I knelt inside his thighs and his hands fisted the sand, wanting to touch me, to secure me there.

I stopped.

I met his eyes and knew he did not know what I would do next. He was begging me without words.

Without any indication of my next act, I rose up and then lowered myself upon him in one slow slide and began to ride him. He screamed, but it was not about pain, and I did not stop. He was bucking under me and when I knew he was at his moment of release, I increased my actions and brought him home. As he found his peace, I took a sizeable amount of energy from him—not too much, I had always been careful about that—but I had been hungry. I left him wordless, lying in the desert.

A fair exchange, I thought.

When he reappeared at the cave's entrance, the two humans were chattering and refreshed. They advanced on him and he waved them off. I snorted. Nathaniel still underestimated me. He would continue to want me. He would burn for me as I had for the Sidhe king. It would have been better for him if he resisted the urge to pressure me into another round of sex.

I then snorted at myself. I had been perfectly willing to play my part. And his high sex driven energy had been pleasing to me. There was no pressure. I had initiated everything that happened out there—except the scream.

CHAPTER TWENTY-ONE

TIME TO TALK

The next day, after dark, Nathaniel brought us back to the building on Dagon's land.

"Dagon has asked that no one come outside for a while. No running out to see who is arriving." He lifted an eyebrow at the human sisters. They nodded.

When he left, Nathaniel left Ka behind with her sister, and I was surprised and touched by his decision. Nathaniel liked variety and he liked to take his sources fairly hard, but apparently he did not feel good about acting that way with the two humans who were so clearly awaiting Dagon.

The house had been re-provisioned and there was again crystal clear water and fresh food for the sisters. I went to the computer to read about the various accounts of the passing of Dagon's mate. No account identified her as his "beloved" mate or anything even vaguely similar to that. It was obvious the Shadakon clan understood that theirs had been a political alliance.

Dagon showed up late that night. Io and Ka were asleep and he put his finger to his lips when he entered. I stood and then knelt to him.

"My Alpha," I said softly. He raised me to my feet and looked at me.

"You have been having adventures, Danu. And you were unavoidably in uncomfortable circumstances.

Uncomfortable," I thought. *As in, expecting momentarily to die either painfully or perhaps quickly and mercifully. But finally, nevertheless.* I shrugged my mostly healed shoulder. There was still a dull ache there at times, especially when I slept on the ground.

He continued to watch me.

"I would like you to offer me access to your memories, especially of the last few days."

He knew I was aware that once accessed he might follow any thought into the past. That "especially of the last few days" was an untruth of omission.

"There are things you may not want to see," I said. "But there are also things that a mere description could not catch. Including an interaction between the Sidhe king and a being he called a "sky dancer.""

"First for the good news," he said. Settling himself on the divan at one end, he extended his arm and caught my hand lightly. He drew me to him to facilitate what I knew would be a deep reading. He settled me gently, my head on his lap and the rest of me presumably comfortable and supported.

"And the bad news?" I asked.

"Hmmm …" said Dagon. "It is my task to decide which is which. Or if any of your experiences should be defined so rigidly." He stroked my hair and for the moment I relished his touch. I closed my eyes.

"Now, Danu," Dagon said.

I opened my eyes and saw the flickering flames that beckoned me to fall into his eyes. I began my deep breathing, willing calm although fear flickered around the edges of my mind and I tried not to think about what that fear was attached to.

Dagon had grown even more powerful in the years we had been apart. He told me that he had read me when I was asleep in the drawer on his ship. That hadn't hurt, or at least, in a way that I could recall later. This might be different.

"Shhh, Danu. Be easy. I will try not to hurt you, my love, but do not resist me."

Usually I did not know after a certain point what Dagon was viewing.

I went away and floated in space, content to await my summons to return from the quiet darkness.

This time I saw the memories that he lingered on as he viewed them, one being me riding a screaming Nathaniel in the desert. And me at the moment of understanding how his mate had died and then overriding his mental command for me to not notice that I no longer had the small dagger in the sheath that I wore. And, finally, me checking that and finding only the small stone in the sheath.

He withdrew from my mind abruptly. We looked at each other. I asked, "Did you continue on to see the Guardian in the cave and her conversation with the Sidhe king? Did you sense and see that there is much water there?"

"I may have to go back," he said. "I seemed to have gotten distracted. Do I have to find a new second, in addition to everything else I must do?"

"Nathaniel saved our lives," I said. "Yours, mine, and the two humans sleeping in the other room. He spent his own money to secure your favourite humans and save them from a brutal debut on the energy Registry. He brought us to an unknown place of safety, which turned out to be of great significance."

"I told him not to touch you," he said in a growl.

I took a deep breath. "He did not touch me. I touched him. I ordered him to lie down naked in the desert. And then I rode him," I said defiantly. "And then I fed from him."

"Why?" said Dagon, seemingly calmer.

I sighed. "He returned Ka to her sister in good condition. He had not taken from her. He arrived with food that they both were used to eating. Io had had to catch and kill and eat raw, disgusting, blind cavefish. She did so to be able to nourish me.

She did that because she knew I was important to you. I am not sure how she feels about me beyond her promise to you to preserve me. She took me to a place in the cave that I believe she was already aware of. There was a Guardian. I might have died shortly after I was brought before her. I invoked the Sidhe king and they talked, or communicated, with one another."

"I was in deficit. Nathaniel arrived well fed. He asked me to ease him and take from him. I could have given him minimal service in a few moments, or not at all and merely taken sustenance from the humans. He reminded me that I had touched him, kissed him, in front of you but you did not seem interested. So, he had flown on, hard for his troubles. I decided to handle things differently this time."

We looked at each other. Dagon put his hand lightly on my throat. I did not freeze. I continued to look at him, noting that his eyes had darkened.

"Would you drive me out into the desert, Dagon? You are the one who brought me into sex play with you and your two humans. And I know that at some point you were pleasured by a number of Sidhe." He jerked.

"I also know that you had been in contact with the Sidhe king over the long weary years that I yearned for you. When, in spite of everything I tried, I could not let go of you. And when you finally arrived on Exterra, you did not want to even see me. Would this be revealed if I read you?"

"You do not have the power to do so. You do not have the skill either."

I noticed then that he was idly rolling an object in his hand. It was out of my frame of vision, but I knew it was the dagger. The dagger that had killed two Shadakon that I knew of, but might still be capable of bringing death to more.

"Dagon! Do you flirt with the end of your own life—or mine?

Or do you still wish to accompany me to death?"

We looked at each other for a timeless time.

He drew the sheath from under my shirt and placed the dagger back in it. Then he tucked it against my skin. My breath stopped at the touch of his fingers. He stroked my cheek and my tears slipped down and reached his fingers.

I said nothing.

"Why did you not contact me?" The pain was washing over me now. I had lived as a solo warrior, fighting against wanting what lay in the past. Wanting someone who had left, never to be seen again. But meanwhile he was in touch with the Sidhe king. Meanwhile he recently had availed himself to a Sidhe gathering and sexing while I lay alone in my hill house. I was not important enough. I was no longer useful enough. He had easily let his love for me go.

He had followed my thoughts although I had not organized them. I felt the blackness of despair come and take me then. He picked me up in his arms and walked outside into the darkness. He carried me into his home and laid me on his bed and locked the door. He held me until I eventually awoke.

I had no idea where I was. As I looked around, I guessed, and was horrified. *What would come of this?*

"You can transit to the small house later. I want you here, as my mate, in my house, in my bed. She never slept or sexed in here with me. We came together in the beginning but her ... tastes ... were different than mine. We quickly tired of each other."

"I never forgot you, Danu. You were living with the Sidhe and seemingly forever attracted to the Sidhe king you called Fiórcara. I also appeared to be forever attracted to you.

You did not fit in my world and did not want to. You still don't. I am what I am, and you are what you are. Only one thing ties us together."

I reached out and touched his heart. Mine was pounding out a message. *"Come to me, Dagon. Let me come to you."*

"Yes, Danu. There is that. And there is this …"

He drew off my shirt, baring my nipples that pointed at him, begging him to touch them. I moaned. He touched me skilfully and then stopped to take off both his and what was left of my clothing. He touched where I wanted him; was ready for him, and he moaned. And then he had me. He had me. He had always had me. I was his.

Later we lay cooling from our efforts.

"And yet I do not have you," he said calmly, resuming our conversation. "You come and you go. You frolic as the Sidhe king invited me to do. However, for whatever it's worth, I think he got me drunk, or high. Because I could not leave, could not protest anything that was done to me—did not want to protest. And the Sidhe king was present, overseeing it all."

I laughed. "How long did the party last?"

"I thought it was one night. I think it was closer to a week." We looked at each other and smiled.

"Yes those long Sidhe party nights," I said. "Now you know." He laughed.

I felt safe and loved by him—at the moment, still drifting and satisfied from our activities. "You may want to complete your reading of me, Dagon. I believe you have seen the difficult parts. And I also think you should read Io and Ka—especially if you do not know their history. Io was familiar with the cave; she knew what she could eat there and how to obtain it. She knew about the Guardian …

"First I will claim my power over my mate's faction of the Shadakon. I will show her my ritual respect. I do not want more secrets in my mind to complicate my thinking."

"Ritual respect? Lore had died and Morag had disappeared. Had they been given some Shadakon send off?"

"Neither was my mate.

"But I was once your mate. Would you have done so for me?"

"I had set you aside formally before I came to, …" He whispered in my mind, *"Kill you."*

"Ahhh. But this mate was still formally your mate? Will you make some public gesture of loss?"

He nodded. "Why does this information not hurt you as much as knowing that I stayed in touch with the Sidhe king? Or that I put myself in their hands and enjoyed what followed?"

I was silent, going within to check the true answers to these questions. "You came to kill me because you loved me. It was a dark possessive side of your love that had hurt us both before. But not bothering to send word, being unwilling to even let me see that you were still alive—that you were thriving…" I stopped, overwhelmed by the feelings that rose in me. I took a deep sustaining breath. "It meant to me that you no longer loved me." I hung my head "I believed that," I said.

"And now?" asked Dagon very quietly.

"I know you want me. I have been actualized as a Sidhe. The Sidhe wield great power by their sexual attraction and its effects on others. However they often are indifferent to their effects on those who come to them. I am no longer human, or just Shadakon, or Sidhe. However, perhaps my human heart refused to be changed over. I do not just want you or want you to want me.

I love you, Dagon. I have and will continue to offer my life to you. Even though it puts me in jeopardy. Again and again."

I turned my face from him then. He could not give me what I craved. This had been proven over and over to me.

There was deep silence between us. "You mentioned reading me. I do not think you have that skill. But I would show you if you want answers. You will know the truth of them, because you can sense defence and the significance of silence or missing information."

"I would show you, Danu." He turned my face to his and we lay together, our heartbeats synchronized, our bodies at the same level of satiation.

I looked into his eyes and mind-spoke him, "*Show me Dagon. Show me your love for me.*"

I saw a brief scene: me standing on one side of an electro fence at the pleasure fair, he on the other. Our hands were moving in a slow arc towards each other even as he was jolted by an unfamiliar feeling of wanting to provide protection to me. He wanted to get me out of the environment of the fair and its tawdry pleasure tents; he wanted to take me home. And we had flown there, me in unexpected bliss, but him as well.

Another scene: I was locked in Dagon's small dusty basement room undergoing my trial by hunger by the Council of the Shadakon on Exterra. I had told him earlier that I hated him. That I thought he had set me up to be tortured in front of him. But all the while my heart called out to him and I eventually did as well. He felt the ongoing scorn of the other Shadakon, and the hope in most that I would fail and so he could be eliminated as well. But he never set me aside in his heart. Perhaps he sustained me, in ways the Shadakon could not understand. Certainly he was prepared to die for me that day. I took another steadying breath.

"I would see farther into our relationship," I said.

He showed me a scene further along in time and our history. He and I stood on a beach on an island where I worked with the Mothers in their hospice. I was there waiting out the last few days before midsummer.

He knew, through adequate information, that I had lay down under the Sidhe king and taken pleasure with him not far away in broad daylight. We had been seen and that information was made available to other Shadakon. His position as Alpha, and maybe his life, rode on whether this threat to him could be eliminated. Even so, he had resisted what Morag laid out for him to do. He had arrived in deficit, with a very determined Morag at his side. He had taken me to the very edge of my life. He intended to take me to death, and I had surrendered to him. Heart struck by what was happening, I had again offered him that.

But he could not do so. Morag was running to us with her needle gun when I noticed her. It was then that he returned all my energy and more and turned to face her. I transited to Between and the Sidhe king retrieved both he and Morag for a reckoning. Dagon knew then that he had lost me; that I would not return to his side or home or life. He waited, with the patience of someone who has waited for an end to a long life. He awaited death. Although his plan to kill me would have been accepted by the Shadakon as necessary and overdue, he could not and would not do so and accepted the consequences of being brought before the Sidhe king on that day. I now felt his despair—not in facing the loss of his life, but the loss of me. He had stood silent and undone before me and the Sidhe.

"And yet I did return to you, Dagon. Over and over. Right up until you left Exterra. I searched through the ruins of your home. I knelt where we had lain together. I slowly regained myself. Yes, I had Sidhe lovers including the king, but I could keep none of them.

I thought once that I had you, that our hearts were joined and that we would be one." I sadly wiped the inevitable tears away that ran down my cheeks.

"A little more then, my love," said Dagon. "The Sidhe king had suddenly appeared on the Shadakon communication net after years of silence.

We Shadakon were slightly disturbed by our new planet's persistent droughts and shrinking waterways. We did not bother to adequately investigate the amount of water that was being transported off planet. Perhaps the Sidhe were more aware of this. The king had exchanged pleasantries with me and then inquired as to the health of the planet. He had told me that Exterra was thriving thanks to the efforts of many, including the Shadakon. There were long silences in our conversation during which I begged without words to hear about you, Danu. But you had been claimed as Sidhe. I had no right to imply a claim on you—even by gathering information about you that you did not know I had. I knew that the Sidhe king knew my unvoiced feelings. Fiórcara, your dear friend, and also king of Sidhe, had laughed once during my pauses and said, 'She is still healing from you. Would you bring her fresh pain?'"

"It was then that I decided to stay away from you forever," said Dagon. "Even when I came to Exterra, I tried to honour that as what I could still do for you. I knew that to do otherwise would only bring you more pain."

"And the party with the Sidhe?" I asked.

"The Sidhe king invited me to his home when I first arrived. I assumed that there was some diplomatic intention. And well there might have been," he said laughing. "The Sidhe tie themselves to others in their own way. I was given a cup of the elixir of life. I suppose in thinking back, that it tasted different than what I had been allowed before. Later other Sidhe arrived, including the most beautiful and powerful female I had ever seen."

I knew then that he had been entertained by the Sidhe king and queen. I smiled, remembering her skills.

"I would have been more disciplined; I would not have acted as I did with her in my usual state of mind. But that night everything disappeared except her. I was dimly aware of others present."—*Of the Sidhe king being present,* I thought— "She took her time with me. So much time. I drank many cups of elixir until all I could see were her blue eyes and all I could feel was the burning within me. When she finally came to me, I was without thought or concern. Then I understood the state you were in after your visits to Between.

Fiórcara, my Sidhe king had shown Dagon the full power of Sidhe and why I did not, could not, resist it. Perhaps he thought to challenge Dagon's rules of possessiveness and even his boundaries of what he might allow in pleasure. Perhaps he had done this for me, and some long-range plan. Perhaps he did it because he could—he could observe and take from the proud Shadakon, undressed and undone. I tried not to guess my king's actions.

Dagon and I were in a peaceful place. Knowing that he had missed and yearned for me

It fixed nothing, and it fixed everything. We loved each other. He loved me. (In fact he had used those words before I did.) The confusion and difficulty between us was enhanced by being different kinds of beings: he was Shadakon through and through; I came as to him as a human, changed when exposed to him and the energy he shared with me, and then slowly further changed into being recognizably a Sidhe. The first hybrid, for want of a better word, that had ever been accepted into the Sidhe ranks. I was not good mate material for an ambitious Shadakon who was a good leader for his people; though knowing me may have developed his compassion for others. I thought of Io, curled in his lap, believing in the safety he provided.

And both he and Nathaniel had come through for her, rather than abandoning her and her sister to the registry and the rough appetites of some of the Shadakon. Most of the Shadakon.

He and I would not rule together here, or anywhere else in the galaxy. I could possibly stand at his side as an advisor—in the role I was in now. We would be under constant observation from Shadakon intent on climbing the ranks to gain power.

He stroked my hair and sighed. "I know, Danu."

He had said that to me on the last day he was on Exterra before the Shadakon exodus. I thought it meant that he understood the pain of parting that I felt. I knew it did. And he was very familiar with that pain within. He felt it himself. He had continued on, leading his clan onwards away from a planet that no longer had sustenance for them.

"And what future do you see in front of us?" he asked.

I waited to answer, knowing that I was making it up as I went, but also knowing that I might actually have some power to see into the future.

"I have seen this planet restored to greenness and blue water. I know that the Sidhe will have a part in making that come into being. They may well buy this planet and expend a lot of energy here. Whether that would mean that the Shadakon and their humans would continue to live here, I do not know. But if humans were allowed on the land held here by the Sidhe, they might be used as farm labourers. It would be seen as a better option by most of them than the life they live now. They would prepare the ground for seeds to grow and water to flow. Reversing the dying of this planet without intense intervention is beyond even the Shadakon and Sidhe's concept of the immediate future. I knew that the humans would have to be taught other ways of walking on the land than what they had done in their past. There have always been humans who were not takers, but rather connected with the life force and taking no more than they needed.

They did not overpopulate. They walked lightly on the land and perhaps the Sidhe had watched them over the eons."

I thought then of the Indians of the Americas who had been pushed into extinction by the aggressive Europeans. I thought of the Aboriginals in Australia who had lived and thrived before the Europeans came and claimed their lands for penal colonies and sheep stations.

I recalled the two words that I had heard in the first circle I had made on the land.

"*Sidhe*" and *"Australia."*

"And in the more foreseeable future—like next week?" Dagon asked.

"I must talk to Fiórcara other than through a green stone, affirming as that is," I said. "You might ponder what deal you could offer to the Sidhe if this planet comes up on the market. Do the Shadakon want to buy a dying planet?"

Dagon shook his head. "We would not invest in a dying planet or depleted and dying humans. Many of us are ready to leave now.

"So why haven't some left already?"

"We have not found a suitable planet anywhere near here."

"So the Shadakon may have to take on the role of shepherds, at least for a while? Another place to be reluctant heroes?"

We looked at each other.

"Perhaps. I need time to see how I can present this idea," Dagon said musingly.

"And I need to have a clear communication channel with the Sidhe."

"I will arrange that. But be aware that unknown others may be listening in," he said.

"I would bet everything on that fact," I said. I gathered my scattered clothing and transited to the small dwelling that I was familiar with.

CHAPTER TWENTY-TWO

WE ALL DO WHAT WE MUST DO

I didn't see or hear from Dagon for the next week.

I kept myself busy, familiarizing myself with the trans-planetary communication system between the Sidhe king and myself before I contacted him. Io and Ka readied themselves for Dagon each morning and were obviously disappointed as the day wore on. I took sustenance from them as quickly as possible. Neither seemed interested in raising my interest in them sexually, and this proved to me that the attentions they had given me in Dagon's presence were, in fact, for the purpose of pleasing him.

Meanwhile I followed the coverage of the upcoming funeral. It seemed that it would culminate in some grand public ritual, the details of which I could not translate nor guess at. I suspected however that there would be pain. Since she was beyond pain, it would fall on him to grant her some last public offering of his own.

Meanwhile I was making a list of questions that I needed answering:

Did anyone own the planet other than the piecemeal short-term titles of private interests?

Did anyone still hold water and mineral title rights, or had they been allowed to extinguish with no further interest on the claims?

Were the humans native to this place or had they been imported?

I was considering all this when Io came into the room where I was working. She obviously wanted a few questions answered as well.

"Will Dagon not come back to us?" she asked directly.

I told her that I believed that he would but he had much to do at this time. She nodded.

Nathaniel had told her that we all were staying out of sight of Dagon's mate and her followers.

She and her sister must have overheard somehow that his official mate was now dead.

"Io, we must talk, or something deeper than talk. You were familiar with the cave we stayed in, you knew how to catch the little fish you could eat."

She made an expression of disgust.

"I know you did not want to eat them. But you knew how to catch them."

She was silent, perhaps sensing what was coming next.

"You also brought me to the Guardian." I said calmly, but she looked up to see if I was angry.

"I would have died if I had not known to offer her my respect," I said. "And if I hadn't had a sign to prove myself." She put her head down.

"I already know these things, Io. I do not have to search your mind for this information. But I do need to know where you and your sister came from. Why you are familiar with the cave. Will you tell me?"

She backed away from me. It would fall to Dagon then to extract this information, I would not push her to give me the answers—he could and would. They would comply in the end, willingly or unwillingly.

The leave-taking of Dagon's mate was today and he had been completely absent from me. I knew that his silences were often significant. I knew that something was going to happen that I could not foresee. The Shadakon perhaps had more than one type of trial. I watched the live feed in growing apprehension. A long double line of Shadakon in dark garb had formed in front of Dagon's partner's bier. Dagon stood at the foot of the line with Nathaniel behind him. Dagon was stripped to a brief wrap of cloth around his waist.

He looked composed and shut down.

At a signal I did not see, the double line separated and Dagon walked up the centre. The Shadakon on either side had weapons in their hands: flails, short clubs, weapons with sharp projections … None looked immediately death-dealing; that they provided great pain, however, was obvious. I had not seen what his mate had hit me with when she broke my collarbone; perhaps it was a short club like what I saw being used now.

Dagon walked slowly and determinedly up that long line. As he passed by, he was beaten and whipped, clubbed, hit with tools that caused his blood to run freely. He surely could have walked faster! When he could no longer see clearly to move forward, Nathaniel touched him lightly from behind and provided guidance. Some of the blows landed on Nathaniel, although he was dressed. Neither of them changed their pace.

At the end, Dagon was at the end of his endurance. Nathaniel stood beside him in front of the bier, and they both knelt briefly and bent their heads. There was an approving roar from the crowd. Dagon had provided public evidence of his loss and the value he placed on she who lay dead in front of him.

I was horrified and slumped to the floor. He had not mentioned this. This was so … Shadakon!

The bier was lit and the remains (and evidence) blazed briefly and then dissipated into drifting smoke. Wood for such an event would have been incredibly costly. Finally everyone left and the square was dark. The live feed ended.

I sat on the floor, unable to move, unable to go to him, to provide what he needed. Eventually I heard a flitter arriving. I slipped out and saw Nathaniel lifting a limp body out. It was wrapped in a sheet, more red than white.

He carried it in and had the humans remove the pillows from the large divan where he gently placed Dagon. I moved to read what state he was in and Nathaniel let me, but interrupted after only a few moments.

"He is broken and bleeding. His skin is ripped off in many places. Her family no doubt had suspicions that they could not formally raise. He could have moved faster, but he stood them down today."

"He needs blood. Strong blood. Yours and mine, Danu. The human sources will provide for us. We will provide for him. For my Alpha." He grabbed Ka and Io by their arms matter-of-factly and pushed them none too gently against the wall. He took from one and beckoned me to the other.

"This is not a time to be squeamish, my Sidhe queen." As I took what was a reasonable amount of energy from Ka, I saw him drive his fangs into her sister and gulp down blood. She sagged in his arms. He gestured to me and I sensed anger and fear in him.

"I have never done this with a stranger," I said backing away. He shrugged and continued to look at me.

"Your blood is the strongest, Danu. You know this is the truth."

I thought of Io determinedly killing and then forcing herself to eat the cavefish. I moved to her and said, "Close your eyes, Io. I have to take care of Dagon." And then I drove now sharp teeth into her neck and drank her young human blood until I knew I must stop to preserve her.

Nathaniel just nodded. He went to where Dagon lay and unwrapped the sheet from him. I gasped in pain. I could see broken bones and deep wounds. Large bruises were spreading across his body. He was failing as I watched. I bit into my hand and put it to his lips. He made no motion to take what he needed. I whispered in his ear, "Dagon, I would be one with you now.

Take my blood, my love, please do this for both of us."

He frowned and then lapped weakly.

"More, Dagon, more. There is as much as you need."

He grabbed my arm and pulled blood and energy from me. I did not stop him. Eventually Nathaniel pulled me away and presented his own bleeding wrist. He too provided until his head drooped. Dagon passed into what was now normal sleep. We looked at each other in relief.

"Are you injured as well, Nathaniel?"

He shrugged. His shirt was stuck to his back with blood, whether his or Dagon's I did not know.

Io and Ka had somewhat revived and were looking at both of us in alarm.

"Which of you has the most healing skills?" I asked. I did not ask if they had healing skills. I now knew that they had lived on the land and had practical knowledge of what could be used. Io approached me tentatively.

"Go draw a basin of warm water and find some soft clean cloths. If there are herbs in this house that would serve in healing, add it to the water."

I was not surprised that the herbs she came back with were the same as what Dagon used to put in my soaking pool in his old house on Exterra. Healing herbs ... for the mind and body.

Ka was standing apart from Nathaniel watching him warily.

"Draw a bath for Nathaniel, Ka. Wash his wounds. Comfort him however you can."

Io and I spent a long time gently sponging away the blood off Dagon. I could see his wounds closing and I searched and found him with my mind. He was drifting in relative comfort. "I will lay with him now," I said. "Help your sister if she needs assistance with Nathaniel. I had heard soft gasps from the room the pool was in. Put him to bed between the two of you.

He preserved Dagon's life and therefore your own once again. He is Dagon's valiant second.

CHAPTER TWENTY-THREE

A SMALL BUT SIGNIFICANT CHANGE

I woke up to see Dagon looking at me. His eyes were almost pain-free and his body, while still bearing evidence of his sacrifice, was healing. He smiled at me.

"You wouldn't have wanted to know about this ahead of time—you may have tried to transit me off somewhere! But these dues had to be paid. The ritual is old and can be required by the family of a mate who dies under suspicious circumstances. I was in my mate's presence when she sickened and died. Extensive tests showed nothing other than heart failure. But ..."

He reached out and stroked my cheek. "I remember little after a certain point. Did Nathaniel bring me here?"

I nodded. The human sisters were in the kitchen, probably eating a well-deserved large breakfast. I heard them laughing together and relaxed. We had not become monsters to them then.

Dagon studied me carefully. "You took blood and energy from them as did Nathaniel. So that you could give me generous amounts of your Sidhe blood?" I nodded.

"And did Nathaniel also contribute to my healing?" I nodded again.

He wrapped me in his strong arms. He moulded to my body even as he gently entered me. "No big moves, Danu." We floated together as the heat gradually intensified between us. "Ah, my beautiful Danu," he said. "I only regret that I do not remember your gift to me last night."

I smiled. I turned my head away from him, baring my neck. He kissed me there. And then he licked me, his tongue feeling ever so much as that of a great cat.

I shivered at the slight roughness and then again when he rubbed his fangs lightly back and forth across the area. "Please, Dagon," I said. "Please take what you need."

He gently so gently entered my skin where my heart's blood pounded just beneath the surface. He lapped, delicately, and I entered into blissful heat. We rocked together, safe for the moment in a small harbour of a turbulent sea. I wanted to be nowhere else. I wanted nothing else.

Eventually Dagon got up and, walking carefully, went to the room where Nathaniel and the two humans had spent the night. They were in the kitchen and Nathaniel was sprawled in the middle of their bed. His naked body gave evidence that he had not been spared in his walk with Dagon. It was clear by the marks he bore, that some considered him part of what had happened to ...

"*Mara*," Dagon said in my mind, sighing. "*Her name was Mara. Nathaniel had to walk a dangerous path with her. She drew him to her, but he was wise enough to know that it was a strategy of hers that he must avoid, if possible. He may have had her, or she had him. I think it might have been unavoidable for him. He knew better than to open his mind to her, and he was strong enough to prevent that from happening.*"

I thought back to the scene in the desert, Nathaniel immobilized by Dagon, his body and mind fighting but eventually overcome by Dagon's forced reading of him. I shuddered. *How powerful was this lover of mine? What was his true ambition?*

"*I am ancient enough that small games no longer interest me, Danu. When you met me, I was asleep, content enough in my small life. I would say that you have had a large part in my awakening.*"

Nathaniel opened his bright amber eyes and took in Dagon. He rose in one graceful move, seemingly not concerned with his lack of clothes.

There was a fresh set beside the bed and he took a moment to pull them on. He stood before Dagon and I sensed deep emotion; relief being the loudest one, but beneath that ...

I smiled and tried very hard not to broadcast what I had glimpsed. Surely, however, Dagon knew.

Nathaniel had deep feelings for Dagon. I struggled for a word, because the word love did not describe the usual feelings between Shadakon. But something bound them, and perhaps had made him more vulnerable (as I was also) to Dagon's readings.

"Brothers in arms." Nathaniel said. Then he knelt at Dagon's feet.

Dagon raised him in a heartbeat and clasped his forearms. "I will never forget," he told the younger Shadakon. And then he said something I was not expecting. It rocked me.

"My lover is a Sidhe and now you know what that means: she can never be my mate and we all understand that. I must move forward. She has a planet to save." Here he looked at me and raised an eyebrow—*Yes?* "I have been confused and angry about the connection that has grown between you two. One of her powers is passion and she has tied you to her, more successfully than Mara ever managed to. In some ways, my own actions made it necessary that ... that there was a semblance of connection between the two of you. It was she who suggested sharing her blood with you, not me. But I agreed in the service of all of us staying alive after we reached this planet."

"So now you want her," Dagon continued. "I would not have my possessiveness poison what lays between us three. If she comes to you or if you come to her, you both can decide what happens next. I rescind my command to you to not touch her. She has already confided in me"—I shrugged at this—"that she has pleasured you in the desert within the limitations that I set. If there is a next time, I will not be standing between the two of you.

She has recently reminded me of the fact that sexual pleasure is just that, and for the Sidhe, something given casually."

"*Oh, my love,*" I thought. "*There was nothing accidental or casual about who came to you when you were in the Sidhe king's home. No one less than his eon's old powerful queen. I will not stand between you and them! No one could. But you, too, have been marked and made Dagon, by two much more powerful than me.*"

We three stood silently. Nathaniel did not look at me but I felt him appraising me in mind-silence.

Then Dagon turned to go. "I need you at the main house in twenty-five minutes Nathaniel. Feel free to feed before joining me. I will have a brief word with my humans."

CHAPTER TWENTY-FOUR

I WANT TO STAY ... BELOW

Dagon was busy in the coming weeks. He eventually came by for a pleasurable morning feeding with the human sisters. I came in to find them so engaged and put a finger to my lips.

"*I would pass on this my love. I need to go see this world. I would travel deep in the earth with adequate equipment. I would dive in the dying or dead seas.*"

I rubbed my arms, imagining the lifeless water sliding along them and sighed.

"To do so you need a guide," he said calmly.

I knew we would come to this. We both needed someone that I could trust my life to. There was only one. "Nathaniel ..."

"And how will you source energy, Danu? Will you take from the Registry? There are men there of course if you prefer that."

"There is one human female I would try to find. Her name was Ker. I thought that was a remnant of a name. But it is perhaps all the humans have here."

"If she still lives," I added. I remembered that I had given her name to Dagon earlier.

Dagon looked up at me from what was an interrupted pleasant activity—what I might have once called breakfast.

"Would you automatically hold me responsible if she was gone or dead?"

I shook my head. Life is dreary and short for those who earn their living on the Registry. "I would take her with us, feed her nutritional food, learn what she knows and in the end ..."

"In the inevitable end, Danu?"

"If she cannot be given a place of sanctuary, I will end her myself."

Dagon regarded me with seemingly no emotion. "Would a Sidhe do this?"

I looked back, holding back the rising anger within. "I ended seven ships of humans, most of the crews blameless of being where they were. I gave others a faint chance and some took it; most did not. I directed a beam of power that was not retrievable or survivable; I did it for a planet that was shortly going to die. I find myself in the same situation now. I am here on behalf of the Sidhe. None of them would grieve an unknown and expendable human energy slave."

Dagon continued to look at me. "But you will, Danu. I know you will if it becomes necessary."

I bowed my head. I would not deny that. I had to walk a fine line between the ambitious and ruthless Shadakon and my own directive to save, if possible, this planet. Where the humans factored into this, I did not yet know. What parts Dagon and Nathaniel would play, I also did not know.

Dagon cut my musings short. "I will have the equipment available for you by tomorrow and Nathaniel will be ready to fly. I will send Ker to you. Do you wish to reacquaint yourself with her in deficit?"

He gestured to his two sources that were patiently waiting for him to return to their expected pleasures with him.

I sat on the end of the divan. I watched him stroke them in turn, building their energies higher and higher. He rose over one and took her. She was gasping in her bliss when he pulled a significant amount of energy from her. Without looking at me, he began with the other.

"*With Ka!*" I thought. "*Her name is Ka.*"

He smiled at me then, the pure look of a predator.

I could hear him in my mind purring as he leaned into his prey. Her eyes were on his and she was willing as he took from her, as he entered her body and mind and extracted what he wanted.

"And now your turn, Danu." I saw the panther and the bright flames in his eyes. I shivered, knowing that this would not be gentle. And that I did not want it to be.

He laughed. "Danu …" His voice was deep and raspy in his chest. "I so enjoy it when you see me, truly see me."

I had a momentary thought of fleeing him.

"Ah, Danu, I would enjoy that: to chase you down. The further you would go, the more pleasure I would have in eventually taking you to ground. Although whether it would be a pleasure for you—I do not know."

I stood before him. The humans had quickly left the room, sensing and avoiding what was building between us.

He stood and began what could only be called a stalk towards me. He circled me, smelling my unavoidable fear and desire blended into one fierce feeling. He growled.

He was dangerous. I wanted him that way. I began to slowly take off my clothes as he watched me, as a cat in the tall grass might watch someone thinking to take a dip in a jungle pond, unaware of being in a big cat's territory.

We were silent, not even using mind-speak. If I loved this Shadakon then I must accept him as he was. I had chosen to be here, and I had gotten my wish. I was on his world and in his keeping.

I faced him, my breath coming in short bursts.

My body wanted his—wanted him as my Alpha Shadakon. He closed the distance between us in less than a heartbeat. He took me to the floor and joined with me as the great cat he currently was. I felt his teeth close on my neck to secure me although he did not use his fangs. He purred and bit and licked me as he continued to drive into me until I cried out and heard him roar above me.

Eventually we both lay still, still intertwined.

Still cat then, I thought. I felt him smile in my mind.

"Ah, Danu. There has never been and will never be anyone else like you." He wrapped his now human arms around me and gifted me with energy such that I saw it as sparkles in the air around us.

"Time to go to work," he said, rising and donning his clothing. He left me lying on the floor.

In the morning I rose early. There was extra clothing laid out beside me. Next to these was a small device containing all the information I had sourced about the geology and water resources of the planet and the property claims on the land. I heard the flitter arrive and gathered myself to face the arrival of the pilot. Nathaniel.

He swung down, having seen me come out, bearing my extra gear. There was a human, a woman in the back seat. I recognized her. She looked even paler and more tired than before.

"Do we have ample provisions for her?"

Nathaniel smiled. "I followed my orders. I think she fears me though; she has not accepted food from me. It's possible she thinks I would immediately eat her."

I made contact with her. She was silent and braced for what always came. "I would have you eat and drink, Ker. You will accompany me, and yes, I will come to you for energy.

But not right now. Be easy. I would break bread with you, even if I can no longer eat it." I reached into a nearby container and drew out fruit and the dried meat that Nathaniel had brought to the human sisters while we stayed in the cave. I broke off a piece and offered it to her in my hand. She was still but then reached out to take it and eat it. The pale green fruit was also accepted.

"Now sleep, Ker," I said. I put my hand on her head and induced sleep.

I turned to Nathaniel, saying, "Show me more. Show me where the humans still live on the ground. Show me where the water was withdrawn. Show me everything."

He made no thought or comment about my choice to not avail myself to Ker. We flew on in silence.

I saw mountains beneath us. We landed beside what had been clear, deep lakes. There was still shallow water and vegetation around some of them. *The water was still being conserved in the mountains then*, I noted.

Flying in a large circle, we landed on a windy plateau. There were ancient survivor trees here, some showing just a flicker of grey-green life. I knelt before one, Ker now awake and standing and witnessing without comment and Nathaniel slouched in the flitter. I dispassionately felt my hunger growing. It seemed right—I was synchronizing with the hunger of the land. I felt light and stripped down. I identified with the endurance of the world around me. There was a particular strength in that.

The sun was fading into an eerie cloudless sunset of purples and golds. Ker sat beside me, having eaten several times that day and possibly noticing that I had not. I felt her hand tentatively touch mine and her fingers curl around my own. I waited. I was very good at waiting. I breathed calmly and felt the fear and anger in her mind settle and something else replace them.

She was looking out at the sky as the blue faded into purple and the first stars began to shine in the dusk. I listened for what I had wanted since I left on this journey. We sat awhile longer and then she said, "I have never seen this place before. I know that it is in trouble and that is why you are here. It is beautiful. I would provide for you now, Danu, if you wish."

So I took from her, gently.

Nathaniel said nothing when we returned to the flitter except, "We should return now." That silence was not broken until we arrived where I was staying.

"I will keep Ker with me," I said. "Let us start again tomorrow."

Some days I spent time tracing titles and the tangled trail of how the water of this planet had been traded away for credits. Not surprisingly it did not lead to either the humans on this planet or the Shadakon. There were some humans still on this planet involved in the lower levels of the water trade, and they were also involved in managing the Registry. But where had the big investment come from that organized taking a planet's entire supply of water? I suspected the multinational, multi-planetary businesses, whose names and CEOs changed regularly. Old Earth then. I snarled involuntarily.

I called Fiórcara, my Sidhe king. He looked out at me from his screen, appearing unsurprised to see me. I thought I saw Céadar standing behind him and my heart jolted—I missed his calm energy. I returned my attention to my king; he was studying me carefully.

"So, Danu. You are there now, with he who you love. And your heart reaches out to Céadar. You who seemingly cannot resist me—and usually do not want to." I knelt, and hoped he could see that.

"It has been, ah, intense, here my king. I am ready to show you what I know about this planet. It is painful to be here, to live on human and Shadakon energy. If I could just sit beside the tree and have a cup of elixir ..." I bowed my head. I did not think Fiórcara could read me—through a screen, across time and space. I suddenly only wished that I was before him. I felt my body kindle.

He smiled. "Better, Danu. It isn't for lack of passion though that you are suffering?"

I then realized that he could truly find me here. "My king, you once told me that being an ambassador would involve using my sexual passion. And loving the one that I engaged with would be part of that assignment. I did not think I could do that, but I have, at least partially. I do not love him"—I intentionally did not use the second's name—"but he has won my admiration. Once again I am entangled with two males, both powerful and both dependant on each other."

"There is great strength in threes," said Fiórcara thoughtfully. "As you well know, Danu. Seldom have you been content with only one lover."

I thought back to the information that I had gathered about Dagon's night with the Sidhe. I could only guess at the lines of power that had been spun and strengthened as he lay unprotestingly, looking up at aquamarine eyes. And later ...

Fiórcara laughed. "It was truly a fine night. The rough energy of the Alpha Shadakon was to her liking. Once again you brought her to a new truth."

"I brought her?"

"Ah, Danu ... he would never have returned to Exterra if not for you. It matters not what he said or even what he told himself. Surely that quickly became evident to you."

"You waited to put me in play," I replied.

He smiled. "Time is what you and I and the Shadakon and Sidhe have a lot of. But the earth-type planet you currently are suffering with—not so much. I will require some proposals, as detailed as you can provide. Fantastic suggestions will be equally considered."

He put one finger to the screen and I felt it touch my cheek. Then the screen went dark. I was to fly with Nathaniel in the morning. I had heard nothing from Dagon in many days. I tried not to make any more of that than the fact of it. Ker was comfortable enough with us, although the sisters were standoffish. Ker now ate foods she had never even known existed. She drank unlimited fresh clear water. She bathed. But there were no herbs or attendants for her. That had all been a performance for Dagon, the day they readied me for him.

I requested additional clothes for her and a brush and comb and other simple grooming aids. These were provided without comment. Someone had decided on drab clothing for her but that suited me. It would be better to be unseen on the land, if possible.

In the morning she would sit at the table and wait for me. I smiled at this. I had offered to break bread with her; perhaps she still saw me as requiring a morning meal. Her energy was not stirred up with passion but her numb sadness faded as the days passed. The arrangement satisfied us both.

We flew to another ocean. Much of the dying away had already occurred; the water beyond the shallows was blue, clear, and seemed lifeless. I put on gear that was considerably more advanced than any I had used before. I was breathing a mixture that did not require waiting to rise slowly and I had a re-breather to extend the time I could stay below.

When all was ready, I saw Ker watching, but noticed Nathaniel was indifferently looking elsewhere. I started to put on the large fins, but then stopped and returned to him.

He looked up surprised.

I took my courage in hand. I knew that I would feel worse if he refused my simple request. And yet ... and yet I knew that every time I did a deep dive, I risked my ending, alone below the surface. I was not so much afraid as sad to be facing this alone.

I felt this particularly strongly today.

"I would have you watch for me."

"Cannot Ker do that? I will be right here." He raised his amber eyes to mine with no emotion.

"She can. But she will only slightly miss me if I do not return," I said.

"And you think I will?" We beheld each other. "Why would you expect that of me?"

I could have made a plausible excuse: that Dagon would want the details. But I didn't. I continued to study him.

"Perhaps you can lie comfortably before what might be your last minutes of life. I cannot."

He said nothing. He simply reached out and grabbed me firmly. He brought me to his lips, and then hesitated, even as I involuntarily opened mine. He held me there until tears gathered in my eyes. Punishment then. I closed my eyes to spare myself his look of disdain.

He closed on my mouth instead and I gasped as our energy spiralled up. I shook in his tight grip.

"What now, Danu? Would you smile and turn away?"

I shook my head, my body informing him of the truth.

"A little pre-battle sex then," he said. He pulled me into the flitter and wedged us both in the back. My swimwear required little effort to work around. He did not bother with removing more than was necessary of his own clothing. "Is this what you want then, Sidhe?"

"I would have accepted a kind hug."

He laughed then. "Has anything that passed between us suggested kindness? Have you observed me acting in that fashion?" His amber eyes were over me and flames danced there.

I knew then what I had only thought about before; this Shadakon would soon be an Alpha—or die. He already felt it growing in him. If he moved away from Dagon, they both could be. But his days of being a second were coming to an end.

"I want you, Nathaniel. It is that way for me. Do what you will." I opened to him and he knew that I was telling him the truth.

He swore at me then, in a language I did not have. I remembered a horrible day when Dagon had cursed me in an old language and then broke my arm. I had not avoided what came next because I believed I deserved his rage. And here I was again. Time slowed. I felt the lines of fate extending out from this moment.

"Please do not hurt me," I whispered. "I never used my passion to hurt you. You requested a second round with a Sidhe and I obliged you. I thought you could use that lesson. Overall it was more pleasurable than painful," I said.

"And the kiss you bestowed on me in front of my Alpha?" Nathaniel asked.

"I was grateful to be alive. I was not thinking past that."

"And our interaction in the desert?"

"I managed to make you blameless. I took full responsibility for that later with Dagon."

"And then he granted you, us, the freedom to act as we would. Do you think he believed that I would take up that offer? Or that you would?" Nathaniel asked with seemingly little emotion.

"I think he did believe exactly that. As he said, I am not and cannot be his mate. Even now he may seek another after whatever politically expedient time period passes. He knows that I am a Sidhe and we have both come to some sort of peace about that."

"So what arrangement do you have?" Nathaniel asked. I sensed a quiet fury building in him.

"He has allowed me to love him; and he to love me. Just that," I said. I said it even as my breath caught in my throat and my hands clenched on emptiness.

Nathaniel let go of me and gestured that I should get off of him. I climbed down from the flitter, straightened my suit and walked to the waterline. I wanted to be calm before I entered the water. Instead tears ran down my cheeks. Keeping my back on Nathaniel I put on the awkward fins that would drive me effortlessly once under the surface. I prepared my mask, checking the flow of air. Heavy with counterweights, I cautiously moved the last few feet to the edge.

"*Stop!*" I heard both his voice and mind-speak to me. I paused, wondering if this could get any worse.

Nathaniel waded in to stand beside me. He drew me into his chest and I felt his heart and my heart beat together. "I would like to try this again, Danu. Have a safe dive and come back to us."

I dove in and sank through the sunlit water.

I might have dived in this sea for months and not happened upon what I saw this day. The water was crystal clear and as I neared the bottom I noticed a small amount of seaweed and simple life forms. *Good. Everything here wasn't dead—yet.*

I began swimming parallel to the shore, slowly edging out deeper. I was soothed by the water's gentle hold on me. I breathed as a trained diver, slowly and with pauses between the top and bottom of my breaths. I was deep in a meditative bliss when I looked down to see something in the depths below. Streamlining myself into a vertical dive, I dropped down and down—onto a temple. It was stone and had a lot of what looked like dead coral on it, but its covering life forms were mostly gone now and I could see what looked like carved human figures—female figures.

They beckoned with their stone arms and stood in poses that promised sexual connection and bliss. I had seen something like this in a book long ago. Had they been Hindu? Buddhist? I sank deeper until my alarm rang. It was time to return. But I yearned to see more. I hesitated. *How long?* I couldn't have said. I floated in the water column drawn to stay here. By the time I felt the sensations of low oxygen levels, I knew I was deep and in trouble.

I headed up. It is what one does, even if one knows that the surface is unattainable. Up I finned, and then as my vision grew dark I pulled the cord that would bring me up rapidly. But I would not be conscious for that reunion with my world. Or this world. I thought of Fiórcara. And the gentle Céadar. And Dagon! ... *I am so sorry.* And in my last fleeting thoughts ... Nathaniel.

It was Nathaniel who swam out to retrieve me. I bobbed gently on the surface, face down and feeling no pain. On another part of the planet Dagon suddenly gazed down at his Maker hand and went terribly silent. He called Nathaniel who didn't immediately answer. Dagon went to find a flitter.

Nathaniel brought me to the beach and pushed the water out of my lungs. I struggled weakly to breathe but perhaps I was close to crossing the void to wherever I might go next. I saw faint stars and smiled. He bit his hand and offered it to me and when I did not take from him, he drizzled his blood into my mouth.

I believe I remembered a deep moan. "I cannot let you go, my Alpha requires you to be well." Then he slapped me and I did take some note of that and gasped, swallowing the blood in my mouth. He bent over me and his energy swirled around me. "I require you here, Danu. Do not leave us so easily." And I believe I again heard something close to a moan.

I took his hand and lapped from it as he cradled my head. I saw his eyes above me. I fell into those bright amber flames and then slid into a natural sleep.

Nathaniel put a tarp up to shield me from the sun. Preoccupied with this, he handed Ker some water and food. She had sat with me, her hand in mine, offering what she could.

"Danu needs nothing but rest and time now," he told the human who he had not bothered to exchange words with at their first meeting.

In due time, Dagon appeared. He strode over to me, read my energy level and then turned to Nathaniel. In full Alpha he stood over him as Nathaniel knelt beside me. "How did this happen?"

"I do not know. I am not a diver. Danu checked out the equipment before she entered the water and everything seemed fine. She did not reappear—we were not timing her. It seemed too long and I began watching. When I saw her bob to the surface, I swam out and retrieved her."

"And you then revived her with your blood?"

"Yes." Nathaniel said stoically.

"And is there more that will come out that you might want tell me now," asked Dagon.

Nathaniel sighed. "Yes, Dagon, yes, damn it. Danu asked me to watch her on her dive. I said that the human Ker could do that; she seems devoted to Danu. Then Danu came to me. Came on to me. I knew she was frightened of going into the water. She wanted … she wanted something real before she risked her life."

"Something real?" asked Dagon quietly.

"She wanted me. She told me she did, but she did not have to tell me, as it was obvious. I started to have some brief sex with her, but decided that it would cost me more than it was worth. That no matter what you had said, you would not approve of my actions."

Dagon nodded. "You are right in a way. It is hard for me to accept Danu as a Sidhe. She was once my Shadakon mate.

I flew her as an Alpha—and she wanted me to. Then she spent more and more time in Between and gained new powers. She saved my life and Morag's—twice. Once when we were locked in our basements, experiencing the Hunger and the second time when we stood for judgement in front of the Sidhe king. She stated to him that she would not pick one of us to save. That she would join us in whatever fate he would administer. I saw her say farewell to Between that afternoon, a place that had invited her in, that enjoyed her presence. I realized then that no matter what she had done, that she loved me—and that she was a Sidhe, and I had tipped the balance she had tried to hold. She could no longer live in my world."

"She is responding to the emerging Alpha in you, Nathaniel. She wants you that way, as a powerful Shadakon. Not as a momentary distraction in the back of a flitter. I have watched this develop. So …" He said finally, "You dismissed her and she went alone on a deep dive on an alien planet. Is that the end of this story?"

Nathaniel shook his head. "I knew I had hurt her. I knew she had come to me for comfort. She asked me for a hug."

Dagon just raised his eyebrow. "Asked you for a hug? You who made it immediately clear that she must make good on her bargain to allow you to taste her Sidhe blood? And then you who marked her but did not seal the wound—so both she and I could see that? So, Nathaniel, gentle warrior, what did you do then?"

"I gave her a hug before she entered the water." They looked at each other.

"So, Danu transforms another Shadakon," said Dagon with a sigh. "I'm going to take her home now. Should I leave Ker for you?"

Nathaniel looked at Ker and asked, "Would you help me here while I pack up and also allow me to take you? I have given Danu blood and am in deficit." Ker looked astonished and then nodded.

"Better have some more food and water then," he said.

Dagon shook his head, picked me up and headed for his flitter.

CHAPTER TWENTY-FIVE

MISSING PIECES OF THE PUZZLE

I awoke in Dagon's bed. It would seem that whenever he had no idea what to do with me, he took me to his own space to give us the quiet and safety it provided.

I would never wake to have one of the many servants in his house seeking to serve me and gain my approval. I would not rise and put on whatever was required by the role of being this Alpha's mate. Our time for that had come and gone on Exterra. I had not been accepted by most of the Shadakon there as being Shadakon, or Dagon's mate. Once my Sidhe abilities began to manifest, I had had to withdraw from him—at first for a month in high summer, but later permanently. It no longer mattered that he had forced my leaving. It would have happened in any of a thousand ways.

He was gently stroking my body and I knew, removing any traces of Nathaniel and replacing them with his scent and touch. I had been asleep but my body awoke and was tuning to his. He leaned over me, making eye contact. I sighed.

He frowned and then said. "We can talk this out then. I expect to hear about or see you and Nathaniel grappling in the flitter," he said. "He told me his version of that. I only want to know that he has told me the truth. It is what I require of him as my second, and it is what I require from you as my lover. So before I request you to show me, I would ask you what happened and why I felt you dying—again."

"We were doing a lot of flying and landed where I requested. Ker was serving as a source for me; I did not concern myself with how Nathaniel fed. He always seems ... well fed."

Dagon nodded; content that this was moving towards what he wanted to know.

"I decided to enter the sea we had flown beside.

I was preparing for a dive and I suddenly became fearful. In light of what happened, I was right to be. I did not want to go to what I felt might be my death, without someone to witness me. Not to stop me, just to stand on the edge of the water and want me to return."

Dagon was silent but nodded.

"When I was a diver on old Earth, I always knew that I might not return to the surface. I had hardened myself to the fact that no one would care if that happened. But Nathaniel and I had had a connection. It was sexual most recently, of course, but he had seconded for me in my fight with Lore and then carried me out and preserved me as I was dying from my wounds. Of all the Shadakon present that night other than you and Morag, he wanted me to survive. And then he became closer to you."

"Were you distraught because of his treatment of you today?"

"He let me know that I had disregarded him or treated him indifferently on a number of occasions. That was when I knew that he had been aware of our tie, no matter how either of us may have acted recently. Otherwise he would not have cared. It saddened me that, once again, my Sidhe passion had complicated what might have been a friendship. I was, in an obscure way, pleased that he rebuffed me, because that also showed me his depth of feeling. He could not use me as a convenience, even one who came to him to be used." I stopped and sighed.

"I was upset when I returned to the edge of the water and made final preparations for my dive. But he stopped me and told me that you and he required me to return to both of you. I began my dive in a calmer state than I otherwise would have been in."

"And the hug?" asked Dagon, straight-faced.

"I asked him for a hug, for a moment of kind physical contact before I went below. At the last moment, he granted me that."

"Hmmm. So what happened to cause you, an experienced diver, to not heed your alarm to return to the surface?" Dagon seemed to have taken in the previous information without anger.

"At the limit of what I should do, given the air I had, I saw a temple below me. I saw a stone goddess that reminded me of things I had seen in pictures of archaeological sites on old Earth. Something not unlike what was in the cave here. The remnants of an Old Earth civilization, now gone and covered with the sprawl of overpopulation there. This planet has obviously been settled in the distant past. Or maybe it was the source of those who later thrived on Earth. Before the ruins were grown over with jungle and, later, the soya plantations."

"Ka and Io are descendants of those people, Dagon. I imagine that residual populations stayed here, retreating to the far edges of survival. They were eventually plundered for the Registry trade. They both have the ability to shut their mind to me, and seemingly to distract you from reading them. They have been in your presence for—years?"

Dagon was thoughtful; his hand no longer moving over my body. "They were a gift," he said. "From Mara."

"They are a delightful distraction. Whether they are more than that remains to be seen. But to return to what we were speaking of earlier. Once again I must take responsibility for attempting to force contact on Nathaniel. I did not have his consent and my emotional needs did not justify trying to force him to comfort me."

"I hear that," said Dagon. "And your accounts are basically the same. You are becoming clearer, Danu, about what you can and perhaps should do with your Sidhe powers. But he is able to make his own choices. I gave the two of you permission to do what you would."

"He did not believe that. He thought, and maybe still thinks, that I am a tool for testing his loyalty to you."

Dagon sighed. "Let us make peace now, Danu. The kind that holds us together in difficult situations." His hand dropped to make contact and then slowly moved down my body. He covered my mouth and my sigh with his own. We were together. My actions and Nathaniel's had not changed that. We moved towards our release and little peace.

The next morning, Dagon and I walked back over to the house where the sisters lived. They fluttered around him excited, but then caught his mood and retreated. He sat on the divan and pulled Io down on his lap. He put his arms around her and then tightened his grip slightly. I had meanwhile gotten my hand on Ka's arm. She struggled with more strength than I might have thought she had at her disposal, but I settled her between us without letting go of her.

"One sister at a time," he said gently. He laid Io's head in his lap and looked down at her. I felt her fight to resist him. "Ah, my beautiful little human, do not hurt yourself or make me do that. I realize now how successfully you have avoided my curiosity and observations. This will happen today. The only question is, how will it unfold?"

Dagon was silent although I sensed the intensity he brought to bear on the small, delicate Io. I had seen Nathaniel surrender more quickly than she did. I felt waves of anger building in Ka. They had prepared themselves for the various forms of taking that they would endure from the Shadakon, but they had not expected this.

I turned to Ka. "*Breathe with me, Ka. Settle yourself. We mean you no harm. But you already know that we have no idea who you are, where you come from, what you can do. I am here for this planet—possibly your original planet. Or at least one your people lived on for thousands of years.*"

I sensed Io go limp in Dagon's lap. He was in then. Without comment he gently laid her aside after a few minutes and turned to Ka. There were tears in her eyes, but Dagon remained matter-of-fact. He positioned her and, brushing aside her tears, locked onto her eyes and went within. She surrendered more quickly, perhaps realizing the futility of resisting. When he was done with the second sister, we picked them up and carried them to their bed, settling them close to each other.

Ker watched very quietly from the other side of the room. In what was truly an act of courage, she approached us and whispered that she was ready to provide information as well. I could have been the one to do that, but Dagon was far stronger than I was. Dutifully, she lay down beside him; he bent over her and I shivered. I too well remembered those dancing flames in the dark amber of his eyes. She opened like a flower, with no resistance to the process. I marvelled at the change in her since we first met.

Afterwards Dagon paced. He had unavoidably drawn energy from all three. Ker now lay curled on a blanket with a pillow in the corner of the room. She often slept on the divan with me, although neither the Shadakon nor the Sidhe sleep long or deeply.

Dagon finally sat and turned to face me. "I should have known that this planet was more complex than just an out-of-the-way place with a secondary population of humans." He sighed.

"The original people here were no doubt transplanted from old Earth, but not, I think, by humans. I'm guessing the Sidhe had a hand in it. However it could have been the original Visitors."

I thought then of the Sidhe king, my Fiórcara, easily naming the Guardian in the cave: "*a sky dancer.*" How he had communicated with her and, later, used his influence to secure my safety.

"There may have been several settlements," said Dagon. "They lived lightly on the land. And the land was rich with water and life then."

"Then after centuries of peace, the businessmen came," I said bitterly. He nodded.

"They brought with them bond-humans. Slaves basically, with no rights here and no power to return. The men worked in the waterworks plants that dug deep wells into the aquifers and also siphoned off available surface water. The women become breeders and prostitutes. When the project had run its course, and the waters of this planet were depleted beyond recovery, the businessmen welcomed the Shadakon and set up the Registry. They could now transform the last useful product of the planet—the life energy of the humans—into credits."

Dagon was a predator, but I saw him hiss in disgust. It was as though the humans had not just fractured into Shadakon and Sidhe and human, but more likely that another strain of human existed or showed up in the gene pool. Those who became the first power brokers. They were beyond personal or casual cruelty to their fellow humans. They treated them as things, as they did their environment and the well being of the planet. The others, the followers and supporters of them, seemed to sleepwalk through their lives as their doom approached. The fungus drug was helpful as well. Perhaps the last sweep of anything useful here was to bare the entire surface of the planet and mine whatever was accessible. I had no doubt that the fungi had been modified in a lab on old Earth.

We both sighed. "And now what, Danu?" Dagon asked.

I was silent as various plans and ideas arose in my mind. "The Sidhe king asked me to submit any proposals I could come up with, even if they were fantastical. I am going to report to him and make some suggestions. You can be part of that, Dagon.

But be aware that he can read me through the distance between us—not just with his stone, or through a computer screen."

I smiled then. "You may have made yourself available to him and his queen that way as well."

He went very still then.

"You have not nourished yourself today, Danu. I have taken from all three sources. Sit with me for a moment."

And so I sat, but I was not good at sitting. And we quietly joined as everyone in the house napped in recovery. We held the energy between us until we came to our mutual release and bliss. And then I took; he gave. And with that energy now within me, I was ready to face the Sidhe king.

CHAPTER TWENTY-SIX

A PLANETARY PUZZLE—WITH DISTURBING ANSWERS

I placed the small green stone beside the computer screen. It flickered with faint green light. I keyed in the connection with the Sidhe king and the stone's glow intensified. I called him by the name he had given me—and immediately he was on screen.

He looked at me intently. "You did not check the stone lately or you would know that I also wished to be in contact."

I nodded. "A significant oversight my king." I belatedly thought that I should kneel to him.

"Do not bother to kneel, Danu," he said. "You have obeyed at least part of my prime directive to you, which was to stay alive and return to me. But I believe that you required help with that. Once more you required rescuing."

He studied me carefully. I opened to his reading me then, because he obviously could do so at a vast distance, and I did not wish to hide anything from him, and because what was to be seen was important. He saw me hanging in the clear water, the temple deep below me. He saw—and I saw for the first time—Nathaniel working frantically over me, as his blood offering ran down my chin and was lost. I saw him slap me—hoping pain might still reach me.

"*A resourceful lover,*" Fiórcara smiled. "*The Shadakon handle pain creatively. My queen might want to see this later.*"

He returned to the scene of me hovering over the ruins of the sunken temple. "*Why did you linger so long, Danu?*"

I was open to him and revealed my truth without a qualm "*I wanted … to stay and serve Her …*"

The Sidhe king was silent. "*Dakini,*" he whispered in my mind. "*You are in tune with that, Danu.*"

"Dakini?" I asked.

Fiórcara, my king, was not just reading me. He was showing me what most interested him in my mind and we were able to discuss it.

"*Yes, Danu. As your power and control grow, we can converse at deeper levels.*" He sighed. "*We always did, Danu, but for you it seemed wordless.*"

I pondered that. "Dakini?" I questioned again.

"*The sacred feminine was part of the beliefs of the ancients in many cultures on old Earth. In India, temples were erected with explicit depictions of physical love. They practiced tantric sex, a way to focus and intensify sexual passion into religious ecstasy. In the early times, all women served Her, spending one night a year in one of her many temples, offering themselves to whatever man came to be with the Goddess and had anything of worth to offer in turn. It was uplifting to the women who served, and perhaps granted them health, fertility, and happiness in their marriage. Or not,"* added the Sidhe pragmatically.

"Later the practice of serving Her was taken up by women who were temple-trained in music and dance and erotic arts. They had great prestige and power in their community. Some had rich patrons and birthed children, but turned their infants over to others to care for. Sometimes they later brought their daughters to the temple to be trained and to lead their own lives of pampered service."

As the male sky gods and their hostility towards females and goddesses moved across the land, the temples fell into disrepair due to lack of offerings. The remaining dakinis were then seen only as prostitutes."

"Stop!" I didn't want to pass by an important part. I showed him Ka and Io dancing with each other for pleasure and to tone their bodies. I showed how adept they were at pleasing Dagon and how long they had kept him at bay from scrutinizing them, reading them. And finally how much resistance they put up to him before surrendering to his reading of them recently.

I showed the Sidhe king Io confidently leading me back into the darkness of the cave.

"Dagon said that he had seen in her mind that there had been colonies of people planted here or who got here well before space travel was even a concept to humans. Well ... to the human descendants of those who no longer remembered the Visitors and their technologies firsthand. I wondered if the Sidhe had had a hand in this. And if that was why they now had interest in this planet that was growing inhospitable to humans, the Shadakon and Sidhe. Perhaps the Sidhe had invested in it originally and brought humans who were better stewards of the land."

Fiórcara, my Sidhe king, was mind-silent and we sat in Between time. I heard the restless dry wind outside the building I sat in.

"Ah, Danu," the Sidhe king said aloud softly. "You are a treasure in so many ways and when I met you, you did not even partially know your worth. At first it was your fierce will and compassion that drew me. Then your irresistible body and the skills you wielded with it. I also saw early on that you were a strategist and used both rational and irrational sources to come to conclusions vital to us all." He paused.

"Then one night, I heard you proclaim yourself as 'Goddess' and I knew that was true.

I deferred to you willingly. You chose Céadar as your consort, the night before midsummer's eve, a night when we may have all perished. I accepted that too. I had entangled myself with my queen. I did so in defence. I felt that you and I had grown too close and you were too complacent about your hold on me."

"You flew an entire planet's life force. They showed up for you; beings from the bottom of the ocean that had never seen the light. Miniscule lives that stopped whatever they were doing to heed the call—your call!"

"You flew alone; you returned to Céadar—it was my task to accept that." He was silent again.

I knelt to him then. "*I was not the only one who suffered through my changes. Dagon was another. There would be more.*"

"A little more, Danu," said Fiórcara, gesturing me to rise and returning me to the matter at hand. "*The humans who now live in the grey city?*"

I sighed. I showed him what Ker had shown me earlier: dwellings with no pride of place, exhausted human workers sitting listlessly. I showed him the business of the Registry and how few children survived the organ traders, how few pregnancies resulted in even fewer live births. He hissed. He did not care for humans but he hated cruelty to any being.

"Could some of these be put to work to renew the planet?" I asked. "Could the sheep be separated from the takers who had stripped the planet of its water, vitality, and now might strip mine what would be left? All those minerals in the bottom of the dwindling seas ..."

"It is hard to tell who might be an openhearted human, and loyal to the Sidhe," he added.

"I'm sure some winnowing or sorting process could be devised," I suggested.

"Wanting to return to the land and attempt to bring it back to life would only appeal to certain types of humans." I showed him Io bringing the rock down on the squirming translucent cavefish, her fingers bloodied in her sacrifice to catch them. I showed him as she returned the unusable parts back to ones still living in the pool. Then, although I had barely been able to watch, I showed him her eating them raw, with a considerable act of will. "She had been living on fresh bread and fruit and delicacies. In less than a day, she reactivated her survival skills."

"Assuming that the Sidhe are even faintly interested in this project, what is the status of ownership of this planet?" he asked.

"Only broken portions are now owned under local law. The entire planet was never leased or bought. The takers probably figured it was an unnecessary cost; they would strip out what they wanted and then leave with no restoration fees to pay," I said bitterly.

"Buy the planet, ..." said the Sidhe king. "Hmmm ... And what other visible and invisible costs, Danu?"

"It needs a major infusion of water. Somehow."

"And?"

"The new role of the Shadakon who might remain, their sources and the human workers need some defining."

"Indeed. Is there more?"

"The powers that remain here need to be consulted, and their permission secured."

The Sidhe king I called Fiórcara, before I knew his title and even afterwards, (as it was the only given name I had for him) smiled at me.

"A lot to think about, Danu. To buy another planet ... Even though it is ravaged and even further out than Exterra. However, Earth-type planets are not that common."

"Dagon said that the Shadakon were actively looking for another planet. He said they hadn't found a suitable one."

"Yes," said the Sidhe. "But that is more a problem for the Shadakon to solve. Meanwhile."

He beckoned me closer to the screen. He ran his hands down my screen image in front of him. I flared into wanting him. I remembered again that there was no one that I had ever wanted like this. I felt his fingers wrap around to run down my back where he had marked me in passion many years ago. I always responded to that touch. I shuddered.

I was ready for him, although he was far, far away. I moaned.

"Ah my sacred dakini. Danu ..." He touched me in the centre of my heat and I went over the top to my bliss. I stood gasping even as he looked back at me calmly. I also realized that I had no hunger anymore, just the calming energy of the elixir of life.

"Always a pleasure, Danu," he said. "I'll be in touch."

And the screen went blank.

I felt a tremendous need to be out of the small house I stayed in. Without over-thinking it, I called Nathaniel. I knew how to call my Sidhe lovers, and I believe that Dagon and I had communicated at that level, although he might have no words for it. I shrugged. I had nothing to lose.

Fifteen minutes later Nathaniel was at the door with a flitter waiting. I walked out and got in with Ker in tow, without saying anything. The sun was an hour from setting.

"What are your intentions, Danu? It will be dark soon."

"You are skilled at flying in the dark."

"What would you have me tell Dagon?"

"Tell him that I realized that I need to be on the land in the dark, far from the city."

"*You need to ...*" I heard him think. "*Is this one of those Danu-needs-something-and-I'm-a-jerk-if-I-do-not-comply?*"

"It is nothing like that Nathaniel," I said. "There will either be full consent on both of our parts, or I will take in the feel of the land beneath me and the stars above. Only that."

He was silent. "I am afraid of you, Danu," he said unexpectedly.

"That did not stop you from taking me in the barracks," I said. "Leaving me marked in an uncaring act of sex and taking."

"You were with me at the end. Still, you took your revenge on me."

"Surely now, Nathaniel, you know that coming to me involves coming to a Sidhe. We tease and please and torture humans, and apparently Shadakon, with our attraction. But I have a human heart. I want to combine with people who care for me in whatever way they can. I expect no promises from you. But you, again, fought to save my life. I felt you calling me to return. You asked me to and I did. I returned at the moment the balance shifted—and I came back to you."

"I knew my Maker would grieve. I did not want to die that day, although perhaps I realized that it was likely. Some of this has recently been explained to me by my Sidhe teacher. I have an affinity for what lay below me in the sea. It called to me. I may have lived a similar life to those now almost forgotten, as a representative of Her."

"Her … And what happened to the men who came to such as you in that life?" Nathaniel asked.

"Once a year, if they made an offering, no matter how small, they could have their heart's and body's desire for a night," I said.

"And the rest of the time?"

"That depended on the choice of the female," I said. She could later grant or withhold her favours."

Nathaniel put the flitter down on a now bare hill. Two moons were rising, throwing crazy shadows over the white sand. He reached into the back and retrieved a few blankets. He gave one to Ker and also a small box of food and a water bottle. He indicated the back seat of the flitter. She settled in, seemingly happily.

He spread the other blanket out on the fine sand, with room for two bodies to lie without touching. He took off his shirt and bunched it under his head. His strong chest shone pale in the moonlight.

I felt the slow burn of wanting him begin in my centre and radiate outwards. I took off my own shirt. The desert wind did not cool my body.

Nathaniel rolled to face me. "I clearly did not do this right before," he said, "maybe in any of the befores. I would have you, Danu. I would give you this token of my respect, to do with what you wish." He placed a light stone in my hand. It seemed to take up my heat and radiate it back.

"Look at it later. Let the offering not colour what comes next." He studied me calmly.

"Is this your wish, Nathaniel? Do you agree to this?"

He laughed. "It will probably completely change the course of my life. It may endanger my position as Dagon's second, but yes. It has been my wish since I first saw you on Exterra. It seemed to me that all I could do was save you—for Dagon. So I did that. When you were left with me for your protection, I forced you to make good on the bargain you and Dagon made with me: that I could have you and your delicious Sidhe blood. I figured it was my only chance and I moved on it. You let me, Danu. We did what we did and I enjoyed taking from you.

But I wanted you more and more and it tormented me. I thought you toyed with me later; I see it differently now. At edge of the sea before your dive, you came to me and I felt like I finally had the upper hand. I would build on your fear and sadness. I would take you like a registry human, quickly and with no pleasure for you."

"But you did not do that," I said.

"No." The silence built around us. I could hear his heart beating, and mine. I could hear our breaths as we tried and failed to deepen our breathing to slow our climbing arousal.

"And now, Nathaniel?" I was moving into his moonlit eyes that I knew were bright amber. I knew what his body looked and felt like. It was one hand's reach away.

"It is all for you, Danu. Take what you will of me. It has always been for you."

I moved over him then, stripping him of his clothes and removing mine as well. I sat on him and did what I would until he put me beneath him and took me hard. He took me like an Alpha until I called out his name. Until I screamed in the darkness and I heard him howl. Then the stars spun down and I stayed in his arms and felt the rising energy of the earth beneath us.

It wanted to come—alive. It was enduring, waiting, even hoping—for rain. For water running in the creeks and rivers. It held the seeds of its own revival. I felt its whisper, its prayer.

It knew I heard it; I was its hope.

Nathaniel and I mated until dawn. That is how I thought of what we did that night anyway. He did not ask me for energy or blood, although he was aware I was not in deficit. At one point I touched his lips where his fangs would come down and then just turned my head and placed my neck beside his mouth. He licked me and moaned. "It is all for you too, Nathaniel. I freely offer you what you have held back from asking for tonight, much less taking. It is for you and I have been charged with faerie energy today."

He gently slid his fangs in and stiffened in pleasure. I felt waves of the life energy I had received roll over him. He took slowly, as if wanting it to last forever.

Perhaps it would. Hopefully we would live to find out.

In the morning we flew over the outskirts of the city before heading to Dagon's compound. There were some animals in the fields, overgrazing the thin lines of green along ditches with a few inches of water in them. There were wilting crops, alongside the windbreaks of stone fences or buildings. Any water placed on the surface of the ground here probably never got to the roots below.

"Food must be getting more and more expensive," I said. "What do you know about this, Ker?"

She shrugged. "People now go on the Registry four or five times a week. And they are tempted by additional money to offer more. If they falter, someone takes their children or relatives away. When they cannot get up to go to work, someone takes them away."

I had a horrible realization. In my mind's eye I saw the dried pale meat that Ka and Io enjoyed eating and Ker as well. I went totally silent, and Nathaniel noticed. I looked down at a few browsing animals and up to the spread of the city. I began to shake.

"Did you know?" I asked Nathaniel. He, too, was very silent.

"I suspected. I fly a lot and have seen few domesticated animals."

"And you didn't tell me? You brought it to feed the sources. You brought it yesterday for Ker!"

"They have to eat something, Danu. We can't import food for all of them."

"Does Dagon know?"

"I didn't tell him. But he also flies over the city and surrounding countryside."

For the first time since I had stopped eating food, I felt very ill. I put my head between my knees and tried to breathe regularly. The impulse to throw up, to rid my body of something toxic, persisted and I gagged.

"I'm glad we had last night, Danu," was all that Nathaniel said. "I think things will move very quickly now."

I nodded bleakly.

CHAPTER TWENTY-SEVEN

THE RECKONING

I called Dagon well before we arrived. He was standing outside and waiting when the flitter arrived. He looked and me and then Nathaniel and perhaps did not see what he expected.

"You are pale, Danu. Are you unwell?"

"I am very unwell, my Alpha," I said, kneeling before him. "I missed seeing something I should have seen weeks ago. I am horrified at my short sightedness. I have not given you or the Sidhe king adequate information."

I did not see any curiosity that my statement should have provoked. "Or perhaps you both knew," I said flatly.

"Should Nathaniel be present when we speak of this?" Dagon asked.

I shrugged. "It is not news to him," I simply said. "He said that flying over the city and outlying lands, and obtaining provisions for our sources made it obvious to him."

Dagon looked at me sadly. "Ah ..." was all he said.

"The humans are now feeding on each other. Their population is no doubt dropping steadily."

Dagon paced a bit and then looked at me. "The protein is taken from deceased humans. It is ... a form of recycling. We do not have any part in it."

I met his eyes with rage in mine. "The Registry humans are now allowed to go out four and five times a week. Some of those also sell blood off the record. No human, even in good health, can sustain that drain on his or her body. And they are not healthy, Dagon. There is scant produce and domestic animals. I'm sure that's reserved for the well off.

For the flesh and organ sellers. The drug dealers ..."

"When were the Shadakon going to move on?" I asked bitterly. "When the last horse died? You cannot travel without healthy hosts ..." I backed away from him as new realizations arose in my mind.

"There were many different clans and civilizations on Old Earth who faced this demise," Dagon said. "The archaeologists long ago found tool marks on the bones in excavated cooking pots and garbage heaps. Human bones, Danu."

I looked from one to the other of the strongest and best of the Shadakon. They knowingly took from human sources that had fed on the flesh of their own dead. The sweet spiced dried flesh. And more than that: they had both drunk from the blood of many human sources. The actual blood protein of their hosts included the dead protein of other humans already forgotten and nameless.

512

"I need to talk to Fiórcara," I said. "If he knows as well and sent me here to be part of this, then I will willingly die." I felt the comforting weight of the small sheathed knife beneath my clothes. "Or either of you can end me."

Dagon was silent. He had told me long ago, when he gifted me the small poisoned dagger that it would bring final relief to me, if I found that necessary.

I was not done with Dagon. "This is why you chose not to directly communicate with the Sidhe king! You had a sizable piece of information you were not ready to share."

I dashed into the communications room and placed the stone beside the screen. It was dark. I went through the complicated series of entries to connect me to the Sidhe, but the screen remained dark. Finally I called his name. The faintest flicker ran across the stone and then it was dark again.

I turned to face the two Shadakon who I held in my heart. I snarled in a way I hadn't since I had transformed to Sidhe.

I transited across the desert to the back of the cave, thinking only to grab the green stone as I left.

I had not brought a light. The glow on the walls was enough for me to see the niche where the Guardian watched. I knelt before her, waiting for her to respond to me—however she might. I opened my mind to her, knowing that she could access me anyway.

Time passed. The light in her chamber gradually grew brighter. I sensed a powerful and ancient presence before me.

"Rise, Danu, friend of the Sidhe king."

I stood. She was no longer bones in the niche in the cave wall. She stood before me, a timeless, beautiful goddess. Her skin, like the glow of the cave, was a vibrant green. Her eyes were dark and I knew she saw within my mind—and heart. I shivered in her presence.

"So, Danu … you were drawn to the temple where I once presided—where I still preside. You stayed overlong. Your final sacrifice was close, temple sister. Only a flicker of remaining will to pull that cord and leave was left, even as you began to die."

I nodded. "I yearned to stay."

"But you returned to someone important to you. A young, yet ageless, consort."

I nodded again. "He bade me return to him. He worked to return me to life."

The being in front of me nodded. "And he paid the price the ritual demands, and came to you. What was your worth, that night?"

I had completely forgotten about the small stone Nathaniel had given me. I found it where I had quickly stuffed it in my pocket and drew it out. It was too light to be a true stone.

I rolled it in my hand—a small piece of amber. Fossilized tree sap from the Baltic Sea of old Earth. The heart blood of some great tree that lived and died without interference from man and then was covered over with sediment and dark water, to harden and eventually float to shore. It was the colour of his eyes.

I held back a sob. This was a gift of great cost, but I had carelessly put it away. He had told me to put it away …

"And if it had been any less a gift?"

"I would have accepted a pebble from his hand," I said sighing.

"This is more than acceptable," she said, extending her hand. I placed the stone in her green palm and sighed again. I decided to ask my questions, before whatever fate ahead of me unfolded.

"The human population here are starving. They are consuming their own. The protein may or may not be harvested from the naturally dead. Where will this end?"

"All death is natural, Danu," said She before me. "An individual or a civilization comes to the end of its life and then, by one means or another, dies. Before that happens, in the final days, people take desperate measures. The life force drives all on to endure and survive as long as possible."

"Why would this concern you, Danu? Surely your Shadakon lovers will preserve you. They will take you with them when they leave?"

I shook my head. "I was sent here by the Sidhe to assess this planet; to see if it could be restored."

"Can it, Danu? What would be the cost to those here? I see you have dealt death to the humans before in sizeable numbers. Some you offered compassion to. Others not so much …"

I stood in silence.

"When you were a human, you ate meat of other beings?"

I nodded.

"Was the flesh and by-products of still other animals included in their food? Even added to the food of those that were vegetarian by nature?"

I whispered, "Yes."

"Did you have a problem with that?"

I stood silent. I shook my head.

"And now, although you do not wish to avail yourself of human energy, you have accepted it as necessary."

"Yes," I said. I remembered Dagon then, refusing to let me take refuge in silence. A wave of sadness passed through me. I had said goodbye to neither of them. I looked at and felt my Maker hand. It held steady. He would know the same of me—until I reached the end of my energy.

"You would come here and die, Danu? What would you accomplish by that action? I have a whole planet dying around me. Another death would not necessarily please me. You have already indicated that you would do so if I wished. That is enough."

I saw myself hanging over the temple, yearning to enter it, and stay.

"Yes. I will call the Sidhe king now. I believe this project has overwhelmed you." She spoke or made a sound and the stone flared to life. For my benefit she allowed me to perceive what passed between them. "*I have your Danu with me. She came offering her death as a sacrifice. It is not acceptable to me. I have enough death here already. You can see for yourself what she struggles with. She is not easy with the natural consequences—plague, starvation, self-annihilation ...”*

There was no immediate answer and then I sensed Fiórcara in my presence. My body was sure he was here and even on this terrible day, I was kindling as I always did.

The Sidhe king was in front of me. *Had he transited from one planet to another!*

“That is not important now, Danu. Although you must have known that my queen does not travel by spaceship.”

I knelt before him until he put his hand on my shoulder. “What you are asking both of us, Danu, is to intervene in a very large pattern—the death spiral of a planet. Your death is not required as proof of your commitment. This is an unusual situation. However, the Goddess has manifested differently today. You are in the presence of Green Tara.” He bowed low to her.

“Take us to speak with Dagon, who even now has Nathaniel in the skies searching for you. Had he thought to ask his human source Io, he would have known where you were, of course. The Shadakon see themselves as outside the pattern of fate and circumstance. You never did. That’s when I realized you were not truly of that clan.”

He nodded and bowed again to She who stood before us in her manifestation of timeless strength and beauty. Then he took my arm and nodded at me, and we were in the centre of Dagon’s home, in a great hall filling with Shadakon.

Dagon knew the moment I arrived. He called in Nathaniel from his search and strode to the dais in the front of the room. He had already called a meeting of the Shadakon.

He thanked everyone for gathering on such short notice, but that there was a matter that could not be put off any longer. He would explain what he could and had also asked his Sidhe consultant to attend. To his pleased surprise, he had said, the king of the Sidhe was also attending. He asked everyone to provide every courtesy to him and listen to what he would say carefully.

I didn’t hear every word; it felt like many words were missing as I went within, trying to formulate what I would say. That I could say.

I heard Fiórcara in my mind. *“Speak about a cooperative effort to save this planet! At least some of its humans, and the Shadakon ... I will fill in any necessary details.*

I was in deficit and unsure how to continue forward. But go forward I must. I flew the slight distance to where Dagon stood, joining him, but well to one side and not touching him. I knelt quietly until he raised me.

I stood and looked over a gathering of Shadakon. Some of them had undoubtedly been in the hall the day that the clan yelled for my death at the hands of my mate. And also at another time when I fought Lore to preserve his position as Alpha.

I no longer felt as sure as I had then. Then I had believed, I had felt within, that all would come around well. I was not so assured now.

“Shadakon, I greet you both as a Shadakon and Sidhe. I have endured the trial by hunger to claim the first. I was later accepted by the Sidhe in a decision that they said had never been made before. And, yes, before that I was human; a human that did not fit with other humans. But knowing differently now, I stand before you with those bloods mixed within me."

I sensed the beginning of restlessness.

"And I stand before you in deficit." I heard some hisses from the middle of the room.

"It would seem that this is my second trial. For I will not feed off humans that eat their own, whose blood carries the protein of those who recently had names—human names. All the human sources here are now drained of energy and blood and then turned into food for the temporarily surviving others. And, I suspect, many who aren't quite dead meet the same fate. The planet no longer provides the necessary nourishment to them.

There are a few animals and wilting crops to be seen—those that exist are for show. You are feeding off the dead." A low murmur swept across the crowd.

"The planet can be rehabilitated. It will be long and costly. It needs to be replenished with water—a lot of water. It needs foresters and farmers and such to nurture the returning life. There are still seeds in the ground and perhaps a scattering of surviving animals. Not enough to feed a large population of humans for a very long time. The humans could work the land, and live very frugally off their proceeds. They would have to be monitored. As their vigour returns with hard work and nourishing food, they could be shepherded by the wolves who have always watched over humans—taking no more than was expedient. The Shadakon could return to being the predators they are and were ... who came to the humans in the night or woods and ran them as the prey that they are."

There was a sharpening of interest now.

"Most of the humans are already useless," someone shouted. I let time pass before I answered. I searched my heart to see if I could say what I needed to say.

"The ones with the will to survive will be divided into work groups. They will be augmented by humans from Old Earth who are still managing to survive in the remaining marginal areas there. In time, these will become separate clans, with different languages and skills. They will benefit from the survival skills of indigenous peoples—African, Australian, Amazon basin peoples living in threatened reserves."

"And the others?"

"The Shadakon are searching for another planet. Meanwhile, neither they nor the humans have anywhere to go.

If there is a little water, then those in the cities here can be taught greenhouse and hydroponics agriculture. Plants like to eat the calcium and nitrogen and such sourced from dead bodies. There will be plenty of that. The Shadakon will meanwhile import foodstuffs."

There was silence. I shrugged. "Or fly away with no destination in sight, in ships full of half-dead humans."

"And why would not the rest of the galaxy return to plunder the planet again?"

Suddenly the Sidhe king stood on the other side of Dagon, his keen green eyes looking out over the Shadakon. The silence was absolute.

"Because the Sidhe will buy this planet, as we bought the one we currently reside on, once called Exterra. We will hold the title. But we will not do the killing to prune the herd or chase away human businessmen." He hissed. "You will do that. We have already proved that this was an amenable agreement between the Shadakon and Sidhe on Exterra."

"The humans were all chased away and killed off. We had to leave."

"Yes. And here you are, still thriving."

Dagon then took control of the remainder of the meeting. There were meetings scheduled and an investigation of those who ran the Registry and the body recycling businesses—food and organs. I was sure that this group would be healthy and could provide a helpful protein contribution.

I felt myself fading, the edges of the room disappearing in a hazy gloom. I felt the beginning of the true pain of the Hunger. I wanted no Shadakon-tainted energy. I felt the Sidhe king take my hand and then there was a longer stretch of black than I had ever remembered before and then—I was in Between on Exterra.

I sat propped up facing Fiórcara, his face was calm but not sympathetic.

I fought to stay focused. I would ask for nothing from him. He had sent me away in a spaceship that took weeks to arrive. In that time I had bonded with Dagon—or perhaps Dagon had bonded anew as I had never stopped feeling that I was part of him. Meanwhile, Nathaniel's ambitions grew quietly in his own heart. I also got to experience the life of a source, kept in a drawer and used without the ability to make a move. Or to even be able to think about consent.

Finally, I had made a bargain much as the women on the Registry had had to make. I gave myself to Nathaniel. I made the usual trade that women make who turn themselves over to whatever demands a man has—in return for safety, for the ability to live another day.

"Not just to preserve me—but also Dagon!"

"Yes, Danu. We have spoken of this before. You love even those who may not be loyal to you. It is your weakness, and your strength. Few can remain unchanged by what you bring them.

"If I had known I could return …"

"Yes, Danu. But if you had known that, they would have known that too. Instead you have not one but two powerful Shadakon leaders—an alpha and one near alpha—wishing to protect you. One would restore a planet for you; he has already proven that."

"Dagon will soon be challenged by his second. Only one Alpha will walk away from such a decisive battle."

I shivered in pain and in hunger and turned away from his deep green eyes.

"One more question, Danu, before you drink a cup of elixir that will bring strength and healing. On awakening, who do you want with you?"

"Both," I whispered, picturing him and Céadar in my mind. "I would not choose."

"So it shall be. Happily, here you are a Sidhe as are we."

He handed me a familiar wooden cup filled to the brim with a cool draught of elixir.

It smelled green and of things far away. I drank it to the bottom. And then I fell swiftly down below dreaming to a place of healing and silence.

CHAPTER TWENTY-EIGHT

I GET A NEW JOB DESCRIPTION

When I awoke I knew it had been a long time since I had lay down. I was thirsty and Céadar handed me another cup of elixir. This was lighter and more familiar to me.

Fiórcara was not present. I tried not to appear surprised and in truth was content with who was in front of me. I loved Céadar although I did not speak of that to him very often.

He took the now empty cup from my hands and put an arm around me. It was warm, sun-warmed, and felt strong and dependable. I leaned into him, sighing.

"Ah Céadar—I had no certainty there. I could not see the path ..."

He laughed. "Our king has gone off to get provisions for your new planet. The largest gift will be water. There is now the water from many sources in the galaxy in orbit around it. Meanwhile he has been consulting with human lawyers to make sure the contracts cannot be broken."

"And Dagon?"

Céadar sighed. "Dagon's rule over the Shadakon has been shattered. Some are leaving, perhaps even back to old Earth. Many are resisting the information that you gave them. They are still using the sources on the Registry, although the ownership of that has changed hands. There are strict limits now as to how often a person can serve in a week. So the offerings are getting smaller. There are now children and old people who respond to a call for a source."

"And Nathaniel?"

Céadar smiled and touched my cheek. "You were busy in your time away. You now have another knight who would save you if he could—and he did recently. Another rescuer, Danu.

Nathaniel is working to organize the humans who are willing to try to survive and replant and protect the land. They are getting better rations, so their ranks are swelling."

"How long have I slept, Céadar?"

"An Earth year perhaps." Céadar shrugged.

I pushed my feet down and put weight on them. I started sliding down into a boneless heap and Céadar grabbed my arm. He pushed me back up on the sleeping platform—my sleeping platform, for surely this was my hill house.

I had many questions that arose when I thought of the balance between Dagon and Nathaniel. "Will Nathaniel have to challenge Dagon? Will they have to fight until one of them falls?"

Céadar bent his head, perhaps to avoid eye contact. "That is the way of the Shadakon," he said softly.

"And if our Sidhe king were to die or cease to be available—would his queen take his place?"

"Such a thing is unlikely, Danu. But if he ceased to be, his queen would need another confidante and consort. She would not rule alone."

"And that would be you, Céadar, would it not? You are the king's second and already well-acquainted with the queen?"

He looked at me with his beautiful moss green-turning-fall eyes. "These are strange questions, Danu. Why do you ask them?"

It was my time to sigh. "Dagon gave me to Nathaniel much as the king gave me to you. It was not a random choice. Although I struggled against the arrangement, it came to me later that it was a true gift to me."

"How so, Danu?"

"I resented Nathaniel, even though earlier on Exterra he had brought me back to life with his blood, and then had sheltered my injured body and guarded us all when we could not fend for ourselves. On my arrival to the new planet, he immediately let me know that he would have me. He was part of a bargain we had struck to prevent the relationship between Dagon and I from being obvious and inappropriate to his subjects. On our arrival, Dagon stood with his Shadakon mate beside him. I stood to the side, with Nathaniel's claiming arm, unasked for, around my waist."

Céadar looked at me without speaking. In his eyes and quiet mind, I sensed an invitation to continue the story or be silent. He waited peacefully.

"Nathaniel was more than adequate as a sexual male with a purpose. I did not fight against what we both knew would happen. I was hot and sad at the same time when he took from me, something I had only shared with one person before—with Dagon. And then he left his mark on my neck, not bothering to lick it closed. I saw this as a further challenge to Dagon and a mark of disrespect to me."

Céadar knew that when in deep passion, I had shared moments of slight pain with my lovers. He had participated in such a session with Fiórcara lying on the other side of me. They had both marked my back that night and I knew he remembered it with pleasure.

"There are marks ... and marks," he said. "Yet you fear for Nathaniel's safety as well as Dagon's?"

"I would be the loser no matter who won a fight to the death," I said.

"I am a Sidhe," Céadar explained. "We do not fight with each other for power or sexual connection. Besides I am tied to the king as surely as you are. I am his, whatever else I might be.

I would have fulfilled his plan for you whether you initially wanted me or not. I would have glamoured you, and interfered with your true consent. You would have come to me eventually."

I looked at him and he looked back with his calm forest-deep eyes.

"But you did not have to do that," I said. "I accepted you whole-heartedly."

"Yes, Danu. You and I both know that is true. What might have begun as duty quickly turned to true affection. Perhaps Nathaniel now feels the same way …"

I remembered the look in Nathaniel's eyes as he bent over me at the water's edge, his wrist streaming blood that I had refused or been unable to swallow. He wanted me to return to him. I made the decision at that moment to open to his gift of blood and life and what he offered me.

Céadar smiled and brushed my lips with his own. "We do not always know who we should …" he paused and smiled, "… who we should love."

Then he kissed me again and I lost thoughts of what might be or had been. I reached up to his sun-warmed skin and strong arms. He took me up slowly, pausing to watch me watching him, me wanting him more and more. At some point I moaned and called his name. He smiled then and brought himself to me and I knew I was back home.

I walked around Between, regaining my strength after my long rest. I drank the elixir of life and savoured the taste of the life freely given in it. I felt the nervous energy of what I had taken in while with the Shadakon fall away to be replaced by a deep peacefulness. On the third day of Between time, Fiórcara, my Sidhe king, appeared beside me.

I was not lacking in being pleasured but I gasped as I felt his energy. He smiled.

"Awake and ready for your next task, Danu?"

I knew somewhere in my mind that I must ask many questions and receive information.

But all thinking seemed to be suspended. I just looked at him—and fell into his gold-flecked eyes. My body … my body had missed him even as I had moved towards others. He offered me something beyond what could be found in anyone else's arms. It was why I had left the Shadakon I loved to return to him again and again. He was sun and wind, earth and water. I had always known that he was one with the life force of this planet. Now I knew he could transit across space, and terra-form a dying world. He was not unlike the green goddess he had conversed with on my behalf in the cave.

I did not take my eyes off of him as I saw his hand slowly reach out to touch me. Something within me wanted to savour every moment between not-yet-touching and touching.

He smiled. "Once you needed the fall elixir to achieve this state. You asked me to join you in that and I declined, saying that I had no need to alter my consciousness. Now you are here, between moments, with me. Your eyes and mind are opened."

His hand reached and wrapped lightly around my arm. I sighed.

"Has Céadar been remiss in bringing you back to your body and its pleasures?"

"No, my king. We have a lasting pleasure between us."

"But you want me now?"

"You promised you would be here when I awoke."

"Ah faerie promises … you know they are not always as foolproof as others would like." He studied me. "Would you compel me to come to you, Danu?"

I shook my head, turning aside so that he might not see the tears on my cheeks. As if he didn't know. "No, my king," was all I could manage.

"Let us take a walk, Danu. Neither reject nor be impatient to receive the energy I share with you." He tucked my arm into his. I shivered at the increased touch.

"I am teaching you something now, Danu. It will ultimately be your great pleasure, but you must learn to mask your passion, if necessary. You may stand between two Shadakon who would kill each other to secure you. I know you would not want to know that you threw the balance to one or the other. It must work out without your influence. Do you agree?"

"Yes, my king. I know that Dagon gave me to Nathaniel; perhaps not unlike you gave me to Céadar—and him to me. It seemed necessary at the time. But with time I have reconsidered that. Dagon could have left me in deep sleep, to be revived at some convenient time. Instead …"

"Good, Danu." Fiórcara ran one finger lightly up and down my arm. I blazed with this slight attention.

He laughed. "You are not making this lesson easy for me." He led me into the grove and I leaned up against the sheltering tree there.

"Nathaniel was young and impatient. He said he had wanted me for years; he had saved me for Dagon over and over again when we were on Exterra. During our first connection he took me as an uncaring Shadakon—he drove me up to sexual wanting and then took my energy and blood. I had only shared blood with Dagon. I had made no real consent to Nathaniel—and then he left his mark on me!"

"Yes," said Fiórcara. He reached out and touched my neck in the exact place Nathaniel had taken from me. "Sometimes we cannot make full consent. The outcome has to determine if in fact we would have given it, if allowed. You did not consent to me the first midsummer's eve. You did not come to me then, but I knew you would make your way back to me. That you would come of your own free will and offer full consent." His eyes were on mine and I knew he could already see the whole story of Nathaniel and my mating dance together. "Then what happened?" he encouraged me.

"I punished him—with sex. I didn't think I could do that. You had said that my predatory skills would draw in any male, I didn't think that I would use those skills against someone."

We were now both studying a picture in my mind's eye. Nathaniel was lying still on his back in the desert after I had finished with him.

Fiórcara smiled. "The Sidhe are known for this. We are not always considerate of our pursuers."

"*But then?*" He shifted to mind-speak, as did I.

"*He had his own small revenge. I feared diving the day I almost died. I felt my death close—and I was right, but it would have been by my own choice. He had started to take me uncaringly when I went to him for some comfort before my dive; seeking some sense that I was in control of my own destiny."*

Fiórcara smiled. *"Did you ever truly believe that, Danu? You surrendered to death in the hands of a professional predator—who had taken you home to enjoy at his leisure. And then you surrendered to me, who did not offer you a home at all. You did earn your right to be in this home with me, however. And I believe that you surrendered to Nathaniel, and he to you, later.*

We were now watching as Nathaniel and I lay beside each other out in the desert and he presented me with a ritual offering to allow him to come to me: a small, exquisite piece of amber.

"Yes. You allowed him to come to you as a suitable lover, Danu. And you forgave him his missteps and received him as a goddess. He will never forget that night ... as long as he lives."

I heard what he had just said. Fear knifed into my heart.

"He told you he understood the cost, Danu, and that he was willing to pay it. But assume nothing. The future, in this case, is not locked in.

That is one reason that we are spending this afternoon in what for you is perhaps painful anticipation."

He leaned forward and ran his thumb down my lips; they opened for him without my bidding. He continued down, touching the place where my heart's blood beat close to the surface. Then to my now healed arm, that Dagon had broken in a storm of jealousy and powerlessness to control me many years ago. I moved imperceptibly.

"Hold, Danu, hold." Catching my eyes completely, he continued to touch and touch until I wept. *"Ah, Danu of so much passion; what do you want from me today?"*

"When I first said this, I did not know your power. I now know more ... but certainly not all. But I stand by my first choice. I would have all that you would bring to me," I said.

He smiled at me in the sunshine. He swept away my clothes and then his own. I realized then that he was an ageless power much as Green Tara was. He lay me down on the grass and I was his. I would make any offering to him that he requested.

"Only your full surrender, Danu," he said calmly even as he brought me up and up into a spiral of desire. "And I have had that since our first midsummer's eve together." He continued with me until I called the name I had for him: heart's friend, and then begged with no words at all. I felt the energy of the planet rise up and take me. I woke up later to find myself in the grove in twilight, a cup of elixir beside me.

It was only a few days later when the Sidhe king showed up at my door and smiled and shrugged at Céadar who was at my side. Céadar walked out without a complaint.

"It's time for you to go back to work," the king said to me. "Are you ready to return to the desert planet?"

I had many concerns, not the least having no choice but to return to using humans for my nourishment. I also wondered about the status of the balance of power I would discover between Dagon and Nathaniel. I wondered if one or both of them had missed me. Dagon was still my Alpha, who I had been mated to, but that time had passed. We continued to have heart-ties, but I felt the draw and invitation from Nathaniel. He was a rising Alpha to-be—if he lived. I sighed.

"You will not have to draw energy from the humans, Danu. I will provide you with an alternative that is planet-sourced. As for your lovers—I suggest you step back from choosing one over the other, no matter what the situation you find yourself in. You are Sidhe. Sidhe share their passion, and I suppose their love, with whom they choose. You understand that now and know that when Céadar walked out a moment ago, he would not spend time worrying what you—or we—were going to do. He went to find something else that needed his attention. At one point in your continuing friendship, you stepped back from him, to give him more room to do what he might want to do. In doing so, you assured your place as one whose door was open, and that you might indeed wish to re-join with him later. Again, a very Sidhe response. I have enjoyed watching your interactions with him. I also enjoy taking in the energy of your passionate nights together."

The Sidhe king knew that I had eventually understood that he partook in the energy raised by the sexual activities of those around him. He enjoyed watching in person and by experiencing mind-to-mind. All the Sidhe did, but I now could sometimes feel his presence. I was not sure how far his abilities reached. *Could he monitor me on another planet?*

"I monitored, but I decided not to interfere," he assured me. "I feared for you when you were unexpectedly brought to the Guardian. I hope you have a conversation with that human, Io, about this.

Did she truly want you immediately dispatched of by She–Who–Waited, or had she been instructed to bring you to Her? An interesting story either way. And how did she know where to take you, such that she walked so confidently in the dark?"

"But all this will be worked out 'on the job,'" Fiórcara said and took my arm.

And I was back on the desert planet. Except the extreme dryness and aching pain of the land had been somewhat relieved. There were signs that water had recently run in the gullies and dry streambeds. The sky was grey and there was no greenish yellow cast to the wind.

"It rains hard here every night," the Sidhe king told me matter-of-factly. "It clears in the morning. It will do so for the next hundred years, although eventually we may taper off the rains to several times a week. The water needs to soak into soil that has little capacity to absorb it. That will change."

He transited us to a small circle of green around a pool of water that seemed to be staying put. Already green shoots were coming out of the ground, the tallest ones being as tall as I. He placed his hand affectionately on the bark of one.

"This will break up the soil and feed the many others who come after. It is a trail-breaker—not particularly useful to humans, but very valuable to what must happen here."

He waved to me, as if he was introducing us. I went to my knees, touching my fingertips to the surface of the water and then rose to touch the base of the tree. Its energy was—fierce. It had found a place to survive and was going to do so.

Fiórcara laughed. "You awoke the will of this land. It will now live—with our help."

When I looked back, I saw my footprints pressed into the now moist ground.

"I will take you to Dagon now. No doubt you will be in the presence of Nathaniel soon as well. Control the evidence of your desire, Danu. You must walk a narrow path.

I cannot tell you how it will work out. Since you love them both, this might be very hard for you.

But do not let your heart mislead you. Wait for this to unfold."

"But first …" He took my hand and plunged it into the earth. I felt only dryness and the sun-heated grains of sand.

"Deeper," said the Sidhe.

Then I felt what he felt. Down below was great heat and energy. The interface between the heat from the core of the planet and the surface rock and soil was a place of melting and shifting. I felt true fear then and sought to bring up my arm.

"No, Danu. Or you must continue to take questionable nourishment from the humans. There is almost unlimited energy here. What you need and take will not be a hardship to this world."

He had linked his fingers with mine and began to draw a wisp of the molten earth energy up and into our linked hands. I expected to be burnt but surrendered to what would come next. I trusted Fiórcara. Instead of feeling burnt, the core of my sexuality at the base of my spine began to glow and energize. It was unbelievably pleasurable and I shuddered.

The Sidhe king had stopped accessing the fiery plume of energy but I could not. I wept when he pulled our hands from the sand. My body ached to continue to merge into the heat and fiery darkness.

"Yes, Danu. You are close to being undone and losing yourself. You must stop well before you want to. This energy may last you for days. Do not be over-eager to return to it too often. Soon there will be a sufficient life force that you can more safely tap."

I wanted him. I wanted him. My body was aglow with the need to discharge some of the deep earth energy.

He shook his head. "This is how you will arrive before Dagon. It is a different and stronger version of midsummer's eve energy. He may be angry with you for leaving him to deal with the fallout of your talk to the Shadakon. He may want to refuse you. But he will not be able to do so."

We stood in the centre of the courtyard of Dagon's home and fortress.

"Call him," Fiórcara said.

I stroked my Maker hand and noted that it flared. Close then. I reached out to him, using the link we had not used in a long time. Perhaps my increased strength made it possible.

He quickly appeared, glowered at us both, and turned his back.

"Go back to wherever you go when you are not here, Danu. This world is in reclamation thanks to you. But I have lost my place as leader. I have no workable suggestion for the Shadakon. They are used to the Registry and the ease of finding sources by merely exchanging credits. But now the Registry does not send attractive enough humans such that it is pleasurable to drive them to heights of sexual energy. They send old men and young girls. Broken down breeders. And no one sells their blood."

"As it was, we were going to hell. But on a daily basis, it was pleasant enough for the Shadakon. Now we should believe that the humans would learn to grow their own food? Oh! And there is no more drug source. The fungus has almost completely disappeared."

He was pacing in front of us now.

"We were all well-off. But we must now import food to feed what human sources there are. Many of us, of course, have some humans stashed away. But sharing is now problematic." He was speaking directly to me.

"I no longer have need of human sources, Dagon.

I will not be a strain on your hospitality—if in fact I am welcome here." I stood calmly, feeling the deep earth energy radiating through my body. I dispassionately noted that he was aware of me and trying not to engage with me. *So be it*, I thought.

"I am not even sure why you are here, Danu. But perhaps it is because Nathaniel has less comfortable accommodations to offer you. Or perhaps you do not enjoy watching him taking his truly Shadakon pleasure with the remaining hosts."

I stood like a tree. I reached down into the earth and felt the fire that had briefly reached up to me. I thought of the temple that I had seen through the layers of blue clear water. I thought of the darkness of the cave that Dagon's own human source had led me unerringly through. I waited in Between time.

He finally sighed. "Sidhe king, I apologize for my lack of hospitality. I will speak to you today. Tomorrow though, you may need to renegotiate with the new Alpha."

I stood like a stone. I put away all signs of the fires that raged within me. I would not make this worse. The Sidhe king had warned me that my neutrality was essential for a best outcome. If I swayed in pain, I hoped that it was not noticeable.

Dagon ushered us into a small private room and shut the door.

He sighed. "The plans that were put into place are actually activating effectively. It is obvious that the planet is reviving with the huge amount of water it is now receiving. I saw a small cloud the other day in the desert. There are plants coming up—more than I expected. The human mentors the Sidhe brought here have taken the first groups of humans into the deep wilderness. They are still reliant on airdropped rations of food and water, of course, but they are building small rock-ringed settlements. They are alive. As far as I know, the Shadakon are not preying on them.""There is a large group of Shadakon returning to Earth.

There is always room for more death dealers there." He sighed. "I will not return to old Earth. In the end, there should be one Alpha here. It will be hard to kill Nathaniel; it would also be hard to give up my long life …"

I attempted to remain utterly and completely still.

"Do you have any preference, Danu? Would you be more satisfied to see my knife in his heart? Or his in mine?"

I looked deeply into his dark eyes and saw the flames burning there. He was under duress, but graceful in meeting his fate. I loved him as much as I ever had at this moment.

I raised my chin. "I was a Shadakon before becoming a Sidhe. It would not be acceptable for me to ask for clemency for either of you. I will not have my hand on the blade. I will ask neither of you to stay your hand. However, if you or he dies tomorrow, a part of me will die as well. My heart will feel the blade."

"That is the truth," I said, turning from him. For a moment I wished I had never held onto my love for Dagon. I regretted that decades after he had left I had not accepted that he was gone … forever. But I had not and still could not.

I had been willing to travel with him—anywhere—to extend our time together. I also realized that the Sidhe king had worked to reconnect us. Dagon had foreseen additional pain between us. But now neither of us would be spared this.

"I would go somewhere quiet," I said. "The two of you can talk as you will." I walked outside, where the stars were beginning to brighten in the sky. The courtyard was purely ceremonial. There was nowhere to sit, no place of comfort. I stood pondering my next move.

When I heard a flitter arrive, and then the sound of voices in the outer house where perhaps Io and Ka still lived, I knew that this day could get worse—had just gotten worse.

Nathaniel walked over and stood in front of me. He was now ready to be an Alpha. It was in his walk, his stance, his scent. He was in his glory. I remembered noticing the changes in Dagon when I first saw him after he transformed into an Alpha.

He gently turned my face up to his and only said, "I am sorry, Danu. I will be standing when this is over tomorrow."

I was not so sure. Dagon had stood down a lot of contenders in his long life. It might be that both would fall, never to rise again. Or Dagon would stand in a circle of the heart-blood of Nathaniel, his loyal second.

I shook my head. "I cannot wish either of you to be successful. Either way, I will take the blade." I gestured towards the room where Dagon and the Sidhe king were in conference. "Perhaps there is an answer in there. I can only offer you my sorrow."

Nathaniel looked at me with some surprise. "Dagon was your mate and still is your Alpha. I took you against your true will and attempted to hurt you when you came to me in fear and needing comforting. Why would you care overmuch if I perish tomorrow?"

"You later came to me as supplicant to the goddess within me. You paid the price and I willingly took you as a lover. In my mind, we mated that night, that one night, under two moons. Our passion fed the planet and gave it hope."

I turned away to attempt to hide my tears. "Nathaniel, this is not helpful to you. I am going back to the cave. I will entreat the Guardian there, who is sometimes compassionate, to let this come around without either of you paying the ultimate price. Once again, I will offer my own life."

He just looked at me in the starlight.

Did he have any idea how strongly I had felt about the night we had—before the truth of this planet and how its humans were living drove me deep into myself? Before the Sidhe king returned me to Between to heal?

"I did know, Danu," he whispered in my mind. "Sometimes I thought it was only my fantasy. But I knew better."

He turned and walked over to the small closed door.

CHAPTER TWENTY-NINE

THE CAVE OF PAIN

I transited to the mouth of the cave and its small creek. It was running more strongly now, indicating that the deep aquifers that fed it were being replenished. I decided to walk up the creek bed into the back of the cave, hoping my body would not attract the small—or larger—flesh eaters that I had seen Io catch by waggling her fingers.

The footing was good enough. My eyes adjusted to the faint luminescence on the walls. I went forward until I sensed I was in the round chamber where the Guardian waited. I knelt, prepared to wait.

At first I heard only the drip and faint flow of water. Underground time ... the drips were hypnotic and soothing.

When I had thought that I was wrong, that the Guardian would not respond to me without the Sidhe king standing beside me, I heard the sound of almost breath with faint words under it.

"Once again you are here, and once again you come offering me nothing I want. I appreciate the work the Sidhe and you have so far accomplished, but why are you here tonight?"

I was silent, afraid to make real what was happening by catching it in words.

"Oh ... then I will see ... for myself."

I felt cool hands on my head and saw beautiful green feet in front of me. She was alive and vibrant and very old and powerful. If anyone could help me ...

"You love and want them both: an Alpha and his second who is ready to challenge him for that position?"

"Yes, Goddess."

"You are pledged to the Sidhe king but are also heart connected with his second?"

"Yes, Goddess. But that is of little consequence to the Sidhe."

"Yes, Danu. But of more consequence when his queen arrived."

"For the most of my human life, I had held no interest in sex or sexual passion. I didn't believe I was capable of experiencing it and refused to fake my pleasure to reassure a partner. When Dagon brought me to my first sexual bliss I was astonished. I was even more shocked when I realized that it was my heart's desire that we be truly mated. We were each other's Makers." I held out my left hand and felt her stroke it gently.

"But then the Sidhe king summoned you."

"I held him off for a year—and there was Sidhe trickery. But I knew immediately I would have made my way to him eventually"

"Do you regret wanting and going to either of these?"

"*No.*"

"*Do you regret Céadar or what you learned at the hands of the Sidhe queen?*"

I smiled in memory of us at the hot springs, her long fall-silvered hair brushing my breasts as we kissed.

"*Ah ... but later when she wanted to end you?*"

"*She felt she was preserving the Sidhe and correcting a major error of her king. She apologized to me afterwards.*"

"*Do you regret lying under Nathaniel, in full consent in the desert?*"

"*No, Goddess. He set aside his Shadakon arrogance and assumptions about passion. He came to me humbly, seeking the Goddess. We stayed together through the night and when I rose, I felt that we had mated—if only for a brief time.*"

"*The Shadakon are intent on fulfilling their familiar pattern—challenge, fight, one or both die. There can be only one Alpha.*" I felt her mental shrug. "*You pit yourself against the dying of a planet and the heartlessness of a Shadakon ritual. Yet even the Sidhe king obviously favours you. What would you pay so that both could survive?*" Her voice had deepened and I wondered if I now was in the presence of the fierce Guardian.

"*I have offered you my life.*"

"*Yes, Danu. Yes. You have offered your life twice. I do not want it. But I am interested in how much you would pay to preserve your two Shadakon. How much pain you would accept before you chose one over the other? Or perhaps abandon both to their fate?*"

"*You have paid in minor physical pain.*" And here she ran one finger down my long-ago broken arm and along my collarbone. "*You have paid in loneliness and sadness. But how long would you stand between me and one or both of your lovers if the price was everything you could bear—and a little more?*"

"*What must I do, Goddess?*"

"*It begins now.*"

I felt pain in my body everywhere that I had ever been injured. I had broken my ankle once as a child and walked home on it, not wanting to draw attention to myself. It began to hurt as it had when I hung onto a fence panting, before forcing myself to go on.

The pain of holding my finger over a flame as a child, wanting to know—and finding out—what I could bear. I had never told anyone.

Then the many small, sharp slashes of slipped knives. The empty-tank aching lungs of dives I had barely returned from.

Depression while on the ship, such that I had considered stuffing myself in the disposal chute and sending myself out into space.

The trial by hunger ... I had hoped never to feel agony such as that again. That I had paid in full that night.

The feel of broken ribs grating together as I struggled to breathe after fighting Lore. The feel of my blood and life draining away.

Standing before Dagon with both arms injured, one broken by him due to his seemingly uncontrollable possessiveness of me.

The pain of condemning crews of incoming spaceships to death. Seeing them bloom into flames as we watched.

Knowing I would never see or be held by Dagon again; breathing to induce calm after yet more tears for him even decades after he left Exterra.

And finally, the dull thud of Dagon's mate's club as she broke my collarbone.

Each of these became a small fire that spread and spread to merge into a single inferno of pain. And the pain was not lessened by anything I could do.

I lay on the floor of the cave, understanding that there were worse fates than death. I felt the sheath and knew the small green stone was close. But already I doubted if my body functioned well enough to retrieve it.

I was quiet for a long time—attempting to deep breathe regularly and float in the calm sea of Exterra that I evoked. But any control I had could not hold. In time I sank into my own hot agony and breathed as shallowly as possible. When thirst and hunger were added to my pain I attempted to poke one hand even slightly into the dirt of cave floor.

I imagined the heat below and attempted to pull a thin strand of core energy up.

Suddenly I was hot and glistening with sweat. I was overcharged and wanted only to meld with that fierce energy. I must have achieved separation and for a moment I felt only intensity and not pain. I sensed that the Guardian came to me then and read me and my condition.

"Time has no measure here, Danu. They will still be in the last hours before fighting an eternity of time from now. I'm glad to see that you can recharge yourself. You will be conscious and aware until the end then. Choose one or none and all this will end."

I began calling the Sidhe king after a forever length of time. I wondered if birth was like this—but I believed that I was birthing the nightmare of betraying someone I loved. I would die with the answer, whatever answer, within me.

The Guardian laughed. *"Take out your message stone, Danu."* But I could not. I knew somehow however that Fiórcara was aware of my predicament.

Still later I screamed. I screamed until my throat felt like the desert was inside me. When I finally fell silent the Goddess returned to me. *"I will make this easier for you—which of them do you now regret?"*

I had no answer for her. I hoped they did not feel that my absence at the challenge meant that I was indifferent to the upcoming fight. Fiórcara had told me to hide my passion. Overwhelmed by pain, my pleasure centres joined in, in a horrible orgasmic spasm of intensity. I felt the sand in my wounds—*were they now open and bleeding?*

"Why do you not beg for death now, Danu?" I sensed the presence of the Goddess I would not. I would endure as this planet has endured.

I was a Shadakon. Shadakon do not kill themselves or agree to an easy death.

"Neither do Sidhe," I heard a voice say. "Do you have enough proof, Guardian?"

I was afraid to move. Even slight movement caused further agony. I dreaded trying to open my eyes, expecting sand and pain there too. I dimly saw the Sidhe king—and Dagon and Nathaniel. I felt their horror at my condition.

Dagon was first by my side. He put his hand on my head and took away some of the pain. Nathaniel was beside him. The Sidhe king stood observing the two attending to me. He smiled at me.

"Through the eye of the needle, Danu. Once more you stand firm."

CHAPTER THIRTY

THE LEAVE-TAKING

Dagon and Nathaniel took me to Dagon's house. I was placed in an empty room where I slept away the day. Dagon's bed and sitting room was next door. Nathaniel moved into the room on the other side of mine. I assumed they visited the beautiful humans that Dagon continued to maintain.

Later I woke to find myself between two large Shadakon warriors—without clothing on. They had quickly divested me of the shirt I slept in. Then they both worked in tandem to awaken my passion. They were persistent and relentless. I no longer remembered the false release and heat of pain. Here was only pleasure and more pleasure. I called out Dagon's name and then Nathaniel's. And then I just called out, lost to anything but what we three had brought into being. Soon after I heard a hoarse roar from Dagon and then another roar that Nathaniel made when he let go of everything and made his claim.

Eventually we talked. Dagon had acknowledged Nathaniel as an Alpha—but did not stand down from his own position. They simply declined to fight. Nathaniel would be in charge of the newly hired humans that were attempting to live and help the planet recover. Dagon ruled the Shadakon in the city at present. It seemed likely that he would lead them onward—somewhere. Meanwhile the humans were put to the task of growing vegetables. There was no animal protein, so they were now involuntarily vegetarians for the foreseeable future. As their general health and nutrition improved, they were able to resume being hosts on the Registry.

I continued to source my nourishment from the deep earth energy. But increasingly, green things were sprouting up.

In addition, the Sidhe had brought seeds from both Old Earth and Exterra and gave them to the humans on the land. The young plants were kept safe and watered under sun shields and behind fences.

Some of the humans were again growing the three sisters: squash, corn and beans. And in other areas the plants of the outback of Old Earth were slowly growing their bulbous root reservoirs—emergency water supplies for the humans. The people in the new circles of huts now hid when they saw a flitter fly close. The food drops became less obviously from a high-tech civilization. The food was wrapped in bundles of plant fibre; the water came in large, reusable pottery jugs. There were dull-coloured blankets and a few chickens and such to see what might survive. It was too early to say if the humans would enhance the planet or become its problem again. But meanwhile, small trees that sprouted spontaneously were thinned carefully and moved to other favourable locations. It rained hard every night, the water falling from giant chunks of ice kept in a low orbit around the planet. They were brought lower and the water was finally melted and free to fall precisely on land and sea.

Nathaniel was often away from Dagon's compound near the city. One day he offered to fly me on a tour of his various projects. He told me that we might be gone for weeks and I passed this on to Dagon. Dagon had kept his unspoken promise to me—to refrain from killing Nathaniel—and so far, had let us combine as we would.

I decided to take Ker with me. I thought that it was time to see if she could accustom herself to life outside the city. I no longer needed her as a source, although I was not sure if Nathaniel would need her or not.

In the first settlement I saw men working under the sun, digging their waste and any compost they had into the rows where they would later plant food crops.

Along the stone fences gradually growing bigger as they worked the land and moved the rocks to the side, were grasses and native plants.

Nathaniel put the flitter down behind a small hill. We walked in, him imposing in form-fitting black and high boots. He had asked me to wear my purple dress, which had been intended to impress the inhabitants of this planet. He looked very alien—wilder than the Shadakon who had previously opened his door to two human sources with about as much interest as someone receiving a fast food order. I stood behind him, my purple tunic dress floating around me as I had intended it to.

The people dropped their eyes to him and me and knelt. He put his hand on the head of the leader and made polite conversation. Were the seeds sprouting and growing? The little trees mostly thriving? Did they have enough to eat? Were their roofs holding back the nightly rain?

I sat silently, observing. In a short while, the leader beckoned two teenaged women to stand before Nathaniel. They trembled in fear, or perhaps more. He stroked the black hair of one of them and turned her face up to look into his. With his hand only lightly on her shoulder, he took from her. He repeated his actions with the second. He then thanked his host and we walked back to the flitter where Ker was waiting.

This was dignified and mysterious. Where was the Shadakon who took blood at every opportunity?

Our next stop was a small, rounded building standing by itself on a hill that faced what once again would be a sea. The basin had already begun to fill with the gifted water. It was peaceful. Two moons were rising although soon the rains would begin. I watched the sky turn steely grey and lightening move in those clouds.

Nathaniel settled Ker in the flitter, with water and food.

She was studying various subjects on her small computer. At present, midwifery seemed to be of most interest to her.

He took my hand and quietly led me to the door. "Enter my home, Danu, if you wish."

I dropped to my knees in front of him. He was Alpha—and appeared as a reddish gold lion. He let me be there for a while before I felt his hand on my head.

"Rise, Danu. But know that yes, here I am a full Alpha and I have not come to you like this before. I would fly you now," he said and laughed. The rain was hissing down outside. "Tomorrow then."

We looked at each other carefully. He moved towards me purposefully and I used my Shadakon and Sidhe ways to move just to one side or the other of him, brushing up against him or deftly moving back. He smiled and I could see that he wanted me. In fact I wanted him more and more, but I delayed.

He moved so fast that I couldn't see his hand that trapped both of mine effortlessly. He brought me up on my toes, supporting me with one strong arm as he visited me with a version of my own game. I gasped, flaring under his touch and he smiled some more. Moving me to the wall he positioned me the way he wanted me, face to the wall, arms and legs spread. We said nothing. Ours was an intense dance of silence.

I wanted him. I wanted him as an Alpha. He bit lightly but effectively into my shoulder, pinning me there and then took me. I shouted when we began but then fell into wanting more and still more. After several more changes of position, he took me to the bed and finished me there. I called his name as he called mine.

The rain drummed on the roof. We were never quite done with each other. We would lay languid and easy with each other but then he would begin with me again.

I only wanted more and more of him.

I remembered the pain I had endured to stop what might have been his end and shuddered. He had heard my thoughts and ran his hand down some of the then worst points of pain.

"*The worst and the best one,*" he said within to me, "*was when as a child you held your finger over the flame. And your satisfaction in standing as much as you did, and telling no one.*"

"*Why that one?*" I thought back.

"*Because you were in training to come to the Shadakon, and to me even then.*"

I shivered. He rolled me over and took me again. The night was long and before the dawn I dozed. He woke me as he rubbed his fangs lightly, ever so lightly, back and forth across my neck. He said nothing, waiting for a go-ahead or refusal. I moved my hair away but still he waited.

"*You have become a most considerate lover,*" I mind-spoke sleepily. I heard a deep rumbling in his chest. It could have been a purr. "*I want exactly what you want now,*" I thought, and then felt the slightest prick of his fangs. Soon he lapped slowly and happily and I swooned in bliss.

We visited many other settlements. I had brought Ker along with me. As Nathaniel talked with the elders, Ker disappeared into one of the huts. I listened and heard only the low murmur of women's voices. But then there was a shout - a woman's birthing shout as she brought life into the world. Soon afterwards Ker reappeared in the doorway, a small bundle in her arms.

I had never seen Ker happy before. Accepting, even content, yes. But there was a glory in her today as she gazed down at the newborn.

"Danu!" She showed me what was in her arms. I then understood the cost of immortality.

It clenched in my heart even though up until this moment I had never considered the matter of children. Of protecting them and teaching them and watching them grow up in strength and beauty.

What if the children of man were taught from an early age to feel their connections to the land? What if, safe from the bombarding empty temptations, they could grow up as part of their brother and sister beings and the land beneath their feet?

I saw a tousle of birth-wet dark hair. I saw this new human's dark eyes open slightly, squinting into the first day of her life. I was drawn to the pure energy of all of this—the joy on Ker's face, the satisfied mother, now leaning against the door frame, having done the strongest magic in this world or any other—to bring through life. To cherish and protect.

I knelt before the new mother. "Blessings on you and those you love," I said. Rising I turned to Ker. "If they would have you here, do you want to stay?"

I did not need to read her; her eyes said it all. Then I felt my heart open to an even larger lesson. She handed the baby back and ran to me. She flung her arms around me—me who had unavoidably used her as a commodity—and placed her heart against mine. I felt her tears soak into my dress. Then she dashed to the flitter to gather up her computer that might help her provide information when dealing with difficult births. Nathaniel and I had not discussed allowing the humans access to technology but what she had only held tutorials, as she had no access to the outer worlds. In time, it would cease to work and be reverently buried somewhere.

I looked at Nathaniel and he shrugged. He was not here to enforce Sidhe directives. We walked away together.

On the last day of our tour Nathaniel and I sat overlooking the small sea. The rotting bodies were gone now, their elements absorbed into the great cauldron of life.

We did not speak of what was between us but I knew we would.

Nathaniel sighed. "And now I will walk through what Dagon walked through earlier—wanting you and not being able to truly have you."

"You have truly have had me, Nathaniel. And will again and again if that is our wish."

He watched the horizon, much as I had when I sat on my log on Exterra, wondering what would come next. I had not known then and did not now. He put his arm around me, and this Shadakon, this once arrogant taker, asked for nothing more of me. We would not struggle against each other then.

He sighed. "Dagon has summoned us to return. Events require that he and I make decisions about the immediate future of the Shadakon."

CHAPTER THIRTY-ONE

THE COUNCIL OF LIFE AND DEATH AND LOVE

We arrived and were greeted by Dagon. He extended a hand to me as I disembarked and held mine only for an additional heartbeat or two. He nodded, observing without word or direct thought that I was in my purple tunic dress, the one I had wished to be wearing as I stood beside him, so many years ago. The one he had carefully taken off of me on my first day on his planet.

The Shadakon did not age, although they did assume the look of greater wisdom and authority as they lived through the ages. Those who managed to live on. Dagon had taken on the mantle of calm self-control beyond what he once practiced.

"Please join me after you have refreshed yourselves," he said. "I will be in the small meeting room."

I rinsed the sand and, yes, the scent of Nathaniel away. Not before Dagon had taken in that information though. And I could not rinse away the deepened bond between Nathaniel and me.

For the first time since I learned that I could do so, I imagined my hair longer and darker. When I looked in the mirror I saw that it was as I had wished to be. I braided it in a single thick braid down my back, leaving a few lighter red notes. I no longer felt like who I had been even two weeks ago. I knew I was not. It was not just the bonding that Nathaniel and I had achieved. It was also a result of seeing the joy in Ker's face as she held a new precious human life. It had made me question a lot of things, like my once automatic distain for most humans.

I searched through my clothes, choosing dark pants and the inevitable white long-sleeved shirt.

For all the years, since I had arrived on Exterra, I had worn the same style of clothes, even when I lived in Between among the Sidhe who dressed in the colours of the season.

I had nothing like that here. I thought for a moment and then entered Nathaniel's room. In his closet I found a fitted dark jacket that fit, a little long, but adequate. I joined the Shadakon Alphas in the meeting room.

As I had expected, Nathaniel wore his all-black uniform; it gave him a remote and authoritarian look. I appeared, as I had meant to, as his accompanying second.

Dagon took a moment to take in my changed appearance and then nodded. "The two of you make this easier," he said dryly. "It is time for one of us"— he looked calmly at Nathaniel—"to leave this planet. I have seen you, Nathaniel, working to establish life here and monitoring the humans. I believe that you have a home here already." Dagon gestured in the direction of the shallow sea. "I never felt a true affinity for this place. I cannot imagine it green and fertile again. You seem to be enjoying your role as the tall, dark stranger."

I laughed in my mind. That title had been given by one country western singer on Old Earth to another who had stolen his wife.

Dagon sighed. "No doubt I will be proven wrong in my doubts in the revival going on now, for the Sidhe have chosen to reveal powers that we were unaware of. Powers to gather and transport the water of comets and icy moons. They have harvested more than enough water to restore this planet."

"Most of the Shadakon in the city are not very interested in monitoring or motivating the humans in their task of becoming hydroponics farmers. Approximately half will return to old Earth. Others will seek jobs as enforcers on other worlds. We have found nowhere to live in any great numbers. Perhaps that is in our very nature.

We were never meant to flock together, but rather live in isolated packs. Even in these times …"

He knew that my job lay in remaining here, and that Nathaniel had easily assumed the role of outrider.

"There needs to be an ongoing presence and maintenance of the spaceport. The Sidhe have approached me to provide, ah, security for the requirements of those activities. My heart is not in that work. I too have taken a … second; I too have chosen a female. She is familiar with the work that needs doing here. She will oversee and be in contact with me."

Then he turned to me and I suddenly felt that we were only people in the room.

"I will fly soon, Danu. I will not retrieve you again if I can help it. My life has been transformed again and again by you. I now wish only for the predictable life of my kind. I wish to be free of you and your … love. If in the future I stand up to a challenge, I wish to not have love stay my hand."

I heard a whisper of the Guardian's voice in my mind, *"How much pain are you willing to bear, Danu? Do you now regret your love?"*

I felt his words like a lightning strike in my mind. The accompanying thunderclap deafened me. I saw his mouth continue to move and his thoughts, now meaningless, cross my mind. I could take in none of it.

I fled the room. In front of my computer, the small, dark green stone beside me, I called Fiórcara.

His image came up and he was observing me intently without speaking. Finally he said, "It appears that you have chosen to ally yourself with one of your lovers. How is that working for you, Danu?"

I tried to restore my breathing. We slipped into mind-speak.

"They haven't returned to the plan to try to kill each other. For one to definitely end the other.

"Then you have achieved another strong shift in the world of the Shadakon. But preserving Dagon is not enough is it, Danu, my devida? You want him to continue to love you."

I was wordless and without thoughts.

"You want all of us to love you, Danu—whatever the cost. Dagon did not want to begin again with you. He had paid the same price as you in your absence. Earlier he begged me without words to tell him anything about you, to mention your name. He was proud and spared himself from my obvious answer. He knew that I had no intention of doing so."

"Danu, I left you alone and longing for me in your empty hill house. Céadar was welcome to come and join me and my queen and other partakers. You I left to learn more about wanting. And waiting."

"But I too wanted you—even as a beautiful and willing Sidhe lay in my arms. Céadar, your smiling Sidhe lover is seemingly exempt from your charms. But do you notice that when you are in need of kindness and passion that he is always available?"

I did not argue. The truth sank into me. I could not say if the hurting built up more or not. I was completely motionless, trying not to set off a collapse of will that would leave me completely undone. I looked up at Fiórcara.

"Just a little more lovely, Danu. Even now a new Shadakon Alpha believes that you were fated to be by his side; that you trained yourself to endure pain to join the Shadakon and ultimately him."

"He may have a piece of the truth," mind-spoke Fiórcara. *"Just as all of us have a piece of you. But you are now in pain and so you come to me. What are you asking of me, Danu?"*

I just shook my head.

"Do you think of using your small dagger, Danu?"

"Would you convince me not to?"

He sat before me, his beautiful green eyes on mine. I felt his wanting me and I kindled, in spite of what I had brought to him. We sat together, separated by space and the years that he had lived and learned in and I had not. I suddenly was very afraid of his answer.

He smiled then, *"Good, Danu. You would not attempt to compel me to answer then."* He paused, *"I mean the real question under your question. You do know what you are asking me, do you not?"*

He wanted me to find my own reason to live on. He would not give me advice or promises to convince me to put that final solution aside. He did not make reference to his connection with me and the wild times we had and might still have—if I chose to live through this pain, make my decisions as best I could, and carry on.

"Yes, Danu," he said, switching now to speaking. "In spite of all your drama you are the student dearest to my heart. I will give you everything I can. But I will not allow you to force me into actions of your choosing. Kill or do not kill yourself. I will mourn if you do. Such a loss of bravery and beauty."

"And passion," he said smiling and I felt my body glow in response. "Ah yes, the gossamer net of your wanting and passion."

"Be well, Danu. Do the best you can. It is all we can ask of ourselves …"

The screen went dark.

I returned to the small room where we had gathered to finalize what had to be done.

Neither Alphas seemed surprised at my reappearance and I wondered if the Sidhe and I had conferred outside of normal time. Both Shadakon seemed to be waiting for me to speak.

I found a small place of calm. "Dagon I would speak to you later of what you said earlier—if you allow it. If we are to finalize the fate of this planet tonight though, let me return to an unsolved problem."

They looked at me. Obviously they had not thought much about what I brought up next: the humans! "What about the humans?"

Dagon shrugged. "Most are fairly healthy now. But there are too many to bring along when we leave."

I thought of the drawers in his ship and shuddered. "How many too many?"

"Possibly five hundred give or take."

"And some will have to stay here to serve the Shadakon who maintain the spaceport?"

He nodded. "As few as two hundred would do. Hopefully the best food producers among them.

"Can we evaluate the others again for suitability to live on the land?" I asked Nathaniel.

He looked at me carefully, as did Dagon. Dagon at one time questioned me taking in Ker and letting her see who I and the Sidhe were. I had said that, if need be, I would end her. Dagon had challenged me as to whether I could do so. Now there were three hundred humans in limbo, the survivors of the Registry and even the organ trade. Women who had never seen a living baby put back in her arms, or watched a child grow up in safety. It was not their fault; other more powerful humans had enslaved them. But they lacked the hope and passion for life to live in the wilderness. They had chosen to stay in the city and turn away from further chances.

"One more sweep then, Danu," said Nathaniel. "Some who must stay under stricter observation. It would be a crime against the others to introduce greed or claims of privilege to the fledgling humans."

I nodded.

"And the rest, Danu?" asked Dagon.

"A farewell party," I said sadly. "A cup of kindness ..."

We all looked at each other. Dagon got up and left without a further thought or word to me.

Nathaniel and I continued to sit.

"Who is Dagon's second who will manage this planet's spaceport? Do you know her?" I asked.

He merely nodded. "Some say she could be his daughter, or some close relative. You will see it when you see her. She was not on Exterra and has kept herself in the shadows until now."

He, too, got up and left me to my thoughts. I thought of serving a dinner, extravagant beyond what the humans had ever eaten. With generous amounts of delicious drink that brought pleasure and light-heartedness. And then tiredness, and a quickly arriving death. I knew it would only be a short time of realization that they were not the chosen ones for anything besides an immediate ending.

I knew then that I could handle no more. I was not prepared for the sight of Dagon returning and shutting the door.

I held myself tightly, trying to protect my heart. I could see the hard resolve in him. I had angered him in coming dressed as the second to Nathaniel. I was not, of course—I was a Sidhe. I could not be a part of his Shadakon life.

He laughed, answering my unvoiced thoughts. "You will have to sort that out with him later. He is just arriving at realizing how having you around will complicate his rule here."

"Dagon!" I was trying to stay open to what he had to say to me. But the pain was washing over me. "Would you dismiss me now from your life? In this room, in this way?"

He came around to sit beside me but not touch me. "In the end, you had to choose, Danu. You may have spared my life, or his, but you could not continue to have us both."

"More than momentarily," he said, and smiled briefly as we both replayed the night I had awoke between them. "But your obligation was always to this planet. Perhaps it will be called 'Danu's World,' for surely you fought for it to the edge of your life. Nathaniel may be doing what he is doing out of feeling for this land and its humans. Or maybe just for you. But for now he is willing to do the work you need him to do."

"*Please,*" I whispered in his mind. "*Dagon, I must endure on and on. I will not avail myself to your dagger although the thought came strongly to me today. But to watch you walk away today and have to pretend that I am accepting of this ... I cannot do this.*"

"Who would you pretend for?" asked Dagon calmly.

"For you my love, to let you go as you once did for me when you left Exterra."

I saw tears then, and knew he could not pretend that he could walk past me indifferently without paying the price.

I knelt before him them and bowed my head. I would have stayed there forever if he did not lift me into his presence. Time passed, neither one of us being able to move forward from this moment.

"*Please.*"

At last he raised me and I fit into the curve of his body, my head on his heart. *Would this truly be our last touch?*

"*Please!*"

CHAPTER THIRTY-TWO

PREPARATIONS

Dagon allowed himself to hold me. I shivered against him. *Was this the outcome I had wanted?*

He finally pushed me back so he could see my eyes. I saw the familiar flames in his dark amber ones and sighed. *What had I done in going to Nathaniel?*

He shook his head. *"We have come to this point before, Danu. It is too late to regret that you are now a Sidhe. You need him to complete your task here and you have ... secured him. I am not the farming type. I am not overly hopeful that those humans living on the land will not morph into what they became on old Earth. I watched it the first time."*

He rubbed his thumb across my lips and then lightly traced down to my neck. He lingered there, knowing that I had willingly shared my blood with him many times, as well as recently with Nathaniel.

"But did you partake of his at the same time?" he asked while watching me, looking within.

I shook my head. *"I have one, and only one, Maker. Maybe this will be the moment that you renounce me as I once did you."*

The tears built up, interfering with my attempted deep breathing.

He sighed. "In the end, it did you no good. But enacting that with another—that might cut our bond. I do not know," he said musingly.

"I will not." I said this with inner conviction. "You were my Maker and my Shadakon mate and Alpha."

"For the foreseeable future ..." he said quietly. "One night he may ask and you will have another answer."

I just shook my head. "This was the gift's darkness and light that you bestowed on me. I can sex with and even love others, but I cannot un-love you. If I could have, I might have on the floor of the cave at the Guardian's feet."

He nodded. I felt the heat in both of us and knew I did not want to be in a room near Nathaniel in Dagon's home. I did not want Dagon's pretty human sources nearby either.

"What do you want, Danu?"

"Fly me, Dagon. Fly with me under the moons of this world."

"It is predictably raining tonight, Danu," Dagon said. "It will do that for the next hundred years or so."

"So, let me take you somewhere, a sanctuary of sorts," I replied. "And we can fly at dawn—if we have the strength to."

He smiled then. "I know you can source energy from the planet, although not yet from the life force here. You will have your provisions with you. Give me thirty minutes. Wait for me here."

I knew he went to avail himself to energy from the two sisters, Io and Ka. I knew that they could be a valuable addition to the humans attempting to survive off the land. But I doubted that Dagon would give them up. They were beautiful and devoted to him. They had some part to play in his fate, although I could not say what. Meanwhile they watched and waited, pleasured and fed him.

When he returned, he simply shut the door and turned off the lights. I took his arm lightly and transited to the mouth of the cave of the Guardian.

We stood in the almost white sand that the cave river had created over the eons of time it had carved its channel here. It ran stronger now. We were far enough under the overhang of rock to be untouched by the hard driving rain. Space water—pouring down from above and over the entire face of the planet, trickling and rushing, soaking into the ground. Landing on the surface of the still overly mineralized water of the sea to freshen it and make it suitable for life again.

We took off our own clothes. This was not a coy courting—we were long past that.

"You like beaches for these events," he said. I saw in his mind that he remembered our last final parting on the beach on the small island on Exterra. My breath stopped.

"Please do not leave me before you actually go. If that is later today, then so be it. But not now, Dagon, not now."

Our eyes saw well enough in the darkness, even without moons or stars. Our hands and mouths did not need to see. I fell into him then, merging as if I had never stepped away from his side. I felt him smile then.

"I am still an Alpha, Danu, although perhaps preserved by your sacrifice. Or saved from the fate of killing someone you cared for. Either way, I am Alpha and will come to you as one tonight."

I saw him began moving towards me stealthily in the dim light—*to get within pouncing range?* In spite of my trust in him, a tiny sliver of fear knifed into me. I backed up instinctively although knowing this would only activate the predator in him.

"Yes, Danu," he said low in his throat. "That touch of fear. You did not have it when we met. You had no idea that fear should have been your only reasonable response to me. And during the trial when you were forced into the Hunger? Even more then."

"Ahhhhhhh." He was now growling and had moved to mind-speak.

He was advancing and I was backing deeper into the cave.

When we were in almost total darkness I stopped, my back against the faintly glowing wall. He put an arm on either side of me and he bent towards me. I felt his tongue rasp against my tender skin. As the pleasure spread out from that contact, he nipped me hard. I gasped.

"Perhaps I will get this right tonight, Danu. We have danced around this before. You can ask me to stop anytime. But if you do, I will withdraw from you and await the end of the night rain to fly back. Do you understand me?"

"Yes" I said aloud. I knew that we were making a contract. I had no other choices than yes or no.

"Do you accept, Danu?"

"Yes," I said. And that was the last word I spoke until much later.

He touched me where he would; bit me where he would. I held back but eventually the first scream echoed in the cave. He was biting up my inner thighs, slowly and intently. I feared and desired what came next. I could barely believe what thoughts he showed me then.

The Sidhe queen was bending over him, as he lay unable and unwilling to move. She touched and touched him while he drank more elixir. I sensed the king's presence close-by. Her touches turned ... rougher. And she bit him much as he was now biting me. The unwillingness to stop—to want to stop—had claimed him. He was then in the hands of the faeries, and particularly one who, her king had told me, enjoyed playing with pain. Her king had warned me that she would go further than I might enjoy. And then he had shrugged. Another lesson I might receive ...

Dagon had learned his lesson at her hands well. His bites and touches fell only slightly below true pain. I would not tell him to stop—if he would in fact stop—because I wanted him.

I wanted him and whatever he would bring to me.

He drew blood with a bite. I shook under him. *"A little too much. I will close this now."*

"No!" I saw him above me, appraising me even while he was deep in his animal persona of big cat.

He smiled then and bent his head and slowly sucked my welling blood.

"There! There!" I was lost to what we were building here.

I felt his bliss building as my Sidhe blood energized him. I too was swept up and up, carried by his passion and my own.

He took me. And took me. Until he roared and I screamed out his name.

I heard a whisper in my mind then. *"Ah, Danu ... this is more to my liking. He is magnificent. I see why you fought so hard to preserve him."* I knew then that the Guardian had been present with us.

We flew into the dawn. The land was refreshed and no longer smelled like death. The greenish yellow powder had been washed away, perhaps killed by the moisture. The sun came up, reflected on a few clouds. We flew until I could go no further. And then he swooped on me and as he had on our first Alpha flight, he took me to the ground. The rising sun was in his eyes and the flames were bright. When we were again finished with each other, we lay on the ground and there was nothing in my mind.

He leaned over me then and with infinite gentleness he kissed me. After our night it somehow undid me more than all of the hard passion we had shared.

"Take me back to my home, Danu. Our time together is finished."

"For the foreseeable future …"

"No, Danu. Do not wish for that. I do not."

I took him back. And then I transited back out to Nathaniel's house. I was not sure if I would be able to gain entry. He had invited me in earlier, but if it was locked or if he had rescinded his welcome I would be standing outside without another plan.

It opened to me and I entered.

I could not bear to see the sky anymore. I did not go outside until hunger racked me. Even then, I purposely took little, even though the Earth energy was powerful and enticing. I would take one small wisp of energy and then I flew—different directions every day. I saw the humans in the fields. I saw plantations of small trees, tucked behind stone walls and in gullies. I saw spontaneous green slowly rising up into the light. It was good. My heart was dead in my chest. Dagon was not unreachable because of distance and need to be elsewhere. Not yet. He was unreachable because he willed it so. I could not present myself in public in the pain that I was in. Both Dagon and Nathaniel had to work together until they officially parted.

Time passed. One day I heard the roar of many ships taking off. I had not brought the dagger or the stone and had thought only briefly of both of them. Now I wondered if I had finished enough of the job here to … merely cease to be. Not a drama involving other people. Not in Nathaniel's house or Dagon's although I would have to return briefly there to retrieve my small lethal dagger.

I wondered if anyone had dealt with the city-bound humans. I wondered whether the ones that walked onto the ships to travel with the Shadakon would walk off again—or just tumble in space once their life energy was depleted and they were jettisoned as dead husks. I had stepped back from my job. Perhaps the Sidhe king would turn away from me.

Give me a decade's long lesson of his displeasure. Or maybe just for the foreseeable future …

The rains came down every night and I grew used to retreating to the front of Nathaniel's house to watch the grey clouds mass and the rain begin. The weather had at first merely been rain or no rain but now local winds swirled around me. The air too was reviving.

I sat uncaring. My hair had slipped out of the braid and I had made no repair of it. It hung long around my face in auburn tangles.

I cannot tell you how much time passed. Eventually something else would happen, but I hardly cared now.

★ ★ ★ ★

Eventually a flitter landed at dusk. I watched it without curiosity. I assumed that Nathaniel would step down, and he did. Clad in black, he cut an increasingly formidable handsome figure. No doubt the humans shivered when he arrived and finally exhaled when he left. He stood in front of me and observed me for a while. I had let him down. He had made no complaint about my sudden disappearance with Dagon—at least not one that I knew about. He had not come here immediately to reclaim or disown me, even though I had used his home without permission.

He sat down beside me in the dust. He took my hand and it laid motionless in his.

He sighed. "I came prepared to be angry. You are perhaps more trouble than you are worth." He sighed again. "But you are injured and in deficit. I cannot say I understand because your effect on me was minor until we came here. But I remember that Dagon stood by you during your trial—and would have received a deep punishment if you had failed. You stood beside him as an Alpha as his mate.

You stood up for him through great pain, including your sacrifice in the cave."

I shivered. In my last hours in the cave with Dagon I had opened completely to him.

I had known the cost. Somehow I had held onto faint hope of re-joining with him. This time he had wanted me to understand that he would not accept another meeting with me. It felt like death. Only he would go on and, perhaps, so would I.

Nathaniel followed my thoughts. "You could have allowed the challenge to go down. He might have succeeded in taking me down, then you would not be in this pain."

I shook my head. "I am a Sidhe—I go to who I will, if it is also their wish. The life force and primal energy of the planet flows through me. It will not be leashed. I love. I loved Dagon—but not only Dagon. However he brought me into a new life, one filled with passion and energy. With struggles and complexities. And then the Sidhe took me from him."

"That is not right," I added a few moments later. "I left him to go to my destiny with the Sidhe."

"And me, Danu?" I could finally see him. His gentleness had unarmed me. My hand moved slightly in his—a claiming?

"I waited in the temple for you to come," I simply said.

"And now?"

"I hid in your house. I lied to myself that I hoped you would leave me out here to my deserved fate."

Nathaniel smiled. He looked at me and my tangled hair. "Do you have a brush?"

I nodded. "Actually you have a brush here. I haven't used it."

"I can see that," he said.

He went and retrieved it and then brushed and brushed, carefully separating the matted curls. When he had restored it to his satisfaction, he braided it in a large braid on one side of my face. He then pulled on it and brought me close to his lips.

"Do you want this, Danu? Do you want me?"

I saw the flames rising in his amber eyes. For the first time in however long since I had come here I could feel my body. It felt diminished and far away. I did not say yes or no.

"One step at a time then," he said. He pulled me to my feet even as the first gusts of rain came down. "I think I'll let you call the dance tonight. Please enter my home that you have already been living in. You already know that there are both lights and candles. There is a shower, which you should probably use. Then come to me. Nothing or anything will happen after that."

I wandered off to shower. I left my hair braided as he had chosen to arrange it. When I returned he was on the bed. He was unclothed, lying easily on top of the blanket, his boots neatly put aside and his uniform slung over a chair. When he looked up at me, he rolled to one side and indicated the empty space. He did not reach out to me but smiled a slow lazy smile. He was becoming accomplished at this. At being an accommodating partner rather merely someone accessing a host.

"All for you, Danu. Or none of it. I think I have this down now."

In spite of myself I smiled. I dimmed the lights but left them on. "I want to see who I am with," I said. I remembered Dagon saying that to me after he had strayed. I added the final part, "As if I could forget."

Nathaniel lay still on the bed. I reached out and ran a tentative finger down his chest. He closed his eyes. I ran my fingers through his hair. My braid lay across his body.

He breathed slowly even as I felt his passion rise and I saw my effect on him. He purred deep in his throat. Relaxed and playful then. I increased my touch and felt his muscles ripple under my hand.

"Please touch me," I said.

"Where?"

"The braid—my mouth—with your mouth."

He smiled. And did that and more.

Nathaniel decided to visit a human settlement before we returned. It was the one where I had set Ker free. He may have thought it would cheer me up and encourage me to return to my work here. He sat the flitter down and soon after a figure came running over the hill to meet us. It was Ker. She was tanned and looked stronger and ... more alive. She flung herself into my arms.

Nathaniel stood back and smiled faintly. She had my hands and was dragging me off in a different direction than the settlement.

"Look, Danu! Look!" She scampered up a slope to a sheltered cliff face of sandstone. There was a stylized picture of a woman holding a baby scratched into the soft rock. Another knelt in front her—more a goddess for she was surrounded by what looked like flames.

This planet's version of the creation myth. And my purple dress had morphed into soft flames.

"That is you, Danu!" she said proudly.

"It is not exactly me, Ker. But thank you for showing me." A little more of the ice around my heart melted.

When we returned to her village, Nathaniel was already there, standing calmly, courteous yet powerful. Two young humans were pushed forward towards him. He took from them with a hand placed briefly on their heads. Everyone in the village looked pleased that their offering was accepted. So it had once may have been, I thought. I then wondered if he could procreate with these people—even as his distant ancestors had done. He caught my thoughts and frowned.

"No, Danu. The Shadakon made the decision not to procreate a long time ago. We all accept the process that prevents that. It is irrevocable." The young teens looked sleepy but were still on their feet. Hopefully they would be excused from working for the day.

"You and your humans," he said, shaking his head. "But that brings us to something you need to think about. The ships have left with their sleeping hosts. The remaining Shadakon are enjoying the bounty of the number of humans on the Registry."

He licked his lips, probably without thinking about what that signalled to me. Nathaniel was now Alpha, with Dagon's second managing the spaceport.

"We can have who and as much as we want. But realistically, there are too many of them. You, and I suppose, I, have to winnow down their numbers. Some will be second choices to go back to the land. But most of the rest will either be sullen workers—or they will cease to be. The Shadakon would probably enjoy being given carte blanche to take the excess hosts to death. But there would soon be an uprising if the humans stopped coming home after their call-outs."

I froze. I had managed not to think about this for quite a while, but it was still here as my responsibility. Meanwhile, another thought floated up.

"Did Dagon take the sisters with him?" I asked.

Nathaniel was studying me. "Yes, he did. I think he will continue to favour them."

I nodded. Whatever knowledge of the land they held had left with them.

CHAPTER THIRTY-THREE

DANU'S BANQUET PLANS

Eventually we returned to the city where Nathaniel had his own accommodations befitting an Alpha.

I checked in with Fiórcara, the Sidhe king. I sat at a keyboard, the small stone beside me. The moment the connection was made the stone flared brightly. The Sidhe said nothing, only looking at me.

I breathed deeply. "See what you will, Fiórcara. I am open to you."

I saw him look at my memories of Dagon and I in the cave. I again saw what he had shown me, even as he inflicted pain on me—the Sidhe queen bending over him, her touches welcomed by him even as he willingly endured pain from her hands.

"Yes, Danu. She had quite a night of it. He was not immobilized the whole night, however. She willingly sampled his Shadakon energy and fierceness. I see that he brought some of that lesson back to you. I also see that you have paid for your last night with him. And will continue to pay. But perhaps the worst is over, although ... You are not thinking of loving now. You are thinking about killing ..."

I sat in deep silence. The thoughts of what I might have to do on this planet were within, but I refused to bring them forth. Nevertheless, I saw him find them.

"First you intend to reassess the remaining humans?"

"Yes. But I already know that only a few will be accepted in the second pick."

"Yes. You know that I am mostly indifferent to their fate. I, like Dagon, have little hope that they will not revert to their arrogant, plundering ways.

However, that may take a long time, and meanwhile they are doing a good job in replanting and tending to the emerging life. But their food is still dropping from the sky. If and when the first animals find homes on your planet—will they not just eat them? And eat the last remaining one as well? The Shadakon are like wild predators. They take what they need. Incidental kills are rare. The humans are like dogs in a sheepfold. They kill for the joy of it. They kill and leave the bodies on the ground ..."

I did not argue the point.

"But, in spite of your hands-on knowledge of what humans did on Old Earth and would have done on Exterra—you have compassion for them?" he asked.

"I am of them. One of the human mothers dared to lie down with a Visitor. Or, possibly, awakened in a lab, having been implanted with his DNA. And even though her child was not like those of her neighbours—she sheltered and preserved her. And that was my beginning."

"The children were beautiful. The young maidens were beautiful." He sighed. *"They quickly overran their environment with their fecundity."*

I sat quietly. I saw the small, dark-haired infant held carefully in Ker's hands. I felt the delight of the mother and her attendants. She would have more children if she could.

I continued to sit quietly.

"So there needs to be a few hundred less humans. The remaining Shadakon will pick out the ones they favour. You and your Alpha will look through the remainder carefully, pulling out a few more. One hundred or so is less than what dies every day in an average city on old Earth—shot and run over; sold for parts and killed in skirmishes they no longer dare to call wars. Your humans will get to have a party and celebrate the changes on the world that they lived on, that their relations had previously helped destroy.

If at the end those smart enough attempt to flee—they will die close by on the land, nourishing it with their bodies. They will be useful."

I continued to sit quietly.

"I have nothing to use to achieve painless death, my king."

He smiled. *"Perhaps the Guardian will help you. You definitely have her attention. She is comfortable with dealing death—or life. You know this firsthand."*

I shivered.

"Are you more generous when offering up your own life, Danu, than those of humans who have been maimed by their circumstances?"

I looked into his bright green eyes. No pity, no sympathy, no cruelty either. I yearned to sit in his presence again in the healthy, green world of Exterra. I felt his hand fall lightly on my head. I felt his energy swirl around me. His hand slipped down my sides, lightly mapping the invisible marks on my back that he had placed there on a night long ago. I shivered and kindled to his touch.

"And what do you sense from me, Danu? What is my state of being at this time with you?"

"You want me," I whispered aloud. "You have always wanted me."

"Yes, Danu. Through all of your wanting others this has held true between us. You are Sidhe and I am bringing you through to your full potential. And our rewards of this work with each other are the same: a hot wanting that can be only momentarily satisfied. You caught me in your net a long time ago. I did not struggle against it and now I am here, you are there—for the foreseeable future. As I can be, I am yours. I will do what I can."

The screen went dark.

I went outside of the dying city and accessed the planet's source energy deeply. I no longer feared being caught by it as I once had. It was a dry pure energy that I felt flickering up my spine.

I transited to the cave—directly into the inner chamber. I knelt and bowed my head. It was almost completely dark. I heard the slow incessant drips and trickles of the coming-alive cave. When I had almost forgotten the reason I was here, the air lightened and I sensed a presence. Still, I remained where I was.

Then came the whisper in my mind that I had learned to listen for.

"Danu, once again you seek me out. Your last offering was unexpected and very acceptable."

I saw Dagon and I up against the wall, he taking me without pause and me glorying in it.

"Yes, Danu. You are a woman of many passions. And passion once again brings you to me. You want something."

This was not a question and I did not answer.

"I have seen that you can set your arrogance aside, human-Shadakon-Sidhe. I suggest that you do so now if you are asking for something from me."

I sighed. *"It has fallen on me to attempt to balance the numbers of humans on this planet. Most of the Shadakon have left; the rest have more than enough as nourishment for a long time. I suspect that it will be the humans on the land who will ultimately be their available food. They are already producing young. But, meanwhile, feeding the unneeded city humans is a use of funds that would be better spent elsewhere."*

"You are not quite ready for the gift you are asking me for—for a quick peaceful death for the humans?"

"Not yet, Goddess."

"Do what you must do and return. I have what you are asking for. Choose wisely, Danu."

I felt her energy withdraw. I rose and transited out of the cave—to the courtyard of Dagon's once official home.

Once again I realized how unwelcoming this space was. Although the stone tile work was subdued and beautiful, nothing grew here and there was no place to sit or be comfortable. I expected to sense and find Nathaniel but another figure in black approached me quickly.

I saw dark wavy hair, dark amber eyes. For just a moment my heart lunged forward even if the rest of me did not. The Shadakon female before me was tall and lithe and carried herself as if she bore arms—and I did not doubt that she did. Obviously this was Dagon's second, first in command in his name here at the spaceport city.

I knelt to her. "Please forgive me for trespassing. Much has changed since I was here last." I shivered.

She left me down long enough to make her point. I had not been wrong in kneeling to her.

"I assume that you are Danu," she said, touching my head briefly to permit me to rise. "It is to the Alpha here that you must pledge your allegiance to ... although I sense that you have done so informally earlier." Her nose flared slightly and I assumed she could still read traces of his scent on my skin. She used her device to call Nathaniel and he flew to arrive quickly.

Nathaniel had said that this might be Dagon's daughter, or some close relative; I didn't doubt it. Her build, her bearing, her voice ... each brought him to mind. I crushed down the grief that was inadvertently evoked by seeing her.

She gave me a brief sharp look and I knew that she, like Dagon, had no trouble hearing my thoughts.

"I will introduce myself," she said sharply, before Nathaniel could do so. "I am Inanna of the second-born generation of the Shadakon. Dagon is another. We did not spend time together in our long lives but he sent for me after he declined to fight Nathaniel. His rank exceeded mine and I came to see what he offered. I think it was just curiosity then—perhaps he realized that he and Nathaniel would not be able to work together indefinitely."

She looked at me and smiled and I was not warmed by it. "You guaranteed that, Danu. Foolish connections will not be among any mistakes that I make with you. But neither do I intend to be an obstacle to you and the work you are doing here. Someday this may be a Shadakon-held planet. After you and the Sidhe have restored it, of course."

I smiled, realizing that she had preconceptions that would be unhelpful to her later. But, for now, her unquestioned superiority over the Sidhe and me could go unchallenged.

"What do you want here, Danu?" she continued haughtily. "Do you expect to live here? Retrieve you meagre possessions? Walk through the rooms Dagon lived in, in a futile search for him?"

"All of these, Inanna of the Shadakon. I also came to do work with Nathaniel, the Alpha here on the planet. But I am willing to leave your side quickly and get back to my business elsewhere."

She smiled again and, again, I felt as if a cloud passed over the sun though I knew there were no clouds here to do so. I held that image however, rather than broadcast my thoughts to her.

"Then I release you to do so. I expect you will be gone by nightfall."

Nathaniel had been standing calmly observing us.

"No." he said. A somewhat quiet "no" if one did not know him. I had never seen him act in anger, but this calm was not what it seemed.

I knelt to him then and he left me there while he dealt with Inanna.

"You have exceeded your power here, Inanna. Dagon deeded this command centre to me and asked me to provide accommodation for you if you wanted or needed that. However, I intend to be here when I choose—and have Danu's company—also when I choose."

He raised me then and stood close to me. I could have stepped back but did not. I felt our energies rising. He put his arm lightly around me and although the first time he had done this unexpectedly in front of other Shadakons I had resented it—now I settled into his touch and he smiled.

"First a catch up. Then business, Danu," he said aloud. Inanna turned on her heel and left.

"Would you come to me first, Danu? Before you walk around here, searching for traces of Dagon and your old life together?"

He stood calmly, every inch an Alpha. I could almost see the tip of his tail twitching. I made the mistake, or maybe the right decision, to look and be caught by his amber eyes. I saw the flames of him wanting me there and my body answered swiftly such that I almost slipped to the ground. His claiming arm around me supported me while I returned to my balance. He took me by the hand and led me inside.

We were in neither the room that Dagon had called his own, nor the one once assigned to me. This one looked out of large windows into the setting sun and the far away rebuilding sea. He left momentarily and returned with an armful of clothing.

"For you, Danu. It is obvious to me that you are indifferent to clothing.

Your old faerie clothing is here, washed and repaired as needed. And some newly made outfits. It seemed more appropriate that if you wished to dress somewhat like me, your jacket should not have rolled up sleeves. And although you arrived in finery, you should not have only one dress—or no dress, since your purple one seems to have gone missing. Your dagger, however, is still here."

I stood looking at him in amazement. There was so much information in what he had just said! He had thought to have clothes designed for me. He knew I would eventually come to him as a safe place, much as I had used his isolated home. My dagger was here! My Sidhe purple tunic dress was not. I pondered all the above.

"Where would you have me stay and sleep, Nathaniel?"

He smiled. "For the immediate now I want you right here. With me. We may or may not sleep." He had a slow, easy grin that suggested much and my body clenched around that thought.

"But you will be here and elsewhere. This is but one place for you; somewhere to stack up the clothes that I ordered for you. So that when you eventually need clothes again, you will know where they are."

"But first," he said, "clothes must come off." He pulled me to him and matter-of-factly stripped me out of my garments. He still stood before me in full uniform. I shivered in front of him. I wondered what direction he would take this.

"Please take my clothes off, Danu—if you want any of them off." He stood and watched me process this.

I finally approached him and gestured for him to sit down. I then eased off one boot and sock—but not the other. I kneaded his foot deeply, digging with my thumbs into his heel and footpads. I took my time.

He head was back in pleasure but I also knew that the other foot was probably aching for similar attention. I ran my tongue along his arch and bit gently at the bases of his toes. He hissed in pleasure and growing frustration. I felt him shudder and attempt a normalizing breath.

"Soon, Nathaniel you will beg. Not yet, but soon. Meanwhile you will get almost all of it. To have it all ... you must want me to the core." I stripped off the other boot so that I could get his pants down. His right foot, the neglected foot, remained socked and, I imagined, clenched.

In a seemingly practical manner, I took off his jacket, shirt and pants. I started on his lips then, nibbling and lightly kissing him. When he opened his lips I retreated, as I could, just enough to avoid full contact. I moved down his chest, avoiding the right side.

I slid down and lightly bit his thigh. He moaned and arched slightly.

"Ah those unreachable itches," I said. "You did not have anything planned for this afternoon, did you?"

It was not a question and he moaned.

I finally returned to the abandoned foot, taking off the sock and massaging and biting it.

"Danu, please!"

"What Nathaniel—not enough toe work?" I redoubled my efforts there.

"I beg you, Danu. I beg you." He was shuddering and hard. I could have played on, but I now truly appreciated Nathaniel as a lover. I abandoned his toes. I applied my energy to using my mouth to pleasure him. I would have lingered there as well.

He leaped up and grabbed me and took me to the bed. He rose over me and I saw his bright amber eyes and the flames ... the flames. We were within each other's minds when we joined our bodies. I wanted him as much as he wanted me. What was happening was a mutual desire that burned through both of us.

At one point I noted that the sun was setting and the light was falling on us golden and warm. Then the rains came and we finished in the downpour we heard beating on the roof. I called his name when my lips were free to do so. I heard his roar echo in the building.

So passed a satisfying afternoon and evening.

At some point his side of the bed was empty. I appreciated that he did not bring in a Registry host into our shared space. I well understood the daily needs of the Shadakon and their passion for human energy; I had experienced it myself and had thought I would miss it. Instead I had missed the calm energy of the elixir of life. I still did.

The core energy of this planet was hot and dry and I had to guard against taking too much. It burned hot within instead of calming me.

I transited outside to replenish myself this morning. I plunged my hand into the loose soil and reached down and deep with my will. When I was close, it reached upwards for me. Earth energy was always reaching up to find an easy way the surface. I was just another conduit.

I returned and first entered the room I had once stayed in briefly. It had been restored so that no item of mine remained and even my energy was seemingly not present.

Then I visited the room that Dagon had brought me to on occasion. It, too, had been cleared and cleaned. The bed was now a neutral place, with a new cover on it. I touched the place where we had laid and felt a faint echo of our passion. There was a small rock beside the bed on the table. Perhaps this had escaped attention of whoever had been sent here to remove anything of the past—of Dagon.

I was attracted to it and picked it up. I would have replaced it in its place: a simple rock, left there for whatever reason. I turned it over and sat on the bed.

Dagon had known that I had returned to our old home on Exterra after he was gone. It was by then a tumble of stones. It was his farewell gift to me—the house destroyed so that I would not linger in our broken past too long.

This stone looked like those stones. I knew that it was one of his home stones, picked up in a very unusual gesture by the practical and forward-moving Dagon, leader of his people.

He had known that I would find it here. And somehow it had remained here in spite of the efforts that Inanna had made to erase him. But if he ever returned—perhaps he would be offered his previous room with whatever he may have left behind: a small unimportant rock that he had gathered somewhere.

On the back, inscribed in fine inked script was "Te amo para siempre."

He had left one object and taken another: my purple dress that I had presented myself to him in when we finally had privacy to be together. That had drifted around me as I fluttered down into his arms in the small barracks room.

Crying is release. Crying can temporarily free one from pain. I had brought him pain over and over again and he did the same to me. I could not love only him; I would not pretend to. I was Sidhe. Dagon was a Shadakon Alpha. I could not cry yet.

We had tried very hard to rid ourselves of each other. He had made his finest attempt most recently, when he told me not to wish to see him again. That he did not wish for that.

I had believed him.

He had been lying to me, perhaps to himself as well. Yet here was this small rock, a piece of Exterra, from his home where we first joined. Our shelter for the time we had had to be together.

Our passion had never failed us.

And where was my sea purple tunic? Moving onward in space, a memento tucked into the saddlebag of his latest fast horse? He would allow himself the pain of that then.

"Oh, Dagon!" I felt the slightest flare in my Maker hand. Still alive then—and he would know the same of me. I tucked the stone away.

I sped onward to the pleasure house where Dagon had enjoyed his beautiful human sisters. It had been emptied. Everything was tidy. Perhaps Nathaniel still used this as a place to bring hosts.

There was one item of silken clothing remaining. It was what they had put me into after my bath when he first brought me here. Bright and translucent, it had felt like donning butterfly wings—and it had been Dagon's pleasure to take it off of me. They had had similar outfits that they had worn.

Small and delicate sisters—would he allow them to sleep together in one drawer? Would he awaken them and let them move or dance and keep him company on the long flight? They trusted him. If he had to use them up ... I hoped they did not realize that until it was finished. More tears that I could not shed pooled in my heart space.

He was Shadakon as was Nathaniel. I could now feel the underlying disdain that the Sidhe had (although Fiórcara had not shown it to me) for people who ate other people. Not just tapped into and enjoyed their pleasure and heat like the Sidhe did. But took from them—sometimes until they were dead.

I had done that. I could still do that.

But now I pondered how to kill off hundreds of humans and not even use their energy. Could I do that? I had before. I was saving a planet then. Now I was preventing, or at least delaying, the damage that the humans might cause on this planet. I didn't have to like it; but it had to be done.

I could have arranged to sell their body parts, although those dealers were long gone off planet—or resting in her soil. The unchosen humans would be buried with honour; they would form the basis of a new sprouting forest, a sacred space. A reminder of death and life's intimate arrangement. I could do that.

CHAPTER THIRTY-FOUR

THE LAST OF THE CHOSEN

Every day I would sit with as many of the remaining humans as I could. Nathaniel had picked out those who had skills applicable to maintaining and enlarging the hydroponics and outside farms. The ones who even had had a pet, and could conceivably learn to tend to life stock. He lined up tutorials about various helpful skills. One hundred humans were moved into a special community within the city walls and encouraged to work as hard as they could at their assigned tasks. Nathaniel was imposing but, for the wiser ones, they may have realized that his displeasure was not the worst thing that could happen to them.

The number of Registry hosts, mostly young and strong, was kept high. There were liaisons growing between some of the women and the Shadakon. I remembered a translation I had read a long time ago when I was researching the Visitors and their subsequent offspring with the humans: *"They found the women of the earth comely and laid with them …"*

Nathaniel had told me that no Shadakon was allowed to have offspring; that all had voluntarily accepted this. I wondered if that was true. Time would tell.

The others, ah, the final group of humans; even with nothing to trade and nothing to steal, they still tried to set up little areas of power, forcing those around them to give in to them. I would sit in a room with one or two of these connivers. I could often see into their hopes—to gain power—without even looking into their minds. They were contemptuous of their own kind and thought they could strike a deal with us. Some flattered me, or tried to, complimenting me on how I looked, and spoke of what they could do for me—or to me.

Everyone was asked to supply irrelevant details that we coded on our records and then left them feeling that they had succeeded in fooling us.

Some choices were more difficult. Nathaniel was often surprised when I advocated for someone who looked broken down and at the end of his or her life. But I deemed them useful, like one woman who had learned to sew and knit as an ancient hobby taught to her by her grandmother. She could oversee the making of clothing and more readily understand the tutorials about how to do so. Soon the fast-growing weedy plants could be lightly harvested as a source of fibre. One day the supply airdrops would not bring blankets, but possibly still needles or awls.

A lamed man was an unlikely choice, but he had made and played an instrument much like a guitar. I spared him, knowing music would get the humans through hard times on the land.

And so it went.

Eventually there would be banquets for the ones remaining in the city. First the farmers and then the hosts, and, finally, the unchosen—those who perhaps thought the city would be theirs again to have and run. Even now, they were planning how to force the growers into feeding them, and the women to pay them from what they earned working on the registry. They thought we had underestimated them but we certainly had not.

I returned to the Guardian. I took the small green stone. As soon as I arrived I was in her presence—that of Green Tara. She looked solemnly at me.

"So you and your Shadakon Alpha have decided who lives and who dies?"

I shook my head, "No, Goddess. They are all mortal and all will die. Only the blood of the Visitors changed that for some of the humans."

"But some will die immediately after attending your banquet?"

"I know the Shadakon would enjoy taking all of them to death—slow, fast, frighteningly.

It is in their nature to prey on humans. They would do this without suffering from their actions."

"And yet?"

"I am the one choosing the humans' immediate fate. Everyone on this planet would have died except the Shadakon who left and the hosts they took with them—and even they were cutting it close. The humans were in a death spiral. On behalf of this planet I am offering up a peaceful death rather than one of slowly starving, with the fungi growing on and within their bodies, or one of being taken in bloodlust. It is what I can do for them." I bowed my head.

"You are partially human, Danu. You too might die by your own hand."

I had been ready for this. Ready to speak about it anyway. "I have a way to bring the Sidhe king here to us, if he will attend. I will take his advice in this very seriously."

I called the Sidhe king by the only name I had for him. I held the small green stone and pictured him, here with us on this planet. I bowed to him, asking him to forgive the fact that I was summoning him.

In the next moment he was in front of me. He bowed to the goddess, still manifesting as Green Tara and slightly lifted his chin to me. Although I had seldom done so, I went to my knees before him. He drew me up and read me. By the time he finished I was swaying on my feet. He kept one hand on my arm and his energy swept around me. *How had I not realized how powerful he was?*

He smiled and wrapped his hand around the one I held the green stone in. It blazed and my arm was translucent and green. I felt the energy spread through my body like a tsunami.

It crashed over the barriers of who I thought I was, and memories that I might want to hide from him. I saw him see the small stone that was in a pouch around my neck. I saw him read the inscription on the base and smile.

"*Gossamer nets, Danu. You thought he escaped you this time. Perhaps not … But you have summoned me—summoned me, Danu! Across space and time. And I am here although I could have refused to comply … perhaps … I will have to consider that.*"

But we are speaking of death today, not love or even the joy of passion you bring to me," he continued. "*Death then … So, Danu … you intend to kill a small number of humans. Why you? Why not let the Shadakon have their fun with them—run them down and rip their throats out? You would gain immense popularity from that choice. You no longer want to partake in human energy, much less lethal contract. Why the pain over this decision?*"

I looked at him in disbelief. Once again he was offering me a choice that would result in me being responsible for dooming a portion of the people in front of me. Shadakon, human … it was the same. I could not choose one person I loved over another. It was the same dilemma that had resulted in me laying in agony in this cave, reliving every pain in my life to try to offer up something that might keep one of my Shadakon lovers from killing the other.

"*So you do love them, Danu—these humans who shunned and bullied you for your entire human lifetime.*"

I saw the infant in Ker's arms. I saw her draw her first breaths and feel the wind and sun on her. She had not sinned against the planet; she could be raised to love and feel part of her home.

"*Possibly,*" said Fiórcara. "*There were those on Old Earth that lived lightly on the land. But still, they harvested firewood faster than it could regrow in drought years.*"

I saw a flash of the abandoned cliff dwellings. I knew the inhabitants had had to leave because they had used up the area around them.

"*Keeping the humans' numbers down is critical. Hence the Shadakon, our lions and wolves. Hopefully they will decide to stay here and help you with your long-term plans. I think Nathaniel will be more than willing to prune the human flocks. He enjoys the chase and the takedown, and the blood, of course—but you know that. However, for some reason you have not assigned him the task you face. What is your plan then, Danu?*"

I switched to talking. I was sure that the Other with us could easily follow our discussion. However it seemed disrespectful to exclude her with silence.

"I will have a dinner for the different groups we have separated from each other in the city. The farmers and growers will be first; the registry hosts the second. I will speak to both of these groups about their valuable part in restoring this planet. Those selected to die will be last; I will congratulate them about their drive to improve themselves and restore the city to what it was. I will assure them that, in some ways, their contribution will be the most significant. Then they will eat and drink and grow sleepy and die. Any that escape that will be hunted down before they can reach the other groups."

"So there may be some running and the Shadakon wolves enjoying that part of the job?"

"There is always someone who refuses the cup," I said. The Sidhe king looked at me steadily.

"We are about to find out, Danu," he said softly. "The substance that the Guardian is offering you kills humans. It has been used several times before on Old Earth before She and the Sidhe abandoned that project. You are human as well as Shadakon and Sidhe, Danu.

I once watched you step into the Touch-me-not, not knowing if your next breath would bring agony or if you would be spared that. Will you toast with your doomed humans the same way—the ones you least approve of? Will you take that cup from Her hand, Danu? Or will you turn aside and let the Shadakon have their fun? You may become intimately acquainted with death soon. You have survived your brushes with it before, however ..."

"Then I will be buried with them and form the basis of a later forest. It will be known as sacred land and be kept from plundering for as long as the story lasts."

The Sidhe looked at me with many emotions up. One was sorrow, another, perhaps, was pride, and wrapped around us was the intense passion that we generated when together.

The Guardian spoke up. Green Tara had disappeared and this was the fierce woman of bones and will. "The drink for all three groups will include your blood, Danu of the Sidhe. It will be intoxicating to them. You are already aware of that." She gestured to the Sidhe king. "The third cup will also include this." She held up a small vial. The green contents swirled as if they would climb up the glass walls. "Make sure none falls into the hands of anyone who might realize the value of it."

I reached out my hand but she held it out of my reach.

"And what will you pay to receive this, Danu—a peaceful death for the humans rather than the usual ones that plagues or violence bring? What do you have that you want to keep almost more than carrying through with this plan?"

I suspected that they both know the only thing I could offer. The thought of losing it was like a blade in my heart, but I pulled the small pouch out and shook out the small insignificant stone. The stone that was my only proof that Dagon had not left content to never think of me again.

I dropped it in her hand and saw the small piece of amber that Nathaniel had given me was there as well. He had never asked me what I had done with it, but I had mourned not having it. Perhaps this was how humans felt about their possessions and dreams; they would hang onto them even as they pulled the other humans and all around them down to their death. I put Dagon's hearth stone in her hand and shakily drew my own back.

She met my eyes. "So be it, Danu. Return on the day when you need to use the potion. Do not leave it to fall into another's hands.

I wondered who she referred to and the image of Innana came to mind.

She smiled. "Keep your enemies close but your weapons even closer."

Fiórcara stood beside me in full faerie. I wanted him such that I would have followed him onto the moors, over the cliff ... my blood burned for him. I knew that he was aware I wanted more from him and it occurred to me that I might not see him again. I froze, trying to appear as I had been the moment before that thought came to me.

"Ah, Danu," sighed Fiórcara. "You test yourself and me over and over. Show me a little of this planet that you are so committed to. Show me your humans."

We flew over settlements where the humans were working at a steady pace, making furrows in the ground, fertilizing them with whatever organic material they had and carefully planting things: small native plants and larger ones that might eventually become trees. The one settlement that was near the sea had stacks of retrieved bones that I had previously seen on the bottom in the shallows. Those who could not put in a day's work in the fields were methodically pounding them to powder to be added to the ground.

"Who knew that you were a farmer at heart?" said Fiórcara.

I shook my head. "I have studied tutorials.

But some the information seems to be coming from these humans, from ancient memories perhaps. We let them follow their instincts."

"Show me, Danu. Show me where your heart lies here."

So I took him to the shore where I knew a temple was submerged in deep blue water. I showed him the yearning I had felt—to stay and serve. I had almost died that day—not because I yearned for death, but rather for the calm presence that lingered there.

"The humans will not be temple builders for a long time. But this planet is the temple you are restoring for them. I hope it will not cost you everything." He pulled me to him then and I felt light and life flowing into me like living water. I shuddered in wanting and pleasure. He did not ask what I wanted; we were long past that. I fell into his bright green eyes above me as I lay on the ground of this world. It did not rain this night and the moon shadows criss-crossed our bodies as I took and gave everything. Everything.

And then he was gone.

CHAPTER THIRTY-FIVE

THREE BANQUETS

Within a few days, the first banquet was held, the one for the farmers and growers. Nathaniel had been generous with funding and there were gifts of durable clothing and even bandanas, which made me smile; he had obviously watched a lot of old movies. There were bountiful amounts of fruit and vegetables ordered off planet at extraordinary cost. There was a small amount of animal protein—not human as had been in circulation earlier, but, I assumed, some small creature that grew fast and flourished in captivity. I had mixed up a festive drink to share containing my Sidhe blood; Nathaniel had sampled a mouthful and moaned. He kissed the palm I had sliced and licked it gently.

For the time being, all festivities went well enough. The humans looked unexpectedly grateful. Little did they know that their gratitude would be greatly increased in the coming days.

Two days later there was the party for humans on the Registry. All were able to be present and some wore off-world clothes, indicating they were special to the Shadakons who had ordered them these gifts. Perhaps soon some could come off the Registry, if that was the will of the Shadakon they spent time with. I thought of Dagon's two sisters and how gentle he was with them. I hoped they still felt safe with him.

There was conversation and hopefulness in the room that day. I presented the drink and all raised a glass, including me. Then the coupled humans drifted off to find their Shadakon lovers, and to enjoy the effects of my blood that would certainly amplify their pleasure tonight.

On the sixth day, we gathered the remaining humans. There were those there whose eyes were calculating both escape routes and how best to handle this event.

Most, however, seemed oblivious.

Those who had deduced which group they truly were in did not bother to inform the others. This, too, indicated to me that we had chosen well—they were the ones aspiring to the Alpha rat position in this half dead city.

There was great interest in the drink I served up and assisting Shadakons took it to all the tables. I had gifted these humans with a larger amount of my blood than the first two groups, and had had to ask Nathaniel to assist me in gathering it as both my palms were still healing. Holding my eyes with his, he had produced a small black knife and made a deep cut above my heart and held a cup there until it filled. He had again moaned and started to lick it closed until something in my eyes and mind stopped him. I did not know whether he and I would be together at the end of this day. I could not reassure him otherwise but now I could give him what he most desired: my Sidhe blood.

He put his lips to the small wound, and sighed and took a little more. And then we both took shelter in our bliss for a little longer.

I had retrieved the small green vial and, with Nathaniel guarding me, had poured all of its content in the drink, rinsing the vial in it after. The vial sat empty in my hand. Perhaps I only imagined the green energy instantly spreading throughout the liquid and inching up on the edges of the bowl.

When everyone had a glass in front of them, I spoke, thanking them for their contributions in the past and in the future. I raised my glass but one of the more attentive humans stepped forward and bowed. He asked me to exchange glasses with him, as a show of my humanity in common with them.

I had expected no less. I smiled and did so and drew him to my side at the podium.

It was then he knew that he would have no escape.

I raised my glass to him and the others and drank it down. The man raised his glass and appeared to stumble but was instantly supported by Nathaniel who was aware of the drama unfolding. Nathaniel appeared to hold him lightly by the arm, but was actually slowly crushing his arm bones. The man drank. Everyone drank. And then I …

I ceased to be. I floated in warm darkness; my last thought being that this truly was a mercy.

I awoke in the cave, in the presence of Green Tara and the Sidhe king. He knelt beside me and offered me a cup of the elixir of life from Exterra. It was green and vibrant. I had missed this for so long! Then Nathaniel stepped up and calmly gave me energy sourced, as I well knew, from humans, but with the addition of his caring for me. I accepted that too.

I slept then. Cave time passed. I would wake briefly and hear the running water, the lifeblood of this planet, and smile. I was always alone but there would be a cup of elixir of life beside me—and then on one awakening, two small objects beside it: the piece of amber and the small home stone. I returned them to my empty pouch around my neck taking deep comfort from them, later adding the green stone to the collection.

I was sitting up and contemplating trying to walk when Nathaniel, Fiórcara, and Green Tara came to me. Much time had passed since the banquet and I had seemingly become a legend since. I learned that a few desperate and clever humans had attempted an escape but were effortlessly swooped down on by the Shadakon. The dead were taken and offloaded near one of the bigger settlements. Nathaniel had chosen a space ringed by hills and had the humans dig shallow pits; I would have called them graves.

With a few words the bodies had been laid to rest facing up, the direction that life takes.

Soil was reverently placed over them and some sapling native trees were planted nearby. Areas for paths were left open and one went down to what was slowly becoming a small lake where one of the human settlers had left a flag flying. It had the yin-yang symbol on it; life and light in death, and death and darkness in life—a fitting tribute.

I was changed by my experience, both in handing out death and by falling into it. I assumed that, in the end, my Sidhe and Shadakon bloods had preserved me.

Inanna could have become a problem to me, but her ambition spared us both further difficulties. She requested and was granted leave to go to Dagon's side and help administer another planet.

Nathaniel now was full Alpha here. He was imperial and I knew better than to openly challenge him, but as time passed I yearned for a different kind of lover. I yearned for Céadar's quiet male presence and how he came to me. I missed seeing green in all directions.

I requested to return to Exterra and the Sidhe king arrived, and, taking my arm, took me home.

CHAPTER-THIRTY-SIX

OTHER LESSONS

Of course, as time wore on I realized Exterra was no longer my home either. The sea still chimed on the rocks of the island I had lived on, and when midsummer's eve came I flew in joy to hear the whales and all the little lives join in. However, I had flown alone, and no one came for me afterwards. There were no notes on my table, no unexpected arms reaching for me in the night. I wept then, but I did not call out to anyone.

I had seen Céadar holding the hand of a beautiful Sidhe as we all rose to build the cone of power, and I had seen the Sidhe king with his queen alongside. Their beauty stopped my breath, as it always had.

I placed silver in my hair for I no longer felt young. The pain that I had borne seemed to still echo within me: loss, loss, loss. I may have proven at the end to be one of the long-lived ones but not, like the Sidhe and most Shadakon, immune to pain.

I was lying quietly in a meadow one day when Céadar appeared beside me. He bent down and for a moment it was like it always had been with us. But then a slight cloud came over his bright gaze and I knew I had not been wrong to leave him be.

He smiled. "Ah, Danu—if I could have come without complexity to you I would have. But what we had is no longer in service between us. I did not want to seem to offer something I could no longer provide." He looked fully into my eyes then and, for a moment, was with me.

"*I came to see you,*" I thought. "*So I see you, and I see how it is …*"

I did not want to weep. Surely, after all I had been through, I would not weep in front of this generous, kind Sidhe, who had pleased me so well. I wept anyway.

I turned my face away but he gently turned me to face him.

I saw his forest green eyes and for a moment I did not see Céadar, but an older Sidhe who looked back at me.

"So, I will not even be able to remember your face? That was just a face that served at the time? The young lover to accompany the human fool?" Anger now intertwined with my sadness.

I took two handfuls of long grass into my hands and clung to it, feeling like I was being blown away by a strong wind that I could no longer resist. I no longer knew if anything that had shaped me in Between was true or just a game the long-lived ones had played. Or if I had merely been undergoing training, my experiences better enabling me to do their bidding. I fell away somewhere and the bright day darkened and I lay still. I did not want to be—anywhere.

★ ★ ★ ★

I awakened somewhere warm and kept my eyes closed, trying to not-think. It was already long proven that this was not one of my skills.

I heard a laugh and one hand slid easily down my back and on the other side so did another. The marks visible only to the Sidhe burned coldly and I gasped. I had been out of touch with my body for a long time.

I knew the two I lay between: he who I had called Fiórcara, and another, once so dear, who had given me the name Céadar to call him by. I knew now that I did not know them at all. One could travel from planet to planet—perhaps both could. What they did when they were not briefly paying attention to me—I had no idea. They touched me and called up my passion and I did not, could not, have refused them. Nevertheless, some deep glamour that had held through everything that I had experienced with them both was gone. Maybe it had been sweeter for them when I offered my heart as well as my evoked passion to them.

Not so unlike the Shadakon, I thought.

"We are both the children of the Visitors," said the Sidhe king. *"And you are too. And you want us the same way. You came back to Exterra specifically to be with Céadar, but you wanted him to come to you. You would wait. So now you have wanted. How is that working for you, Danu?"*

I wept. I wanted to go away again, but Fiórcara held me, both in his arms and mind. I was kindling to them both and trying to resist it.

"Ah ... so now we will play out the innocent human lass lost in the woods? About to become undone by the faeries who happened upon her? Do you want to run now, Danu? Take to the stars perhaps?"

They held me down easily and prevented me from shifting or flying. Then they took turns doing what they would to me. But first I had to consent did I not?

"I never required consent," said the Sidhe king, pausing momentarily. "I liked you having to give it to me because it meant so much to you. To me ... not so much." He ran his long finger down my now sweat-slicked chest, and smiled. "We can have a long night of it, Danu. Do you consent to that?"

"Yes." There was nothing else to say anymore.

"And me, Danu—your Sidhe lover who held you even while you wanted someone else. Who saved your life when you were on trial—do you consent to me having you as well? Having you as you no doubt wanted me to since you set foot here again?"

"Yes. Yes!"

"Ah," said Céadar who no longer quite looked like my earlier Céadar.

"Do you bring any impediments, Danu? Old lovers tucked into your heart that you can turn to at some critical moment? Obsessions about humans planting crops?"

"Or whose neck Nathaniel is no doubt lapping from as we speak?" The Sidhe king spoke calmly but there was an edge under his words.

"No, my king. No, you who is second to my king. I give you who I am now. I will take what you give me."

Both laughed and continued on with me. On and on and I went, higher and higher, unrelieved and slowly but surely being pushed over some boundary that I thought I could hold. That I would not break and weep and beg for what I wanted from them.

I succeeded for a while. But then I surrendered and my pride and my sense of apartness from them fell away. I called their names and shuddered as first one and then the other would do something new to me—and then veer off when my release was a heartbeat away. I was just there, with them, and then there was only one of us and no longer three. We leapt into the void together. I was in the matrix of light and darkness, being and not-being. For the first time I felt the full power the Visitors must have had, perhaps still had. A planet was insignificant; its life, if it generated life, was inconsequential to them as to how it lived and died. That their children had profoundly influenced Old Earth was of no matter to them. If they watched, it was from far away. I felt the contractions of release sweep over us and I knew the universe felt them as well. There was no pain here, no regret, just energy radiating out and out in ever spreading patterns.

When I, at least partially, returned to who I was, who I had been, they were both quiet at my sides. I held the hand of each of them and felt the complete peace that we had achieved still moving outward from this place and time.

I could not have what I wanted. I could have this, even if only this one time.

"Thank you," I murmured. I felt them both smile in my mind.

"*Our pleasure,*" I heard in two voices in my mind. "*Tonight you have touched on more of what you inherited from your mixed bloods, on who you are and can be. Your humanity died within you when you drank from that cup.*"

"*You, too, are a sky dancer, Danu,*" mind-whispered the Sidhe king. "*I knew for sure the night you drank the autumn elixir with me, and then later with all of us. You are not planet-bound. Your attempt to escape my home and Céadar was perhaps not as much an attempt at dying as an ill-prepared fledging. The timing was very wrong, but your instincts were true. You yearn to peacefully serve much as the Guardian did and does. But timing is everything, Danu. You are potentiating but have not completed your transformation. Your teenage-like connection with Céadar is now too limiting to both of you. He once appeared as your Shadakon heart's desire, but you caught the fact that he changed to be more acceptable to you. You chose to forget that day. Now it is time to remember again.*"

I stayed between the two, feeling some fear but also some feelings that I had no words for. I felt protected and embraced by whoever they were.

"You will be leaving us soon, Danu," said Céadar. "Do you still have an unmet wish?"

The Sidhe king laughed. "Still willing to be a knight for Danu? Well you have your lessons in this as well. I am going off to do whatever I do that you don't know about, Danu." He winked at me. "But perhaps Céadar will accompany you on a picnic before you go. The two of you still have things to talk about."

So shortly afterwards I found myself on a familiar log on an island surrounded by the sea. Small waves rolled in; there were more life sounds now. I stripped out of my clothing and walked to the water. It was warm and smelled like life.

I felt minds sliding by; one was far away but recognized me and gave a subsonic rumble of pleasure.

It was the whale mother but she was now in courting mode.

I wrapped myself in the frilled purple seaweed that had served as a model for my dress. The dress that now was still flying on, or perhaps had landed somewhere—on yet another world where Dagon and the Shadakon might prosper. The memory didn't hurt as much as I thought it would. I rolled and unrolled myself luxuriously and then looked up to see Céadar, or the Sidhe I called Céadar, wading naked out into the sea. I swam swiftly to the shallows and stood before him, a small piece of seaweed gracing my arms and hair.

He stood and watched me. When I got close, close enough to touch, I stopped and looked at him. He was ancient, I saw now, but no less beautiful. His power was all around him and the air and the water around him seemed to fizz. He was more, much more than I had thought that he was. I remember choosing him as my woodland god, the night before we all almost died.

I had chosen correctly. He was no less than that. He had let me see him that night, and let me see it now. *King in waiting*, I thought softly.

"Merely king," he responded. *"No less than that. We both ruled different kingdoms and decided to join in our efforts on this world. You believed that the Sidhe do not get jealous, and we generally do not act on those feeling, but I suppose there is a human part of us as well. When you lay in my arms and yearned for him I felt ... the sadness of that. You were not with either of us, yet came to me for company. I wasn't sure that I was grateful. When you asked me if I would become king if Fiócara died I thought you were close to understanding, but you let the thought go ..."*

"I did realize that he had claimed you and intended to mentor you.

I fell into my role—it was better on some days than others," he explained. *"And then you returned here—apparently to see me. I wanted that—that you would see me, and not just as your friendly Sidhe. But you sat apart, waiting for me to do what I had done so many times: come to you, soothe you, and watch you turn to Fiórcara again."*

"Let us leave the water," I said. We walked up the beach and I sat beside our clothes. I was slowly taking in the information I had been given. That had been all around me and that I had refused to see.

I slipped to my knees in front of him. I saw and kindled to his beautiful Sidhe body, however he might arrange himself with me. I felt his far-reaching energy and quiet power.

"I am still the Fool," I said. "You have held my life in your hands and my heart as well. You were available and I discounted you for that, for being someone who was useful and pleasing to me. Céadar, I am sorry. I wronged you. I am glad that you allowed me to see you now."

"You are a child of the Visitors," he said softly. "Do you think where we went last night was an illusion?"

I shook my head. It had felt endless and had quieted something that had burned in me since I started watching the stars.

"Yes, Danu. That is how we can come together. You knew this the night before the midsummer's eve when our collective energies knocked the stealth ships out of their death orbits above us. It is why Fiórcara did not question that you had been goddess and me god. He, however, is wiser than I am. He knew you would not be able to remember who you were with to achieve that."

I looked into his fern green eyes then and wished for one more chance to come to him—as he deserved.

"Do you want to leave the galaxy again so soon, Danu? It requires a large energy expenditure."

I laughed, although shakily. "I would be honoured if I felt the leaves digging slightly into my back and felt your breath mingle with mine. As above so below," I said, quoting an ancient saying.

"You have no idea how ancient," he said, answering my thought. "But continue."

"What we do here, as well as what we do as larger versions of ourselves, both are the gifts of choice and honouring what is within. The energy we generate touches the universe."

"Are you asking to join completely with me, Danu? Can you truly lay down your gathered sadness and yearning for others?"

"It was not always so, Céadar," I said. "There were times that we were one whether here or in the stars."

"Yes, Danu. But you always managed to forget. Over and over."

I felt the tears gather in my eyes and let them fall without turning away from him. "Give me one more chance, Céadar. Hold me to it—to see you through whatever we may do or become."

"I can do that, Danu, though it may complicate your life. I will not spare you any more than Fiórcara has. Do you consent to that?"

I looked into his deepening eyes. I knew I would say yes. That I wanted to say yes, no matter how it might change my life and me.

"Yes," I said.

He smiled and kissed me gently as he often had, but then he continued and I felt the full force of this Sidhe king. There was ecstasy and madness and all that he could bring.

I was glad that the earth supported me from being pushed beyond this reality. I felt the edges softening …

"Into the sea then, Danu," he said, lifting me and carrying me back into the water. We sank into the glittering water and I kept my eyes on him as his turned the colour of emerald seaweed. I opened my mouth caring not if water rushed in, but all I tasted and felt was him and the water that fizzed around us. He took me as a man but also like a supple sea creature. He wrapped me in his coils and held me while he had me. Later we surfaced and rolled and he took me whenever I went up for a breath. It was short lasting but so intense that I could not have stood a moment more. This time I did not fight my surrender but joyfully let go all I was, knowing that I too was now a deep-sea swimmer. We swam and mated and I heard the songs of the whales around us chime in in approval.

When we returned to shore it was to star and moon shine. I sat on the log beside clothes that I barely recognized as anything of mine. My hair was long and free flowing and I knew it was no longer grey. He gave me another honeyed kiss and I leaned into him, to smell his now ocean scent of spent desire and satisfaction.

"This would be a hard act to follow anytime soon, Danu. You do know that you helped manifest this?"

I sighed. "I will return to my planet. If I invited you, would you come to see what I am doing? To see who I am there? And, if so, what name should I use for thee?"

"I will always be Céadar to you, Danu," he said. And kissed me as I now knew he could.

And was gone.

CHAPTER THIRTY-SEVEN

BACK TO THE BUSINESS OF REVIVING A PLANET

When I returned to my desert planet, I realized I had no idea how long I had been gone. I transited with Fiórcara to Nathaniel's desert home. The shift between Exterra and here was long and I rubbed my arms to bring back warmth to them.

Not as cold as my first journey, I thought wryly.

Fiórcara looked at me. "A problematic practice run," he said.

"Could Céadar have brought me here?" I asked him.

"Yes ... and no. This requires the perfect trust that you have given me and I can count on as we weave through space and time. If you fought me, we might both die," he explained nonchalantly. "If you doubted him—for an instant—you would both die. I understand that he allowed you to see him and his greater place in things. He has been very patient with you, Danu. But you realize now that you greatly underestimated him. He let you see him in various forms but you believed in only one. He had joined as fully as you let him—but until recently, only once as your god. A fine night for him. But even so, you wept the next day over your Shadakon. Often you are looking in slightly the wrong direction, Danu, the direction of how you want things to be rather than how they are."

I met his still emerald eyes. I did not look down, although his effect swept through me.

He smiled. "Good, Danu. Hold your own until it is time to completely let it go. None of us are done with each other." He smiled and kissed me and as it often was when we parted, it was gentle and carried no sting of passion. He laughed.

"I am going to leave you with the memory of your last time with he who you call Céadar, I think it will provide you with many pleasant details to relish again."

That was when I realized that Fiórcara had partaken in the passion we had raised.

"Of course, Danu. King's level passion—I would not have missed it!" And then he disappeared.

I used Nathaniel's home as a base, flying as far out as I could in each direction. Some I could have transited to, but chose to fly instead until I was absolutely sure of the shifting landmarks.

The sacred forest, that happily didn't contain my body, was shoulder high in green sprouts. Some were transplanted trees and seedlings, some part of the planet's plan for what should appear here. The ragged yin-yang flag fluttered softly. It was peaceful here, more peaceful than anything these humans had ever experienced in life. I wished only that, if they had souls, that they were in peace now.

Next I went to the village where Ker lived. She arrived quickly as if she and I had a connection that would bring her to me. Perhaps we did. A child with black eyes and black messy braids ran alongside her. I smiled. Ker chatted briefly but I sensed there was something she was not telling me. I took her hands.

"Tell me Ker. I know that you want to. You are smiling so I suspect it is a good story."

She met my eyes and then glanced over her shoulder. A strong, young human man stood there, holding a hoe or something that could be more threatening.

"Ker?" I waited, wondering if I would have to force a reading on her.

"I promised, Danu. To make a life with that man. To live with him and welcome any children who come." She stopped abruptly.

"There is already a child coming, is there not, Ker?"

I laid my hand gently on her only slightly rounded belly and felt the beating of a small, determined heart. "Is he the father of this child?"

She nodded. "We were going to wait until the end of summer celebration."

"To be promised to each other in front of your clan before bringing your daughter into being?"

She hung her head.

"Ker. Life on this planet and in your circumstances will be hard. Not all children will live long enough to be born and of those, many will not survive childhood. But life is a gift, when it does not arrive in hopeless situations. Be happy. You have been practising and will be a good mother. I hope you have chosen well in your partner." I stood and looked at him and was pleased to see that he squared his shoulders and came to me. He knelt and I allowed it and raised him to look into his brown eyes.

"I bless the three of you and your union now. I do so in the power granted to me."

I took both their hands in mine and sunk my hand into the earth. I pulled until I felt a determined wisp of energy rise up to join with me. It was golden and strong and I let them feel that for a moment.

"If you will, call her Sola," I said, and transited away.

CHAPTER THIRTY-EIGHT

ΛLONE

I was again sitting in the front of Nathaniel's desert home when he arrived. I had felt his coming for weeks—first his wondering if I would return and then his growing certainty that I was near. He had waited for me to call him, but I was still carrying the memory of Céadar and I and our last union, and I did not want to see Nathaniel as less than anyone. He was a beautiful and powerful Alpha Shadakon and I thought of the connection between us with some growing hunger. But he could not join me in the stars, or take me past them. I wanted to have a quiet heart when next I saw him. Once again he stood in front of me, assessing my state with a certain amount of distance. It occurred to me then that in my absence he might have chosen a more accessible partner. He might have come to un-invite me to this place. And, in fact, that was up in his mind. I sighed. I saw his power and beauty and was braced for what would come. Once again my behaviour had guaranteed me that I would live apart.

"Once more I find you here," he said quietly. "Living in my space but not inviting me to join you here."

I started to rise but he pushed me down lightly.

We would not be casually together then.

I knelt at his feet, head down, awaiting his next action. Much time passed. I felt the faint touch of water in the wind and smiled, the planet was coming alive. This was partially my victory but I could only take in the pleasure of this quickening world.

Just as I had greatly underestimated Céadar, so Nathaniel saw me as a desirable Sidhe that he might hold claim on; though not so confident enough in his claim that he risked killing my Shadakon lover Dagon. "You have been gone a long time, Danu. Much has happened since you left." I said nothing. Dagon's training stayed with me. I heard Nathaniel say something softly in an unfamiliar language. He stood, his hand on my shoulder and once again I wondered if I would have to deal with the formidable Shadakon possessiveness. I had thought he understood. I realized that, again, I had understood only what I wanted to see. But I truly felt that he had missed me, no matter how he had satisfied his thirsts and desires.

We stayed like this while the wind moved; the sun transited across the sky. Nathaniel had gained much patience; he would not be moved to sudden violence by me or anyone else. His would be a calculated decision and perfectly executed.

He brought me up abruptly. We stood facing each other and I saw the flames in his amber eyes and his considerable anger towards me.

"Will you not say something, Danu?" he finally asked me.

"I am here now, Nathaniel. I was using the time before you arrived to clear my heart and mind. I realize now that this place is as close as to what I can call my home. I no longer belong on Exterra, although I can visit. With permission of course ..."

"And you expect me to accept you coming and going without a word?"

"I expect nothing. I have, in the past, expected too much; it brought me, and those around me, pain. I have not seen what was plainly before me—because the truth was not what I wanted. I will tell you this Nathaniel. I see your beauty and strength, your wanting me and also your anger—I accept that. I will not let you or anyone else kill me, but everything else is on the table.

I slipped off my tunic and stepped out of my loose pants. I shook my hair, which was now longer, and quickly arranged it into a thick braid. I put it in his hand and he pulled me towards him and I knew then that we were safely through the previous moments.

We passed a long evening reacquainting ourselves. He was increasingly a confident and skilled lover and I moaned for him, but it was only after we had sated ourselves and lay together that he turned towards my neck and I felt his warm breath on me and knew what he still desired from me. He lay perfectly still, not asking, and for that reason I was able to gift it to him with an open heart.

"I know, Nathaniel, I know. If I could, I would release you from wanting me this way. But you have experienced Sidhe blood that only I can provide for you. And although it ties you to me, I offer you that which you have waited patiently for, without taking or even asking for."

Then he lightly kissed me there, even as his fangs slid across my skin. We both shivered. His fangs entered me so easily that I could not say when the kiss ended and his taking began. The bliss hit us both and we rocked together. *Another kind of bliss*, I thought. *No better or worse. As above so below.*

I thought I heard a faint laugh in my mind.

Time passed and passed; for me, the Shadakon, and Sidhe this was of little consequence. However, the chosen human hosts grew older and eventually they were offered other jobs. Other humans filled in - women who didn't fancy working with livestock or bending over all day. Young men, too, filled in the gaps in the Registry ranks.

One day Nathaniel reported to me that there was a surplus of animals and birds around the city and we decided to move some out onto the land, emphasizing to the settlers that they must be kept enclosed and gathered up if they escaped. I now saw men behind ploughs drawn by oxen, putting in both imported and native seed crops. The humans were proving themselves competent in surviving on this world. The rains continued to fall every night. It was now common to see small bright bodies of water here and there, surrounded by plants and small trees. The seas reflected the bright sky but showed no sign of life. But then one day, I saw a small piece of seaweed that had drifted in, and I thought I saw some beings darting in the waves.

Nathaniel was managing the star-port and those who came were often Shadakon who were passing through to more distant destinations. A few stayed and interacted with the humans both in the city and in the outlying areas. My last visits with Ker and her group had felt more distant than before. The humans now feared the Shadakon and probably had a reason to; they no doubt resented the contributions that were required of them. They did not realize that the alternatives were wars and plagues to keep their numbers down. We were no longer gods, or if still gods, dark ones. Much later we might become even more frightening than that.

I went on a rare visit to Nathaniel's compound one day and heard the sound of laughing young women's voices coming from the room where Dagon had once entertained his human providers. I stayed briefly in the courtyard and then transited to what was occasionally my room and gathered up my possessions—some extra clothes and boots, a beautiful blue dress that I had never worn gifted to me by Nathaniel and my small dagger. I took these to Nathaniel's desert home that he seldom went to anymore.

Did Dagon wonder if my thoughts reached out to him, curious about how his life was proceeding? There was a faint spark in my Maker hand.

Nothing else.

And Fiórcara,

And Céadar?

I sometimes took the green stone out and held it in the hand. It was dull green and nothing more than it seemed. So I was surprised one day when I placed it on the ground in the sunshine and it shimmered with faint light. I pictured Fiórcara and Céadar, I saw them both in my mind's eye, both smiling. *"Ah, Danu—you finally have decided to open communication between us. I hope that this is not another emergency but rather a social call."*

"All is well here, my kings," I mind-spoke. *"The planet is greening up and the water is slowly returning to its natural state of flowing. The sea basins are filling and I believe I saw some plant life along the shore the other day."*

"Good. The Sidhe are getting weary of harvesting water all over the universe for your project. Perhaps it could rain every other night now."

I nodded. I wasn't sure who had spoken to me.

"But this is not what you wanted to talk about."

I sighed. *"I have no one to fly with on midsummer's eve—not with the life of this planet or anyone else. Passion is missing from my life. I can live without it, but some days ..."*

"Your Shadakon lover is busy these days?"

"It would seem so." I thought to them.

"Are you waiting for him as you waited for me?"

I knew this was Céadar who asked me this.

I was silent.

"Are you waiting for me as you waited for me before?"

I was silent. I was thinking about his question. *Did I want him to show up and comfort me? What if I asked him to come—and he refused?*

"There is only one way to find out Danu." I heard his gentle voice in my mind, even though I knew that he was more than capable of saying no.

I was silent.

"Well it has been interesting talking to you, Danu."

This I was sure was Fiórcara.

"Please!" I said aloud. "Céadar, please come and review my project." But then …*"Please lay with me and take me where we three went before … where you and I went, Céadar."* I surrendered then. *"Please, Céadar, my newly-discovered king, please come to this world and to me."*

Fiórcara laughed then. *"Well, you have been waiting for that for as long as a faerie's forever,"* he said in an aside to Céadar. *"I will leave you two to work on these details."*

I looked at Céadar and saw him as he had been when I first saw and refused him. I saw him as the handsome and undemanding friendly lover who I returned to again and again when I was lonely. Then I saw him as he had appeared on our last meeting. I saw his timeless face and also the forms he had taken as we frolicked in the sea.

I set aside pride and expectations. I set aside even guessing at the answer I might get. I dropped my hands from around my heart, where they had been hovering.

He smiled. "No protection, Danu?"

I shook my head. I met his eyes and felt his deep green energy swirl around me even though we were a galaxy away.

"When?" he asked.

"Now."

And within a couple of deep breaths he was beside me.

He had brought gifts for the planet and, I knew, a gift for me as well … the places he could now take me. But first we went to visit the humans' settlements. He appeared as he had to me earlier: clad simply in green, with various packages hanging from his belt. He doled out handfuls of seeds—some for the children to strew, some for the adults to plant more carefully. He touched the young humans gently and they drew around him.

Ker stood apart, large with child again, looking worn and well used, but happy. She was a human with a brief lifespan; her children would soon replace her.

I took him to the sea. The bones were gone, dredged up to augment the farming efforts. The shore was clean and uncluttered by life debris. He bent down and took up a handful of the clean sand and let it run through his fingers.

"Are you intending to stay here for the whole process, Danu?" He spread his arms out under the cloudless blue sky.

"I do not know, Céadar. How long did you live in your kingdom?"

"My kingdom was land that was named and lost and reclaimed again. I lived in the area of Sumer on old Earth. I believe every stone has been blown apart by humans many times there. When there was nothing but desolation from endless wars and poor use of the water, I had to leave. I was fortunate to be offered a position on what the humans called Exterra.

That, too, had been scourged and had to recover. It was not as thorough a job as was done here, however."

"Humans are like locusts," he continued matter-of-factly. "Once their population reaches a certain peak they become aggressively voracious. They change in a few generations from peaceful creatures that live in a small area all their lives, to flying hordes that swoop down and destroy the land, leaving little to recover. They can now take, and have taken, whole planets."

I said nothing. I cared for the humans working so hard to survive and bring their children into the world here. But I knew that Ker and her mate would have this child and then another if they could. So would all of their neighbours. Eventually the web of life would begin to unravel from the incessant taking. This world would have to have predators and prey to stay in balance, but at present the most problematic balance to maintain would be to limit the spread of the humans.

"Fortunately you have the Shadakon to assist you," he said, following my unspoken thoughts. "If they leave this planet, you will face a difficult decision, Danu."

We stood together, looking out over the empty sea.

"I am here now, Danu. Is there something else you would have me see?"

I turned to him. "Why did not you tell me you were more than a simple Sidhe, who Fiórcara had given me to?"

He smiled. "Do you want me to touch you, Danu?" I shivered.

"Yes ... and will you answer me?"

"Yes, if this answers some of your questions." He took me loosely in his arms and I saw in my mind how on another night he and I, Fiórcara and his partner had combined and went to the stars. We were all one that night.

I realized that he was a frequent other partner to the beautiful female Sidhe who, I later realized, was Fiórcara's long-time queen. She had made reference to his skill as a lover. I wondered now how well and for how long he had known her.

I then saw the night that I was connected to the life force of Exterra after drinking wild elixir of life, granted to me by a tree unknown to me. Céadar had immediately realized that I was well outside of my usual state of being. He had been my consort on a night when I was goddess and he was a forest god. He had said that he wished to fly me in that midsummer's eve cone of power as his queen. I had not taken his statement seriously.

I leaned back into his chest. I did not see any of these things because I thought I saw the shape of things. I had been focused on Fiórcara.

"Yes," he said. "You certainly were." He shrugged. "Fiórcara thought that my attempts to keep your attention were somewhat amusing. When we came together as three you understood—that both of us could transport you. But over and over you turned away from the knowledge that I was equally part of that."

"But now you are here," I said, and turned to him. He kissed me and all my carefully held preconceptions again fell away. I gasped at the power we were raising and pulled up some earth energy to fund myself—hot and golden. He smiled and took me to the water's edge. There he removed our clothing and pulled me in after him.

It was no surprise that we ended up swooping down and down to the now ever-deeper temple. Céadar swam languidly in and out between the pillars. The feeling of peacefulness was strong here and I breathed it in, not needing diving gear, weights or air this time, but just to be in touch with Céadar. I imagined a ghostly supplicant coming to me here, hoping for a glimpse of the goddess in me and the god within himself.

I looked at Céadar, with the flickering blue tones of the deep water making him appear as an ocean deity. I watched his hair, now blue, floating around his face.

He came to me. He took me to the white sand in the shallows and began. I would give over and then realize that there was more and still more to surrender. In the end I had no name and no will except to continue for as long as I could endure.

Céadar laughed in my mind. I heard him say something he had said before: that the Sidhe needed little sleep and that only another Sidhe could hold up to their passionate marathons. I knew that Fiórcara used to have me until I was completely taken to ground.

But Céadar had obviously held back from what he could bring me—he did not this day. I called his name and moaned into his mouth, and neither of us stopped or even slowed until night fell. Eventually we were lying together side by side, spent for the moment, watching the stars wheel overhead. I remembered thinking quietly, as I had when I was lying beside him once, that I loved him and felt safe in thinking so because he was asleep.

"Yes. I knew you did. You had moments of lucidity." He laughed. "Interspersed with long, complicated over-thinking about people who were no longer available—or never had been."

"You are not available," I said calmly. "You never were completely. That was one reason that we could come and go from each other."

"True," he said. "I am often not. That part you got right with me. But today I am. I came across time and space to you. If you like, I will be your consultant on this world."

"Would you be more than that?" I asked.

He was silent. "Perhaps later. You are still in an active learning phase.

And there is the fact of the imminent arrival of the large red-haired Shadakon Alpha who will be here momentarily." He kissed me as I now knew that he could ... and disappeared.

CHAPTER THIRTY-NINE

ALL MUST RISE, LIVE, AND THEN …

Time passed, measured by the ever-freshening new streams and rivers. Ker's village was thriving although she was now only present in the bloodlines of her children. She had died quietly, and her partner went shortly afterwards.

I had visited her frequently at the end and she had made a very private request of me. Her body was depleted and she harboured a relentless cancer. We both knew her end would be difficult, as the humans had not yet discovered a pain-reducing herb on this planet. She was worried mostly for her family—that they would remember her broken by pain. I granted her something I had not done for a very long time and which had no attraction to me. But on the day I saw her begging me with her eyes, I took her to her death. The energy of a human life within me was discordant and I later went into the desert and grounded the energy back into the planet. Her husband was beside me and I had touched his arm, knowing I would probably never see him again, and I was right.

Céadar would come and stay with me for long stretches of time and we would fly and later transit across the countryside. Some of the domesticated cattle had escaped to form herds of now wild-born offspring with formidable horns. In a similar fashion, the chickens had returned to the wild and now flew strongly where they would. Once they had been jungle fowl (before their domestication on old Earth), and they returned to something like what they had been before. I had asked Céadar to bring two small predators, much like a fox, from Exterra and he appeared with wicker cages and some scrabbling small animals. He had brought their food as well—small mouse-like creatures.

We released them all in the memorial forest and watched them melt into the shadows. The mice that escaped being immediate food for the foxes would go on to establish themselves. I now understood why the animals and some of the plants on Exterra had seemed like Old Earth life forms—they were. The Sidhe had taken on repopulating the scourged planet with creatures from old Earth. I had not seen anything like a reptile on Exterra and assumed that the Sidhe were less fond of this kingdom of beings. Natural selection would fill the niches in the tree of life.

The Shadakon in the cities continued to have their human farmers and gardeners to grow the food the humans needed. Various cereal grains had also escaped the fences and grew wild in the now well-drained highlands.

Nathaniel and I had eased apart. I sometimes went to him for debriefing about the Shadakon and their plans for the planet and had not been surprised to find him in the company of an attractive Shadakon woman on my last visit. He introduced us and she, who he introduced as Alta, gave me an appraising look. Nathaniel just laughed. Pulling her close he had said calmly, "Danu and I rule separate parts of this planet. We would not be here now if she had not restored it to life and we all can be grateful for that. But she is not interested in things Shadakon, and that includes me."

I dropped my eyes, grateful that he could voice this so calmly without rancour. I tried to recall our last intimacy. *Had I known it was the last? Had he?*

He mind-spoke me then in the whisper of under-speak. *"Ah, Danu, I said goodbye to you several times as you lay in my arms. And then one day after you had left, I realized that we had had our last time together."*

Now I stood before him again and saw his eyes, his wonderful amber eyes, looking at me without flinching but with slight sorrow.

His gaze slid momentarily down to the base of my neck, lingered for a moment and then returned to his partner at his side. I felt the phantom memory sting of his fangs there, and the bliss that had always followed for both of us, and attempted to hold stillness in my own mind. We had had a good run together and had not inflicted pain on each other.

I thanked him then, for his good management of the planet and the human population around the Shadakon city. The travelers who arrived here were fed however they needed to be, entertained and provided good service for the substantial amount of money it required to linger here.

I suddenly felt the need to ask Nathaniel about Dagon. It came upon me without warning and I drew a deep breath and tried to dampen down the reaction I had to it. My connection with Nathaniel would become only more and more distant. If we both stayed on this planet, officially now named Danu's World thanks to some paperwork that Fiórcara had done, we would only meet if there was a planetary problem. I would ask now, or perhaps not again for the foreseeable future.

He bent slightly over his companion's hand and whispered something. He then slowly dropped it and turned to me.

"I think we need a minute or two of privacy, Danu."

I could not read him. He walked with me to the suite where Dagon used to take his sustenance and pleasure. It had been changed over the years and was not painfully recognizable.

"I have something for you," he said. "An office or outer base or whatever. I suspect you now sleep on the ground or anywhere you find yourself. Like the humans, you have gone feral."

He then gave me both a keypad and an old fashioned key to a lock that I knew was on the door of his desert house. He had not been there for decades, but there was always the fact that it was his and not mine. Now it was mine.

"My new partner will not want to go into the wilderness anytime soon. If she does, I'll build her another house, exactly as she wants. But for now we will be here, availing ourselves to the city and its offerings."

I looked at him carefully and sensed him and strident human energy around and within him. *He was taking blood regularly. It was no longer my business; had never been my business.*

"You are right, Danu—never your business. You put your money on Dagon and later on the Sidhe. How is that working for you now?"

I did not want to reveal my loneliness and my questioning of why I was still here and how long I would have to remain. But then my mind treacherously showed him something long packed away in a box at the desert house: a sheer blue dress, the very one that he had picked out for me when I lived with him in his estate.

He flinched. We both took deep breaths. We were now in unknown waters. I knew he was still vulnerable to me; he knew that I had not let go of an item that tied me to him. And I was a person of very few personal items.

"Why, Danu?" he whispered in my mind.

"I am a Sidhe, Nathaniel. I do not let go of all the strands between me and another." And then I told the truth and surprised myself with it. *"One never knows when another may be useful ... again."*

"And even though you have just told me this painful truth, there is more is there not? You wanted to ask me about Dagon, an Alpha I surely should have killed a long time ago.

But he and I may soon correct that which you interfered in so long ago. The Shadakon are building an empire, with humans firmly controlled within it. Like the Sidhe, we are buying planets. Political consolidation is the order of the day now, Danu."

"Many would choose an indirect approach," he said, seemingly mildly. I shuddered.

"But Dagon and I go back a long, long way. Neither of us would dishonour the other or ourselves by arranging for poison or an accident ..."

He waited then. He waited for me to cry or beg or attempt to make a deal with him. Our "few minutes" lengthened. I sat as still as possible as I would have sat on the bottom of the ocean, breathing out the last of my air as a large shark circled lazily and intentionally above me.

"So do you want to know when, Danu? Because you are in luck—it will be here."

I did not want to know, did not think I could attend. And yet I could not possibly stay away. Friendships and loves were supposed to continue until they were used up or changed, the bonds slipping away, not broken in intentional death.

"It is our way," said Nathaniel with a gentleness that hurt more than any other way he could have come to me with this information. "One of us is no longer necessary; neither of us will step back from being Alpha. I think you and I both know that I will be standing at the end of that day."

And for the second time in a few minutes my mind betrayed me again. For a moment I saw the small, sheathed dagger, which had quickly killed a Shadakon warrior who could be forgiven for her wrong assessment that I had no useful weapon. I had the edge of knowing her weakness, a weapon I could use even while she held it in her own hand, a poisoned dagger that I brushed down against her thigh just hard enough to break her skin. Nathaniel was very familiar with it.

After my fight to the death with Lore in the council hall, he had carefully picked it up off the floor and presented it to me later. We both knew what that little dagger could do; we both knew it had been Dagon's, and we both knew it was in my possession here.

We both also knew that it had been removed from my keeping without me realizing it by Dagon, who then killed his formal mate with it before returning to me again.

"I must now require you to attend. And come wearing the dagger so that it is visible. If you attempt any trickery in this, I will punish you so that you long for final death, and no Shadakon or even Sidhe will step up for you."

"I would not put it in either of your or Dagon's hand."

"I will not leave that to fate and to your shifting Sidhe ethics," said Nathaniel angrily. "He and I will both examine it and verify that it is in your holding. The poison has not been replicated. Whoever wins the day—receives the dagger, to do with what he chooses. Others will be sure to carry this out, if I am not available to do so."

"Wear your blue dress that day, Danu. You can dance in celebration or sorrow but you will witness what you put in play." He grabbed my hair suddenly—he had always loved securing me for his attentions—and pulled my head back and slightly away. I could feel his breath on my neck and for many reasons, I shuddered.

"You will submit to me in this," he said calmly. "You can call it what you want at first, but there will be a moment that you surrender to me and give me what I crave from you."

I realized that if he had known before our last embrace, I had not.

"Yes, Danu. There was no easing apart. I kept myself from coming to you because I could see that I had worn out my welcome. But it was not painless for me. That is a soothing story you tell yourself."

I met his eyes. I saw the fires there, blazing up as we looked at each other. Even with the terrible news he brought me and the calm statement of what he would do if I attempted to interfere, I knew that he spoke the truth to me and it was the least that I could do in return.

The air in my tank ran out. I sensed that the surface and safety was unreachable now. I felt merciful darkness in the corners of my vision but Nathaniel gave me a slight shake as if to prevent me from escaping the full experience of what would soon happen between us. He brushed my lips with his and when mine parted, making their own decision about this, he simply leaned in and kissed me until he had to hold me up to continue. His fierce passion swirled around me; I, who now took in no energy except that of earth, air, fire and water, felt the power of it. It was the kiss of a great cat and I felt his fangs come down. He met my eyes to make sure I could not later say I had not given permission.

"Well, Danu," he said. "You must say the words."

I just said, "Yes," and felt him drive his fangs into my skin and then slowly lap my faerie blood. I wanted him as he was taking me, but he did not offer anything of himself to me and by the time he was finished, there were tears silently running down my cheeks. My bliss was empty as he had offered me nothing but his wanting and then satiation.

"Yes, Danu. So we started and so we finish. You do not 'have me' although I paid heavy dues to remain free of you. I took you indifferently in our first encounter and it appears that was repeated today, in our last meeting here."

I thought about myself lying on the floor of the cave, paying by experiencing every significant pain I had ever hosted in my body. I had begged the Goddess to intervene in the upcoming battle between the two of my lovers and she had named my lifetime suffering as the only price she would accept.

He shook his head. "You did that for Dagon," he said coldly. "You knew I could take him then."

It was my turn to shake my head. "No, Nathaniel—not then. Perhaps now, although I have not seen or communicated with Dagon in many years." I shakily rose to leave.

"Oh no, Danu." He took my arm and although I could have transited him to the other side of the planet I stood motionless, allowing him his last power over me. I felt like I was in shock. He had taken from me as he would have used a host; there was no offer of kindness or even momentary pleasure from him other than his initiating kiss.

We stood quietly and then he wrapped his arms around me and for a brief moment, opened his fierce Shadakon heart to me once more. I felt his arms slide down mine and although I could have, should have left then, I did not. I fell into his amber eyes and the blaze that was there and soon he laid me gently down and for a brief time, we were one.

"In two weeks, Danu," he said on arising from me. "Be here in your blue dress, with your dagger by your side."

And then he was gone.

I returned to the desert and the building he had gifted me. It was intact, with only some fine sand sifted into the corners of the windows. There were minimal tools—a shower, a brush and comb, blankets on the bed, a knife. And a small wrapped box.

When Dagon left he inexplicably took the purple tunic dress that I had had commissioned for myself before I left Exterra. I had wanted to be able to appear as Sidhe, at least as an important ambassador when we landed. But that plan had not included Dagon and I falling back into a hot bond of passion while on his ship.

It had been clear to me and Dagon—and Nathaniel—that we were all in danger if this became obvious, and my state would unavoidably have been obvious. So I stood at the welcoming event for Dagon, held tightly by Nathaniel and identified as his ... sexual conquest, I suppose.

I had only worn the purple dress three times: once when I stepped off the ship to be presented to the Shadakon as a conquest of Nathaniel's, then again when Dagon came to me afterwards and I floated down into his arms. The last time I wore it, Nathaniel and I toured the humans and arrived back at Dagon's house still scented with each other. Dagon had let me know clearly before he left the planet that he did not want me to wish to see him again. But he had taken the dress.

The dress in this box had been gifted to me, along with other clothes by Nathaniel. Perhaps he had understood the significance of the purple dress. His choice for me was shimmering deep blue. I had never put it on; it lay in my lap like a bit of the ocean here that I hoped was coming alive. I suspected that the Sidhe, who brought the water still needed by this planet had included gifts with it—eggs and young of life forms. Would there ever again be a whale sliding serenely in the shallows as I had encountered on Exterra? I ran the fabric through my hands and sighed.

Again I had been caught up in Fiórcara's manipulations of the Shadakon. He had put me on that ship, knowing that Dagon still wanted me and that I wanted him, even after all the years between. He had sent me and then let me know, subtly, that this was now my place and Exterra was not. Now Céadar and Fiórcara visited me here, or communicated long distance with me. I well understood the anger that had obviously ridden on top of Nathaniel's still wanting me.

The Sidhe knew that their lovers would never forget them, and I had been named as a Sidhe, although my blood-line included Shadakon and, of course, human. I was vulnerable to both as once human. I craved the energy of having a Shadakon Alpha lover, and I had surrendered to two Sidhe kings who used my vulnerability as they would.

I put the dress on. It caressed my body and showed too much skin. I did not want to appear at a death match, in a celebratory dress. I would need to alter it then.

I drew out the small green stone that I kept in the sheath of that small deadly dagger. I placed it in a beam of light that came through the feathery bushes that now grew in the lee of the house. It caught the light and my intent and the green intensified to a green blaze.

Fiórcara appeared in my mind, standing easily and looking unsurprised. "*I wondered when he would tell you,*" he just said.

I rocked back in surprise. "*How long have you known?*" I asked.

"*Oh, Danu, someday you should avail yourself to technology again. I understand that you have been on ... a retreat from such things. The passage of the sun across the sky and all that. And of course, you have been busy overseeing the reviving of a planet, but still ...*"

"*I went to speak to Nathaniel about other things. He did not immediately tell me.*"

"*And when he did, there was a cost, was there not, sweet-blooded, Danu?*"

I skipped over that for the moment. The cost had not been my blood gift but rather his withholding of affection as he availed himself to me.

"Ah yes, Danu. You endured a lifetime of pain to attempt to avoid the pain of being left by someone you love. Those of us who have come to you understand that all too well."

I moved on. I was afraid he would smile and disappear before I got to my request.

"Request me," he mind-spoke. *"You never seek me out for pleasant, easy conversations, why would you start now?"*

The matter-of-factness in his tone almost undid me. Fiórcara never offered me sympathy or any other showing of feeling that would give me false hopes that he could extract or protect me from whatever I faced.

"Nathaniel saw in my mind the sheathed dagger. They are going to fight in hand-to-hand combat to the death." I bit my lip and dispassionately tasted my own blood.

"And?"

"And Nathaniel demanded that I attend and present the dagger so that both would know the other could not use it." I absently wiped at my mouth and looked down, surprised to see my hand was red.

"And?"

"And he requested that I wear a dress—a dress Nathaniel picked out for me after Dagon took my Sidhe purple one with him, past these stars. A blue, silky, sexy dress that I am being compelled to wear at the death of someone I love or loved at the hands of someone else I love or loved."

"How can I or anyone help you through this Danu?" Again, this was spoken softly but without undue emotion. Nevertheless I wept.

"I need an outer garment of spider web and drab, dried foam on the edge of the water. I will not celebrate that day, no matter what the outcome is. I want to appear as I am—Sidhe and beyond the actions of the Shadakon."

Your power grows, Danu of the Sidhe. You will attend and you will endure. You know, and I am sure Nathaniel explained this to you, that this is their way.

You knew this even in your first interactions with Nathaniel that he would not always be a second to Dagon. He is fair to deal with and has not inflicted great suffering on the humans he and his clan depend on. It could be far, far worse for them. He will continue to be our ally if he survives."

I was stopped by that. He had known, before I did, about the upcoming challenge and had thought about the consequences. Neither of us said anything more.

"Anything else, Danu?"

I wanted to speak to Céadar. But once again I was in pain over others. I would not ask him to come and comfort me. Or worse, refuse my invitation. I took one deep breath—after another—after another. *"But surely someone would stand with me on this day. I was Sidhe and part of those who owned this planet. Would not someone stand beside me?"*

"Who do you want beside you, Danu?"

I tried to continue to keep thinking, to be attentive. This was an important request I would make. *"I want you and Céadar,"* I just said.

"*And my queen, Danu? I believe she would like an outing to another mostly-Sidhe ruled planet.*"

I could then see in my mind's eye the ancient Sidhe and his beautiful (and dangerous) queen. And Céadar and I—a Sidhe presentation of strength and official interest in the combat that would occur in front of them—on their planet. I was not unaware that there would be two Sidhe couples in this scenario. I smiled faintly.

"*Good, Danu! You see the larger picture now. Not the heart-broken lover of two Shadakon Alphas intending to kill each other. But a Sidhe responsible for the coming to life of your planet—and her royal consort.*"

"*Can I speak with Céadar now?*" I saw more clearly now the possibilities of support and show of strength for me and the Sidhe. Fiórcara smiled. "*He should really give you his own stone. Perhaps a blue one, as you and he both enjoy the ocean.*" Here he smiled and once again I knew that he had participated in the energy raised as we raised our passion in Exterra's and this planet's sea. "*But yes, he is here awaiting your attention, as usual.*"

I turned, as it were, to Céadar. He was standing easy and no doubt had heard everything that passed between Fiórcara and I.

"*Should I not have listened?*" he asked, raising an eyebrow. "*I would say that you launched a conference call to both of us.*"

"*Céadar!*" I simply could not continue. My heart ached and I did not want to bring that to him. He had never caused me pain; he had waited while I disregarded him and his offerings. Now I wanted him, wanted his uncomplicated arms around me and later his invitation to passion almost beyond endurance.

"*Danu. I continue to wait for you to come to me with a calm heart. We have done well recently. But I do not expect today to be a day like that. I well understand the conflict you are in, and what you will have to stand and witness.*"

For a moment I saw a flash of Fiórcara's queen in Céadar's arms. Did he or had he yearned for her in a way that could never come into being?

For the first time since I had met him, I saw a shadow of sadness cross his eyes. "*Ah.*"

"*We have very long lives, Danu. It is inevitable that we cross each other's paths and yes, surrender to passion with many.*

But we are Sidhe and we learn to step back when it is time to do so."

"*Would you come to me, Céadar, prior to this sad event? Will you remind me again that I, too, can stand as a Sidhe, not overpowered by my heart?*"

"*When, Danu?*"

"*When my Sidhe garment is completed. I want to be covered to my feet and fingers. Dressed in Beauty but not available to be casually looked at.*"

"*I will be happy to make those wishes come true. The bigger one, of being overpowered by your own heart—that I cannot help you with.*" And then he was gone.

Two weeks ... I tried to remember if that was a long or a short time. Very long when one is seasick or wishing to disembark from the small scut space freighters I had worked on. No time at all, I suspected, when I thought about an outing when Céadar and I had flown to view the planet and bring plants and animals to thrive here now that the water flowed again.

Both horribly long and a blink of an eye; the time of the date of the challenge between Nathaniel and Dagon drew closer. I lay and looked at the stars overhead. Rain still thundered down a few nights a week in most places. The high plains got less now and the areas around the equator more. Soon the seas and vegetation would regulate the weather around them.

Céadar came bearing gifts, the largest one being himself. Within moments of arriving, and putting down the package containing the dress (and other things I didn't even bother looking at), he just took my hand and took us to the edge of the sea. Stepping out of his clothes he stood looking at me, waiting for me to be present.

He was so beautiful, smooth muscled and poised, as only an Otherly one could be. He wanted me and his body proudly showed that. I had the impulse to go to my knees in front of him and did before I could over-think it.

"Either you have decided to lead the dance today, or you are acknowledging me as a Sidhe king, perhaps your Sidhe king—or both, Danu. What are you showing me, Danu?"

"Will you be my king, Céadar?"

"Ah ... a seemingly simple question. But from you, I think not so simple. Your first allegiance is to Fiórcara, as you call him. What if we both called you and requested your presence and anything else you might bring to us? Who would you go to?"

I knew then that he had had to find his own way through this very issue, possibly with Fiórcara's queen.

"She was not always Fiórcara's queen," Céadar said quietly. "She is that now and has been for ages. It suits her and him, and in truth I would not want to answer to her needs and wants full time. But yes, you have guessed or read the truth of it in me. Once she and I flew over the unbroken forests of old Earth. She made garlands from the flowers that grew in the meadows we rested in and bound me with them. I could have broken the green stems that held me, but not the feelings she encouraged me to enter into. I am happy that occasionally we can still lie together, although that has fallen off since you left and Fiórcara does not have to hide his intentions to come to you."

"But know this, Danu: if I become your Sidhe king, then Fiórcara could be an occasional lover and mentor, but you would take out the blue stone that you have not looked at yet, and call me first."

"Do I have to answer now?" I asked.

"You started this, unless you are merely kneeling to adore and administer to my body. It is eagerly awaiting your attention, no matter how you answer—or do not answer. Make your decision with a calm heart and mind, Danu, when that is possible for you. That means: not now."

I sank back down on my heels and kissed that part of him that I craved. He did not disturb me at my task but moaned and then sighed as I brought him across to his bliss. Making a Sidhe moan was no small feat I figured. He laughed at the thought in my mind and carried me to water's edge.

His eyes were bright forest green and his energy wrapped around me. I was begging before he touched me and sighed into his mouth when he kissed me. There was no arrogant taking here, although he took and I wanted only more and more from him. We were lying in the shallows, now in human form. I always remained who I was. Céadar, however, enjoyed coming to me in various forms, as Fiórcara had. Today I had recently been wrapped in glistening coils of what I assumed was a sea dragon.

He laughed and wrapped his now very Sidhe arms around me and rolled me beneath him again.

"Ah, Danu," he murmured. "There seems to be no end to this." He did a little teasing, maybe torturing me with his mouth and laughed as I quivered, unable to move. I cried out and he disregarded it completely. The only rescuer who might come was in fact creatively bringing me on and on until I did not know my name much less his.

I did not think about Nathaniel or Dagon this night. Or Fiórcara. I did not think at all. Dawn found me weary. I started to pull up some energy from the planet but Céadar stopped me.

"This planet's plants and life force can now sustain you, Danu. We will both breakfast in the memorial forest."

We transited there. The trees were now overhead and the ground beneath them shady and hosting shade loving plants. He pulled me down beside him there, under an unfamiliar tree, and put one hand on me, one hand on the tree and indicated that I do the same.

"*Tree this is Danu, she who is restoring your planet. If I am not mistaken, you are an original inhabitant here and have re-established yourself without much help from the other beings here.*"

I felt the smooth bark under my hand and the determined roots that stretched out in all directions beneath us. I got a strong message and smiled. "*It wants to remind me and you that the humans buried here were gratefully received. It wonders if it could do me the honour of consuming my body when I die.*"

I was silent then; it was a simple question, but it would require me having someone to carry out my wishes after I died.

I heard the next part clearly. "*We are all kin here, Danu the Restorer. Any tree would do. The grasses on the hills would do.*"

Then I understood the request. That I would stay here for my whole life and that I would pledge myself to this web of life. It didn't seem that hard to answer and so I did.

"Yes. I may travel on occasion but I will always return."

"*Then drink deeply, Danu and your king,*" the tree indicated. Céadar took a small cup from a pocket somewhere and put it in the way of a golden trickle of sap now running down the smooth trunk. We both drank and I almost fell into a swoon of pleasure. The elixir of life was wild and strong here.

"Like Damascus steel," said Céadar. "Tempered. Only the truly strong survived the long thirst here. You do know that this tree indicated that I was your king."

I nodded. "Trees don't lie," I said. "And they don't over-think."

He laid me down there then, and no doubt the trees and all other life participated in our passion.

CHAPTER FORTY

WHAT MUST BE...

"It is today, Danu," said Céadar.

Dawn was just touching the rim of the sky. I rose and stood under the shower and raked through my hair. Then I unpacked the Sidhe gifts that I would wear this day.

There were leggings of filmy lace, not unlike the spindrift on Exterra's shore, and a tunic top with sleeves that went to my fingertips. And then there was the bright blue obligatory dress. I put it on underneath and then tried it on top. I looked at the filmy fabric soberly and then tore the skirt repeatedly so that it hung in ripped blue petals around me. Céadar said nothing. I put on the shoulder strap of my dagger and it hung in its accustomed place. I frowned and shortened it, and hung it over my heart. I took out the green stone and found it glowing. Fiórcara was momentarily in my mind then.

"*We are underway,*" he said. "*A few Sidhe moments more.*" I laughed in spite of the heaviness of the day.

Céadar approached me with something in his hand. He placed a smooth aquamarine coloured stone in my hand. When I looked at him with appreciation it blazed.

"Now you will have a choice, and we will see who you summon."

I put both stones in a small pouch and hid it under my clothes. I would be surrendering the dagger today. I would put it in Dagon's hand or in Nathaniel's. My hands shook at the thought.

"Do you wish me to help you in any way? Do you want to alter your appearance?"

I imagined my hair swept back from my face, secured with something. I looked around, momentarily despairing of my lack of belongings.

Céadar combed out my hair slowly, then went outside and, with permission from the plant, took a long supple twig from the small tree that grew against the house. He peeled the flexible bark off carefully and twisted it into a strong twine, then used it to secure my hair at the nape of my neck. Then he kissed my neck, where I had offered my heart's blood to both Shadakon again and again. Céadar wanted nothing from me—except my promise to turn to him in times of joy as well as distress or loneliness. Only that—and to be able to stoke both of us to hot passion.

I leaned against his strong smooth chest and sighed. "*If only we weren't going where we were going ...*"

"You have been traveling towards this day for many years. Now it and you have arrived together. You bought them both some time. I have no idea how that choice will affect you today."

We were still standing with his arms lightly around me when Fiórcara and his queen arrived. She looked around dubiously, seeing no doubt the lightly greened hills, showing only the promise of a faint spring. She was dressed, as she often was, in layers of gauzy fabric with subtle weavings of colour showing here and there. Her eyes were bright blue. She turned to me and took in the shredded blue dress atop my faerie finery and frowned but then smiled.

"It's a perfect way to present a dress that one is being compelled to wear." She shredded a few more sections more thoroughly and curled them to hang separately like small breeze-driven waves. She then added something to my hair. It had an elusive smell and I suspected that it was a moonflower, brought across time and space to be with me today.

Had she known that a vine had grown behind Dagon's house, and that it sometimes scented our nights together there? It too, I supposed, was perfect somehow.

When we arrived there seemed to be surprise at our sudden appearance. Perhaps Alta, Nathaniel's partner, had thought I would stand cringing behind a pillar where I would not be able to see until whatever happened was over. Instead, she had a regal delegation of Sidhe, the owners of this planet, to contend with. I saw her take in the fact that I was accompanied by a king and queen and had ... another king by my side.

Both Fiórcara and Céadar were dressed as royalty. Both wore greens with soft napped fabric, and in Céadar's case—a bow over his shoulder and a small quiver of arrows. Ceremonial perhaps, but I was sure that he was completely competent using it. He had probably shot more humans than any other targets. A space was quickly cleared out for us in the front row.

We all sat around the edges of the open space in the centre of the fortressed home that Dagon had built many years ago and, I assumed, Nathaniel and his partner Alta lived in now. Perhaps she would not want to after today.

Nathaniel approached us, glistening with sweat from his warm up and stripped to form-fitting short pants. He was magnificent and I saw that he knew this. He went lightly down on one knee and bowed to the three Sidhe and then cast his eyes on me. I realized then that he had never completely seen me as Sidhe royalty, but only enough of one to have intoxicating blood. I had showed him some of my power but had stayed my hand many times. Our last meeting was an example of that. He approached me and held out his hand.

None of us moved. Fiórcara's ancient queen gave him a look that would have stopped anyone who was paying attention. He was, and paused. Then he returned to her and Fiórcara.

"Danu has a dagger that needs to be accounted for during every second of what is to come. I need to take it from her now and let Dagon examine it to ascertain that it is the original and therefore bearing poison. And then it needs to be in another's safekeeping.

None of us moved or spoke. Céadar leaned forward slightly, as if he was interested in these facts. I knew that he was assessing Nathaniel to throw him off balance and would soon do so.

"You are fighting the Shadakon Alpha Dagon today in this place," he said calmly. "And you would tell my partner that she is to surrender this dagger to you—so that both you and Dagon will be safe. I think if she does so, she may hand you Dagon's death."

Nathaniel scowled. "Do you wish to do this, Danu?" he asked me.

"No. I will not surrender this blade, which is mine, a gift from Dagon long ago. I have used it in my defence, and proved to both your and my satisfaction that it brings death to a Shadakon." I raised my eyes to his and saw blazing anger.

"*Not a good way to begin this*," I mind-spoke him in under-mind. "*For so many reasons ...*"

He strode away and returned with Dagon. He, too, was stripped down to minimal clothing and his energy was up. He looked at the four of us and smiled a bitter smile.

"So the owners of this planet have come to learn who they will have to negotiate with after this day." He immediately realized then that the Sidhe who had come to him one night was Fiórcara's timeless queen. He looked at Céadar and doubtlessly remembered him as well from Exterra. He bent one knee and his head to us all and I shivered. His eyes had slipped past me without a pause.

After an almost Sidhe-long space of time, he spoke.

"Nathaniel was reminded recently that you still possess the dagger." He pointed to it, as it hung between my breasts shrouded in fabric like sea foam. "I suppose that he is afraid you might toss it to me or leap out and deal out some personal justice."

"Can you hold it and not put it into play, Danu?" Dagon asked quietly.

My mouth was dry and I wished only to nod and deal with keeping my tears in check. But Dagon had taught me well and my spoken answer would acknowledge that to him.

"I will not use it in any way or hand it over to anyone," I said softly. "Nathaniel has told me that the winner will receive it. I did not agree to that."

"May I see it," he murmured.

I drew it from its sheath, holding the blade carefully away from my skin. He studied it, and then me.

"Ah ... I had this in my keeping for a very long time. And then you too were unable to put it down or lose it. Why is that, Danu?"

I wanted to tell him it was because it was all I had of him and the troubadour in his tapestry. And I didn't really want to tell him—though the truth was doubtlessly available to him in my mind—that it continued to be my last hope, even when there was no longer hope at all.

I held on to tears that were determined to fall. My heart felt like a rock in my chest. I realized then that I could not say for sure that Nathaniel had loved me, or if he had mostly craved my Sidhe blood. I knew that Dagon had held me in his heart, in spite of the hazards that we presented to each other.

"When a knight fought another in a tournament, he often was aware that of those who watched merely for the entertainment of seeing someone die or be gravely injured that day, one would hold him in her heart." Dagon said.

"He presented her beforehand with a token that showed that he fought for her, as well as whatever other issues were being decided. I would give you this, Danu. I have carried it almost as far, as you have carried my dagger."

He put out his hand and there was a small scrap of purple silk in his hand.

I knew exactly where it had come from. I reached out for it and my fingers brushed his Maker hand. It burned under my touch.

He bowed a little lower then and simply said, "Don't forget what is most important to remember, Danu, no matter how this plays out." He heard me gasp in my mind.

He stepped back and kept his eyes on me. "I will say this aloud then. "Promise me Danu that you will not use that blade today."

I nodded. I said, "*I promise,*" in my mind. I was beyond speech.

"*Te amo, Danu,*" he mind-spoke to me before he turned to go.

There was a table set in plain view that contained various weapons. They could choose what they would and if they lost the ones they had, they could try to return to get another. The table was on the edge of a circle drawn in salt on the ground. If one of the contestants went over that line, it would not be seen in a good light. If it happened more than once, the contest would be called for the contestant remaining in the circle. The winner would choose the fate of the other. No Shadakon would intentionally leave the circle before the match was finished; but if this occurred, it would be wise to end his life, as the loser would be humiliated and perhaps capable of attempts to regain his pride by ending his opponent by less than honourable means. Poison or "accidents," Nathaniel had mentioned, equipment malfunction perhaps—there were many ways to end someone over a long lifetime.

All this was explained to us by a Shadakon official, perhaps in more detail than usual due to the presence of those who were not Shadakon. Nathaniel and Dagon had once settled the fact of both being Alphas peaceably, but the Goddess Tara, or perhaps her other more bellicose form, had intervened last time. I had not asked her this time. *Why had I not asked her!?*

I heard Céadar speak softly in my mind. "*Because you would arrive over and over again at this moment. There is no avoiding this, Danu.*" I heard the gentle finality of his statement.

There was a large crowd assembled now, and their attentions seemed to be divided between the contestants and the Sidhe who sat impassively in front of them.

"A few rules for you, Danu." It was Fiórcara mind-speaking to me. *"You may not transit today unless we all go together. You may not faint—I can keep that from happening as can Céadar, and one of us will. Your eyes will be open and you may show your pain but not leave. Do you understand?"*

"Yes," I whispered silently. I wondered if he could, in fact, keep me from seeking sanctuary in the darkness of fainting.

"Oh yes, Danu. I have always asked for your full attention and received it. But were you to attempt to slip away into unconsciousness today ..."

Suddenly my head was full of white pain. I could not escape it and I could not bear it. My hand reached out to Céadar and he took it but did not in any way interfere with what I was now learning.

"Please!" I begged silently.

"No drama here today, Danu," mind-spoke Fiórcara. *Nothing to draw attention to yourself or us.*

You would dishonour both contestants and draw the wrath of the Shadakon you share this planet with. You must surrender to this, Danu, and bear it as you have held up in all of your other trials."

I saw in my mind the council hall on Exterra and Dagon holding me, taken to death by him, him holding over his head while the crowd roared their approval.

"Yes. He has seen you dead. Now it may be your turn."

I cannot give a blow-by-blow account of the struggle that went on in front of me. The crowd was engaged and roared at each slight wounding—cheering for Nathaniel. I saw no one present for Dagon except a very old human sitting as still as a stone on his side of the circle. After overlooking her significance for a while, I realized that she was Io, one of the beautiful sisters. He had kept them at his side then and cared for her into her old age. The rock that was my heart softened slightly. I was so glad to know this about him, and promised inwardly that I would approach her at the end of this.

The first rounds went swiftly, with neither gaining any true advantage. Both now had numerous flesh wounds, where a blade had shallowly slid by or where the steel nailed glove that Nathaniel had chosen had raked Dagon's skin. Dagon was, of course, in fighting trim, but I also believed him to be a better strategist. And I had seen him easily take Nathaniel down to the ground and force a deep reading of him very much against his will. Dagon, I believed, waited patiently to close on him.

My fingers clenching the purple token were numb. It sat in my lap, not obvious, but many—without knowing the history of it—had seen me accept it, and there had been hissing. Did many in the crowd remember that this had been their chosen Alpha and that he had left the planet rather than attempt to kill the newly risen Nathaniel?

Céadar sat beside me, like a strong, tall tree on a windless day. Likewise Fiórcara and his queen sat and observed carefully with no emotion evident. I knew that his queen had interest in pain in the service of passion and possibly other applications;

she had worked her sex magic on Dagon and found him pleasing. I felt her smile in my mind at that thought, and then knew they were all monitoring me.

The day wore on. Weapons were hooked and tossed out of the circle and replacements were taken from the table. Both were staying closer now and waiting for the one chance to break through the other's defences. Try too soon and the aggressor would discover that it had been a feint and that he had moved too soon. Lore had taught me that well … even as I broke her arm she had dealt me a deathblow with only an elbow.

I watched and at times my eyes burned from looking into the sun. Just as theirs did I was sure. Mine, however, were blurred with tears.

A break was called at midday. Both had to agree to it, Nathaniel declined for both. I knew then that he was depending on his younger body. Both were ancient but he had turned as a strong younger man and still had the benefits of that. However Dagon was taller and had a longer reach of arm and leg, as well as ancient patience.

They circled and circled. The crowd was mostly quiet now. They knew, as the predators that they were, that the end would now come swiftly.

Nathaniel suddenly stepped forward and stabbed Dagon deep into his abdomen, intending no doubt to bring the short sword blade up through his heart.

But Dagon leaned forward slightly and placed his hands, almost gently, on either side of Nathaniel's head.

Nathaniel screamed as Dagon took his life's energy.

Dagon then took Nathaniel's lifeblood until his spent body slumped to the ground. His own wound bled and then slowly stopped as the new energy infused through him. He looked around at the crowd who were silent. He then used his well-honed speaking voice, making good use of his timing and pauses.

"Your Alpha called this contest and I had to accept. I also had to kill him. I know you all understand this—it is old Shadakon law. He was a fine warrior and would have served you very well for a long time. However, it came to this. I will accept your loyalty now."

Almost everyone knelt on the spot.

My relief and grief rushed in, forming a standing wave of intensity. I continued to clutch the purple cloth in my hand, and watched it tremble as my hand did.

My companions did a surprising thing. Rising as one, (and Céadar pulled me up with him gracefully), they bowed to Dagon.

Once Fiórcara had threatened Dagon with death and would have made good on that threat. Now on this day the Sidhe formally honoured him.

Nathaniel was left to quietly finish dying, not that he needed any more time, but it had to be clear that no one attempted to revive him or interfere with the judgement that he was, in fact, forever dead. I numbly saw his body finally rolled into a blanket and taken away. Alta stood like a lightening-blasted tree to receive it. I got no read from her—a good Shadakon warrior, she honoured him as she could.

When Dagon could walk again he came to me. "I know that you chose not to give up the dagger and I also know that you did not agree to handing it over to the winner. So I will ask you, and not in any way command you now. Would you gift it back to me, Danu?"

He met my eyes. He was flush with Nathaniel's life energy and his blood.

This was an honouring that he had made to his opponent. I saw the flames flaring in his dark amber eyes. He saw but did not react to the fact that my one hand still had Céadar's in a tight grip.

The tears, long held back, flowed down my cheeks. I was caught in Between time, a moment that lasted far longer than the time that was swirling past the others here. I took the strap off my neck and undid the knot that had kept it short and against my heart. I handed it to him.

His fingers brushed mine again and I knew then that we were, in this single moment only, as one.

I felt us touch, mind to mind. I knew he did still love me. He knew that I still loved him as well. No matter what had been said, what stance of bravado either of us had taken—this was true, for the foreseeable future.

"*Para siempre*," he whispered in my mind. He stepped back from me and was gone.

Io hobbled to him then, across that circle of recent death, and clung to him. He touched her gently and she released him and her gaze went to me. She looked up at him, seemingly asking permission and he smiled. She came to me, looking slightly awed at the other Sidhe.

"Io! Here you are. Do you have time to see your planet now?"

She looked back at Dagon and then nodded. "He will be busy for some time here."

"I will come for you soon," I said. "If that suits you and Dagon." She nodded again.

We Sidhe finally transited away. Céadar placed me on the dusty blanket on the bed in what had been Nathaniel's outpost house. The house had proved to me that he had cared for this land enough to be on it, outside the comforts of the city. I wept until I was numb and after awhile Fiórcara and Céadar had a conversation that did not include me. It was Céadar who came to me and, sitting beside me, caught my attention and held it gently.

"Nathaniel forced this contest, driven by his ambition. Dagon would have won, no matter what the outcome was. He has a quiet heart and, I think, was prepared to die if it came to that. And it came close to that."

I shook my head. "You are a Sidhe, and do not believe in accidents. Nor does Dagon.

His timing is his finest skill and he took it to the edge as I have seen and experienced him doing many times. His strategy held throughout the long day."

"And now, Danu?"

"And now he will probably take Alta as a mate, if he does not already have one. They may or may not enjoy each other. But he will consolidate his power and presence here until he finds a suitable second to administrate this planet. That might end up being her."

Céadar looked at me patiently and even perhaps with humour. "Danu, think of the rest of us for a moment. Do you require ... my services?" He raised an eyebrow at me. "Do you want to stay alone and suffer your emotions that are now no longer called for? Perhaps just sleep and stay in the darkness for as long as you can?"

I remembered then the day that Dagon had attempted to kill me and I had transited to Between. Fiórcara had retrieved him and Morag and asked me to choose which one—but not both—would live. I declined, casting my lot with them to suffer whatever judgement the Sidhe king would make. Later that day, I drank a cup of elixir of life handed to me by Céadar and afterwards willingly came to him for the first time.

Céadar was holding a cup out to me now.

I was, again, offered an invigorating and slightly altered cup of the elixir of life from this planet by Céadar, and I accepted it eagerly. I felt the energy surge through me and when Céadar looked down at me I reached up for him.

We ended up, as we often did, on the edge of the sea that now was definitely quickening. There was phosphorescence in the shallows—lights that darted and floated up towards the moonlight

"I am yours," I simply said. "As much yours as I can be anyone's. You are my king, and I think that Fiórcara is king to both of us. You are his, as am I.

But this ..."—I indicated us still entangled with the salt drying on our skin and then gestured to the horizon—"here I am yours, hopefully again and again."

He smiled and bent to cover my mouth to end further unnecessary conversation.

EPILOGUE

Loyal Io stayed by the side of Dagon as he finished healing. After it was clear that he was ready and able to resume his role as Alpha leader, she asked him about me and my promise to show her the planet.

He summoned me and I went and retrieved her from his residence. He was not present when I did so, though he had given me a few suggestions as to her care in our communications earlier.

Alta was behind closed doors—whether in grief or as a requirement of formal grieving. Dagon had participated in the Shadakon funeral rites, speaking briefly about Nathaniel's bravery and loyalty. Although he did not say it directly, and would not have been understood by the resident Shadakon clan if he had, Dagon indicated his sadness that it had come to the point of no return for Nathaniel. I knew the depth of connection that had been between them—brothers in arms ...

Céadar and I took Io on a tour of the human settlements, saving the outlying ones populated by the Old Earth groups last. I had always assumed that Io had come from a transplanted First Nations group from old Earth, one that had hung on here until they were at the very edge of survival and then were plundered for the Registry. I believed that Dagon had had first choice of them and had taken the sisters before they experienced the heart and mind numbing experience of being on the Registry and providing to indifferent Shadakon users.

Her bright eyes and still bright mind missed nothing as we visited, including the numbers of children being born. "We had a way to space children," she simply said. "It should be implemented here."

Our last stop was to a settlement deep in the rolling high hills of the planet. Interestingly, there was a cave entrance on the plateau we stood on that just might connect with the one she had seemed familiar with decades ago. When we arrived, she stopped and sniffed the wind and heaved a deep sigh.

The people here lived in what had been called tepees on old Earth. Their homes were made of the hides of the wild cattle and straight branches, tied together at the top. The people seemed to take no more than what would be naturally replenished each spring by both the birth of new cattle and the straight spring branches and I had allowed them to do so. They moved frequently so as not to overuse the land by their presence.

Those who came to greet us from a distance looked much as Io had in her youth—they had glossy straight black hair and golden skin. When they gave her a ritual greeting in their language, she responded and was understood. Céadar and I sat and watched the people gift her and feast with her and knew that even if she returned with us, she would return here soon to eventually give her bones to the earth. When it was time, I told her that Dagon had suggested to me that if she wanted to stay now, she could.

It was the second time I had seen her cry. The first was when her sister Ka had been rescued and kept by Nathaniel. She, like I had done, merely shook her tears to the ground as a blessing of water.

I promised that Dagon would visit her here—a promise I felt safe in making. But in truth, when he did come a few weeks later, she had already gone on, to wherever her people believed they would go at death. I had brought him and watched him kneel briefly beside a small cairn of stones. I loved him again in a way that did not endanger either of us.

He did not have to tell me, although I would learn when I established diplomatic connections with him again, that he was taking Alta as his mate. I did not ask if he loved her, or if she loved him. I knew she would be very suitable to the Shadakon. I hoped she would not hold darkness in her heart and the desire to kill him later. He had laughed then in my mind and, for another brief yet timeless moment, we were one. I savoured that and then put my hand on his arm and transited him back to his home and fate. His eyes were on mine in the moment before I took him back and perhaps we both wished we could go somewhere, at least briefly, to be lost together. But it passed and we landed in his courtyard, the place of Nathaniel's dying and he turned and walked away.

"Te amo, Dagon. For however long para siempre will be for us."

BOOK FOUR

Danu Crowned

CHAPTER ONE

BEFORE THE BEGINNING

Time for me, once seemingly human, passed slowly on Danu's World. Some of the trees that had dared to come up as spindly saplings o were now leafy green overhead. Creatures that were mostly transplants from Old Earth and Exterra took shelter under them. Faced with a new empty world of opportunities, the small lives multiplied so we also had brought their predators to hold a balance here.

Dagon and I were still each other's Makers—bound by exchanges of blood as mates even though he lived in the Shadakon holdings by the spaceport with a partner who he may or may not have cared for. The Shadakon understood and approved of marriages of convenience. Dagon had killed her husband in a ritual fight to the death that was forced on him. I knew he had grieved his brother-in-arms, Nathaniel, who he had had to kill. Hopefully he was kind to the widow, now his wife.

I had, as my main companion, Ceádar, a gentle Sidhe friend and lover who only later I discovered was a displaced Sidhe king, pledged to be second to Fiòcara while on Exterra. Ceádar visited me here, transporting across space from his planet to mine, and helped me in my long restoration project. The Sidhe are not monogamous, and I had long periods of time with no companion to dance the life dance with on midsummer's eve or to hold me through the empty nights.

I had said goodbye to Dagon. It was he who was clear that he wanted no further contact with me other than diplomatic necessities. I still missed him, an ache that was amplified tonight as I stroked my palm where we once had exchanged blood in bliss.

I could feel him nearby and it saddened me when I could not deny my feelings.

CHAPTER TWO

THE CALL

For several seasons, I felt that some change was coming—change always comes, but I
felt this arrival keenly. I hadn't seen or heard from Fiòcara or Ceádar in a
long time. Meanwhile I continued to check on the humans and monitor their
activities. Some of the settlements were surrounded by trees now, and the people
wore woven garments made from the fibres of plants they harvested. I still gifted
them with some tools, and, of course, seeds and useful animals. The Sidhe had
gotten behind my project to make it possible, bringing space ice to replenish the
missing water on this world, and then fish for the seas and small beautiful beings
like butterflies and fireflies and other insects. Some life forms, like crocodiles and
snakes, were conspicuously absent, but I did not question their choice of gifts and
all seemed to function as a living unit.

I sourced my nourishment from the life force of the plants of the planet, an
elixir I gathered ritually and stored to use as needed. I could also draw up the hot
energy of the planet's core after Fiòcara showed me how. It was harsh and overly
potent but necessary for me to use to sustain myself in my early years here.

But tonight, I was sitting beside the sea, my Maker hand in my lap, slowly
tracing over the mark that only some could see. I was thinking about Dagon—his
dark eyes with amber flames that danced within when he was excited as a lover or
hunter—or both. Dagon and I had bonded by sharing blood simultaneously and
with intent; the Maker mark was the only visible sign of this. I recalled his tall
lean body, so unlike the Sidhe, and his strength. He could easily out-fly me, but
waited and let me believe, for a while at least, that I could outdistance him. I was
remembering just such a night, under Exterra's smaller moon. How I had wanted
him, how I had surrendered joyfully to him as my Alpha. He had swooped on
me and pinned me to the earth, like a raptor might take down a sparrow, his eyes
with their dancing flames looking down on mine.

I had not been afraid of him then. Later he taught me that he could, and would,
hurt me.

Still later he tried to kill me—but at the last minute, relented, resulting in my
permanent exile with the Sidhe. I was not safe with him, due to my Sidhe ways.

But in spite of everything, we reunited many times as lovers though no longer
as mates accepted by his clan. The last time we were together and I referred to a
future in which we could continue to be together, he had warned me not to wish
for such a thing anymore. I sat for a timeless time in the desert then, grieving him
but honouring his request until he left the planet.

He had returned eventually, and almost died in front of me when challenged to a fight to the death by the then rising Alpha, Nathaniel. Dagon had whispered something to me after his victory that had been our own private vow of renewal.

"Te amo para siempre."

I will love you forever.

I knew that I would, though I was not sure that he would continue to honour that tie that had been between us.

The sky darkened slowly and, I admit, I called to him then, using our bond to see if he would respond to me. I realized that it was unfair and probably futile; he had another life and possibly even another love now. Certainly he had many sex partners. My loneliness did not justify seeing if I could reach him and bring us together again, but as the stars brightened in the darkening sky and there was no response, I bent my head and wept. I was undone, alone on a desert planet, burning with the building energy of late spring. I was Sidhe. I was not meant to be alone now, although my entire earlier life as a human I had spent behind closed doors avoiding all contact. Dagon had taught me about the power of wanting someone, of wanting him. The waves did not drown out my sobs although there was no one to hear me or be concerned about my state of being.

I heard a faint sound—a soft but obvious landing of someone nearby, and a sigh. I did not look up. I assumed that my mind was now torturing me with a construct of what I most wanted.

"*I may not be what you most want,*" he thought and it was a whisper in my mind.

I could only see his outline but I felt the power of his Alpha energies swirling around me. He had continued to grow in strength since I had first met him.

"*Yes. Few would dare to summon me without permission, Danu.*" I felt his high arrogance and bent my head. He deserved my apology. Once again, I sought him thinking only of myself, hoping he could relieve me of my sadness and loneliness.

I said and thought nothing but he could read my under thoughts easily. He was silent—both in words and thoughts. It was then that I knelt before him, as I had as his mate when he first became Alpha of the Shadakon of Exterra.

I wanted to feel his hand on my head or shoulder, giving me a sign to stand and be welcome in his presence. He left me kneeling in the sand and I stayed there, aching, but not begging.

Time passed and the only sound was from the waves that were building with the tide and sighing across the dried sand.

"*Dagon. Whether you stay or go, I am yours tonight if you want me. I have fought against calling out to you for months.*"

"I know." He had switched to speaking and his voice was deep with under messages of desire. Still he left me kneeling in the sand before him.

I remembered the afternoon he came to me on another beach and bent gently to my mouth, even as he prepared to take my life energy, intending to leave me empty and dead forever. I was an inconvenience and confusion to him. I was not faithful and yet we were tied to each other, bound by passion and the ritual of our mating. It occurred to me that he might act in a similar way now. That he might end me here tonight.

He was partnered with a Shadakon female and they ruled the part of this planet that the Sidhe allowed them to—the spaceport and the traffic there. His previous partners had all tried to kill me. The Shadakon were fierce in protecting their sphere of control. Coming to me was problematic for him.

I felt his hand fall lightly on my shoulder. I did not wipe the tears from my cheeks but met his eyes that glimmered in the moonlight. He left his hand there as I rose and I kindled to his energy. I had been alone a long time. Not as long as when I first met him—then I had been alone all my life and innocent of true passion with my own kind or any other. Then he had intentionally and professionally, awakened a force that overwhelmed both of us and changed the courses of both of our lives.

I wanted him like that first night. I shivered under his touch and he sighed and ran his fingers lightly down across my breast and continued down over my tunic to where I ached for him.

"You want nothing else but this, Danu?" He sounded almost business-like and more tears slipped down my cheeks.

I wanted him to love me. I always wanted my partners to love me. But Dagon … Dagon and I had had something unique and dangerous.

If we began, we would want more than this moment, this night. I would anyway. He was a fierce leader of a clan that had killed and taken since their beginnings. Vampires took. Whether a little bit or all, they took from the store of life energy in their human prey—or, as it turned out, another of their kind, or a Sidhe. And although I was all and none of these, I was vulnerable to him in that I could not resist giving over all to him. I would not have to be entranced or manipulated into surrendering, I would do it of my own free will.

"Where is your Sidhe king?" he asked dryly. "Or both kings?"

I shook my head. I had not called Ceádar or Fiócara in what was probably a long time. Either could have arrived here without announcing themselves, but they had not. I sensed that they were involved in other actions and currently less interested in Danu's World and in me, Danu. I had been accused before of not asking for what I wanted. But surely it should not always fall to me to make contact? Instead I was here, on the edge of a quickening small sea, with an ex lover who had told me not to wish to be with him again.

"What of you?" I asked. "If you were content where and who you were with, why did you answer my call?"

"Do you truly want the answer to that, Danu?" Dagon asked. "I will give you a clue then. It is approaching midsummer. You have faerie blood. It is part of your allure." He stood watching and taking in the effect of what he had said on me.

When I had been young, a teen struggling to come to grips with awkwardly turning into a young woman and what that meant to me, a man had offered to relieve me of my ignorance regarding sex. Afterwards, he had let me know that it was not a particularly valuable thing that I had given to him. He wanted nothing more to do with me and I felt the same. I had hidden out then and later bore the speculation of my crew members that I was more interested in women, or no one. I thought they were right until I had met Dagon, until he had taught me about pleasure and more pleasure.

Now he stood before me, offering to take what I would gladly give him, but giving nothing in return?

I felt like I had run out of air, far below the surface of the water where I had once dived with confidence. I had misjudged and now there would be merciless consequences. I sank to the sand and huddled there, with Dagon still looking down from his height on me. I had no further thoughts or expectations, or hopes.

I felt shame heating my cheeks where the tears had made cool tracks. I was an unwise creature—not human, nor Sidhe, nor Shadakon—who had simply overestimated her safety margin. When meeting a predator, that usually results in painful consequences. The situation was in his hands now. I stood.

"I will swim now. You can go. I apologize for taking your time." I spoke calmly. I wondered numbly how long I would have to swim before my strength failed me. Perhaps the sun would rise, but I would not retrace my path. I knew that this small sea was wider than my ability to stay afloat. I took off my minimal garment and took a step to the edge of the incoming small waves. I was glad that the whale who had befriended me on Exterra would not be present to witness my decision or come across my body later.

"If you wish to die tonight, why not gift me with your intoxicating blood first?" Dagon asked, so softly that the cruelty was not immediately evident.

"Would you take what I have and give nothing of yourself?" I only asked. "Would you cause me more pain to see what I can bear before I beg you to care, to love me, if only briefly, or end me?"

He took my arm and then we were both lost. He drew me into his chest and wrapped his strong white arms around me. I put my mouth up to whatever he might give me and he brushed my lips and began to build the fires in both of us. He took off his own garments and the evidence of his wanting me shined in the moonlight. He took me down against the moist sand and entered me like he still lived there, within me, all along. We both moaned and then he set a rhythm that intensified until I called his name and lost my own.

"Danu!" I felt his release.

I had one hand in his hair and I was touching the starburst scar on his chest—the place that he had been staked so long ago. We had just finished and I wanted him again and again. This time he drew me down over him and looked up at me as I rode him to our mutual ecstasy. The tide had continued to come up the beach and we finally moved away from its salty touch. The stars were lower in the sky although dawn was not yet arriving.

"Now, Dagon." I moved my dark red hair aside and placed my neck against his mouth.

His fangs came down immediately, or maybe they had been down all along.

He slipped them beneath my skin and we both entered into a bliss that lasted until the first faint colours of dawn. He sipped rather than immediately taking what he could, and each time jolted both of us through the shared energy of our bond. And then, without me asking, he bit into his own palm and offered it to me. He was offering to renew our Maker bonds—something he had intentionally not done in any of our later partings. I tasted his wild life's blood and my own as he gazed at me without blinking. I drank enough that I could feel him diffused throughout my body and mind.

"We are both undoubtedly crazy," he said, replacing his clothing and handing me mine. "There are many reasons to not have done any of this, and no reason that I can think of to have done so. Except ..."

"Except ..." I said, but was unable to frame a thought of why it would be beneficial to him or me later.

"Except that this planet will need a united governance to deal with the changes soon to come."

Dagon and I both suddenly faced Fiócara who was standing slightly down the beach from us. We immediately knew he had vicariously partaken in our activities and that if he had not approved he could have stopped us.

Dagon sighed. "In for one faerie, in for them all I suppose. I won't ask you, Danu, if your invitation was on behalf of only you, or for the betterment of the Sidhe, I believe you acted on your own. If I could have kept my heart hardened, I know I would have seen you swim out from the shore. I am not a swimmer. I could not have rescued you, even if you hoped I would. And I sensed no hope in you."

"Once again, Danu chose death over being abandoned or punished by you." Fiócara said calmly. "This time you rescued her. I suppose that she and you are making some kind of slow progress."

"Ceádar and I wondered why we did not hear from you, Danu. I decided to make the trip. I am aware of your ties and am accustomed to you returning again and again to Dagon, and then coming back to me. I am not sure whether Ceádar has the same long perspective on your loving as I do."

I hung my head. Even by Sidhe standards, I didn't seem to be able to behave appropriately.

"It is the fact of your choice being a Shadakon who has tried to kill you several times that is the complication for us who are Sidhe. Well ... and also that you chose two Shadakon lovers who had to fight to death over who was to be the Alpha. You may have been included in the benefits to the winner."

I started to protest but was silent instead.

Dagon had been surprisingly silent as well. What the Sidhe king said was true: I had been involved with both Dagon and the warrior Nathaniel, who had been his second and who challenged him to a ritual fight to the death to claim Alpha status. I, and the Sidhe, had witnessed that long day that ended in Nathaniel's end. Now Dagon turned to Fiócara.

"I thank you for not interrupting us," he simply said.

Once he would have been furious. But Fiócara and his eons long queen had entertained Dagon in their hill house without me present. He had learned firsthand the ways of the Sidhe and how they joined easily in each other's activities with both body and mind.

"I wouldn't have missed any of it," said Fiócara. "Such events are delicious to me. Danu is passionate as we both know, but the blood bonding has its own unique element of bliss. I thank you for both of your performances."

"Of course, re-bonding with Danu means I can access you more easily, Dagon," he continued offhandedly. "But that has been our arrangement since the beginning of our negotiations."

Dagon bowed slightly to the Sidhe king. *Why had I thought that the Sidhe and Shadakon were done with each other?*

"I must return, Danu," said Dagon. "We will be … in touch again soon. Not that you asked, but my Shadakon mate has gone off planet, no doubt to satisfy desires that I have no wish to fulfill. I thought I would have a peaceful time of contemplation. But as usual, I am again entangled with the Sidhe and you. No doubt you or your kings will fill me in with the details later."

He touched his palm and I felt it in my own. He turned from us and was gone, swiftly flying back to his fortressed home.

I was now in front of Fiócara, my Sidhe king and lover. He had repeatedly taught me that I could not possess him even though what was between us was intense, and I think even for him, unique. Now he stood in the growing light, assessing me.

CHAPTER THREE

FIÓCARA LEAVES HIS MARK

"May I offer you the shelter of my home and some elixir of life?" I asked Fiócara.

I was still stunned by what had just occurred between Dagon and I, but could feel the effect Fiócara had on me intensifying. I always wanted him—even when I was frustrated and angry with him. One night, he had punished me for daring to leave Between (the hidden dimension and wild part of Exterra where the Sidhe lived) against his direct orders. When I had transited across the boundaries of Between, he had morphed into a giant hawk and took me to ground as I flew in the starlight. He ripped my clothes away like fur or feathers, and drove his hawk's beak into me again and again as he easily held me down. I bled and cried out, but in the end I wanted him and he took me. As I lay beneath him he warned me that the next time I disobeyed him he would not spare me, and I believed him. Now he plied his erotic power and I trembled before him. I thought I should apologize to him as well but he held up one long thin finger and simply said, "We expected you to do no less."

It served him then that I had called and re-engaged with Dagon.

I took his arm and transited us to my home, a small building overlooking the sea that Nathaniel had gifted to me when he and I had parted. I seldom used it for anything more than a place to store a few things and to avoid the rains that the Sidhe had arranged for this planet. They came hard, three nights a week, replenishing the waterways and the small seas. Earlier, human water miners had taken all the water they could reach and sold it off planet. When I came, the ground was sand with only the bones of rocks and some barely surviving plant-life. There were deep empty canyons. Now water glinted in the bottoms of them, and the humans on the land found water when they dug their wells. I knew it would rain tonight, would pound down hard on the roof of my dwelling thanks to the Sidhe work of securing and positioning huge chunks of space ice in the planet's orbit. Depending on what Fiócara intended on this visit, I would give him what I could. I knew that that included me if he wanted that.

"Ah, Danu, I can easily slake my usual desires elsewhere. You live too far away now to serve as more than an occasional lover. And then there is Ceádar. I believe you recently asked him to be in his full power with you. And you admitted regretting that you had disregarded him as merely another beautiful Sidhe." He raised an eyebrow and caught my gaze. He smiled.

"Yet, even fresh from a hot night with your vampire lover, I feel you responding to me."

I said and tried to think of—nothing

"There is one thing between us that few understand about you—although Dagon took a page from my queen's book of passion when you and he were together before he left this planet. Green Tara was quite happy with your offering to him of accepting pain and passion."

Dagon and I had flown to a cave where I had taken shelter before, when Dagon's then mate was trying to kill both of us. There was a timeless presence there, a goddess with the powers of bestowing life and death. I returned to her several times to make desperate deals with her, paying in pain for what she offered me. To my surprise Fiócara seemed to know her and they easily communicated together. On Dagon and my seemingly last night together, I had taken him to the cave and he brought me passion and pain beyond where we had gone before. Green Tara, like Fiócara, had participated in our raised energies and she was pleased and told me so later. Apparently she had told my king as well.

From the beginning, lying with Fiócara had been a mixture of pain and bliss that took me beyond anywhere I could have ever imagined going.

"Get the elixir ready," Fiócara said calmly. "I have something to do outside."

He soon returned with a full handful of thin, green spring shoots off the bushes outside the house. He split the bark with his fingernail and peeled it off in a twisted thin strip. After each thin branch was stripped, he gathered them and began to braid the bark into a strong twine that he wrapped around the folded over larger ends, so that he had a serviceable handle. He bit off a few of the longer branches and delicately chewed on all the ends to produce softened tips.

I watched him in curiosity and then growing fear. He heard this of course and smiled up at me, his beautiful spring green eyes shining guilelessly.

"I think it is time for you and I to renew our bonds as well," he thought directly to me. He swooshed his new tool experimentally against his other wrist. It made a sound like nothing else I had ever heard, and left faint red marks.

"Pour the elixir," he said.

Moving his cup to the side, he brought mine in front of him. "Will you take this cup from me, Danu? I would slightly change your perception of our connection, although you are more sensitive now than when I first met you. We will not bother further with words. Do you accept my offering to you?"

I looked at the new tool in his hand.

I had no doubt that if I agreed, he would use it on me and I would surrender to him as surely as I had to Dagon.

"Perhaps even more deeply, my Sidhe lover," he thought back, having heard my under-mind realizations.

I looked into his eyes and sighed and thought back, *"Yes, my king. Yes, my lover. I surrender it all to you with no restrictions."* So we had first come together and so we would continue. My bond with him was seemingly unbreakable and I would not wish it any other way. Ceádar understood this, although I knew he hoped my feelings were deep for him as well.

"Yes," thought Fiócara, smiling. *"You never gave me reason to doubt you."*

Saying that, he bit down and made a small wound in his own palm and dripped some of his potent Sidhe blood into my cup.

"You have already tasted my blood and know its effects on you."

I took the cup, looked into it briefly and then drank deeply. He drank from his as well and moved mine away. *"More later, Danu."*

Soon, so soon, I was in a place I had been many times before—laying beside him, craving him, wanting only that he would touch me. A glow suffused my body, and slowly deepened from pleasant warmth to an ache.

He was smiling down at me and my clothing was gone. He ran one finger down, across my lips and between my breasts and then down to where the fire had begun to burn in my core. I wanted him. I wanted it all. I shivered under his touch.

"I will take your thoughts as a further agreement that you will accept whatever I bring you."

It was not a question but I breathed, "Yes." Early on he had made it clear that he wanted my consent to whatever he might do to me.

He replaced his finger with the fringed ends of his newly made tool. He trailed it over my breasts and belly, and ever so lightly across my place of wanting. He ran it up from my ankles, along the soft skin of my inner thighs. I shuddered, wanting him, wanting whatever he was planning to bring to me.

"Ah, Danu. You are privy to some of the secrets of the Sidhe. My queen is not the only one of us who uses pain in the service of bliss. Pain is, of course, just more intense feeling. Where the line lies between pain and pleasure is a personal boundary."

He seemingly experimentally brought the flogger's supple branch tips down on the skin near my breasts. It left a flash of pain that faded quickly.

He paused to gently massage my nipples and then abruptly brought the lash down again, harder this time. I moaned, attempting not to cry out.

"Oh, Danu. You will cry out and beg me. Although at the end, we might both be surprised at what you beg me for."

This time the fringed edges landed directly on my nipple. He paused and then lashed the other side. I bucked beneath him and he laughed and held both my hands above my head with one hand. Not that I was fighting him, but he was seeking perfection in the pattern he was leaving on me. Like the scrapes on my back that he had left me with one night, he wanted the evidence to show to others and me. He hit with a soft criss-cross motion over my belly, over and over again. I knew the marks would fade. But they would be forever perceivable to me and to another Sidhe. And to Dagon.

"This is not about Dagon," he thought to me matter-of-factly. *"Do not bring him into this. I did not interfere with you and his activities on the beach. This is between you and I."*

At one point he raised me up gently and gave me more elixir. I drank thirstily and he laughed. *"You know this will open you up even further to the experience I am bringing you, Danu, but I would expect no less from you."*

When he laid me back down on the bed, he gently spread me so that I was open to his eyes—and to the lash. He laid his patterns up and down my thighs as I cried and called his name.

"Fiócara! My true friend!" It was the name he had first given me to use to call him—I was gasping now and begging him.

"*You are begging me to …?*"

I cried and thrashed while he paused, waiting for my answer. I did not know what I was begging for. For him. For all of him and whatever he would do to me.

"*Yes. A little more then, Danu. And then I will enter into your pain and take you the rest of the way…If you have not already begun without me.*"

He would lash a less sensitive area with enthusiasm and then quickly return with a light but more devastating touch to my most tender parts. After several of these, I began to scream. And then I fell away into a place of intensity but no additional pain. I reached up for him, grabbing his shoulders and he smiled and came to me.

I felt the life energy of the planet surge into me. We were one, and one with the energy of the planet.

It was not gentle. Neither of us held back and I noticed at one point that we were no longer inside. The rain was beating on us and neither of us paid any attention to it. We were one being. Once again, Fiócara had showed me as much as I could bear about communing with a Sidhe king.

Still later, I had drunk to the bottom of my cup and felt him holding me firmly but gently against him in the dark. He was stroking skin that felt sensitive but not painful. I fell into what might have been sleep or might have been a deep recovery. When I awoke, the sun was up, drying the puddles of the night before. Fiócara was gone. Two empty cups sat on the table beside me and the small, exquisitely fashioned flogger was beside them. The tips had a faint reddish stain.

I looked down and saw—nothing. No marks, no broken skin. But I knew that I had been marked and that he and I and possibly others would perceive it and understand it for what it was.

I had been taken over the edge.

CHAPTER FOUR

A CAREFUL BALANCE

I walked the shoreline of the sea for several days, pondering what my part was now in the developments of the two nights I had spent, being taken and combining with both the Alpha leader of the Shadakon and my Sidhe king. I waited to see if clarity came, meanwhile watching out to sea, hoping to see new life. I was surprised to spot some seabirds and the glint of silver scales in the shallows. I swam out in the salty water, glad that I was not in the desperate state I had been in, when I considered making the sea my way of dying. I could see these thoughts as over-dramatic now, but at the time they were the truth to me, and I would have carried out what I willed to do.

Letting the salt dry in my hair (my home had a small fresh water shower that I occasionally used), I finally did what I knew I had been stalling and avoiding doing.

I shook the bright blue stone out the small buckskin bag that usually stayed around my neck. It was my call stone to Ceádar, the Sidhe who I knew cared deeply for me. I was not sure if he, too, could monitor my actions on this world; I knew that Fiócara could and did and had.

Had Ceádar also been witness to what I had been doing? And would that be a problem between us? The truth was, I didn't crave Ceádar as I did Fiócara and Dagon. I had never felt driven or desperate when in his company. And yet I missed him, not just his effects on me, but how he was with me—quiet and without drama. It was he that I went to now, for advice or just kindness. I would not be silent about what had transpired here.

I put the blue stone down on the sand in an intense beam of sunlight. It shone with the reflected light of the sun but then brightened even more.

"*Ceádar,*" I thought on an outgoing breath. I waited.

I felt his presence and his clear calm mind. "*Well, Danu, you have kept yourself busy. I am somewhat surprised that you contact me now. And you still unsatisfied? Is there something I can offer you that they did not?*"

It was a fair question. I had not thought beforehand how this interaction would proceed. I decided that I had only my intuition to guide me in my wanting to be in contact with him.

"*What happened was intense, and if you monitored that, you know that Fiócara took me to a place further than I have gone before. But that has been the history of our connection. He is my king and I am his, and I also somehow belong to Dagon at times.*

But both are content to mostly let me live my life without them. I did not expect Dagon to renew our Maker vows, but I could not have refused him either."

None of this answered Ceádar's questions and he remained silent.

"It is soon midsummer here and I wish to fly a cone of power in honour of this strengthening life force. I wish, if you agree, that you would be my king on that night."

"Why?" he thought. It was like a pebble dropped into a small pond. The possible answers spread in ever-widening circles.

"Because I am the only one who would accept your invitation?" he asked quietly.

I was shocked. Once again, I had hurt this gentle lover, although I wasn't sure what exactly I had done. Midsummer was not at the same time on Exterra as on Danu's world. They were in spring, the Sidhe's powers waxing with each moon phase.

But here I faced the turning of the energy from growing to ripening and then to the resting time of fall and winter. I wasn't sure how long I had been alone, and thought that that fact was not reassuring. I needed connection with someone who knew me and accepted me as-is without trying to change or challenge me. I needed a friend who was a lover rather than a master. I acknowledged Dagon as an Alpha and Fiócara as my mentor and king.

"You once asked me to be your king," Ceádar thought to me. *"You asked me to remind you if you forgot that I was, in fact, a Sidhe king, and could show you what that meant. I have done so. Was it not enough for you?"*

"Ceádar!" I suddenly felt the crashing loneliness of possibly not being with him. That he might not continue to be part of my life. I looked up and saw a desert planet. I felt like my heart was an equally inhospitable place. Ceádar brought the rains and the renewal. Dagon and Fiócara were like fierce weather moving across the landscape—but then gone in the morning.

I had recently felt sadness and hopelessness in my pursuit of Dagon. I knew our connection was only a small reprieve. I had been intentionally taken to the edge of what I could bear by Fiócara. He had some plan in mind, molding me into one with greater endurance perhaps, but I knew I would not sit by his side, or he by mine. He was out of my league forever as an ancient Sidhe king.

"I am out of your league as well, Danu. I chose to modify what I brought to you. I had to learn to acquire a quality in myself not highly prized by the Sidhe—patience. I allowed much that Fiócara would not have accepted from you.

Now though, newly renewed by both of your 'lovers'"—and I felt the sting in that thought—*"you get around to calling me. Why, Danu? What do you truly want from me? It is quite possible that I cannot provide it. In which case, we should respectfully step back from each other—for, as you say, the foreseeable future."*

"Please come." I hadn't expected to say that, but there it was.

"You want to renew with me as well? Renew whatever it is between us?"

I sat as motionlessly as I could. *"I can't do this with us on different planets. I need to see you, look into your forest eyes. I don't care if you don't touch me. But please don't take the long step back from such a distance."*

Ceádar was silent.

"I am begging you now, king of the Sidhe. I did not intentionally set you aside. I became used to my loneliness until it crashed in on me and I could not bear it anymore. I take no comfort from the humans, although their babies and children are briefly beautiful. Both Dagon and Fiócara took what they knew I would give them, but passion does not make up for a connection of kindness and enjoying each other's company. You came to me that way—in the beginning and from then on. I have slept in your arms without you requiring anything from me. You waited for me after the midsummer when we saved Exterra ..."

My thoughts went back to that terrible night. In the days before midsummer's eve, I had gone out on the land and attempted to get the attention of all the beings who lived on Exterra. There was a human stealth fleet gathered overhead. I had no doubt that they meant to bring death to us all—another scourging of the planet's higher life forms and Sidhe and Shadakon as well. We flew to create a cone of power that I focused and disabled the humans on those ships that did not voluntarily leave. The ships blossomed in a final deadly blooming on our scopes. We were saved, but I was wracked by the destruction I had delivered. I had fled to the beach, but Ceádar was waiting for me when I came back from a midnight swim. He had rescued my clothes from the rising tide. His arms and lips were warm and I returned to him from the place beyond sadness that I had gone to. He had restored me and gifted me with a loving midsummer's eve.

There was a long silence before Ceádar responded.

"I promised myself that I would not offer you solace after you had a rough experience with another lover. I broke that promise to myself many times. The Sidhe pleasure each other without further expectations. You wanted more from me—and less.

You wanted me to care; you wanted me to accept you in grief and self-doubting. Meanwhile Dagon tried to kill you. That was our first night together, if you recall. You had drying tears on your cheeks instead of easy laughter. I was not wise enough to step back after that night. Maybe it would be easier for both of us if I do now."

"Please," I whispered aloud. "I will not threaten to give up my life here because you have spoken your truth. But this project, this life—I do not feel any reason to continue. I don't care what Fiócara has planned for me. He sent me here, and I have served his purposes well. But now ..."

I heard the wind blow across the newly thriving sea grasses behind me. It flowed around me, without touching me. I felt nothing, but beneath the nothing something was crushing the breath from me. I had again been oblivious, assuming that Ceádar was a given in my life. He had now gently told that this might work for me—but not for him. I did not cry, or make a further sound. I assumed that he had broken the connection and was gone.

In an eerie replay from only a few days ago, I sensed him near me, but did not open my eyes. If this was something I had conjured, I would not be able to bear the pain of seeing nothing but the blue sea and the rest of my days stretching before me.

I felt his strong warm hands on my shoulders and waited another moment to look up. If it had not been him, I would have surely broken in such a way that could not be repaired. I saw his forest green eyes of spring and his slightly curling brown hair with highlights of sunbeams. His body was, as always, strong and warm.

He held me at a distance, looking into my eyes. I was wearing what were rags of clothing, something that kept the full strength of the sun off of me, but were graceless and faded. Nathaniel had had clothes made for me. That had been a long time ago. I had turned into someone who was as wild as the humans that I had left on the land. I shivered under his touch, not in immediate wanting but as a wild thing might. When he raised one hand I flinched slightly, hoping for his touch but fearing it equally. He laid it on my head and ran his hand down my tangled auburn hair.

"Danu," he said gently, "you have been alone too long. We, I, left you here while we dealt with other urgent things. Old Earth is now truly dying. She has gone well beyond the tipping point and, if more than simple life can retain a foothold, it will take a very long time of regrowth, and man may never return to her.

Our Sidhe brothers are weary and undone and need to come away for good. Some will come to Exterra; I don't know what the process of choosing who will go where will be. But some must come here if they are to have a chance of a healthy life. Many are bitter and heartsick and need to recover themselves if possible. They will need guidance."

I looked at him and although I understood all that he had said, I could not immediately put together the rest of it. They must come here? They would need … a king? Fiocara had given me the job of repairing (with much Sidhe assistance) this planet—for their eventual relocation?

Ceádar had been promised to be king here, not a second king on Exterra. Once again, he would use his skills and powers to their full extent. I had once asked him to be my king here, but he had not agreed at that time.

Someone had to communicate with the Shadakon and placate them, someone who was a reliable conduit of information to Fiócara. If Ceádar allowed me to be by his side with my pre-existing allegiances to Fiócara and Dagon—his previous tolerance for my situation might serve Fiócara as well. If Ceádar put me aside, then another plan was doubtless already coming into existence.

Fiócara had given me to Ceádar. Although our connection was not forged immediately or easily, still we became close and lovers.

I was silent. He continued to look at me, following my thoughts as I put together the facts I had had, but had not been able to understand their place in the scheme of things.

"Did you see and understand this, Ceádar?" I asked.

"The answer to that is not yes or no," he said softly. "I think initially he thought that I could use you to further our plans in the future without getting caught by you."

"But he knew you as well as he knows me," I said. "He knew you carried a flame for his queen and allowed you to be present and, yes, to make love to her, but only if he was part of it and it suited his purposes. He knows you do not let go easily."

"That would be a yes," said Ceádar.

"Did we have any choice in the matter?" I asked.

"That cannot be answered either yes or no either," he said. "But I have a different question for you, one you should ponder before answering.

Knowing now, that you have been a seemingly willing participant in Fiócara's plans, would you have chosen otherwise—to not have come to me, flown on midsummer's eve with me, stayed by my side when you were gifted by the wild elixir of life? Given that time cannot be set back, would you now choose to forget me and Fiócara and live your life here as a newly-arrived Sidhe, with little knowledge of this planet and none of us or Dagon?"

"You know I wished for death rather than forgetting! You were there, when Fiócara took my ability to transit rather than take my memories. You know I fled his queen who would have done what Fiócara could or would not do—wipe out my memories and leave me unwelcome in both the Shadakon and Sidhe world." My anger finally rose to my defence and I shook with it. He stepped back from me.

"There is only one choice here, Ceádar. I was given to you by Fiócara and you, better than I, understood the full implications of that. There is now a beautiful mostly empty world here for the weary Sidhe refugees. But if you no longer want me as a responsibility and yes, friend and lover, then take my life. I have no doubt that you can do so as quickly as the Shadakon can. I do not want to walk this land, not knowing what I have done and become here. I do not want to be a mind-damaged sort of Sidhe. Doubtlessly you and Fiócara have discussed this possibility because here we are again. I don't know how it came to pass that once again I turned to Dagon. I do know that I have no way of refusing Fiócara and that he deepened that recently. If I could take back those actions I would. No bliss in someone else's arms is worth losing you. But I have limited power in the game I am in, whether I seemingly have free choice or not. I now think that none of us have true choice in many situations where we think we do. That is a cruelty of bad logic and should be set aside. We do what we do. We are who we are. I am Danu who takes many lovers and, against all reason, actually loves them. It is my vulnerability and Fiócara has used it well. He was intrigued that I surrendered to him when he could have glamoured me and taken what he wanted. Perhaps you were as well."

I stopped. I waited, like the forest waits for the coming fire or raging storm—nowhere to go. No way to escape my fate. I looked into Ceádar's beautiful eyes and at his strong browned body. I wished only that he would touch me kindly one last time.

Time paused. There was no Between here, although later there might be, but time for the Sidhe is not that of clocks or devices. If time did not pause, perhaps we did. I knew that until he turned his back on me, or even moved to take my mind or my life, that he was still my Ceádar.

He had given me that name, which was old Gaelic for cedar, to call him. He was and had been my life-saving cedar canoe, carrying me safely across rough waters. He had brushed aside my sadness, as was once done by the original Pacific coastal people of old Earth, who used fresh fragrant cedar branches to brush away sadness and hopelessness. He had gone to the stars with me. In time, I might have learned to transit between planets, but meanwhile, in his arms we had gone to hang in space watching the slow spirals of light and darkness. I was, in a curious way, content and accepting of this gifted timeless moment.

"I cannot leave you," he finally said. "I will not take from you who you are. Whether this is the will of Fiócara or not, I will accept my part in standing beside you. I will be king here and you will be who you are—queen if you wish, although the Sidhe might have difficulty with a queen who also stands beside a Shadakon. But we will face that when it comes."

He had been to my home and he transited both of us to it. The two empty cups and the small tool that Fiócara had fashioned were still beside the bed. He very calmly moved all aside and lay me down and joined me. He had only one more question for me, and it was an easy one to answer.

"Do you want me to come to you now, Danu?"

And I did. I did.

CHAPTER FIVE

NEGOTIATIONS

In the morning, I put on my most serviceable tunic and long pants after enjoying the gift of a fresh water shower flowing over my body. Solar energy fuelled the pump. I seldom used the available lighting, preferring candles or darkness. Ceádar had looked over the energy source and determined that it would be adequate for powering his computer, which also had its own source that could be replenished on a sunlit day. He had picked up the flogger and, after raising his eyebrows to get my attention, had placed it on a shelf.

I heard his thought about it though. *"Would you want me to use this on you, Danu?"*

I froze. *Would I?* It did not seem to fit with what we built up between us. But he had been present when he and Fiócara had once taken turns pushing me further and further into wanting both of them. I had been angry at them both, but in the end begged both to finish with me. The next day I was aware of some slightly stinging marks on my back as I sat at my station and worked. I could sense that Ceádar was aware of them as well. His thoughts were ... exciting to both of us.

"I don't think that has a yes or no answer," I said, using the language he had recently used in explaining what he had known about Fiócara's plans for the future here. "However, I can't help but notice that I didn't immediately say, 'No!' But let me ask you the same thing: would you want me to bring it to you?"

"Perhaps," he said mildly. "Let's wash it off and let it dry in the hot sun."

And so I swished it in water.

"See how it feels when wet—on wet skin," he said. I brought it down over my inner arm and yelped.

"Good to know," he said calmly. We looked at each other.

"I think we have more immediate things to talk about," Ceádar said. I had poured elixir for both of us and he seemed to be savouring his. "So different than that of Exterra," he said, sounding like some long-ago wine connoisseur.

Ceádar smiled. "What we take in, we should appreciate. This would be, a wine nouveau. Complex and aggressive—I can tell that you gathered a significant amount of this from native plants."

"I love their tenacity. There are already groves of trees."

I thought then about the Peace Grove where we had planted the bodies of the humans not trustworthy enough to be put out on the land. They had held positions of self-created power in the city. Their fellow humans were hurt by their indifference and cruelty. I did not want them or even one to build an empire and use other humans unkindly. I had poisoned them and myself to achieve this last winnowing. Green Tara had given me the substance to put in their celebratory punch at a dinner I had hosted. It was swift and painless and the few humans that realized that it was past time to flee, were quickly mopped up by the Shadakon guards. I recovered from it, but perhaps I was now less human than I used to be. Plant life flourished where the bodies had been buried. The planet had been so waterless that the humus in the soil had disappeared, however, those small beings that make soil were only waiting to flourish again.

Ceádar had followed my thoughts and he turned me towards him. "You do not like to cause death, but you do so."

He smoothed his thumb over my lips and laughed when I opened to him.

"Sex and pain and death—not so different," he said. "And then there are the times when you seemingly are willing to go to your own death."

Ceádar had been present when I transited to Between, away from Dagon and Morag who had come to the small island when I assisted in the hospice. I had immediately understood why Dagon stood in front of me, and I accepted my imminent ending at his hands. But when Morag came streaking towards us with a needle gun full of pain and slow death, I transited to Between. Fiócara had retrieved them both and asked me to decide their fate. I refused to ask for their deaths and he shrugged and let both go. I never saw Morag again—Dagon forced her to leave the planet. He and I cautiously recovered our connection, but I never again was part of the Shadakon world.

"It was always present in my mind," I said. "The solution of ending it all quickly and with some control when in a seemingly hopeless situation."

"You needed that door then," Ceádar said. "You have more choices now. You have time to wait and see if your situation comes around to more what you want," he added. He smiled at me and I wanted to dive into his spring eyes, like a pool found unexpectedly in the woods, to float and be easy with him.

"Maybe I want the same thing," he said. "To let you lead the dance."

We looked at each other, with the same question—"*Now*?"

He sighed. "No, Danu, this has to be a short visit. I am taking note of what you need though. You need Sidhe clothes that are appropriate for you as our representative here. Not quite queen level dazzling, I know that dazzle isn't your style, but some shades of green or blue, and more than one so that you can switch them off. I also suggest that you tame your wild red hair a bit. I will include in my order for you, something that might confine your hair a bit, if you want to wear it."

"Are you going to speak to Dagon?" I asked.

"Soon, I think. Fiócara will as well. You will see Dagon before we do though. You may give him some advance information—such as what I have told you. The Sidhe own the planet; talking to Dagon is merely a courtesy, but we need to work together closely. You should check on the situation in the city around the spaceport, and the humans there as well, and find out whether the Shadakon are preying on the humans on the land." He looked at me softly and my heart melted for him.

"You will combine with him, Danu. I know this. I would say, it is inevitable, so be easy in your own mind. Fiócara has put you in this position and you are still connected to Dagon. Once I am here more permanently though, we must talk about where your primary loyalties lie."

He held me briefly, forehead to forehead and I felt his power surround both of us and gasped.

"Do not open the dark door," he just said. And then he was gone.

I flew over the settlements, noting lush crops in the fields and children playing in the creeks and small lakes. I landed in a few places and talked to the people there. Their languages were already evolving away from any I knew, including English. I could communicate with them mentally, of course. I would pick a bright looking older child as my "translator" and he or she would speak for me. As a gift for this service, I would briefly search their minds and tell them that with hard work, they could achieve what they wanted—a fishing net perhaps or a much-desired tool; I would later make that happen. I saw corncob dolls that made me smile—so they were once made on old Earth.

I would also sit and be silent with the elders and access their thoughts. There were beings that came in the night and left people who had been safe and asleep in their huts asleep outside under a tree or a haystack. Usually they recovered uneventfully.

Sometimes, however, they did not. I would talk to Dagon about the activities of the Shadakon.

Nathaniel and I had monitored the early settlers closely, and had imposed birth control measures. It was now taboo to have a baby while an older child still nursed or within three years if one's infant died. Infant and child mortality was still high and the humans did not live long, so this was adequate control at this point. I preferred them not to be killed by demons in the night, but humans have always had their demons close by.

After several days of taking care of my business, I did note that there was not one word from Dagon. With a calm mind, I touched my Maker palm and invoked him. He was immediately in my mind, with an intensity that did not bode well.

"Why are you contacting me, Danu?"

I sat calmly, listening to the small waves work over the strand. It was, as usual, a very bright blue day, and I could sense the under-mind of the life force—animals calling to each other, trees and grasses whispering in the wind as they gave up their pollen and early seeds ripening.

"There is more than one answer to that, Dagon," I mind-spoke to him. *"I do not wish to assume anything or assign meaning to what passed between us. But there is the fact that I have received firsthand information about changes on Old Earth and the resulting relocation of the remaining Sidhe. You and I are both are in a position of power on this planet—you more than I, although I do represent the Sidhe when my king is not present."*

"Kings are not present," corrected Dagon in mind-speak.

"Just so. But now I will ask, since I have heard no invitation to join you in any way, do you regret what passed between us recently? I do not. No matter what else I might be doing, I carry you in my heart."

"You offer yourself to the Sidhe kings." I could hear and feel the anger beneath his thoughts.

"Yes. And they offer themselves to me. Have we made no progress in our connection that jealousy must come in, if not immediately, then later? You are ..." And here, again, I was overcome by pain. Why had the Sidhe put me in this role? Why could Dagon and I not have a night of bliss without the wolf of possession and jealousy coming to him later?

"That is also more than one question," he mind-spoke more calmly. *"Do you want to come to me, or shall we roll about on the beach again?"*

"I would like to see how the city humans are faring and talk to you about the Shadakon's interactions with those outside of the city." Dagon was silent for a moment and did not reveal his under-thoughts. I felt his energy turn very Alpha, however. I waited.

"You are asking to know what is Shadakon business, I am not sure that you will be allowed to do so."

"Allowed by you?" I asked.

"Yes, Danu. By me."

"Even though I bring you fresh information from old Earth?" I asked. I felt him sigh and give in at least partially.

"Transit to the open space outside my home. I know you are familiar with where I am asking you to arrive."

I remembered Dagon bleeding from a wound that had been just short of reaching his heart. He had killed his friend and second Nathaniel in front of all of us in a called ritual fight to the death. He had not wounded him physically but simply laid his hands on either side of his head in a gentle hold and took him in one breath. Dagon had then taken his still-living blood, to replenish himself and in honour of his opponent. Later he had taken Nathaniel's Shadakon partner as his mate. *How could I forget that place?* I thought sadly.

I landed in the centre of what had been a terrible place of death of someone I cared for. I had, however, been relieved that it was not Dagon whose heart's blood was spilled and he knew that.

Today he was standing very still, dressed in black with a black cape over his shoulders. It was decorated with various medals and was obviously part of a formal uniform. I was wearing what passed as my best attempt at being dressed—a tunic and loose trousers. At the last moment I had put purple and lilac notes of colour in my tangled curly auburn hair. I had done this once when I wanted to look Sidhe and desirable to him. I knew he would remember.

His eyes swept over me, lingering on my hair and then my lips. I shivered. I intentionally looked into his dark amber eyes and saw the flames there leap at our contact. He was immediately next to me without seeming to have moved. He put a finger under my chin and caught my eyes fully. I did not struggle or protest in my mind.

"You are daring much, Danu," he said calmly. "This is my part of Danu's World and I am in control here.

You would not suffer due to lack of energy or blood from others, but I could put you somewhere apart from the earth. Unless I am mistaken, cut off from your sources you would starve, much like a Shadakon.

I stood in front of him. I shielded my thoughts now. Pain and sadness were part of what swirled within me. Anger as well. *Would we have to play this out after every parting?*

He heard it all of course. We were each other's Makers and had recently renewed our bond. Perhaps he knew what I had done with the Sidhe since we parted. As always, although I knew that I could not stay by Dagon's side, a part of me wanted to. Wanted to promise to change and be loyal only to him.

Those promises melted as midsummer drew nigh. He could not fly with me to honour the life force here. He would not be welcomed by the Sidhe and it would certainly endanger him with the Shadakon. Our lives touched at times, but no longer overlapped. *And yet …*

"And yet here we are again," he said and I heard the dusky note of desire in his voice.

He tucked my arm in his and walked towards his personal living place. Once again I was in the room that was obviously his, rather than shared with anyone else. His smell, his energy, infused everything. I wanted to rub my face on the comforter on the bed and breathe his essence in.

He laughed. "Danu, you must be half-crazy with loneliness. Your desire has, if anything, intensified. You can rub your face on my chest, and anywhere else on my body. I'm sure you have things to tell me, but let us first do what works between us." He was taking off his clothes and then turned to me and removed mine.

"My Alpha," I murmured. I knelt in front of him but looked up with a question in my eyes. He put his hands on both of my shoulders and I cupped his man parts and took him in.

He growled but stood quietly as I did what I would. After I had tasted the length of him and slid my mouth up and down, he trembled and pulled me up to him and then threw me lightly on his bed. He held my hands above me with one hand and touched and touched until I begged him to come to me. He took me hard, his Alpha energy driving both of us up and up.

"Yes, Dagon," I said when I sensed we both were close. I felt his sharp teeth slide into my neck and the bliss of my faerie blood pushed him over the edge and took me with him. We lay while the diminishing ripples of desire swept over us. I had looked up at him and sensed the big cat, pleasure rumbling in his chest as he held me in place with his teeth.

"Ah, Danu," he sighed. "We both know this cannot go on indefinitely. When the Sidhe come, and, yes, I know already that they are coming, there will be a king residing here. I assume that will be Ceádar. And perhaps you will stand by him, although I'm sure he is as confused about that as I am. My mate will eventually burn through enough credits that I will require her to return or to void her contract with me. I am very rich, and she will probably return and you and I will be where we have been many times before. Not that she wants me—she never did. However, she will not allow herself to be set aside for you, or even tolerate your presence. Every time you and I come together we tie ourselves closer to each other. I don't know why I offered you to renew your Maker bond with me. I guess, like you, even in our hard times, I wanted to feel you within me. Within my heart ..."

I rubbed my cheek against his chest and slid down to behold his temporarily satisfied man part. I breathed deeply and sighed.

He moaned. "Let's talk while we still can. He sat up and pulled me up as well. He touched some of the purple strands of my hair. "You are entrancing to me, Danu."

"I am Sidhe, Dagon. It is what we do. However you know it is more than that."

He shook his head as if the clear the haze of passion from it and walked over to his computer station.

"I know the Earth is dying quickly and will no longer support its population of humans. Most of them have no credits to go anywhere, although those who do will try to force those anywhere within reach to take them in. There are mining planets and others that nominally support life. Exterra and Danu's World, due to the work of the Sidhe, are the most desirable. We, the Sidhe and Shadakon, will have to unite to control what otherwise will be a tsunami of human refugees. I had not thought out that the Sidhe on Old Earth would leave as well. They are united with the land; such a leave-taking would only be done in total desperation. I can only partially imagine their states of mind."

"I think that many of them will end up here," I said. "I cannot imagine Sidhe who are bitter and disconnected but I think I will soon find that out."

"Will you take on more humans?" Dagon asked.

I thought long before I spoke. "Maybe a final winnowing to bring the old skills here, but no huge numbers. Can the Shadakon make use of more here or elsewhere?"

He smiled and suddenly he was all predator. "We could definitely make use of them, especially if that use ended up in being allowed to chase them down and take them to death." I shuddered. "My humans would be traumatized, and so would the Sidhe."

"Don't be so sure of that, Danu. The Sidhe permitted us to chase down and take to death any human straying into their lands of Exterra. We did so with relish. No Sidhe seemed concerned with our actions; in fact they were paying us to do so."

I looked into his eyes and shuddered. *How had I survived my first week with this being?*

"*That is the great mystery,*" he thought back. "*I have held your life in my hands many times and could not do what my nature drove me to do. We are alone on this planet together. If I hunted you—I would eventually find you.*"

"Perhaps not, Shadakon," I murmured. "But I understand you. Neither you nor the Sidhe have any love for humans, even though you have made an exception to that in your life." I thought then about the beautiful sisters who he kept in comfort and he had had affection for. One had lived to old age and he had continued to care for her to the end.

He sighed. "So ... I am now back on the planet that I did not intend to live on again. I am the leader of all the scattered Shadakon clans, including those on Old Earth I suppose, although I have not communicated with any there for a long time. And on this planet, that I admit has become a welcoming space, I am once again with you, with my uniform lying on the floor beside the bed. Soon, I suspect, my Shadakon mate will re-appear with her demands and expectations. You and I may or may not pull off feigned indifference to each other."

He paced and whirled to face me. "And I must feed, Danu. I did not take enough energy or blood from you to sustain me, as you well know. Perhaps this is a good opportunity for you to observe how some of the humans in the Shadakon's care fare these days."

He flung on his clothes and gestured to me to dress. He then made a quick call, and within minutes there was a knock at the door. A Shadakon guard stood there, with his hand lightly on the shoulder of a young woman. Dagon drew her in and she looked at me with surprise in her bright blue eyes.

"My friend wishes to enquire about your wellbeing," Dagon said to her. "Then I will feed and sign off for you."

She continued to look at me. She was young but not too young to not have experienced offering sex or being a blood host.

I sat down with her and asked if I could take her hand. She seemed puzzled at this request. She obviously did not expect to give permission to whatever might happen here with me.

"Have you come to this Shadakon before?" I asked.

She nodded.

"May I look within to see how your health and life is?" I asked her.

She shrugged. "I have one more assignment to attend today before I am off the Registry," she said.

"This won't take long," I assured her. Dagon was staring out the window, not involving himself with what I was doing. I took her hand and noted that she did not do physical labour with it. She was slim and not well muscled, however, she seemed healthy and obviously ate nutritious food.

"What is your name?" I asked. She flinched. I realized that her real name was all she might own. "Never mind," I said. "You may keep that to yourself. I will think of you as 'Sky.'"

She smiled. "That is a good name."

I took her hand. I did not have to do so but I liked to make physical contact before reading someone. "Close your eyes, Sky," I said.

I saw that she lived with others in a building complex that was adequate and that she had her own small room with kitchen and a bathroom and shower. There were clothes in her closet and food in her cooling unit—fresh vegetables and a small amount of some sort of meat. This was very different from the way the host humans had lived when I first came here.

I looked for children and noted that she was aware of places where children were kept, but she had nothing to do with them. She was, at present, chemically blocked from fertility.

There seemed to be no lover, although she hoped to connect with a woman friend later.

Dagon interjected. "*The young beautiful humans are blocked from fertility and are not allowed to take human lovers. That makes them more receptive to the Shadakon they come to. When they fade a bit, they are released from these limitations. Some partner and have children then.*"

I said nothing. They were still at the beck and call of the Shadakon, who wanted them ready for whatever they wished from them.

"*Do you fear anything?*" I mind-spoke to Sky.

She shuddered. "Some do not return from their assignments. We are told that they did not please. I do whatever I can to be pleasing."

I withdrew from her mind. "I will have more questions of you later, Dagon," I said. He nodded and glided over and laid hands on the young human. She trembled in his grasp but faced him and he pushed her lightly down in front of him. She reached for his pants and he undid them matter-of-factly and then put his hands on her shoulders. She worked skilfully to please him, taking him deep and making small sounds that might have been pleasure. Somehow, though, I doubted it. Her life was on the line and she would preserve it this way and any other way that he required her to.

He pulled her up and took her to the wall. Baring one of her shoulders, and pushing aside her clothing, he took her even as he drove his fangs into her neck, drinking deeply and accessing life energy as he finished with her. He licked to close the wound and steadied her as she regained herself.

"I will sign off on both of your requirements to serve today, and also for providing blood. You are very satisfactory to me. I may ask for you again. How can I do so?"

She rattled off a string of numbers that was apparently her identification on the Registry. He walked her to the door, where the waiting guard took her away.

I was shaken. We had just had, what to me was meaningful sex and yes, loving. To see Dagon take her as unemotionally as he did was difficult for me and I felt various feelings of sadness and anger. I knew he had done this in front of me on purpose. I had watched him partake of the sisters as he built their passion before taking them—this was different.

"This is how men take whores." I said. He nodded.

"You have watched Nathaniel take humans this way. In fact, he took you that way," Dagon said dryly.

I nodded, unwanted tears spilling down my cheeks. *Men had once worshipped goddesses and the women who served them. They understood that what was freely given was a true gift.*

"Yes," said Dagon. "But soon men felt it diminished them to care for women. Their wives they kept locked away, producing sons to be heirs. The women and their girl children were—expendable. And as for Nathaniel, since we are discussing old issues; he wanted to have you, and even after he proved how he would come to you, you turned away from me to go to him, my second. I allowed it because I thought it would happen anyway. He did save your life and in the end, he let you know your true importance to him.

Nathaniel had demanded my faerie blood after he told me that he had challenged Dagon to a fight to the death for the ultimate Alpha rule of the Shadakon. Dagon had tried to avoid this, and I had managed to stop it once earlier. But in the end, it happened as it was going to happen. One must kill the other. And yes, I had suffered for them both as they fought.

"In some part, Danu, I had to kill him because of you. You came between us and weakened my authority again and again. He saw me as weak for allowing you freedom to do what you would do. This is not just a Shadakon way of looking at the world. It is possibly the way males, all males, look at the world and the females in it."

Dagon had fed well and I could feel the extra life energy swirling around him. He looked at me speculatively and I shrank back from him.

"Oh, Danu, do you think I am different from other males? Do you think your Sidhe kings are? Fiócara arrived before we were even done, and did he not reinstate his hold on you? And then, if I am not wrong, Ceádar arrived soon after. All of us attempting to leave our mark on you ..." He reached out and stroked my belly where the criss-crossed lash marks had been laid down and then ran his hand down my inner thigh. I felt the marks flare under my clothes.

He came up against me and now I, too, was at the wall. I could have transited away, and he knew that. He caught me with his eyes and I went down and down into the flames and grew hotter and hotter. He ran his hands down my arms and I shuddered and wanted him in spite of the pain he had just brought me. Softly, so softly, he touched my cheek and then let his hand slip down to my breasts.

"Fly, Danu, fly," he said. "Or stay and be taken by an Alpha who wants you right now."

He bent to my lips and took them and whatever I might have meant to do, I arched towards him and his renewed hardness.

"Yes, Danu. Whatever else you are, you are a woman—a female, anyway. And a part of you wants me just as I am, taking you even after taking and feeding on a human woman. The Sidhe are not squeamish about sexing in front of each other. Why should you be?"

He nuzzled the area on my neck where he had recently taken my blood and ran his fangs across me and I—I only wanted more and more of him. He gave me energy then, some of the human energy Sky had provided. It had been decades since I felt this and I did not protest. He laughed then and stripped off our clothes again and had me until neither of could raise our heads off the pillows.

"Well then," he said, running one finger down my midline and stopping at my point of pleasure that he tapped seemingly absentmindedly. "A good start to our day, Danu. Now what do you want to do?"

"Will you show me the city, Dagon? And will you tell me about the Shadakon who go to the humans and prey on them in their settlements?"

"I will allow that, Danu. You are as always what I desire and you have endeared yourself to me today with your skills. I will show you what you want to know."

"Can you show me what is happening on old Earth?" I asked. I feared getting the answers but I felt I needed to know.

He went to his computer and entered long strings of codes and then turned me. "Where first, Danu?"

"The Pacific Northwest," I said. I had once owned land there, supposedly held in trust in a nature preserve. The screen revealed a thick haze which made seeing the ground difficult.

"Wildfires," he just said. From Pan Estadas Unitas to Alaska. Here and there the land was torn and rent with what must have been the result of devastating earthquakes and landslides. They had removed the water from the deep aquifers that lubricated the faults and slow slippage. Now there were roads that led to gaping holes and blackened and smoking remainders of cities.

"More?" he asked.

"The Amazon," I said, knowing already that I would not like what I saw. There were a few small islands of green in the midst of criss-crossed red dirt roads. Smoke hung heavy over this land such that my throat ached in sympathy.

"Are there any humans left there?" I asked.

Dagon shrugged. "They have nothing to eat."

The enormity of what I was seeing and also the importance of restoring this planet hit me such that my knees gave way. I wept for the beautiful life force that had been Earth.

"The oceans," I said in a whisper.

He panned to Hawaii. Its hills were still green and it looked relatively unscathed, but dead sea-creatures of all sorts were piled on its shores. The water had a reddish tinge and even the waves that broke cleanly in the bays were red in the sun—and empty.

"Red tides and various algal blooms due to the warm water," Dagon explained. "They strip the water of oxygen and release toxins when they die.

And of course the solar and nuclear radiation is playing a part as well …"

"No more." I said. I felt the enormity of what I had seen and realized that we must fight the humans bringing their sickness here or anywhere else they made a beachhead. Shadakons feasting on humans seemed less unacceptable to me now.

"Yes. They carry the seeds of their own destruction. So if some of us go out into the wild lands and take an occasional human—is that so bad?"

I shook my head. "After they have restored the land here, a choice will have to be made about them."

I had not asked a question. Dagon was silent.

"I can assure you that the Sidhe are pondering the same problem," he said dryly.

"Will you show me the city around the spaceport?"

He nodded. "Tie back your hair and wear this." He handed me a set of black clothing. "You will not pass careful observation. But perhaps it will limit the necessary damage control I will have to do."

"Can I not be by your side as the Sidhe representative?"

He shook his head no. "Yes, but this will cause fewer waves. Better to apologize later and do what one wants than get permission... it is an old human saying I believe."

CHAPTER SIX

THE SHADAKON

Dagon made a call and moments later a flitter arrived. He told me to wait and went and spoke with its pilot, who climbed down and left. We took off and flew over the city.

"You could have done a fly-over, Danu," Dagon said.

"Would I have survived it?" I asked dryly.

He laughed. "Probably not."

I saw fields of crops that looked healthy and well tended. There were humans in the fields running equipment and looking efficient.

"The humans you chose have kept the system going," Dagon said, "and we still have hydroponic crops as well." He indicated long sunlit sheds. "If you still fancied eating greenery I could get you some." I smiled. I remembered the meal he laid out for me to prove to both of us that I had turned. Delicately braised squash and plum wine. I had mouthed it, wanted to appreciate it but had been unable to swallow it.

"Yes, Danu." I felt warmth in his remembering our early times together.

We landed and walked towards an animal enclosure. There were small … what I assumed were meat animals—something like rabbits. They had runs and hay to burrow into and seemed content enough for the short time they would be alive.

"We are careful; our humans are very careful, not to let any of them escape," Dagon assured me.

Perhaps both of us remembered places on earth where escaped rodents meant the end of the local populations of plants and animals.

"Australia comes to mind," he murmured.

We then took to the air and alit near a large plaza or square surrounded by shops. There the humans bought food and clothing and other small items they wanted.

"No free lunch?" I asked.

Dagon shook his head.

"What about those too old to work?"

"We, or the humans, find them something they can do. If they are useless then they are eliminated." I though of Io, old and by Dagon's side when he fought.

"She was never useless," he said gently. "She was my …"—he used a word in an old language that I was not familiar with. He finished in mind-speak. "*She was my bond-servant who I gave freedom to.*"

I had seen him at her cairn, his head bent in honour of her. It had touched me then, and it did now.

Finally, we went to a building that Dagon said housed Shadakon and humans that they had chosen as informal partners. The human women were well dressed and had an air of some authority about them. They looked at Dagon with hunger and at me in curiosity and then dismissal.

"I would be a fine catch," he said, smiling at them but not pausing. "Had you continued on with Nathaniel, you might have ended up here." I shuddered. They were concubines, and any power they had was borrowed and easily withdrawn.

"Yes," said Dagon, responding to my assessment. "They would see she who you named Sky with distain, although they all have spent time on their knees."

"Might she end up here?" I asked.

He shook his head. "Very unlikely. She would have to learn to hide her hatred of us better."

"You knew that ... and proceeded with her?"

"Danu! You have probably killed almost as many humans as I have. You have seen into their minds. They want to be in control but they will never again be in control of us; the days of the torches and stakes are over. If they can surrender to us as their masters, they are more attractive to us. Did Fiócara not teach you that? You surrendered to him. He was intrigued that you could for a time resist him, but in the end, chose not to—that was when he had you and you had him."

I was silent.

"Sky does what she does from fear of me and all the Shadakon. I definitely could decide her fate in a heartbeat—as I could have decided yours," he said. "She is skilled but there is no passion. Still, taking that has its own flavour. I enjoy being Alpha, Danu, as you realize. As Nathaniel grew close to assuming that role, his energy also attracted you. You initially remembered him as kind and helpful. I would imagine that your later memories of him are of a different type.

"You answered my call," Dagon said calmly. "It started with us, at the pleasure fair. You came to me. I was inside a fence, minding my business, soliciting clients for the afternoon. I merely wanted a payment of their credits and of some of their life energy for pleasure and nurturance. I took you to my home, to spend a longer time with you before taking it all." His eyes glinted. "I knew immediately that you would never go back to your ship."

"Ah, Dagon. I wanted you without concern for my next breath."

"I know, Danu. I know. You still do. And now that you have totally distracted me again, what else do you want to know or see?"

"Maybe some numbers. How many Shadakon live here permanently?"

He was silent for a moment perhaps pondering how much he wanted to tell me. "About five hundred. The visitors who come and go make up another two hundred or so."

"How many humans?"

"There are about six hundred working humans plus older ones and children."

"Do you have the means to blast a Sidhe out of air above your city, much less more threatening arrivals?

He looked at me with no thoughts up to read—he was shut down and I could not get any information from him. "Why do you need to know?"

"You were part of the team that saved Exterra. The Sidhe have become more sophisticated in using psi to deflect or kill those who would come to overthrow them. It matters not how desperate the arrivals are, but would what you have here be effective?"

"Fortunately, there is not much left of the military complex on old Earth," said Dagon. "It is hard to launch ships without electricity or a communication grid. Not many humans with the necessary expertise show up for work in such places anymore. There have been missile strikes back and forth to take out other each other's bases and command centres. Electricity generation failed in most places years ago."

I was silent. I had to have known that this would come; it was underway when I left. I guess I had hoped that sanity would somehow prevail and that the humans would pull together.

I must have known that by their very nature, they could not. They had been gifted with intelligence—but not far-seeing intelligence—and aggression by their ancestors, the Visitors. The Visitors had also left their legacy in the Shadakon, or vampires, and in the Sidhe, or faerie—all of whom fiercely defended their territories.

Happily, the Sidhe had taken on the preservation of the life force while the Shadakon had been the humans' fearsome shadows. Ironically, the Shadakon were now preserving themselves and a human population, with a firm control over the humans they needed to sustain them.

"Yes, Danu. You did know. That was another reason why you had no intention of getting back on your ship and returning to old Earth. Dying or passing as someone you despised were your only options. Dying seemed most likely, by your own hand or someone else's. But now you have other choices, you do not have to choose dying anymore."

And so my Shadakon lover echoed what Ceádar had recently said to me, and I knew that there was caring in Dagon's statement, and Ceádar's as well. No more thoughts of swimming out in the moon's path until I perished; no more offering up my own death: I was here for the long haul. This planet could shelter and nourish its inhabitants; my part was to keep a guiding hand on that, if possible.

Dagon flew on and landed in a familiar place of a ring of standing stones. When he and I and Nathaniel had first come here, it had been a parched desert. It was here I had had a vision of restoring the planet and what that might look like. There was now vegetation around the stones, although the grass in the centre was short and soft. We were drawn there and Dagon lay down, putting his body in touch with the earth.

I took off his clothes and then mine. The grass touched our skin and I felt the earth energy entering me. The afternoon slanting sun put a glow on his pale body. I knew what he was doing: he, the proud Shadakon, was surrendering. Not exactly to me, but I would stand in for her. I straddled him but did not complete our connection.

"I have a requirement of you, Shadakon Alpha." I noted that I spoke formally and not entirely as myself.

Dagon moaned. I allowed him to feel the entrance of where he most wished to be.

"I will invite you in as far as you think you want to go, dark warrior, if you pledge to serve the life force here. If that means working with and cooperating with the Sidhe, then I require that of you."

He said nothing. He put his hands on my breasts but with unexpected strength I put his palms to the side and willed him not to be able to move. He had done this to me in the past. I had not known I could use it as well.

I moved slightly above him and saw him swell with desire.

His head thrashed back and forth.

"I wish you to commit to this place, Dagon of the Shadakon. I will take your desire for me and fulfill you, but only if you come completely to me."

I felt the earth energy, the fire energy from below search for me and find me everywhere I touched the earth. I felt like I was glowing, then perhaps burning. I wanted him; but would he accept and commit?

I gave him a taste of the energy that was entering me—I kissed his lips and saw his eyes widen in surprise.

"I would share some energy with you, Dagon. You will be satisfied with our union."

His body arched to mine but gained no ground. I was over him, waiting, hoping he would give voice to his surrender to me—to the planet.

For what seemed forever we stayed like this. I wanted him and he wanted me—of that I had no doubt. *Did he want it all? Would he commit to it all?*

"Yes," he said in a whisper. "I will serve the life force here. I commit to this planet and this goddess above me."

"I surrender," he said. I slid down his length and took him as hard as he had recently taken me. I bit him and even drew blood although that was not my intent.

"Take it, Danu. Take of me what you will."

I did.

The stars rose before we sat up and regained our normal selves.

"What have you done to me, Danu?"

"I don't believe I did anything more than I always do, but there is no doubt that you surrendered and committed. You brought us here, Dagon. As surely as I came to you in the fair, you came here to the goddess."

He shook his head and threw down the packet that was my clothes from the flitter. I gathered the black clothing he had had me wear and handed them up to him.

"I think we can find our ways home, Danu," he said gently. "Be well, my love."

CHAPTER SEVEN

MIDSUMMER'S EVE

The season moved forward as it must to middle summer. I had decided that I would fly with whomever on this planet wished to join with me that night. I swam in the warm sea and extended an invitation to whoever was living there now—the ancient kingdom of algae and sea wrack, and to the shining silvers that I glimpsed in the shallows now. I wandered through the Peace Grove, touching bark and leaf and saying, "Two more suns."

I flew over the settlements as a mysterious shadow in the sky and touched down to run my hand across ripening grains. I saw no circles of desolation around the humans—they were being careful to only gather dead and downed wood. I allowed those who sprang from the peoples of the plains on Old Earth to harvest saplings for their conic tents in the spring. They were careful to use what they had for as long as they could. All in all, I was content with the humans' behaviour.

I felt most touched by the desert plants that had somehow held on and now bloomed in exotic colours after the spring rains. The Sidhe now allowed more rain in some places, less in others. I did not want these elder desert survivors to be crowded out.

Finally, I went to the cave and walked carefully into the dark, kneeling in respect in the faintly green-lit inner room where the fierce goddess seemed to stay, guarding the entrance to the ever-deepening rest of the caverns. After remaining quietly for a timeless bit of time, the light brightened and Green Tara, the seemingly more compassionate manifestation of the goddess, was before me.

"Ah, Danu." Her voice was a whisper in my mind. "*Do you come to me to make another desperate deal?*"

I remained kneeling until I felt her cool hand on my shoulder. "*We are well pleased that you brought the proud Alpha Shadakon to surrender and commit to this planet's life force. His promise may not hold, but it was a worthy attempt.*"

"Goddess, it is a day until midsummer's eve. I will fly the cone of energy to honour the life of this place and I have invited any who wish to join with me."

"*Even the disgusting to you—pale swimmers in these clear pools?*"

I bowed my head. "No, Goddess, but I will amend that mistake before I leave."

"*Perhaps if you feed them, they will pay better attention. The creatures of the dark should not be slighted.*"

I nodded. "It was the oversight of someone who lives in the light, Goddess. But no less an error for that."

636

She smiled. *"You have a good heart and do not lie. I am pleased that you did not defend yourself here before me."*

I pondered the information she had just given me.

"But who will fly with you, proud Danu? Must you be a lonely queen this midsummer's eve"?

"I invited a Sidhe king. But he and Fiócara are involved in the exodus of the last of the Sidhe from old Earth. There is much to do and I am seemingly holding my own here."

"Seemingly, Danu. But if your Shadakon lover had not relented in his rejection of you recently, you would be returning your elements to the planet."

I said nothing. A force that lived in the dark in a cave somehow knew, as Fiócara did, of what I did here?

I heard a quiet laugh. *"Danu, do you think that I am confined here? You found me underwater. And do you not think I was present when you brought your Shadakon to the sacred circle?"*

I sighed. "He piloted his own ship to arrive there."

She laughed and the sound hit the curved walls and returned in soft ripples of laughter. *"Ah, Danu, he cannot protect himself against you any more than you can disregard him. You are blood bonded. He honestly told you one of the things that draws him to you and his honesty made you sad—that he wishes to drink from your life-infused faerie blood. But he spared and protected you long before you had that power over him. 'Te amo para siempre!' He has said that to you—over and over again."*

I nodded, momentarily overwhelmed by hearing that promise again.

"Well, Danu, you do not seem to have any wishes for me. Did you perhaps have something for me?"

I was silent.

"You will invite the small blind ones before you leave, and no doubt gift them to catch their attention. Did you think to invite me as well?"

"Goddess!" I was stopped in a moment that stretched forward in silence. "I did not ... I am not good at this! This is your world. Please be with me and with us. I meant no disrespect!"

She put her hand on my head. *"I have no doubt about your loyalty to me, Danu. You have proven yourself. I enjoy watching you prove your loyalty to this planet. You have a large and probably overwhelming task ahead of you. Dance with those you have protected and brought to life. You are precious to me."* The light faded abruptly and her touch was gone.

On my way out I knelt at the now large pool where I had once watched Io "fishing" for blind cave fish with her fingers. I used the same technique, but allowed them to bite and draw blood. When the pool had spreading circles of pink in it, I gently scraped them off.

"We fly tomorrow night. Join us in spirit, if you will, with whoever else shows up."

I picked up hunger and confusion.

"The waters bring more food to you now, do they not?" I was pressing my fingers together to staunch the blood flow.

There may have been a silent acknowledgement of that.

I flew back to the edge of the sea. The sound of the small waves was soothing. I was as ready as I could be. I may have dozed but awoke slightly to notice that the hard sand beneath me had changed to soft sinuous curves. I was wrapped in the sea-form of Ceádar who was looking down on me, waiting for me to come to awareness. I did not have even my usual scant clothing on.

"Did you start without me, my Sidhe king?"

He laughed and tightened his hold on me slightly. Pinning my arms he bent to my lips and contented himself with taking me slowly but surely up to the edge of bliss. I struggled half-heartedly to free my arms.

"Tonight I call the dance, Danu. Tomorrow you can if you wish." He adjusted his supple body that now included hands and calmly and attentively took me, touching everywhere he would and securing me to make his access to wherever interested him possible.

I eventually begged. And then I wept.

"Anything else on your mind tonight, Danu?" he asked, perhaps too calmly.

"Ceádar!" I attempted to rub up against whatever form he shifted to.

"Sometimes pain does not have to be heavy-handed," he said. "Although I did stop by and pick up your new tool."

He glided us both to the edge of the water and rolled a few times with me while I sputtered.

I was locked with him, eye to eye wanting, needing us to join. The water did nothing to cool me.

"You have three choices, Danu, of where this will fall," he said, dipping the flogger into the salt water and running it lightly across my chest. "As I recall, it hurts more when wet."

I looked at him and knew he would wait a long time for an answer.

"My heart," I finally said.

Watching me, he dipped it again and then brought it down across my chest. I gasped.

"And now where, Danu?"

"Your heart."

He smiled at that and handed me the lash. I dipped it and used some force. His breath caught but he never lost contact with me.

"And for the last choice?" he asked huskily.

"Throw it out to sea," I said. "Let the fish do what they will with it."

He embraced me completely then and brought us both to bliss.

In the dawning we arose from the shallows to go to my home and partake in the elixir of life. I expected to see Fiócara standing on the shore beside us, but we were alone.

"Are you disappointed, Danu, in entertaining only one king?"

I looked up at the Sidhe who, long before he revealed his full Sidhe powers to me, I had called The Beautiful One. "Surely you know the answer to that, Ceádar. But I am a little apprehensive about throwing away his painful gift to me."

Ceádar laughed. The flogger lay on the tide line in the rising sun. I sighed and picked it up and we walked to my home. Ceádar had obviously stopped by there before finding me on the beach; on the bed was a gauzy green dress, suitable for little besides flying in. My heart stopped momentarily. Fiócara had dressed me similarly before our first flight. And before that, Dagon had purchased a dark lilac one for me that I had flown with him in.

I looked up in alarm—knowing that my Sidhe king could take in all that I had thought. He looked at me gently. "I promised not to take your memories. They are part of who you are."

I thought about the gauzy blue dress that Nathaniel had given me that I had never worn until he had demanded I would to attend the fight to the death between him and Dagon. I had shredded it, and worn it over my concealing and obviously Sidhe clothing.

I felt the tears gathering. "All this about a beautiful dress."

He drew close and kissed me then. "We will make new history tonight, Danu. Joyful history."

"But one thing holds true for all those dresses in your mind: your lovers saw you as beautiful as you are, but they couldn't help imaging you wearing something colourful and beautiful, too. You change yourself little over the seasons."

He reached out and touched one of the purple locks I had recently put in my hair to catch Dagon's attention. "The Sidhe love colour, the colours of life. You do not have to wear this, but I hope you will. I will particularly enjoy taking it off of you after the flight."

I turned back to the dress that lay on my bed. Beside it was a silver circlet worked into a wave pattern that curled and uncurled around the brim. I touched it with one careful finger.

"Again, Danu, a gift, not a demand, from me. But if you chose to wear it tonight I do request that you allow me to comb out your knotted red curls. I have brought familiar herbs from Exterra for you to rinse your hair with, which might make the task easier.

He tangled both hands in my curls and brought my lips to his. We had had each other into the dawn, but I suddenly felt the heat grow between us.

"Let it build, Danu. Do not be afraid of walking through the day wanting me. I enjoy sensing that in you. Particularly when you are wanting *me*."

I looked at him and licked his lips suddenly. He moaned satisfactorily.

"Then let us both announce our wanting each other," I said. I eyed the evidence of his desire under his tunic.

I dragged my attention back to the beautiful circlet that glowed in the morning light.

"This is faerie silver," he said. "The Sidhe were the first silversmiths and made many fine ornaments for ourselves and the humans that we favoured. This has been in the earth for a long time. It was brought to us by one of the Old Earth Sidhe arrivals. They are trying to take away what they can."

I looked at it again and I attempted to shut down my thoughts. But I was thinking that it was something a queen might wear; I was thinking that he had politely declined my request for me to be his queen here; and then I had renewed my blood bond with Dagon. All this I tried not to think about.

"We both know, Danu, that what isn't spoken is obvious," he said, still holding me tightly. "You will be my Midsummer Queen here if you will accept that. Let the future sort itself out on another day. This is a day of joy, of renewal of a nearly extinct life force and all her children here."

"There may be one who flies above and around us," I said. He looked at me and waited.

"I spoke with Green Tara and she asked if I intended to invite her—as a courtesy of course, since this is her planet, too. I would not be surprised if she shows up."

He looked me in quiet amazement. "Any other surprise guests?" he asked.

"Well, Fiócara may show up. And … well, Dagon recently committed to the life force within the standing stones that we will base our cone upon. I did not invite him, but Green Tara might—she enjoyed taking in our passion one night when we sheltered in her cave."

"Are you done now?" Ceádar laughed. "Fiócara, now king of Exterra, has stepped back to avoid influencing you today. He has gifted me with the full possibility of being your Sidhe king without any distractions. If Dagon has the courage to show up I'm sure he'll enjoy the energy, if not the aftermath. Would you like a few Sidhe females transited in for the event?"

I growled. He brought me closer until my heart was hammering against his.

"Perhaps something to take the edge off," he murmured, moving the dress and circlet carefully off the bed. "I must admit this is comfortable space to do what I intend to do to you now."

I sighed and then I gasped and then, very soon, I called his name.

Eventually I had a shower with human made soap and then Ceádar poured a blend of sun-steeped leaves and flowers through my hair and down my body. He sat me down to dry in the sunshine and found the brush and comb that I seldom used and gently teased my curls apart until they rippled like flames in the sunshine. He then brought the dress and slipped it over my head and, lastly, held the circlet of silver out to me.

"Danu, will you be my Midsummer's Eve Queen? I nodded even as I cried. I wanted to be Ceádar's queen. His strong, clear energy grounded me and did not bring sadness. The tears were of joy, a strange feeling for me. Joy. Passion was present between us, but this was quieter, steadying.

He slipped it on, catching some of my side curls so that they did not hang in my face.

He kissed me, my first kiss as his announced Midsummer's Eve Queen and I felt it through my whole body and heart.

He just smiled.

As the sun set, I transited us to the circle of stones. He walked around smelling the air and sensing whatever he would.

"The circle called to you in your first days here," he said.

I nodded. I hadn't even noticed the circle of stones until after I asked Dagon to put the flitter down.

"And it activated your Sidhe calling stone?"

"Yes. I made a small circle of intent and asked whether the planet wanted to live or just sink into its mineral sleep. And then I saw those from before going to the lake to drink fresh water. I knew what I had to do, if possible."

"And this is where Dagon again brought you recently—and you, or maybe not exactly you, forced him to choose to intentionally commit or not commit to the planet and its life force."

"Yes," I said, continuing to be amazed at the details that were available to him—from my own mind or this place.

Suddenly I was afraid. Always there had been many to share the chant. There had been music and the beating of a small drum.

"I don't know if I remember the chant," I said. "I always remember it only as it arises from my throat. But there were many others present to fill in any errors I might have made."

"Danu! You formed the cone and brought all the energy of the beings of Exterra into it. You didn't know their names, or if they ever had names. You didn't know their name for 'home' but you knew what it meant. You are able to do this."

Then I knew he was right. But I also knew that he needed to fly me, rather than me fly him. He would have accepted it, as Fiócara had the night we all almost perished, but I knew that no matter what my part would play here in the future, Ceádar was to be king of this planet.

I walked with him around the stones, finding a pace that felt good as we circled three times. Then I simply raised the hand that held his and said, "Inhabitants of this world, your world, I bring you Ceádar, my Midsummer's Eve King and soon-to-be Sidhe king here. He will protect your home and he will lead the dance with you tonight."

Ceádar looked at me with surprise and then picked up the pace until my feet were no longer on the ground. The moon would not rise tonight, nor would the rains come to this area, but a green glow was brightening around the circle. We were in the air now, and the chant poured out from my heart, blending with Ceádar's deeper voice. I heard or sensed many voices, many of them from the original kingdom of Flora here, but also from the new arrivals. There were small voices from the underbrush and even the feral cattle and birds came in.

We all want and need to be home and to know that our home will provide for us in life and welcome us into the ground at death. We all celebrated being home tonight.

Ceádar flew us up and up until, like my first cone of power that Fiócara had flown me in, I was still but the world and sky whirled around me. Under us, the green glow brightened. Finally, we gave a shout of gratitude, Ceádar using a word that I could almost hear and repeat. Perhaps at the end I did. Then we turned the energy back to the earth and her life force. Ceádar took me to ground in the centre of the circle and after carefully divesting me of the green dress, left hanging on one of the stones, he powerfully planted me there until I could not speak; I could not think and only felt part of one thing, taking in the circle energy and circulating the life force through me and out again into the ground.

When we stopped, or paused, the green glow still hovered over us.

"Welcome, Ceádar," the green voice in my mind said. *"What lovely purpose you put this place to, Danu. I so love celebrations of life. I didn't think this planet could have such an event again. Thank you, Sidhe king and all your companions for the huge job you are doing bringing water and life back here. I wish you a long and happy reign."*

"Thank you, Goddess," thought back Ceádar. *"But I am far from being named king here. I am a king and perhaps this will be my home to protect for the foreseeable future. I wish that."*

"Mere formalities," responded Green Tara. *"And, Danu, I hear your unvoiced hopes as does your Sidhe king. But the future has not been set. You may have a hand, in that you may have to do something that you would rather have died than done before. You may also have to choose to commit, as you brought your dark lover here to do."*

"And, speaking of which," she said. *"I thought to bring him for my own company. I have no doubt that he will please me as I have observed his stamina and willingness already."*

She reached out her hand and tucked it around Dagon's elbow. He looked stunned, perhaps already in goddess-induced ecstasy.

She placed his hand on her glowing green breast and he shuddered and was lost.

Ceádar and I grabbed my dress, vacated the centre of the circle, and transited off without a backward glance. I wondered how Dagon's second surrender to a real goddess would change him. Most people might say it would be the best possible event in their lives, and continue to search to find it through mystical practices. The same logic had people looking for Sidhe for even one night of passion.

But I knew that it tied one to a world apart from where one lived and loved and died. I knew she would give him more than he could imagine, and also take the same from him.

But then, we were on the edge of the sea and Ceádar was moving me purposefully towards the water. I put my hand to the circlet, fearing that it would fall off, especially if the glint in his eyes truly indicated that he was still energized and wanted to take me further out in every sense of the word.

"Don't worry, Danu," he said. "Your Sidhe silver, will not come off until you intentionally take it off."

I was stopped by that. "Would you have me wear it always?"

"That is your choice, Danu, always your choice. But if you put it aside for long, it may disappear, like faerie gifts often do. Tonight though, you will not lose it nor think for a moment to take it off."

And then he dove with me, holding my hand as we streaked deeper and deeper. For a moment I held my breath but then remembered I had no need to while with Ceádar. He swam us down into the depths but although it was night, I could see in the glowing indigo light. We swam down to the temple, where I had wanted to stay and disregarded my low oxygen warning when I dove here and discovered it the first time. Now we entered the temple that was surprisingly intact. The marble floor was smooth and the power of the place was unmistakable. Ceádar approached what appeared to be an altar and placed a small object there. It appeared to be a small, unremarkable stone.

"It is a home stone from old Earth, from a site such as this. Perhaps it will aid in forming a power grid to help Old Earth maintain some life and promise of an evolving future."

"Once again, Sidhe king, you demonstrate why you should reign here. What a lovely gesture. But now, we both have passion to pursue this night."

Green Tara laughed and her presence disappeared.

As we swam into the shallows I saw phosphorescent glimmers of light streak by, and larger shadows perhaps chasing them. When I looked back, the temple was covered with a new growth of waving seaweeds. Once again I realized that I truly did not know what this Sidhe king could do.

"How far do you want to go and know, Danu?" he asked me in my mind. *"Don't immediately answer that. Do not say 'Bring what you will' unless you truly mean that. You cannot claim later that you spoke in innocence."*

We were in the small waves on the edge of the beach now and I could breathe air again.

"I am still innocent or ignorant of most of your powers," I said.

"Not entirely," Ceádar said, securing me with a coil of his sea body that he obviously liked to manifest. "Perhaps I was not so much the frail canoe that the name I gave you suggested to you, as the sea beneath it. But I thought the name was manageable for you at the time.

I shuddered as he slowly tightened his coils of glistening blue green scales around me. "So shall we leave it at that tonight, Danu? Or will your curiosity lead you forward as it has in the past?"

"Bring it all," I said.

"Say that again, Danu, with a few more details. I do need to know that you know, as much as possible, what you agreeing to."

"I do not know what you are; what being a Sidhe king means, or in your case, a specific Sidhe king who is wrapped around me, means. But I will say it again—bring it, Ceádar. Bring me what you so carefully avoided showing me when you were my gentle companion who comforted me."

And so he did. I cannot hold all the images of what happened that night. At one point we were within the thundering rain of space water and suddenly the clouds were speared with lightening that went through our bodies. Ceádar held me; had he not I knew I would have perished. I trusted him. Abruptly, we were far above the storm and then in outer space and I felt the wisps of light of stars and I felt cold so cold until he took me into himself, to his warm core and beating heart. There he held me and I learned his secret.

He was Sidhe, a carefree Sidhe, and he loved me. He loved outside of space and time.

I was not sure I loved him enough. Often passion had overridden my feelings—Yearning for other people, yearning for Fiócara, yearning for a Shadakon who persistently had tried to hurt or kill me. And this one, had waited, gaining, as he said, a skill not particularly valued by the Sidhe: patience.

I was undone. The rest of our endless night was spent holding and driving each other up to bliss and then holding each other again. I loved lying surrounded by him in whatever form he took.

When I awoke in the morning, surprisingly in my bed, I knew it had not been a dream and there was thin circlet of silver on my head. And I was once again alone.

CHAPTER EIGHT

WE BRIDGE ACROSS
SORROW—FOR NOW

Eventually I shook out the green stone, that promptly lit up and I saw Fiócara in my mind.

"A good midsummer's eve, Danu? Ah, I see you are crowned. I am sure you made a beautiful Midsummer's Eve Queen this season."

Did he not know? Or was he testing me in some way?

"I do know, Danu. I wonder if you fully know. Ceádar made a precipitous choice in gifting it to you, a Sidhe who is still openly consorting with a Shadakon Alpha. If you think the larger contingency of Sidhe would accept you in your dual roles, I believe you are fooling yourself."

I sensed anger in him. I thought he would be pleased that Ceádar would be free to show me more of himself.

Fiócara was silent—too silent. For the first time since I had been in his presence I was truly afraid of him. I also went silent. I had thought he would be pleased—for Ceádar and me. We could work together, if not as king and queen, then as king and consort, to ease the transition of the refugee Sidhe who would be soon arriving.

Fiócara left me in silence to feel my apprehension grow. When he again mind-spoke to me, I felt an iciness of distain that I had never felt from him before.

"Ceádar, as he has you call him, has been with me since the beginning. He is not as casual in his connections as he has led you to believe. I knew, and he knew I knew, that he yearned for my queen. I could do nothing about that. She craves power and when he lost his territory on Earth and came to Exterra, he became my second. She later came to me and stayed. It was her choice. It was perhaps not his choice to continue to want her, but he did, and she did not discourage him. And so we often shared with each other temporarily. I would have stepped back and let him have her, but I could not offend her. She is older than I am and possibly more powerful."

He paused to let me take this information in and then continued. *"Danu. You now know the secret of his heart—that he loves you, has loved you from the beginning. He was so careful not to reveal himself to you, knowing how tangled your heart was, but on midsummer's eve you asked him to bring who he was to you—what he had hidden before.*

A heady night it is, as you well know. But now that you know, if you intentionally hurt him—I will hurt you in return. I will do something Ceádar could not do: I will banish you from this world and Exterra. You will then learn what being a solo Sidhe is truly like."

I shuddered. I had no doubt that Fiócara could do exactly what he said he would do. This was the ruthless side of the Sidhe that so many humans had discovered when searching for an enticing Other.

I answered too rapidly. *"I would never intentionally hurt Ceádar,"* I said. Even as I said it, I knew it was the wrong answer.

"Everything you do now must be totally intentional, Danu. You were gifted a planet by the Sidhe and it was brought back largely by our efforts as well as paid for by us. You have been a good enough manager. Perhaps putting your name on the title was an error, but that can be remedied."

I wept. I knew it would have no effect on him but I could actually feel the pain of his focused unkindness in my body. The marks he had placed on me ached anew. I could not help but think that he regretted taking me on as his student and, even more, pronouncing that I was Sidhe. Now he was being protective of his friend, a Sidhe king who Fiócara had deep ties with, call it whatever a Sidhe might or might not call it.

"If I offered to come now, Danu, and ease your pain the way you have begged me to do so many times, would you say yes?"

I shook my head. *"My king I could not refuse you if you arrived, but if you are offering me a true choice, then no. I feel your Sidhe scorn and it hurts deeper than the lash. I do not want to open myself to you this day or for the foreseeable future."*

For just a moment, so brief that I could barely believe it could contain information, I felt a wash of profound sadness.

Then Fiócara smiled coldly and said, *"Good, Danu. We understand each other then. Do not use this stone unless you are in dire straits and Ceádar does not respond."*

I put the stone back in the bag. I considered throwing it into sea but feared that he would let me do so. This was not a moment for precipitous behaviour on my part. I also knew something that Fiócara allowed me to know: this was part of his gift to Ceádar, so that I would not be tempted to choose between the two of them anymore.

I waited several days before attempting to talk to Ceádar.

I did not trust myself to not immediately reveal what had passed between Fiócara and me.

When I thought of Fiócara the pain of his scornful words was still physical. Perhaps he had prepared me in advance for our conversation. I thought of him taking me deep into pain and then transforming it into total bliss. *Was that all a plan to control me and my emotional reactions?* I would not bring this to Ceádar intentionally but he would know soon enough. What he thought of his fellow king and friend's action, I did not know. The Sidhe were in a delicate situation, triaging Sidhe arrivals from Old Earth to determine which should settle on Exterra, with fewer responsibilities, and which could come here for a working cure.

And so, I let time pass. I also did not contact Dagon, although I would have loved to hear how he had fared with Green Tara. Let his returning mate be mad at a goddess rather than me. I realized that I had been given a cover story that was so outside reality that it had to be believed. I smiled and left him alone.

Finally, sitting on the beach with as calm a mind as I could muster, I shook out the blue stone and called Ceádar. He was immediately available but not smiling when I saw him clearly in my mind. I flinched slightly and waited for yet more difficult news.

"*I see you still wear your circlet, Danu,*" he said quietly. "*Have you been tempted to take it off?*"

I shook my head and vehemently thought, "*No!*"

He looked sad for a moment. "*Obviously Fiócara spoke with you. I wished he had not, but he does what he will do. I do not want you as a lover or a queen or even a friend if you feel that you are forced to be any or all of those. I showed you what was in my heart because I thought you finally wanted to know. If I have put you in a difficult situation, I am sorry, Danu. Midsummer's eve magic was on both of us, with a strong boost from Green Tara.*"

"*I do not want you to comfort me for Fiócara's revelations.*" I turned my face away, but of course he was seeing me with other than his eyes. "*I need to tell you what you already know. I will not come between you and Fiócara.*"

"*We all need to come together and set some guidelines between the Sidhe and Dagon and the Shadakon. I won't have Sidhe murdered because they blundered into his territory. But we have to devise a work plan for them as you did for your humans,*" Ceádar said. "*I never imagined that Fiócara would not be present and working with us.*"

I sighed. "*Come then, with or without him. Shall I set an appointment with Dagon for tomorrow or the day after?*"

I am not asking this out of any possessiveness. You wear my crown, Danu, and I would know if you chose to set aside even before I saw that it was not on your flame-coloured hair. But things seem unusually confused around you right now. Nevertheless, we must proceed. So, yes, please secure time with Dagon. If it is later than two days, let me know. Otherwise I, or we, will see you tomorrow."

I went to the edge of the sea and swam out until I was very tired. I turned around while I still had the resources to return to the beach. I just hoped that tiredness would quiet my mind. The stars were brightening in the sky when I returned and with as much calm as possible touched my Maker hand and called Dagon.

He was immediately present and, once again, I felt that my contact with him was following the same course as with everyone else I contacted recently. I waited for him to acknowledge me, which he did not immediately do.

"*A booty call, Danu?*" This was an Old Earth term that he had obviously kept in mind. It meant, calling someone—not for a date or dinner or walk or talk, but a late call, and it was specifically to ask to come over and have sex.

I had not had booty calls in my human life but I was familiar with the term and knew it implied indifference to anything but immediate benefits.

I did not think I could be stunned three times in one week by my lovers, but obviously my status was rapidly changing.

"No, Dagon. I apologize for the hour. I am asking if you can receive one or two of the Sidhe and myself to talk about the arriving Sidhe from old Earth. Without giving details that I am not clear on, I believe that the Sidhe want you to be protective of them if they stray into your territory. They have been, up until very recently, in hell. If tomorrow is not convenient please give us another time, but time is of the essence for this meeting."

"And you must attend this meeting?"

I bit back any response that I could possibly hide from him. Once again though, I felt pain roll over me like a giant unexpected seventh wave.

"Yes, Dagon, I am the representative of the Sidhe here. You know this."

"Tomorrow afternoon is fine. Do you want to meet here?"

I felt the cold control in his tone.

"We will accommodate your schedule and situation. Would it be better for you to meet us away from your area of control? We could meet outside of my desert home, or inside if the rains come. You could come by flitter or fly. One of us could transit you back if the weather turns harsh."

I was congratulating myself for remaining civil and helpful in spite of the effect he was having on me. My Maker hand stung like some small poisonous insect had bitten it and the venom was quickly spreading while I waited for his answer.

"My mate has returned, as I predicted. She has already heard that you were here in what she thinks of as her home. As all my formal mates seem to act, she is wishing to punish someone and knows better than to take me on directly. Sky is no longer available. I did some research and discovered that she had died suddenly—probably poisoned. Her last call out was to this place. She did not live long enough to see me on that assignment and in fact, it was not me that requested her. It would better if you did not come here."

"I'm sorry, Dagon. But I must say, I was your formal mate, and although I did things that hurt you, I would never have killed you or anyone you might have cared for." I thought this out after I said it, and realized that it wasn't entirely true.

I heard Dagon sigh. "I know what you mean, Danu" He was silent for a moment, his anger seemingly ebbing. "You wear his crown. Are you intending to stay clear of me and any others that might catch your eye?"

"I don't know, Dagon. I know you still have the power to hurt me by wanting to refuse all contact. I think it is safer for both of us for us to act diplomatically, if coolly, towards each other and for me to continue to wear the crown until it feels so light I do not notice the changes it brings. Or until I take it off and am probably exiled by Fiócara from this or any other Sidhe planet. I have been warned ..."

I hadn't meant to tell Dagon this. I was silent.

"In that case, I will insist on your presence at all further meetings. And, Danu—you and your Sidhe king were beautiful on midsummer's eve, but Green Tara moved me beyond even the passion of the Sidhe. I had nothing to regret that night and everything to try to remember for the rest of my life."

I felt him smile then, and he broke the connection.

In the morning I awoke to a warm kiss. I didn't have to open my eyes; I could feel Ceádar's presence and my own response building.

He sat down on my bed—I had swam and walked late into the night, trying to quiet the tension that was building within me and had ended up wanting the comfort of the soft bed for the remaining hours of darkness. I feared seeing Fiócara and I also feared not seeing him again, our last bitter connection being what I now remembered most strongly about him. I knew that if Ceádar did not know the particulars of what had passed between us, he now could merely read me as I lay, temporarily comforted by him.

Ceádar sighed. "I know enough, Danu, to know that Fiócara hurt you. I do know that. I also know why—it is part of a long story that seemingly had to resolve as it did. He knows me well enough to know that I was deeply hurt by his queen and the fact that he allowed events to unfold as they did, including bringing her to Exterra and allowing her full queen status, although they had been apart for … a long time. She never spoke of what she had left behind. She called him to retrieve her after assessing that he was her best choice for ongoing security and power. He has since understood what allowing her choice to be by his side has and is costing him."

He paused to see if I was paying full attention and then went on. "He thought he owed me somehow, to set things straight. As you know, Danu, one person cannot do that for another—set their life straight. I knew on the night that we flew together to practice midsummer's eve and then returned to Fiócara's hill house that I wanted you more than her. It was a turning point for me, but a long, slow one. I had no intention of letting you close, as once again, you were someone I wanted who wanted Fiócara more than me. I was careful not to show you, but then you began acting as if you understood things not directly revealed to you. When you chose me to be your god to your goddess, on a day before our likely annihilation, I thought you knew why you chose me. But Danu of the complex heart, you were juggling many connections. Again and again I fell into the role of comforting you."

"Although it will be difficult for me, I will now accept the crown back, Danu, if you feel that it is merely a measure of control by me. I will never forget you flying with me and wearing it," he said with no trace of anything but sadness in his eyes. "I have told Fiócara that this is my choice and that I wish no further attempts at interventions by him between you and me."

He sat and stroked my hair and then reached up to remove the circlet that I had not removed since he placed it there. I distinctly felt my heart breaking.

"Please, Ceádar, don't do this." I had had not felt so sad since I held the frail Lucia, the girl who the Sidhe rescued with me from a renegade Shadakon prison in the forest. I had once held her and whispered, "I'm sorry," as she slept, because I was entering the Hunger and they had jailed us together. I knew that some point I would take her. And then take her again and again, eventually using up all her life energy, and breaking the rule of the Shadakon who lived peaceably enough with humans by not taking without true consent. We were both doomed, but Fiócara had rescued us from that dark fate. Later she came to the hospice where I worked, asking for me and ready to die from an incurable disease. I held her one more time as her spirit went out on the falling tide. At least I felt that I had done what I could. Now my choice to do what I could, to live and love past the present difficulties was seemingly being taken from me.

"Do you want to retain it to protect your pride in this coming meeting?" Ceádar asked quietly.

I shook my head. The pain was threatening to eclipse me. I wanted to go—to the stars, to the bottom of the sea. I had finally seen and sensed Ceádar to the full extent that I could; he had held me in his heart.

"Can you so completely misunderstand me, Ceádar?" I turned my face away and tried to breathe but there was no air, no comfort, no way forward. "If you must take it back, then take it. I will not remove it, even if you order me to."

I felt the last of the air, the last breath in my lungs and slowly exhaled. Then the darkness came for me. I heard from a far distance …

"Oh, Danu. Dagon is arriving soon here. How can we stand together now to deal with our business here?"

Dagon was in fact, standing with Fiócara outside in the sunshine. I learned later that he had felt my pain in his Maker hand and come early. Now he correctly assumed that Fiócara had had a heavy hand in the pain he felt in me. I had told him more than I should have, or perhaps not. He stood in front of Fiócara taking his measure.

"I have no doubt you can best me, Sidhe king. But one who I love lies helplessly in pain. I have put her in that situation before and lived with my regrets ever since. I have abandoned her many times and yet she opened her heart to me and reunited with me—a predatory creature, a vampire. But you, shining one, have come between her and he who even I can see loves her.

She deserves no less than your apology for whatever you actually said and did to bring this so far into the wrong or I will not work with you. I do not care if the wounded Sidhe find their place here. She has told me you threatened to banish her—she who you tied to you with passion that she could not refuse! You have provoked her to try to take her life. Now you must do whatever you can to turn this around. Or I … I am not sure what I will do, but it will not be helpful to you."

Fiócara said nothing and then he came in to where Ceádar was standing beside me, his hand lightly on my head and on the circlet. I was far away, as far as I could get into the darkness. I would not witness this act with any senses of my body. Dagon stood in the doorway, looking anguished.

Fiócara spoke to Ceádar quietly. "Don't do it; do not make this mistake any worse than it is. You told me that once. Dagon reminded me that this is largely of my doing. I am an old fool." He sighed and bent his head. "Can you find her, hold her, and show her again what she so wanted to see in all of us that she loved? You professed to love her—will you now hold her in your heart no matter how confusing that may be?"

Ceádar sighed. "She is not on the planet." He looked down at my huddled form on the bed.

"She wears your crown—you can find her anywhere."

"I'm not sure she wants me to," said Ceádar.

"She wants nothing else," said Dagon from the doorway. "In my recent past I have consumed people, I have drank Danu's blood and given her mine. It is all she wants—the love of you, Ceádar, and probably you, too, Fiócara. She wants to stay tied to me, a mated Shadakon whose lover and mates have done their best to kill her, as have I. Love is all she wants. What she gives—that is another more complicated thing."

He walked outside and stared at the sea.

The two Sidhe stared at each other. As one they lay down on either side of me and perhaps I felt them drawing nearer to wherever I had found to hide. They laid gentle hands on me and Ceádar murmured in my ear—"Never will I ask you to remove or give back the crown, Danu. Please do not give me back my heart. It wants only to hold your own in safekeeping, such as anyone can do that. Males are fools at the best of times. Please accept my apology for hurting you, for assuming that I knew your mind and heart."

Fiócara said nothing for a long moment, and then said. "You saved a planet. You gave me your dramatic but always true allegiance. I thought that driving you from me would open the way for Ceádar to come to you without my shadow on you both. How I wanted to see and sense you flying the first cone of power on this planet! How I would have enjoyed taking in the power of your joining with Ceádar in that circle. But I stepped back, thinking it a gift, perhaps. Now I ask you to return to us, to Ceádar and, yes, to Dagon—to all of us."

I hovered somewhere closer.

"Please, Danu. I am sorrier than you may ever know that you believed my harsh words."

I was back. I was surrounded by streaming light and gentleness. I felt Dagon's presence as well. I opened my eyes and then threw an arm over both the Sidhe. I felt both shudder.

"I knew you were pushing me away," I said to Fiócara. "But I also believe you were telling me something true. The Sidhe as well as the Shadakon, and I suppose, the humans, all have seen me as a stranger and an object of scorn. I have proven myself as best I could but I make only temporary gains. What is true by starlight fades in the light of day. Tell me the truth of full light now. Are you done with me Fiócara? Are you Ceádar? Dagon—have you contentedly returned to your loveless mate and Registry slaves? Let us do this once and finally."

The pain in the room was finally not only mine. I felt them close in around me, hold me, warm me, after being in the cold place I had retreated to. Then it was just Ceádar and I and he enveloped me and his heart found mine and beat in time with it. I felt energy surge into me—perhaps from many sources. Very soon I got up, smoothed my minimal clothes (which I had intended to exchange for something more suitable for a diplomatic meeting). I felt light but not empty, rather, light hearted. The circlet rode easily on my head. We all sighed in relief.

In the end, the negotiations were simple. No new Sidhe would be held accountable for errors of trespass or inadvertent interference with Shadakon dealings. They were under Dagon's direct protection and he would let it be known what that entailed. The Exterra Sidhe would individually bring two or three Sidhe refugees over at a time and they would come with what gifts they could give to this, their new planet. I put no limits on this other than to be ecologically thoughtful about introducing something that might tip the life balance here. No kudzu vine, if such a thing still existed. No zebra mussels or rabbits, or locusts. Ceádar and I would speak with them and assess their individual immediate needs.

Ceádar, when he was not transiting Sidhe, would stay with me here. None of us referred to whatever status he and I might have. I put out my Maker hand and Dagon laid his own in mine. We communicated what we intended to let be known only between us. Then he flew away.

Fiócara walked to the door but I touched his arm and walked out with him. We faced each other and, yes, I felt his power swirl around me and smiled. "You were my first Sidhe, Fiócara. I will not forget your gifts to me."

He looked at me with his momentarily ancient eyes. Gone was the ageless beguiling look. He took my hand and the energy between us rose. "You are strong and ever more powerful. But one thing you should know, Danu, I was lying to you. I knew what would most hurt you and I used it. It may have seemed to me to be in the service of good, but now I know this was not true. I am sorry, sorry about what I said and also that I was convincing enough that you believed me."

I smiled. "I felt your pain for a second although I doubted myself later. I could not hold onto what I knew. I am sorry that I disbelieved myself, but you were very convincing. I believe that what you said, you, at least partially, believed. To threaten to shun me—that was beyond anything the lash could bring. I think we should walk apart for a while. Not for the foreseeable future. But for now."

Fiócara continued to watch me and then nodded. He disappeared.

I went back inside to reassure my king that all was well enough. And then we attempted to strategize what we would do with unknown numbers of heartsick Sidhe.

"Where should we receive the incoming Sidhe?" I asked Ceádar. "My small bedroom seems inappropriate."

We looked at the small space critically. Finally he went outside and busied himself with some task. The light coming through the front window changed, alerting me to the fact that he was doing something substantial outside. He had woven and bent the willow-like bushy trees outside my house into a loose canopy that faced the distant sea. He carried out my few blankets and put them on the ground. He then brought out the small table that I placed my pitcher of elixir of life on and the two cups. I had plenty of elixir to fill the pitcher with after they arrived.

He added a bowl of water with strewn aromatic leaves floating on top. Returning inside he disappeared the flogger and pulled the bed into a more neutral state than it had been in earlier. Then he kissed me deeply until I almost fell back into it.

"Wear your desire as finery—but also change into one of those official dresses now."

He pulled off my everyday threadbare clothes and held out my choices. I went with a watery blue and he smiled and smoothed it down over my body.

"Have a cup of elixir, Danu, it will cool your fires without putting them out."

We both sat outside in the new space, watching the horizon. When we were done he shook out the cups and just said, "Fill the pitcher, Danu." And suddenly Fiócara was standing before us with two slim, almost gaunt Sidhe. Their garments were the colour of red dust and their eyes looked stunned.

"I will leave you all to acquaint yourselves," he said to Ceádar. "Do not expect much today." And he was gone.

The two Sidhe watched the spot where Fiócara had disappeared and then turned back to us. They looked at Ceádar briefly and then me. The taller Sidhe hissed and stepped back. "Human! We did not come here to be under the rule of a human!"

I felt Ceádar begin what might have been an unwelcoming interaction with them. I put my hand on his arm lightly. "My king, please converse with our guests and answer any immediate questions. I will pour some elixir of the life of this planet if they would take refreshment from us."

I turned away and went to the green living bowery that Ceádar had built earlier. I heard a heated exchange in an unknown language that I knew was an original Sidhe tongue. Then I heard Ceádar whisper in my mind.

"I am taking the angry one with me to the edge of the sea. He will be soothed by it. If you would please stay as company with our second guest, I think it would be better to separate them. They are unknown to each other except in the last few days. You will be able to hear his thoughts and speak to him in mind-speak, although some ideas may not translate well."

I turned to the remaining Sidhe who stood totally still beside me. I gestured to the hopefully welcoming green space.

"Would you care to join me in the shade, and have a cup of the elixir of life of this planet?"

He shrugged and turned to follow me. I led him to the place we had prepared to meet with them in. Already our interactions were taking their own shape. These people, these Sidhe, had been forced to the very edge of survival. I would follow their lead in what they needed from us—and from me at this moment.

The Sidhe male looked about and then moved the blankets aside and sat directly on the ground facing in the direction of the shining renewing sea. He did not make eye or mind contact. But he was not here to keep me company and I did not force it on him. I only asked, *"May I serve you now?"*

He looked at me with the palest and blankest eyes I had ever seen. I gestured to the cup and raised the pitcher, my eyes questioning him.

"Pour some for both of us. I will choose which cup I partake from."

I bowed my head but in truth I was attempting to not show the sadness that arose in me. *The proud Sidhe—had they been poisoned? Killed off by competing human farmers or settlers?* I poured two half cups and waited.

He chose a cup and downed it. At the bottom he looked up at me. *"This is a wild new blend. The elixir was made from quickly growing trees and even grasses. This planet was a desert? A wasteland?"*

"The humans took all available water from here and shipped it off planet. It was dying."

I showed him a picture in my mind that I would never forget, of the whirling yellowish wind and wilting and dying plants—even the high desert plants. I showed him how I had sourced planetary core energy to sustain myself for years.

He looked at me with a slightly different look then and perhaps a softer tone. *"The Sidhe King of Exterra"*—but he used a Sidhe term for that world that meant "new home"—*"assisted your king here in devising a way to save the planet?"*

"No," I said. *"I was alone here. I consulted with the king on Exterra and explained the amount of water that would be necessary to restore this planet. The Sidhe brought space ice, and arranged it in orbit such that it rained every day for many decades. It is now scheduled to rain here three times a week at night, more in the central latitudes, and less on the high desert."*

He looked at me appraisingly. *"What is the name of this world?"*

"Danu's World," I said. *"Although that is merely a name that was necessary to get a legal contract of ownership drawn up for the Sidhe. The name could change."*

"And who is Danu? It is an old goddess name from old Earth. She was goddess of Eire, the emerald isle."

"I chose that name when I was very young and living on Earth. I thought then that I was a human—a human that did not fit with other humans, not that I wanted to.

But that is a long story. May I pour you some more elixir?"

The weary and incredulous Sidhe held out his cup. I filled it this time. We sat comfortably enough in silence, watching the sea after that.

Eventually Ceádar returned with the angry hearted Sidhe. They had gone for a swim, and the new arrival's clothing had been washed in salt water, restoring its colour to a neutral grass gold.

Ceádar's curls were wet, his clothes dry. He whispered in my mind, *"This is going to be complicated ..."*

I laughed. *"How could it not be, my king?"*

I turned to the returned Sidhe.

"May I pour you some Elixir?"

I offered him civility but no explanation of who I was or why I was here. Perhaps Ceádar had already done so, or not. I would not explain myself unless I was asked politely. I knew that the Sidhe had never felt the need for politeness towards humans. These last refugees and witnesses to their world's murder by the humans would definitely not feel compelled to treat me kindly. Yet I wore Ceádar's crown—that made me more than human for that reason alone. I would wait and see how our interaction progressed, if it did.

But I did not have to wait long. The Sidhe I had sat with grabbed his companion's arm and they had an intense under-mind dialogue that I could not follow except for hearing my own name mentioned once. The still angry one turned to me.

"Ceádar explained to me that you wore his crown, and that you were Sidhe and human by blood and that the king of"—and here I heard the Sidhe word for Exterra—*"has claimed you as Sidhe. I do not understand that. But I now know that you were largely responsible for saving the life of this planet—yet again necessary due to the ignorance and indifference of humans. I doubt that you did it with us in mind, but this is a great offering to us. I apologize for my anger and rudeness towards you. It was obviously misplaced. I will gladly accept some the elixir of life from this new place."*

I smiled and poured his cup to the brim. Without thinking I leaned in towards Ceádar and he wrapped his sun-warmed arm around me. I felt us both kindle and smiled. It was going to be a long day ... many, many long days.

Ceádar mind-spoke to the Old Earth Sidhe in a language that I could read the emotional components of, but not the exact content.

Ceádar turned to me. "Do your humans have the ability to make some natural fibre-sourced tunics? I think it would be good to be able to offer fresh clothing to our arrivals. Later they can make or import from Exterra their own choices of garment."

I nodded. "Do they know about the humans here? Perhaps that would not be a choice they would make—to wear human-made cloth."

He turned to the guests. "There is so much for you to know about this world. We do not want to overwhelm you. You are welcome to explore and search out where you might eventually want to live. But you need to know that there are two separate varieties of humans living here."

The more obviously angry Sidhe hissed softly.

"One group lives in the city near the spaceport. They are under the control of the Shadakon who live here and maintain and enforce their rules of commerce and travel. The Shadakon leader is in cooperation with us and understands that the Sidhe own this planet, and that the humans are here only as long as it works for the Sidhe owners. The other group lives on the land, under the overseeing of Danu, my queen." He said this calmly although I had a jolt of surprise at his words.

"Danu chose humans who may be able, at least for a while, to live in harmony with the life force here. They did all the early work of raising seedling trees and transplanting small native plants to give them their best chance to survive and then be planted out. They raise a few crops and have animals for food as well. This, too, is an experiment that may be eventually ended."

"There is much empty land to share at present. We will show you whatever you wish to see when one of us has time to accompany you. There is no reason not to fly and see for yourselves. However, do not fly over or into the Shadakon holdings. We have asked their leader to excuse any accidental trespassing; however, do not test this intentionally. The Sidhe and Shadakon work together on this planet, but they are fierce predators as you know."

The visitors took this information in silently. Then the angry one spoke. "There are no humans or Shadakon on [Exterra]. I would rather live there."

"That would be between you and the Sidhe king there. You can put that request forward."

"Danu and I will swim now. Rest here if you wish.

Explore and return when you want more elixir."

"I would gather my own elixir."

Ceádar turned to the angry Sidhe and spoke clearly so I could hear, but also in under-mind to our visitor. "I am king here. This is my queen. We will do what we can to make you comfortable. Neither of us is surprised at your heart-sickness—how could you not be in pain? But this is our world and we, and especially Danu, have worked ceaselessly to protect and restore it. She and I require your civility and patience. Exterra, as you might know, was populated with both Shadakon and humans before the Old Earth humans forced our hand and we barred them from coming anymore. We destroyed their fleet that had come to scourge the land to ready it for plundering—again. The Sidhe have never had a world to ourselves since the beginning of our existence. The only one now that exists for Sidhe only is Exterra. The king has suggested that the more able Sidhe could come and assist with the transforming of this world. At some point, we may create a Between as sanctuary for ourselves, and some untouched wilderness for the little lives who now live here. For now, Fiórcara and I are the gatekeepers for these two worlds—your two Sidhe kings."

Ceádar looked at me. "I would swim with you now." To our guests he said, "We will return at dusk. Be welcome here."

Soon we stood on the edge of the dry sand and small rising waves. I was pleased with how I had held control and not let my own anger rise. I was still susceptible to sudden sadness and anger, having been dismissed and misunderstood by the ones closest to me recently. Always early bridges are tentative at first ... a woven cord across a chasm and then more re-enforcement done carefully over time until one could walk across with only a little trepidation. Fiócara and I were still at the slender grass rope stage. Dagon appeared to not want to cross over to me at all at this time, and I sensed there would be no welcome if I showed up in his mind or life.

And then there was the crown that was still seemingly firmly attached to me. I put my hand up to be sure, because I could not always feel it. It was warm and curiously soothing to run my hand along.

Ceádar drew me to him and removed the overly fancy but beautiful dress and draped it across a rock along with his tunic. He laughed.

"You and clothes. Should we make this a world where no clothes are worn? Thing is, there would be little subtlety between you and I."

I could plainly see that he wanted me and I was giving off my own signals.

"Yes, Danu," he said. I could hear the honey tones of want in his mind-speak. He then matter-of-factly wrapped me, first in his arms and then in iridescent coils and moved us to the shallows. He bent to my mouth and slowly, slowly moved over it and parted my lips as I lay willingly caught and eventually panting.

"*Please, Ceádar,*" I thought to him. "*Please have me, Ceádar. Please be one with me.*"

"*When?*"

I sank my ineffectual teeth into his arm. He bit me back in a more tender place. I was not wounded but definitely warned if I wanted to take it in this direction …

"*Now, Ceádar, my king, my lover, my planet-maker.*"

He smiled and, holding me firmly, he was suddenly within me and we were one being. I wept at the intensity, a power I only recently knew was part of him.

"*Is there more?*" I gasped.

"*Ah, Danu … another question I have wondered if and when you would ask. What exactly is your question though?*"

I was beyond questions or even words.

I could feel him sliding in and out and I could feel what he felt as he buried himself in me. Both feelings were exactly matched by my own, and beyond what I could bear for more than a moment. I wept in his arms even as we both went over into bliss.

We returned to the beach when the first star was brightening in the amethyst sky.

We put on our dry clothes and returned to my home. The quiet Sidhe was asleep, curled on the flattened grass in the bower in front of my home. The angry one was gone. We poured a cup of elixir and settled down to watch the sky darken.

It was almost peaceful that night.

CHAPTER NINE

THE REFUGEES

Ceádar and I spent time thinking and talking together about how we could both help and put to work the arriving Sidhe. We needed to know how they had sheltered on Old Earth and also what skills they could share. There were no mature forests with gnarled roots here that would provide good shelter for hill houses, and few came with anything in their hands except a few bows and arrows and a carrying bag—and means to harvest elixir of life.

I was concerned that they might inadvertently over-harvest in some areas. The young trees might not be able to stand repeated tapping of sap and energy. I decided to make a map of useable plant and tree areas for this project, and set some of them to collecting elixir in areas that I chose for them. I also experimented with tapping and tasting some of the thorny desert plants. Many of them had surprisingly abundant energy with a pungent taste that reminded me of the deep desert. This was more than adequate to provide nourishment and energy, but had to be mixed with sweeter sources. I flew out and over a lot of land and then could transit back when I had bearings. I asked Ceádar if I should take a work party with me, but after considering that, he asked me not to—that he would go with my maps and set them to harvesting elixir in small amounts from various places.

"These Sidhe have been starved for the last parts of their lives. They had to subsist on the failing energy of the dying forests. Sidhe are careful to stay in balance with the life force, but these may not have lived in balance for a long time. They are hungry and need extra energy to heal, both physically and in all the other ways. I will take them out and put small groups in harvesting areas. They will return in the evening and we will, for the present, keep the elixir here and blend it with the less delicious sources." He made a wry face. Neither of us had enjoyed the desert-sourced elixir although it satisfied thirst perhaps even better than that of the fast-growing vegetation.

"I think I need to observe the angry male Sidhe. Some may be pushed past their own self-control. One thing you might do is take histories or information from any who chose to sit down and talk to you. Many will not. But if we discover their unique skills we can place them on the land more easily. And those who are particularly enraged should not be near you or the humans on the land."

I knew it saddened him to have to say what he was saying.

I also knew that my apparent human appearance—slightly taller than the usual Sidhe female, and with my auburn curly hair I was set apart visually. We had not mentioned my Shadakon heritage. One day in the future they would hear about that, or observe me with Dagon and have to come to grips with another aspect of their so-called queen. I was more than happy to leave that for later.

So day by day, Sidhe arrived. Fiócara had sent bales of simple tunics woven and assembled by the Sidhe on Exterra. We had decided that offering them human-made clothing would be an insult to them and he agreed. I still had not communicated directly with Fiócara—I left that to Ceádar who was, as much as possible, available and with me when the new arrivals came. They gave me no names and I knew not to ask for any. However, I attempted to categorize them by some feature so that I could tell them apart.

That was not easy. They all arrived in dusty worn-out clothes. With blank eyes and shutdown hearts and minds. I would offer elixir and answer simple questions. Ceádar took them to the sea to swim if they wished, and provided clean garments when they came out of the water. All carefully folded and kept their old clothing. It was the rough touch of home and they used them for pillows and no doubt smelled the fading smell of Old Earth as they fell asleep.

I had worked out a flexible style of intake. Some Sidhe I asked if they could answer a few questions and they said no. Those I offered shelter to rest or sleep and continued to provide elixir as frequently as they wanted it. I was relieved when the first gathering group returned with barrels of fresh material to be blended before being offered. The Peace Grove had provided heavily for the newcomers. Now I particularly appreciated the tough native trees that had sprung up there and spread their roots far in all directions. I thanked them carefully and was reminded that they continued to benefit from the bodies below that were the remains of the humans we could not turn loose on the land.

I had killed those humans, after a lovely banquet and speeches of appreciation on my part. Then the doomed humans drank a punch infused with my faerie blood and the green contents of a small vial given to me by Green Tara. They dropped where they sat, as did I, having shared a toast I felt I couldn't refuse. Perhaps a significant part of my humanity fell away that day and the days that followed as I recovered.

There were a very few Sidhe who asked to see the human settlements and those I transited to one or two sites.

The humans knew and remembered me but no longer knew the history of how their families had met me. I was a strange visitor who they provided with very careful respect. I often sat in silence with the elders and read what I would from their minds. I sometimes brought the children something—a handful of seeds or a shiny rock I had found in my travels. The humans had not re-invented money, instead they bargained among themselves for what they needed. I was gifted some wooden drinking bowls that I took to serve elixir from. One of the Sidhe, appearing younger than the other males, seemed to enjoy the human children in one group that we visited. He looked so wistful that I wondered if the Sidhe had in fact managed to procreate in their last years on old Earth. I gave him permission to return and interact; it would have to happen sometime and I would keep an eye on him.

I was enjoying a momentary quiet moment when I was jolted from it by an intense feeling in my Maker hand. Dagon was communicating with me immediately and I felt his anger behind his carefully chosen words.

"We have a Sidhe arrival here. He was captured in town. I don't know what he has done, but I suspect he is here to harm us and may already have done so. Some Shadakon he was near have sickened. You need to gather him and explain that there will be no second chances. If he has in fact harmed us, we must insist on justice from the Sidhe."

"I will contact both Ceádar and Fiócara immediately. Can you hold him?" I could easily guess which Sidhe this was. He had arrived in toxic anger and has shrugged off any attempts to help him settle.

I called to both Ceádar and Fiócara, shaking both stones into my hand. Ceádar had to wait to gather up his charges before returning. Fiócara responded and I could feel the distance and coolness in our connection. I continued on with him, as neutrally as I could.

"Fiócara, I am calling you because I must. We have a renegade Sidhe here who intentionally entered the Shadakon city and may have injured some Shadakon by some means. We have offered him every courtesy—he was unwilling to accept Ceádar's or my guidance and has stayed away, harvesting his own elixir although we asked the new Sidhe for the time being to take nourishment here with us. We are trying to spread the taking of elixir so that a few areas are not over-used." I then waited.

"And your king cannot resolve this?" Again I heard faint scorn and turned away from it without openly reacting. Of course I was reacting. An ache spread across my heart.

"I suspect that you and Ceádar may have to do some deep work with him. Perhaps, and I cannot believe that I am suggesting this but … perhaps do something like you did for me a long time ago—make the pain more distant. Make it bearable for him."

"You had to agree, Danu. You had to place yourself in my hands." I felt his connection turn more gentle towards me. He had brought me through, from a bitter and almost powerless human woman newly turned Shadakon, to what and who I was now. I felt a blaze of gratitude towards him and then I felt his power intermingle with mine. I sighed.

Dagon was still waiting for a reply. I returned to him without having an answer yet—but my job here was to interface and provide diplomacy between his kind and the Sidhe, and the humans.

"Dagon, I have reached both kings and both will be attending as soon as possible. Where do you wish to meet with them or with us?"

"I have him here and here he will stay until this is resolved. I have put a command on him so that he cannot transit or fly. I will not probe to discover what he has done for a short time. But if more Shadakon sicken, I must. I also may have to destroy him if he carries an illness in his body that he intends to spread."

Ceádar arrived with his work party and waved them towards the beach. Fiócara was standing in front of us.

"What now, Danu?" he asked me.

I touched both of them lightly and let them read what Dagon had mind-spoke to me.

"This must be attended to now," Fiócara said, seemingly calmly, though I knew he was locked down. There were so few remaining Old Earth Sidhe. He might have to make a hard decision to keep one from endangering the fragile balances here.

"There are four more arrivals this afternoon," he said to Ceádar. "Danu and I will go to Dagon and begin to sort this out."

I was shocked. I did not think he wanted to be in my company and I was not sure I wanted to be in his.

"This is beyond small misunderstandings between you and I, Danu. You have a job and I need you by my side when we go to Dagon. That is not debateable." He simply took my arm and transited us to the courtyard in front of Dagon residence. He was waiting for us, pacing and looking darker than usual.

Dagon looked at me, still crowned, and Fiócara and shook his head. "Follow me," he said without any further greeting.

In the small meeting room, where I had had many difficult conversations with both Dagon and Nathaniel, there was a blanket on the floor and the unconscious Sidhe lay limply on it. Fiócara knelt and put his hands on both sides of his head. I also knelt and touched his arm—it was hot and his life energy seemed chaotic.

Fiócara frowned. "I must do a deep read of him. You must provide me with additional energy as I do so, Danu. Dagon, if he starts to come out of your induced state of sleep, do more of what you have already done. He must not leave here until we are all sure that he is safe."

He put both hands on the Sidhe's motionless head and time slowed for me. He reached out at one point and took my arm and I felt a significant amount of my energy transfer to him. I sat, feeling the light dim for me but not struggling against it.

Fiócara said something that I was sure was an oath. "Feed her, Dagon," he just said without looking up. Dagon laid one hand on my shoulder and as gently as the lover he sometimes was to me, he infused me with life energy. I sagged against him even as I kept the link with my king open. *"Ah, Danu,"* he murmured in my mind. *"I would like to be doing this under more pleasant conditions."*

Fiócara didn't respond to our side conversation. I saw the Sidhe shake and then he went completely limp. Fiócara had broken through. We all understood the effort it had taken.

"He must be isolated and unconscious until we know what to do with him," Fiócara said wearily when he rose from his side. "Dagon, he infected himself before he left old Earth. He is one of the last of the Sidhe kings—from the Amazon kingdom. They survived longer than most and had knowledge of jungle plants and poisons. He is not dangerous to other Sidhe—at least not physically. He was and is dangerous to you and yours. I don't know whether the effects will wear off, or if what he carries is lethal. Even if it is my choice to end him, I cannot do so until I gather more information. There were others with him brought to Exterra. They cannot be allowed to come here or even be on Exterra near the spaceport which is still visited by Shadakon."

"Is this also dangerous to humans?" I asked, suddenly realizing that if the Shadakon's food source was interrupted, this rage-filled Sidhe, with what he carried, could eliminate both Shadakon and humans and possibly create a Sidhe-only world.

Fiócara looked at Dagon. "I am sorry. I never thought that this could happen. I will do everything in my power to make it right. Danu or I should take a reading on the affected Shadakon if you and they will allow it. As for affecting the humans, this would disrupt your stay here. The Shadakon might spread it to the humans by using Registry hosts."

Dagon just looked at Fiócara. "My clan may not accept help from the Sidhe," he just said. Especially if said Sidhe spread a plague on this world."

"Maybe in this case, they will have to receive help they have not agreed to," said Fiócara. "Their memories of the event could be altered or erased."

Dagon hissed at Fiocara. I felt the energies building between them.

"The Shadakon are not aware that Danu wears a Sidhe crown. Such things are not of interest to them. Some are aware that I have allowed her in my presence over the years. She can remain here; I will try to keep my official mate from murdering her. But she cannot be an identified Sidhe queen. And if she is not; then she must decide if that changes how she and I connect."

I shivered. Ceádar had been so happy over the last months. Now I was to be absent. And not wear his crown, an act he would feel immediately. And deeper, if it was off, how would I feel about being with Dagon?

"I said I would not take it off," I said numbly. "That if it had to come off, Ceádar would be the one who removed it." I looked at both of them seemingly calmly. Both looked back without any helpful suggestions to my seemingly small dilemma.

"Fiócara can you keep it in your safe keeping? I don't want it to disappear. I don't want Ceádar's faith in me to disappear ..." I was silent.

Somewhere deep within I was afraid, very afraid. There was not one single cause for it. Perhaps my easy honeymoon was over.

"*Perhaps,*" mind-spoke Fiócara. "*But surely you remember that we pleasure with who we will. My queen would not expect me to turn to her alone. And she definitely has no intention of denying herself pleasure.*"

"*You've been together since the dawning of your history,*" I thought back. "*Ceádar has waited a long time for me to see him. I am not in a hurry to take off his gift.*"

Fiócara swept the crown off my head. "I will talk to him," he just said. "This situation is more important than what you do or do not wear on your head.

And wearing or not wearing a crown does not make you a queen, Danu." He then disappeared.

Dagon and I looked at each other. Something undiscussed occurred to us simultaneously. *Would Dagon and I be safe from the toxin or plague that affected Shadakon?* I looked at the Sidhe's limp body and numb mind and shuddered.

"*We need to take him and the others to Green Tara.*" We had shared this realization as one mind as well.

CHAPTER TEN

RETURN TO THE CAVE
OF GREEN TARA

Dagon left me with the unconscious Sidhe and went to find those Shadakon identifiably affected by him. He arrived soon after with four Shadakon. They were weak and barely on their feet.

"How many can you transit, Danu?" I could easily take two at once, but we had four Shadakon and Dagon and the unconscious Sidhe. I took two at a time, transiting to the soft sand in the month of the cave. I walked alone into the darkness and knelt when I got to Green Tara's chamber. I saw only the bones of the fierce Guardian and spoke to the darkness.

"I have brought some sick Shadakon and a Sidhe who brought illness or a toxin to them. He is from Old Earth and is, I believe, not in his right mind. I have never heard of such a thing in the Sidhe, but the Old Earth Sidhe have been tortured by the dying of their planet. I do not know what we are up against except that the Sidhe infected himself intentionally before leaving old Earth. If you can help us, please tell me what you might require of me and what to do."

There was complete silence. I waited, outside time. I could have been there an hour or a day. I did not question or complain but knelt on the floor of the dimly glowing cavern.

At last the light brightened and I saw Green Tara, her scantily clothed body lush and green. She placed her hand on my shoulder and I felt ... euphoria. My body felt more alive than it had a moment before.

"*You have brought the Shadakon Dagon?*" Her voice was a throaty whisper that may have only been in my mind.

I suddenly realized that, although I had been trying not to think about going to Dagon while we had the chance, Green Tara might invite him for another round of pleasuring. A thought of jealousy or maybe disappointment drifted quickly across my mind.

"*The Sidhe has infected four Shadakon by intentionally entering their city and making contact. Dagon, too, could be affected. And I could too, as I have Shadakon blood. And if this also affects humans, the course of this planet has been altered.*"

"*I will come with you to the entrance,*" she mind-spoke to me.

In a moment we were there. Dagon was sitting down and I immediately knew that he was not well. The other Shadakon were lying quietly but I could hear that their breathing was slightly laboured. The Old Earth Sidhe lay as if dead.

I wondered if Dagon had enforced a continuing deep sleep in him or if the toxin was affecting him as well.

Green Tara went to Dagon first. She touched his face gently and he opened his eyes and smiled at her. She ran her hands along his body, sensing what she would. She then bent down and kissed him on the mouth. I felt his life energy rise. She then went to the other Shadakon, passing her hands over them, lingering over some more than others. Finally she went to the Sidhe. She ran her hands up and down his body and then matter-of-factly opened his pouch and examined the contents. I heard her hiss.

"He has brought a toxic fungal life form with him. He harbours it in his body and also brought spores that he probably blew towards these Shadakon when he was in the city."

"Will the affected Shadakon recover?"

Green Tara was silent and I felt time stretch for all of us.

"The Sidhe brought death. He let his body take up the poison. His breath, his touch is poisonous. There will be more victims. Some Sidhe may harbour the toxin without realizing it. Also, some Shadakon may seemingly recover, but still carry this darkness."

I looked at Dagon. I had spent time with this Sidhe. He had sat outside my home and Ceádar had spent time alone with him. Dagon looked better than he had before Green Tara had kissed him but I knew that he still had low energy.

"I could be carrying this?" I asked softly, with dread. "I am part Shadakon. My job here is to help the arriving Sidhe find a place here." I did not say, but thought, *I could be a danger to Dagon and the Shadakon! And possibly to the humans on the land who were actively restoring the planet.*

Everything I had struggled to bring into being could be undone by one anger-crazed Sidhe. I felt a weakness surge through my body and allowed myself to slip down onto the sand. I do not know how long I was there, without thought, my heart breaking over and over.

After some unmeasured time, Ceádar and Fiócara were present. There were additional Shadakon laid on the soft sand of the cave floor. Green Tara moved among them, passing her glowing green hands over them but not saying or thinking anything I could hear. Ceádar moved to my side and touched my cheeks gently. I dispassionately noted that I felt weak and disconnected. There was something I needed to remember! I struggled to sit.

"He was part of the gathering of the elixir of life.

He said something on his first day that I took to mean that the Sidhe had been poisoned and that he feared that from me. But he could have taken a lesson from that and added the toxin to our communal elixir—elixir I partook in every day. But worse, could all the Sidhe eventually carry this in their bodies? In which case, they soon could have all-Sidhe planets." I shivered and lay down again.

"There is more, Danu. You might as well know now, as you face the full scope of this." I heard sadness in Ceádar's quietly spoken words. "Some of the human settlements that he was allowed to be near are sickening. He apparently covered a lot of ground that we were not aware of. Some of the outlying humans are ill as well."

I lay completely still, as if this was merely a very bad dream, and if I did not wake myself up in it, I would be safe and in Ceádar's arms. He stroked my hair, seemingly not concerned that I was not wearing his gift.

I turned to Green Tara. "Goddess of light and darkness, life and death. I know that you have the means to easily kill and have allowed me to benefit from that power. Now I implore you to undo this monstrous act. I am sorry that this proud Sidhe king"—and here I indicated the limp pale form on the ground—"came to this solution. I believe the Old Earth Sidhe were poisoned by the humans. Perhaps they were well aware that the Old Earth Shadakon were indifferent to their fate. Maybe the poisoning was incidental, due to the large amounts of mercury and life threatening chemicals released into the waterways that got taken up by the trees. I want to hate him, but hate brought us to today. But even if he was a willing sacrifice, he was not on side with the life force. He is a broken Sidhe."

I took a deep breath. "I am in touch with the entire life force of this planet. I love the Sidhe, a Shadakon, and, yes, the humans. I am hoping they can grow up past their aggressive childhood and live peacefully here. I would give all that I have to preserve the affected ones. I know you have refused to accept my death before. But the stakes are higher now. I would give it all over."

Suddenly Green Tara's eyes were looking directly into me. "Would you give up the lives of your lovers as well?"

I blinked away tears. "Their lives are not mine to give. They would have to make that decision." I dispassionately felt a cold pain spreading from my heart down my arms and legs. I could no longer turn my head.

It was very silent around me now.

I felt Dagon in my mind, begging me not to make deals with the Goddess. He knew of a previous one I had made, to prevent he and Nathaniel from fighting each other to the death. My offering had been successful but I had paid by experiencing every pain I had ever endured in my life. And in the end, they had fought later, and Nathaniel had died at Dagon's hands. Dagon, too, had suffered that day. I knew that he had been closer to Nathaniel than to any other Shadakon.

"Well," murmured Green Tara. "I do like offers. Does anyone else have one for me?"

Dagon got to his feet and walked carefully over to me. "You have taught me to love, Danu. It is my people who are most at risk. The Shadakon. The humans have done this. We thought we could ignore what they did and do what we wanted to them. The night that Exterra was almost flamed into a dead planet I realized that Danu loved us all, even if we did not love or even like her. She even warned the humans who had arrived to annihilate us. Some lived to question the choices that had brought them there."

He looked down on me and I saw tears in my fierce Shadakon's eyes. "I will give up my life as well, if you will undo this spreading horror." He sat down next to me and took my hand. "I committed to the life force of this planet. If the solution needs my ending, then so be it."

I remembered being poised over him, both of us awash with wanting but both choosing to be intentional. I remembered the earth energy of this world entering him and me. I saw the flames dancing in his eyes and I went within and felt that he spoke the truth without hesitation.

Green Tara then turned to the two Sidhe kings. "And you. You brought this event into being by bringing heartsick Sidhe to this world. Will one, or both, of you be willing to pay with your life for the continuing life of those on this world?"

Ceádar came to my side, and with seemingly no concern for the connection Dagon and I had spun, took my other hand. He put the silver crown, which I had not seen in his hands, gently on my head. He smiled somehow.

"I will not allow my queen to go on without me," he simply said. "A part of me would die anyway if I lost her."

We were all silent. No one argued with any of our choices. Green Tara stood up and smiled. "But not you, Fiócara? You were the one who arranged for the transit of this poisoned Sidhe."

Fiócara stood like a tree awaiting the blade.

I saw for a moment his vast span of life and the changes that he had seen during it.

"You may have me, Green Tara. But you cannot have both of the last Sidhe kings. I will willingly accept whatever fate you bring, but Ceádar must then stand back. He will be a good leader for the Sidhe. If he loses Danu, he may be sad for a long time, but then, so would I. We four are intertwined, with none of us being more important than any of the others. This world was Danu's joy and I take full responsibility for not assessing the full extent of the craziness of this Sidhe. This situation arose from my inattention and inactions. I will bear the cost." He bent his head to Green Tara.

Green Tara seemed to change then, and I could perceive that she and the fierce guardian were one in the same. "As I told Danu, I am weary of death, having lived amidst it much of my long existence, but the sacrifice of giving up what one wants more than anything else—that excites me. Danu was ambivalent about living when she offered me her life earlier. But all of you passionately want to continue on—to complete the transfer of the remaining Sidhe to safety, to see this planet restored to a rich life force. Even to give shelter and another chance to the humans. Even the wild predator"—and here she stroked Dagon's cheek—"is committed. I can do no less."

"I will neutralize the toxin—it will be short acting in its effects and then be rendered harmless by this life force. This planet did, after all, fight off the previous fungal infection. All the affected ones should be taken to the sea or a tub of salt water and immersed. Anyone showing symptoms must receive this treatment. Eventually everyone will recover unless they are not given to the sea."

I imagined groups of cringing Shadakon entering the blue water. None swam or took an interest in the water. I could see the humans evolving a new version of baptism after being part of this. I looked at the unconscious Sidhe king sprawled on the sand. "And him?"

"I would have Ceádar take him to my underwater temple after he is restored. But before that, I suggest that you, Fiócara, wipe out these days from his mind. If you cannot do that, then you must end him. He will serve here humbly without knowing the horror he unleashed, or he will die honourably of his Old Earth wounds."

The green glow left the cave. Ceádar started to lift me up but I pointed to Dagon and his clan members.

"Help him get them to the sea, Ceádar.

I can wait, knowing that eventually all will be well."

He assisted Dagon to his feet and gathered two more Shadakon and transited to the sea. The remaining Shadakon looked around warily but did not attempt to leave. I made my way over to them.

"You must all be vigilant about symptoms appearing in the Registry hosts or your human companions. The Shadakon had a part in this near-disaster. You must pay attention to missing or ill clan members; we will help you any way we can."

Fiócara, meanwhile, had knelt beside the ravaged king of the one-time Amazon basin of old Earth. He straightened his limbs and kissed his forehead. Then he placed his hands gently on each side of his head—and took his life. I felt a huge wave of sadness move through Fiócara as he said something in the ancient language of the Old Earth Sidhe. I felt the meaning of the word "brother" and then a chant of leave-taking. I lay quietly, not wanting to intrude even by obviously witnessing what was happening. Soon he reappeared at my side, his eyes fierce.

"You attempted to save him and did not hate him for his illness and for that I am grateful. He was, however, too dangerous to be allowed to walk on this world."

"He wanted to return to Exterra," I said softly. "We directed him to ask you. But his bleak heart was set on another path."

"And so he shall," said Fiócara. "We seldom use fire, but his body will be burned and his ashes scattered into the sea." He lifted me up and walked with me towards the back of the cave. "Danu, I need you now. I would thank you for this and everything else you did today but I am almost beyond words. I have seen you in this state; now you see me here."

He was trembling when I brought my mouth to his. He took me down to the soft silky sand and we both buried our fingers in it, pulling up the energy of the planet. He then joined me and we became all of it. I did not know my name or his but I knew I was home. I felt his old Sidhe heart, heavy with sadness and the responsibility of what he had had to do. I knew if it had been necessary, he would have died with me and, for a while, perhaps we did—we died to each other.

"I did not ask for your consent," he finally said.

"Nor did I," I said. We both smiled. My silver circlet crown glinted in the near darkness. I knew, however, that Green Tara had joined us and I heard her laugh in my mind. *"The heat of two great Sidhe,"* she mind-spoke.

"Danu, you bring me such pleasure when you do what you do so well."

CHAPTER ELEVEN

REBUILDING TRUST

We did not receive relocated Sidhe for a while after. I had no doubt that Fiócara was now spending time with each candidate to avoid what had happened earlier. Ceádar and I sat quietly in the bower he had made outside my house that was green and sheltering. Frequently I went to check on the humans to find out how they were faring.

He and I transited a large basin and containers of seawater to some of the humans living away from the sea in the desert. As I suspected, it grew into a ritual of protection for the very young and the sick. After awhile they made their own seawater with some of their precious sea salt that they bartered for, adding it to the fresh waters gathered from stream or lake.

One day while we watched the sea, Ceádar took my hand and, brushing it with his lips, said, "Have you communicated with Dagon since we took the sick Shadakon to Green Tara?"

I looked at him but saw nothing in his eyes to indicate distress or doubt. I shook my head. The relief that came as the days passed and no further illness was discovered had left me languid and drifting. Ceádar and I had swum, availing ourselves to his joy of taking a water form, and even napped in the long afternoons.

"I need to go back to Exterra and assist with the continuing screening of the incoming Sidhe." He was silent but then resolutely added, "It is midsummer's eve there tomorrow, Danu. I would fly with the Sidhe of Exterra."

With the queen who still held a part of his heart, I thought before I could shield that thought.

He was smiling at me. "Yes, Danu. I will be in a cone of power with her again, even though she will doubtlessly be distracted by the irresistible Fiócara, among others." He ran his thumb back and forth across my wrist, relaxed and attentive to my reactions. He had not invited me and we both knew that I was pondering that.

I fought not to look down or withdraw my thoughts. For a moment I saw her in all her beauty and remembered my longing for her. She was a powerful force and did not hold back her enticements.

"I did not think this would be an ideal night for us to arrive and assume hospitality from Fiócara and her," said Ceádar.

I smiled.

My relationship with her had ranged from surrendering to her erotic skills and wanting her as I had wanted no man—to her attempting to kill me. In between those opposites she had let me know that she might be available to me again—or not. A delicious balance, although, unlike Ceádar, I would not have wanted to dance her dance for eons.

"I did not want to dance her dance," Ceádar growled. "She danced me nevertheless. Not unlike you and Fiócara ..."

"I will be gone for four days, Danu. What you do while I am absent is your choice. You are my queen, but you are Sidhe and have a lover who, in spite of himself, continues to long for you. The day that he offered to die for the planet—that day I knew the depth of his connection to you. He has spent the night with a goddess, but that is not who he thinks of when alone. You have seen him take a Registry host in front of you. That was an act done to push you away, even more so when he took you again afterwards. It was seeming ineffective though."

How did Ceádar know all this? I bit my lip to induce pain and block out the other feelings that were a lot like pain.

"*I laid him down in the shallows and sat with him while he grappled with his terror of water—of being submerged. I eased his mind and then quickly dipped his head under and brought him up almost before he realized what had happened. In that moment of trust, he was open to me and I took advantage of that. I wondered if he still harboured dark wishes to hurt or kill you. I now know, and he knows that I know, that he does not. Perhaps in surrendering to the life force here, he truly surrendered to you as its guardian. Green Tara honoured him by allowing him to remember his night with her. Few, probably no, Shadakon, have felt the energy of the cone of power of midsummer's eve, much less the caresses of a goddess. He is a lucky male, in a complicated sort of way. You, of course, are his major complication and this serves the Sidhe well. The Shadakon may have retaliated against us after the rouge king entered their domain but for his quick contacting of us and enforcing peace.*"

"But now?" I asked softly.

"But now I will be gone for four days. When I return, you and I may or may not ask each other questions about our time apart. I can assure you, though, that I will bring home the energy of a second cone of power for your pleasure and mine."

I licked my lips. In the beginning of learning to know Ceádar, he had hidden himself from me. I thought him a beautiful alluring Sidhe—but not a king.

I been given hints and think that part of me understood that he was more than he seemed. But I preserved my stubborn small-mindedness. Both he and Fiócara had watched me approach knowing and then retreat into confusion again and again.

"But meanwhile," I continued on, "I need to hear that you consent to what you seem to be offering me."

Ceádar smiled. It was a particular smile that I knew often led to extended sessions of pleasure giving and taking. "Perhaps I will get your full attention before leaving, Danu." He reached over and delicately picked up the small flogger that now sat by my bed where he had placed it. I shivered.

He leisurely pulled off my tunic, baring me to the breeze. He took his own off as well. The evidence of his intentions was obvious. He laid me down on the comfortable bed that he so enjoyed for activities like this. He bent over me, catching my eyes easily. Looking into his now bright green ones was like looking deep into the forest. Things moved there that could not be easily identified.

"Green man," I said in a husky whisper.

"Your green man," he answered.

My body kindled to his and heat radiated out from my centre. Every light touch he made left a fiery wake of desire. He laughed and kissed me, drawing away to leave me arching to retain contact.

"Ah, Danu," he said. "I love these long afternoons." I heard the unmistakeable swoosh of the lash that landed delicately on my belly, amid the visible to both of us cross-hatching of Fiócara's previous erotic work with the lash. Ceádar brought the strands down precisely in the old marks that we both could see, that the Sidhe could see but not others. My skin blazed.

I moaned.

"Complaints, my queen?" he asked, knowing that soon I would not be able to answer. "Specific requests? Harder?"

He increased the power of his stroke minutely and moved me closer and closer to the edge where pain and pleasure were one.

"Please," I begged. "Don't talk, don't stop."

"*Ahhh*," he mind-spoke and moved the lash down to where my inner thighs were trembling.

Again he laid pain directly over the previous tracks. I moved, unable to hold still anymore.

He stopped and watched me come partially back. He bent to me and kissed me in the centre of my heat, again and again, holding my hands stretched over my head. When I began to break, he resumed lashing me—this time with force. I moaned and eventually I screamed. And then I passed into the place where all is intensity and welcomed. He came to me then and we both crossed over to bliss. I held him to me, not wanting to become a separate being again. I knew that playing his part in this had brought him to his own bliss even before we joined bodies. It was not right or wrong but very Sidhe. He had always known when my interactions with Fiócara had had elements of pain in it. It usually did, although I was not aware of how he affected me because in our early connections I had only shards of memory of being with him—and craving him. These days I remembered everything and even the memory could take me to a place of hunger.

We lay together. The breeze coming through the window touched my body, which was exquisitely sensitive but not painful. He ran his hand down the areas of his recent activities and in spite of myself, I moaned again.

It was a long afternoon. As the sky dimmed, he simply walked out the door, leaving me with the thought, "*Four days, Danu. Do what you will ...*"

I spent that night on the edge of the sea and its whispering waves. I noted phosphorescence in the water—small flashes of life and death dramas. It now smelled alive. There was a line of detritus along the tideline, a resting place for detached seaweed and small stranded creatures.

I watched the stars rise and brighten and did not call Dagon with my Maker hand.

The next morning I swam and did not call Dagon. But of course, I knew I was reaching out to him, whether with full amplitude or not.

As the sun dipped below the horizon on the second day I gave up and touched my hand. It flared at my first touch. Dagon was immediately in my mind; he thought nothing but was waiting to see what I might bring to him.

Finally he gave in. *"Yes, Danu. You are there. I am here. I don't hear anything. Are you just checking to see if our bond still works? Or, dare I say, a true booty call?"*

I sighed. Of all the ways I might have framed my desire to see him—okay, to touch him—that phrase stopped me in my tracks, as he no doubt knew it would.

"I'm sorry, Dagon. I just wanted to know if you were ... well. If the recent events we went through changed things between us."

He didn't bother to answer this somewhat false entry into bringing up what I really wanted. Of course I wanted to know if he was well, but my Maker hand provided that information without directly contacting him.

"Are you crying now, Danu?"

I nodded without confirming it. Why did all of our connections begin with seemingly polite cruelty on his part?

I drew up pride up around me. *"I'm sorry, Dagon. I'm sorry that ..."* And then I was silent because I wasn't sorry that I still wanted to be united with him, that I still saw him as my first mate—now distant but still tied to me with invisible strands, heart to heart.

He too was silent. *"Shall we say goodnight then, Danu? You have to promise me though that you won't take that midnight swim."*

I sat as still as I could. I tried to breathe through the pain in my heart. I could not say goodnight or goodbye. He had tried to break my heart before yet it still beat and loved who it would—a crown would not change that, nor would being left alone under a sky full of stars. I put my hand on my Maker hand and gently stroked it. The pain circuit between there and my heart surged such that I expected to see light tracing its way from one to the other.

Dagon came silently. He stood before me and gazed down at me.

"To say that your random summoning of me is sometimes very inconvenient is putting it mildly. I need to feed and I had a Registry human lined up tonight for sex and blood. They are probably delivering her to my door even as I speak."

I looked up and he easily caught my eyes. There was fierce hunger there, anger, and desire. I watched the flames rise and knew I wanted to give him whatever he wanted from me. I shivered and went to my knees before him, an increasingly strong Alpha Shadakon.

His hand fell on my shoulder and he raised me but still stood apart from me.

"You cannot give me everything I want," he said. "I, fortunately or unfortunately, know that your king is a generous and kind Sidhe.

You deserve no less but, of course, you might find him too nice."

"He told me he was going to be away for four days." I said. "He asked me if I had been in contact with you and then just said, 'Do what you will ...'"

Dagon nodded. "Like I said, generous. He can now afford to be, Danu. He has you ... he can give you some room for your side interests."

"He may be already indulging in his own," I said.

"Ah the beguiling and entrancing Sidhe queen," Dagon said and smiled coldly. "Fiócara has you, she has Ceádar—when it is helpful. And you have me, whether I pretend I'm indifferent to you or not—also helpful to the Sidhe. The Shadakon could have ended a lot of Sidhe lives recently; most really wanted to. Once again I had to move very carefully to maintain my authority. My mate was particularly interested in diminishing me. She, like you once did, has her eye on several upcoming Alphas that I will have to banish or kill, or be killed by, as eventually I must be."

"I would take this gift of time to be with you, Dagon. At very least, I have to ask—to beg," I corrected. "I beg you, Dagon, Alpha of the Shadakon, to use me. To bring us both to pleasure; to take whatever I have to give."

I saw the eyes of the great cat before it springs. The widening of the pupils as the excitement of a take down increases. I faced whatever my fate would be in the next moment.

He took me to the ground and ripped off my minimal clothing. I shook under him but not in fear. I wanted him. I wanted him like this. At the moment I wanted nothing else except to be one with him. He pinned me and leisurely licked my neck. I swear that his tongue was coarse against my skin and I arched to him. I heard him growl deep in his chest—or maybe purr.

He covered my mouth and there was little that was gentle in what he brought. He rasped over my nipples as I moved to him. And then down—he smelled me like the big cat he was at the moment. I had been apart from Ceádar for two days and had swum in the sea. He made a chuffing sound and then plied his tongue, seemingly willingly to do so until I lost my mind.

"Ummmmmmmmm." I could no longer speak or even think.

He returned to looking at me. I saw his fangs had come down and I felt them graze my neck. I moved my head to the side. His eyes were almost black now and I felt the force of his full Shadakon nature.

"*Will you give it all up to me, Danu?*" I heard his deep mind-speak.

All? I wondered. But there was only one answer. "*I am yours, Dagon. Do what you will.*"

He drove his fangs into me then and took until there was blackness at the edges of my vision. Then he secured me with a firm bite and entered me without further negotiations or preparations. I wanted him like that. I wanted him like the storm—a wild primal force buffeting me as I rose to ecstasy. This was not like the grounding we had done in the circle of stones. He took me and then I realized we were in the air, he having me as we spiralled down.

I gave him everything and he took all that was safe to take from me and maybe a little more. I returned to find myself lying on the ground, wondering how long a trip home it would be. I started to get up, but although I could clearly imagine doing so, my body stayed where it was. He had taken me hard. I lay under him now, totally open to the next event in my life—if there was to be a next event.

"Why do you not fear me, Danu? I give you every reason to." His eyes were quieter now, his lust for my faerie blood and body sated. Whatever had driven him to assert himself so fiercely now left him quiet and sad. It had begun to rain. He picked me up and flew with me to my house. He lay beside me and ran his fingers through my hair. I suddenly startled, wondering how he could do so.

I wore no circlet of silver! My panic broke through my sleepy lethargy. Dagon looked about and it was he who saw it. It was sitting on the shelf above my bed, propped up against the small grass flogger.

I had said earlier that I would not take it off. Fiócara had taken it off when I went to attend to the infected Shadakon. Later, without me noticing Ceádar had obviously calmly taken it off when he left for Exterra; he would replace it when he returned. Neither time had been my choice but I understood the practicality of sometimes not being identified as a Sidhe queen, especially if I was not one. I was Ceádar's Midsummer's Eve Queen—the rest was undecided.

But now I was free, by the courtesy of my Sidhe lover, to do what I would. I turned back to Dagon and gave him a drowsy smile. He studied me without smiling.

"I took too much, Danu. For a moment, I thought I would not stop. Could not stop." He rubbed my arms that felt distant to me. Then he did what he had done so many times when I had returned to him—from death or from the Sidhe. He gently stroked and stroked until he had touched every part of my body. I felt him leaving his essence on me, but it was more than that, he was calling me back and reclaiming me.

I touched the starburst scar on his chest and then leaned forward to kiss it. I felt him shudder. "I do not deserve your gentleness, Danu. Nor your forgiveness."

"There is nothing to forgive, Dagon. I wanted you—all of you. This is part of who you are. What you are. But I need you to pour some elixir of life for me." I pointed to where my small store of it was and he brought me a brimming cup and sat me up. I must have fallen asleep before I finished it, but later that night he offered it again. I realized that he had sat on guard, monitoring my return to my body.

I pulled him down to rest beside me and stroked him as I would have stroked a big cat. He was silent for a moment and then I heard the rumbling of what could only be a purr.

When I awoke again it was morning and the place beside me was empty.

It was past midday when I felt my Maker hand come to life.

"I left you to sleep, Danu. I would like to return tonight. This time I will be well-fed and not bringing hidden anger. Over and over, I know you are not toying with me and never have. And over and over I forget. I would to show you another side of me tonight."

"We still have time, Dagon. I would spend it with you, even though I will keenly feel your absence later. I would gladly pay that price."

"I will see you at star rise, Danu." I felt the sweeping feeling of his wanting pass across my body and then he was gone.

That afternoon I gathered the Sidhe here on this world in the green space outside my house. Their bodies seemed quiet but I sensed and sometimes heard clearly many disparate thoughts and feelings.

Where was the king? When could they be autonomous here? Were they now in danger because of the rebel Sidhe's actions?

I let true silence grow, coming in from the edges where the green living trees were anchored deep in the ground. From the faint sounds of the sea, from the deep blue of the sky. I waited and opened my eyes and returned their gazes.

"When I came here," I said both aloud and in mind-speak, *"There was very little vegetation. The seas were salty and dead, the riverbanks held back only sand. The planet was dying. And it was dying because of the actions of humans."*

I felt the blended emotions of anger and sadness from the Sidhe. I let them feel my own despair. I continued. *"There was a plague that blew in the air.*

The wind was yellow and where it blew it left sticky dust that grew and reached into the remaining still living plants and fed. It had a similar effect on the humans. Their thinking was dulled and they did not notice that they had no faith or thoughts about tomorrow. That was perhaps a mercy, because the Shadakon were going to take the healthier ones and leave the rest to die. The humans did not realize it, but they were already eating dried meat that was recycled from dead companions. When I realized the true horror that was playing out on this world, I fell ill. I spent a year on Exterra while a Shadakon who had promised to help me evaluated the humans, chose some that could survive on the land, and continued my work."

"Why would he do such a thing?" The Sidhe who asked seemed both contemptuous and disbelieving.

"I will never lie to you," I simply said. "He was a Shadakon and I have the erotic power and enticing blood of the Sidhe. The King of Exterra claimed me and named me as Sidhe in front of his queen, but that is another story. I made sure that the Shadakon Nathaniel"—and here I shivered to recall his name—"was tied to me. The current Alpha Shadakon, Dagon, is also tied to me; if he had not been, many Sidhe would have died, and due to a lack of information and coordination, many Shadakon as well. Their leader put his position in jeopardy to hold back the first response of his clan."

We looked at each other and for the first time, a few Sidhe males smiled at me. They had observed and felt the interactions between Ceádar and me.

"You wear a Sidhe's crown sometimes."

"I do. Ceádar recently removed it when he went to Exterra three days ago to fly in the midsummer's eve celebration. He and I had celebrated a smaller one here earlier." I smiled when I remembered that night. "I saw his action as proof of his acceptance of what I might do while he was gone."

One of the Sidhe glanced at my bed through the window. I had no problem accepting that he knew that not all of my visitors there were Sidhe.

"This is my home, given to me by the Shadakon Nathaniel who died, in part, fighting for me. Ceádar and I and all of you will create a new home for the Sidhe, and you will find unique solutions to creating your own personal spaces here. The trees are mostly all young and do not have the old forest root systems that are so useful and comfortable to shelter under. On old Earth, people of the land built homes of clay and straw called adobe.

Others cut entrances into shallow caves or buried most of their dwelling in a hill of grass, with one opening facing whatever one wanted to face."

An older-appearing Sidhe turned to me. "There were no root homes in the last decades of old Earth. There were no trees except a few scattered groves in the tropical areas. The deserts were industrial mining areas. The rivers were all dammed and put to work creating electricity, no matter what hardships that provided to the people who had lived along the rivers or the creatures that swam in them."

"You seem to have a joy in the water, Danu. Your Sidhe lover takes you there frequently. He can shape shift, as can Fiócara and some of us to a lesser degree. I knew that you worked to preserve the sick king who died here. We had not known what he intended; he shielded his mind and was absent from us. He took elixir where he would, without regard for your request to return here and pool our resources. We knew he was sick at heart—we all are. But we see this as an opportunity. We thank you and your king."

I bowed my head. I was still part human I guessed. Humans had ruined the water world that Old Earth was once called, and they had killed off most of the inhabitants. Now they too would die.

"You feared the cup I offered you in our first meeting. It hurt my heart, wondering if the Sidhe had been poisoned," I whispered.

The self-chosen speaker was silent, and then he said, "Those of us who sheltered in the Amazon and forests of Africa made trouble for the workers who came to finish stripping the land."

He sat quietly as did I. I could see a kaleidoscope of images: humans hammering something into the base of the great trees, sick and dying hunter-gatherer humans, lying where they fell. No rituals of parting. No returning to the life force. The Sidhe took longer and died privately when possible.

The tears were running quietly down my face. I did not wipe them away and they trickled down to find the earth.

"*I understand the rage of the Sidhe king,*" I mind-spoke. "*I left Old Earth never to return, content to let everyone and everything die without my attention. I have been atoning for my inactions ever since. I fought and will continue to fight for the life force and her children here.*"

"Yes," said the old Sidhe. "But all of us are children of the Visitors. The Sidhe were perhaps the most connected and intact. But all their children now pay for what they did not begin."

I already knew and believed this. The humans had been genetically engineered to be domesticated work animals. The Anunnaki who stayed on Old Earth after the exodus of the Visitors, disobeyed orders and were abandoned to become at first local gods, and then demons. And then … ghosts or uneasy spirits. Their children carried the aggression of their Otherly parents. The Shadakon carried their fierceness and requirement of energy from live hosts. Early on, the Sidhe had made their deep connection to the life force, but they were mostly indifferent, and then later angry with the humans. They retreated from them, and in their occasional contact with them were tricksters or worse.

We sat together for a while longer, and then I said, "There will always be elixir of life available here. We will have gatherings as the time goes by and host events where everyone can get caught up with their companions about how they are doing. In future, we may all create a Between as sanctuary. But I want to show you something now that Fiócara, the Sidhe king of Exterra showed me. It may free you from feeling dependent on us.

I walked into the sunlight and knelt down on the sandy ground as did most of Sidhe.

"The heart of this planet, as all planets, is hot and powerful. It is a hot fierce nourishment that seeks to access the surface through the channels you open to it. You must stop taking before you are filled."

I took the speaker Sidhe's hand and clasped my fingers around his. I plunged both of our hands into the sand and I felt the golden strands of energy seek my own. I felt a golden glow accumulate in the centre of my body and reluctantly, I pulled away. I almost felt the disappointment of the energy that was preparing to come through me to the surface of the planet and meet the air.

I knew the Sidhe felt and understood the seductive power of that momentary union. He leaned back and let go of my hand, looking slightly dazed.

"If you tap this power, you will not need to do so every day or even every other day. And I would not suggest relying on it exclusively. It is of the mineral kingdom and least concerned for living beings. If you take too much—I do not know what it will do to you. It was not an experience that the King of Exterra wanted me to have."

The speaker took the hand of another Sidhe and then a circle was formed of clasped hands. I realized that if such a contact did not immediately kill a Sidhe, the power could be dissipated between many. I smiled. There was so much that we could teach each other.

I poured blended elixir and all drank without wishing to exchange cups with me. One Sidhe lay inertly in the corner of my green shelter. Each briefly touched him and then drifted away, leaving him there. I wondered if I would find him better in the morning; but it was just as likely that I would find him lifeless.

Their graciousness in accepting me was more than I deserved, but I would do what I could for all of them. I shook my green calling stone from Fiócara into my hand and saw and felt him in my mind immediately. There were people behind him and I tried not to see whether Ceádar was one of them and in what combination.

"*Yes yes, quickly, Danu. Not a good time to chat.*" I felt his aroused sexual energy swirl around me.

"*Fiócara, the transported Sidhe have left one of their companions here with me. He is distant from his body; it may be that his heart or soul has already left. I thought to tuck your green stone in beside him. But I would not do so without your permission.*"

"*Why the green stone, Danu?*"

I gulped. "*Ceádar gave me four days to do as I would and I would do the same for him.*"

"*But you have no such consideration for me. This is the day after midsummer's eve. As you know, the Sidhe are even more erotic and enticing then.*

I remembered the small circle of steel chain I suffered in during the all-night struggle I had fought to not go to Fiócara on my first midsummer's eve while staying in Between. I had smeared my body with Touch-me-not, an herb that obliged me by providing agony and blocked his call. The next year though I had willingly been his Midsummer's Eve Queen and the agony and pleasure of that had tied me to him forever.

He smiled. "*Yes, Danu, you are unforgettable. And if I am not mistaken, you have your own plans that you might not want to inadvertently reveal to Ceádar today. I accept your reasons for interrupting me—it will be only a temporary delay.*"

Meanwhile, my body had kindled to the energy that came through a mental link with a Sidhe king on another planet. Without thinking I touched my breast with my free hand and moaned.

"*Yes Danu. Maybe we will have a moment and then I can continue on with the rest of the day and night. Hopefully you too will find some release to your liking. But meanwhile ...*"

I had my hand on my breast although it no longer felt like my hand. I felt his long fingers expertly knead and pull while I mewed and moved to his phantom touch. He touched my lips and they opened to him. He traced around them and I was already silently begging for more. Empty! I was empty.

His-my hand moved down the centre line of my body and I shook under it. Then further until he-I were stroking my centre of pleasure. He continued and continued until I wept. And then I surrendered and let go. Wave after wave of sensation moved through me and I moved with it and made whatever noises came.

"*Well, that should provide a good charge for the stone,*" he thought. "*And it was quite satisfying to me and my guests.*"

This was yet another moment when I realized that I was now more Sidhe than anything else. I tried on feeling embarrassed, but in fact I was still giddy with the pleasure of midsummer's eve energy from Fiócara.

"*Tuck the stone in near his heart,*" Fiócara thought matter-of-factly. "*Check on him and offer elixir if he rouses, or whatever else that might sustain his life, Danu. You are Sidhe and you have sourced from the planet today—do what you will. And now ... I will do what I will.*"

The connection was abruptly broken.

I went out and knelt beside the seemingly sleeping Sidhe. I put the green stone, which was flickering with inner light, on his chest and his hand came up and held it there. I looked into eyes the colour of the shallows of a tropical sea. We looked at each other without words or thoughts. He reached up and touched my lips and I smiled. *These Sidhe*, I thought. *Even half-dead they can bring it on.*

"*Please*," he just said in my mind. I lay down beside him and wrapped my arms around him. The green stone was nestled between our hearts. I sensed that he would stay with us here.

As the sky moved through the shades of deepening blue and then amethyst with brightening stars, I finally left him and sat on a small dune overlooking the sea. I felt my Maker hand glow and I was in touch with Dagon.

I felt gentleness in him definitely not evident yesterday. "*I would have a night together with you, Danu. If this were our last night, where would you want to be with me? Where might you take me?*"

I felt sadness in him. I had my connections and, yes, lovers. He had human women who came and tried very hard to act as though they found him irresistible. In fear they came and in fear they left.

He had asked me why I didn't fear him. That, beyond any Sidhe pleasure I could provide, was truly my best gift to him. I remembered the lovely human sisters who he had indulged and cared for and who had met him when he returned to them with excitement and affection. That had been a long time ago. Io had gone to the ground here after living a long life—a long time ago. I assume Ka had died before her sister.

"*I assume that your places are not suitable,*" I thought.

He shrugged. "*Wondering whether we would die right away or very slowly might add something to your experience. We actually have done that one, and the after sex was good. The immediate pain and desperation—not so much.*"

"*Come here. I have a sick Sidhe outside of my window so we will not linger here.*"

I went to check on him while I waited for Dagon and he was sitting up. I poured him a full cup of elixir and he accepted it and drained it immediately. He shook his head at the offer of more.

"I would sit beside the sea tonight," he said. "I will be fine until morning." He waited a moment then added, "Could you take me there? I am still weary."

Dagon showed up while we were discussing the details, dropping out of the sky as silently as an owl stooping on prey. I could almost see him shaking out his feathers after he landed.

The Sidhe looked at him and said, "Greetings Alpha Shadakon. I was just leaving but think I need some help tonight."

"I am taking him to the edge of the sea. He has sea eyes," I added, without knowing why.

"I would continue to hold the green stone tonight," he said. I smiled and wrapped my fingers around his hand that still held it tight.

To my surprise Dagon took one arm over his shoulder as I did. He nodded and I transited us to the edge of the sea. The Sidhe sighed in pleasure or some sort of relief.

We left him there and returned to my home.

"A comfortable bed then, Danu? You never cease to surprise me."

"I am likely to do so again. I wish for kindness tonight, everything else that may come is welcome, but my heart wants to whisper to your heart."

He shared energy with me and I gave him some of the deep-sourced hot energy of the planet. He hissed in surprise as we blended our gifts to each other into a radiant ball of energy between us. When we could no longer wait a second longer, he covered me and I covered him. After a while I felt something towards him I had usually only experienced with the Sidhe kings.

We were one. I did not want to separate from him or lose him anymore. I did not care what repercussions might come of that revelation. I watched the flames dancing in his eyes when he was above me and I opened to him as I had in moments of great danger to me in his presence. As I had opened to wanting him and the resulting deep sadness as the years went by and I had not heard a word or message from him. I saw tears in his eyes then.

"Danu, I did not want to tell you. But I am being challenged by a smart, strong, rising Alpha. I always knew I could take Nathaniel—I knew him too well for him to surprise me in combat. I cannot say that about this Shadakon. He is hungry, more hungry than I am now. There is nowhere for me to go in my clan but to endure endless challenges and finally into the ground."

At that moment I believe my heart stopped. I was at the bottom of an Old Earth sea, with no air, no tender. The surface was above me and I could see it dancing far over my head. I knew I would not reach that promised breath. I tried to remain calm and still; panic and the knowledge of what was soon coming was around and within me.

"Oh, Goddess Danu! I am more sorry for you than for me. It is how it ends for us. I was so close last time—I had accepted that but made the last effort."

"For me," I whispered.

"Yes, Danu. Much as I might have wanted to detach from you, there is seemingly an unbreakable bond between us. This love is a lot more than what people or Others say about it. It seems so innocent—a taste, a delaying of the ending—and then ..."

He wept. "I would not hurt you but this seems to be part of it."

The weak Sidhe was sitting by the sea, allowing us this time and space. He had decided that, at least for a little while, he would live.

He granted us the courtesy of not having to roll on sand or dust away from my home. We were all doing what we could do.

I could do no less than all I could do for this proud Shadakon.

"Never mind," I said. "Never mind, Dagon. I will continue to breathe and I believe it is now time for me to—"

I reached for him and took his willing man part and made good use of it. He moaned and stiffened and then gave it all up.

"We could do this. We could do this tonight …"

CHAPTER TWELVE

REUNIONS

When Ceádar returned suddenly, I was sitting beside the Sidhe I now thought of as Blue Water. He knew I had given him that name (in my own mind) and had smiled when I thought it.

"It is a good small name for me, Danu. Thank you for wanting to keep me separate in your mind from all the other beautiful Sidhe males."

I laughed. "You clearly are regaining your energies. But, Blue ... were there female Sidhe that came to Exterra?"

He sighed and looked away. "Some have come across. The Queen of Exterra is providing them a place of healing and rest. Eventually some will come here. We can all sleep on the ground and under trees, but after our long descent into death along with the planet, we now prefer to hide ourselves away when resting or needing a safe sanctuary. We would build shelters here before they come—for them to share with us or live in apart as they choose."

I nodded. "Homes are our first priority then."

He looked at me gratefully and I continued, "It would go faster if the humans could provide basic building materials. I am thinking about adobe bricks. They also could help dig the hill mounds and provide saplings and vegetation, if desired, to plant around them. The grass is dry on the hills and is perfect for the required straw to strengthen the clay. The sun is still warm enough to cure it. It rains less in the deserts now, which means that maintenance would not be ongoing every week. The sea bluffs are another possibility. Such homes might need to be refurbished more often but all could help each other."

"You do not live in such a home," he said quietly.

I sighed. "This house was built by another, using modern technology. It was given to me as a true gift—we were no longer together but he knew I slept and rested outside and sometimes sheltered under the eaves here. I accepted it rather than see it sit empty or be torn down. It is useful to me and, I suppose, a gift that still reminds me of the fine fiery lover who gave it to me."

"You loved him as well?"

"Love is a complicated word and I no longer can say with certainty that all that I feel for others is or is not love." I went silent and we sat and listened to the faint sea sounds.

Ceádar had arrived and squatted beside us, listening and not interrupting. He knew, however, that I was very aware of his presence.

The Sidhe I thought of as Blue turned to him and said, "Welcome back, King of this world. Your queen has kept everything going as smoothly as it could. I have decided to live and be useful. I am now going to the sea—though not to your favourite place."

Ceádar laughed and touched him lightly. "You can help me later to bring more life from Exterra to this sea. It is still largely empty due to its high salt content. But we have time ..."

He smiled at the Sidhe who promptly disappeared.

"Your chaperone has left," said Ceádar. I snorted at the idea of protecting one's precious virtue by not being left alone with a male. The humans had valued women who came fearful and inexperienced to their wedding beds—who were still "pure." What was vile with any man not their husband became blessed by the church when the inexperienced young woman or girl bled underneath her husband on her wedding night.

Ceádar advanced on me with a seemingly sinister intent. I had never felt this energy from him before. He often liked to render me helpless as he did what he would do, but I had always gone to his arms (and coils) willingly. Now though, there was a light in his eyes ...

I transited a short distance away. He followed me easily. I went farther, wanting to prove to myself, and him, that I could avoid him.

He was there where I arrived, no doubt taking my destination from my mind.

"This is enjoyable, Danu. A little frolicking."

I rolled my eyes and took off again—this time far into the desert. I was perhaps more familiar with the hiding places on this planet than he was. I could smell the faint smoke of the cooking fires of my plains humans. I was pinned to the dusty ground before I realized that he was close to me. He immobilized me and looked down at me with his full summer dark eyes. I saw the golden sunshine and I ... he was entrancing me!

"Women who run from faeries usually get caught. We assume they want to be caught. Or ..." He looked thoughtful, "We don't care if they want to be caught or not. It becomes a fine game played best on a dark night in the woods with no moon."

I suddenly realized the similarities between the Sidhe and the Shadakon.

"Yes. One can only imagine how much fun the Visitors had with the original inhabitants of old Earth."

I looked up at him with a perfect blend of desire and anger.

"Ah, yes, Danu. You like to keep your options open. Always a back door." I stilled under him. Under our erotic play, if it was play, was a more serious conversation.

"Let's call it an understanding," said Ceádar. His lips were close enough that I felt his warm breath and wanted to taste him.

He casually removed my clothes and looked at me with his golden green eyes. I could have closed my eyes. I could have really fought him, if I had wanted to, but I was lost and only wanted him to come to me.

"It's hard to believe that you have only been a Sidhe for a little while," he said smiling. He touched the edges of my lips with his finger—exactly as Fiócara had when I summoned him recently. I sighed. Ceádar had been present then. Had Fiócara's easy rousing of me been part of his enjoyment that day?

"Of course, Danu. After all, you called him at a busy time. His queen seemed very attentive to your response. She would still like to entertain you in the future."

I shuddered and he laughed. "Well you should, little Sidhe."

He was now touching and lightly kneading my breasts as Fiócara had. I kindled into a blaze of wanting and feeling particularly helpless.

His finger arrived at my place of wanting, hesitated, and then entered me. I knew I would soon plead for him.

"But not just yet," he said smiling and including another finger as I tried to move to meet him.

"And I personally know he did not do this," said Ceádar He moved down and put his mouth on me and I moaned. Slowly, slowly he worked his fingers and his tongue until I cried.

"So, surrender, Danu. I want this. I want to see you hot and empty and begging before I come to you."

I felt the wave below the horizon and knew it was coming for me and that I would be alone and overwhelmed by it. I could feel it touch the bottom and rise up and up. Ceádar also felt it within me ... and stopped what he was doing. He would make me surrender to passion—alone and empty. It hurt as much as the lash. I whimpered and then was silent as I hung between one state of being and another. I went limp in his arms, looking up into his patient and alien eyes.

"If you were merely a human, I might leave you like this: alone in the woods, your skirts over your head, likely to be found by a roaming human.

You would beg him to take you, and he would, but it would not be what you had briefly tasted and wanted. You would know that for the rest of your life."

I continued to look up into Ceádar's green eyes and the wave caught me and I began to tumble in it. But he came to me then and moving rapidly, he caught up and set his own rhythm. When I broke he was with me and I felt the surge throw me high up onto the beach. When I opened my eyes, we were no longer in the desert. Instead we were beside the sea and he had rolled us both in the shallows to wash off the desert dust.

"Welcome back, Ceádar," I said when I could breathe normally again. He laughed. He touched my cheeks where a short time ago helpless tears had traced down. He kissed and tasted my lips and he was present and with me. He kissed my breasts and was already plying his considerable skills. They rose to him and he gave them his full attention. Bit by bit he retraced his previous path until, when he stroked my still quivering centre, it flared in heat.

He entered me then and remained still. I felt our fires merge as one in a slow burning hot desire. I moved but he shook his head. "Let this be just as it is, Danu. Want me and want me and want me for as long as we both can stand to wait."

It was a very long afternoon. Eventually we temporarily finished with each other and swam together.

We did not speak about our time apart but I did relay to him my connection to the Old Earth Sidhe and that I had showed them how to source planetary energy. And then we spoke about partial solutions to their housing. When he met with them and shared elixir they talked of creating shelters and what they would need. The new Sidhe agreed to accept adobe bricks made by humans but did not want the humans to know where they were going to live.

I went with Blue Water and took a few hand tools to set the humans to the task of making bricks. I set up a drying shed, open to the afternoon hot sun but a shelter from the rains that fell predictably. I then went with some of the young humans and Blue to find clay. In fact, they had already found it and were probably not far from remembering or evolving how to do what I was going to teach them to do. We brought the wet riverbank clay back to the village, along with tough grass that I had scythed into short lengths. I had a tarp, something I knew they would find very useful later.

The children helped mixing the clay and grass, laughing and painting themselves with it. I could feel Blue's heart softening slightly towards the humans.

The children were beautiful even, or maybe because, they were smeared with clay. I made some forms from wood, so that the bricks would be regular shaped and easy to put together later. The new wet bricks had to set up for about two days and then we would carefully knock them out of the forms and stack them under the shelter. Soon the humans would be carrying on with this activity.

Blue and I sat with the elders. As I always did, I was silent and let our energies join softly. I could hear them (they did not know how to shield from me) but when I communicated with them with my mind they could hear me. It was clear that they could hear Blue as well. Finally we entered into dialogue.

"*We can see that these new building materials will be useful. But I assume that you taught us how to do this because you want the material we are making.*" There was no heat in this. The elder had seen the situation clearly.

"*I would ask you to make many of these, but not neglect attending to your own needs. I will leave you with the knowledge to make them for yourselves later if you find that helpful and also I am gifting the scythe and forms. Adobe slowly melts in the rain. It must be repaired frequently with a topcoat of clay over grass or branches to increase its durability.*

"*If you are willing, I will leave this Sidhe to assist in moving the clay and grass here. He may not always be available. He is recovering after coming from old Earth.*"

The eyes of the elders shifted to Blue and all bowed their heads slightly. "*Some of us were told stories about how it had been on old Earth. Our people were killed because we were in the way of what those in power wanted. Everything alive on Earth was in the way. We still have stories about the forest people. There was once respect between them and us.*"

More silence passed.

"*I will return here and help you,*" said Blue. "*What do you need in return?*"

"*We enjoy having enough salt.*"

Blue smiled. "*I will bring salt. And then I will bring you to the sea and show you how to gather it yourself.*"

And so this Sidhe, who arrived in life threatening despair, had committed to helping the humans. It was better than I could have hoped for.

Blue looked at me and thought to me alone, "*I remember the children. They came and played with us at the edges of forest and left feathers and shiny rocks in the clefts of trees.*

"*They could see us and were not afraid. Perhaps on this world ...*" and then he went mind-silent. I looked at him and suddenly I remembered being a sick young child. I showed him.

"*I was lying on the high, dry plains of illness and fever. There was music. They came to me—the Sidhe came to me! They kept me company but had to leave me as I was. I never forgot.*"

"*Your heart seemed familiar,*" he murmured in my mind. I felt him reach out and take my hand gently.

"I will stay here," he said aloud to the humans and me. "We will make bricks!" He seemed cheered at that thought.

I left him there after promising to return and check on his progress, knowing that he could get back to my home when he wanted to.

CHAPTER THIRTEEN

THE CALM BEFORE THE STORM

Ceádar and I did not speak about what we had done while apart. However, he now seemed calm at heart, while I harboured a secret that was not easy for me. I did not want to tell him about the sadness I kept as hidden as much as possible from him. He had comforted me many times during the intense and chaotic connection I had had with Dagon and my subsequent sadness and longing, and I did not want to bring it to him now. But Dagon had told me that another fight to the death was going to occur and that this time he did not expect to survive. The thought of him being gone, not just gone and living his life elsewhere, but ceasing to exist, was a constant deep pain.

I walked and swam alone and was relieved to be involved in the brick project. There was now a small shed next to my house, roofed with broad leaves. Inside were many pallets of bricks, transited in small amounts from where Blue and human children made them. I could involve myself in that without thinking. Also I was grateful that the Sidhe male was finding happiness digging clay out of the river with the human children and watching them paint themselves in lightening bolts and spirals. And that he was gently showing them how to make sure that the molds were tightly packed. He would occasionally return to sit in the shade in front of my house and drink elixir. I could see that his vitality was returning.

He had transited a group of young adult humans to a shallow saltwater bay where he showed them how to dig trenches where the salt would crystallize out of the water. Later they eagerly scooped up the valuable crystals and proudly returned with them to the village.

Ceádar listened to me respond to Blue's stories and smiled. "You are close to this Sidhe and have given him a name that he has accepted from you, but I do not think I have to worry about your connection to him. You are friends. Of course, Sidhe friends often combine with their friends ..." He raised one eyebrow.

"But there is something I am worried about. I have waited for you to tell me more about the pain you carry but you have not. I can only assume that it is in regards to Dagon."

My impulse was to transit away and he caught that thought.

"I would not see that as helpful, Danu. I would find you and you know I can. I would rather you and I discussed this without a chase first."

"I'm going to the sea," I said. "Join me if you will."

Blue looked from Ceádar to me and then shrugged. "I'm going to play in the river with the human children," he said, and disappeared.

I sat on a bluff overlooking the sea and remembered sitting beside the sea on Exterra, looking out as far as I could imagine and seeing nothing threatening.

Of course, threats to my well-being followed me to that peaceful place; Dagon had brought the greatest one. Goaded by his Shadakon second, Morag, he had come to kill me or imprison me in the little death so that I would not be a hazard to his—to their—plans for him to move forward in gathering power. I loved him that day but refused to let his fierce second, Morag, take my life or freedom. I fled to Between and never stood by his side again. I had, however, lain with him after that; those bonds were seemingly unbreakable.

But now ... now it was possible I might no longer feel the answering energy in my Maker hand. There would be no mate, no matter how far away, connected to me. Ceádar wanted me as his queen, but I wanted to retain Dagon as my mate, no matter how unreasonable that was. It might serve Ceádar if Dagon was sent to his death by a fiercer opponent, but I ...

I wept. Ceádar sat beside me. Finally he responded to my jumble of thoughts.

"Did you think I was so indifferent to you, Danu, that I didn't know you were in pain? And the more you worked to hide it from me, the more I was sure that it was a heart wound. Now I see that Dagon has confided to you that he will soon fight a determined Shadakon to the death. And that he does not expect to win." He hesitated. "That he does not want to win."

I sobbed. Hearing it spoken made it more real. I turned to Ceádar and slipped to my knees. "You do not deserve this, my loyal lover."

He smiled sadly. "We can revisit that statement later, Danu, but I understand what you mean. You turned to me for comfort and distraction when you and Dagon were dancing your dangerous dance. But you have not turned to me for comfort now and I realize that this is worse. You cannot be fully with me because you are guarding your heart so fiercely. Only when you are overwhelmed by passion are you with me. The rest of the time—not so much."

I felt a double stab of pain was in my chest area. Would I lose Ceádar because I was grieving what was to come?

"No, Danu," Ceádar said and he took my hand. "I will be with you when you want me to be. I will accept your absence if and when you need to be with him. It is what I can give you.

I only ask for one thing." He looked at me fully with his beautiful late summer eyes "Do not come to me when you want to be with him. I am here, I will wait with you to see how the future unfolds, but I will not stand in for the Shadakon Alpha."

I knew that Dagon had never really accepted the bond between Fiócara and myself even after both of them had joined to save me from an impulsive choice to die one night, but Ceádar did accept that I was tied to this Shadakon. I knew he would not punish me as Dagon sometimes had.

"Your connection with him saved many Sidhe, Shadakon, and the humans after the mad Sidhe king from Old Earth attempted to spread death among us all. It could have gone from individual actions of killing us, to setting fire to the planet and undoing all your and our work."

I shuddered and Ceádar continued. "Fiócara helped forge the bonds between you and Dagon even as he drew you away from your Shadakon mate. We often want most what we cannot have."

"You need to do what you must do, my love," said Ceádar calmly. "But I ask that you not hide or pretend with me."

We looked at each other. "Alright—I will try to stay open. I feared that you would find me undesirable in my dramatic weeping state of mind."

"I will feel undesirable if, as time goes by, you do not want me," he said. "But we will cross that bridge if we get to it. I will now trade heart secrets with you, if you like. You are not the only one of us who is harbouring sadness. I, as a long-lived Sidhe, do not value it quite like you do. You see it, I believe, as a test of the depth of your love."

He was right. I was silent.

"When I returned to Exterra and prepared to fly in the midsummer's eve cone of power, I was certain that some comely female Sidhe would approach me and I would have her by my side—if not exactly my queen, at least company for the night. But none came forward and as dusk arrived I knew that I would fly alone. You have faced that, Danu. It is a difficult night to be alone."

I nodded, thinking of the midsummer's eve night I had later transited to the sea and swam out to speak with the whale mother and her half-grown calf. Ceádar had been waiting for me when I returned to shore; the generosity of his offering was not forgotten by me.

"Just so," he said. "When I landed on the central green there was a figure waiting for me. It was Fiócara's queen. I hadn't even seen her earlier. She was dressed in moonlight and her long blonde hair. She said nothing, but removed my tunic and ran her hands over me. I was unable to move or agree or disagree with what followed. My skin burned; I wanted her as I have wanted nothing else in my life." He looked at me to judge the effect of his words on me. I nodded. Fiócara had had the same effect on me. They were very powerful beings.

"She did what she would. I knew that Fiócara was with us but I could not focus on anything but her. She had me all night, until I shivered when she approached me yet again."

"It ceased to be pleasurable. Her touch brought pain and helplessness because I could not pull myself away. She laughed then and Fiócara came forward. 'I will take over now,' he just said and they walked off arm in arm. I lay on the grass undone, still shivering in pain and need. They play a rough game, Danu. I no longer harbour delusions about his queen——Maybe he let me have that lesson in its entirety. She took me like the Shadakon took you: to the edge of what you had to give—and beyond."

"You have taken me to that edge, Ceádar," I said, unable to keep from shivering. "You came back and delivered that to me."

"I am sorry, Danu. You are right. What is intoxicating can turn to something toxic. You and I have gone to the edges of pain. I am not unaware that you welcome that sometimes and you are aware that I want to bring it. But we must act thoughtfully, Danu. I want what we have to draw us together, not push us apart."

"I have acted how you described the queen treated you," I said sadly. "In the end, my Shadakon lovers may not have hated me, but they did not love my power over them. I regretted my actions. It was the first time I felt fully Sidhe and aware of my erotic powers. But then later—I did it again to him." I was talking about the now-dead Nathaniel and for a moment I brought up his amber eyes and strong desires.

We looked at each other and then, amazingly, smiled.

"Well ..." he said. "We must protect each other then."

CHAPTER FOURTEEN

THE SIDHE FEMALES ARRIVE

The new Sidhe worked through the end of the summer and into the fall. There were a variety of houses being built and less and less they came to share elixir and talk with us. They were, with Ceádar's and my approval, gathering elixir from a wide area and blending it and storing it in their homes.

The shelter homes were, of course, wonderful. I remembered the first time I entered Fiócara's mound. The roof was made of gnarled tree roots and there was a platform for pleasuring and sleeping; the blankets were spun from grasses and perhaps spider webs. It was comfortable and I had felt held—by the tree above us and by Fiócara.

We did not have spiders here yet. I sent an order to Exterra—the Sidhe here would need blankets. I knew that for many years they all had lived on the run and probably had had no possessions at all. I wanted to give them comfort. For some of them here, this was just a place to be after a horrible journey of witnessing their true home relentlessly killed. They would only gradually commit to this planet and her life force.

I was shown some of the finished homes; most were adobe, at least in part. Blue had dug back into one of the hills along the beach. The front he had constructed of adobe and after laying the bricks, had covered them with a thick layer of clay that he molded into smooth arches and even a small window. I guessed but did not ask if there was a back exit hidden in the tall grass that served as a roof and surrounded him with life. There was a sleeping platform that could accommodate two. He had also built in a shelf and niche for his elixir.

The entrance door looked directly at the sea, and there was a small path down to the beach with undisturbed sea grasses on either side. There was a deep sense of peace here and I was pleased that he had chosen to live near us. Others of the transplanted Sidhe scattered far. Some, I was told, lived in the sandstone bluffs near the village where Ker had lived and died and whose offspring now scrambled on the steep cliffs. An exclusion had to be put up so that they would not climb up too close and fall in their eagerness to try to see the new neighbours.

We had not received any new male Sidhe since the mad king had almost succeeded in bringing chaos and death here. A few females had arrived from Old Earth to Exterra where they had been given shelter and shown some skills that would eventually be helpful here.

The Sidhe on Exterra spun many types of cloth including some that seemed to be made of moonlight.

With the blankets that I had ordered came new clothes for me that were well made and flattering but were sand coloured and modest. I remembered asking for and receiving such a garment to wear to Dagon's fight to the death many years ago. When I saw them I knew that Fiócara was aware of what was coming. I thought that Dagon might have told him, to prepare Fiócara for changes in the arrangement between the Sidhe and Shadakon in the likelihood of his permanent absence here. I held them to my chest and rocked back and forth, a soundless wail coming from me. Ceádar had noticed but said nothing; he watched me and then went elsewhere.

The day the first female Sidhe arrived dawned bright blue and with just a touch of the fall breezes. Fiócara's queen suddenly stood in the green bower where Ceádar and I were sitting quietly. Beside her were five beautiful, but thin and frightened, female Sidhe.

She waved at them and said to me, "Elixir is always welcome."

I bowed my head. "Welcome, Queen and life-long partner of Fiócara. Welcome, Sidhe, who have come so far to be here."

Some looked down to hide the misery my words brought.

"This planet is still in healing and Exterra is further along, but both were taken down to bare ground by the humans. I am sorry for your loss. I hope that together we can create a safe home." I heard the flat no-sound of guarded minds.

I brought out a large pitcher of elixir and poured myself a small amount and drank it in front of them. I then poured their cups to the brim as well as the queen's.

"Please be comfortable here," I said, meaning both "right here now" and a more planetary "here."

The queen had sat down next to Ceádar. She touched his arm and he very slightly flinched. It was not obvious to the others perhaps, but I had felt it as a deep-mind communication. She smiled and removed her hand.

"Has Ceádar given you an account of his stay with us over midsummer's eve?" she purred.

I looked her in the eye and merely said, "We both visited ones we had wanted to see. It was more complicated for both of us than we had hoped for."

She smiled and turned her attention back to the Sidhe females.

They were silent—both in speech and mind. *Had they had to learn to not think aloud? Had some of them been betrayed into the hands of humans?* I shuddered.

"They will tell you or they will not," she thought directly to me. *"They will probably not tell a male Sidhe what some of them suffered."*

"The male arrivals have built you houses." I told them. "You can choose to live with a companion or by yourself. Later we will show them to you. You can also create your own to your exact liking."

I indicated a pile of blankets from Exterra. "We have few goods here but these are for you. Later perhaps you will make your own or teach the humans to produce them for you."

There was a low hiss from the seemingly weary Sidhe females.

"Or not," I said and laughed. "You will have as many choices as possible on this renewing planet."

"We could go to sea and swim if you wish," I said.

They stood up to go with me, but Fiócara's queen remained seated. I suddenly realized that Ceádar would not be able to go either.

He waved his hand dismissively, "Go take them to pleasure, Danu."

We walked rather than flew. They didn't know the way so we couldn't transit and some looked very weary and pale, even for a Sidhe. When I got to the water I stripped off my clothes without thinking of the effect that might have on them. The Sidhe females stood and stared at me and then looked down at their scant clothing and seemed unable to move forward.

"Swim in your clothes," I said. "Or just wade. Or just sit and let the small waves that come up the beach touch your feet. There is nothing in the water here to hurt you." I remembered the blood red waves of Old Earth that Dagon had showed me on his computer and my heart clenched.

"It is still a little saltier than it should be, so you will find that you float well," I added.

To demonstrate I slipped under the water and then reappeared, floating easily and saw them still huddled together on the beach. I got an under-mind read of feeling exposed, in the open and in danger, and barely contained fear.

"Let us sit in the circle," I said, taking the hand of the one beside me. "I am Danu, and I know you're not casual with your names, but perhaps eventually you will give me a small one that I can use—I do not ask this of you now.

"I was raised on Old Earth as a human, but knew from an early age that I was not like the ones around me. I came as a spacer to Exterra and met a Shadakon. After a very short time together"—I heard confusion and disbelief that I had spent time with him without dying—"it became apparent that I was, by blood, of their clan."

Several were shifting uncomfortably. Happily they were the not the ones whose hands I held.

"The Sidhe king of Exterra was interested in me. He knew, even though I did not, that I carried Sidhe blood as well," I continued.

All were now looking at me in amazement.

"There were children born long ago," I murmured. "They were outcasts of their clans. Some found each other ..."

"I have not been physically harmed as some of you have. I was shunned and kept myself apart from what I once thought were my kind—the humans. They let me know that I was an ugly, sexless thing to be made fun of. I faced a gang rape when I was newly on Exterra but by then my Shadakon powers were rising and they could not touch me. I, however, might have killed them and put myself in great jeopardy." I sighed.

"Being female, even female Sidhe, is complicated; males want us and sometimes resent us for that very thing they want."

A few Sidhe nodded.

"*Sometimes they kill us for the very thing they want,*" I thought and knew they had heard me.

"I will go back with you to my home," I said, trying not to think of what the queen might be doing to Ceádar. "Or we can go into the water now."

They rose as one and came to me; some got only slightly damp, others braved the shallows and swooped down into the water.

Water Sidhe, I thought. *Ceádar is one—and I am another.*

When we finally returned, the queen was gone and Ceádar stood staring out to the sea.

I went and put my arms around him and felt Ceádar's body rigid under my touch.

"*I am sorry, Ceádar, I should have asked,*" I mind-spoke to him alone and stepped back.

He turned to me and everything else around us disappeared. "*Why does she want me to continue to want her?*"

"That is the question for both of us to ask. I would say, there is great power in being wanted. Especially if that wanted person is not equally captured by the feeling."

"*But we want them to be,*" I whispered in his mind. "*We hope they are and are hiding it from us somehow. And maybe from themselves, too ...*"

Ceádar bent his head in agreement.

CHAPTER FIFTEEN

THE SECRET

As the Sidhe females began to settle in, I flew some of them out to outlying human settlements where they could see the small fields and sheltering trees. There they saw seedlings of trees and wild plants that had been carefully moved to the edges of the fields and nurtured until they were big enough to put back out in the environments where they would flourish. I was happy to see some desert plants in the mix of what the humans were tending.

I was in the company of a slight, light-blonde Sidhe with pale, almost icy eyes. I noticed that she could not take her eyes off the human children. I felt a deep pain within, and suddenly I had an answer to a question that I hadn't asked either the Sidhe or myself.

Had the Sidhe in the last terrible years, set aside their no children policy and dared to have and keep offspring alive?

She turned to me and I read terror in her eyes.

"Let us sit down for moment," I offered. I felt my own heart begin to beat wildly and my breath find an irregular pattern. I forced myself to relax and practice deep-dive breathing. In, pause, out, pause. In the moments of silence and no movement I relaxed into that space. Time passed and I heard and felt the wind blow and the far-off sound of laughing children. When I could be present, I looked at the Sidhe in front of me. Silent tears were streaking down her cheeks.

"Tell me, if you can," I prompted gently. "I sense this is more important than you or I."

She lifted her head and I met her icy eyes and felt the full intensity of the female Sidhe; and there was a challenge there.

"Ceádar and I will do whatever we can. We will welcome any to come here."

She silently shook her head. "A very long ago, the Sidhe king you think of as Fiócara made a proclamation: We were not to procreate. Most thought they were incapable of doing so and so having sex was separate in their mind from an action that had once invited offspring into existence."

I waited. I had a feeling I could guess where this might go.

She observed me carefully, looking for a reaction that would indicate that she had made a terrible mistake.

"Still, some believed they still could procreate—and they did," she continued.

It was infrequent. The children grew to young adulthood and then, like all Sidhe, remained the same year after year."

"Fiócara did not kill these children," she reassured me, "but he sent them and their parents far away from the rest of the Sidhe. Life was difficult there, even then. They lived on the margins of the human-held lands and attempted to stay out of sight. Sometimes, though, they chose a terrible solution to try to keep a child alive while banished."

We looked at each other with no discernable thoughts.

"Some put them in the cradles of humans who had recently lost a child. The Sidhe could nurse and eat some foods as babies and slowly went to a fruit and vegetable diet. If they were lucky, they learned to access the elixir of life. If not ..." She spread her hands and then dropped them. No more child. My heart ached when her hands opened to nothingness.

"Are there Sidhe young on Exterra?" I asked.

"No. Fiócara only transited us to Exterra. The children are still on Old Earth and they are in incredible danger. A very few Sidhe have stayed with them—to comfort them in their dying but also to protect them for a long as they can," she said. "It is what a mother does."

"Have you revealed the situation to him?"

She shook her head. "It was a very clear dictate. To defy it would put many in danger."

"I will defy him," I said. But even as I said this, fear blossomed deep inside me. He had told me before that if I disobeyed him he would come and kill me. I had seen him end the life of the mad Sidhe king who had attempted to spread death among the Shadakon. He had done it quickly and efficiently and perhaps there had been compassion on his part.

"Danu, can you get back to old Earth—and return through the deeps of space to here?" She sounded doubtful.

"Not now," I said. "But there are possibilities open to me."

She asked silently.

"I can discuss this with Ceádar and he and I will go and retrieve the remaining Sidhe and Sidhe children."

She looked doubtful. "Ceádar has been below Fiócara for all of his time in our hierarchy. He might not choose to dare his wraith, and I would not advise you to do so either. Whatever fondness he may have for you, Fiócara can and will set aside."

I looked at her without blinking. "Then I will ask Ceádar to teach me how to go there and come back."

"So, you might not tell Ceádar what you intend to do with that information? Without a choice of his own, he, too, might be doomed to face the wraith of Fiócara?"

"So ..." I exhaled slowly as if I was slowly heading for the surface and whatever awaited me there. "I have gone to the deeps of space with the two kings without fear. Earlier, I put myself into a death orbit when I transited to just above the atmosphere of Exterra. I wanted to die that day. But in truth I stopped in a dead zone. I could not have gone to a place that I could not imagine."

She finally smiled. "You are a fierce one, Danu. But that I believe should be a last choice."

And then I knew that there was one more slight possibility: I had a lover with a spaceship.

"Leave this with me," I said. "I know that time is of the essence, but I will examine all possibilities and let you know what our best chance is."

She looked at the children once more and sighed. I could not ask her if she had left a forbidden Sidhe child left behind on the dying old Earth, I already knew the answer to that.

I started with Dagon. I called him and found him very busy with the running of the Shadakon affairs. I sensed that he was putting his and this planet's affairs in order, as much as he could.

"Danu! I have only moments to communicate with you. You know what is coming up for me. I want to have done what I could to preserve the Shadakon and this planet and their relationship with the Sidhe."

"All of that might be quickly undone though," he thought quietly.

"I do not know what kind of company I would be now," he thought softly. *"I was content with our last connection. We had time to talk with each other and spoke what truth we could. But now ..."*

I remembered how he had killed a previous Shadakon mate after she had done her best to kill both of us. I knew that he owned a small medieval dagger with poison on its edges—a poison that worked immediately and lethally on any Shadakon who touched it, even slightly. The mark on his mate had been so small that the death examiner had not found it.

While he was not directly implicated in her death, she had died in his presence, which meant he faced a public Shadakon ritual during which her relatives had a chance to beat him—nearly to death.

Dagon had not warned me about the ritual, about the fact that he would have to walk slowly down a gauntlet of her kinsmen who wanted his death and would inflict terrible wounds on him. Instead I learned what I needed to know on a live feed. I saw him collapse at the completion of his walk, after he knelt at her bier. His second had brought Dagon to me later, and, together, we kept him alive throughout the night with our energy and blood.

He had not told me then. And he was telling me as little as possible now. My heart clenched but I continued on.

"Dagon. I need to use your spaceship to go to old Earth."

I felt his incredulity through our link. "Of all the things I thought you might ask me, including when will I die, somehow I could not have guessed this, Danu. I would give you anything. Nothing has more value than this breath and the breath after it. But they stripped me of my assets months ago, I cannot leave the planet and my credits have vanished. This mate is much more thorough that the last one; even as we speak she is lying in the arms of her new champion."

"But just to satisfy my curiosity, why old Earth, Danu? Why would you travel the long slow way in a ship? Your Sidhe kings are both adept at fast traveling in the deeps of space."

"But I am not ... an adept. And I need to bring back a precious cargo—too much for me to transit in one or two trips. I don't want to put it at risk."

"It?" he asked.

"Them," I replied.

"And why wouldn't Ceádar and or Fiócara help you with this large task?"

"I need to look at you when I tell you this," I just mind-spoke.

Almost immediately he was by my side. The Sidhe who had revealed the secret of the Sidhe females here quickly transited to somewhere else.

Dagon sat and then touched my cheek with one finger. The gentleness of it almost broke me. "No crying until I get the story, Danu. No sexing to distract us although I would not mind that later, if you have a little time."

I looked into his dark eyes and tried to visualize him as a child.

An already tall, much-stronger-than-expected, child. Had his parents been as he was? Had they showed him how to live, avoiding the light and hiding his secret from the nearby humans? Would I, if I had had the choice, have chosen to carry his dark-haired warrior son?

"Oh, Danu! What is this about? Those choices were made by others for the rest of us, a long time ago. Once we could combine and bring forth young, but our young put us at terrible risk and generally the nearby clan died as well as the young welplings."

"But what if one knew that death was all around, and one's clan were doomed? Might not some choose to bring forth life as a last hope? There are always babies born in the human death camps. It is the life force's last hope—the extravagant blooming of dying trees. The clouds of newly hatched locusts that have no food wherever they land."

"The Sidhe have children on old Earth," he said. He knew without asking me. "Why hasn't Fiócara brought them to safety?"

"They are forbidden," I said. "The Sidhe females believe he will leave them to their fates."

Dagon ran his hand slowly and intentionally down from my cheek, alongside my breast and then rested it innocuously on my thigh. This is how we had begun many years ago in an erotic tango that brought me to passion. Predictably, my body kindled and wanted his. He temporarily ignored this.

"So both of us are seemingly willing to face what will probably be our deaths. I used to be the most bloodthirsty and fierce lover you had. You and I both wondered if you would survive your wanting me. But now, perhaps Fiócara has taken my place at the top of your list."

"But why, Danu?" he asked. "Why would this matter to you? These are old Sidhe rules and ways of enforcing those rules. You may be acknowledged as a Sidhe, but you do not feel the rightness or inevitability of their codes. There were enough Sidhe, enough Shadakon and way too many humans. Why would you interfere with this? Why would you endanger your own position here?"

"Who will carry your wisdom if and when you die, Dagon? Who will tell stories of your bravery or quick wit in solving problems? Who will remember that you helped save two planets and their life forces?"

"We do not bring the past with us, Danu. We live, much like wolves do, or did, in the present. No matter what current technology we avail ourselves to, we have no nostalgia.

When we are gone, we are gone."

I looked at him and he looked calm and resigned to these truths. "Who would carry away a lilac dress that I once flew to you in? Who would return with it and put a piece in my hand before your life and death battle?"

"Who has promised to love me forever? *Para siempre*?" I continued. I was crying now. If he disavowed this, then what would I have to carry me forward?

He was silent and waited until I returned to his eyes. "We do not believe in love either. I guess, somehow, I was transformed and now hold other truths. I credit you with that change in me. Sometimes I am grateful and sometimes I wish I had taken it all from you that first night. Or the other times when you stood up to my anger and jealousy. I do not believe in 'para siempre,' but I believe in you. You are my way to the beyond. If any can love from there to the land of the living, I will love you, Danu. That is my promise, as it has been for a long time."

I had climbed into his lap and felt the heat of his wanting me. I threw my head back and felt his fangs graze lightly over the place where he had taken his pleasure from me so many times. He slid in, as gentle as a kiss and as we both spiralled up to bliss, he raised me and seated me on his throbbing man part. We moved together and on to our conjoined finish. I held him tightly and did not want to let him go; did not want to loosen my hold.

He kissed me and gently broke my grip.

"I can hold babies if you can keep your hold on me. I will go to the deeps with you. I have no doubts that you can pull this off. What happens after that is your ongoing problem. But we have to be quick. I do not have much time ..."

Then I asked the question that he would not have answered until I asked. "When, Dagon?"

"Next week," he said. "They are requiring that I undergo 'purification rituals.' This basically means that they will have me stripped and examined and I will feed on only whatever they give me for the last three days."

"Then I will stand in the ring," he continued. "I would prefer that you not witness what follows, for it will be brutal. Short but brutal," he said with seeming acceptance.

"You are not going to fight," I said horrified. "You will take his blade but also take his glory."

"Yes," Dagon said. "You have seen how it will be.

But before that, I will allow myself to be kidnapped by a crazy Sidhe intent on going to a death zone. And return with Sidhe offspring. Perhaps that will balance out my cosmic debts."

He turned me towards him. "I was never a human, although, like all Shadakon, I carry their genetic legacy. I was a wild wolf and ravaged humans, adults and children. Now I will carry babies. I have no doubt that you will somehow pull this off, but I suggest you go to talk to Green Tara. And then kidnap me and we'll carry on. I'll bring a large cape," he said with a hint of humour. "That will provide a satisfying confusing mythology for this planet."

"I have to go now, Danu," he said gently.

He stood to go, but then turned back. "I can imagine a child of mine growing within you. I would feel your swelling belly and talk to my son long before he was born. I would fiercely protect you and him. I will do so now with these Sidhe offspring. I will do my part to stand down Fiócara. It will be my pleasure."

And then he was gone.

I transited to the cave where I could most easily contact Green Tara. I knelt on the soft white limestone sand in the back of the cave.

It was dark. That seemed right because I felt dark. I did not think about what Dagon had told me, but it had permeated my being. I felt sadness like I had once felt deep cold. I wanted to lie down and surrender to it, to sleep the last sleep—but I was needed. And I had a deep curiosity about whether I could in fact get to Old Earth and back, without assistance. And so I would continue on.

The brightening of the cavern let me know that Tara was present and allowing me to know that. I saw her bright green sandaled feet in front of me and smiled.

"Rise, Danu. You are obviously here on some urgent business or other."

"I would tell you. But I want you to know exactly what I know without mistakes of translation. I would have you read me and see the problems I face."

"You have not suggested such a thing before. I believe you have opened to both Sidhe kings who were seeking information. And Dagon, too, early in your relationship when you still thought that it was safe to live beside him. But me—I would know everything, Danu. I would know those things you wish never to think of again. But also those peaks of passion that you may never reach again. I would know."

"I only ask that you do not reveal what you find to Fiócara and Ceádar," I thought to her. "At least, not until I either succeed or fail at what I am asking your help with."

Green Tara was silent and I feared that I had insulted her. I remained standing, looking at her and her black endless eyes.

"You are bold, Danu. You would have me withhold information from the original king of the Sidhe—who is your Sidhe king lover. If you are trying to manoeuvre around he who you call Fiócara, he already has felt the disturbances around you. He is probably watching to see what moves you will make. He is usually well ahead of you in the game."

"Please, just look and then I will ask my question. I have nothing to pay you for your service, but if you see something that I have that would be useful to you—I will agree to it without knowing the cost in advance."

"Ahhh. Once again you bet it all. What an exciting poker player you would be! But Fiócara plays chess, timeless chess. Well, I will do what you ask. Lie down, Danu."

She sank down and sat beside me and then leaned over me. Although I would have said the cave was almost dark and her eyes were black, I could see lights that might have been vast suns or even galaxies. She put her hand on my head and her fingers were icy but I wanted only that she continue to touch me.

Would you be awake for this, Danu?"

I nodded. Immediately a kaleidoscope of images rushed by in no apparent timeline. I saw myself lying beneath various lovers and wanting them in different and exquisite ways. I saw myself as a shunned and angry child on old Earth, and leaving with no concern for anyone I left behind. Then this planet, stripped and thirsty but, as time went by, greening and coming alive. At some point the flow of memories of my life overwhelmed me but I could not close my eyes or stop the process.

Green Tara laughed. "You are fully in my hands now, Danu."

And then she said, "Babies! Sidhe babies and youth! Oh, how well the Sidhe females kept their secret from the king and his queen! And how amazing that they trusted you so fast."

"Time is running out," I murmured.

"And your wild vampire lover is going to help you with this if he can?"

"Yes. Time is running out for him as well." The pain of saying that then rendered me speechless.

"You believe that Fiócara would kill them or leave them to their inevitable painful end?"

"The Sidhe females believe this. Some of them experienced banishment as proclaimed by him, and I have no doubt that his queen would have even less difficulties in ending this problem effectively."

"And Ceádar? You would leave him in the dark and leave, perhaps not to return?"

"It is the only way I can protect him, at least for the immediate future."

"But you would bring them and their mothers back to this planet—one might say, at least partially *his* planet?"

I was silent.

"Are you afraid that he will not help you, or that he will reveal your plan to Fiócara?"

"Yes."

"And that he will be punished as both of you are likely to be—by being banished by Fiócara. As I saw, he already threatened you with this before."

"Yes."

She took her hand away. "So what is your request of me, Danu?"

"Can you teach me to navigate to Old Earth and back?"

Green Tara laughed and her laughter bounced off the smooth walls of the cavern and returned amplified.

"Who taught you to fly, Danu?"

I looked confused. "I flew in my dreams. And later I just ... did."

"And who taught you to transit?"

I thought a little longer on this one. Fiócara had led me to longer and longer transits in a game of chase we had once played under the northern lights of Exterra. And then I had taken my newfound skill and transited to what I expected to be my death, looking down on the light of the setting sun on the top layer of Exterra's atmosphere. I had been sure that I wanted to die that night. I had been wrong.

"And have you gone further?"

"Yes, under the influence of Fiócara's autumn elixir, my Sidhe companions and I went out and watched the streaming stars."

"Were you cold or dead after that experience?"

I shook my head.

"When you transit, do you need to know every branch or tree or hill you might encounter?"

I shook my head.

"So there you have it, Danu: you already know how to do this. Fiócara was in no hurry to confirm that to you. After today, he might have wished to ask me for my silence before you did." She laughed again. "At one time you believed that Fiócara had taken away your ability to transit, and he probably believed that as well. Many have underestimated you, Danu; believe or not, the ancient king you call Fiócara does too."

"You need to have an exact landing place, Danu. The surface of Old Earth is increasingly unstable as are the remaining human populations there. Wherever the Sidhe have hidden their young, you must know it exactly. You must take a mother with you."

"How can I transit all those Sidhe? Dagon has offered to wrap them in a large cloak, but I have never carried more than three people even short distances."

Green Tara smiled. She pointed to a slim boat that appeared suddenly beside her —a double kayak—a bidarka. It was pale green and stocked with blankets. "You'll have to provide the elixir."

"I am to go into the deeps of space in a kayak?"

Green Tara shrugged. "It will hold a lot of people. I'm not sure why Dagon has to go, but I see that somehow he does. An atonement, perhaps, for his earlier lifestyle."

I whispered my last question without thinking that I had only asked for one boon. "Does he have to die, Green Tara?"

She touched my cheek. "We all have to die, Danu. He happens to know when he will have that experience, and he is going to make it into a personal statement."

She traced a tear that slipped down my cheek, seeking the floor of the cave, a small piece of water seeking union with the rest. "Does it seem to you that he is fighting this fate?"

I shook my head.

"And you are not fighting possibly losing two Sidhe kings that you love and even the planet that you have fought so hard for ... all because of some small helpless Sidhe who may already have perished."

"They are important, Green Tara, more important than me or my life and loving; I don't know how I know this."

Green Tara kissed me and we both pulled the boat over the soft sand towards the mouth of the cave. It glided like it was floating on water.

"Retrieve your Shadakon and lay in some elixir. I give you and anyone else on this journey my blessing."

I arrived home as the sky was going through its shades of amethyst and purple and then to a clear dark blue that darkened to black with stars. Ceádar was sitting in the bower, watching the horizon. I had thought to avoid him, and not implicate him in my wild plan.

"*I am already implicated in your wild plan,*" Ceádar mind-spoke to me. I knew then that he practiced courtesy in not usually commenting on my supposedly guarded thoughts.

"Ceádar." I did not know how to go forward from that one word.

"I sought to protect you from Fiócara," I said. "I intend to directly disobey him."

"And your doing that, without telling me, will protect me in some way?"

"You could say you didn't know what I intended to do."

"I could say that. But if so directed I would submit to a mind reading such as you may have experienced today, but maybe rougher and a lot longer. Green Tara is fond of you."

I stood in front of him, finally feeling the fear of losing everything.

"You should touch on that, Danu, before you go off like Wynken, Blynken and Nod."

I smiled at the reference. "There is a boat in the plan. How do you know all of this, Ceádar?"

"Apparently I informed him." The female Sidhe with icy eyes stepped out of the shadows. "Or ... I finished telling him—it appeared that he already knew."

I could sense that they had recently been together.

"And why exactly does Dagon have to go on this adventure?" Ceádar asked with a touch of attitude.

"I'm not sure—he was sure, and Green Tara agreed that he should go. Also that someone who knows exactly where the children are should go."

"You will provide the precise destination I require to pull this off," I said, turning to the Sidhe who had shared the secret with me.

I knew that Ceádar had recently lain with her and accessed her mind while she was lost to passion. It was a well-honed technique that Fiócara had used often enough on me.

"We are Sidhe," she said as perhaps an explanation.

"Yes."

"Does this upset you?" she asked.

"Not as much as knowing that my Shadakon lover will die next week if he returns from this adventure. Not as much as knowing that Fiócara may banish me from this planet." I took a breath. "Not nearly as much as my fear that I will lose everything—everyone. But yes, I suppose it bothers me. I wanted one night …"

"Go now!" said Ceádar suddenly. He thrust a large container of elixir at me. "Hurry!"

I called Dagon and he was waiting at the cave when we arrived. He was, in fact, in the arms of Green Tara and apparently close to ecstasy there.

"Now, Dagon! I believe Fiócara is on our heels."

I saw the air around them flare and then he stepped back from her and immediately got into the boat.

"Show me where I am going," I said to the Sidhe who I had started to think of as Ice.

I pictured the water planet with her one dutiful moon. I climbed into the boat and I pictured us there in the little patch of Old Earth that she had clearly showed me, a little doomed piece of rainforest, patrolled by the very large and hungry crocodiles that swam in its diminished waterways.

I felt the boat rock slightly, as if we were traveling on a dark sea, moving forward over long, slow waves. There were lights beneath us and on all sides. I smiled and remembered a fragment of an old Irish poem: *Deep peace of the running wave to you.*

When we arrived in a place of choking smoke and sun-baked ground my heart sank. Ice, however, strode forward determinedly and called in her original, trilling, old Sidhe language.

Unbelievably, Sidhe came running. They were holding the hands of children and carrying silent babies.

We were almost free to leave when a human who had been running some large machine nearby noticed us and started shouting to get his human co-workers' attention. However, it was hard to hear him over the engine sounds and Dagon disappeared for a moment, ripping his throat out and taking a fast feed before any other humans seemed to have taken in the drama unfolding near them. There was one more Sidhe mother, or maybe grandmother, who was limping to reach us, carrying a silent child and walking on a leg that was burnt to the bone. We put her and all our precious cargo beneath the soft green blankets that Green Tara had provided.

They seemed to induce sleep. They all became completely silent.

"My last meal on old Earth," said Dagon.

I rolled my eyes and then brought us back to Green Tara's cave.

I should not have been surprised to discover Fiócara and Ceádar standing there beside Green Tara. Green Tara indicated that my passengers should bed down on the green blankets and have some elixir of life.

The slim boat promptly disappeared. And then there were only the sounds of mothers murmuring to children, their sighs and then they all faded into sleep. The

Sidhe with the burnt leg lay surrounded by and under a light mist-like blanket. She was in a restful sleep.

I turned back to the Sidhe kings and knelt before them. Neither moved to raise me up but Green Tara did.

She scowled at them both. "I am a goddess of life, of the sacred act that allows procreation, and of the offspring that come to the call of two responsible parents who will take care of those who come to them. Or, at least, of a mother who will do everything she can to preserve her offspring. Death is part of life of course."

She looked at Dagon. "I am amused at the necessary part you played. A Shadakon protector of the Sidhe—it suits you. I would walk with you further into my home here and finish what we started a short time ago. I want to hear how it is that you now have a quiet heart and also why you wanted to be part of this—besides wanting to please Danu, of course, that goes without saying."

They disappeared into the faint green glow that was Green Tara's home but didn't get very far. I could hear him moaning and then begging hoarsely. I smiled sadly. *Everyone was going to get what they wanted tonight but me.*

I felt what could only be fury from Fiócara.

"Ceádar was not part of this," I said licking my lips, now dry with fear. "I take full responsibility."

"Generous, but not true. Ceádar shielded you long enough for you to get past me. He withheld information"—Fiócara gestured at the sleeping Sidhe females and the children—"that he had extracted earlier in the day from a new Sidhe female. He bought you time. Very expensive time in terms of the consequences to him. He, even more than you, understood my full ban on procreating."

I said nothing. He had not asked me a question.

He stepped lightly to stand directly in front of me and put his hand, the hand that I loved to feel the touch of, on my head. There was a moment of connection and rising energy between us and then he gave me unbearable pain. My mind felt like it was broken. I could not find or speak a single word and dimly knew that nothing I could say would matter anyway. In addition to the pain was great sadness. It came from both of us and mingled as a painful brew of emotional and physical pain.

I retched and writhed and then went still. I considered trying to go somewhere, anywhere to escape him.

He took my arm. "No transiting, Danu. No flying and no beguiling. I could keep you in this state for the immediate future—and beyond."

This was obviously a Sidhe version of the Shadakon's little death. When in that state, one hungered and suffered but soon had no energy to do anything to escape or help oneself. It lasted until the punisher restored their prisoner with energy or blood—or did not.

I found some words and put them together in my mind. "*I will not apologize nor ask for your mercy. If this is truly who you are, who the Sidhe kings are, I do not care to be tied to either of you. I do not want to want you, Fiócara. If you would do this to me and to your kind, then you are not who you seemed to be for all the years that I thought I knew you, who I thought I loved in some way or another. You threatened to banish me once before, a threat that you made before I had broken any Sidhe laws or hurt anyone. I left tonight knowing that you might do that, but it doesn't matter."*

I panted and was mind-silent again.

Fiócara lashed me with his mind-speak. *"How could it not matter! What was so important about Sidhe offspring that you would risk all to retrieve them? To defy me? To make banishment a real possibility for both you and Ceádar?"*

I wept. *"It was the right thing to do. Most of the Sidhe of Old Earth are dead. There is room on this planet for more—the ones here are finding their places. You sent me female Sidhe with broken hearts. As they sat under this pleasant blue sky they knew that their babies and children—kept alive at unbelievable effort—were dying. The male Sidhe ache for connection with their females; so you would doom both the males and females here to being dead to pleasure."*

"Ceádar ... today you lay with a female Sidhe who wanted only to return to the hell that is now Old Earth and retrieve a child—her child, someone else's child, it matters not. Was what she brought you joyful? Sidhe are supposed to be joyful!"

He shook his head. *"It was why I decided to help you."*

The pain in my head vanished. Fiócara stood before me with no anger and no apology about the part he had just played.

"I was wrong," he just said almost wonderingly. "We will talk more about this. If you would accept Ceádar's comfort I would ask that both of you go home."

"And the children?" I looked at where they slept easily under piles of glowing green blankets.

Fiócara just shook his head. "They are in the care of Green Tara. Perhaps they are now as they always were: her children. I have to go and ponder how you have changed the deep pattern of this. But you are right—the male Sidhe will welcome happy female Sidhe. If one can invoke feelings of protection for such helpless beings in a Shadakon Alpha, I'm sure the Sidhe will rise to the occasion."

"My queen will be furious, of course. They did not tell her, which was wise of them."

He returned to stand within reach of me. I cringed on the ground before him. He put out a hand and raised me gently to my feet. I felt confusion and pride in him towards me.

He shook his head. "You outmanoeuvred me, Danu, with some help from Ceádar and Green Tara—but the daring plan was yours, and your confidence kept all of you safe while crossing vast and perilous deeps. I have never made a nonstop round trip of the distance that you did today in your debut flight. Your will has kept you on your feet. Soon though, you must take nourishment and sleep."

"And tomorrow will I be summoned to a meeting with you and your queen and discover that I and probably Ceádar will be banished?"

"Not tomorrow, Danu. And not banished. I will wait awhile and see how this unfolds. I will harm no one."

I raised one eyebrow.

"Nor will my queen, Danu."

Ceádar took my arm and in a moment we were standing in the bower, looking out at the sweep of stars I had recently traveled past. He dropped my arm and remained mind-silent.

I felt his distance. And then I felt the emptiness in the place where his crown usually sat on my head. I put my hands up shakily and, sensing I was due for a major heart storm, tried not to come undone. I backed away and prepared to go somewhere, anywhere. Ceádar regained his grip and turned me to face him.

"I sought out who you think of as Ice because she was the last Sidhe you spoke to before you disappeared. There was something she wished to keep hidden from me and I assumed it was a fresh memory of being treated badly by a male. She was also desperately sad and lonely. I took her in my arms and she did not let go. And when she was trusting and open to me, I went into her memories. I believed it was necessary. It is a skill we have—you have it as well. You used it when you worked at the hospice to provide relief from pain. You became the dying humans' mothers, sisters and daughters. You used it to soften their hard passing."

"You used it out of curiosity of what I was up to."

He shook his head. "You still underestimate me, Danu. I knew that there was a deeper sadness that lay over the female Sidhe—far more than the males. But I felt the males' loneliness too, from being rejected by the females. Something was terribly wrong, and they both needed each other. When I felt it in Ice and she made her mind available to me, I took the opportunity. I bought you and her valuable time. Fiócara was following the clues of your sudden disappearance with Dagon. I do not think he expected to discover a boatful of babies and children!" He laughed. "You continue to amaze us all."

"I have no crown," I said dully.

"I did not take it, Danu. It may be that it returned to old Earth, to return to its home ground and be recycled there into its simple elements. Or perhaps you gave it up to satisfy a debt."

The words I had said to Green Tara echoed in my mind: that I seemed to have nothing to pay for her service but—"*... if you see something that I have that would be useful to you—I will agree to it without knowing in advice the cost ...*"

"It was not mine to give away!" I sobbed.

"It was yours to do with as you would, Danu. You may see it again—or not. Knowing that it paid for you and your passengers' safe passage today—would you take back your offer to Green Tara?"

I shook my head, although tears rolled down my cheeks.

He wrapped his strong arms around me and I sagged. He carried me to my bed.

"Ice and I did not take our pleasure on this bed, Danu. I thought you would like to know."

I laughed, realizing how tired I was. I was dozing when he returned with the elixir of life. I sipped and then seemingly napped and then sipped again, as Ceádar held it to my lips in the darkness.

Later I felt his warm skin against mine and knew that he had managed to remove my and his clothes as I slept. I murmured in appreciation. He pulled me towards his heart and it whispered to me, "*I thought I had lost you. I thought I had lost you.*"

Then I knew what his cost would have been.

CHAPTER SIXTEEN
DANU WITNESSES

A few days after I had recovered, I felt my Maker hand blaze. The realization of what Dagon wished to urgently tell me made me feel too unsteady to stand, so I sat on the grass, and plunged my fingers into its tough roots. I hoped they would hold and ground me with their strong survival qualities.

"Danu. I know you are busy with your project and also dealing with Fiócara, but I would not go to my death without giving you a choice, however terrible it may be for you, to attend this last battle of mine."

I felt the world stop. The wind, my breath, the sounds, the smells of the sea were absent. I was in a Between of my own creating—a terribly brief sanctuary. I tried to respond but even that was no longer doable.

I sensed Dagon patiently waiting. When I said nothing he sighed and continued, *"I have been offered one last visit with someone of my choosing. I have not yet put your name down, Danu. I do not want you to feel compelled to come to me under these circumstances."*

"Could Green Tara protect you and take you away? You could be the disappearing Shadakon ..."

"Possibly she could, Danu. I have not asked her to."

"I will come to you, Dagon, and I will also witness what you believe will be your last day."
I hoped I sounded calm.

"The Sidhe will all come. I would not leave you alone in the presence of your enemies."

I realized that that sounded biblical and almost laughed. I did not think I had absorbed anything from the Sunday school classes I attended, much less be able to access it on another planet years and light years away.

"When, Dagon?"

"We fight in two days. I would have you with me the night before, so that your scent and magic is still on me. Tomorrow night then." And then he gave me the details of how and when to access him.

"When the stars come out, Danu," he said and ended our connection.

I sat, lightly rooted to the earth, and this is where Ceádar found me.

He just wrapped his arms around me and was silent. Eventually though, one of us would have to break the deepening quietude that was growing around me.

"What do you need from me and the rest of the Sidhe?" he asked quietly.

"We need to attend," I said first. "Dagon intends to stand motionless, foiling his opponent who intends to gain glory by fighting him to the ground and inflecting many wounds before becoming the victor. It may be short, but I fear that his opponent will take the opportunity to see how much pain Dagon can bear and if, in fact, he will pick up his weapon."

"The Shadakon are a cruel race. Dagon is no longer Shadakon or he would at least ensure that his opponent's man parts lay in the dust." I looked at Ceádar in horror and he shrugged. "You may see that happen to Dagon, but try to hold on to this truth: years ago he was forced to kill his second and brother-in-arms Nathaniel. Neither of them stooped to intentionally inflicting humiliation; that was not part of their battle strategy. Nathaniel died with his body intact, and only his energy and blood going to the victor. If the rest of the Shadakon did not understand—we did. Dagon gave him an extremely honourable death and also mourned him later."

"Nathaniel's widow, and now mate to Dagon, made this happen," I said. "He has always ended up with mates who wanted to kill him."

"Not always," said Ceádar. "You are his true mate and you wish for him not merely power but the true power of learning and mastering himself.

We were silent again together.

"He has asked me to come to him the night before," I said, attempting to breathe deeply and allow the pain to come and go. It didn't go.

"He is strengthening the most important tool he intends to use," said Ceádar. I looked at him questioningly.

"His heart," said Ceádar.

I broke then and he took me to the sea and down into the calm blue depths and Green Tara's temple. I did not see anything unusual other than, once again, while we were there the walls and floor were free of weed and debris. The altar was empty except for one small plain pebble that Ceádar had placed there earlier.

And my crown. My crown sat in the centre, gleaming with a silvery blue light.

I approached it and, knowing that this was what I was meant to do, I picked it up and in slow motion placed it on my curls that waved slightly like a sea creature in the current.

Ceádar returned me to the shore and we sat and watched the horizon; it never seemed to grow nearer, but time spun us onward and we were now somewhere I had not imagined. That I had not wanted to imagine ...

He wrapped his arms around me but offered nothing more. I looked into his eyes and saw and felt desire but he did not bring it to me.

"Go as a hungry invited guest goes to a feast," he said. "Drink from his lips and his loins and lead him to the place that strengthens him for whatever comes next."

I smiled. Ceádar passed as a Sidhe, interested in little but what was happening now. But he was a mystic as well as a powerful lover—of all of me, not just my more obvious assets. I had neglected him as I had yearned for Dagon for years, but his patience had eventually won a place in my heart. I continued to learn how much more there was to him than I could have seen earlier. Tonight I saw another piece— he was patient and even humorous with me. Ceádar continued to defend my right to love as I would. He wanted me—but only when I wanted him as much.

I would wear Ceádar's crown when I went to Dagon for the last time and then when I formally witnessed his death.

When we returned to the comfort of my home, I was surprised to see many Sidhe females sitting quietly, obviously waiting for our return. Some had children with them, some nursed thin babies. Ice sat quietly, holding a little girl who had her mother's almost white hair but had tropical sea eyes. I wasn't sure if the Sidhe children could alter their appearance when they were young, and they might never tell me, but I had a strong feeling that the heartsick male Sidhe who I called Blue might be this one's sire.

Ice stood and came to me and I looked into her child's eyes, which looked back knowingly. I put out a finger and she gravely matched my action, touching me as lightly as a floating feather. I felt the power in her at that instant. These offspring were the survivors; their individual skills and powers had been honed when they were very young.

I hadn't been sure if the Old Earth Sidhe young could follow me in mind-speak, and then this one raised her eyes to me and simply said, "*Yes*" in my mind. She had a clear singing voice and it reminded me of a song I had heard while on Old Earth and also when I attended the death of a human who was obviously known and cared about by the Sidhe. They had sung her out as she died.

She and her mother smiled and both began to hum it back to me.

I had cried a lot in the last few days but these were not tears of pain or sadness. I let my heart open to the marvel of it. It was Lara's song.

They had come to thank me. To thank *me*—a once human woman, who had no interest or affinity for children, even when I was one. I had never questioned the survival rules of two clans that had chosen long ago to not procreate; their numbers set by laws that were so powerful that none of them seemed inclined to question or disobey them.

But then dying became the new law of the land on Old Earth as it gained momentum. The trees that provided oxygen and soil and shade and comfort were ripped or sawed down. Sometimes they were used for lumber, but most were scraped into giant funeral pyres that added to the smoke and heat. The Sidhe did not want to take more than was healthy from the great trees, but in the night, when the machines were silent, they crept to their fallen bodies and extracted the last of the elixir of life that they would ever contribute. They wept as they did so.

I saw these pictures in the minds of the female Sidhe. I saw tiny children who learned to freeze and make themselves as small as possible to not be noticed. Small Sidhe could neither fly nor transit as there was no safe place to practice. I saw large lean crocodiles watching the Sidhe young when they came to the riverside; they did not watch as predators, but as protectors. One frantic mother had found her missing little one safe in a hole in the riverbank that had been dug by a crocodile and who had placed the little Sidhe there without harm. After they hatched, crocodiles brought their own young to the water in their mouths; they stayed close and protected them. This one had done the same for the Sidhe.

"All that was left even temporarily alive flew with us in our last midsummer's eve cone of power," one Sidhe female said. "We had tried to protect each other but we were saying thank you and goodbye."

A silence fell over the room. I remembered that when we had come to gather the Sidhe mothers and their offspring, they were in the midst of large crocodiles. Humans who might otherwise have waded across the dwindling river, gave pause due the presence of these guardians.

I sat and watched them visit with each other. Ceádar seemed to have gone elsewhere but he soon reappeared with a familiar Sidhe in tow: it was the Sidhe I called Blue Water, or Blue for short. He knelt in front of the mother of his child and their child and wept.

"I could not wait anymore for you to come to me. I will leave if you ask me to, but I had to see her." A long silence passed like a dark cloud over the sun. "I should have brought you with me somehow. Or stayed with you." They looked at each other with eyes and hearts full of many emotions.

"I should have found you immediately when you got here," he continued, confessing his missed actions as he saw them.

Ice turned to Ceádar who was standing back and indicated him to Blue. "I went to him for comfort, but I was not comforted. He is beautiful, but my heart was closed to even a short chance at pleasure. However, it all came around. Had I not gone to him, Danu would not have had the time to escape Fiócara's observation. Had she not gone when she did, I believe many here, and all of our little ones, would be dead. The chapter is closing on old Earth. The Shadakon still feed heavily off the excess of the dying populace of humans, but their days are numbered along with their prey."

Blue looked at Ceádar who looked back calmly. They were Sidhe. A lonely and hungry-for-touch Sidhe female had come to him and he had given her as much as possible what she wanted. But she had not really wanted him. It was a recurring theme in his life.

I had thought that in what I thought was private under-mind, but Ceádar laughed out loud. "*It is a recurring theme to most males, Danu,*" he thought back. "*But perhaps some more than others.*"

"I will go now," said Blue. "I have built a fine house and it is yours. I will build another for myself later. Yours will need a few more touches, however. It needs a small room with a window for a small Sidhe who also loves the sea."

Ice looked at him for a long time and then said, "I would see it now. Perhaps she and I will sleep there tonight."

Blue merely picked up a pile of blankets and walked ahead of them to the door. Most of us were rooting for him. I already knew that he cherished his daughter.

By the time the gathering broke up, I was unsteady on my feet with fatigue. The traveling that I had funded with my energy was slow to replenish. I dreaded the thoughts that would come and circle around me when I had no distractions.

Dagon! Dagon! My heart was trying to reach his. My Maker hand burned although no message came through to me.

I turned to Ceádar. "Help me tonight, my king. Help me slip through the circling ravens that are announcing the coming battle and death. I want to sleep or at least rest and gather my strength. I would be strong and love Dagon long into the night, if he wishes that."

He laid me on the bed as he had so many times. But this time he only leaned over me, his beautiful deep forest eyes now touched with the occasional glint of a golden leaf. He was beautiful and he was here for me.

I opened to him and sank gratefully under the surface. I heard his voice speaking softly to me, but all I knew was that the words were loving. I hummed the fragment of the song Ice and her child had hummed to me and I felt his Sidhe heart hold mine. It was whispering promises and I was warm and wrapped in his caring.

When I awoke it was morning. Ceádar smiled down at me, and I knew he had just released me from my induced sleep. He poured me a cup of elixir and turned me towards the shower.

"You have no time to find a creek today. I would again comb out your long, tangled curls."

We sat in the sunshine and he patiently untwisted the odd leaf from my hair and combed and brushed until it stood out from my head like a corona of flame and then he placed the crown upon me. He went inside and returned with several choices of garments.

I did not see me in glad colours, but he suggested otherwise.

"Do not mourn before it is time," he said, choosing a deep green tunic and pants. "Go to him as the beautiful Sidhe he loves above all others. Turn every head as you walk across the open empty space that will be filled tomorrow. Let the Shadakon know that whether Dagon choses to uphold his title or not, he has something that they will never have." He smiled. "At least for the foreseeable future."

"And now," he continued, as if he had planned the timing to the moment, "here are the arriving Sidhe royalty. Are you ready for the queen?"

I shuddered. Fiócara and his queen stood under the deep blue sky of coming fall. She came to me, closer than I would have done to another, but I did not fall back and she smiled.

"Once again, your hold on my king prevented him from taking appropriate action against you. We had pondered the possibility of allowing some Sidhe to procreate. You brought a boat of Sidhe offspring and their mothers past our planet to yours, without consulting us.

Obviously you were helped by Green Tara, who also seems fond of you. Is there anyone not fond of you, Danu?"

"You aren't," I said. *Let it begin now*, I thought. I saw Fiócara lift an eyebrow and observe us more closely.

"How can you say that?" she asked. "You let me pleasure you and in the end, came to me with the same. You thought of the taste of a certain Old Earth flower, certainly dead now, that my own flower reminded you of."

I nodded my head. "I wanted you, the first female who I had ever let touch me—if I can say I let you, but certainly I did not protest or resist."

"But is that not fondness?" said the queen.

"No. It can be many things, including ecstasy. But fondness endures after the sweat dries."

Fiócara was desperately trying not to laugh and Ceádar looked at me in alarm. The queen glared and me and then laughed.

"You are right, Danu. I was never particularly fond of you except when you were in total surrender to me. Call me Sidhe."

"Yes," I said. "You are a magnificent Sidhe. You have taken my breath away even when I was not sure I would draw another one."

She looked mollified although Fiócara knew that I had found a very thin line to safety.

"*As you always do, Danu*," he mind-spoke me, and, I believe, me alone.

"Back to the business at hand," the queen said. "Tomorrow we will once again watch to see if Dagon meets his end. I understand that he is likely to, as he doesn't intend to fight. This will no doubt confuse the Shadakon. But your heart may take the blade too."

She looked at Ceádar. "This one does not like being helpless either." She licked her lips and I felt him momentarily go very still.

"Yes," I said. "You and Fiócara have lived a long time and upheld decisions made when the Old Earth was new and full of life. Perhaps those Visitors who stayed were the first to disobey the do-not-procreate rule. Because both Sidhe and Shadakon are their offspring, as well as the worker humans that were created in the genetic labs of the Visitors to breed a slightly intelligent work force. Very quickly though, the humans bred like, well, humans. It seems they never learned to think forward—and now it is far too late.

The Old Earth humans are now experiencing true helplessness and the humans in the care of the Shadakon are helpless as well. As are, I suppose, those I have put out on the land."

"And the Shadakon—those on Old Earth feast although the banquet is almost over. No one will come for them in the last hours."

I looked at both Fiócara and his queen and bowed low. "I was helpless to disobey my heart-felt conviction to save those remaining Sidhe. They are now my relations and we need all the Sidhe we have and more to hold this planet. It will need, perhaps very soon, a Between to take shelter in. The Shadakon may revert to their uncaring selves and poach the humans who do my bidding."

The queen looked at me. "I hear your easy assumption of power. You have been taking lessons from Green Tara, a true goddess I suppose. But tomorrow your helplessness may come to you, Danu, and hurt you more than I, or my impulsive king, or any other Sidhe could do. The price of loving as you do, I suppose, is accepting its ending. But I would not make your task tomorrow any more difficult. We will attend as two kings and two queens. You wear Ceádar's crown, I see, and it does not seem to weigh on you. You will represent the Sidhe here and do it with as much grace as you can."

"But now," she said. "Can I see those Sidhe offspring?"

I looked at Ceádar. We had not discussed this, although it was now obvious that the moment had arrived.

"The Sidhe females are scattered, some with lovers that they haven't seen in a long time and probably never expected to see again," he said gently. He had no inclination, as I seemed to have, to test or challenge the queen. However she would get no purchase on any feelings of inadequacy that she may have brought to him on midsummer's eve. This was his planet and he stood solidly on the ground here.

"However there is one reunited couple that I might ask," he said after a pause.

Once again I felt how the Sidhe could pull together strands of seemingly unhelpful bits to create a way through. I knew who he would ask. I knew that unless things had gone very badly for Blue last night, Ice would come, partially out of obligation to me. Blue would come because Ceádar spoke calmly to him about pleasuring—or trying to pleasure—his estranged companion. Ceádar made it a reason for easy companionship—that he and Blue could discuss this calmly.

I knew then that I had known how to do this, and that Fiócara had seen it in me early on.

"*Yes Danu*," Fiócara responded, again in perfectly guarded under-mind.

Soon Blue and Ice and their beautiful pale daughter arrived at our gathering. All looked content with each other, so perhaps Blue had not had to surrender his new home and sleep outside in the tall grass.

The queen bent down and looked at the young Sidhe carefully.

"Will she grow up?" she asked abruptly.

Ice looked at her without smiling.

"Now she will," she said. "After she passes through puberty she will no longer grow or change, except as she might wilfully alter her appearance."

The young Sidhe was observing the queen as intently as she was herself being observed.

"*I am glad to be safe and alive*," she mind-spoke to her. "*I watched many die around me. I owe my life to this one.*" She indicated me and then went silent.

Fiócara's queen smiled and said nothing.

The rest of the day was spent with Ceádar transiting the king and queen to show them the new houses and the shacks of new adobe bricks in the human settlements. I stayed on the edge of the sea.

"So it begins," Fiócara had said to him, as they looked at the new industry. For a moment they both saw the early cities of Sumer and Jericho.

I walked the beach as I had years ago as I waited for what fate would bring me. Every time I touched on the ache that was my connection with Dagon, I had the feeling that I could not hold the thought for long. I knew then that Ceádar, like Fiócara earlier, had, at my request, left me with a mental suggestion that allowed me to step back from the full pain. I was grateful. The battlefield ravens did not fly close to me as I walked.

Soon though, the light was fading and I knew I had to go to him. I was already dressed and as ready as I could be for what lay ahead. I ached for him, hungry, as Ceádar had suggested.

I arrived in the central plaza of what had been Dagon's home. There were already Shadakon putting up seating and sweeping the large fitted stones that comprised the surface. I was immediately met by an unsmiling Shadakon male in uniform who, having seen me, beckoned me over to him. I could sense that he found me very desirable and wondered why I would come here. I imagined that many of the last visits were made by humans on the Registry.

He scowled at me and listed off the rules to follow during a last visit.

First, I was not to give the prisoner any object. He would be searched as soon as I left.

Second, He was Shadakon and therefore it was assumed that he might want a blood feed. I could provide that.

Third, I was not to attempt to release him from his cell. It would be impossible, but if I tried we both would die before the eager crowds tomorrow.

I remained perfectly quiet-minded through all of this. *Did this officious Shadakon not know that I would give Dagon energy and faerie blood? And had no one briefed him that the only reason Dagon would be in his cell later would be because he had refused to be transited to safety?* No Shadakon would grab, hold, or even touch me unless I allowed it.

I bowed my head slightly and said nothing.

"You must agree verbally to following these rules and that you understand the consequences if you do not. And then you must make some identifiable sign here." He thrust a compu-pad at me.

This was how it had all begun. I stood lost to that moment of me signing such a device so that I could leave the Pleasure Fair with Dagon and go to his home. The company rep had been more nervous than I was. I already knew what I wanted and that I would pay any price.

I was still paying the price. I made the sign of the cedar tree that Ceádar had once left on a note in my hill house on Exterra. The cedars of Old Earth had been enduring, living on the edge of the sea, bridging sea, sky and earth.

He resumed walking then, and I followed him to the small room where I had been many times. Dagon and I and the Sidhe had met there, and I had met with Nathaniel and his mate, now Dagon's mate, here. Now the doors and windows had been reinforced with steel. It was a cell, with no comforts—no blanket on the metal bench, an open barred window with nothing to shield him from the sun that would come through or the Shadakon outside who watched him, jeering and laughing.

He was waiting for me. There were healing wounds, old and new on his body. His glossy black hair had been cut off and formed a ragged frame around his face. One hand appeared to have been recently crushed. I gasped at the cruelty of what he had already faced.

"Never mind, Danu. Never mind. Glamour us a more comfortable setting."

He looked me up and down, taking in the bright Sidhe clothing, my loose floating hair, and the silver circlet that served as Ceádar's crown. He, too, drew in a long breath.

He took off his coarse shirt and hung it carefully over the window.

"I would not have our last night together watched with cruel eyes," he said, and drew me to him. "I would like you to take off your beautiful forest-coloured clothes, no doubt gifted to you by Ceádar as your indifference to clothing is well-known to me."

I took off my finery and put it in the corner on the floor. Then he reached under the bench and pulled out a small package.

"I pulled in some favours for this," he said.

He shook out a very familiar deep purple tunic and handed it to me. It had a small piece missing from the bottom. I knew the exact shape of the missing piece; it was the piece he had given to me to hold during his last fight to keep his position—against Nathaniel.

"A little crumpled," he said gently. "It's come a long way."

I had first worn the dress a long time ago, when I stepped off his spaceship and met the assembled Shadakon here for the first time. When we had left Exterra, I had imagined wearing it as I stood beside him as the Sidhe representative. But Dagon and I had not been able to keep a wise distance from each other. We never had. So, again, we availed ourselves to passion as Nathaniel was in an induced sleep.

Dagon had me and I had him throughout the journey. But we both feared and, realistically, knew that our connection would be obvious to the keen senses of the Shadakon. So, I had stood beside Nathaniel during my introduction to the Shadakon; he had put his arm around me, possessively, while jokes were made about my connection with him. I was presented as his faerie blood source, complete with small punctures in my neck.

He had not made them—Dagon had. However, I had promised my blood to him later, in payment for his alibi that preserved his Alpha.

And, again, I had had that same dress when Nathaniel had collected from me for the first time. He had done it carelessly once we were housed in a small unit, one designed for high-ranking Shadakon who required a convenient place to satisfy their hunger. I had already taken off the purple dress at Nathaniel's command to come to him and seal the bargain—and, because I was Sidhe and I could—to bind him to me.

I had worn it, again, later that day to join with Dagon—me floating in the air slightly above him, coming down and enveloping us both in the purple fabric, creating a veil of privacy around us, as I had hoped.

And through all that had followed, he had kept it somehow.

With shaking hands, I slipped it over my head. He looked at me with his dark amber eyes and I saw the flames in them rising. I kindled to him but he remained motionless.

"I must leave the dress and you here," he said. "But I will carry the sight of you in it, for as far and long as I may have awareness.

"I want to go with you!" The words burst out before I realized what I was saying.

"Ah, Danu. You have flirted with death since I met you. You think you want to annihilate yourself? But your life has grown more and more interesting. Please do not suggest your death to me tonight. I can only deal with my own upcoming one."

He kissed me then and most thoughts were swept from my mind. But I did clearly hear him mind-speak, *"I'm sorry, Danu, I believe you will be wounded tomorrow along with me. I wish you happiness and healing afterwards."*

We came together then. Thanks to faerie glamour, the bench became his large bed on Exterra with its luxurious pelt of some huge red-furred creature.

Dagon came to me many ways that night, but at the end he came as the great cat that I had loved first and for so long. I heard the growling purr in his chest and saw his eyes widen in anticipatory excitement. He licked and licked and licked my neck with what was surely a coarse tongue. I felt his hardness against my belly and attempted to move closer, to align our bodies but he would have none of that. His sharp fangs bit down into me and pinned me as he took my intoxicating faerie blood. And then when both of us were in bliss, he took the rest of me and we surrendered to each other.

When I could, I opened my eyes to see him looking back at me. Once again, and perhaps for the final time, he had not taken all that he could have in that moment. I was a little drowsy, but not seriously depleted.

"I would give you the rest," I whispered. He shook his head. "I would gift you with the lifeblood of this planet." And then I transferred to him a small golden ball of energy.

"To ease your pain," I said.

"It's time, my love," he said.

The comfortable bed returned to its graceless usual state of a cold bench. I put on my tunic and pants. Dagon handed me the purple dress. "They will not search you, Danu. I can be sure of that."

I slipped it under my clothes. He put on his shirt and the hecklers outside yelled grudging appreciation at how long we had been busy with each other.

I knew what he would say as I left; it was what he had always said when we parted without knowing if it was for the last time. I waited for it, willing myself to stay upright and smiling courageously for him. As I did so my tears flowed. I did not do courageous well.

"Ah, but you do, lovely Danu. You are a warrior and a worthy mate. I am so sorry ..."

"Te amo para siempre, Dagon," I said.

He said it back to me. "Te amo para siempre, Danu."

And then I knocked on the door and the stern Shadakon escorted me outside the gate, where I transited to my home.

In the morning we Sidhe arrived early. Ceádar had, on my request, cut the purple shimmery fabric of my dress from Dagon into wide strips and braided it into my hair. He put the purple enhanced braid on the top of my head, securing it with small wooden pins that he had made. He then put the crown behind it. It was a thoughtful gesture—I would arrive as both Dagon's true mate, and Ceádar's queen.

I wore the Sidhe tunic dress of deep green. The shimmering purple fabric of Dagon's long-kept dress of mine shone in the sunlight, as did my glimmering silver crown. Ceádar was also in green and the Sidhe king of Exterra and his queen wore icy blue.

As we were preparing to leave, Ice and her daughter arrived. They wanted to come with us, to represent the young and female Sidhe that Dagon had helped save.

"You cannot bring your daughter to such an event!" I was horrified.

Ice shrugged. "She has seen Sidhe too weary to fly torn apart by humans, or beaten until they rose no more. There was no sheltered childhood for her, Danu. In some ways she is older than many of us, perhaps reincarnated from Sidhe who passed when the Old Earth was paradise. She has a fondness for Dagon. Apparently he comforted her while I slept in the boat."

"I will hide her eyes if you like, Danu," Ice added quietly. "But I will honour her wish to come with us."

"These offspring are not going to be a force to be reckoned with *later*," said Fiócara. "They already are."

We transited to the central plaza and stood, waiting see where we would be seated.

Dagon's official mate Alta was busy directing last minute details. She saw us and turned away.

I felt Fiócara's anger. It was not fury like he had launched at me. Instead it was old and very cold. He smiled and I wondered if the Shadakon knew what he was capable of.

Seemingly against her will, Dagon's mate turned and looked at us. She saw the young Sidhe and her eyes widened. Ice's daughter looked back and there was no acknowledgement from her that this was an important person that she should defer to. She stared as a child might stare. Except, I was coming to realize, these were not children. They were small, ageless Sidhe.

Finally Alta, who I knew was eager to see Dagon die so that she could stand by and openly lay with her new champion, approached us.

"I will make seats available to you. But this is no place for a child."

The so-called child smiled a smile that could have warned her, if the Shadakon female had been actually paying attention to her.

"This is no place to kill a Shadakon who has helped save planets and has been invaluable to the Shadakon and the Sidhe." Fiócara appeared to speak casually but I felt the ripple of power come off of him.

"You cannot interfere with the doings of the Shadakon," Alta responded in a dismissive tone.

Fiócara smiled again; so did Ice's daughter.

To my disbelief, we were seated behind the table of weapons. On its surface gleamed an assortment of lethal blades and other shapes devised to slash flesh and break bones. We were to sit here and watch as Dagon's opponent used these against a man who refused to fight?

I shuddered. Ice's daughter took in the array and smiled again.

The area was packed with Shadakon expecting a bloody show. Dagon was brought out, stripped to all but a thin strip of cloth. His body had more wounds this morning. His hand, which had been injured the night before, was freshly injured again. He saw us and gave a faint wave. Then he saw Ice's daughter and stood completely still. She met his eyes and gave him a faint smile.

As the official droned on about the rules of not leaving the circle and replacing weapons that were lost in combat with those from the table, Dagon's opponent appeared. He was well muscled and very well endowed with self-importance.

I felt my nails dig into Ceádar's palm. He startled slightly but did not complain.

They were invited to choose a weapon. Both chose long swords. The opponent swished his about experimentally. Dagon held his calmly in both hands.

There was a signal.

I was both attending to the real world details of this event and also sensing what lay beneath and beyond them. Flames of ego-driven greed and bloodlust guttered around Dagon's opponent like a fire that has at its heart, punky wood. Dagon stood like he was connected to the energy of the planet.

He was—he had committed to it, and me, and had done what he could to sway the balance towards life by protecting and preserving this place.

He looked briefly at me and his lips moved. I heard, deep within, the words of his pledge. I sent him life energy and love via our Maker bond.

The opponent began to step forward, but, in seeming slow motion, Dagon laid down his sword in front of him and stood tall. The Shadakons gasped and then roared their displeasure. What kind of fight would now commence?

I saw his opponent's sword make a slow arc and bite deep into Dagon's thigh. The blood welled up freely and ran down into the ground beneath the stones.

Dagon knelt, no longer able to stand. His opponent then performed a precise deep cut to one arm and then the other. Now Dagon would not raise his sword, nor go to the table to find another other weapon.

The Sidhe hissed. This was a public dishonouring.

Dagon bled quietly while his opponent swore and continued to attempt to get a response from him. He slashed him through the biceps and plunged his sword through his side. After watching him stoically bleed, he threw his own sword down and went to the table that we sat behind.

He saw me and laughed.

The Sidhe around me made no movement or sound.

Feeling possibly unnerved by those green and blue and icy eyes, he looked down and studied the objects on the table, searching, perhaps, for the perfect one to use to dole out pain for as long as possible.

We were under a clear blue sky. The bright sun made blue highlights against Dagon's chopped black hair. The sunlight caught the colour of his blood, steadily trickling down, drying in some places and making its way to the earth in others.

The arrogant Shadakon reached for a weapon and seemed slightly surprised. He did not choose it but moved on to another. I could see, even if the Shadakon could not, that something was apparently blocking him from picking up what he wanted. Finally, in a far corner, he spotted a small dagger.

My breath stopped in my chest and I heard Fiócara from a vast distance say, "*Hold, Danu.*"

He picked it up and tested its weight, making curving motions in the air that suggested that Ceádar's comment about what I might see—Dagon unmanned in front of his clan—might have been a foretelling.

He went to Dagon and ripped off his scant covering. The crowd laughed and howled.

"I would make you do this yourself, but I see that you can't."

He held Dagon's cock, which I had recently loved and roused to hot passion, away from his body and plied the knife. In doing so, at the last second he must have let his hand slip down the handle onto the blade. It had little in the way of a guard, as I well knew. It had been in my keeping for decades until Dagon requested that I return it to him. I was sure that any weapon, including this small seemingly ineffective one, had been taken from him long before this contest.

In a heartbeat Dagon's opponent knew that among whoever else died this day, he would be one. His intended action ended before it was begun when the small dagger fell from his now numb hand.

The crowd was silent and then the accusations began. *The Sidhe had sat behind the weapons. Had we somehow provided this knife? Had we affected the fight?*

Fiócara rose slowly and faced the crowd. "We are ambassadors of the life force. We do not use weapons. We do not kill those we might be tempted to kill for simple greed. How will you call this fight? Your Alpha awaits your decision as his life bleeds away. His challenger lies dead by his own hand. There was no honour for him here today.

Dagon's official mate and the lover of his challenger has no tears for either of them." Fiócara pointed at her and she turned her face away. "Dagon's true life-long mate is here and her heart is slowly dying with her mate and Maker. You are all bloody fools to once again try to end the life of this capable Alpha. Through your careless deeds, you may soon need to leave this planet. The Sidhe own it and

Dagon worked within that agreement. It is far from clear that the Shadakon under someone else's rule will be acceptable to us."

Fiócara looked at Dagon whose head was down and whose eyes were focused beyond the horizon. "Let us take him now. Your efforts would be too little and too late."

"Give him back to his faerie lover," someone shouted from the crowd.

And another said, "He has outlived his opponent. He is the winner today, for as long as he may enjoy that."

A tall, stern Shadakon, the same who had escorted me to Dagon the night before, approached the Sidhe and bowed his head briefly.

"There is a mystery here, but Dagon's hand was not in it." He looked at each of us, lingering on the fierce look of Ice's daughter. "You may take him while there is still faint breath in him and do what you will." He turned from us and walked away.

Fiócara walked us to where Dagon lay slumped in the dirt. We were already holding hands and he put his hand gently on Dagon's head.

Then we were in the cave of Green Tara.

CHAPTER SEVENTEEN

NOT DEAD, NOT ALIVE

Green Tara was waiting for us. She must have been monitoring the whole terrible process. She produced a green blanket and we lowered Dagon onto it.

She looked at all of us, one at time, intently.

"Dagon, perhaps, should be dead—but he is not. He has, however, already detached from his body. His spirit wanders now; he may not want to come back."

She stroked my hair.

"Danu, I know that you did not attempt to change his fate line—you had accepted that you should not. But someone here dared to do so."

"I did not like the Shadakon who brought him pain," said Ice's daughter. "He wanted to make it last as long and as horribly as he could." Her mind blazed with a freeze shot of Dagon on his knees, and his opponent calmly wounding him again and again without making a clean kill.

Green Tara knelt before the young Sidhe. "You have seen this before, on old Earth?" she asked gently.

The young Sidhe briefly closed her bright blue eyes and opened them again. "It is the way that the humans treated everyone still alive. They did not kill reluctantly or because they needed food. They left the animal children of the forest canopy rotting where they had fallen. They did the same to the simple humans who had lived there for almost forever. And they particularly enjoyed torturing Sidhe. They killed babies in front of their mothers; they shot us as we crept in to try to get one more meal out of the giant fallen trees."

Green Tara remained kneeling in front of her and neither dropped their eyes. "I am only going to ask you questions about this once, and I do not want you to answer anything I don't ask. Will you do that?"

The young female Sidhe took her time but in the end nodded yes.

Green Tara smiled. "Danu has a problem keeping Sidhe separate in her mind without a small name. Would you like a name she can call you by? You know that she calls your mother Ice and your father Blue. I think you, too, might find a water name suitable."

"You may call me Artica," she said. I shivered. She smiled.

"And may I, for Danu's ease in following us, also address you that way?" Green Tara asked.

She nodded again and then, as if remembering her manners, said "Yes" clearly.

"So, Artica, for awhile longer others will see you as young and inexperienced. But I will not make that mistake."

"When did you first see the dagger?" she asked the young Sidhe.

"I saw it in Dagon's mind. He wished he could have returned it to Danu. But then as his pain continued, he wished he could use it on himself."

"And where was it?"

She shrugged. "In a box in the angry tall Shadakon's room. He had not turned it in and wondered now what he should do with it."

Green Tara laughed. "The opponent's second was in possession of Dagon's dagger? He and Dagon's mate will probably die or be banished because of that detail. Maybe they will be a good match for each other."

"How did you get it to the table?"

Artica shrugged again, as if such details were unimportant. "I transited it. There was a little spot available for it."

"And the reason that the other weapons were made unavailable?"

"I felt that the knife had the most direct line to what I wanted to bring into being."

Fiócara could not hide his amazement. I also listened, having to hear and believe what I had perceived of as a defenceless child explaining calmly how she, a young Sidhe, had manipulated the fabric of the universe.

"I think Fiócara will want to talk to you," I said.

"Yes," Artica said.

"Did you know why Dagon wanted that particular dagger?" Green Tara asked.

"It was a death bringer to the Shadakon. A small sting with it brings death."

"And did you arrange for his opponent to cut himself with it?"

"His hand was slick with Dagon's blood. He couldn't resist feeling it; feeling Dagon's life flowing out through the wounds he had inflicted. I did not cause his hand slide down the hilt to the blade. However ..." She stopped herself, and for a moment showed her inexperience. She looked at Fiócara.

It was an answer in itself.

We all stood silently and then Ice drew her daughter to her and held her tight. Fiócara stood apart from us. I went to the green blanket that Green Tara had cocooned Dagon in. His face was serene and I could not sense his presence.

Green Tara stood beside me and lightly touched my cheek. "You can offer him blood or energy if you like. He may refuse it, but you probably have to know that you offered."

I crawled under the green wrap to lie beside him. His wounds were closing and I sensed no pain or fear in him. I bit my hand and held it to his lips. The drops ran off.

His lips did not open.

I then moved my hair aside and placed the tender place where he had pierced me many times against his mouth. His fangs did not come down although he sighed slightly and nestled in closer to me. I had to try everything, so I attempted to shift energy to him, taking his Maker hand in my own. There was no answering flare between us. Had I felt this when I was apart him, I would have known that he was dead. But he breathed lightly, the warmth evident against my cheek.

"It is your choice to make my love," I said. I could feel the tsunami of grief rising up in the deep water of my back mind. "It was your fate perhaps to save the one who could, and will, break the rules of the Sidhe that she does not even know. That she may have already decided to rebel against."

Artica came to us then and briefly touched his hand. "He is far away, safe from pain and fear. Green Tara is powerful and she loves him, too." She said it as absolute fact. "He may choose to go with her to places we can't go. He has no further place with the Shadakon or here."

We watched him together for a moment. She reached up and smoothed back his glossy black hair.

"His hair is healing too," she said. And then I realized that it now reached his shoulders again.

I walked over to Green Tara. "I asked you for a boon several days ago, and said I had nothing of value to give you in return. You took my crown, but returned it to me to wear today. I do not think you need or want crowns. I now surrender my mate, my lover, to you, Green Tara. He is one of the most precious things … beings, I have ever held. I have been willing to die for him many times, both by his own hand, and to protect him from evil others, not unlike what I witnessed today."

I could say no more but my heart clamoured to be heard. I let it speak to Green Tara while I stood swaying in front of her. She kissed me and I felt the timeless bliss that surely she had brought to Dagon. She assured me that she would stay by him while he decided where he needed to be next. I would not be able to be with him without wanting him to wake and be his old self. She did not tell me not to come. I would have to decide that for myself.

Artica had grown very still as well.

"I didn't mean to hurt you," she said softly to me.

"This has turned out as well as it could Artica. Dagon's cruel opponent is dead in the dust and his scheming official mate will have to ply her trade elsewhere."

"And the angry man who had Dagon's knife?"

I thought about the purple dress, whose streamers were still braided into my hair. *"I called in a few favours,"* Dagon had said. The stern Shadakon had already taken custody of everything Dagon owned, and yet he had chosen to return the purple dress to Dagon. I did not wish the ultimate harsh punishment on him, but his own clan would decide that soon.

"In the end, he did Dagon a few favours," I said with tears dripping down my cheeks. "Dagon's fate unpacked as it had to. I am grateful to you."

"Then we have repaid our debt to each other," she said. "Now we can be friends."

I knew I would have to talk to Fiócara when I could speak and when we had privacy to do so. But right now I ached and stumbled when I took a step. My attempts to nourish Dagon had failed, but my blood and energy had been spilled nevertheless. I felt the ground reach for me, but Ceádar's strong arms caught me instead. Putting me across his shoulder, he reached out for Ice and her daughter. He grabbed for Ice's hand, but it was Artica who calmly took his hand as they transited back to our home.

Ceádar laid me out on my bed and carefully took the pins from my hair, freeing the braid to hang free. He left me in my finery and turned to the two Sidhe still lingering. I could hear Artica from far away.

"I didn't mean to hurt her," she said in a small voice. "I'm sorry."

Ceádar knelt to her. "None of us did," he said. "And we are all sorry."

Ice shepherded her outside, but hesitated, still not taking them home. Ceádar studied her for a moment. "You have come to me before, seeking something or someone. I am not he who you search for."

She smiled and I was witness to it all from the place where I lingered.

"I know," she said. "I just hope I find someone who will care for me like you care for Danu."

"Are you not sure that you have not already found him?" Ceádar said softly.

"He left me there—in hell. With a small offspring to watch die. He was welcomed to Exterra. I could not ask for mercy …And he did not ask for mercy for me and our daughter!"

The rage radiated off her in waves.

Ceádar stood within touching distance of her for a long time.

"We all left you there. All the Sidhe. Blue almost died after arriving here. The clear blue sky, the cool water—all were a torment to him. Danu took him to the humans and together they taught the humans how to make adobe bricks. Blue played with and taught the human children. For a long time, it was the only thing he lived for."

She looked at him and for the first time I sensed a quieting in her. "Why did no one ask? Why did they not beg Fiócara on our behalf?"

Ceádar let the silence grow for a while without answering. "I am old and I had never seen a young Sidhe. I had not been back to Old Earth since I relocated on Exterra. And then when I returned for the male Sidhe. Most of them did not come from what was the Amazon basin. Perhaps not even many male Sidhe on Old Earth knew."

"Blue knew," she said.

Ceádar bowed his head to her. "Allow him to answer your questions. Allow him to beg your forgiveness. If it is possible—allow him to comfort you. I have a heart-broken queen to comfort yet again because she has lost her Shadakon mate. I do it for one reason only."

They looked at each other and Artica looked at both of them. She answered for Ceádar.

"He does it because he wants her. Wants her to be happy and content in his arms. She always returns to him if he keeps his heart open."

Ceádar smiled. They left.

Ceádar sighed and removed my fine dress. He removed his beautiful early fall Sidhe finery. I felt the soft slip of his skin against mine as he joined me and I moved into his arms.

Whether he slept or not, he held me all night.

CHAPTER EIGHTEEN

THE HEALING

When I awoke in Ceádar's arms he was smiling down on me. He continued to hold me without requesting anything and I felt deeply relaxed for the first time in days. This was not complicated. I could want him, or not—and he would wait. Meanwhile, I could feel the evidence of him wanting me.

"Take me to the water," I said.

In a moment I was in the shallows with him, wrapped in his assumed iridescent scaled coils. I stretched out in the sun, as he supported me. I stroked him and he slightly tightened himself around me, and slowly and calmly started kissing me. When I was breathless with wanting him, he brought himself to me and even as we combined, I cried. They were not exactly tears of sadness, nor of joy. I cried and they ran down and joined the sea.

When I could finally talk, I only said, "Again."

Eventually I went to Green Tara to see what was happening with Dagon, but the green misty blanket was gone.

She came to me and slipped her arm around me, not expecting me to kneel.

"I have placed his body in the back of the cave. I will know immediately if he returns to it. He is traveling, Danu, far out in the deeps and also along the timeline of his life."

I thought, then, about the children's stories about enchanted princesses who lay as though dead behind thorn forests or on their bier. Some of them were awakened by a kiss. Perhaps those were the ones who were willing to wake.

I wanted to see him, to hold him, to know that his body had healed. I wanted him to come back to me.

Green Tara sighed. She and I took a few steps and then we were in a massive chamber of pearly cave formations. Her light glittered off crystals and smooth, translucent living stone. It was eerily beautiful. The vast room I was in was totally silent except for the occasional drip; I was in a different flow of rock and time. Dagon lay on his green blanket on a shelf-like projection. His body was intact, his skin had the translucent sheen of the stone around him.

I touched him. He was smooth and cool. His eyes were closed but there was a faint expression remaining on his face. He looked relaxed and peaceful. He had surrendered to death and now here he was, in his own Between, in the care of Green Tara.

Perhaps he would return for this body. And, perhaps, as time passed it would slowly be covered, one drip at a time and become part of the cave.

"*Deep peace of the running wave, Dagon*," I mind-spoke into the emptiness.

"How I love you," I whispered.

I felt, as the Sidhe queen had foretold, the blade twist in my own heart. I sat, leaning up against his resting place, letting the cave time and silence and darkness hold me. I knew that if my wild Shadakon warrior was anywhere, he was not here. Yet I held vigil until the need for nourishment caused me to rise and leave him.

CHAPTER NINETEEN

I AM ALIVE AND AGAIN GRATEFUL

Life went on.

Blue came by to where Ceádar and I were sitting in the gathering darkness one evening. He invited us in person to come to their house tomorrow and then disappeared.

"'Our house' sounds promising," said Ceádar.

In the morning we arrived to find Blue and Artica smeared with mud as they put on the finishing touches of a second room in Blue's, and now his family's, home. There was a small window that overlooked the sea, and a door made of a frame and woven reeds between Artica's room and the rest of the hill house. Ice was watching them with amusement. There was no mud on her face. I assumed that she had been smeared with enough mud to last the rest of her life while on old Earth.

Artica came running to me without her usual composure. She asked me in mind-speak what I thought of their work.

"*I think it might still need some swirls or waves,*" I thought back. She looked at my crown and then ran back to duplicate the pattern in the still wet clay.

"Thank you, Danu," said her mother. "I am still learning to being happy. Thank you for my daughter and for all the other Sidhe young."

All told, we had brought back fifteen young and five adult female Sidhe.

I had a thought that she picked up without me having to specifically send it and she answered me. "*She who had a burnt leg has been healed by us—by Fiócara and Artica actually. She has a limp but can live her life without pain.*"

On another day, while I was sitting amidst some human children being taught by a human elder to weave the supple grass into rough cloth, I felt the unique energy that was Fiócara. Telling the little humans that I'd be back, I walked out into the scrub grassland. My heart was calm but my hands shook. As always, since the beginning, I wanted him.

He smiled. "You always chose to want me, Danu. You were Sidhe before anyone but the Touch-me-not plant realized it. You did and could have continued to refuse me."

"It didn't feel that way to me," I said.

He smiled. "The part that wanted me outvoted your 'rational mind,'" he said with the faint Sidhe scorn he was so good at. "I will not touch you today, unless you want me to."

You must begin it, or fly away. We both know we have a lot of time to have these talks." He smiled again.

"Take off your garment," I said, as I had said to other males—Sidhe and Shadakon.

"*But never to a human male,*" Fiócara thought back to me. "*And certainly not with the welcome that you will soon extend to me.*"

I sighed and took off my own. My nipples rose in anticipation of his touch.

The heat was spreading from my centre although we were standing apart. He was glowing in the late fall sun, his hair longer than when I had last seen him, and streaked with gold and grey. His eyes were the colour of a deep pool. I swayed where I stood. He did not move or reach out to me.

I came to him and touched his face, moving his blowing hair back. He closed his eyes in what may have been great pleasure. I ran both hands down his strong arms and lightly grasped his hands. I placed them on my breasts and we both moaned.

"What do you want from me, Danu?"

I paused in my upward spiral to bliss.

"I want you to tell me what you did, the day of the duel."

He was silent for a moment. "I will do so. Can we do it afterwards?"

I laughed and pulled him to the ground. I felt the fine tendrils of earth energy reach for us both. My inner glow intensified until I had no further thoughts, no words, no name.

We joined there in the sun, and the energy of the planet entered us. I finally wept then, a final realization that I had to let Dagon go—he would never again be my lover. I held Fiócara to me and, even as he came hard to me, my heart, long clenched shut, opened, and then I was with him and no one else.

I rose over him and took him until he cried out. Then we both lay in the afternoon sun while our bodies returned to their approximately usual state.

"Thank you, Danu," he just said. He gave me one of his gentle kisses and I lay in the crook of his arm and was content. "I will give you a gift that you don't have to pay for. There is no faerie deal in this."

I looked at him and wondered if such an exchange was possible.

"You have paid with your heart, Danu. Few love me without fearing me as well. For some reason that was our connection from the beginning."

"I knew what Artica, as you call her, was doing the day of the duel. She had found the knife in Dagon's mind and traced it to where it was. This is amazing, for Dagon did not know."

"Artica has already shown me what a fool I was in my supreme insistence on Old Rule. We Sidhe did not need offspring when our own lives were limitless. We did not need the vulnerability of offspring when the humans pushed over the boundaries we had set. But I greatly underestimated the life force."

"Female Sidhe got with young and had to live outside of my kingdom and protection. I knew they existed, of course. When I left earth, I left the remaining Sidhe behind. Others may find good enough reasons for why I did so, but I cannot.

I suppose I wondered why so few female Sidhe came to Exterra. Rather than seeing me as a king who would help them, they feared and hated me. Some left their offspring on Old Earth with a handful of Sidhe who would stay with them until death came. They came with raging hearts."

I said nothing and he smiled at that.

"My queen may have known or guessed, but she does not have a nurturing nature. She is attracted to females but does not have much curiosity about their lives. You understand that as well as any."

"The female Sidhe trusted you, not me. Once again, the life force passed me by as its champion—in favour of you. You flew the cone that allowed us to end the assault on Exterra. You went across the void in Green Tara's kayak, and found the abandoned Sidhe. You brought them back in a desperate debut flight. Your loyal king stalled me and held out against my searching him to determine what was going on. That was probably the hardest thing he ever did, given our long connection. But he defied me, as did you. And gifted us all with someone who I do not know how important she will be, but her powers are already almost as great as mine—at least as great."

I put my hand on his heart and he removed it and kissed it and continued.

"I could follow what she was about to do. When she blocked Dagon's assailant's mind and substituted the knife as seemingly his choice, that was as clear to me as it was to you. But it was my hand on the hand of his opponent when the knife took him. I felt his arrogance and satisfaction to completely humiliate Dagon, and I was willing to face Green Tara, or any other force, to finish the deed. And I did not want it falling on Artica's shoulders. She was initially angry that I had not given her the chance to do that for you.

She is inexperienced in spite of her powers. I took the weight," he explained.

"Have you checked out the other young Sidhe?" I asked.

"Their mothers still hold deserved anger towards me. In time, you will be a mediator between them and me. You will also take them to Green Tara for instruction, as you no doubt have in other lives."

He stroked my cheek and I leaned into him. Sidhe have great staying power. He was an eons-old powerful king.

We were already in the grass, lying down. I had the passing thought that plants would probably thrive in this spot in the future. The energy we pulled up and that spilled from us was a shimmering golden cloud. When I surrendered yet again to him, I sighed.

He looked down on me with his golden green eyes and read down deep into me. I did not resist. I had no secrets, at the moment, to keep from him.

"Two more things, my forever Midsummer's Eve Queen. Ceádar is being drawn to another's arms beside my queen's. You may have some Sidhe arrangement of an extended family at some point."

I said nothing. I had known that Ice came to Ceádar. I knew he was intentionally remaining as a friend to Blue.

And Artica—Artica and I were connected. Perhaps this was part of it.

"Well taken like the Sidhe you are," said Fiócara. "Not that it may be so easy for you when it comes into being, but a brave start, Danu."

"And one more thing. You will get to say goodbye to Dagon. He will come to you, when he knows that it will no longer bring you grief, or more grief than joy anyway. He has been travelling and has the broadened outlook of a traveller. In fact, I believe it will be more of the 'thank you' than a goodbye, but I will let him tell you that."

I brushed the grass off of me and donned my usual worn-out tunic. Fiócara also rose and with a brief bow to me, disappeared.

"*Ceádar would know of course,*" I thought.

"*Ceádar already knows,*" I heard clearly, "*he has always known. He also knows that you are on your way home—to him. However, he hopes that you will grant him the same courtesy later.*"

I smiled. No one else could hold me so lightly and thoroughly as Ceádar. I felt his gentle strength through my connection with him now.

"*Perhaps a swim, to wash away the day's work?*" he asked. I had no doubt what that would involve.

"*With someone with iridescent scales and a shimmering dorsal fin?*" I thought back.

"*If you wish. Perhaps after some elixir to replenish your energy.*"

I rolled my eyes. "*I drank from the planet,*" I said.

"*To cool you down then,*" he said calmly.

I flew home.

In a very short time I was lying in the shallow water of the now cooling sea near our house. I had returned, not to my house but *our* house. After taking a few tight wraps around me, he rolled in the water, while I sputtered as I always did. He did it again and this time, I knew that he was dissipating some anger.

"*I am yours, Ceádar, when you want me to be. Perhaps even when you don't want me to be. Dagon could have told you how irritating that can be.*"

I could now say his name without a pain in my heart, I realized.

Ceádar smiled. "*It is obvious that you did some deep work today. We shall do some more now.*"

He dove under water with me in his grip and went down and down. In the depths, I saw something big—several big someones—moving calmly in the dark blue deeps.

"*Whales!*" I thought excitedly.

I sent out the name-sound that a whale mother on Exterra had taught me. She answered and came close, her big eye even with mine.

"*I have brought some of my clan, Danu. I was told that you needed whales here. We have had to explain what we needed to eat. That is here now as well.*"

We looked at and into each other with peaceful grateful thoughts. Then she merely moved one fluke, sank beneath me and was gone.

"*Ceádar!* I thought. "*This is amazing. I know it is your doing.*"

"I am a Sidhe of many talents," he said, when we reached the beach again. "I will remind you of some of the others now."

And he did. He did and did and did.

CHAPTER TWENTY

WE ARE SIDHE—
WE LOVE WHO WE LOVE

It was now winter and the sea was no longer warm enough to swim in. I was remembering the Queen's Bath that Fiócara's queen had taken me to. Ceádar looked up from what he doing and gave me a searching look. I felt a light questioning touch in my mind.

"*I am thinking about being warm and in the water at the same time,*" I thought.

"*Yes, and you are thinking about kissing someone besides me.*" His mind was as still as a pond that held the perfect image of a moon.

"*And so are you,*" I answered with now total certainty. He was quiet.

"*We are Sidhe, Ceádar. You have put up with my attractions to others since forever. How can I not grant you the same freedom?*"

"*In that case, Danu, I am going out tonight. I do not do it to hurt you, but am relieved that you are easy with this.*"

I thought nothing. Or, I thought about the beaches of Old Earth as the forever-in-my-mind blue waves rolled in hypnotically. He stood and studied me.

"*You are becoming more and more a queen, Danu. There is calmness in you now, even though you are withholding your feelings about this. I am not leaving. I am merely— going out.*"

He walked to the door and disappeared into the night.

Soon after, Artica showed up in the bower behind the house. She had what I assumed was a favourite blanket.

"Can I stay with you here tonight?" she asked.

We looked at each other. She was coming in the guise of a child needing safe shelter with me, but we both know that wasn't why she was here. She could and had slept or rested anywhere on the planet, including Green Tara's cave.

She eyed me a little more appreciatively.

"No I don't need to be here with a blanket."

She dropped it and continued to look at me. "Ice calls to him and he has refused many times. This time, he did not. Blue is off pretending to be busy, leaving me to look like I don't mind what will probably go on all night—but I do. I feel the energy in my body when adults have sex. It is irritating because it is nothing I can do until I grow up more."

"I am honoured to have you spend the evening with me, Artica. I do not need comforting about this, but your company is always … a pleasant challenge to me."

We sat quietly. Artica wrapped herself in her blanket and faced the sky. We watched falling stars and as the darkness became absolute, we saw the stars behind the stars we usually saw.

"You took us through the space deeps, Danu. You had never gone there before."

"Not quite true, Artica. Fiócara and Ceádar both took me there. We took each other there. I find the void peaceful. If I had failed to reach Old Earth I would have been sorry for those who were counting on me, but I am not afraid to be out there, floating and without pain. When we returned, I had more confidence and less desperation that I might fail. I believe that Green Tara's boat was helpful as well. She is a goddess, Artica, if you don't know already."

Artica nodded. I heard, "*Yes of course,*" in my mind, and I shivered.

"Never be afraid of me, Danu," she said and I kept my mind steady while I pondered her telling me that at such a young age.

"Fiócara told you about what happened during the duel. I could feel every wound hurt you, Danu. I could feel his opponent's rising contempt of Dagon dying as a peaceful warrior. He chose to not fulfill his role as Alpha Shadakon and perhaps had no other path before him. His greatest and only regret was the pain that you went through with him."

"He was beyond pain when the would-be winner arrived with Dagon's own knife to unman him. I did not do it for Dagon. I did it because at last, I could kill at least one male who had such thoughts. I did it because it would have been much harder for you to heal from seeing what was coming."

She watched me for a reaction and then added, "Fiócara thought he took the final action. I arranged it that way. I wanted him to feel responsible for at least one death, since, through his neglect, he would have allowed myself, the other young Sidhe, and those who stayed with us to die on old Earth."

"And yet you are in close touch with him?"

She shrugged. "He is my king and teacher. Ceádar is also my teacher. Ice is right now having a lesson that the Sidhe had to bring to you over and over. She can have Ceádar tonight, but she cannot keep him."

I sat, stunned by this young Sidhe's revelations.

"Green Tara said to me that she would not make the mistake of seeing me as young. You, too, should do that. I was born in hell, as the Old Earth myths describe it—flaming pain, hunger, helplessness. There was always some human nearby who fed on our despair. That is where I arrived. Ice is mad at Blue about not trying to rescue us. I am calmly mad at Ice because she knew where I would be delivered, yet she birthed me there. Perhaps that is under her convenient pain of being mad at Blue."

I shook my head. "Is there something I can do for you now, Artica? Would you like some elixir?"

She came close then and carefully snuggled into the curve of my side.

"I want you not to underestimate me, I want you to be my friend. I will accept teaching from you, and soon it will be time for you to take me to Green Tara." And then she was silent and, perhaps, even slept.

I left her curled up under her blanket and went to the edge of the sea. Ceádar was not here. Somehow the idea of Ice being held by his iridescent coils while he pleasured her was a problem for me. I felt, rightly or wrongly, that he had intentionally taken that shape for me—because of my love for the sea. But the shore was silent and empty, with only the small waves washing up on the shore. The water burned with living lights that darted under the surface, and even glowed on the water's edge where I stepped there.

I remembered summoning Dagon in this spot. He had come to me, initially irritated, but we quickly rekindled our bond. I had promised Green Tara and myself not to summon him. I tried to imagine him traveling swiftly, going where he would and learning what he might learn. He had told me early in our connection that the Shadakon believed that when they died—they were gone. I wondered if he had experienced that, or if his viewpoint had changed.

On this night, while my king and lover lay with a beautiful Sidhe with pale hair and icy eyes, I wanted only to use this time to think of Dagon. To wish for him an interesting journey, if he was on one. I thought of the pale cool body in the cave and ...

There was the pain. I had wanted to tell him ... I had wanted for even a moment, for us to see together that there was no blame, no anger. I did not need him to be who he had been. I wanted to watch him leave with my love.

I closed my eyes and sat as quietly as I could in the chilly onshore breeze.

I was cold, but didn't care. I sat in the space between believing that he was fine, and knowing that he was dust in the wind. I wanted to know which one was true, but begged somewhere deep inside me that he was not now inanimate matter.

I suddenly felt warmer, as if the breeze was kept from blowing across my arms, and I felt a dark gentleness surround me. I kept my eyes closed, not wanting to see that there was nothing to see.

"Ah, Danu," Dagon said softly in my mind. "I know my ending was hard on you. I knew what to expect and merely had to endure it. You kept hoping for the miracle, the sudden twist of fate that would allow you to continue to have me—to be with me."

I felt him lightly raise my chin and then the faintest brush across my lips. I felt no answering rush of heat and wanting. Instead I felt a merging where he and I touched.

He lingered at my throat.

"Dagon, anything I have that you can access is yours."

"I can still reach the most important thing to me, Danu."

I felt myself melting into whatever he was now. Energy. Love. His wild warrior energy was still there, but gentler and touching me without leaving longing or pain.

We sat like this a little or a long time. Stars flared in the sky and slowly the light glowed below the horizon.

"You did not ask what it was, Danu, so I sense that you know, but I will tell you. It is your heart, Danu. I had said this for a long time, but now I realize the truth in it.

"Te amo para siempre, Danu. Live your life in joy. Whenever you are in love and fiercely protecting those you love, I will be there."

"And there is one more thing that you will later understand as I do: there is no inanimate matter. You call up the hot heat of the planet when you make love and it joyfully comes to you. It— we—are all interconnected. Old Earth is dying but her seeds of life have been spread across the galaxy. Perhaps Old Earth life once came from there—from the seeming outside."

I leaned into his shoulder and he circled me in a swirl of energy.

"We will be in touch again, Danu. Be happy."

And he was gone.

When I transited home, Artica was sitting calmly, waiting for me.

"I am glad," she said. "You needed to be alone and undistracted to meet with him.

This was a perfect night" We looked at each other, and perhaps we even looked into each other. Artica had a true fondness for Dagon. I remembered her smoothing his hair as he lay motionless.

I poured two cups of elixir and gave her one. She sipped politely. *Did she already pull from the planet's energies?*

"Danu. I will say it again. Do not underestimate me. It is what I ask of you. Ceádar is on his way here. You can be here, or not be here. I'm going back to my room and ponder what I learned tonight."

She disappeared.

I was going to leave—but then I didn't.

Ceádar lived here. I lived here. We both had had a night of it, although in my case I was cool, my Sidhe fires banked low. He seemed to have burned through a lot of fuel since I saw him last. I offered him the cup of elixir that Artica had sipped from. Then he surprised me.

"I will ask this and accept your answer without further questions. I would offer to show you how I passed the night and receive the same from you. I sense, though, that you had a deeper experience than mine."

I thought of him seeing Dagon, a returned energy being, who lingered briefly by my side. I thought of seeing Ceádar in the hungry arms of Ice. I shook my head.

"I have just one question," I said. "I do not need to know what you do when not with me. But one thing pains me so I will say it: I feared that you would take your companion to the sea and wrap her in your lovely sea serpent body. That thought hurt. I always thought that you took that form because I wanted you that way. That it was between us two."

I hung my head. Obviously I had more work to do to be a Sidhe.

Ceádar drew me to him. I could sense the spent passion on him but that didn't bother me. I trembled.

"Danu. I could not assume that form with someone who could not imagine me like that. It is like a private love word, shared only between us two. When you touch me, I feel your sensuality and water passion. I manifest that for you alone."

I saw a glint of scale and laughed.

"Rest, Ceádar. I am going to see some of the humans today. I will be happy to see you, if you are here, when I return. I think that Artica and I will be spending more time together."

And I transited off to the desert and the humans who lived frugally there.

CHAPTER TWENTY-ONE

MUCH LATER

★ ★ ★ ★

Danu's World continued to heal, the large gaps in its web of life slowly filling in.

There were spiders and bugs and, yes, snakes to eat the bugs. There were smart quick predators in the woods and birds above to eat the mice and snakes. Rats were not on the relocation list, although they were one of the last surviving organisms on Old Earth.

In honour of the protection that they had offered to the Sidhe young, crocodiles had been brought from Old Earth and put in a remote corner of what was becoming the tropical area around the equator. I knew—because I had gone to see the release—that a large mother crocodile now sat on guard nearby her ripening eggs. She would later take them to the water and some of the female Sidhe wanted to be there when it happened. Snakes and crocodiles—I would not have thought they were necessary, but none of us knows or senses what our true part is in the web.

The Sidhe were not at risk from anything that lived, and the humans would learn, or relearn, to avoid them.

Fiócara and a few Sidhe, including Ceádar went back for a final look around old Earth. They were found by a few Shadakon who implored them to take them from the final days of Old Earth's dying and their own. They stood proud but knew that death was riding fast for them. Fiócara surprised them and Ceádar by agreeing, and transited them to Danu's World, leaving them in the Shadakon compound without further explanation. But before that, they had helped gather up some more still-surviving beings to enhance this world—including the crocodiles.

There was no sign of living Sidhe although the sense of their painful dying was still evident.

The Shadakon were dropped off with their kind to make their own fate. The Shadakon forces of Danu's World had been in disarray—they had no formal leader or leader of the guard. One of the newly-arrived Shadakon promptly took up the challenge and announced himself as Alpha. I could then see Fiócara's long-range planning in his actions. The new leader owed him; it was a perfect faerie solution.

The Sidhe females slowly put away their hatred. Fiócara had gathered them to a meeting and most came. He then did what he was learning, relatively recently, to do: he apologized to them, admitting that he was wrong and that he deeply regretted his actions.

He then opened to them and they could see that this was true.

Some of rescued Sidhe young also came and he treated them as equals that evening. He promised them all any assistance that he could provide. And then he did something that astounded me, but I immediately knew that I was ready for it.

He announced me as queen of Danu's World, and Ceádar as its king.

It was as simple as that.